REMY LA[I]

GHOST BOOK

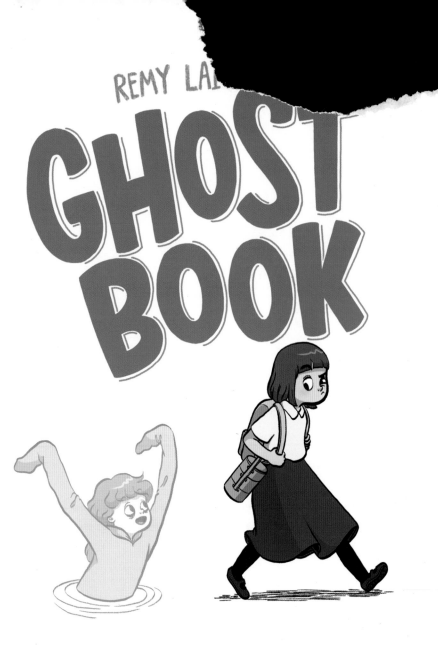

Henry Holt and Company
New York

Henry Holt and Company, Publishers since 1866
Henry Holt® is a registered trademark of Macmillan Publishing Group, LLC
120 Broadway, New York, NY 10271
mackids.com

Our books may be purchased in bulk for promotional,
educational, or business use.
Please contact your local bookseller or the Macmillan Corporate
and Premium Sales Department at (800) 221-7945 ext. 5442
or by email at MacmillanSpecialMarkets@macmillan.com.

Library of Congress Control Number: 2022920245

First edition, 2023
Edited by Brian Geffen
Book design by Lisa Vega
Art direction by Sharismar Rodriguez
Production editing by Mia Moran
Color by Ninakupenda Gaillard
Proofreading by Jill Freshney
Printed in China by RR Donnelley Asia Printing Solutions Ltd.,
Dongguan City, Guangdong Province

ISBN 978-1-250-81041-0 (hardcover)
1 3 5 7 9 10 8 6 4 2

ISBN 978-1-250-81043-4 (paperback)
1 3 5 7 9 10 8 6 4 2

For J Tan

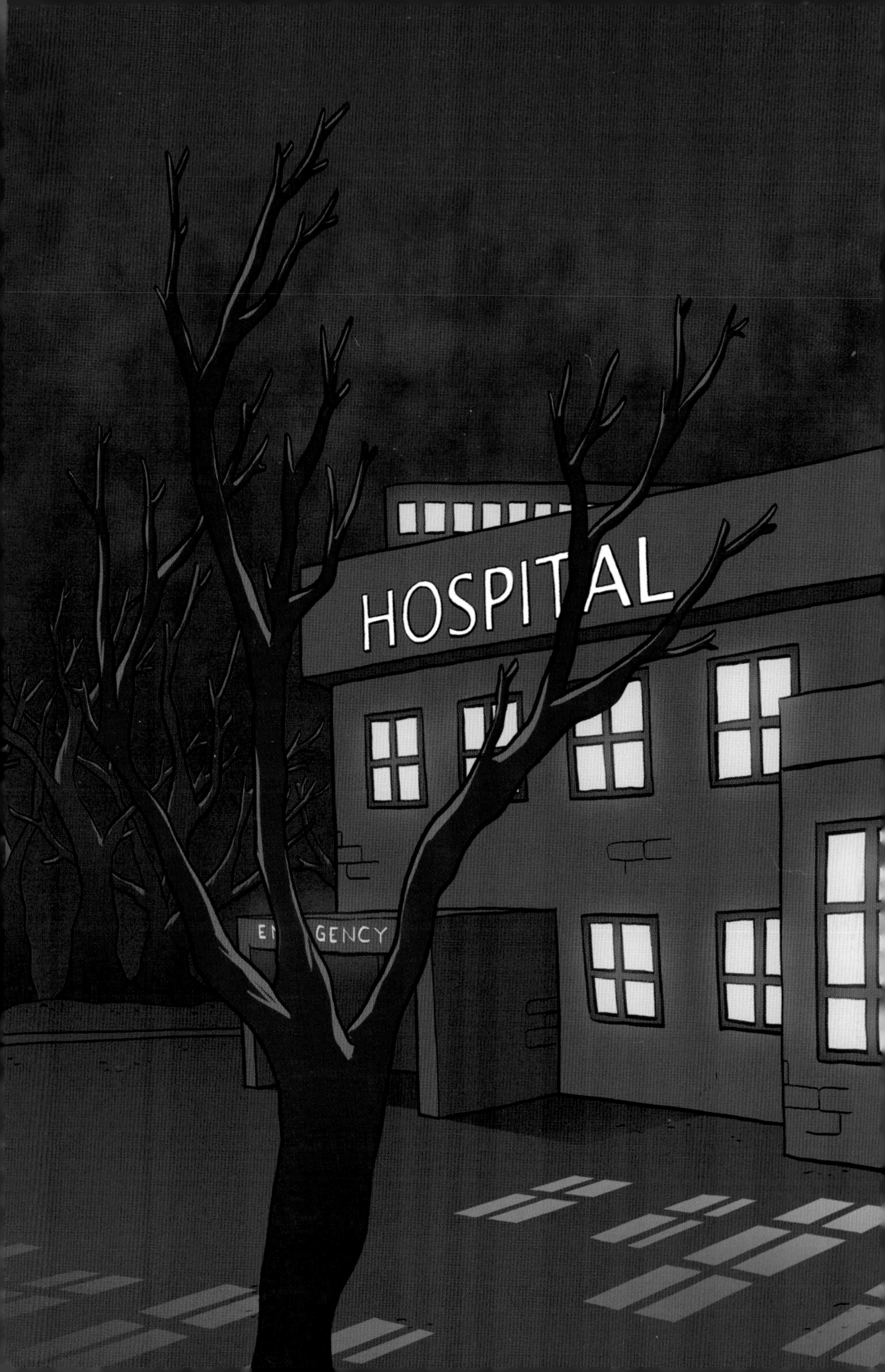
HOSPITAL
E GENCY

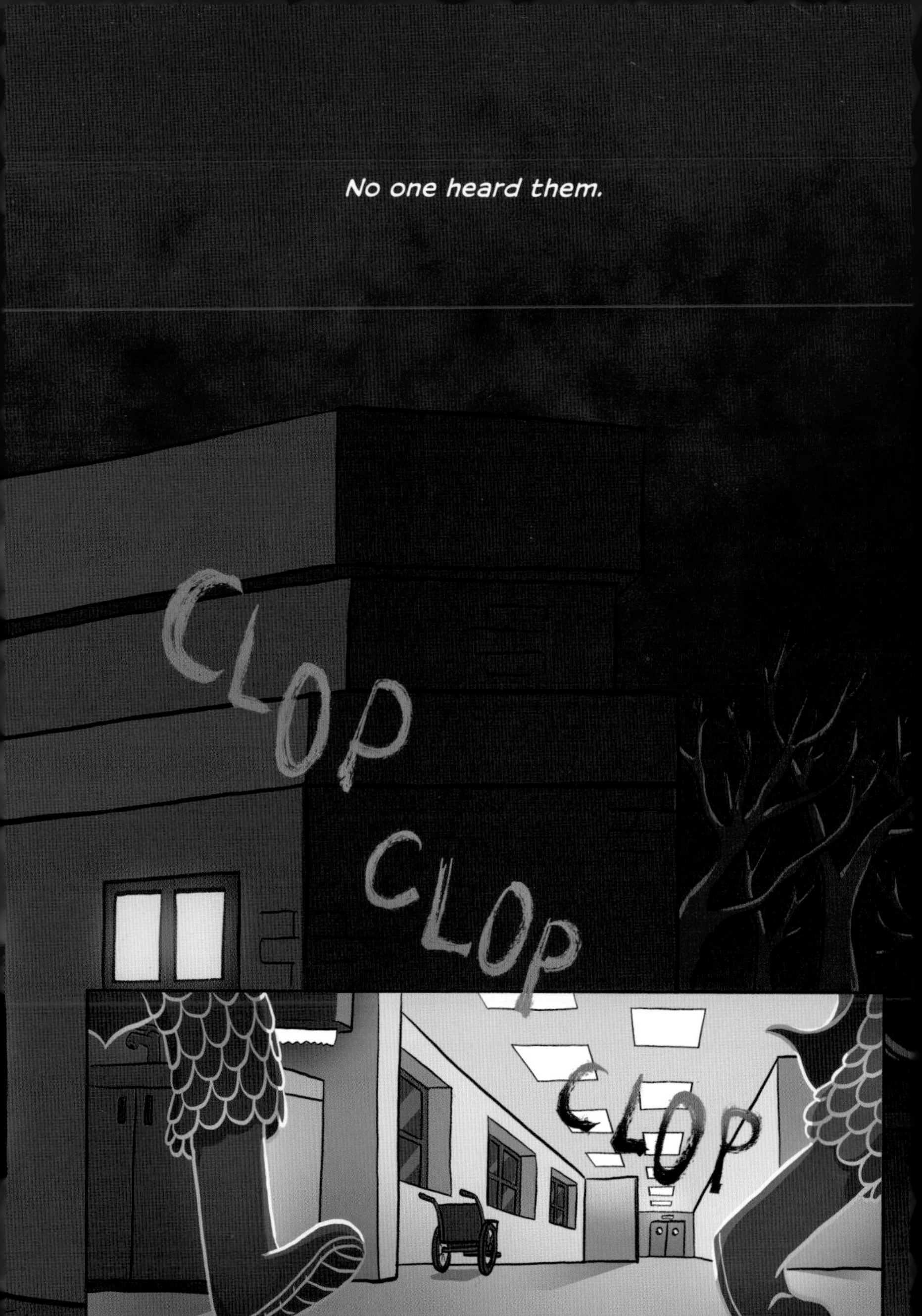
No one heard them.
CLOP
CLOP
CLOP

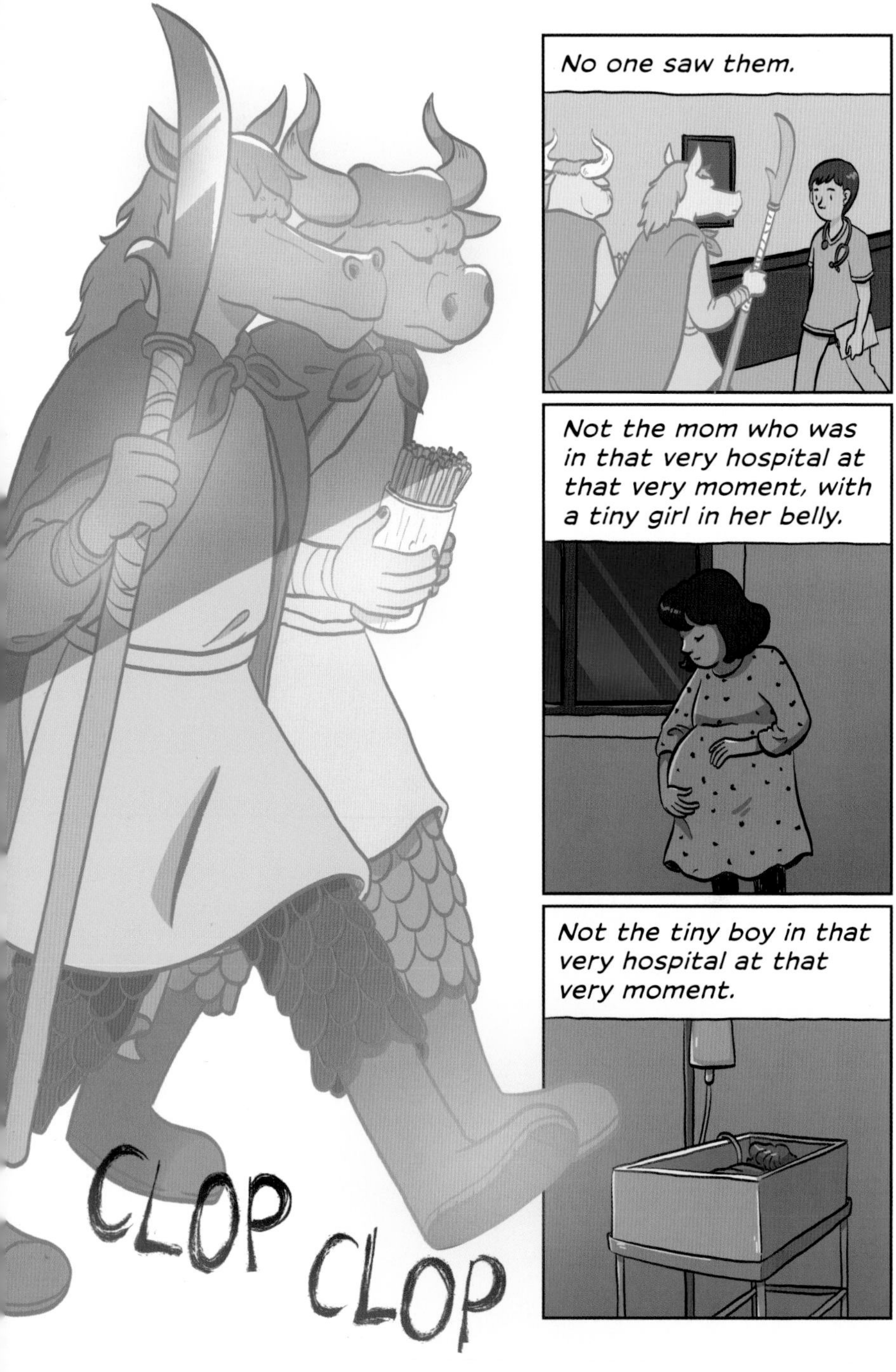
CLOP CLOP
No one saw them.
Not the mom who was in that very hospital at that very moment, with a tiny girl in her belly.
Not the tiny boy in that very hospital at that very moment.

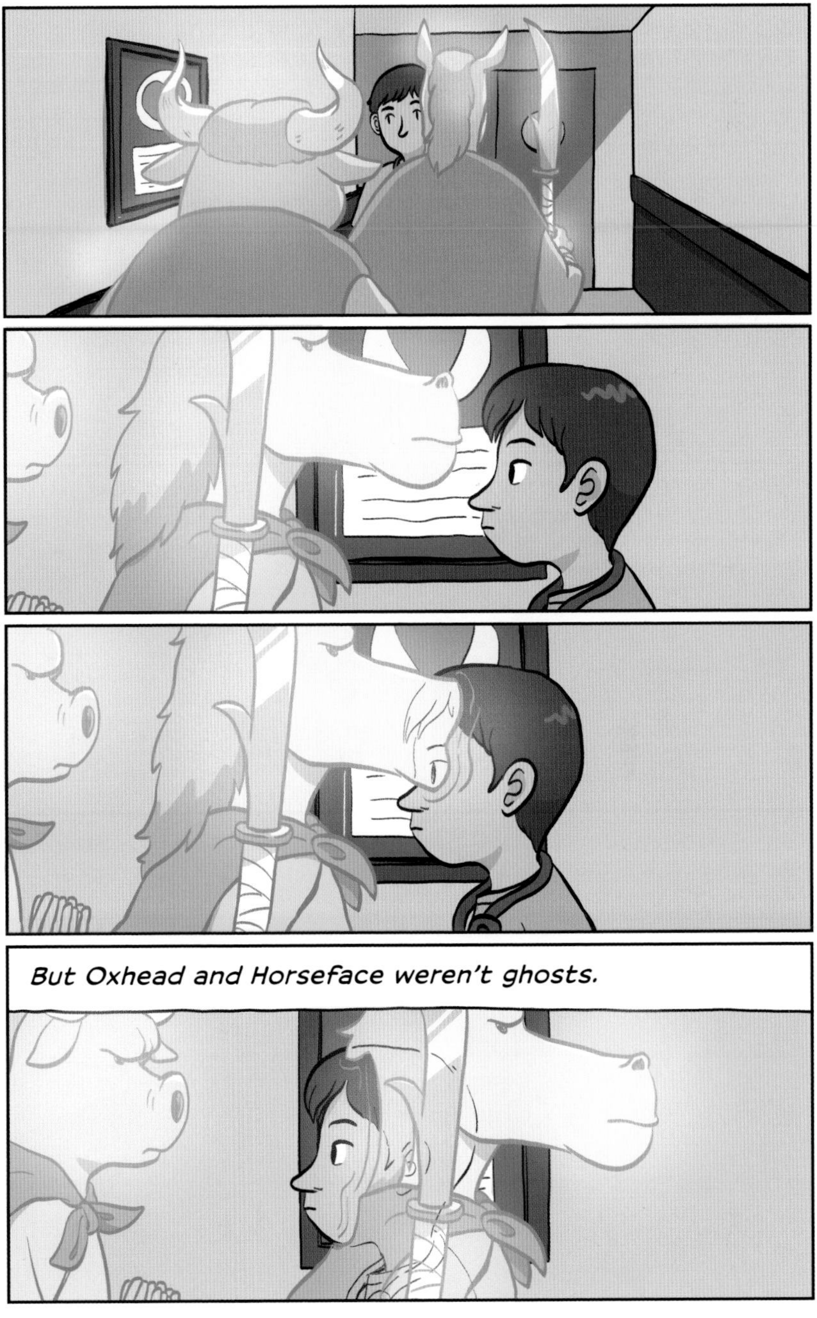
But Oxhead and Horseface weren't ghosts.

Many years ago, at the end of their lives, they didn't cross the Bridge at the End from which no ghost returns.

The King of the Underworld had granted them permission to stay behind.

They were transformed into something not quite human.

And today, the King had given them a task.

SHAKE   SHAKE

SHAKE

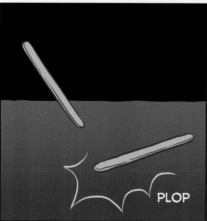

PLOP

Two must die.

4

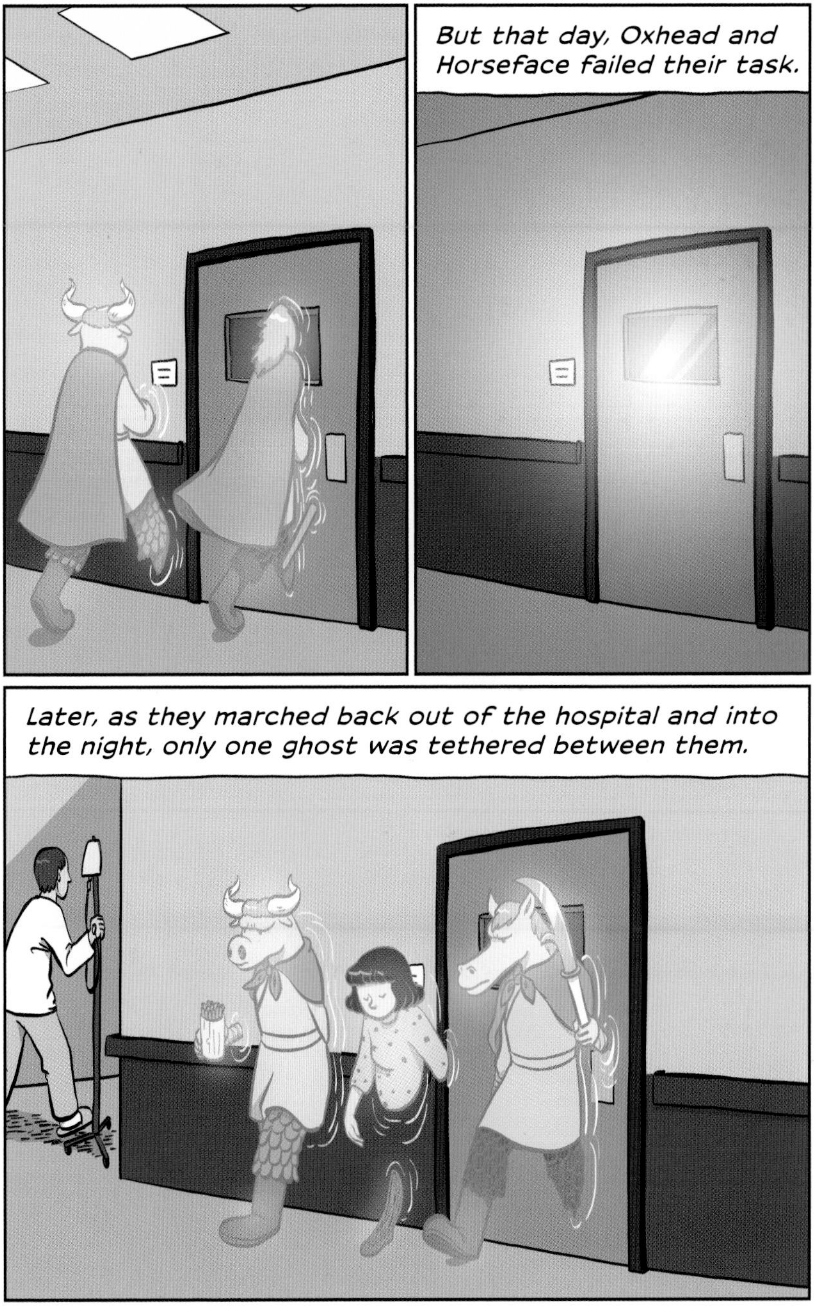
But that day, Oxhead and Horseface failed their task.
Later, as they marched back out of the hospital and into the night, only one ghost was tethered between them.

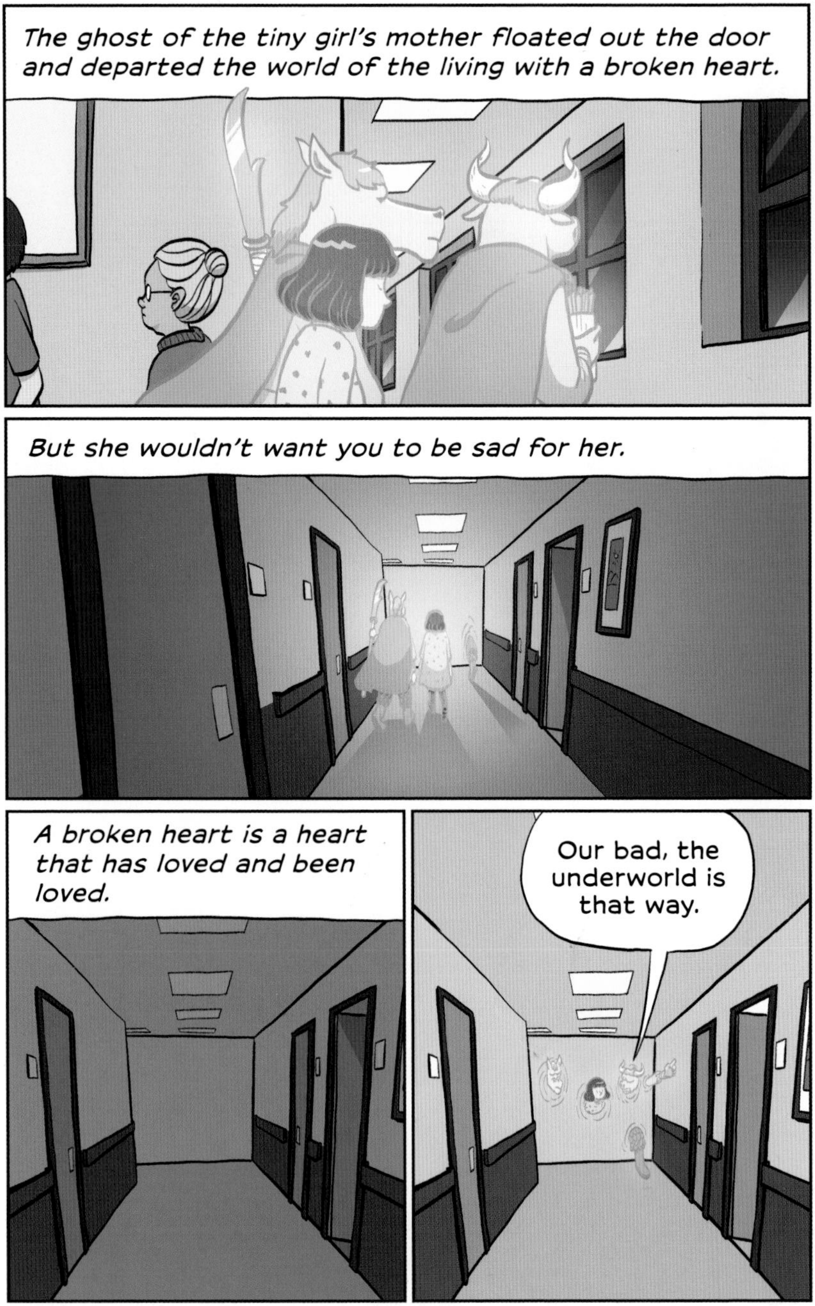

The ghost of the tiny girl's mother floated out the door and departed the world of the living with a broken heart.
But she wouldn't want you to be sad for her.
A broken heart is a heart that has loved and been loved.
Our bad, the underworld is that way.

*Twelve years ago,
the girl lived.*

*The boy
lived.*

One should have died.

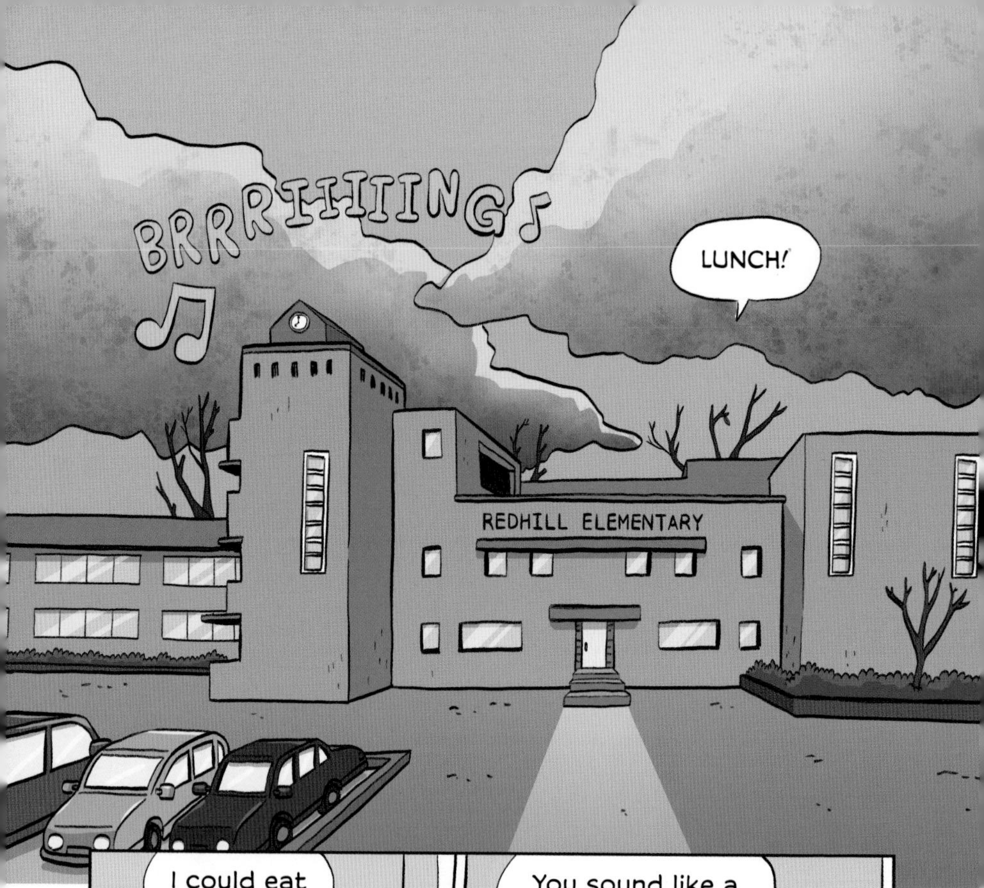
BRRRIIIIING
LUNCH!

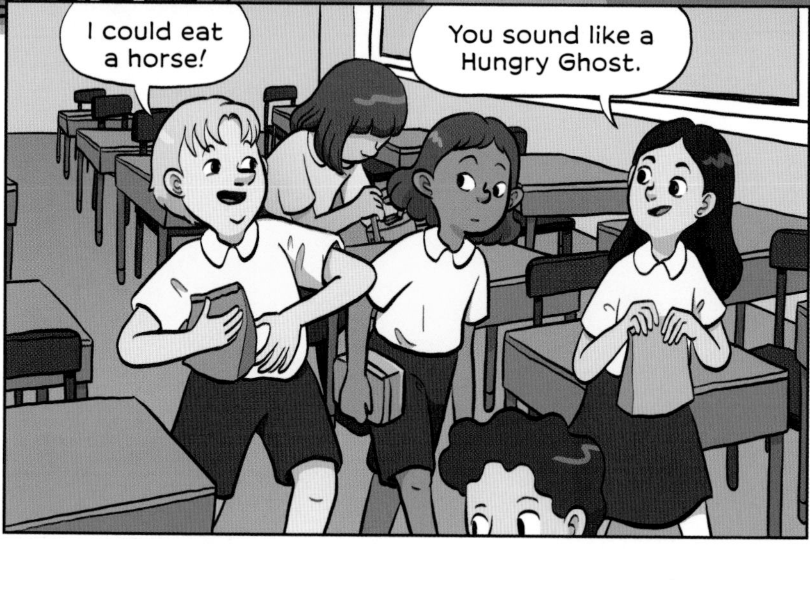
I could eat a horse!
You sound like a Hungry Ghost.

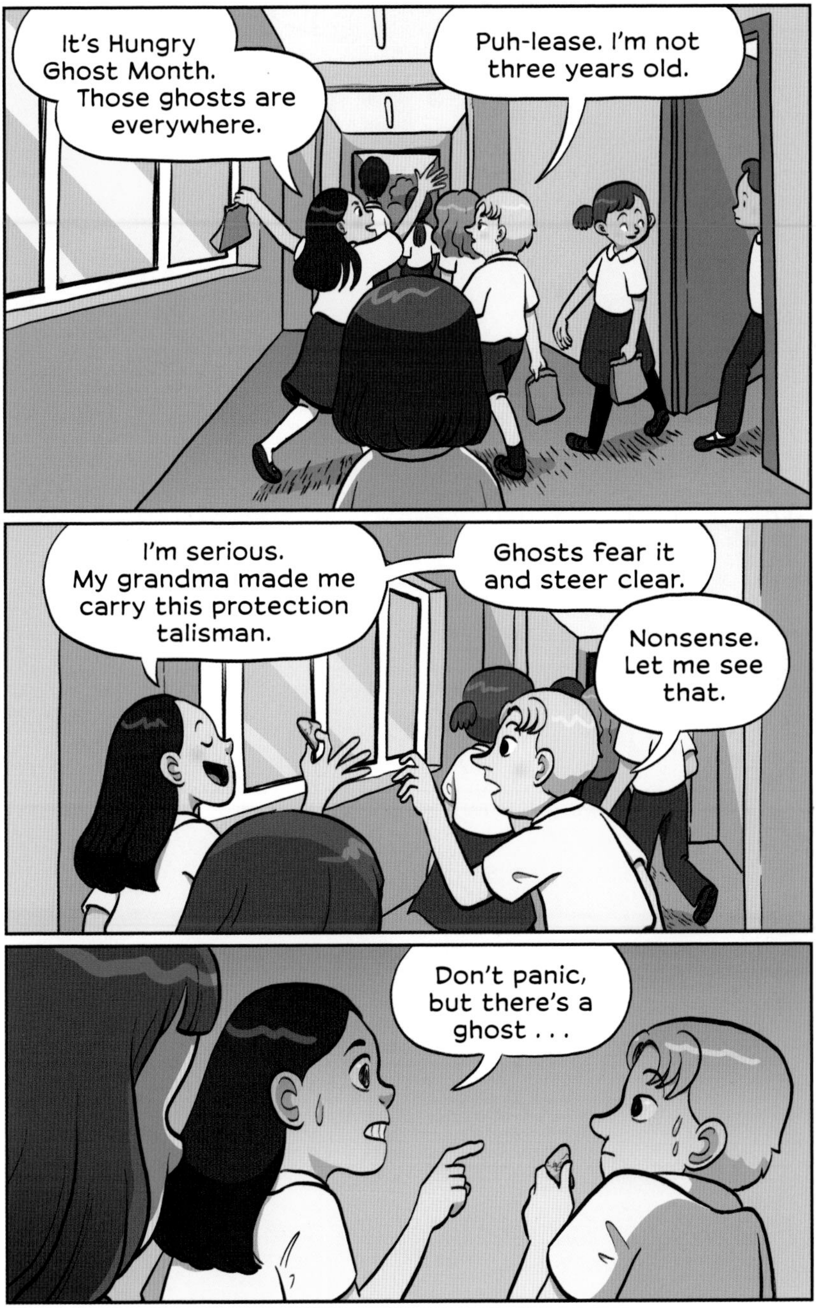
It's Hungry Ghost Month. Those ghosts are everywhere.
Puh-lease. I'm not three years old.
I'm serious. My grandma made me carry this protection talisman.
Ghosts fear it and steer clear.
Nonsense. Let me see that.
Don't panic, but there's a ghost . . .

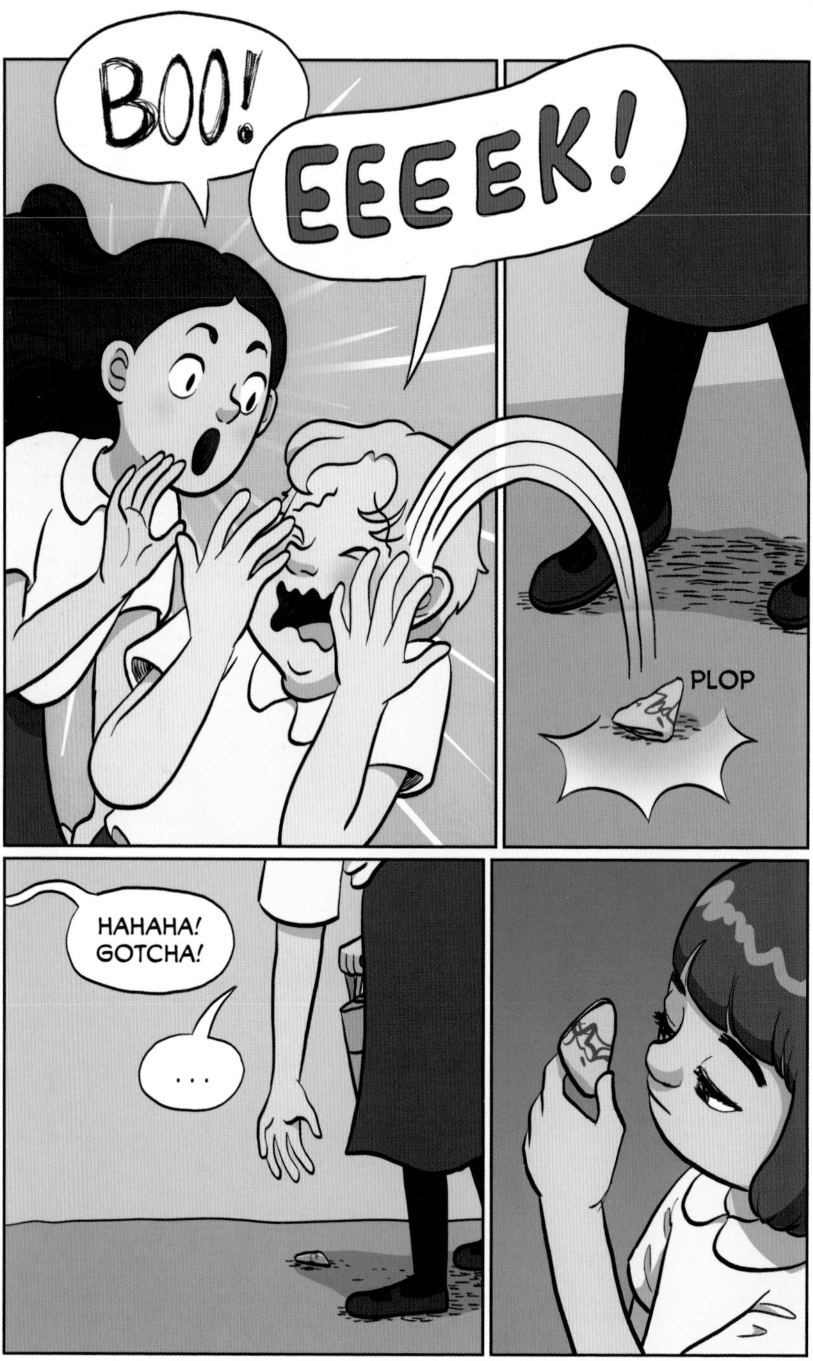
BOO!
EEEEK!
PLOP
HAHAHA! GOTCHA!
. . .

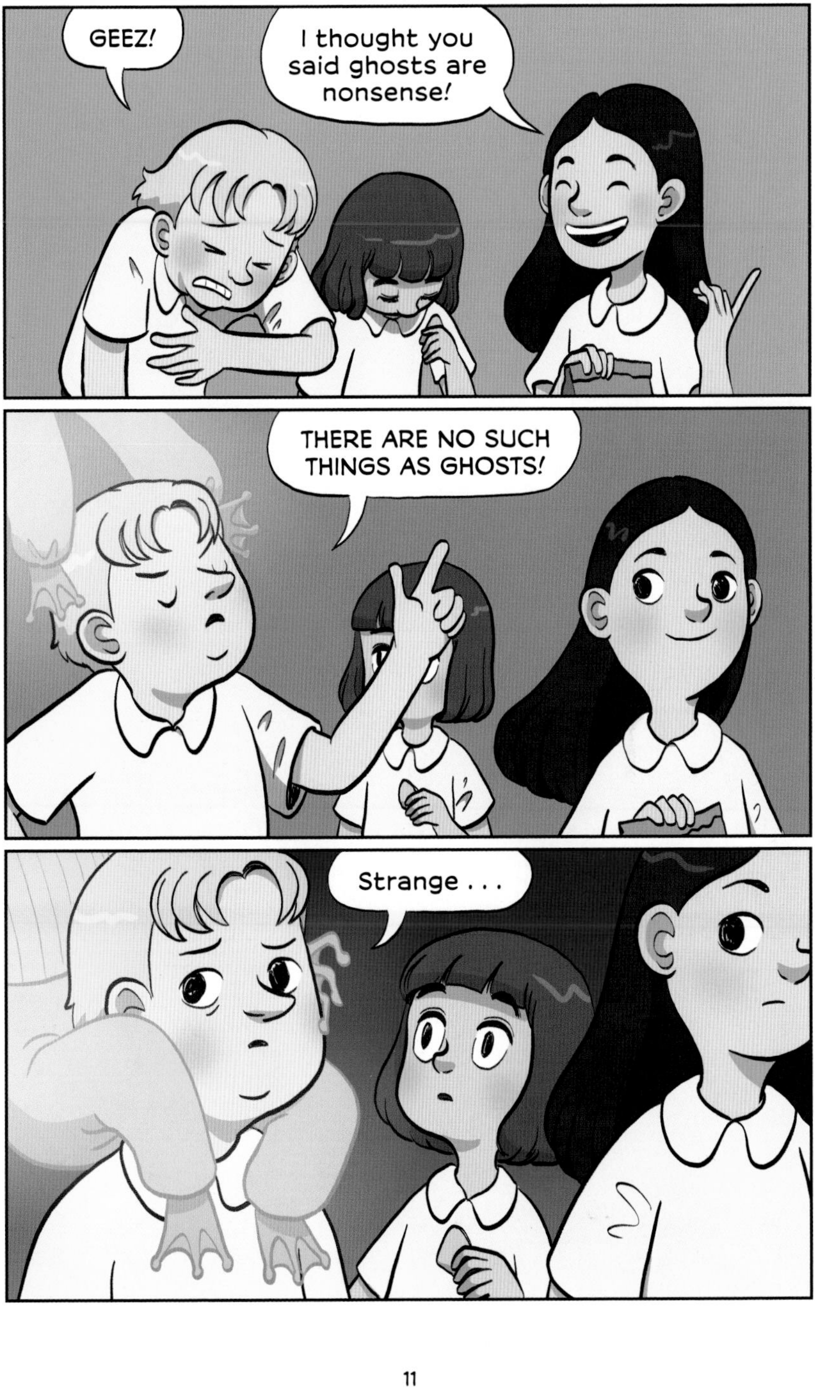
GEEZ!
I thought you said ghosts are nonsense!
THERE ARE NO SUCH THINGS AS GHOSTS!
Strange . . .

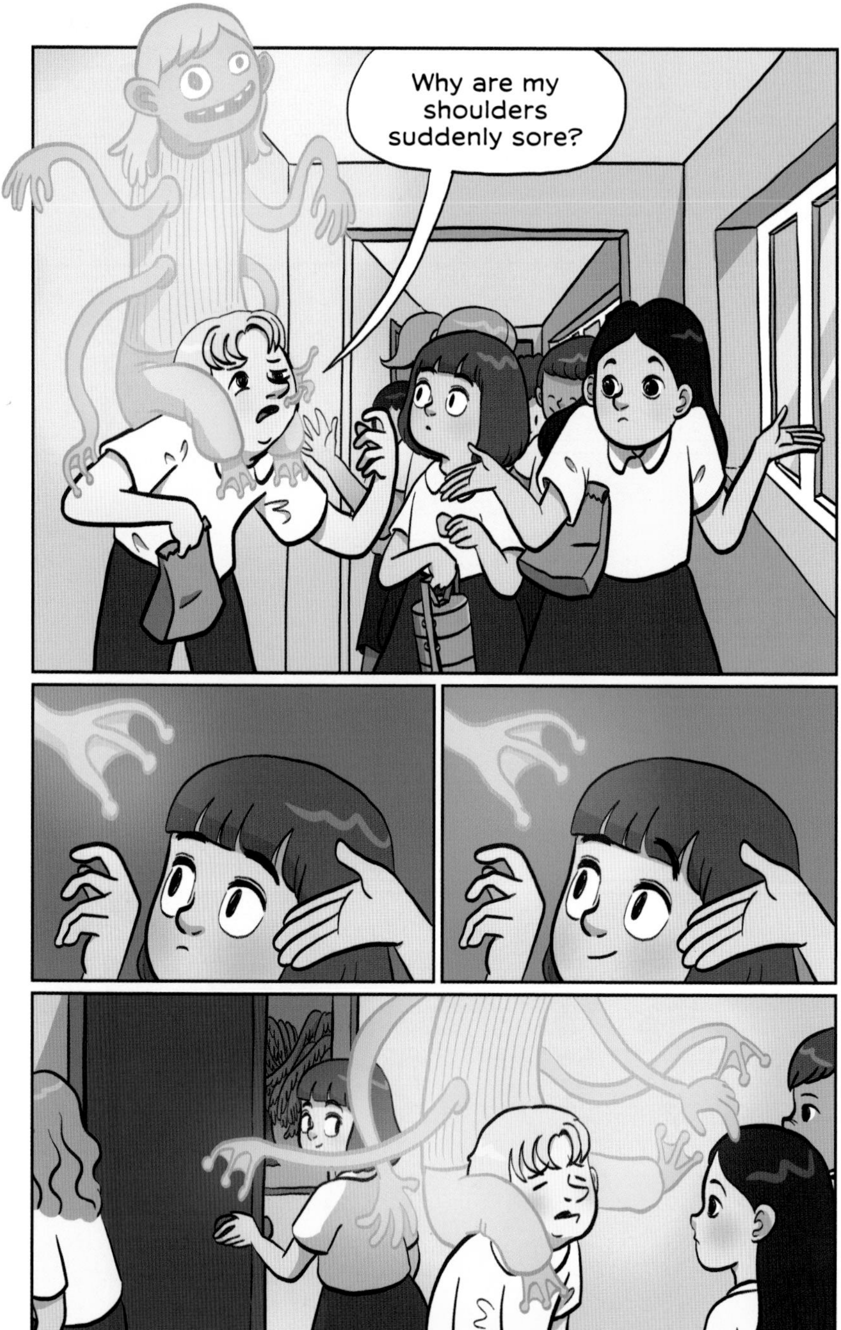
Why are my shoulders suddenly sore?

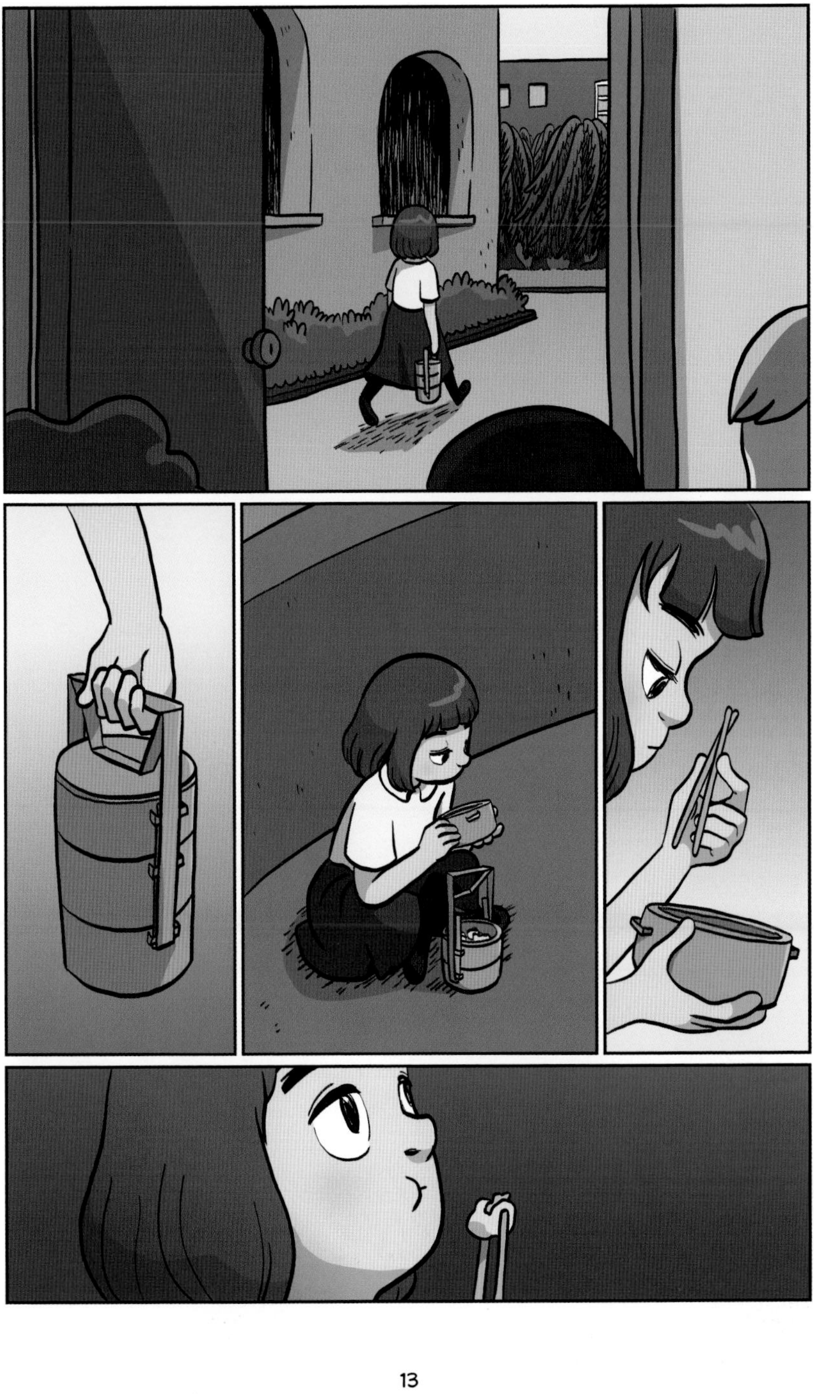

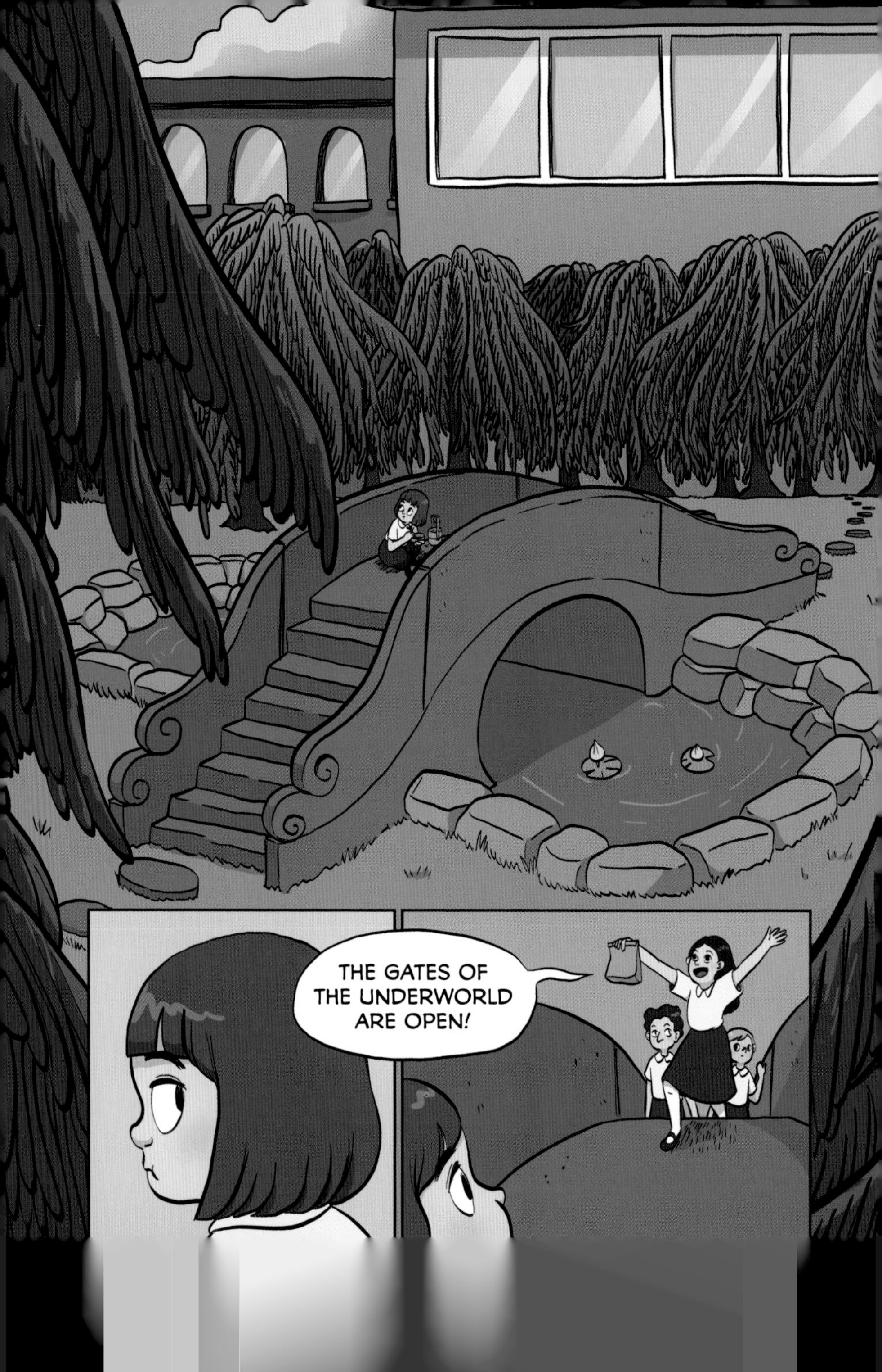
THE GATES OF THE UNDERWORLD ARE OPEN!

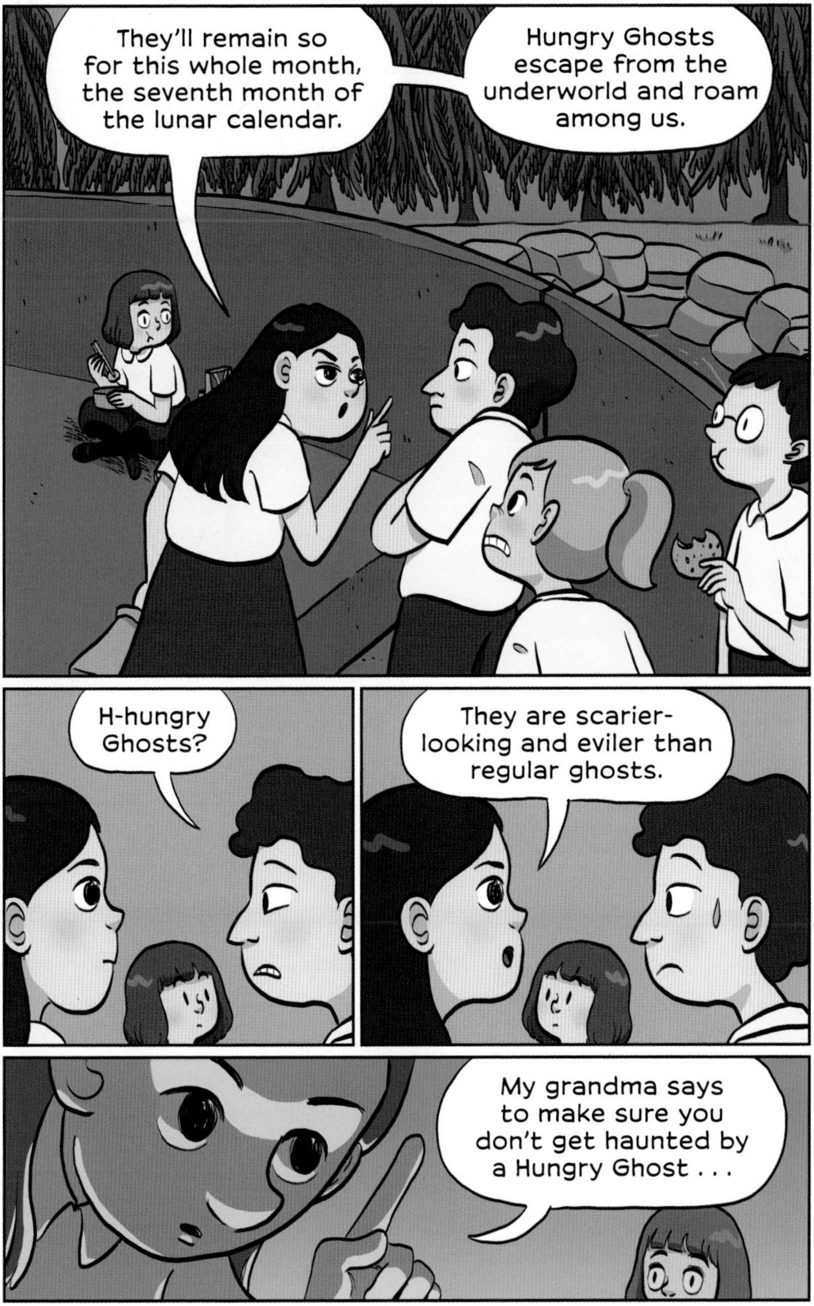
They'll remain so for this whole month, the seventh month of the lunar calendar.
Hungry Ghosts escape from the underworld and roam among us.
H-hungry Ghosts?
They are scarier-looking and eviler than regular ghosts.
My grandma says to make sure you don't get haunted by a Hungry Ghost . . .

DO NOT wear red.

DO NOT hang around
outside after dark.

DO NOT leave
doors open.

DO NOT make loud
noises or ring bells.

Ding-a-
ling!

DO NOT go into
bodies of water.

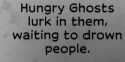

Hungry Ghosts
lurk in them,
waiting to drown
people.

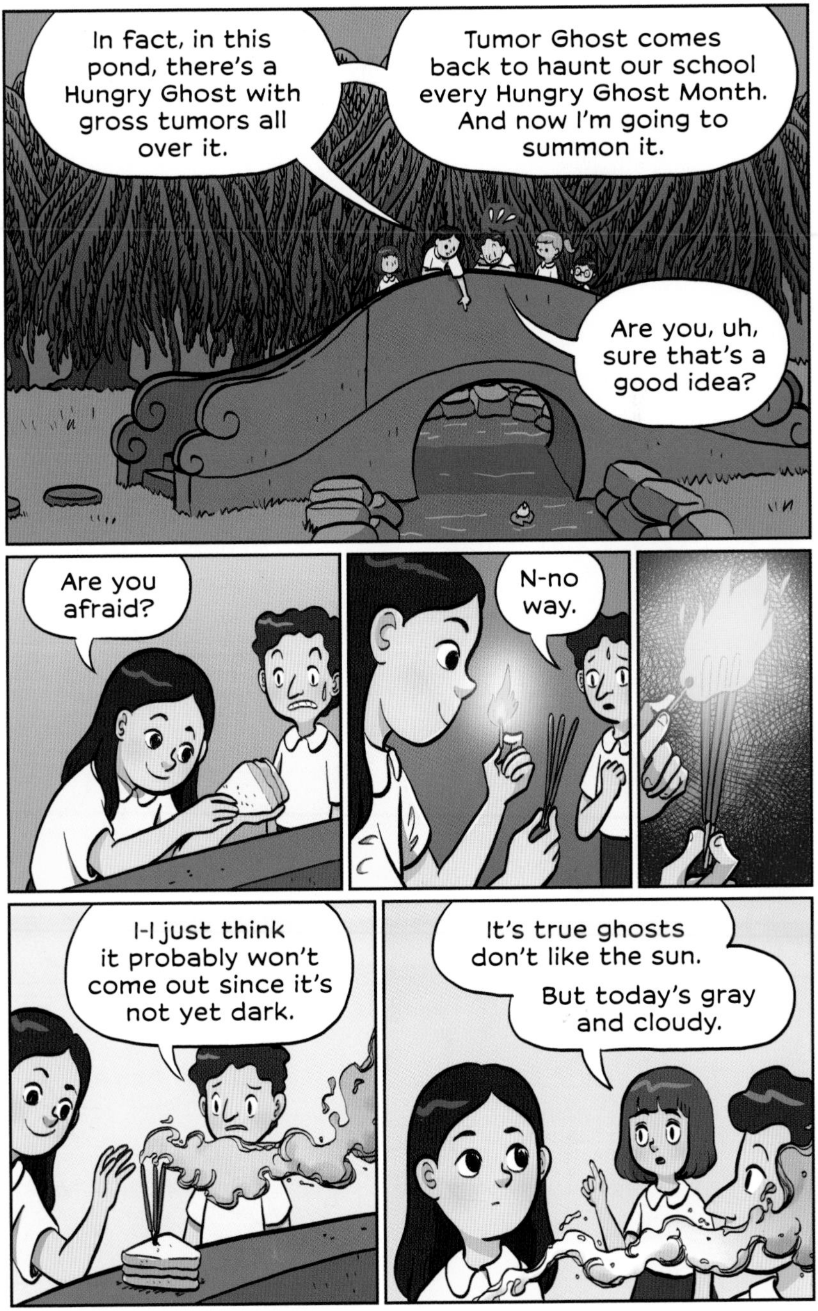
In fact, in this pond, there's a Hungry Ghost with gross tumors all over it.
Tumor Ghost comes back to haunt our school every Hungry Ghost Month. And now I'm going to summon it.
Are you, uh, sure that's a good idea?
Are you afraid?
N-no way.
I-I just think it probably won't come out since it's not yet dark.
It's true ghosts don't like the sun.
But today's gray and cloudy.

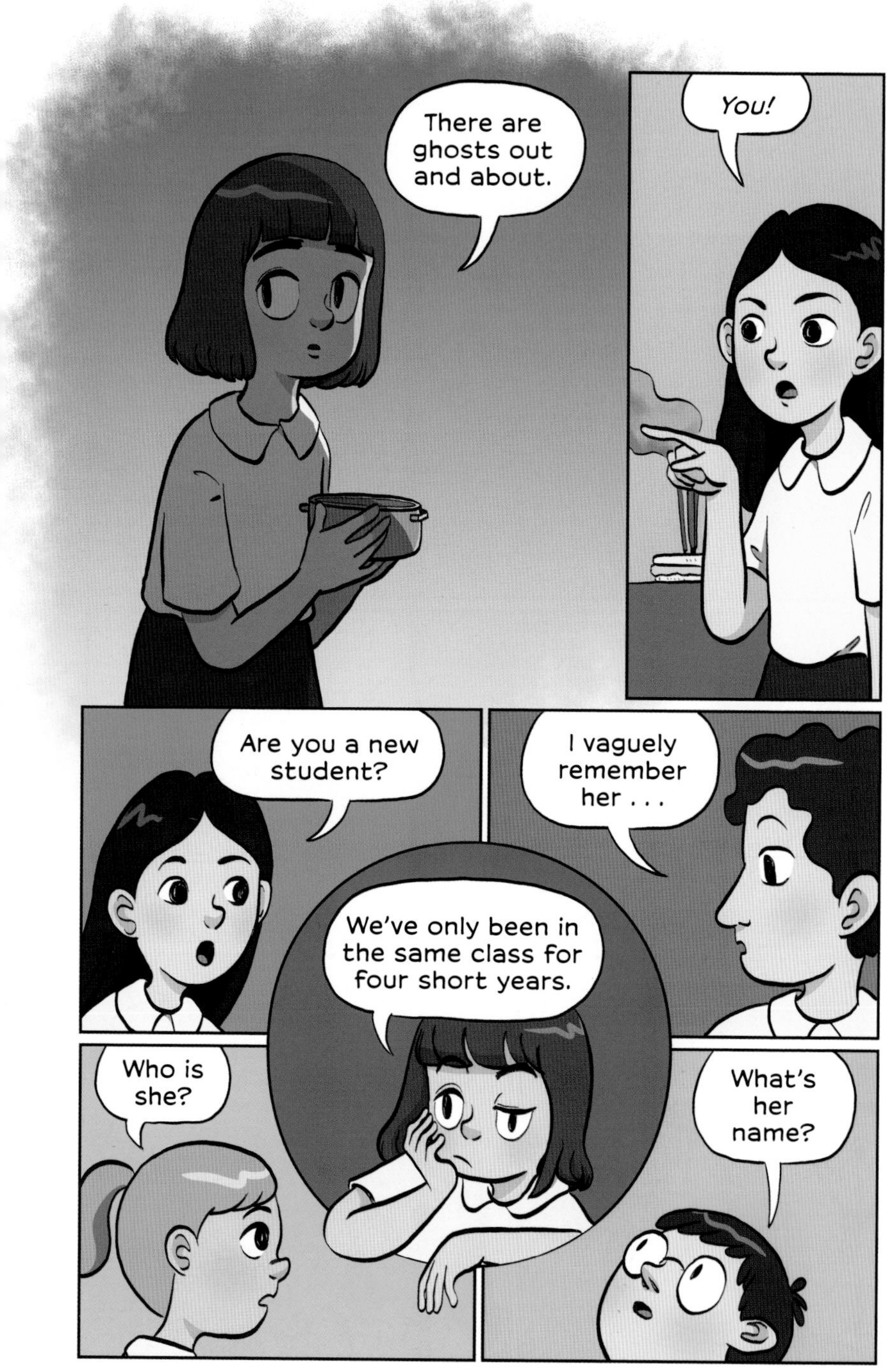
There are ghosts out and about.
You!
Are you a new student?
I vaguely remember her . . .
We've only been in the same class for four short years.
Who is she?
What's her name?

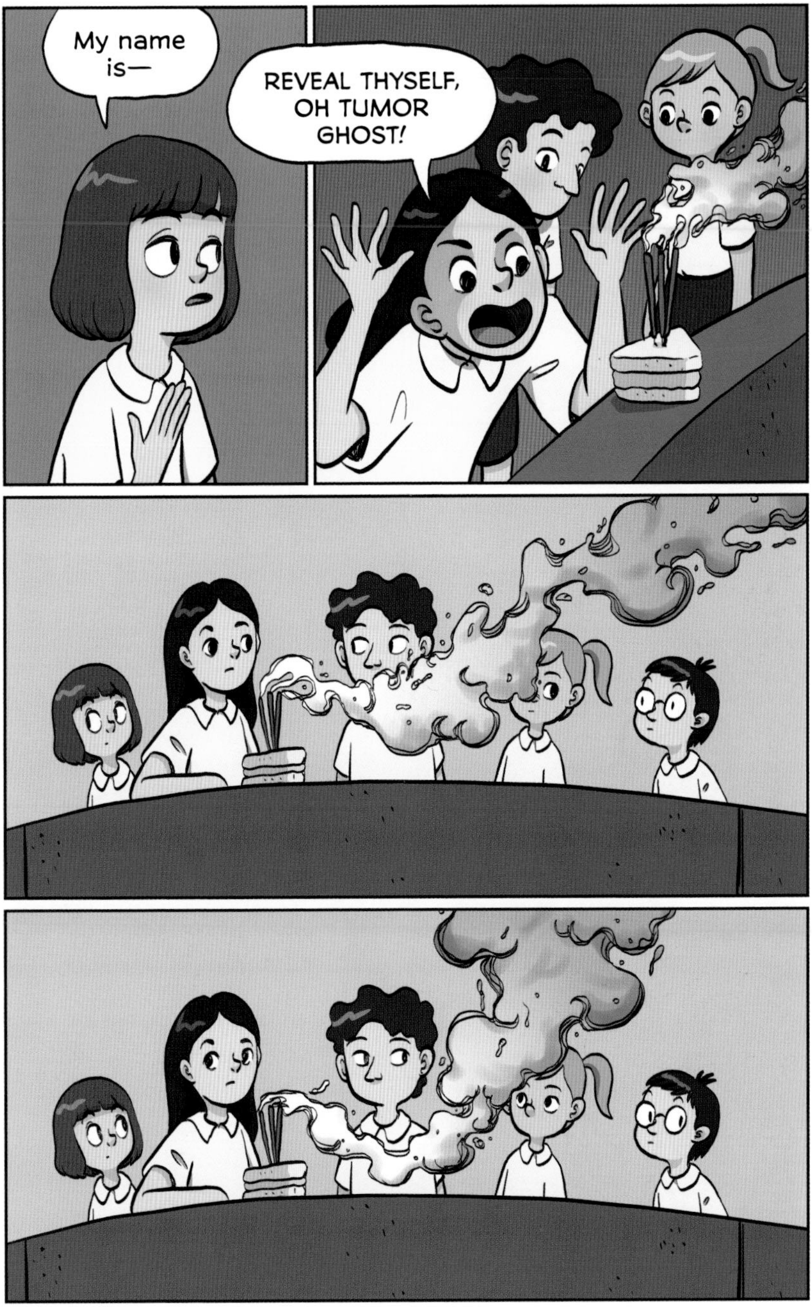
My name is—
REVEAL THYSELF, OH TUMOR GHOST!

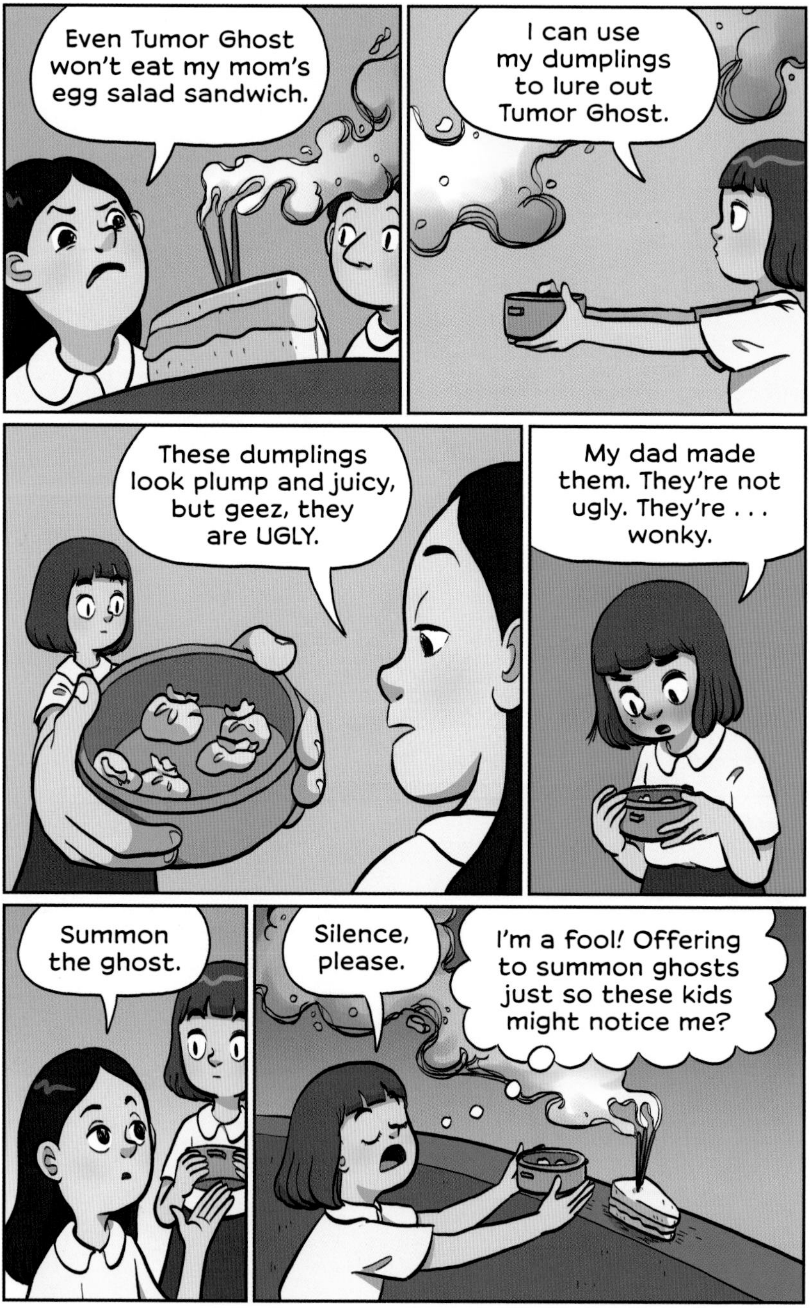
Even Tumor Ghost won't eat my mom's egg salad sandwich.
I can use my dumplings to lure out Tumor Ghost.
These dumplings look plump and juicy, but geez, they are UGLY.
My dad made them. They're not ugly. They're . . . wonky.
Summon the ghost.
Silence, please.
I'm a fool! Offering to summon ghosts just so these kids might notice me?

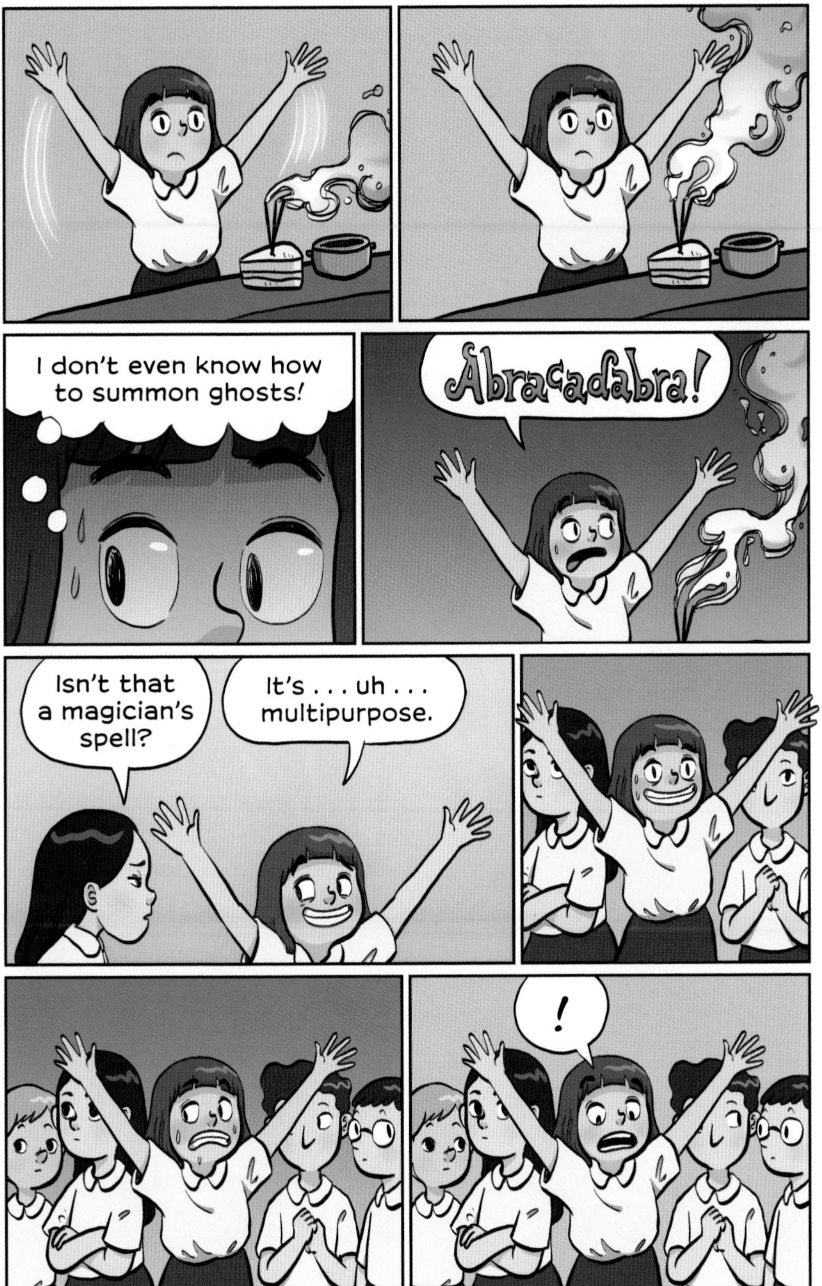
I don't even know how to summon ghosts!
Abracadabra!
Isn't that a magician's spell?
It's . . . uh . . . multipurpose.
!

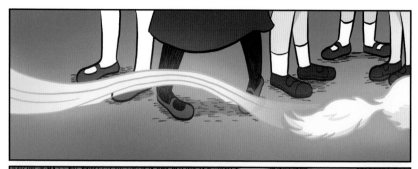

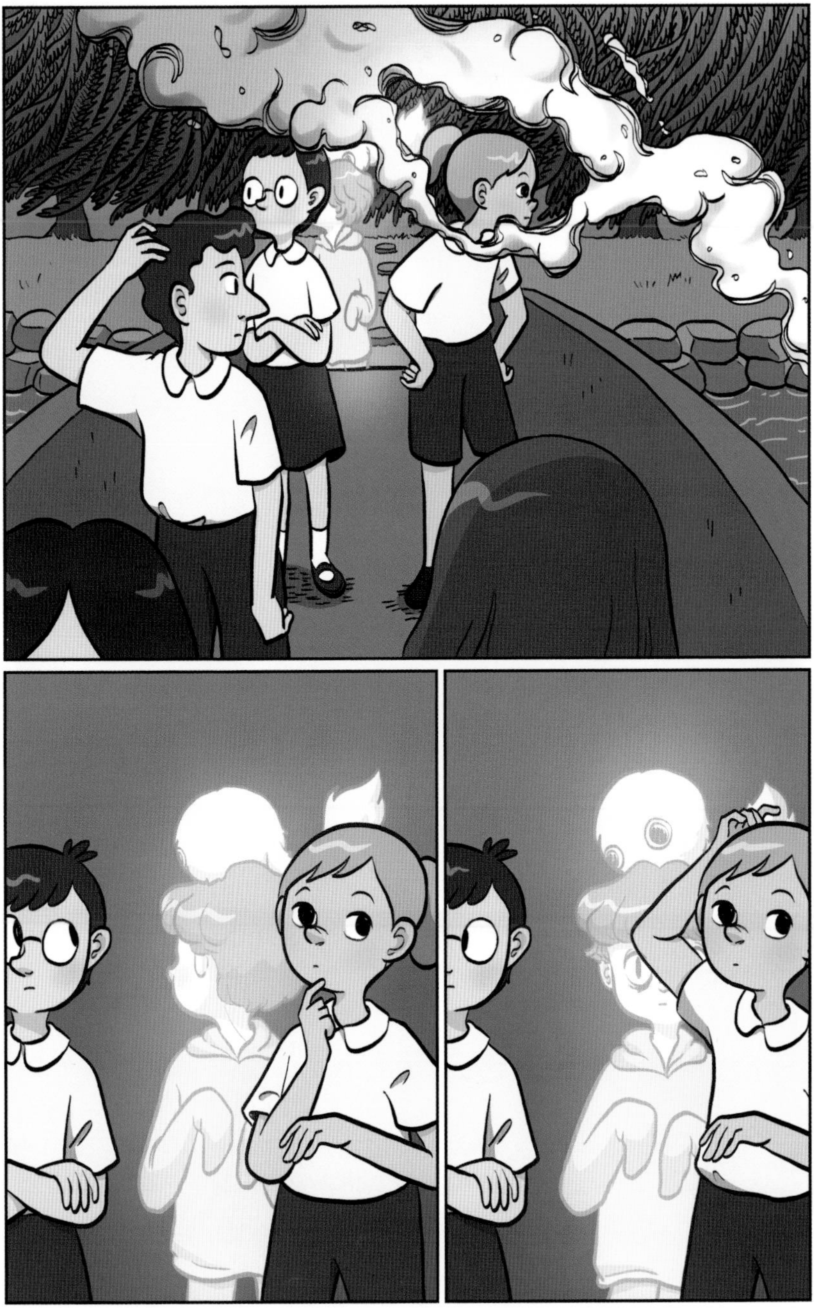

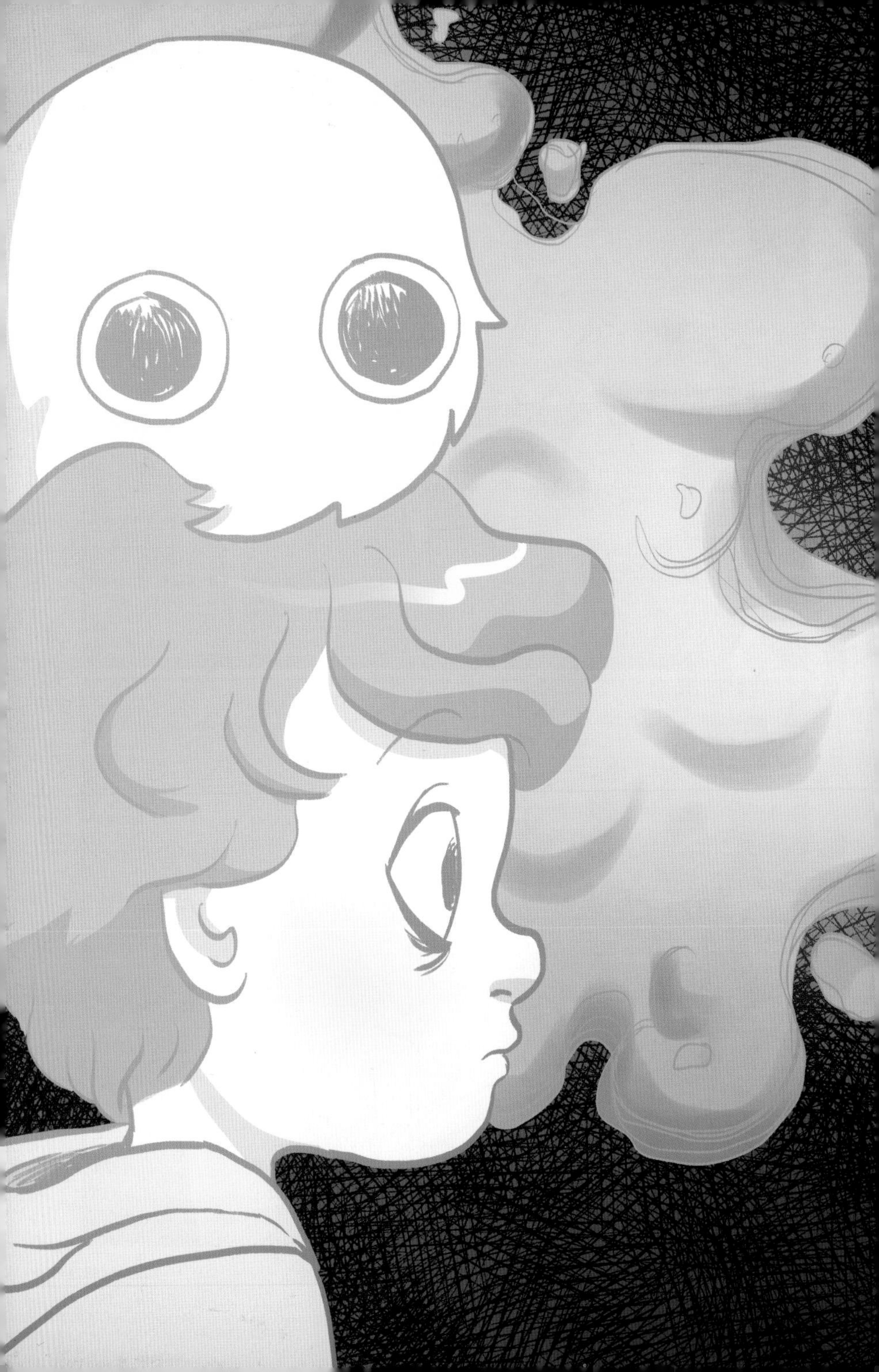

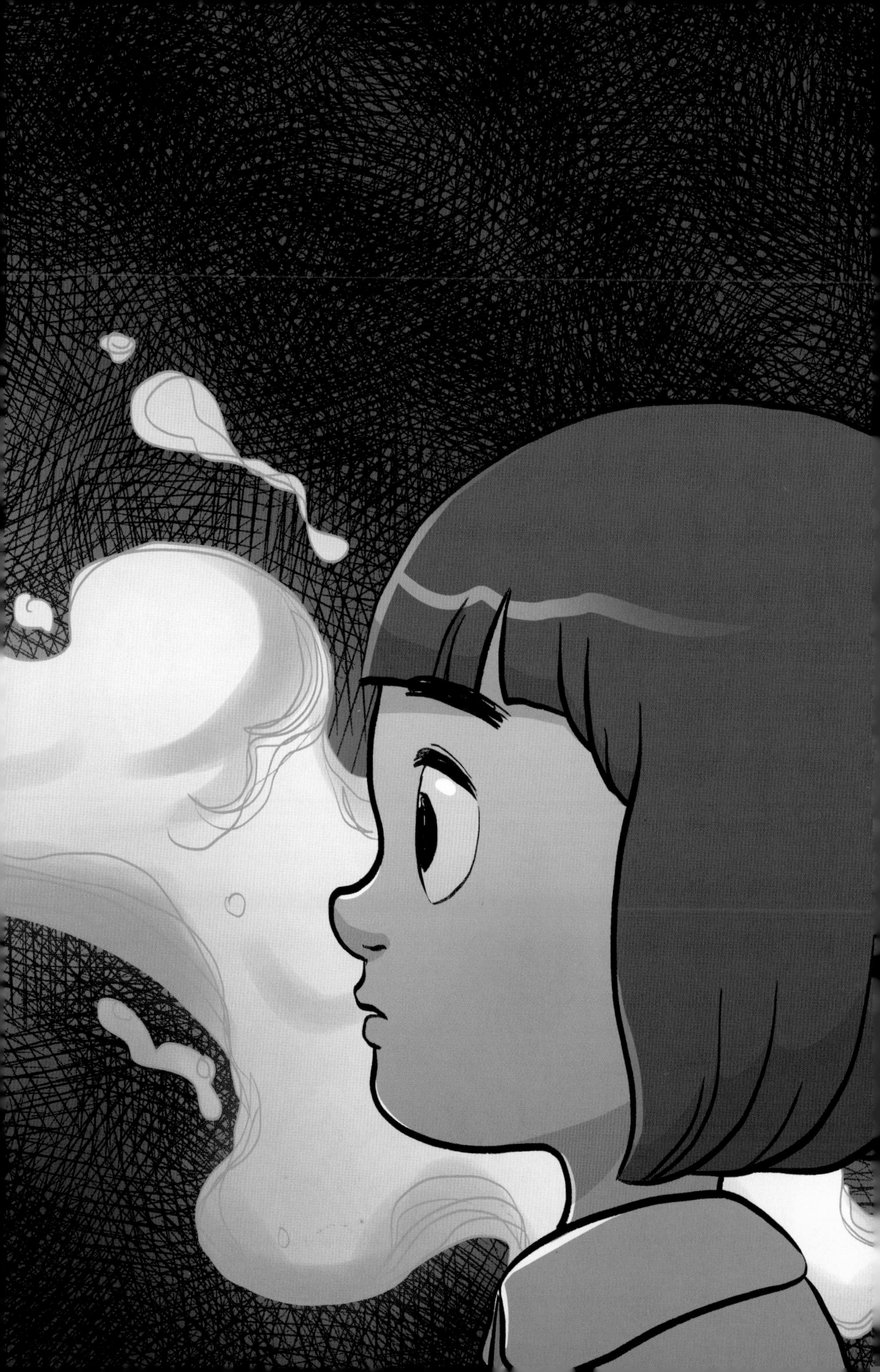

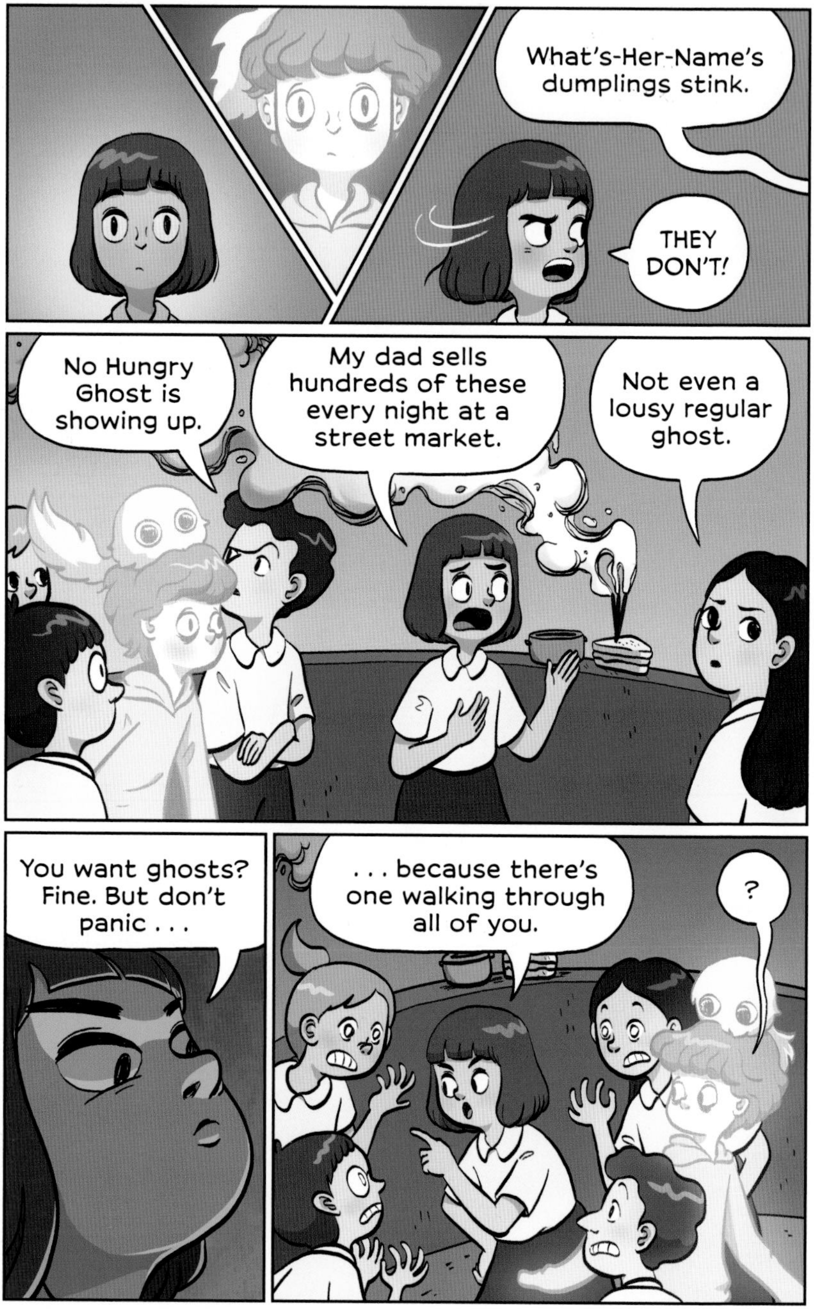
What's-Her-Name's dumplings stink.
THEY DON'T!
No Hungry Ghost is showing up.
My dad sells hundreds of these every night at a street market.
Not even a lousy regular ghost.
You want ghosts? Fine. But don't panic . . .
. . . because there's one walking through all of you.
?

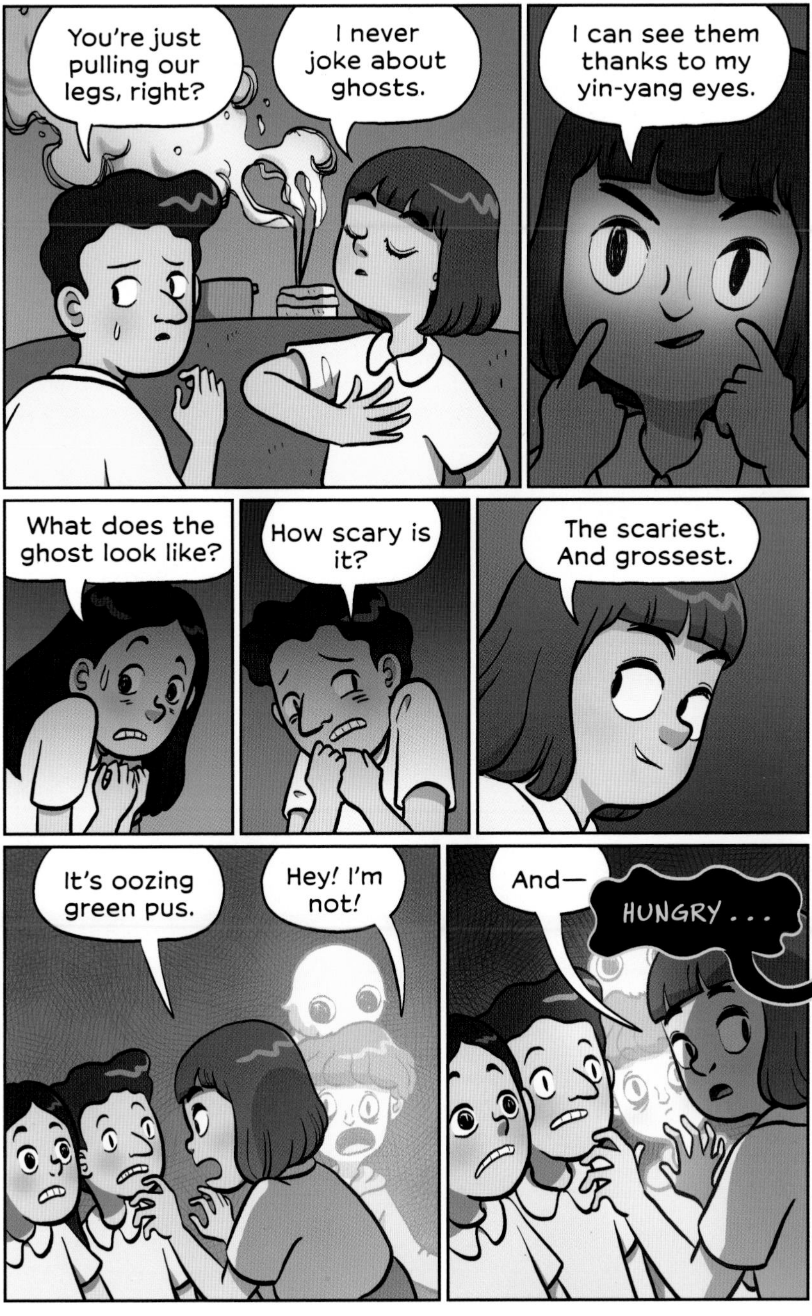
You're just pulling our legs, right?
I never joke about ghosts.
I can see them thanks to my yin-yang eyes.
What does the ghost look like?
How scary is it?
The scariest. And grossest.
It's oozing green pus.
Hey! I'm not!
And—
HUNGRY . . .

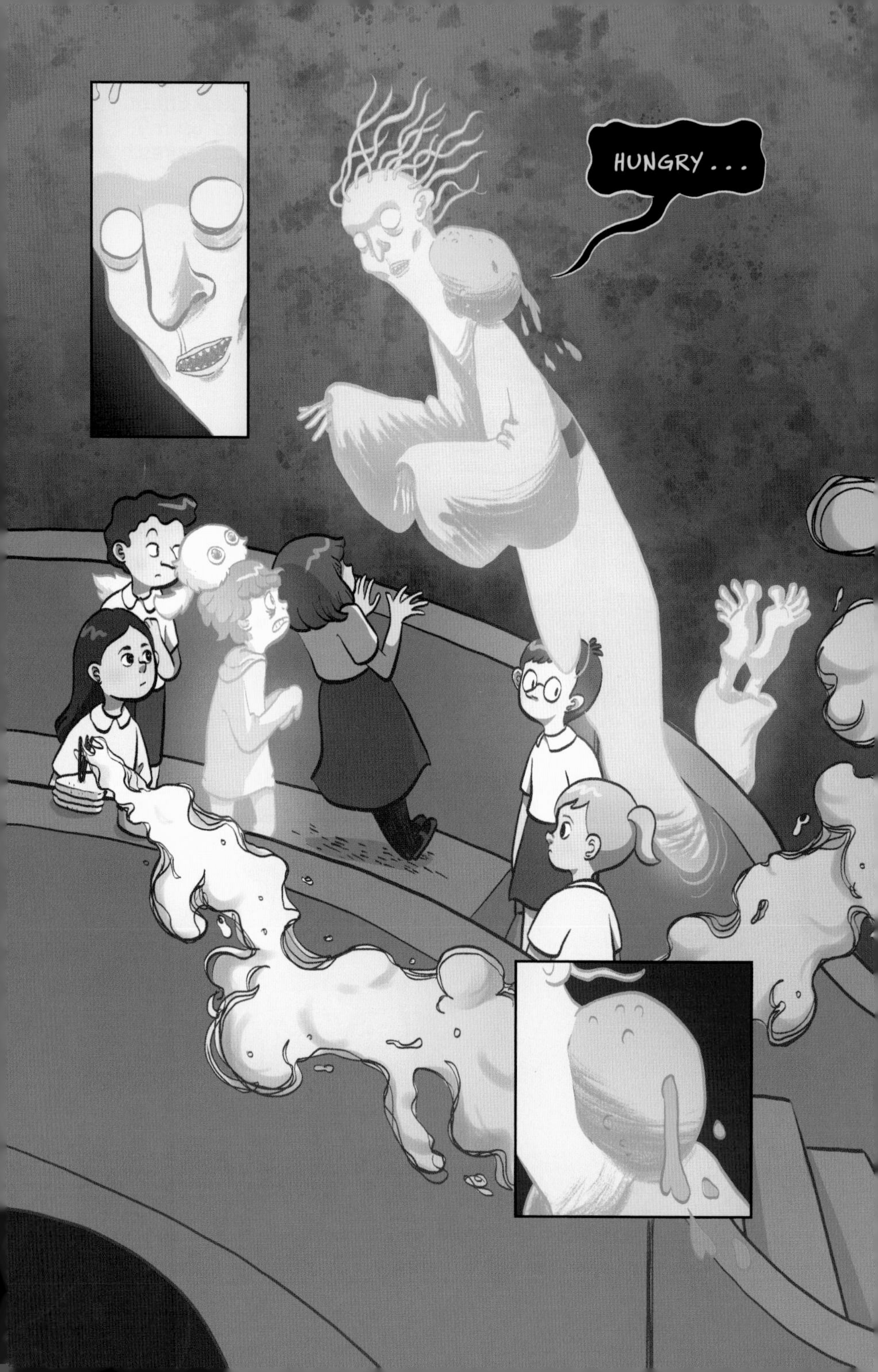
HUNGRY . . .

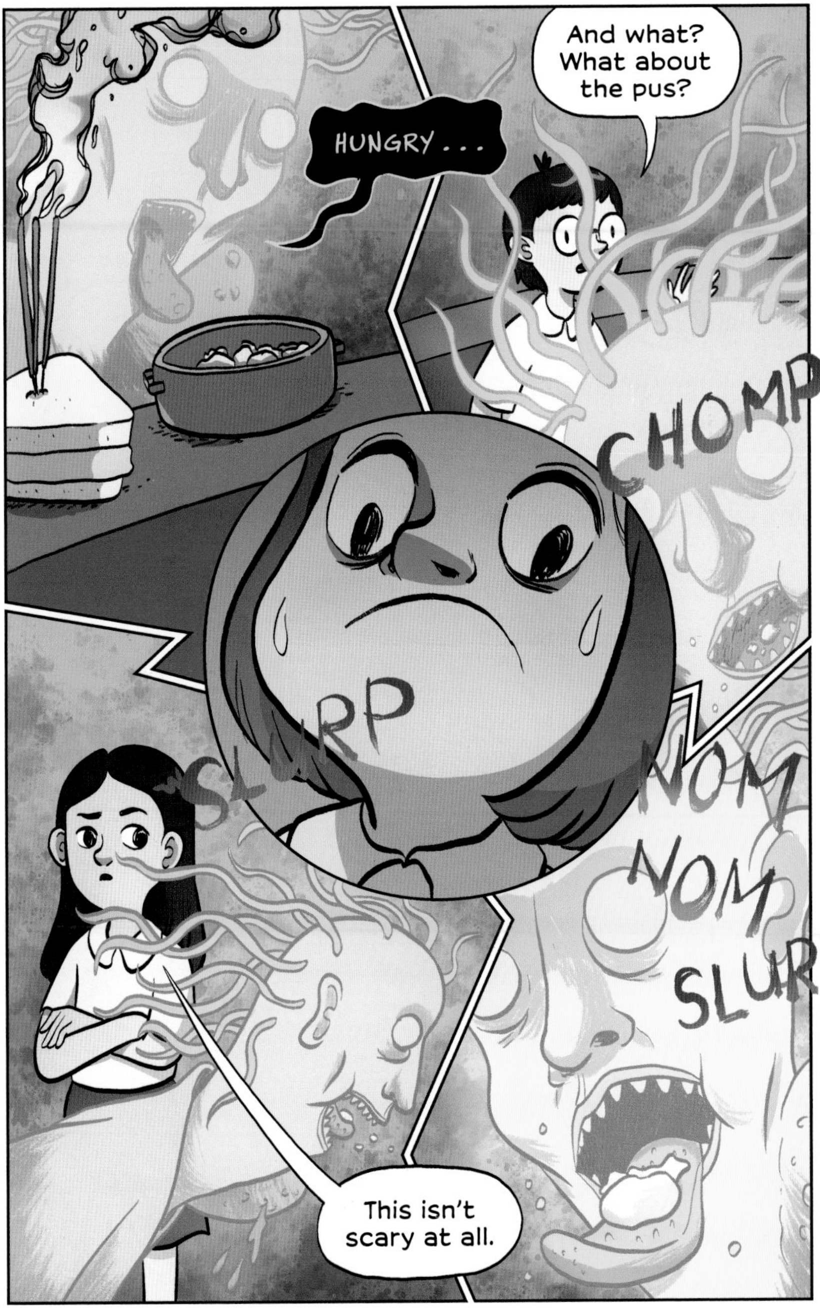
HUNGRY . . .
And what? What about the pus?
CHOMP
SLURP
NOM
NOM
SLURP
This isn't scary at all.

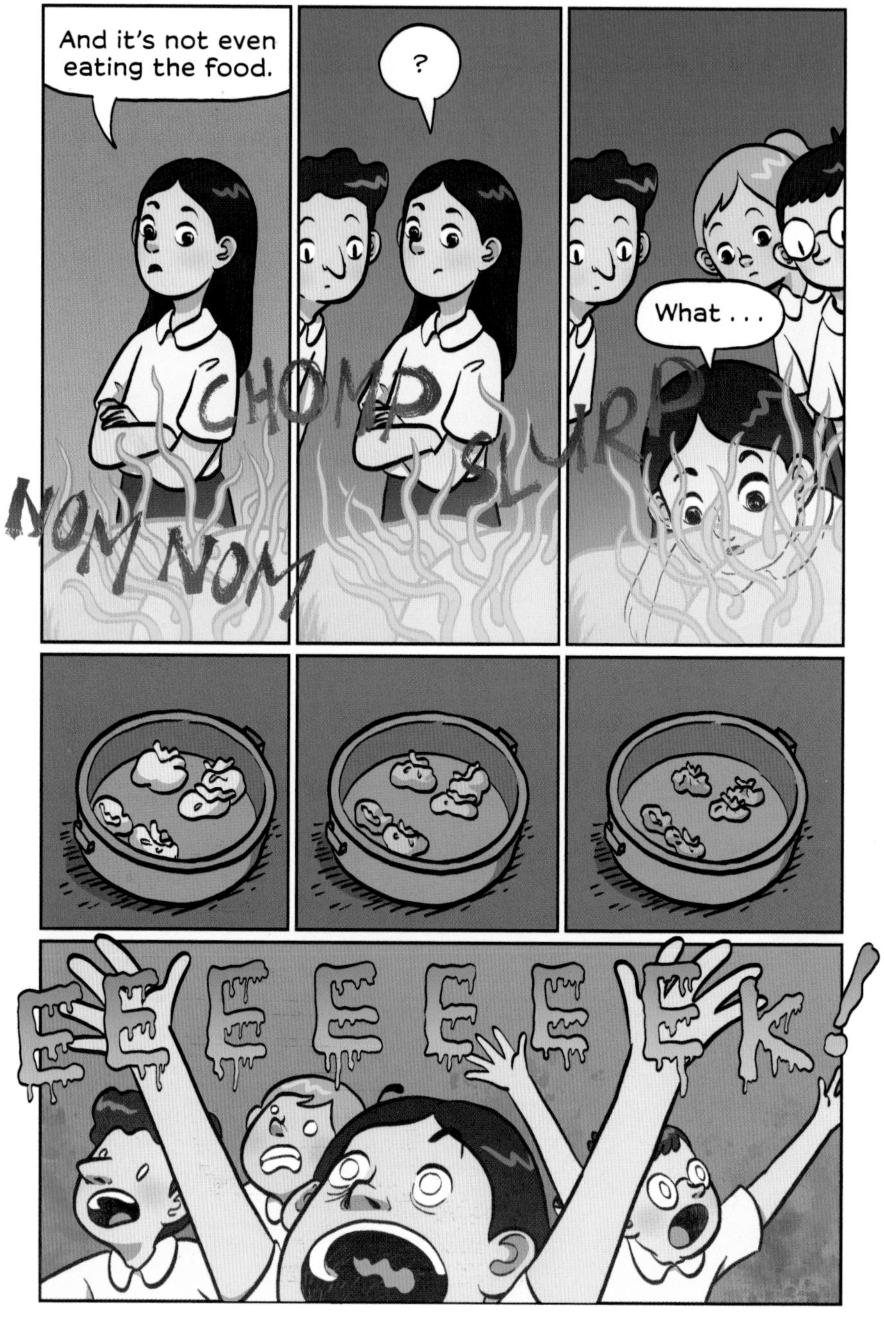
And it's not even eating the food.
?
CHOMP
NOM NOM
SLURP
What . . .
EEEEEEK!

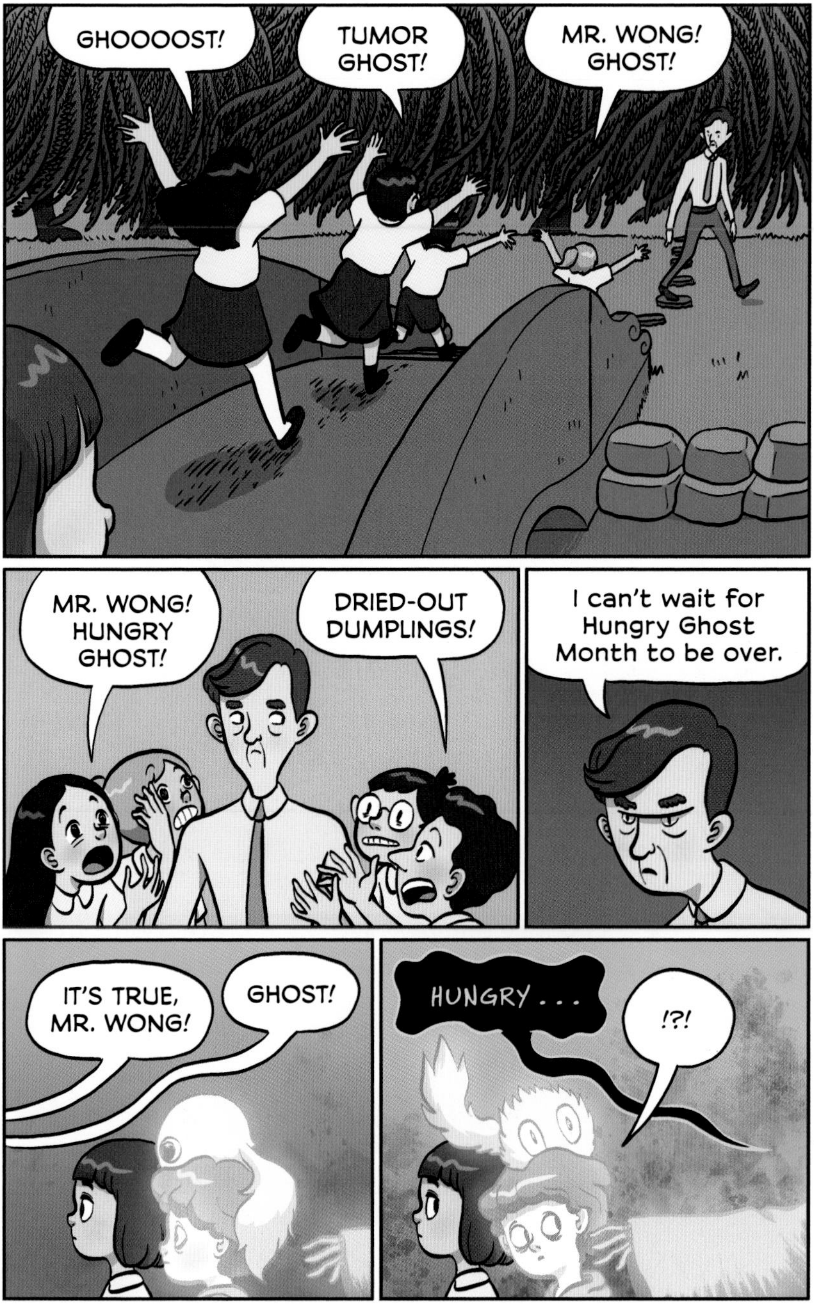
GHOOOOST!
TUMOR GHOST!
MR. WONG! GHOST!
MR. WONG! HUNGRY GHOST!
DRIED-OUT DUMPLINGS!
I can't wait for Hungry Ghost Month to be over.
IT'S TRUE, MR. WONG!
GHOST!
HUNGRY . . .
!?!

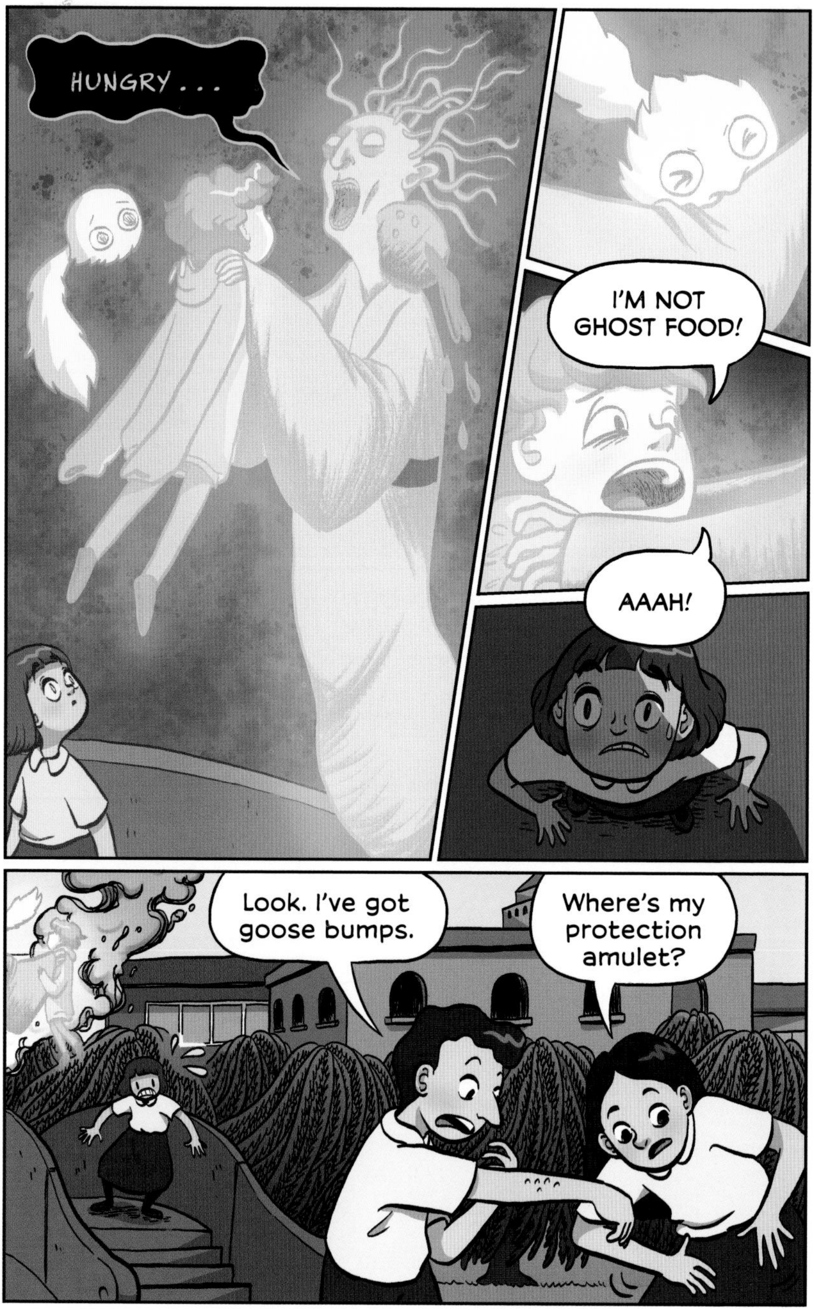
HUNGRY . . .
I'M NOT GHOST FOOD!
AAAH!
Look. I've got goose bumps.
Where's my protection amulet?

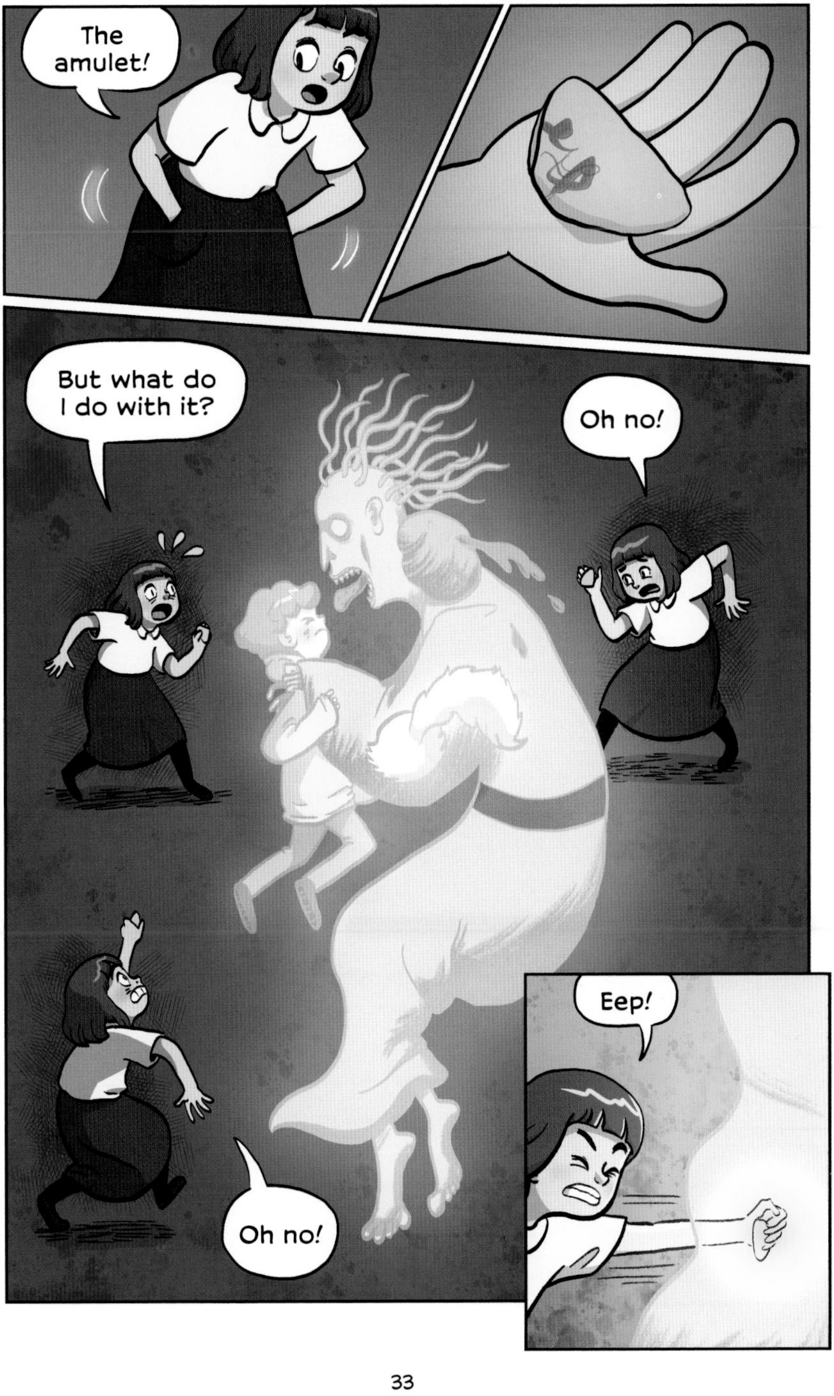
The amulet!
But what do I do with it?
Oh no!
Oh no!
Eep!

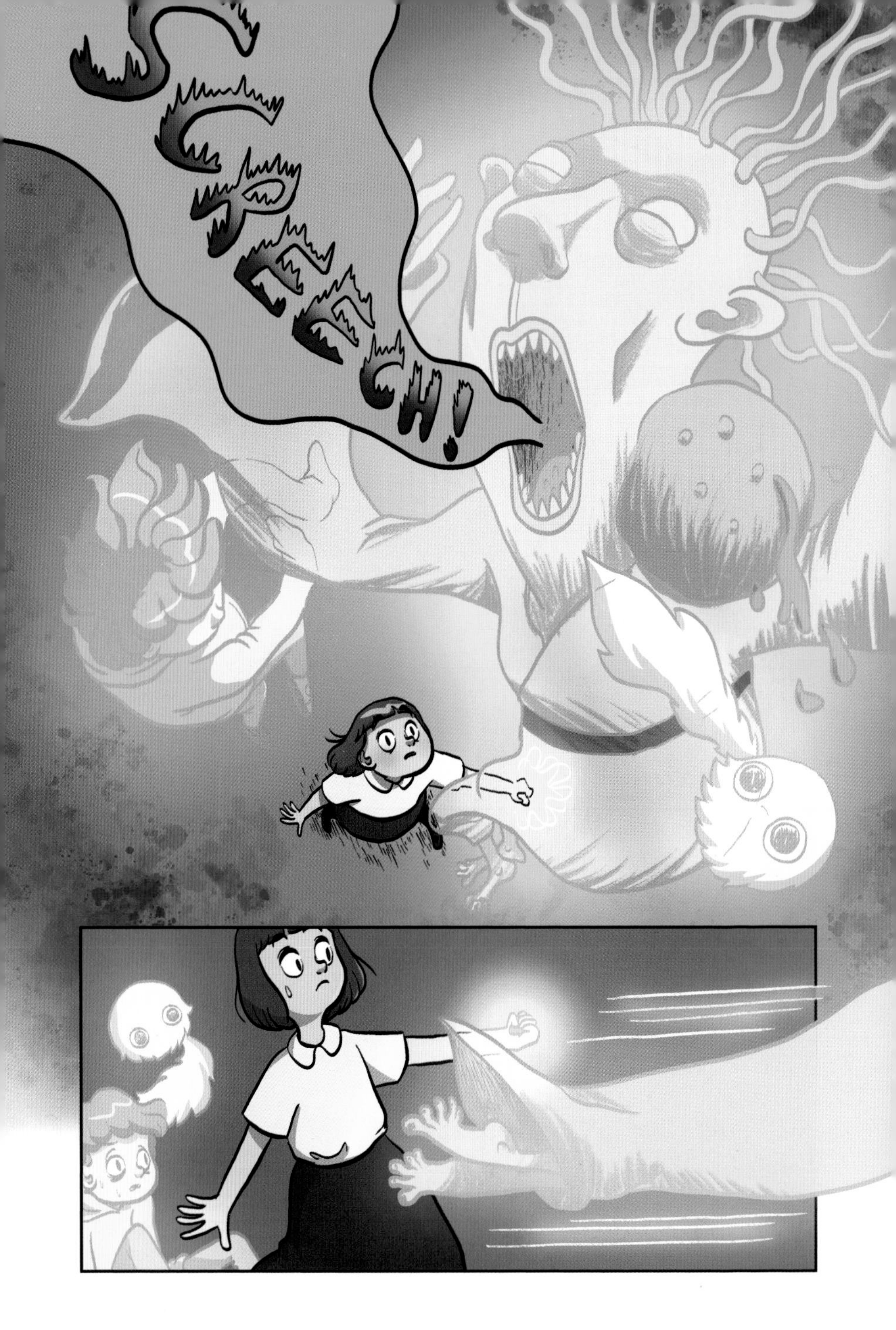
SCREECH!

Whoa.

CLAP CLAP CLAP

What a convincing performance. Do you not know our school has a strict policy against spreading ghost stories?

CLAP

CLAP

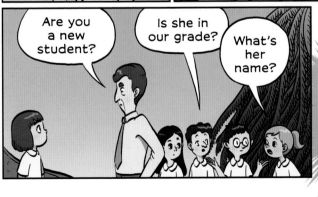

Are you a new student?

Is she in our grade?

What's her name?

Oh, come on!

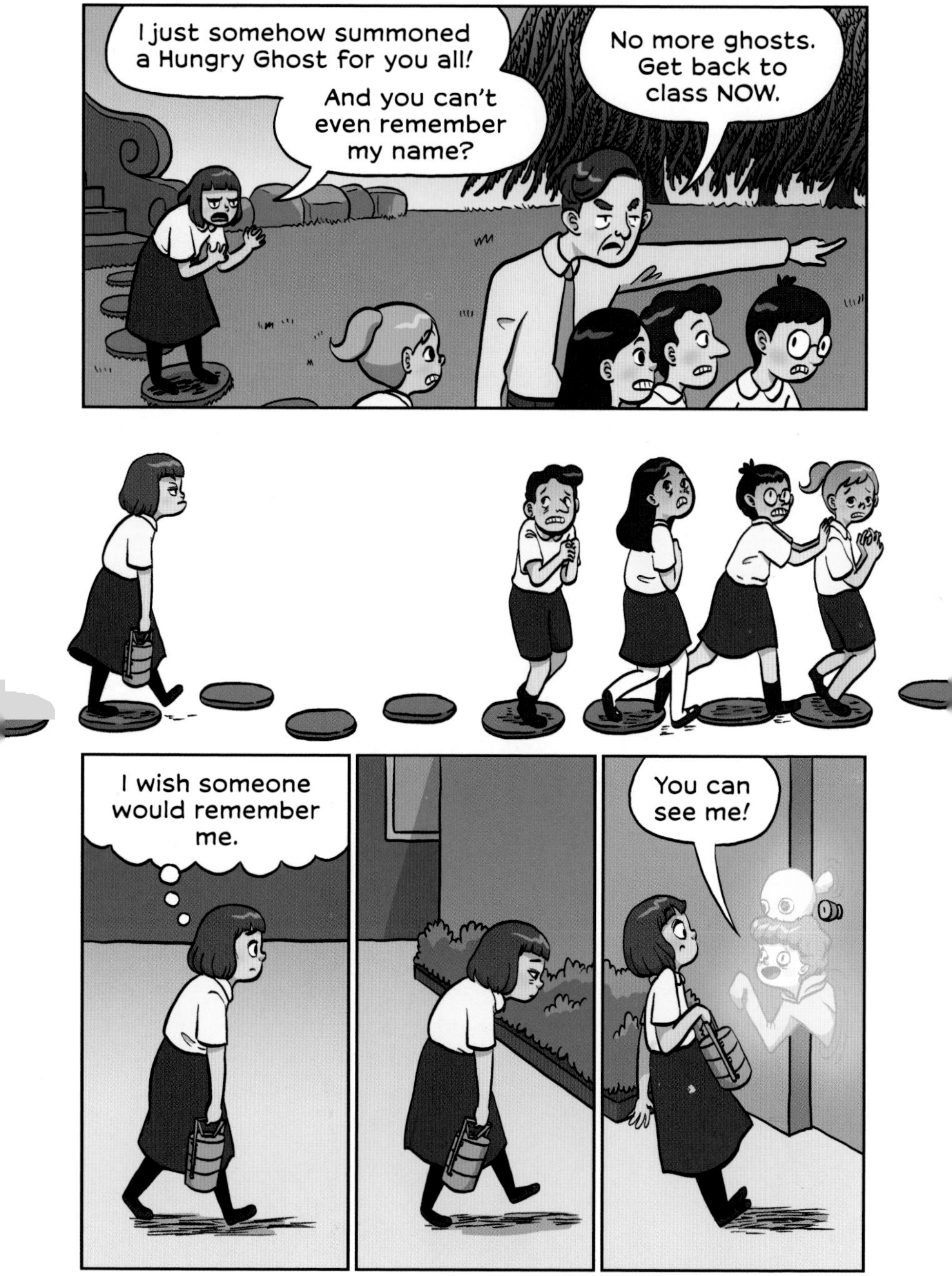
I just somehow summoned a Hungry Ghost for you all!
And you can't even remember my name?
No more ghosts. Get back to class NOW.
I wish someone would remember me.
You can see me!

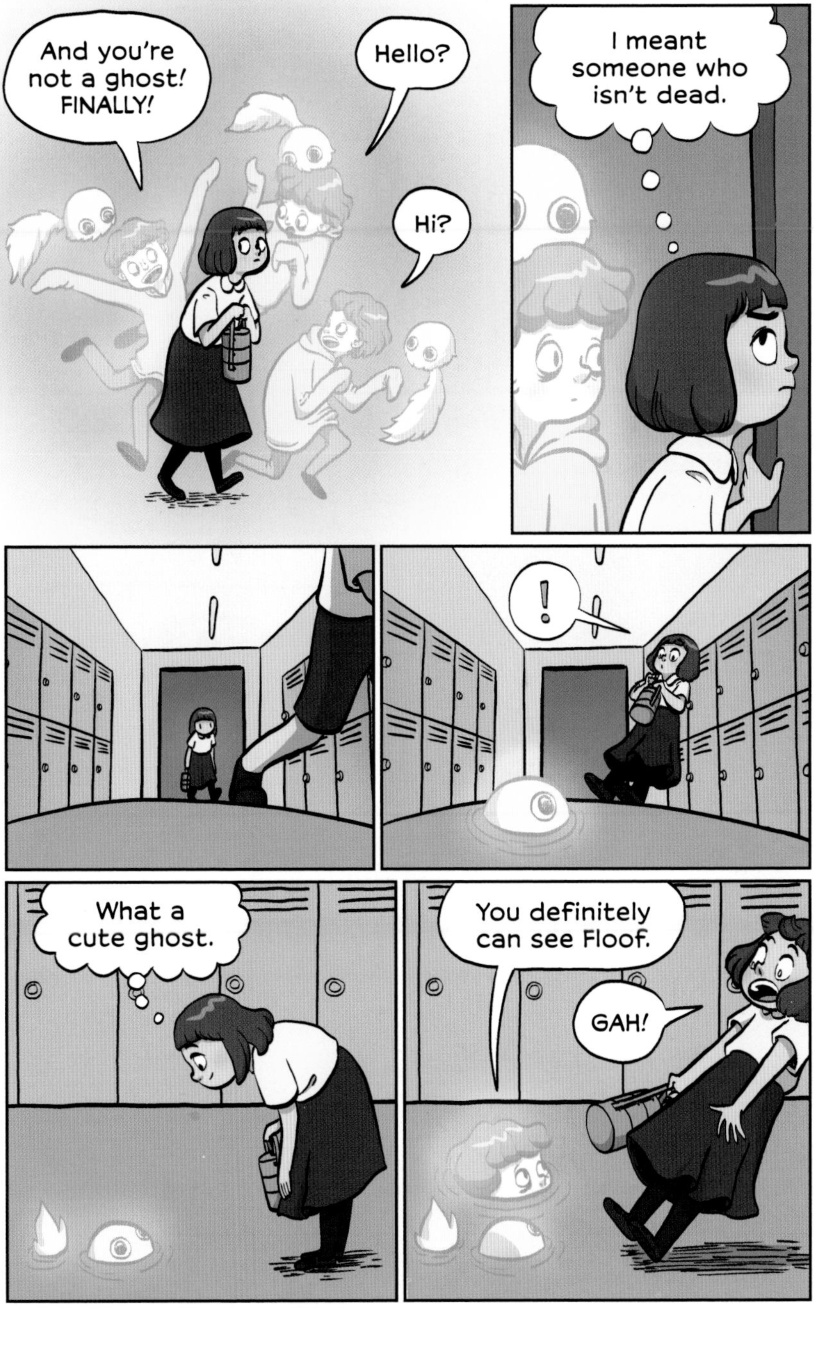
And you're not a ghost! FINALLY!
Hello?
Hi?
I meant someone who isn't dead.
!
What a cute ghost.
You definitely can see Floof.
GAH!

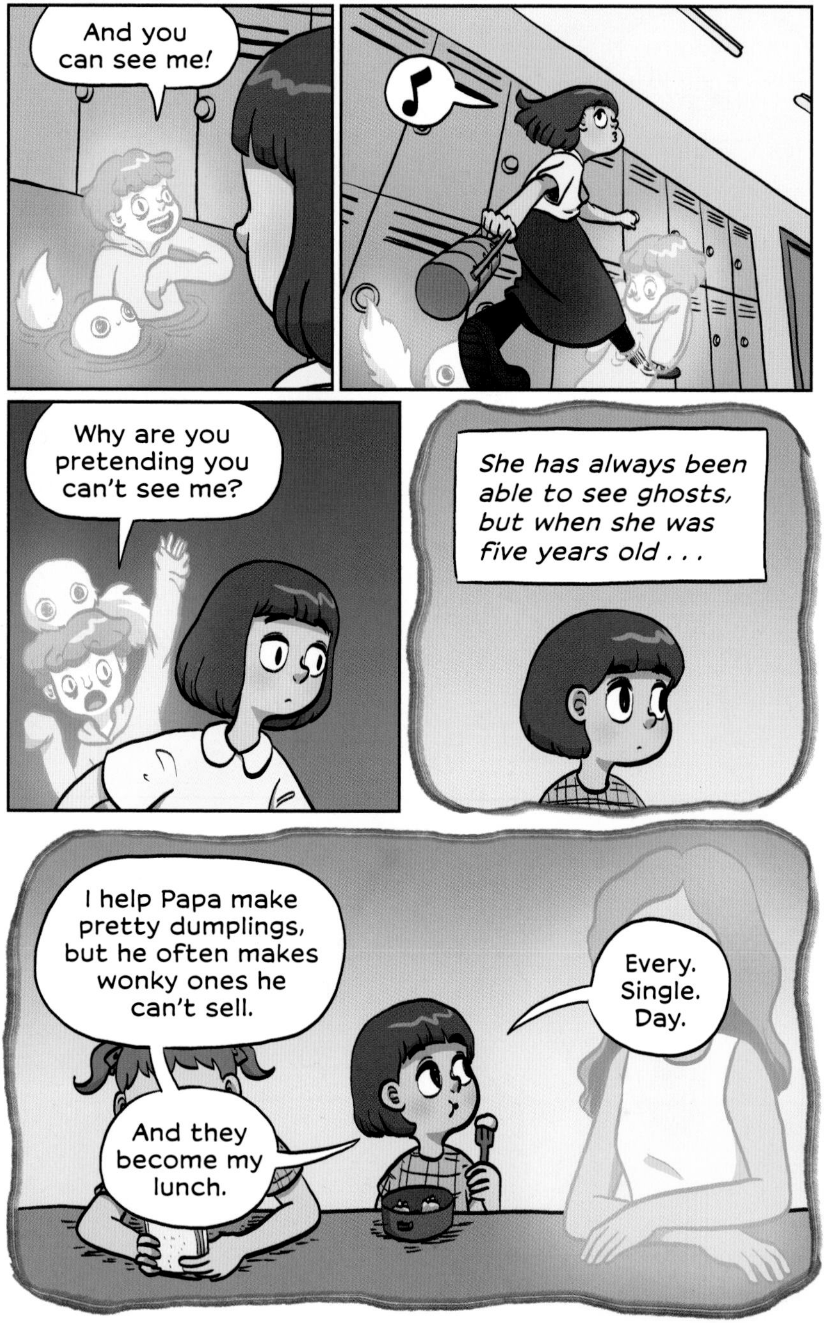
And you can see me!
♪
Why are you pretending you can't see me?
She has always been able to see ghosts, but when she was five years old . . .
I help Papa make pretty dumplings, but he often makes wonky ones he can't sell.
And they become my lunch.
Every. Single. Day.

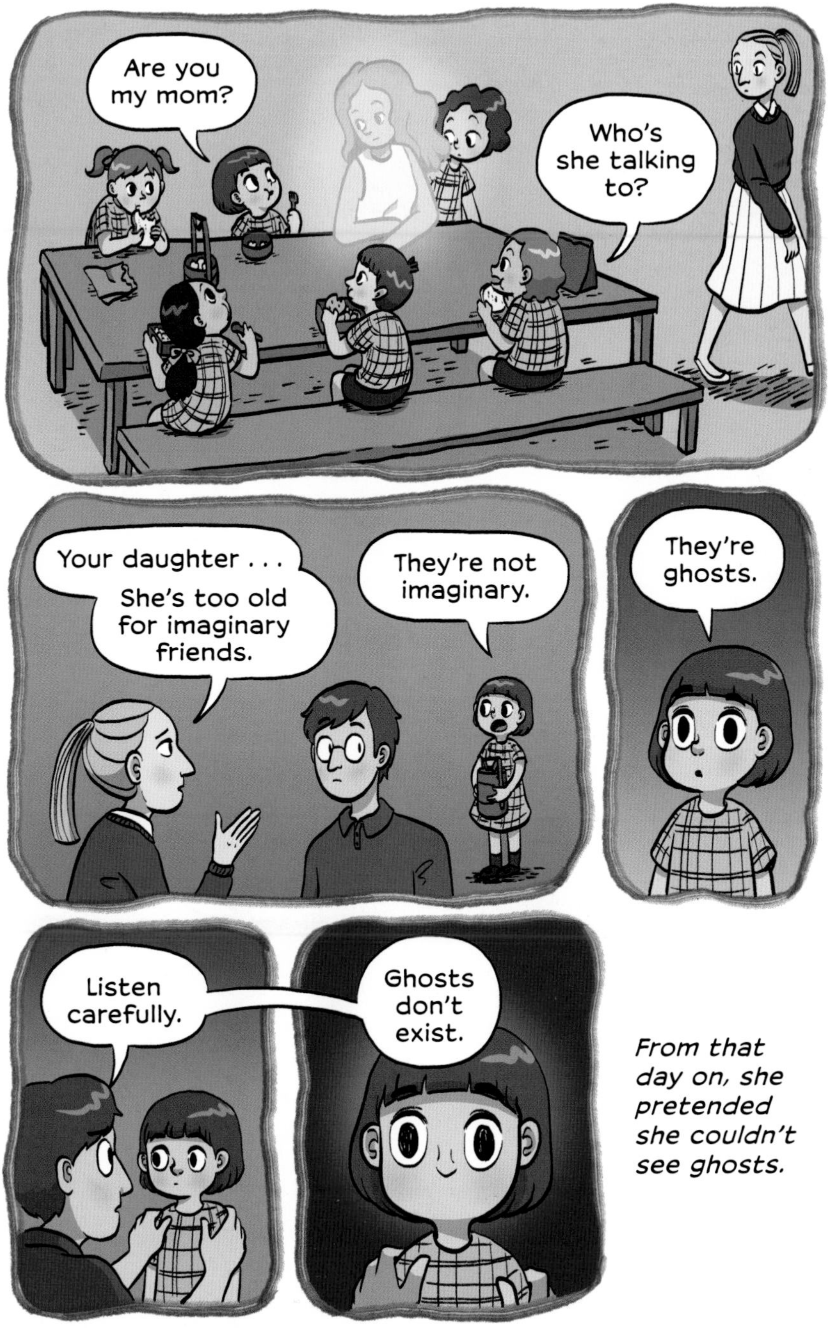
Are you my mom?
Who's she talking to?
Your daughter . . .
She's too old for imaginary friends.
They're not imaginary.
They're ghosts.
Listen carefully.
Ghosts don't exist.

From that day on, she pretended she couldn't see ghosts.

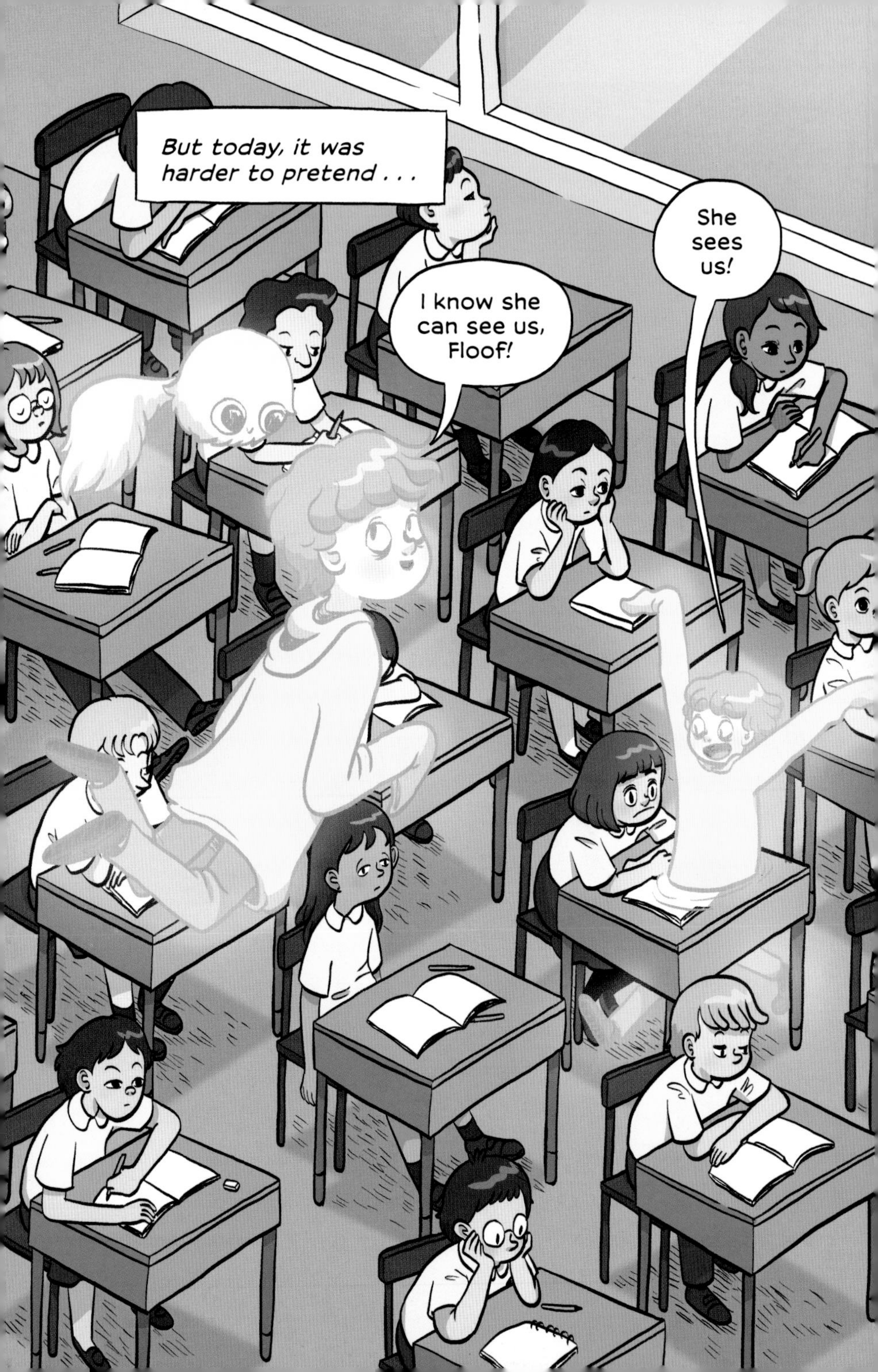
But today, it was harder to pretend . . .
I know she can see us, Floof!
She sees us!

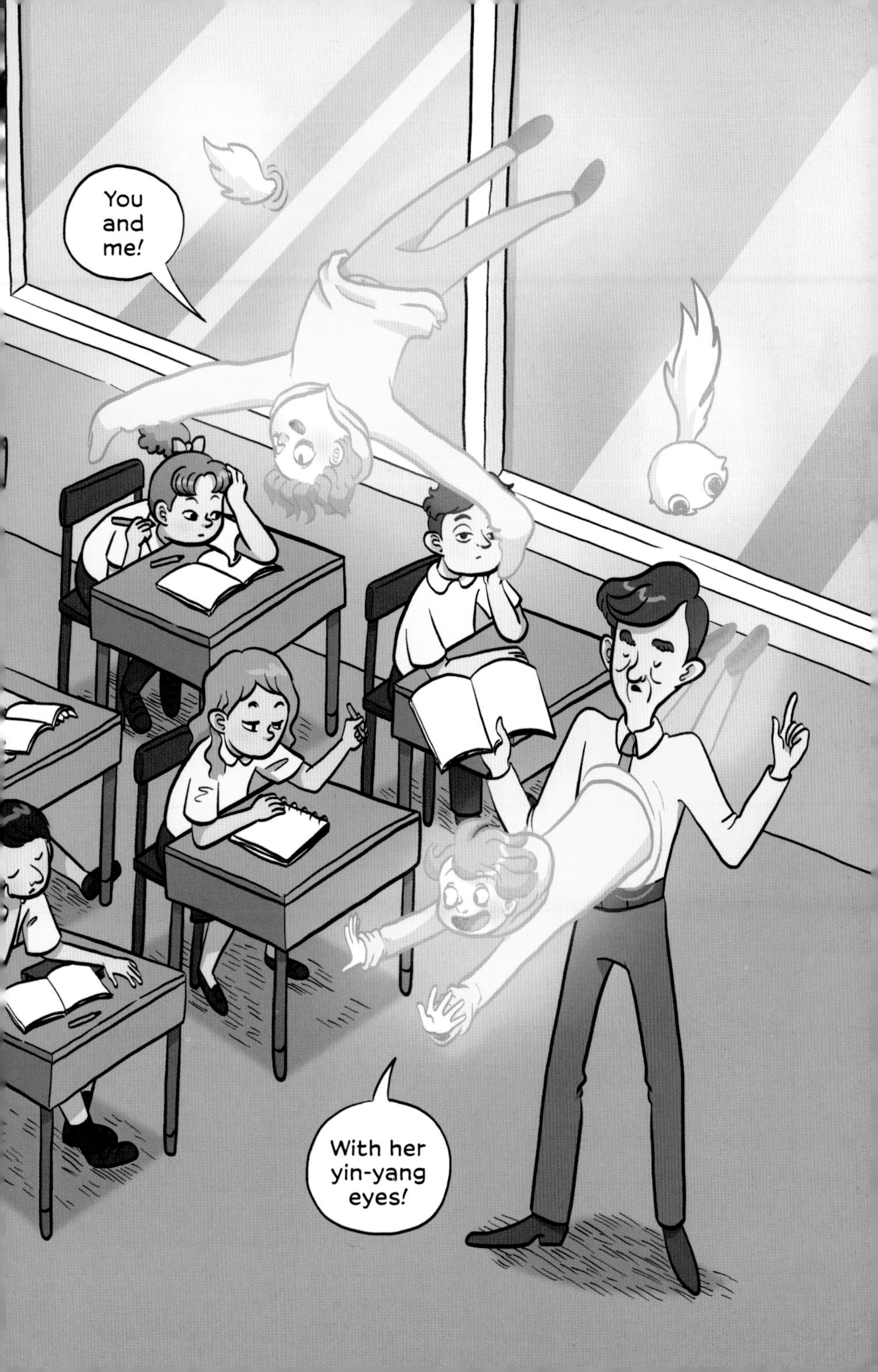
You and me!
With her yin-yang eyes!

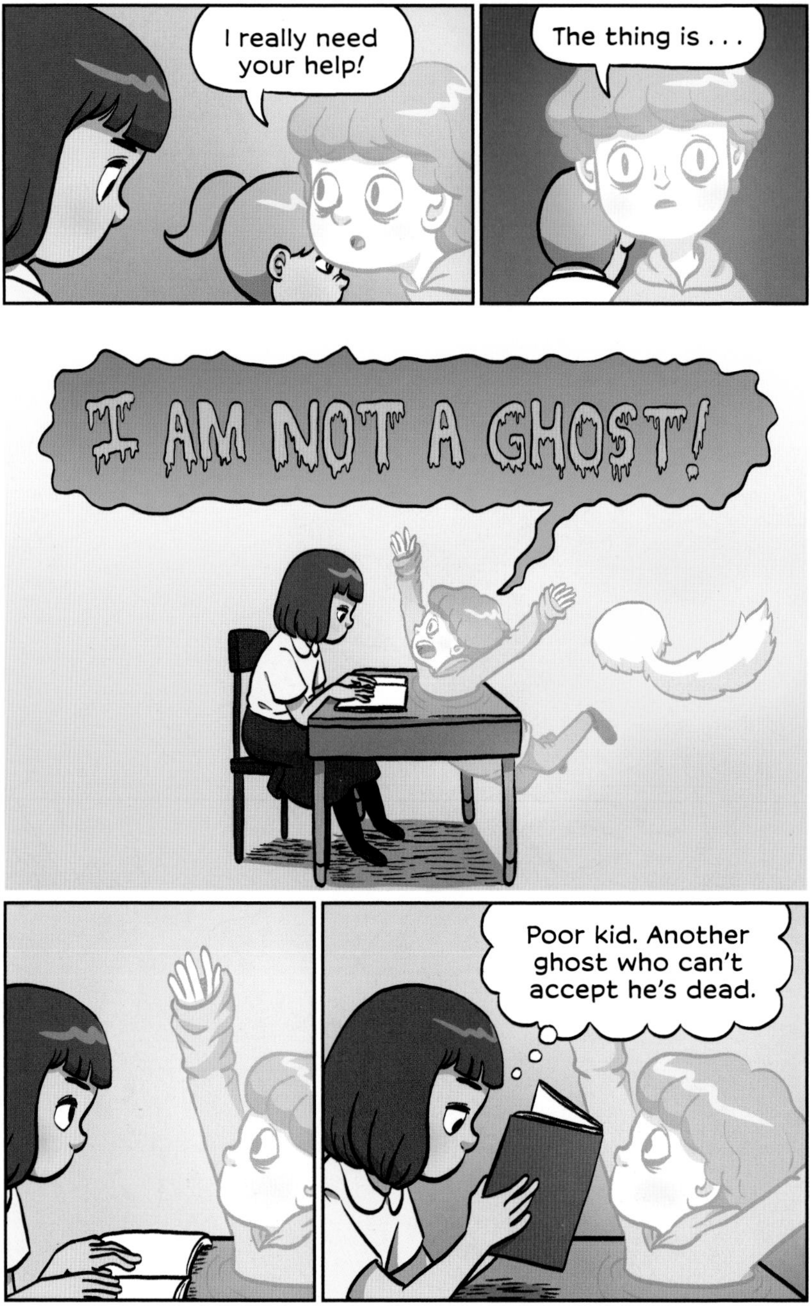
I really need your help!
The thing is . . .
I AM NOT A GHOST!
Poor kid. Another ghost who can't accept he's dead.

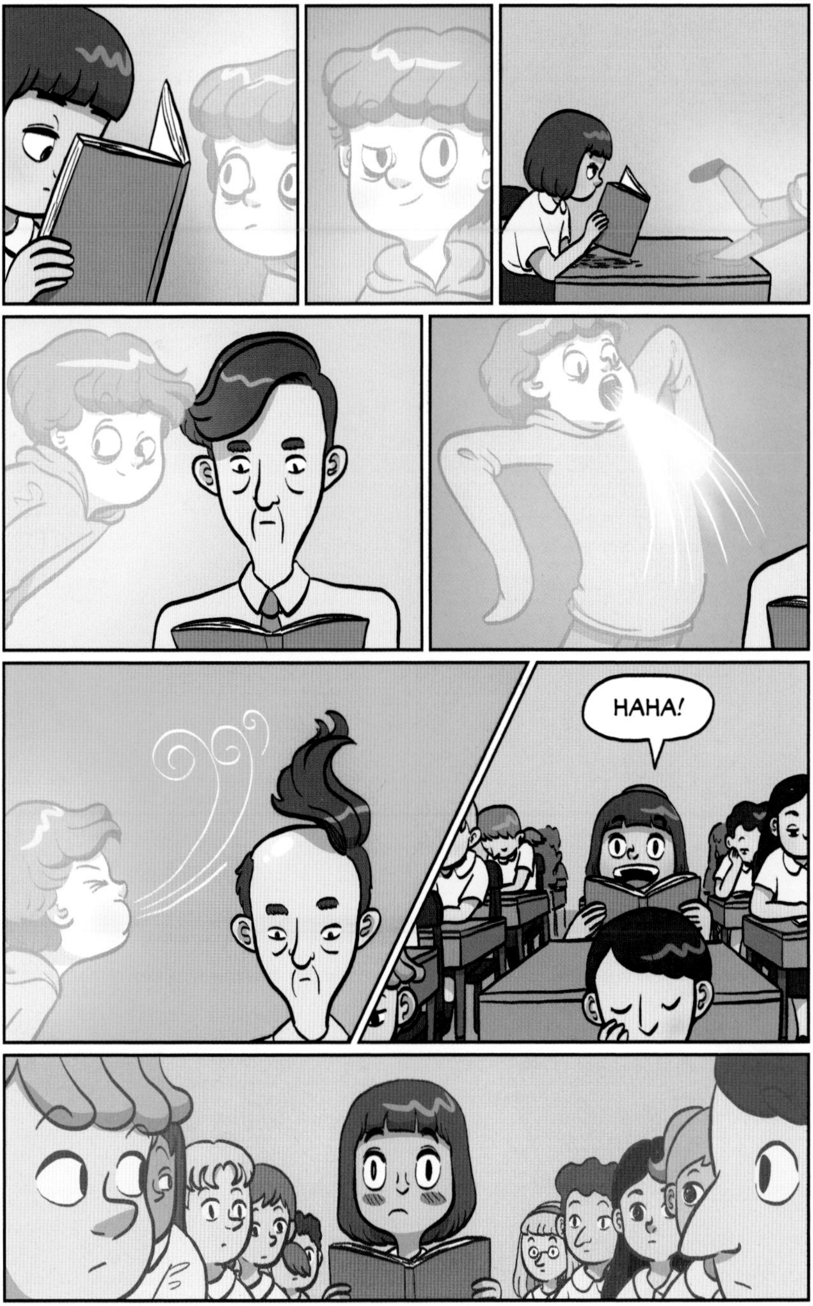
HAHA!

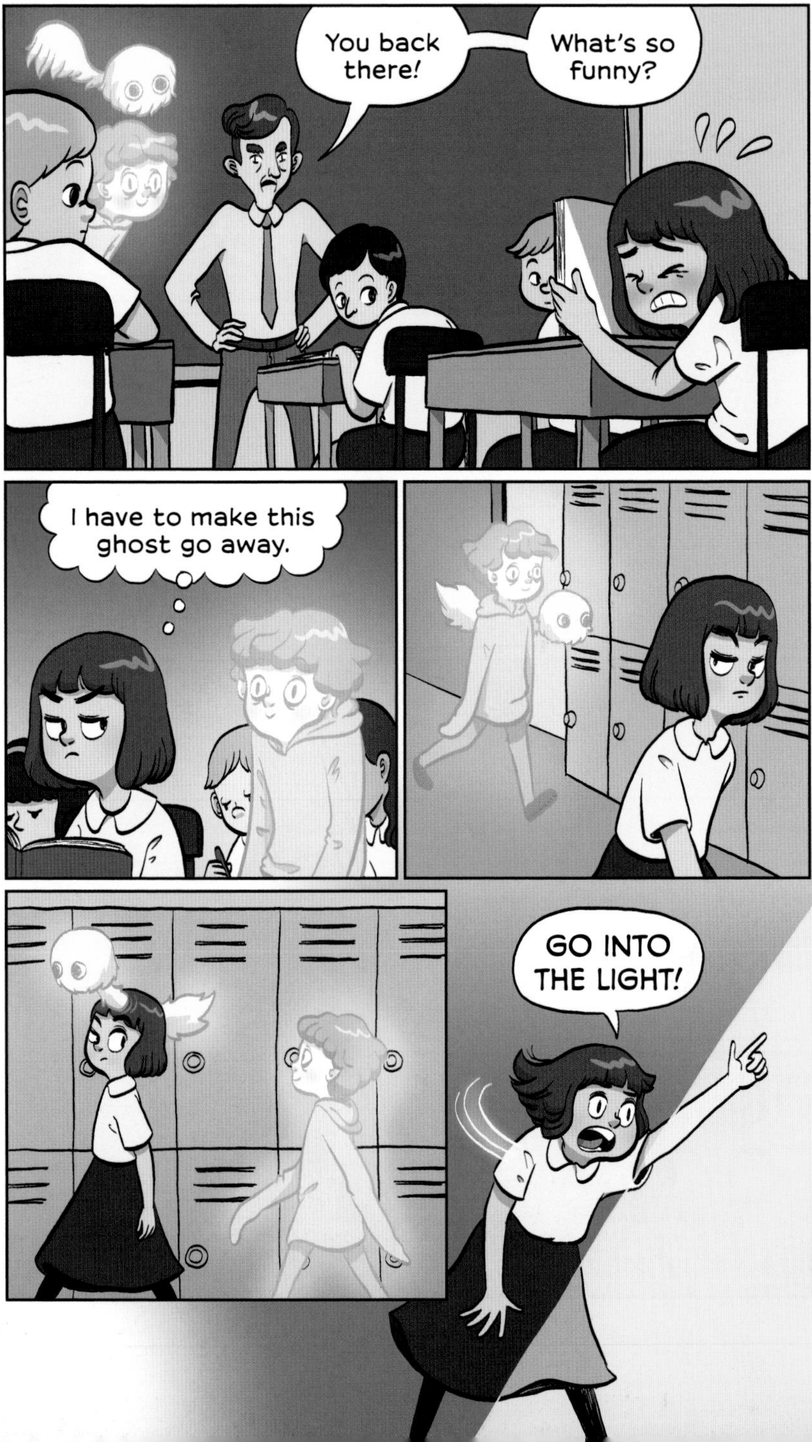
You back there!
What's so funny?
I have to make this ghost go away.
GO INTO THE LIGHT!

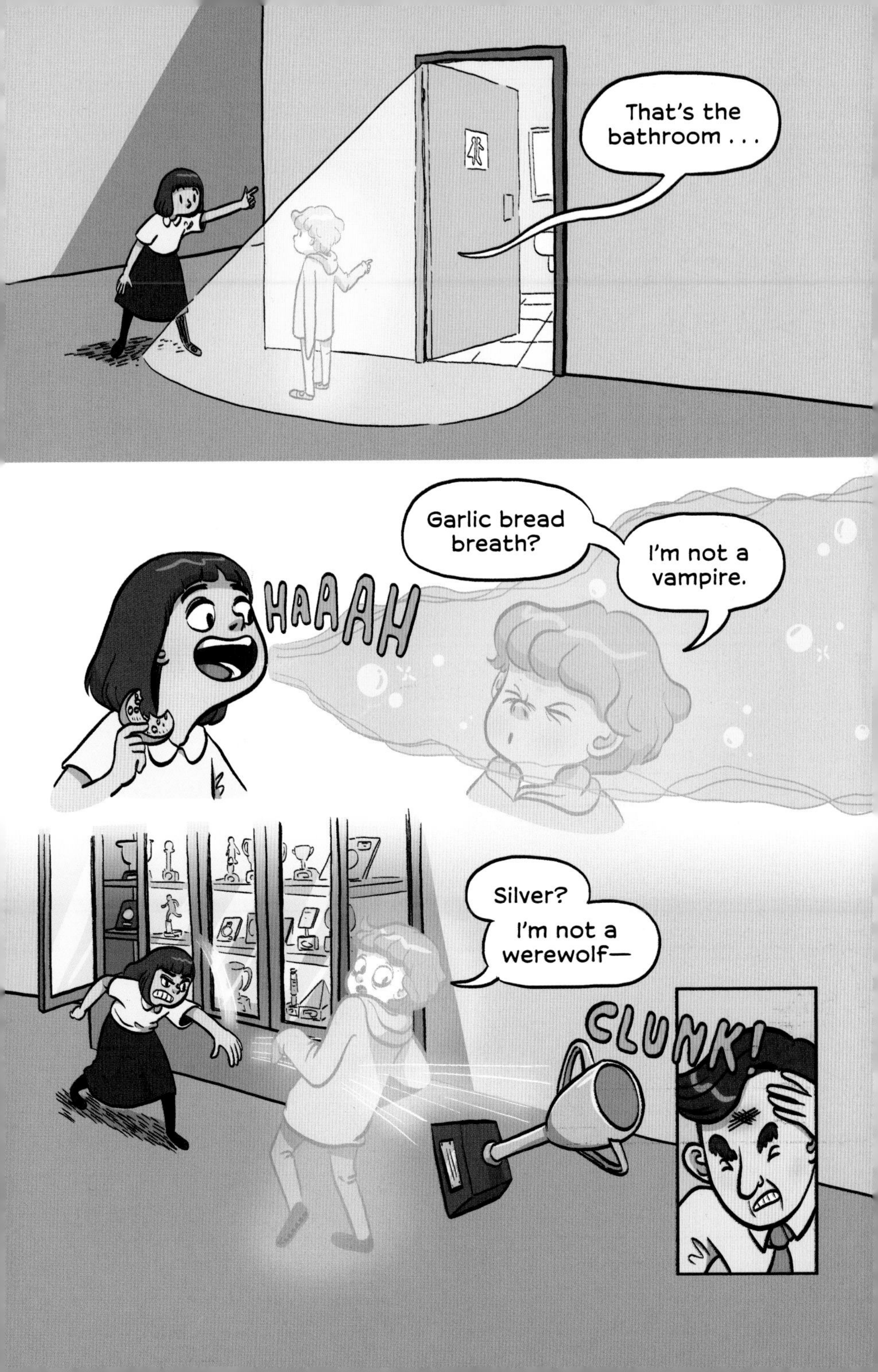

That's the bathroom . . .
Garlic bread breath?
HAAAH
I'm not a vampire.
Silver?
I'm not a werewolf—
CLUNK!

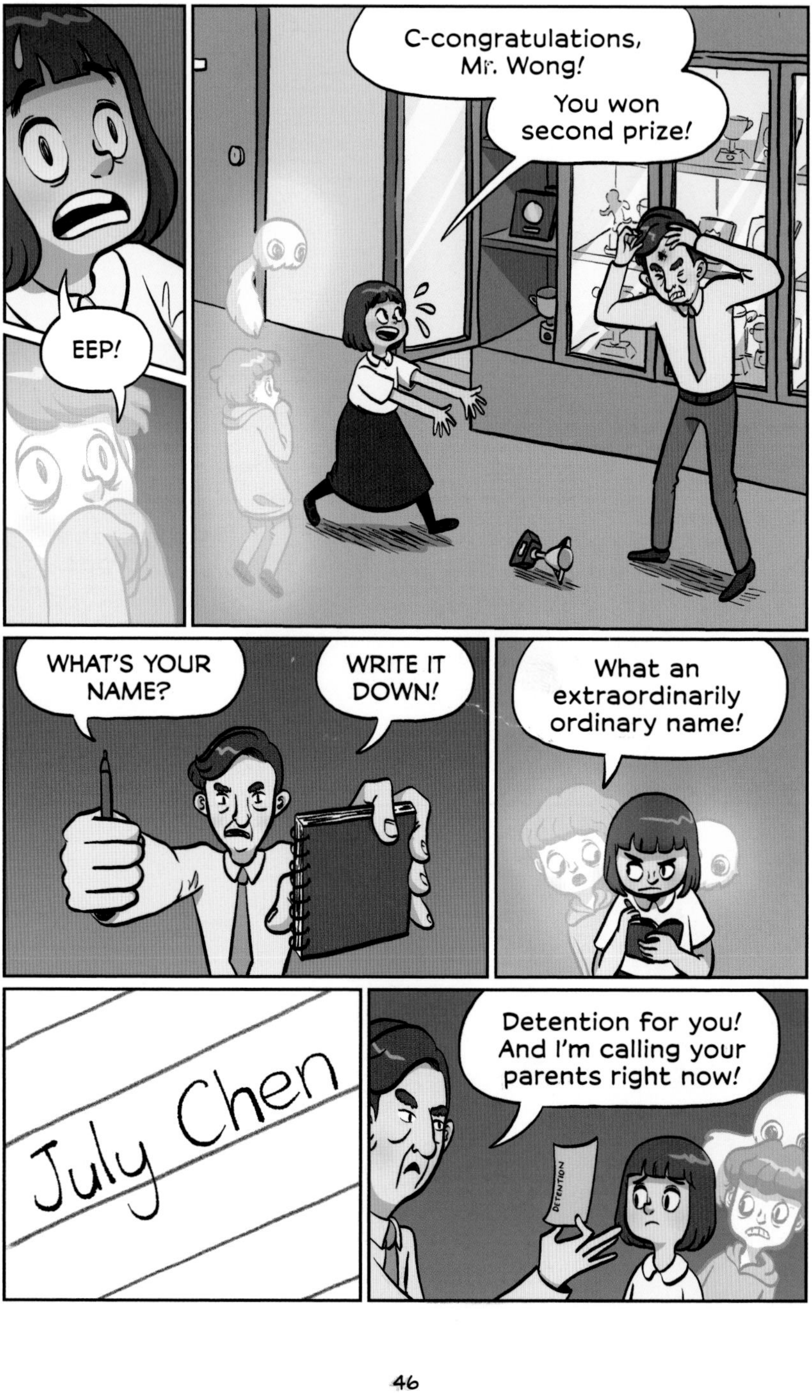
EEP!
C-congratulations, Mr. Wong!
You won second prize!
WHAT'S YOUR NAME?
WRITE IT DOWN!
What an extraordinarily ordinary name!
July Chen
Detention for you! And I'm calling your parents right now!
DETENTION

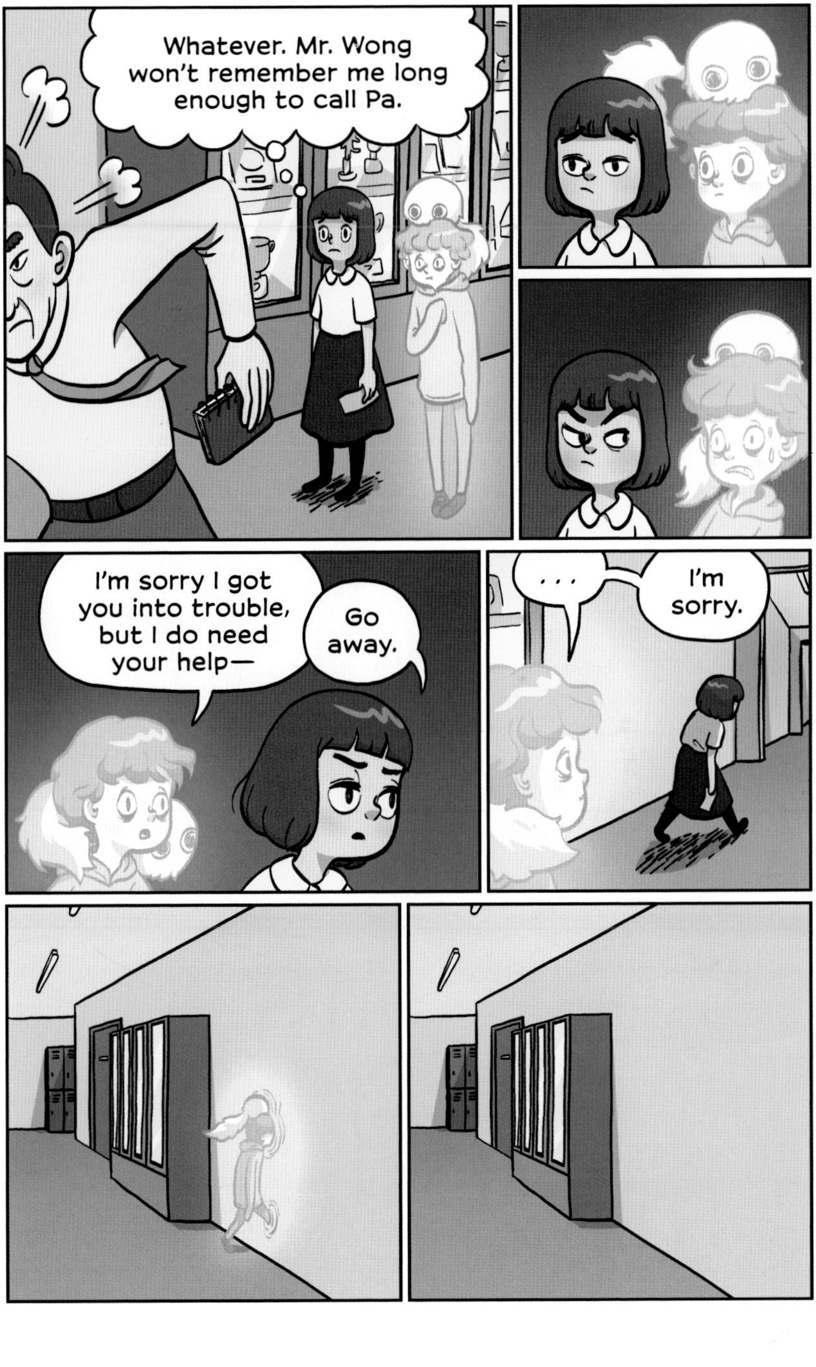
Whatever. Mr. Wong won't remember me long enough to call Pa.
I'm sorry I got you into trouble, but I do need your help—
Go away.
. . .
I'm sorry.

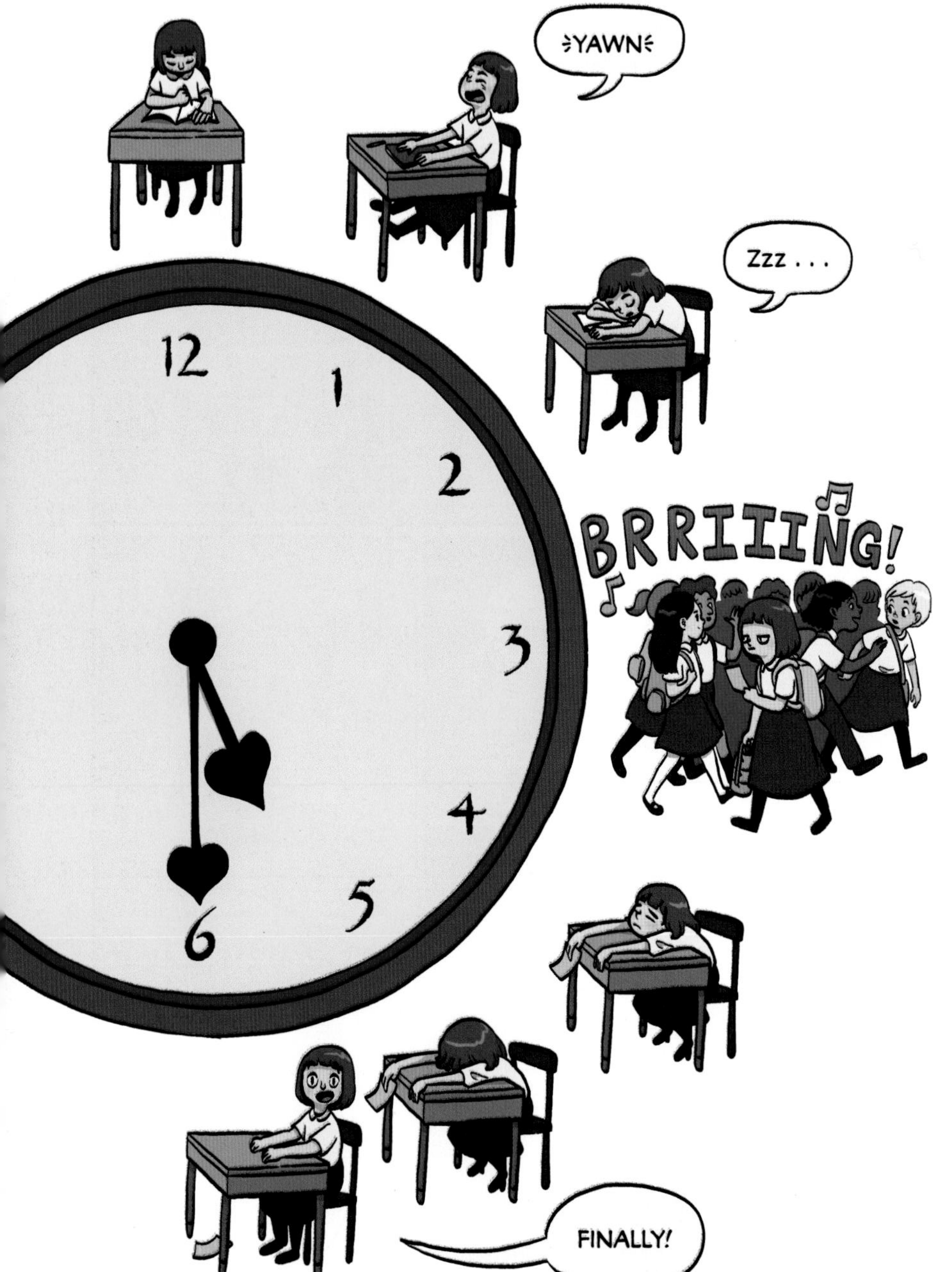
YAWN
Zzz . . .
BRRIIING!
FINALLY!

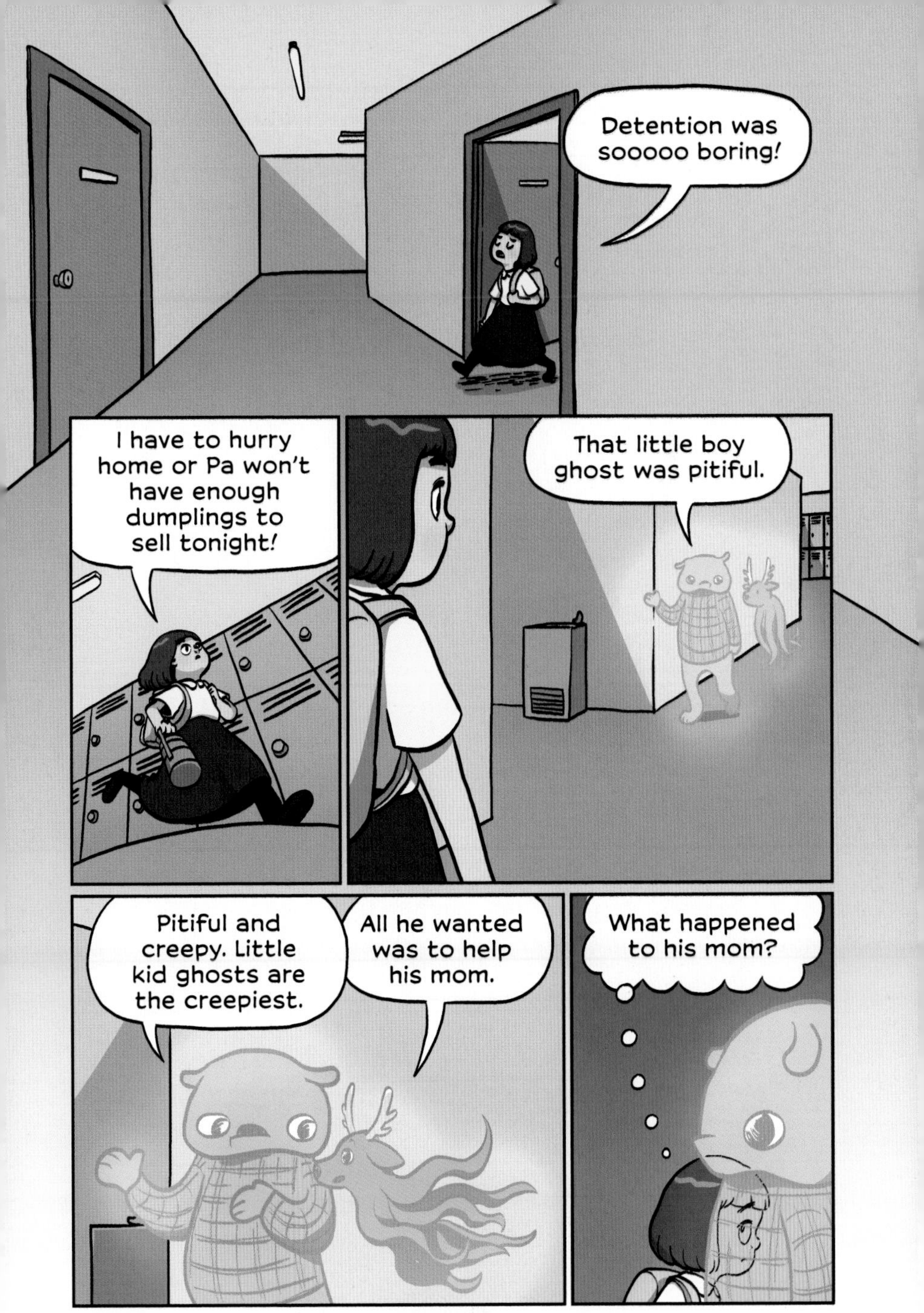
Detention was sooooo boring!
I have to hurry home or Pa won't have enough dumplings to sell tonight!
That little boy ghost was pitiful.
Pitiful and creepy. Little kid ghosts are the creepiest.
All he wanted was to help his mom.
What happened to his mom?

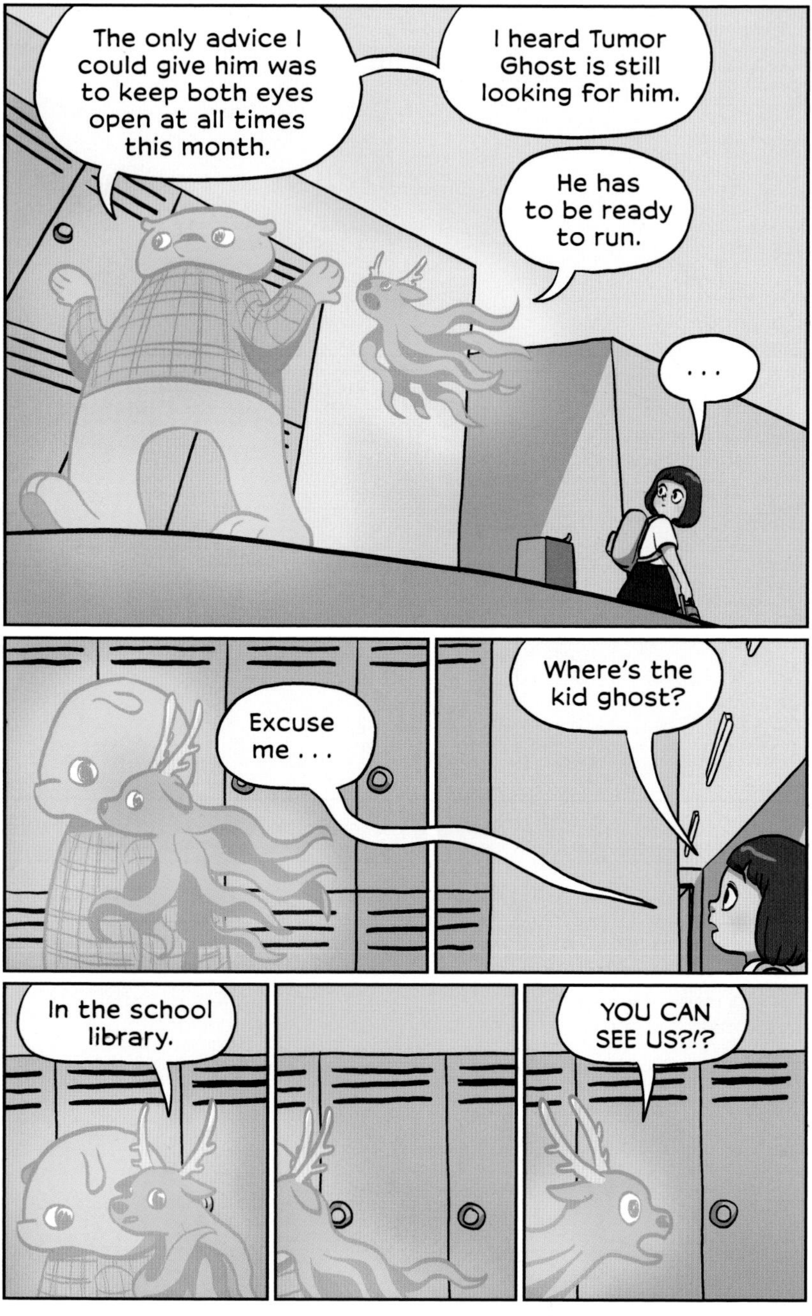
The only advice I could give him was to keep both eyes open at all times this month.
I heard Tumor Ghost is still looking for him.
He has to be ready to run.
. . .
Excuse me . . .
Where's the kid ghost?
In the school library.
YOU CAN SEE US?!?

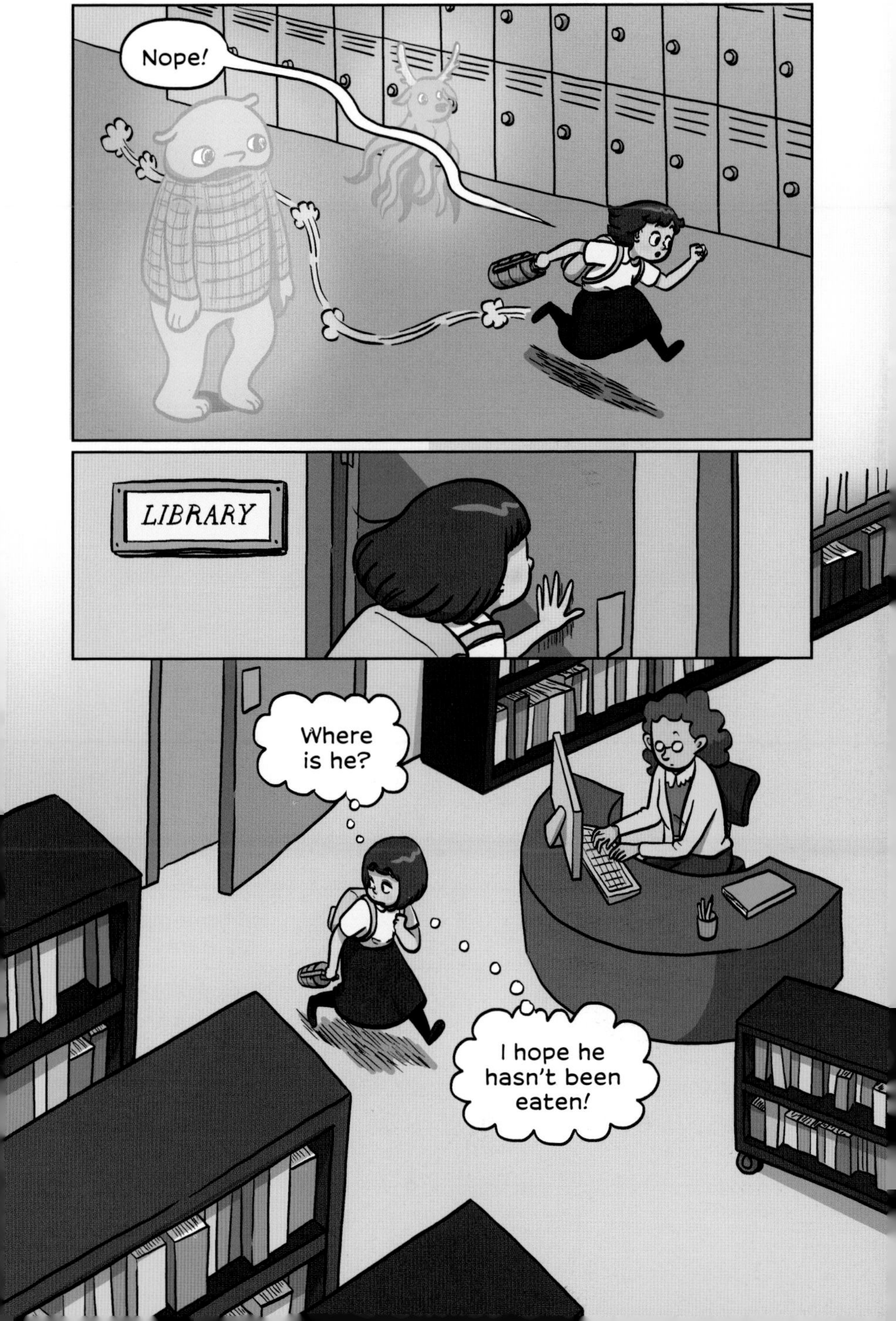
Nope!
LIBRARY
Where is he?
I hope he hasn't been eaten!

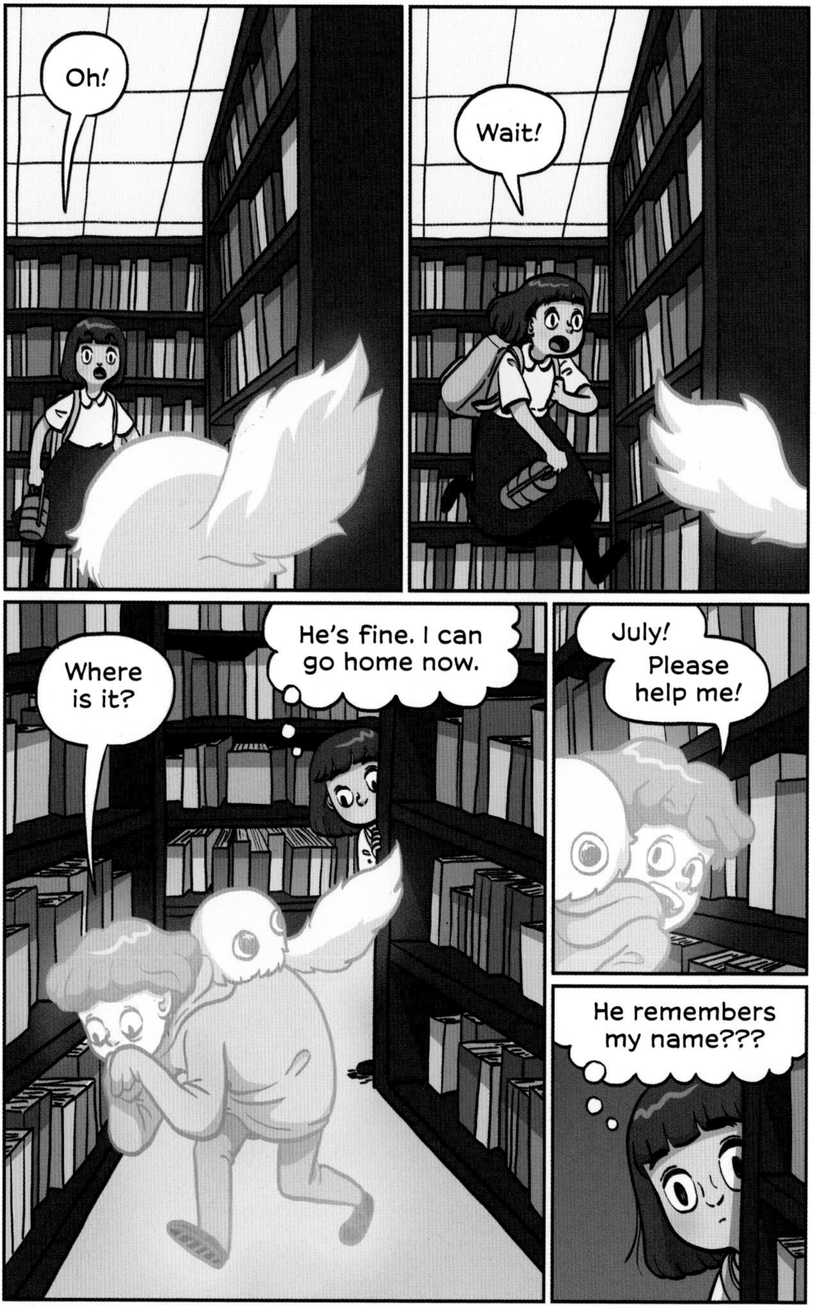
Oh!
Wait!
Where is it?
He's fine. I can go home now.
July! Please help me!
He remembers my name???

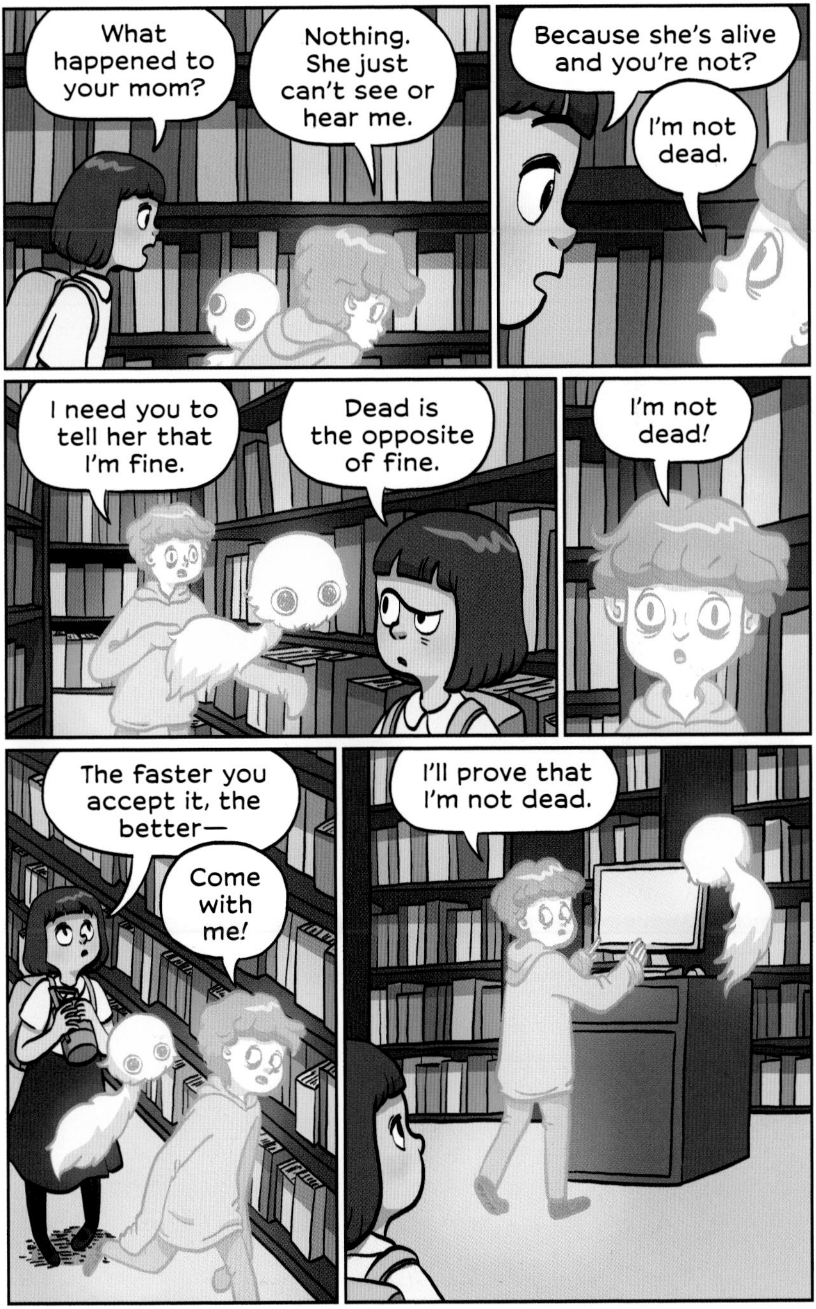
What happened to your mom?
Nothing. She just can't see or hear me.
Because she's alive and you're not?
I'm not dead.
I need you to tell her that I'm fine.
Dead is the opposite of fine.
I'm not dead!
The faster you accept it, the better—
Come with me!
I'll prove that I'm not dead.

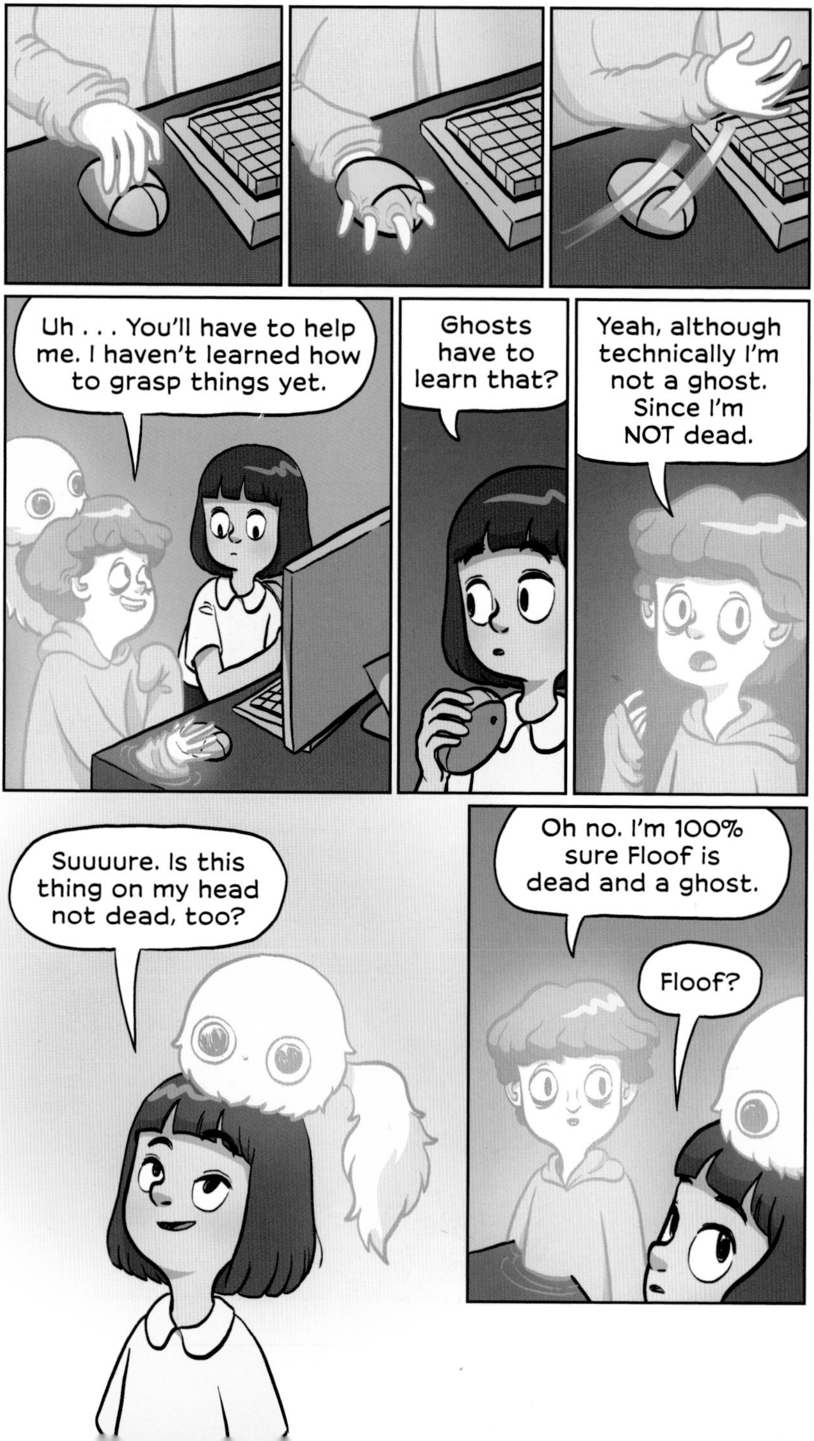

Uh . . . You'll have to help me. I haven't learned how to grasp things yet.
Ghosts have to learn that?
Yeah, although technically I'm not a ghost. Since I'm NOT dead.
Suuuure. Is this thing on my head not dead, too?
Oh no. I'm 100% sure Floof is dead and a ghost.
Floof?

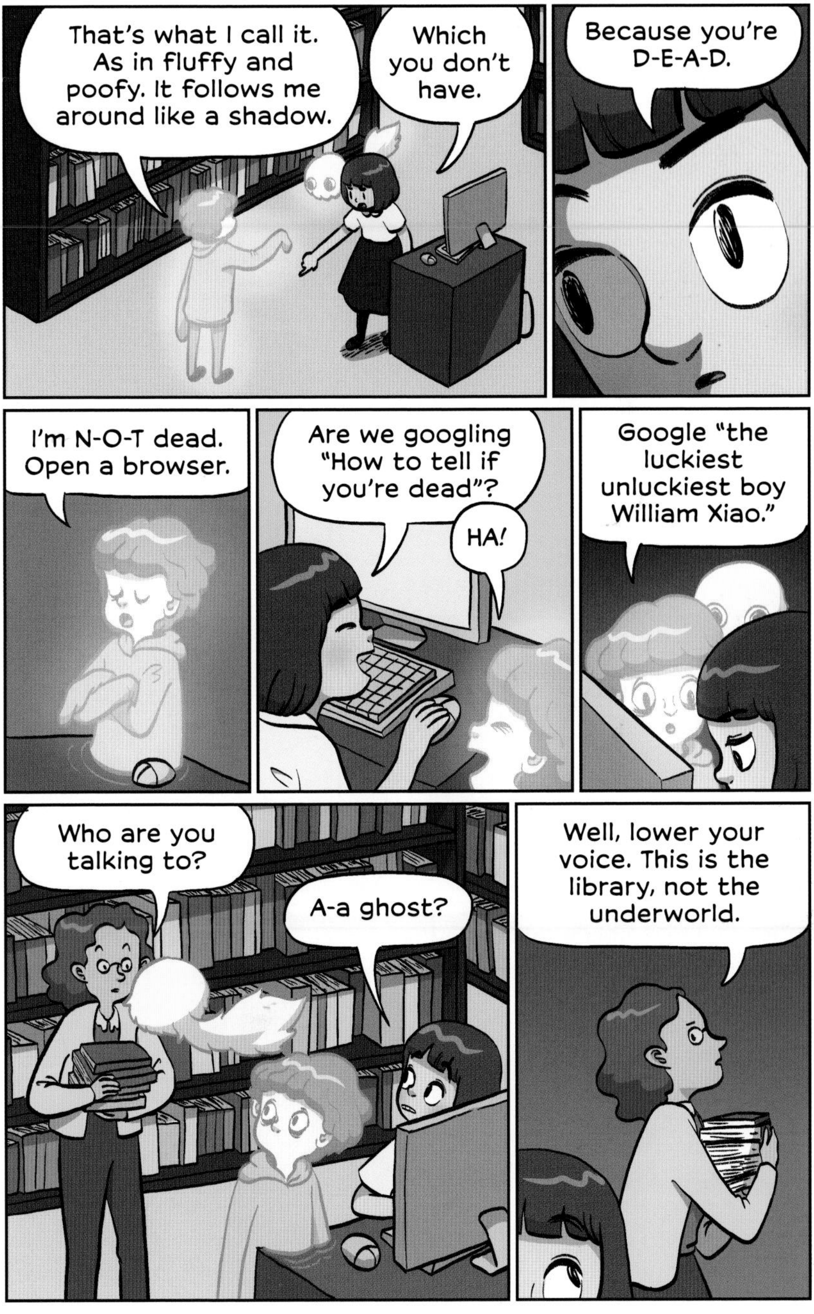
That's what I call it. As in fluffy and poofy. It follows me around like a shadow.
Which you don't have.
Because you're D-E-A-D.
I'm N-O-T dead. Open a browser.
Are we googling "How to tell if you're dead"?
HA!
Google "the luckiest unluckiest boy William Xiao."
Who are you talking to?
A-a ghost?
Well, lower your voice. This is the library, not the underworld.

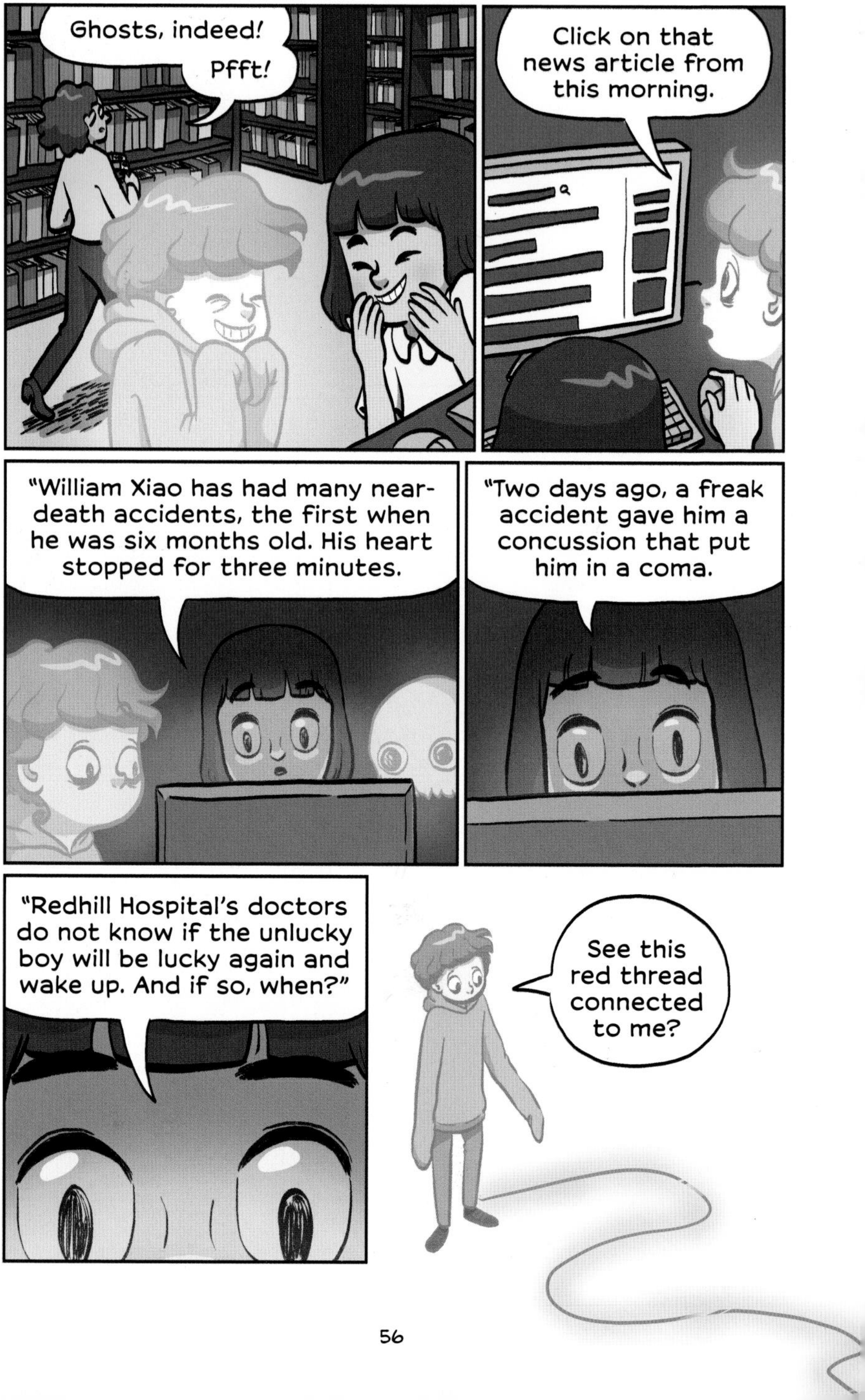
Ghosts, indeed!
Pfft!
Click on that news article from this morning.
"William Xiao has had many near-death accidents, the first when he was six months old. His heart stopped for three minutes.
"Two days ago, a freak accident gave him a concussion that put him in a coma.
"Redhill Hospital's doctors do not know if the unlucky boy will be lucky again and wake up. And if so, when?"
See this red thread connected to me?

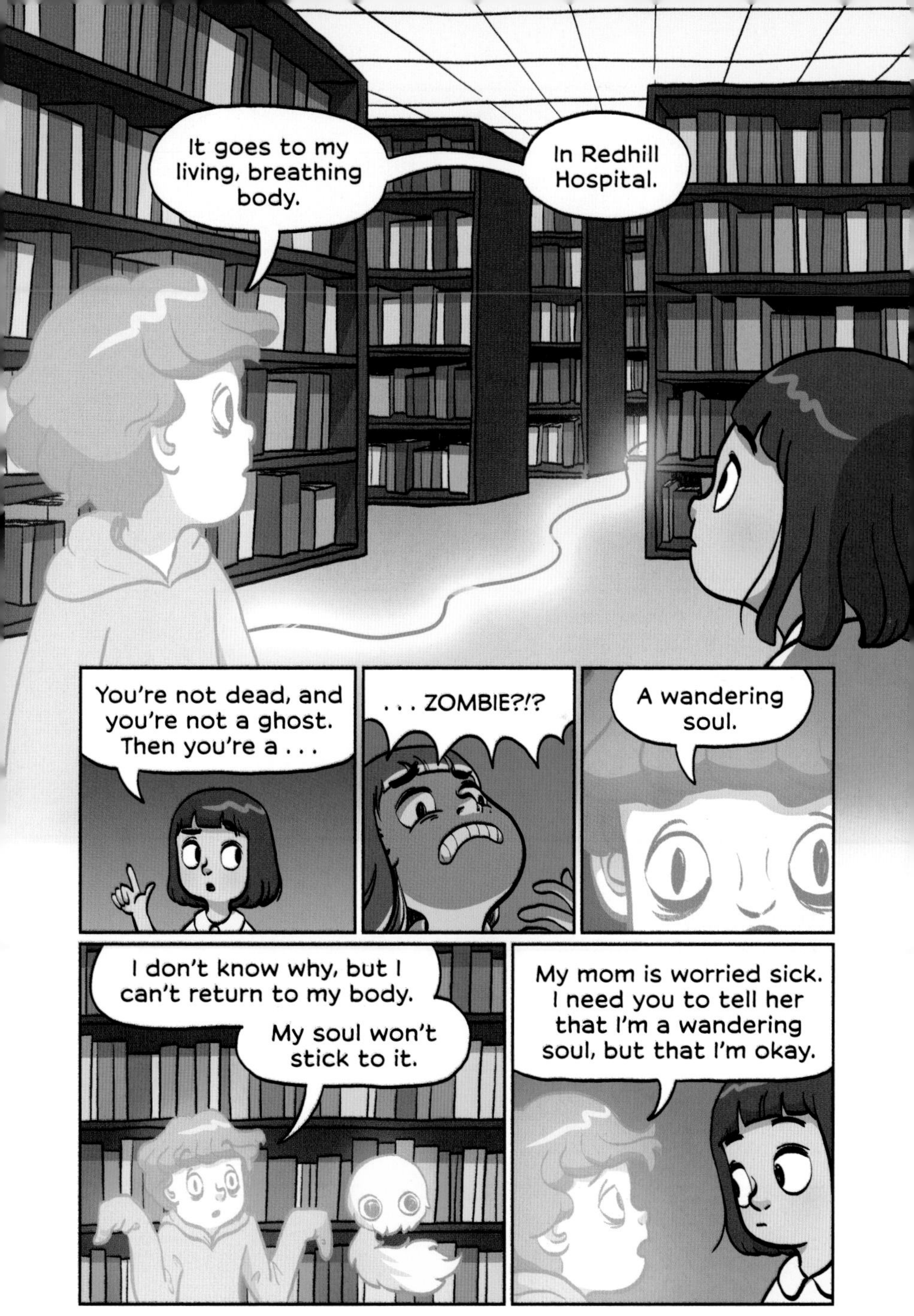
It goes to my living, breathing body.
In Redhill Hospital.
You're not dead, and you're not a ghost. Then you're a . . .
. . . ZOMBIE?!?
A wandering soul.
I don't know why, but I can't return to my body.
My soul won't stick to it.
My mom is worried sick. I need you to tell her that I'm a wandering soul, but that I'm okay.

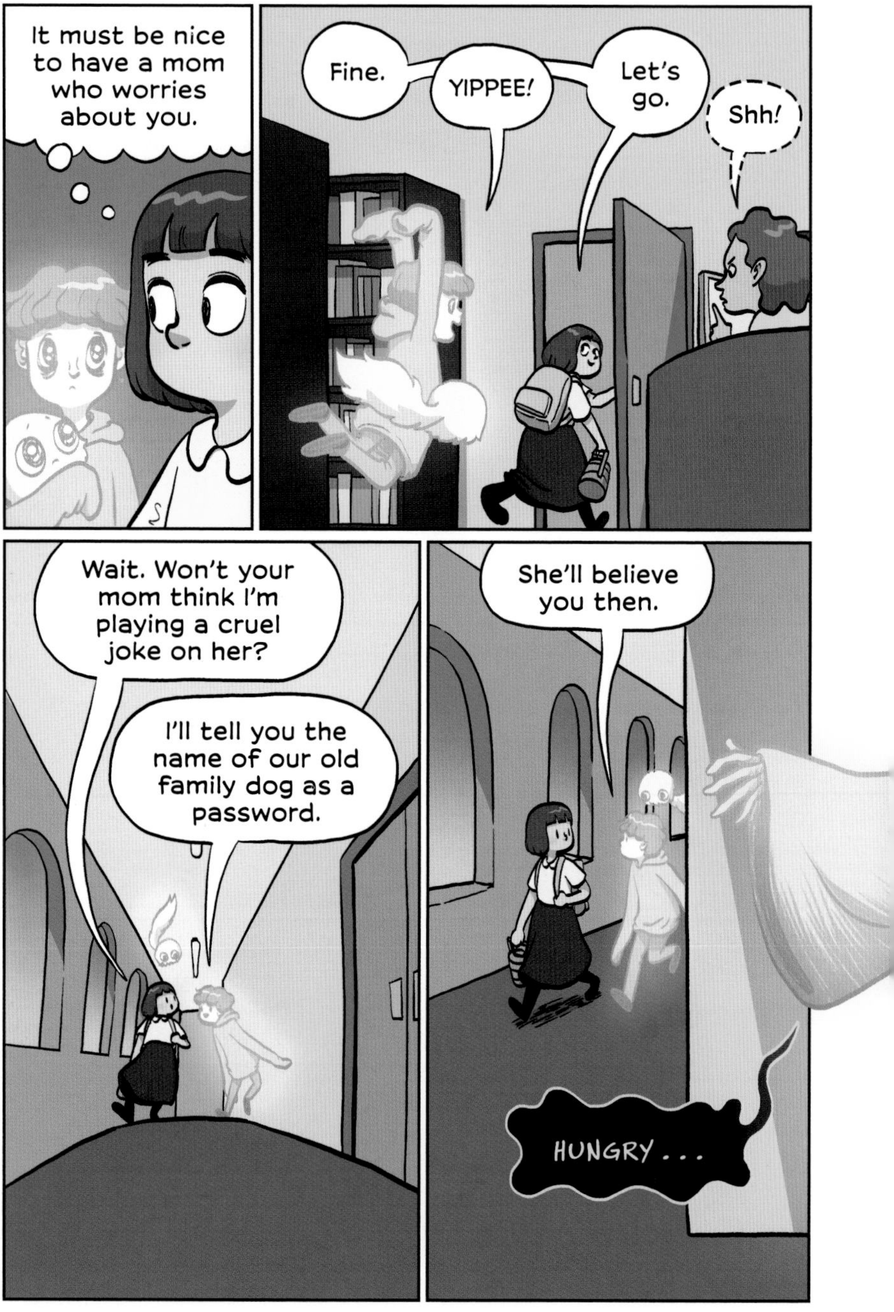
It must be nice to have a mom who worries about you.
Fine.
YIPPEE!
Let's go.
Shh!
Wait. Won't your mom think I'm playing a cruel joke on her?
I'll tell you the name of our old family dog as a password.
She'll believe you then.
HUNGRY . . .

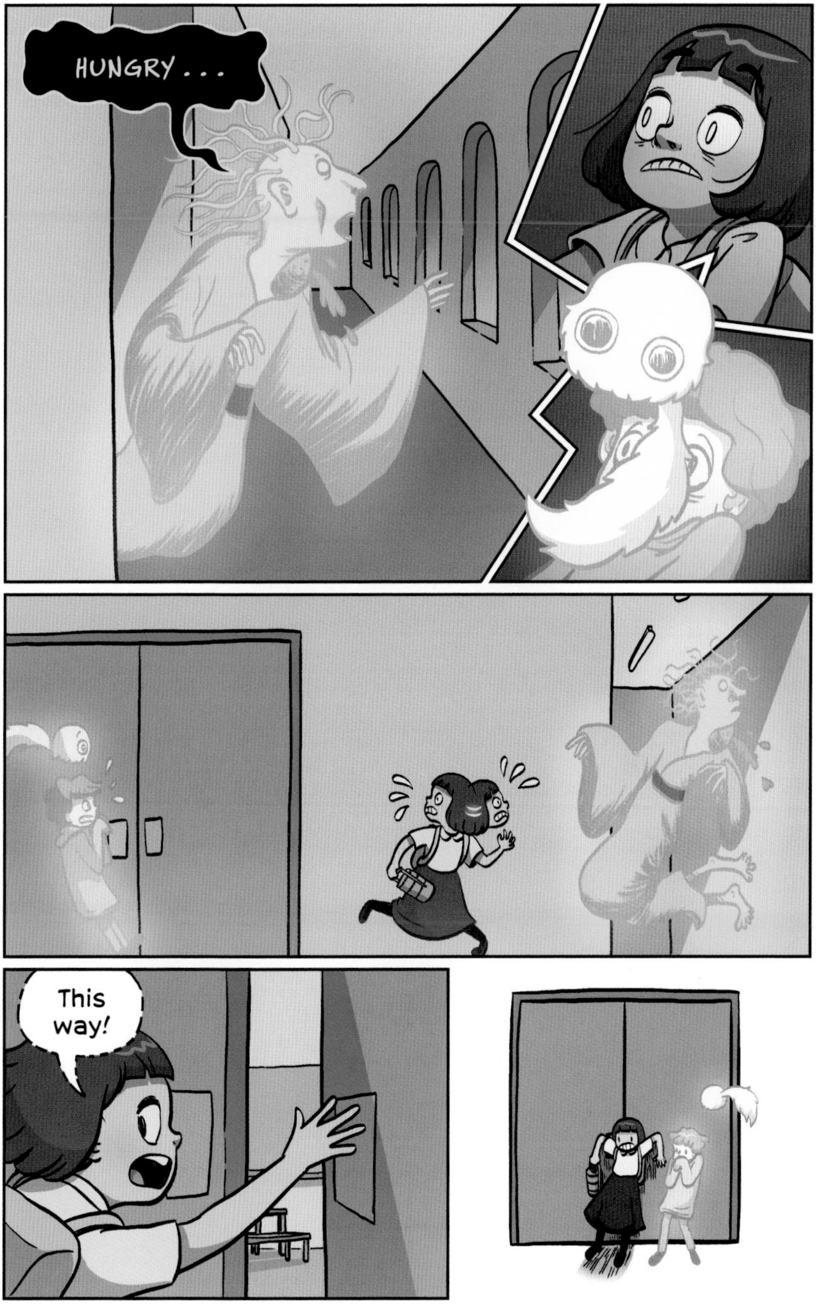
HUNGRY . . .
This way!

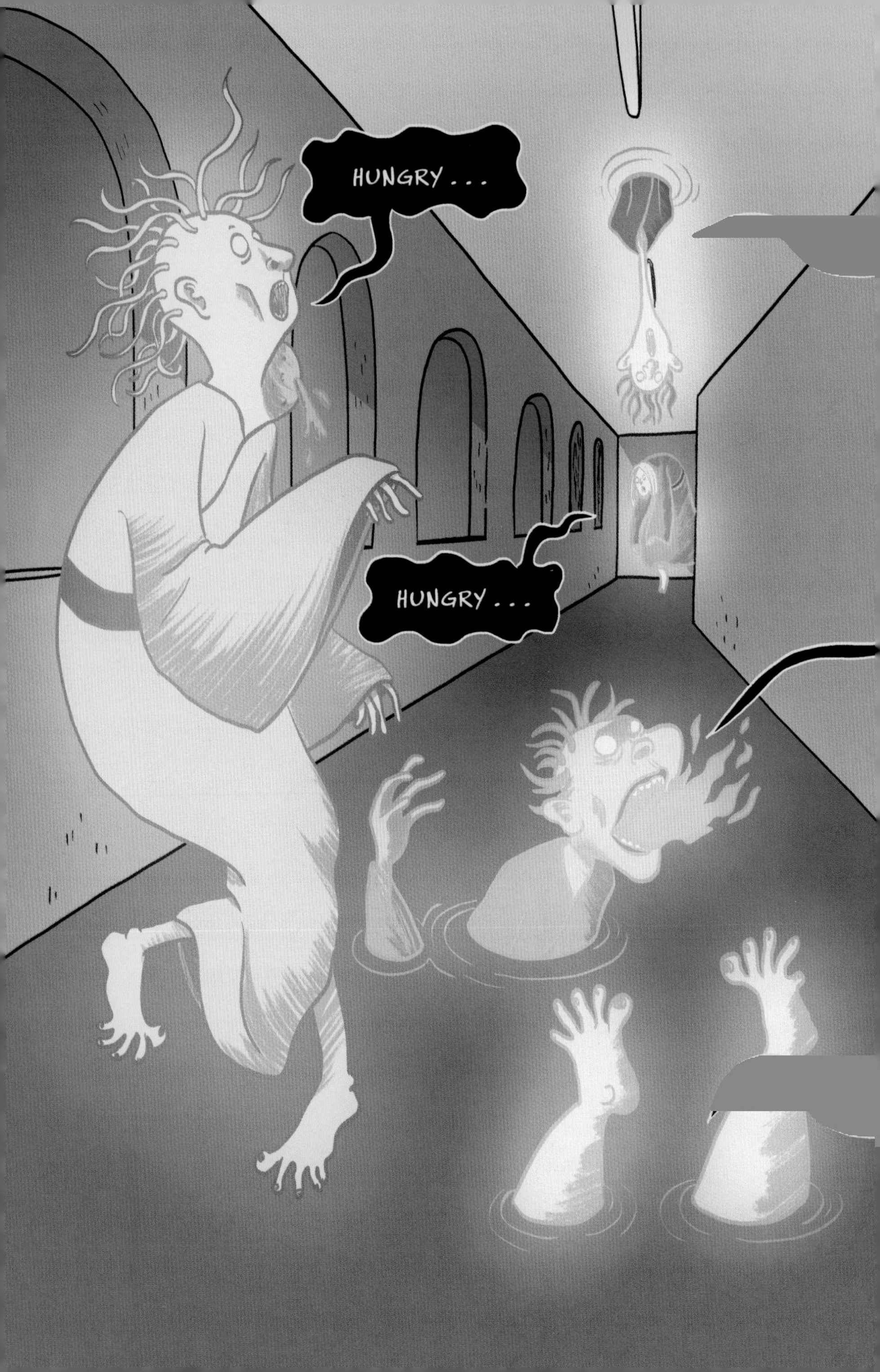
HUNGRY . . .
HUNGRY . . .

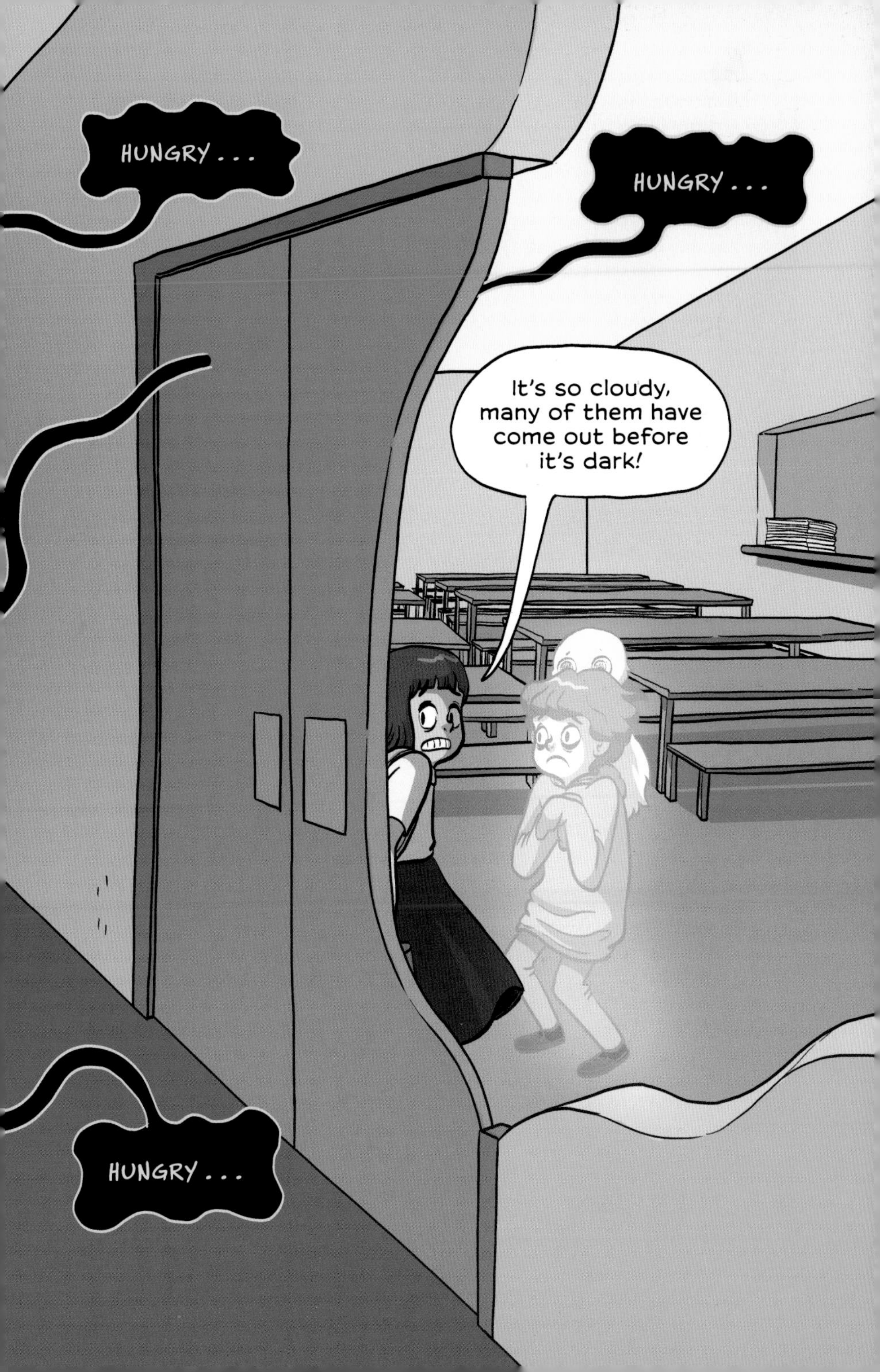
HUNGRY . . .
HUNGRY . . .
It's so cloudy, many of them have come out before it's dark!
HUNGRY . . .

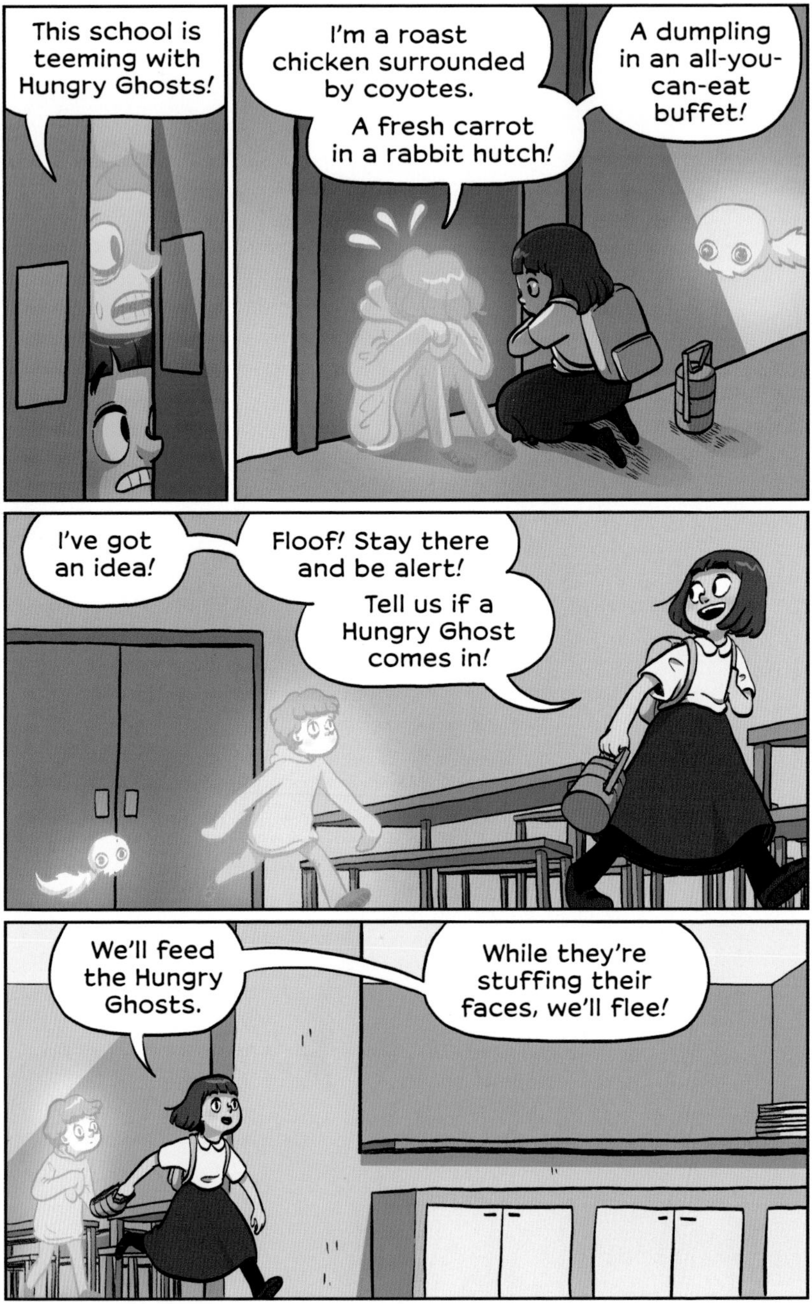
This school is teeming with Hungry Ghosts!
I'm a roast chicken surrounded by coyotes.
A fresh carrot in a rabbit hutch!
A dumpling in an all-you-can-eat buffet!
I've got an idea!
Floof! Stay there and be alert!
Tell us if a Hungry Ghost comes in!
We'll feed the Hungry Ghosts.
While they're stuffing their faces, we'll flee!

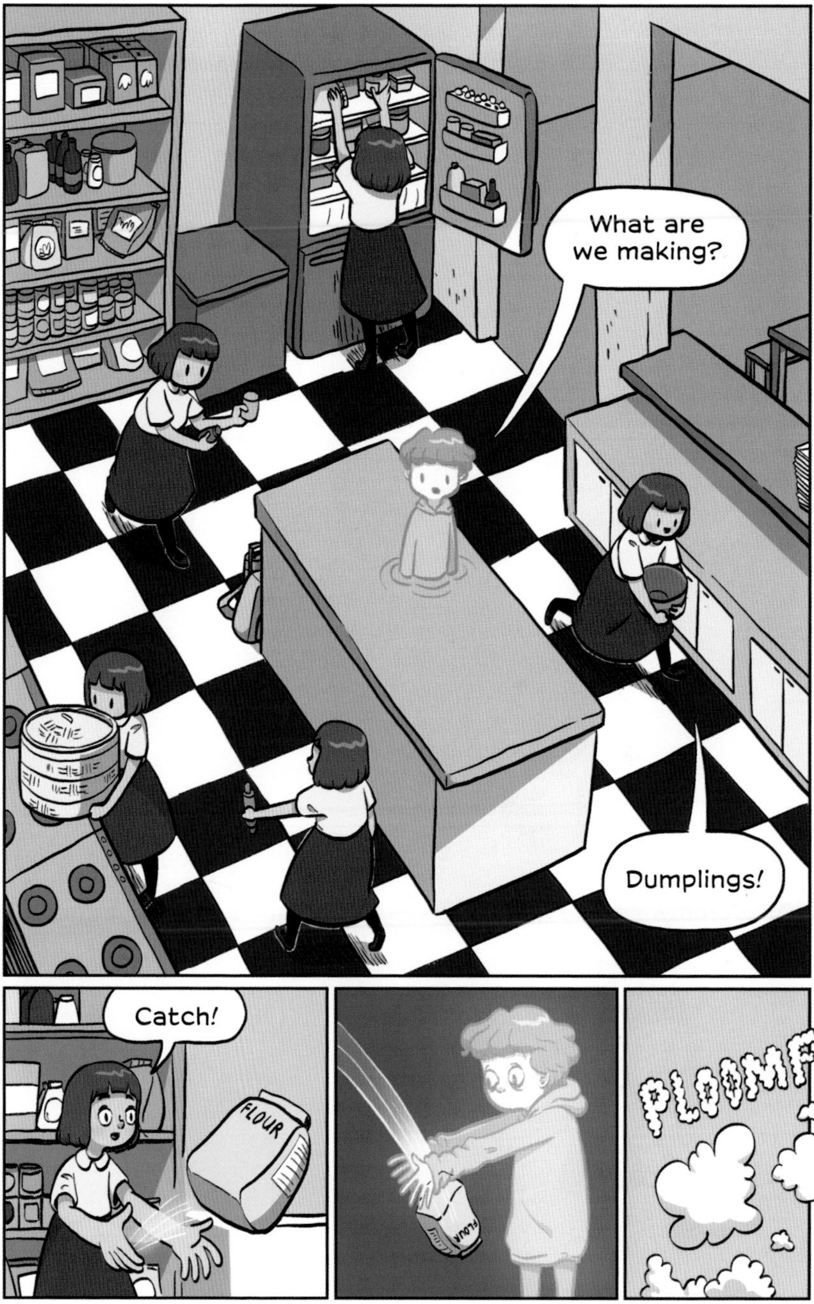
What are we making?
Dumplings!
Catch!
FLOUR
FLOUR
PLOOMF

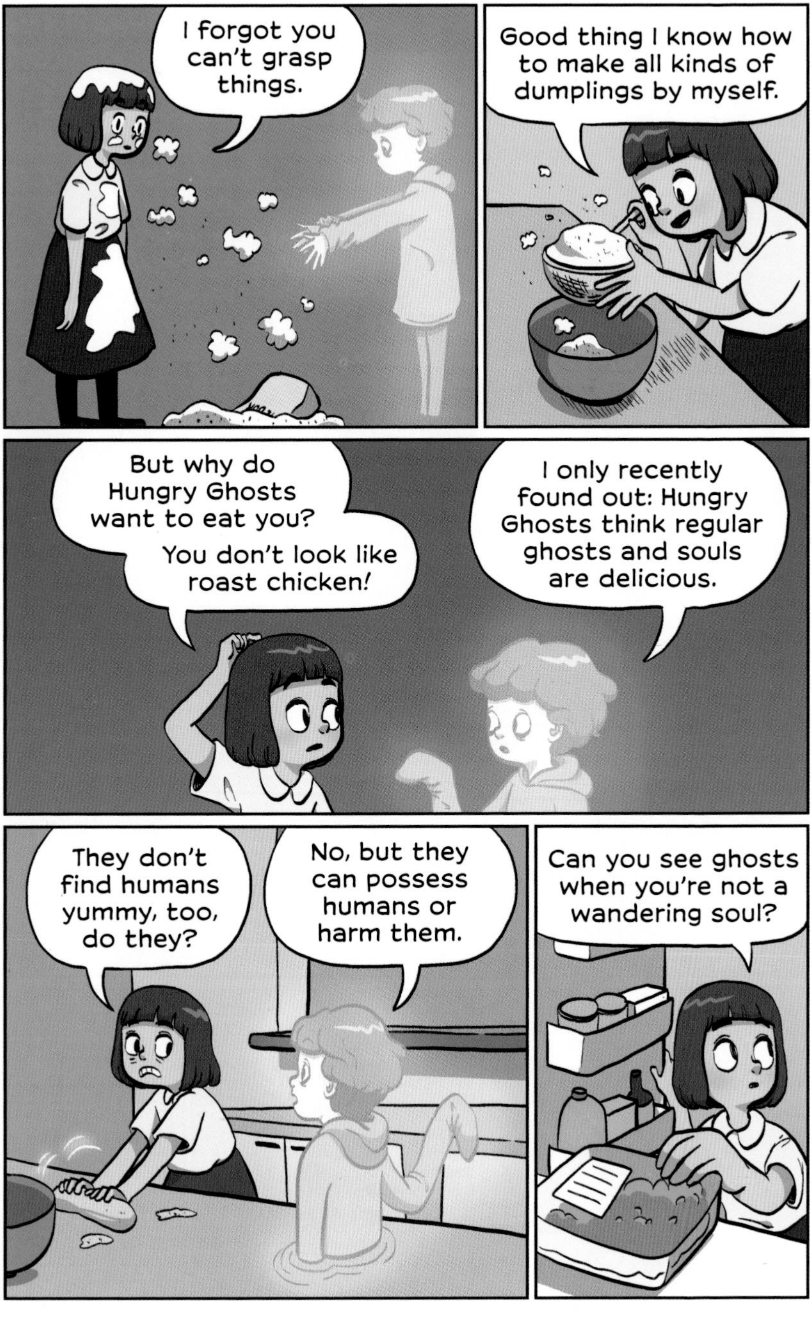
I forgot you can't grasp things.
Good thing I know how to make all kinds of dumplings by myself.
But why do Hungry Ghosts want to eat you?
You don't look like roast chicken!
I only recently found out: Hungry Ghosts think regular ghosts and souls are delicious.
They don't find humans yummy, too, do they?
No, but they can possess humans or harm them.
Can you see ghosts when you're not a wandering soul?

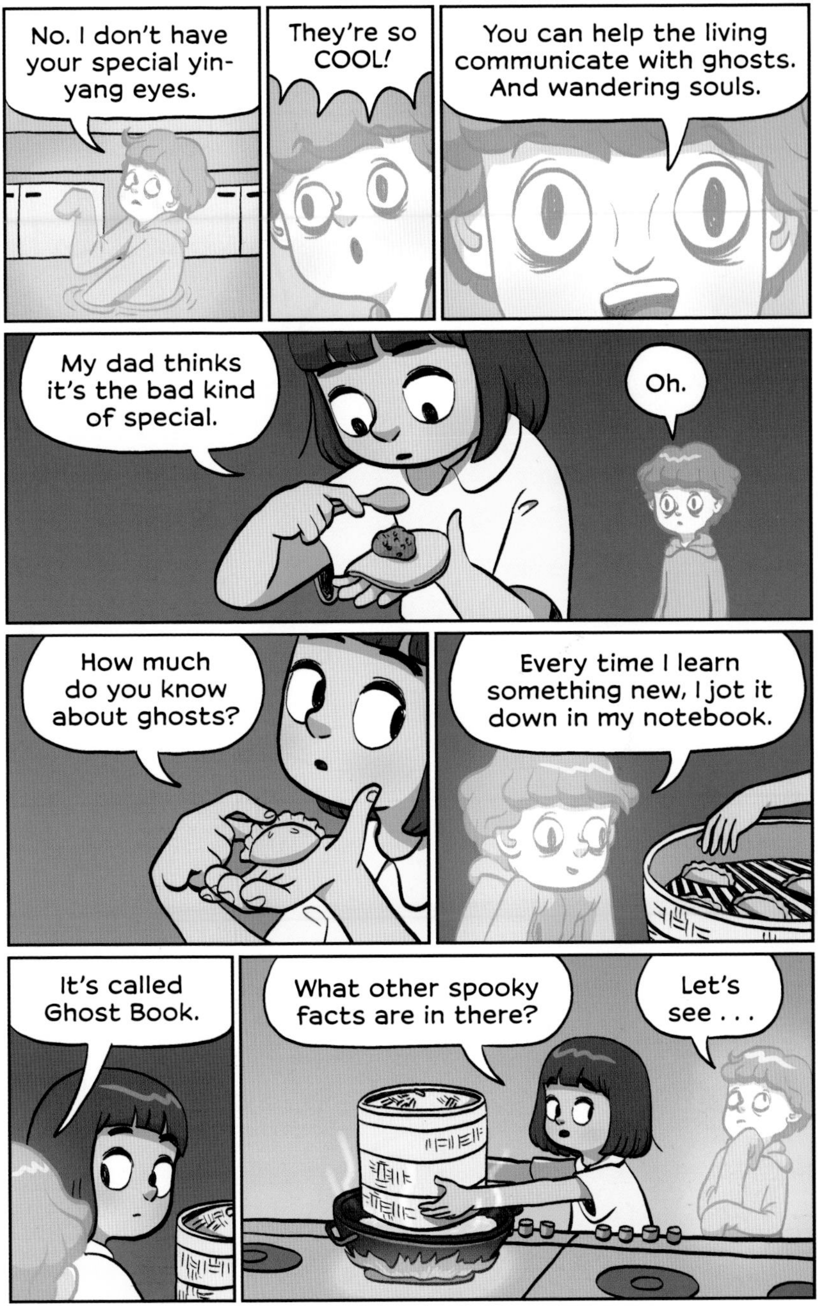

No. I don't have your special yin-yang eyes.
They're so COOL!
You can help the living communicate with ghosts. And wandering souls.
My dad thinks it's the bad kind of special.
Oh.
How much do you know about ghosts?
Every time I learn something new, I jot it down in my notebook.
It's called Ghost Book.
What other spooky facts are in there?
Let's see . . .

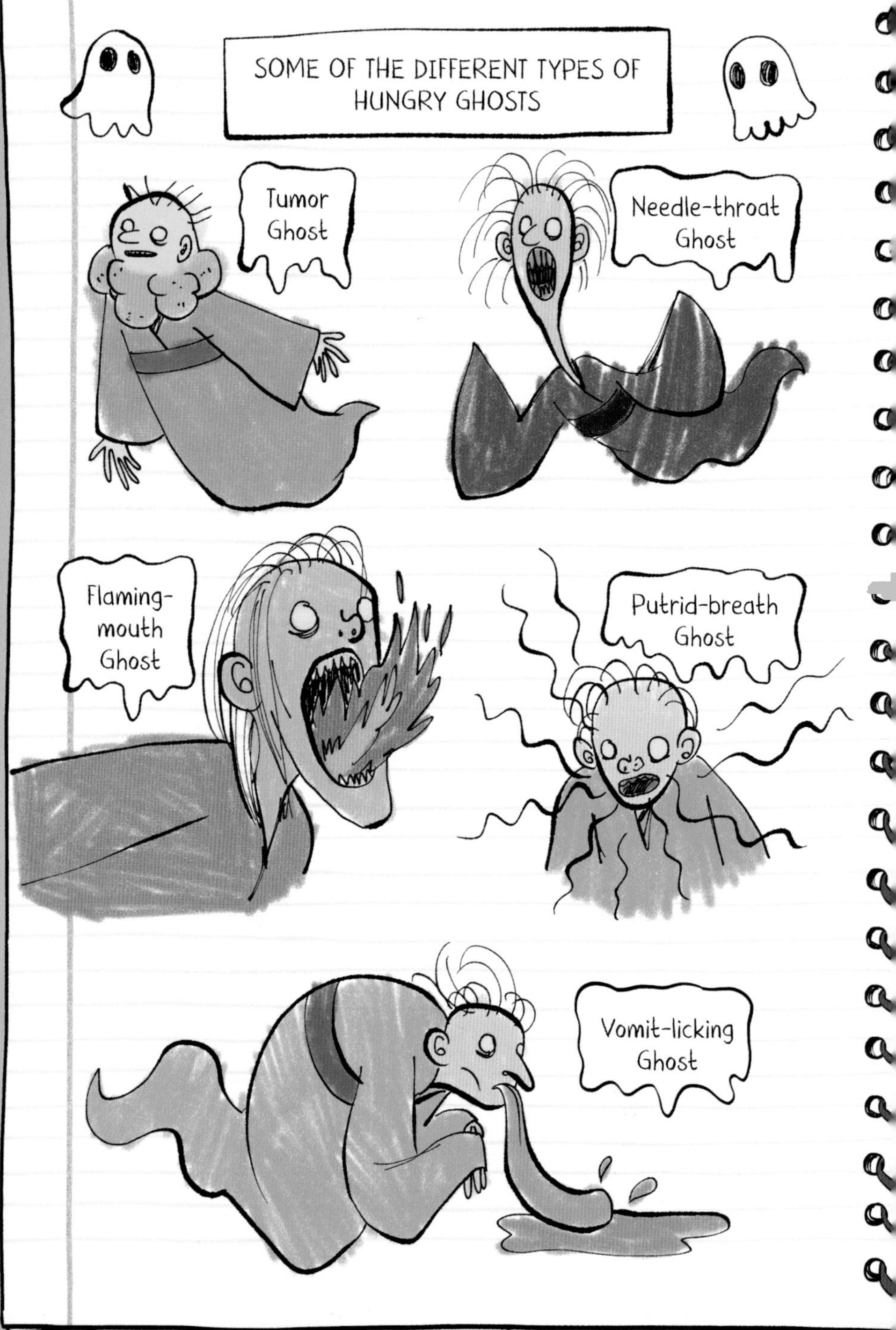
SOME OF THE DIFFERENT TYPES OF HUNGRY GHOSTS
Tumor Ghost
Needle-throat Ghost
Flaming-mouth Ghost
Putrid-breath Ghost
Vomit-licking Ghost

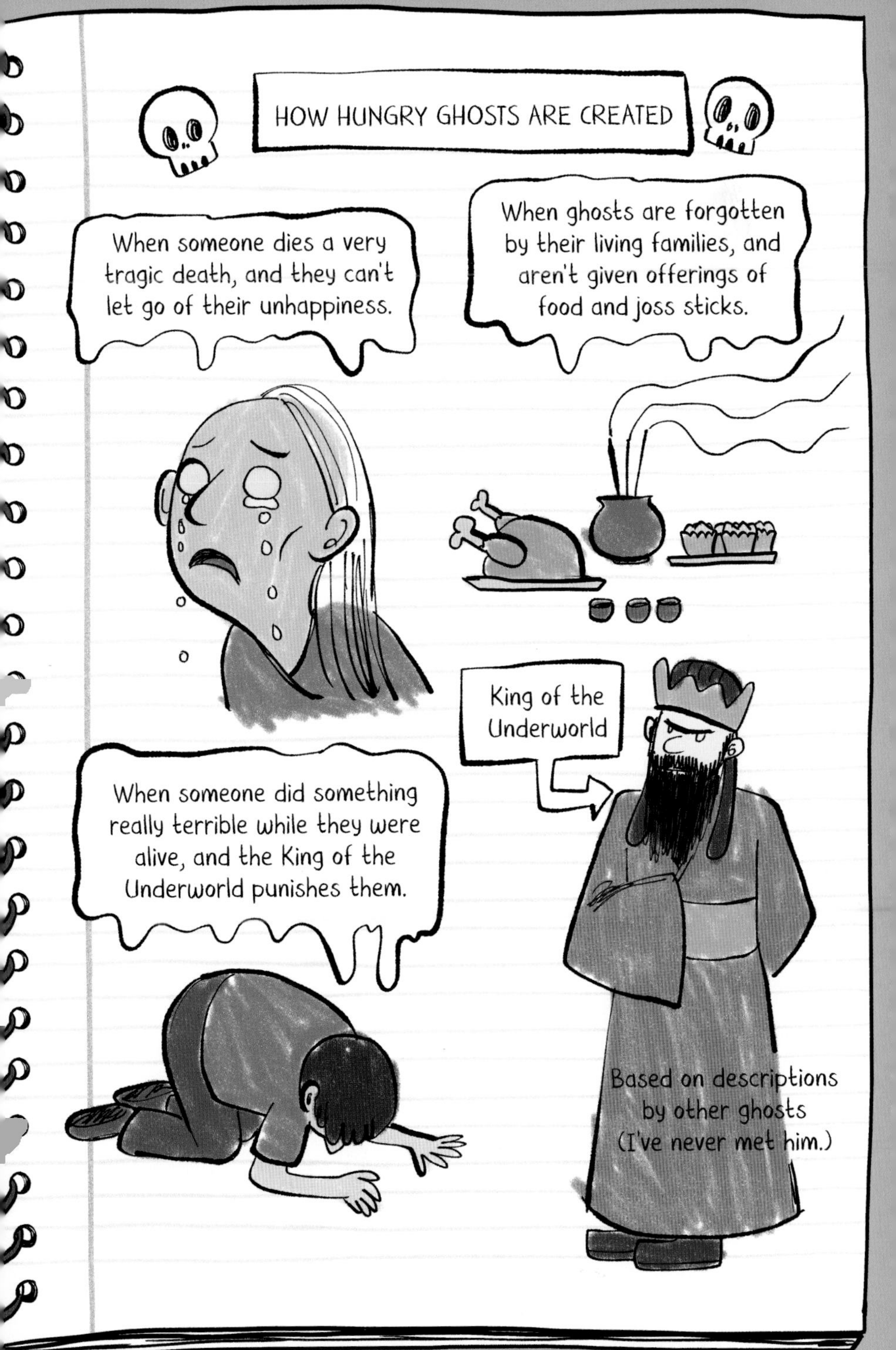
HOW HUNGRY GHOSTS ARE CREATED
When someone dies a very tragic death, and they can't let go of their unhappiness.
When ghosts are forgotten by their living families, and aren't given offerings of food and joss sticks.
King of the Underworld
When someone did something really terrible while they were alive, and the King of the Underworld punishes them.
Based on descriptions by other ghosts (I've never met him.)

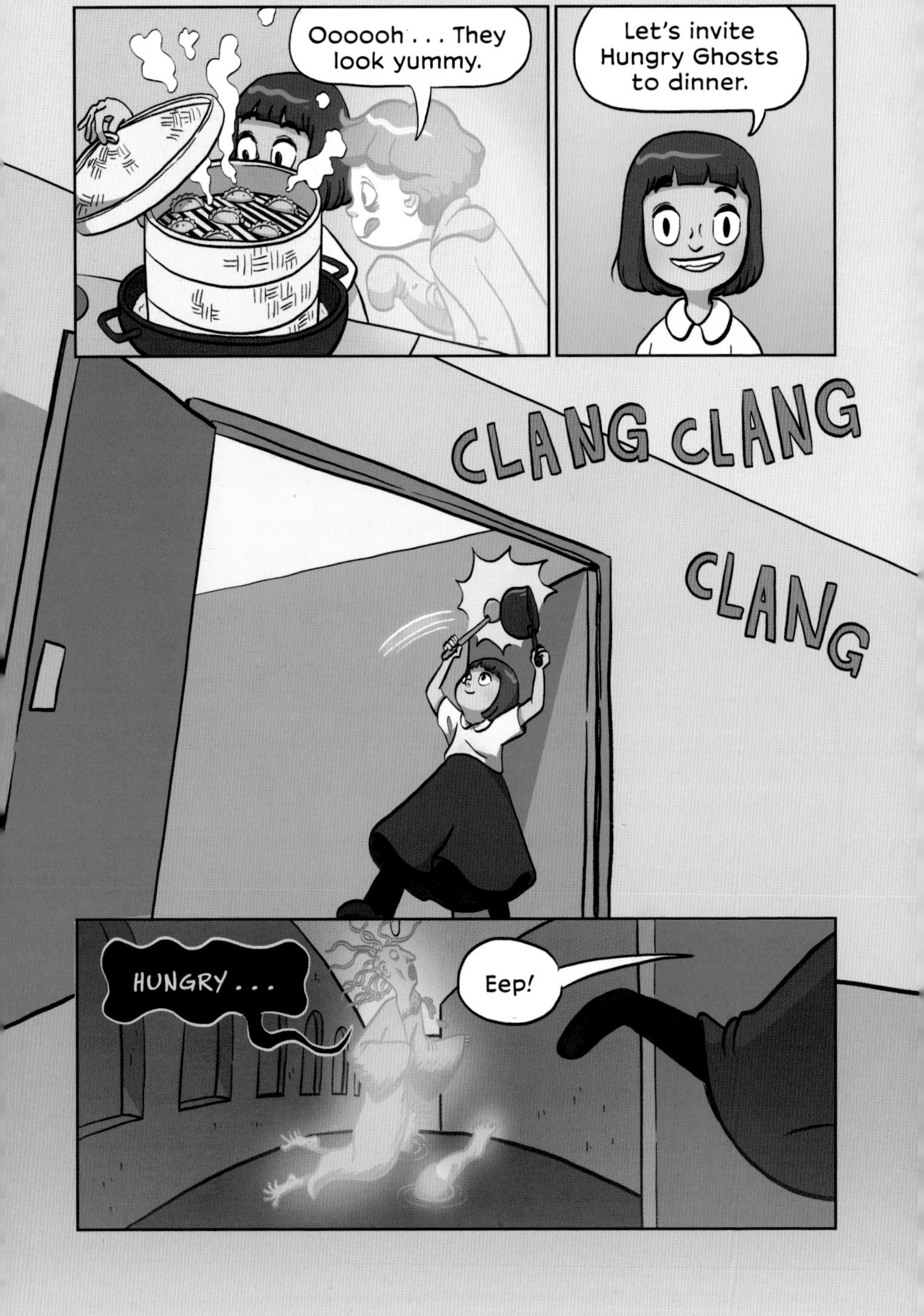
Oooooh . . . They look yummy.
Let's invite Hungry Ghosts to dinner.
CLANG CLANG
CLANG
HUNGRY . . .
Eep!

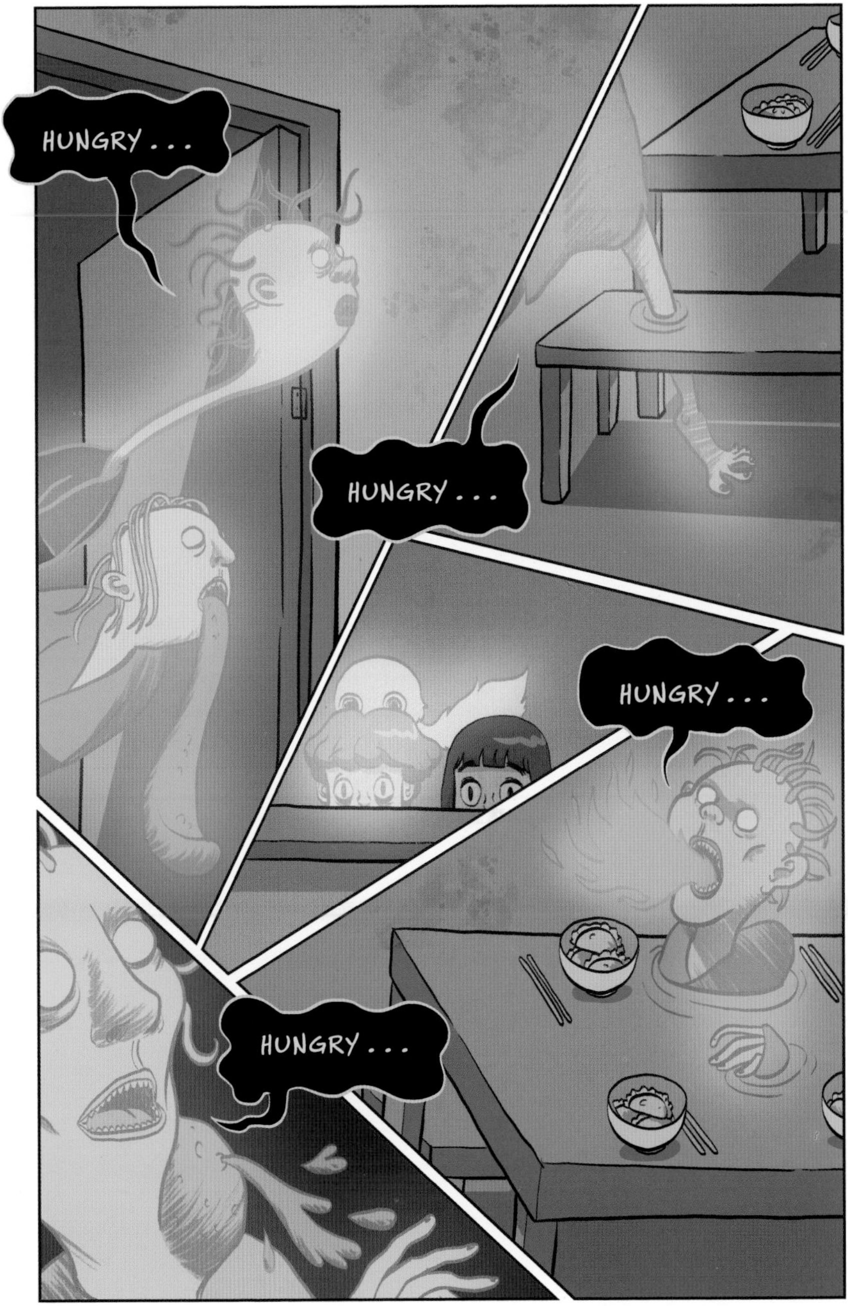
HUNGRY . . .
HUNGRY . . .
HUNGRY . . .
HUNGRY . . .

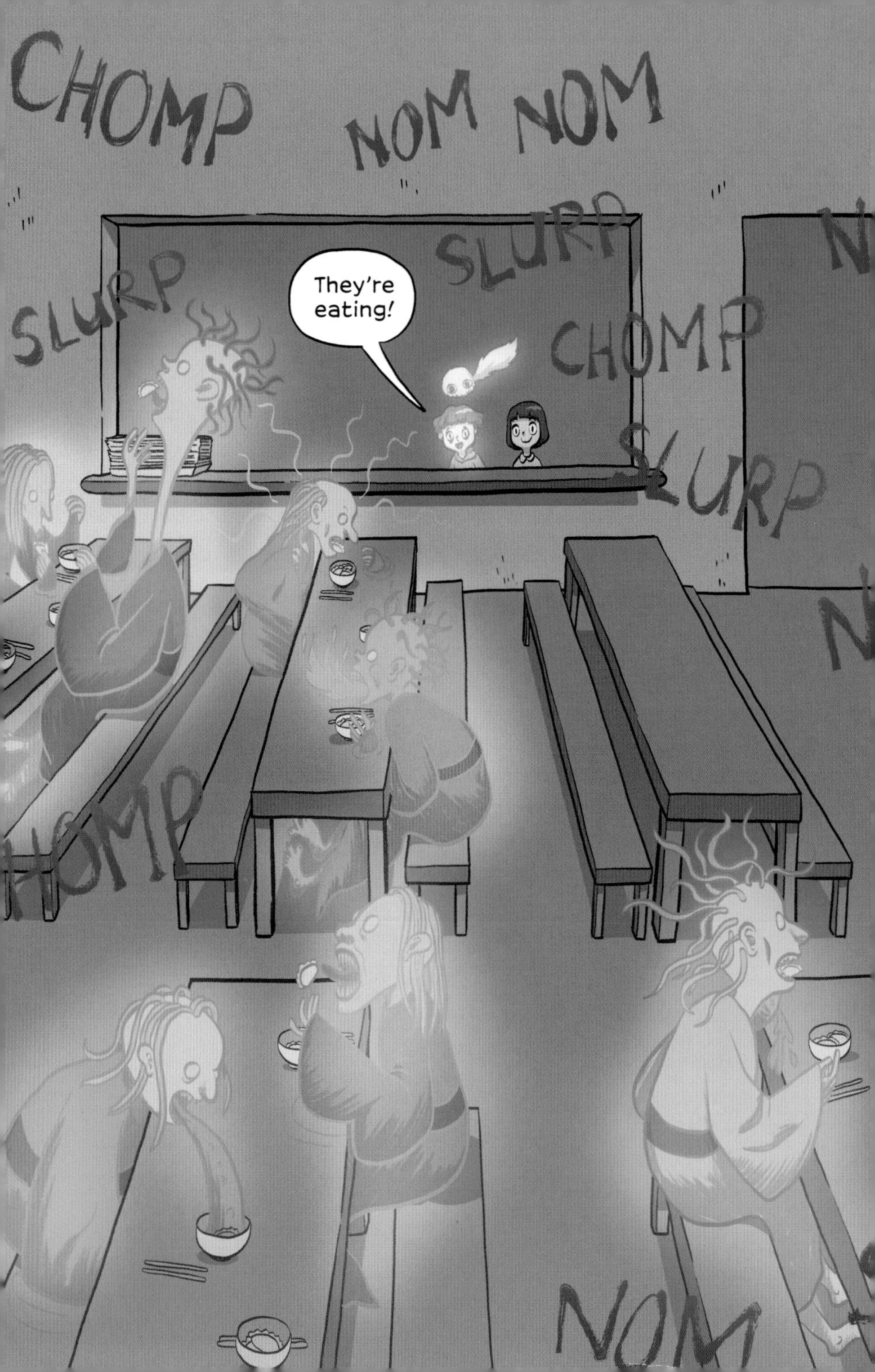
CHOMP
NOM NOM
SLURP
SLURP
They're eating!
CHOMP
SLURP
HOMP
NOM

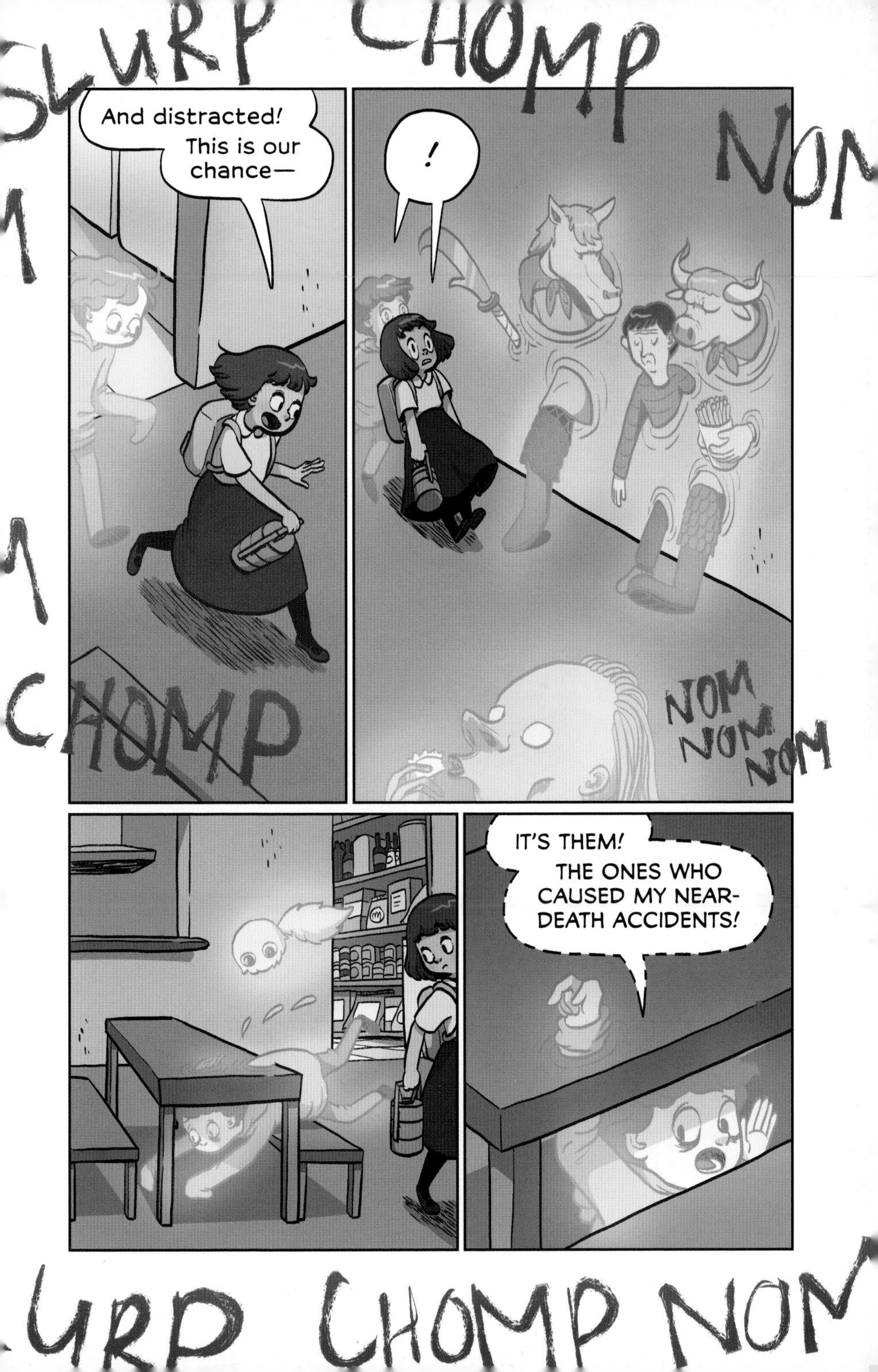
SLURP CHOMP
NOM
And distracted! This is our chance—
!
CHOMP
NOM NOM NOM
IT'S THEM! THE ONES WHO CAUSED MY NEAR-DEATH ACCIDENTS!
URP CHOMP NOM

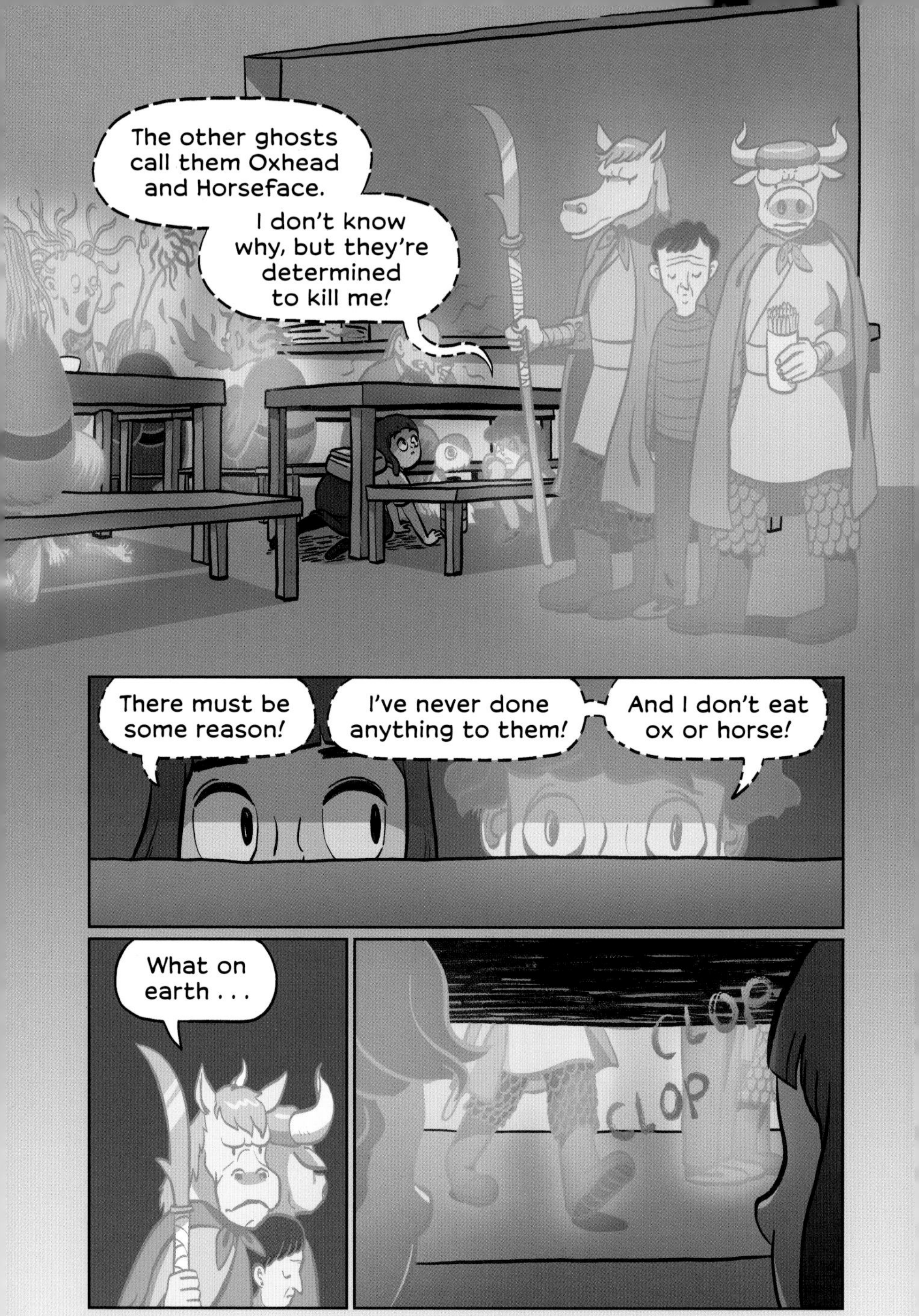
The other ghosts call them Oxhead and Horseface.
I don't know why, but they're determined to kill me!
There must be some reason!
I've never done anything to them!
And I don't eat ox or horse!
What on earth . . .
CLOP
CLOP
CLOP

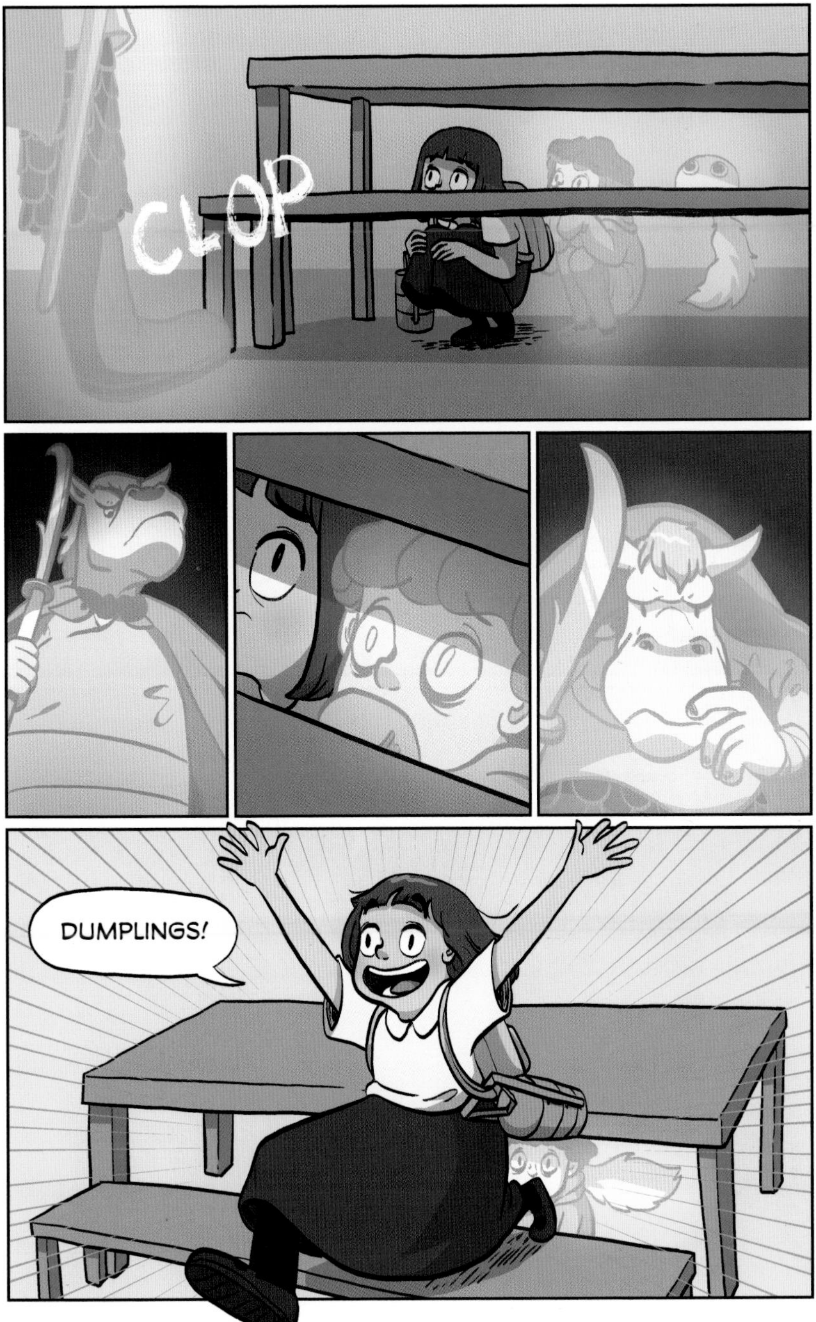
CLOP
DUMPLINGS!

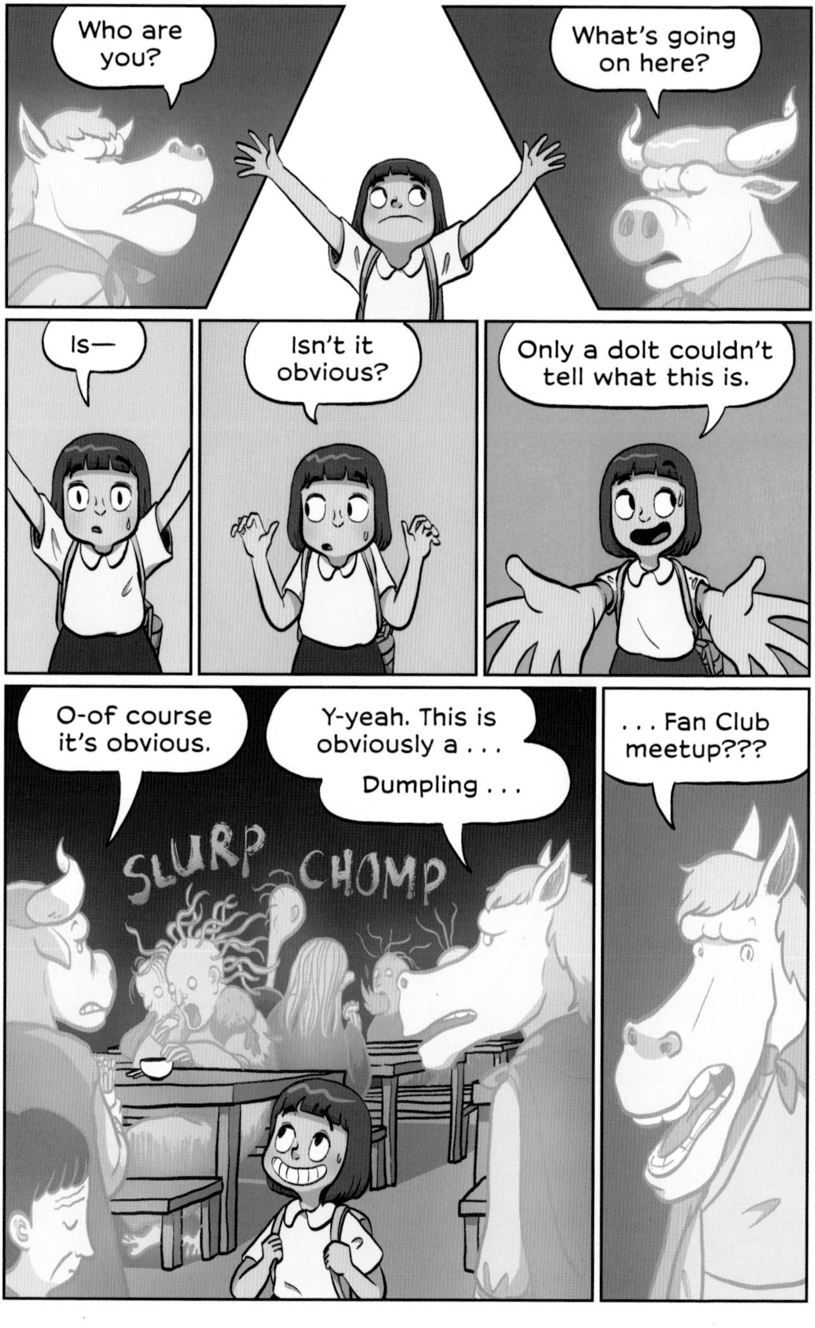
Who are you?
What's going on here?
Is—
Isn't it obvious?
Only a dolt couldn't tell what this is.
O-of course it's obvious.
Y-yeah. This is obviously a . . .
Dumpling . . .
SLURP
CHOMP
. . . Fan Club meetup???

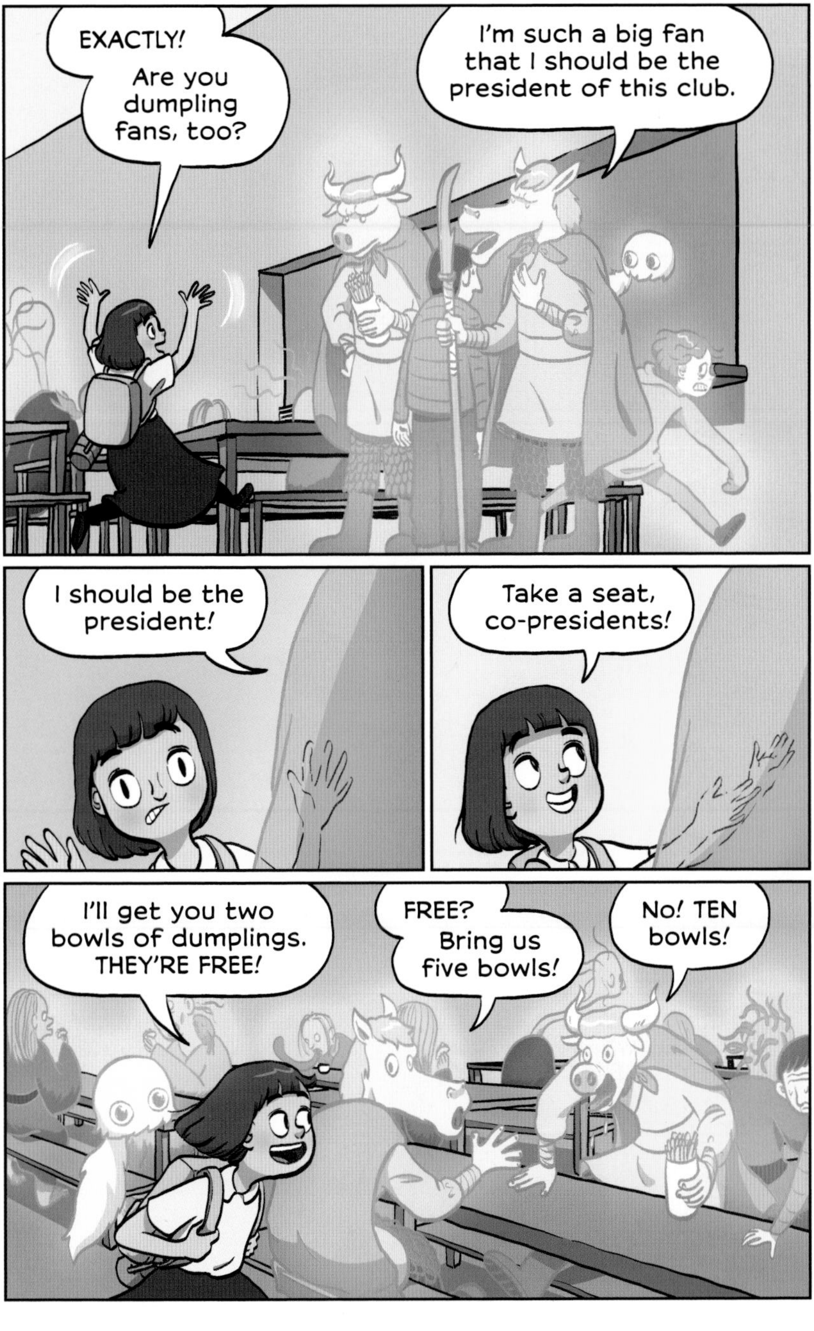
EXACTLY! Are you dumpling fans, too?
I'm such a big fan that I should be the president of this club.
I should be the president!
Take a seat, co-presidents!
I'll get you two bowls of dumplings. THEY'RE FREE!
FREE? Bring us five bowls!
No! TEN bowls!

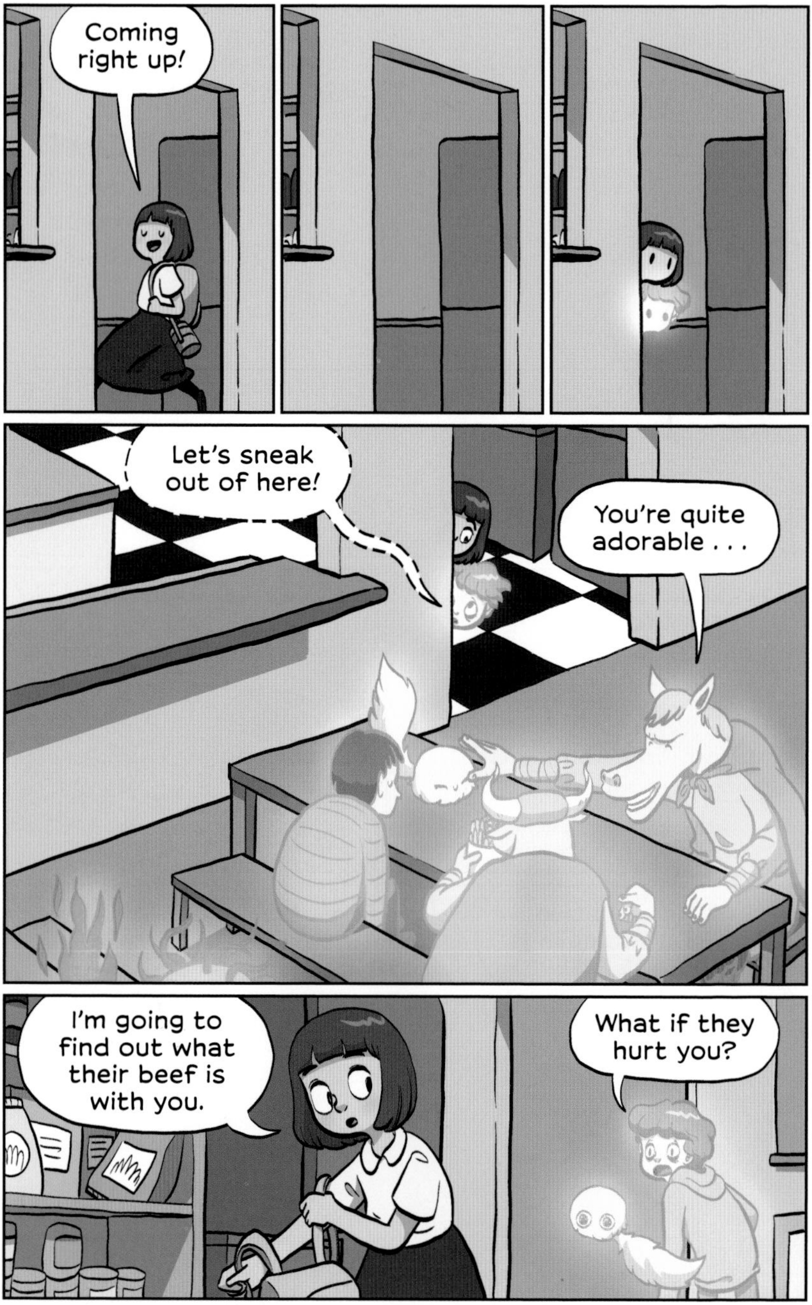
Coming right up!
Let's sneak out of here!
You're quite adorable . . .
I'm going to find out what their beef is with you.
What if they hurt you?

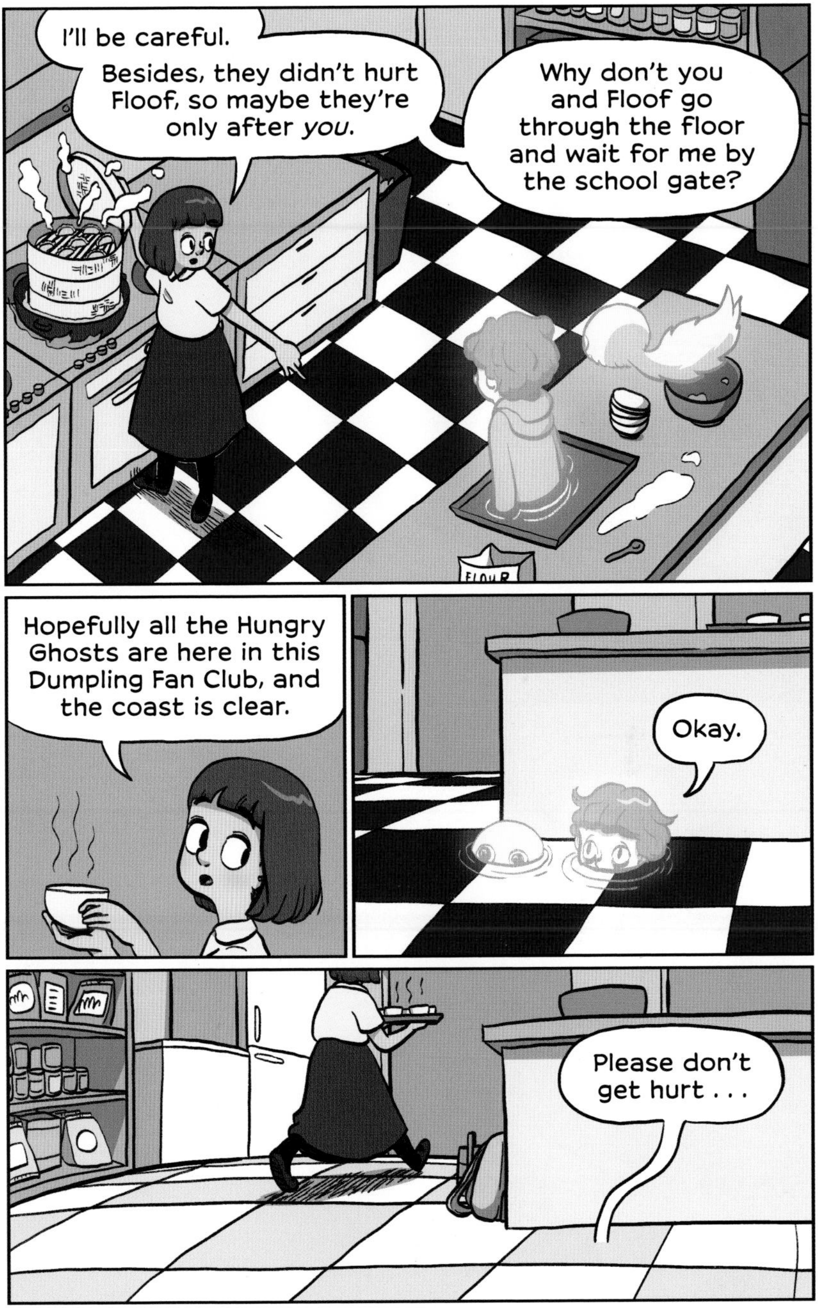
I'll be careful.
Besides, they didn't hurt Floof, so maybe they're only after *you*.
Why don't you and Floof go through the floor and wait for me by the school gate?
Hopefully all the Hungry Ghosts are here in this Dumpling Fan Club, and the coast is clear.
Okay.
Please don't get hurt . . .

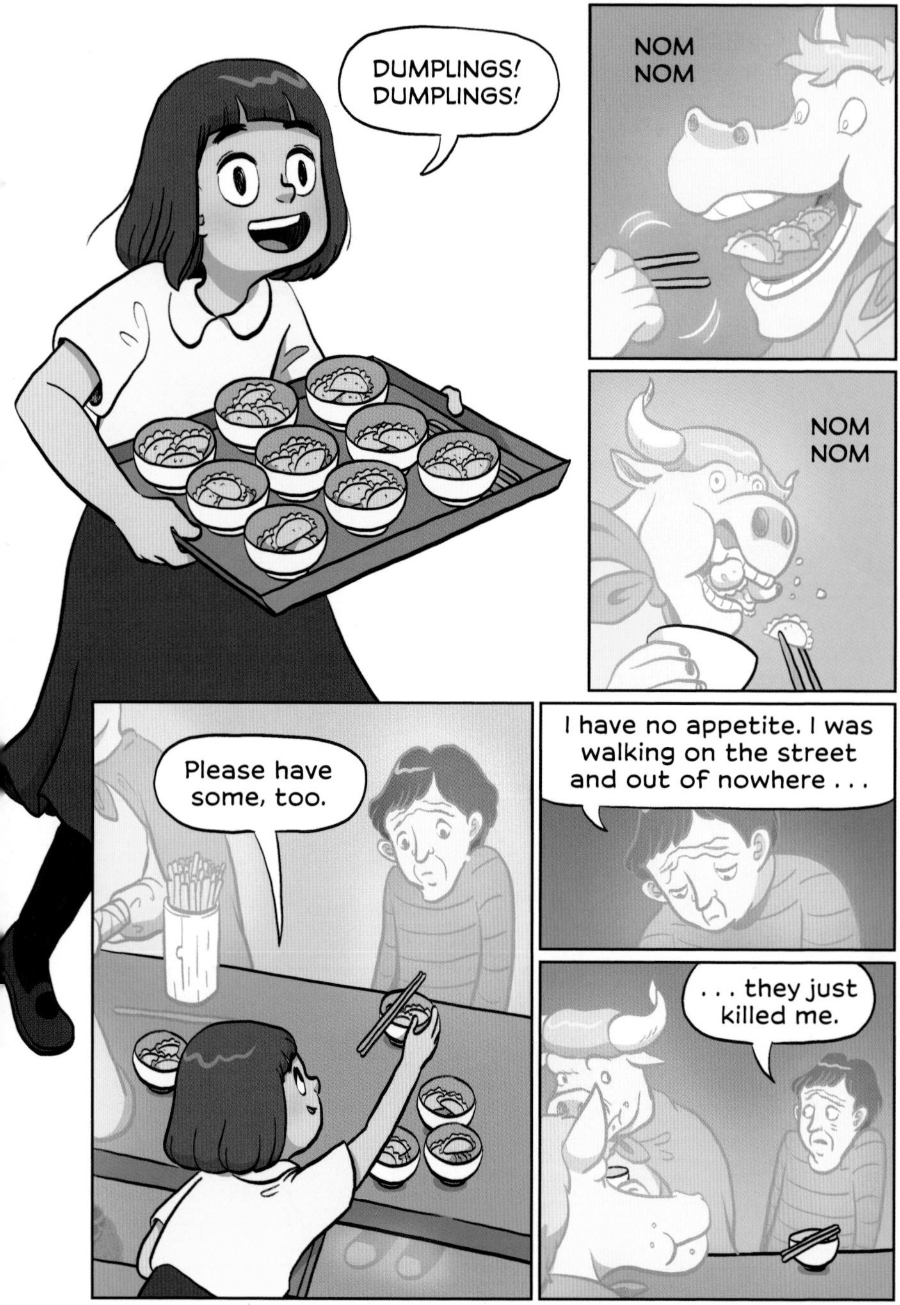
DUMPLINGS! DUMPLINGS!
NOM NOM
NOM NOM
Please have some, too.
I have no appetite. I was walking on the street and out of nowhere . . .
. . . they just killed me.

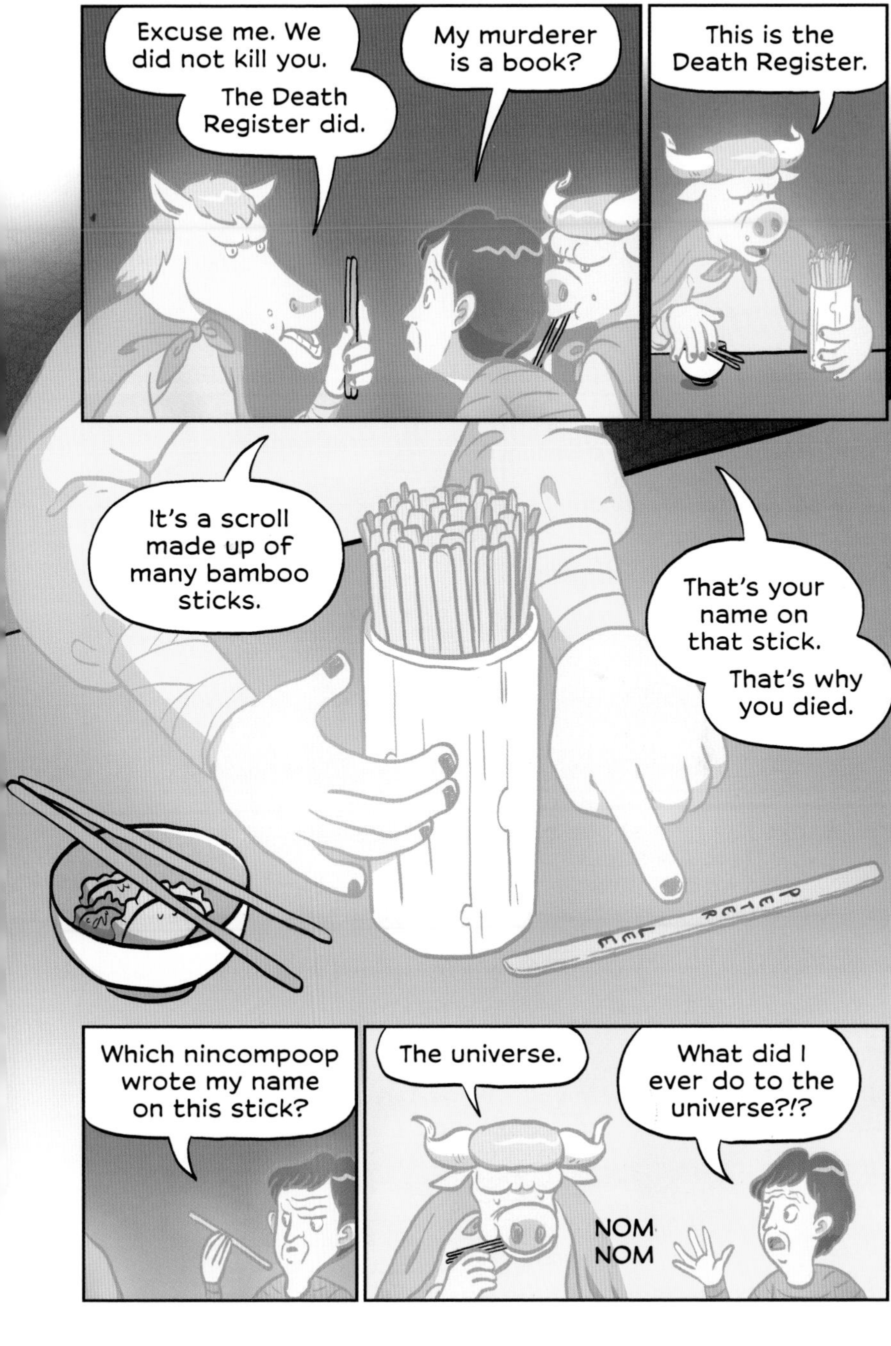
Excuse me. We did not kill you.
The Death Register did.
My murderer is a book?
This is the Death Register.
It's a scroll made up of many bamboo sticks.
That's your name on that stick.
That's why you died.
PETER LEE
Which nincompoop wrote my name on this stick?
The universe.
What did I ever do to the universe?!?
NOM NOM

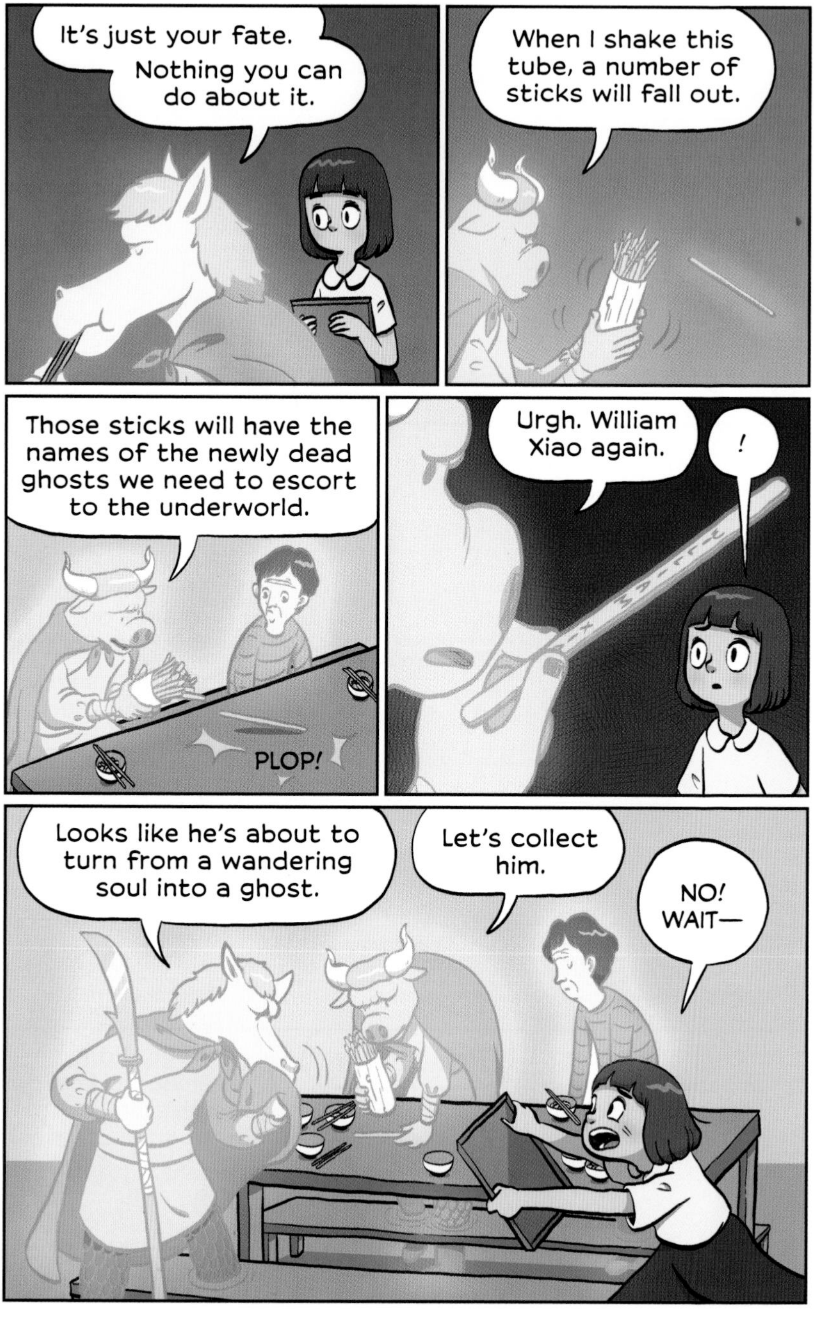
It's just your fate.
Nothing you can do about it.
When I shake this tube, a number of sticks will fall out.
Those sticks will have the names of the newly dead ghosts we need to escort to the underworld.
PLOP!
Urgh. William Xiao again.
!
Looks like he's about to turn from a wandering soul into a ghost.
Let's collect him.
NO! WAIT—

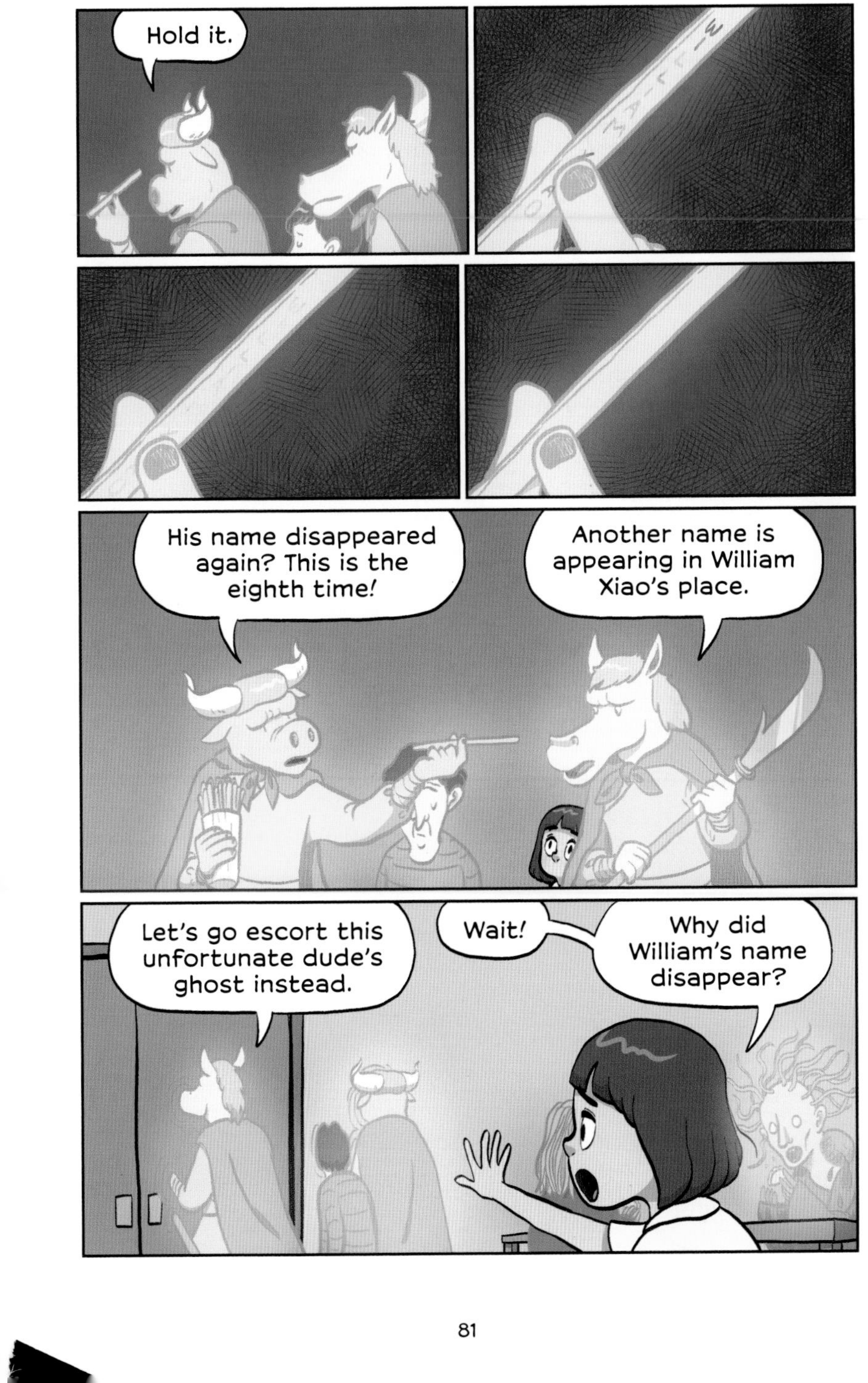
Hold it.
His name disappeared again? This is the eighth time!
Another name is appearing in William Xiao's place.
Let's go escort this unfortunate dude's ghost instead.
Wait!
Why did William's name disappear?

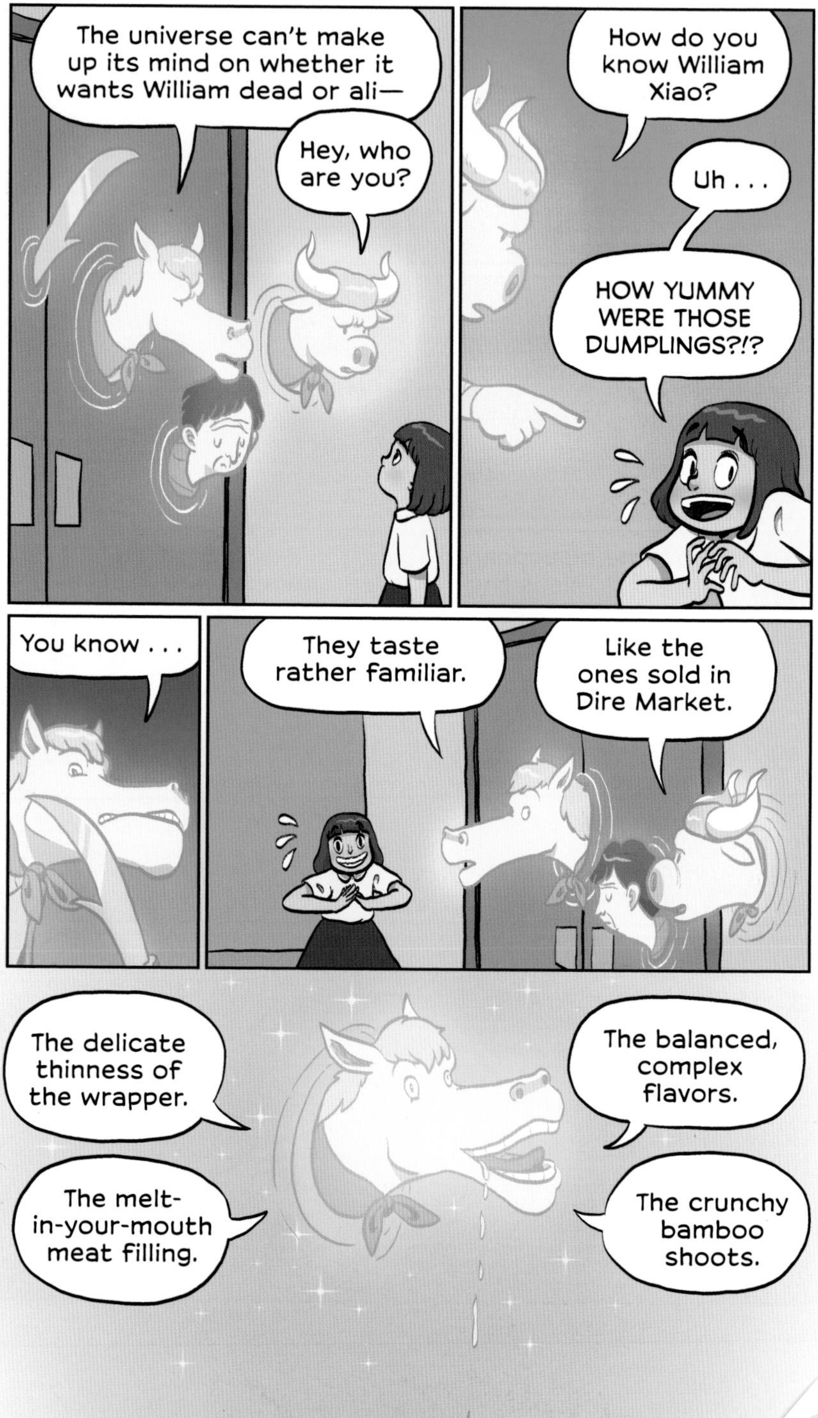

The universe can't make up its mind on whether it wants William dead or ali—
Hey, who are you?
How do you know William Xiao?
Uh . . .
HOW YUMMY WERE THOSE DUMPLINGS?!?
You know . . .
They taste rather familiar.
Like the ones sold in Dire Market.
The delicate thinness of the wrapper.
The balanced, complex flavors.
The melt-in-your-mouth meat filling.
The crunchy bamboo shoots.

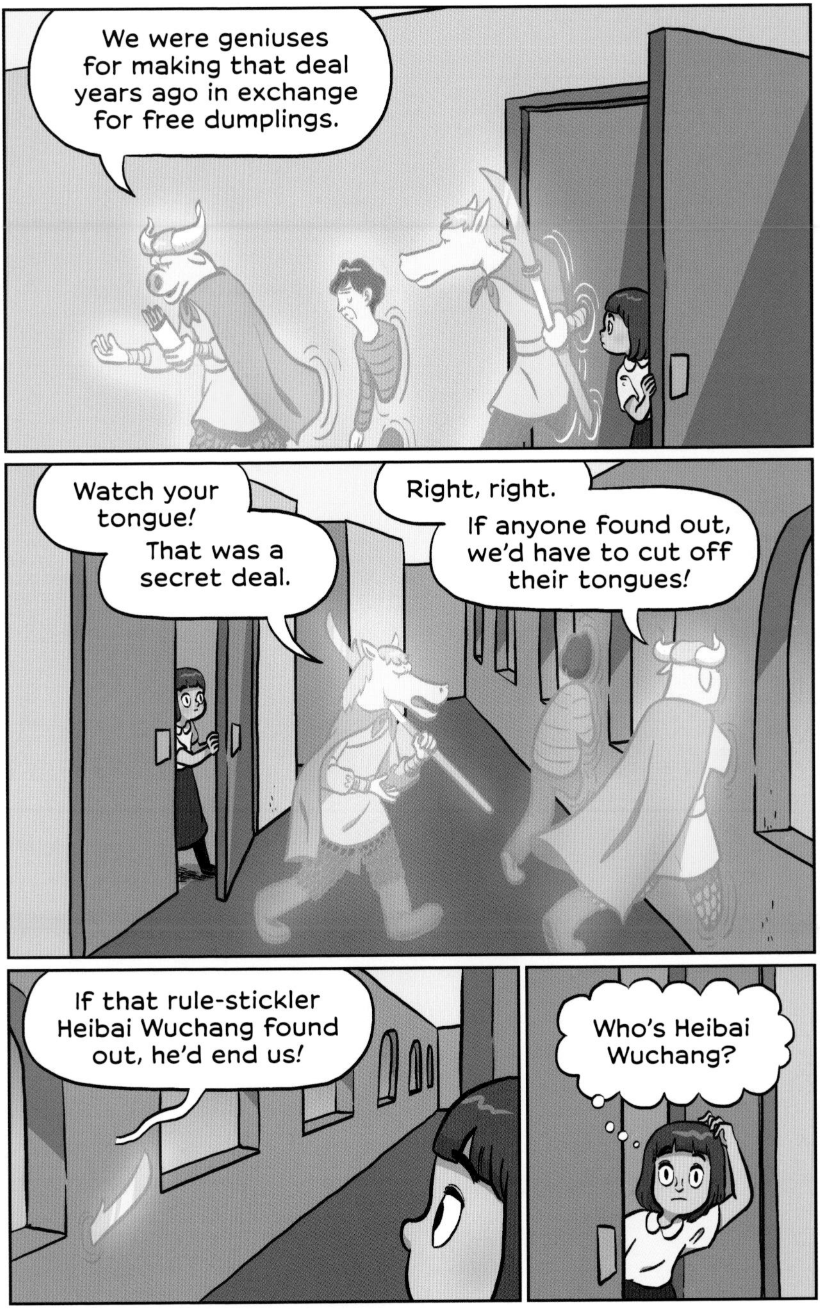
We were geniuses for making that deal years ago in exchange for free dumplings.
Watch your tongue!
That was a secret deal.
Right, right.
If anyone found out, we'd have to cut off their tongues!
If that rule-stickler Heibai Wuchang found out, he'd end us!
Who's Heibai Wuchang?

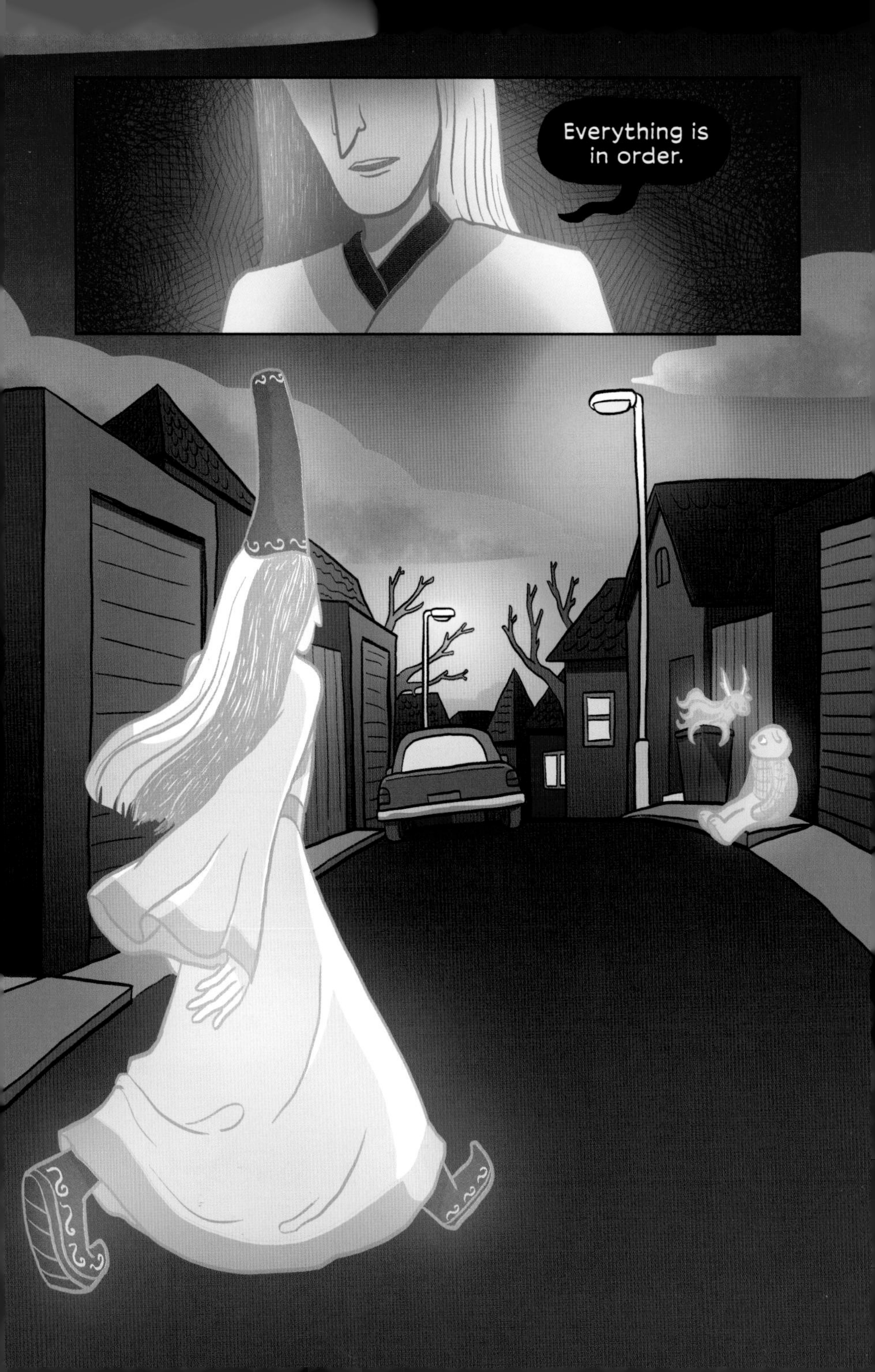
Everything is in order.

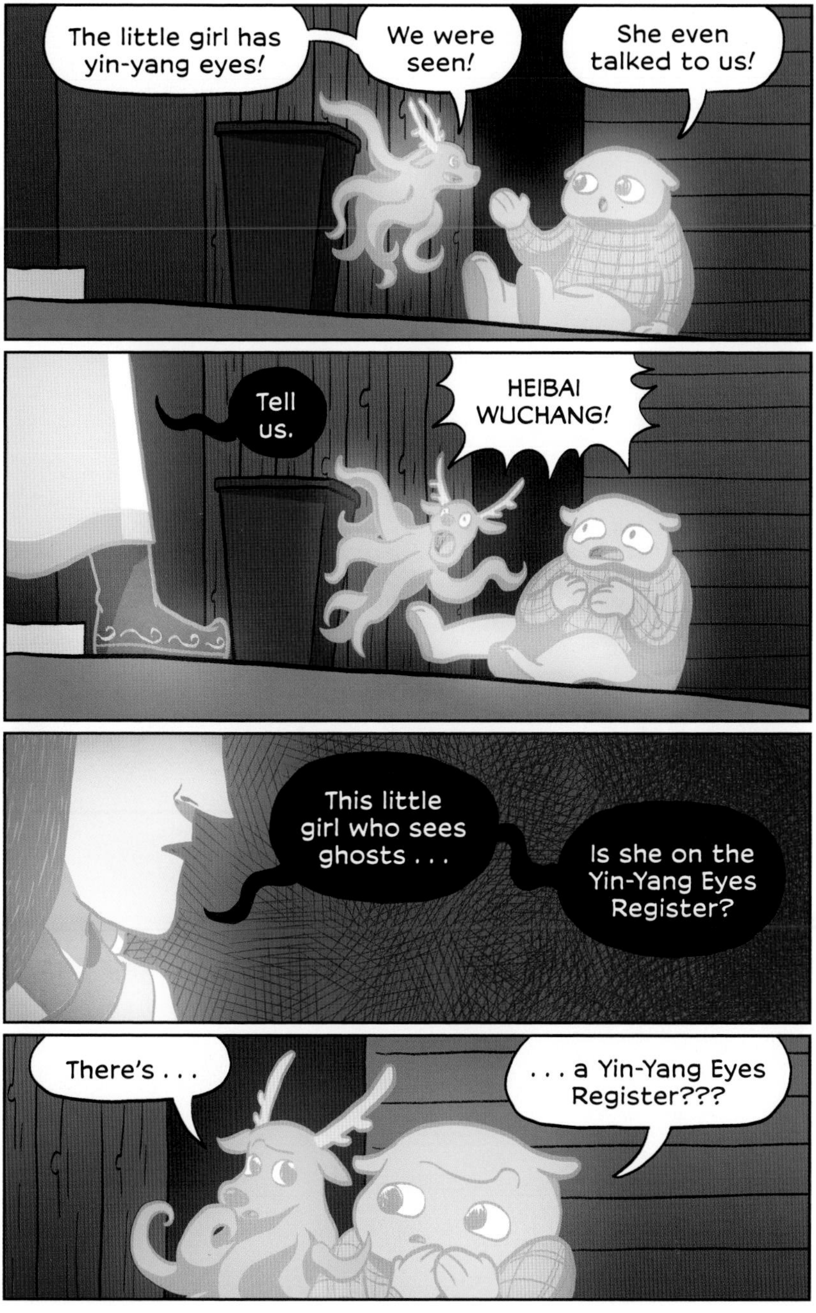
The little girl has yin-yang eyes!
We were seen!
She even talked to us!
Tell us.
HEIBAI WUCHANG!
This little girl who sees ghosts . . .
Is she on the Yin-Yang Eyes Register?
There's . . .
. . . a Yin-Yang Eyes Register???

The underworld has many registers to keep everything in order.

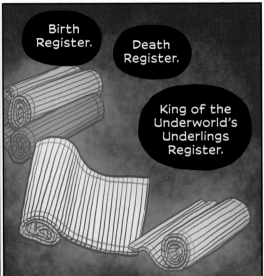

Birth Register.

Death Register.

King of the Underworld's Underlings Register.

Just to name a few.

We've seen that girl around the school before, but she never acted like she could see us.

Until today.

Unacceptable. Anarchy.

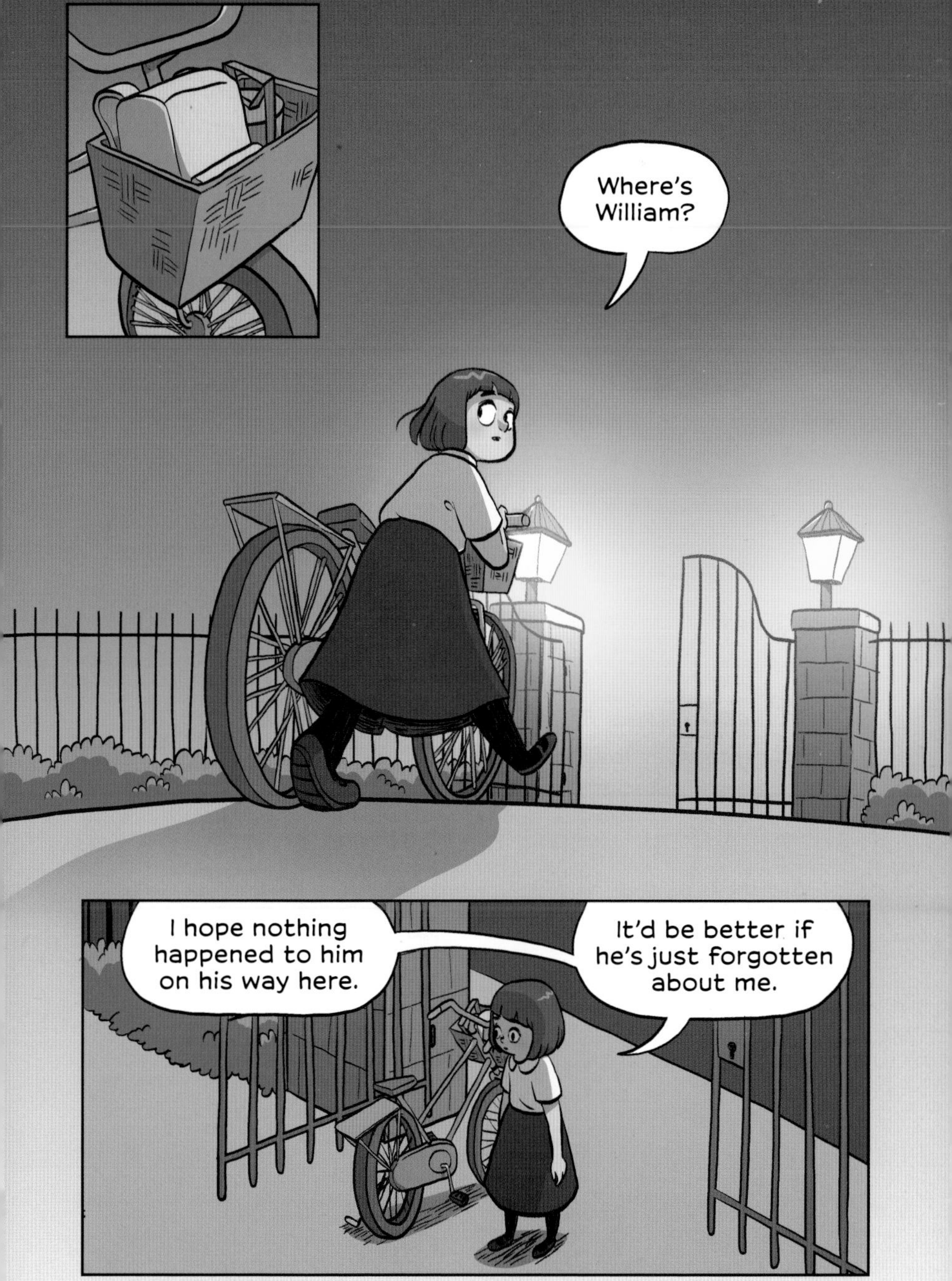
Where's William?
I hope nothing happened to him on his way here.
It'd be better if he's just forgotten about me.

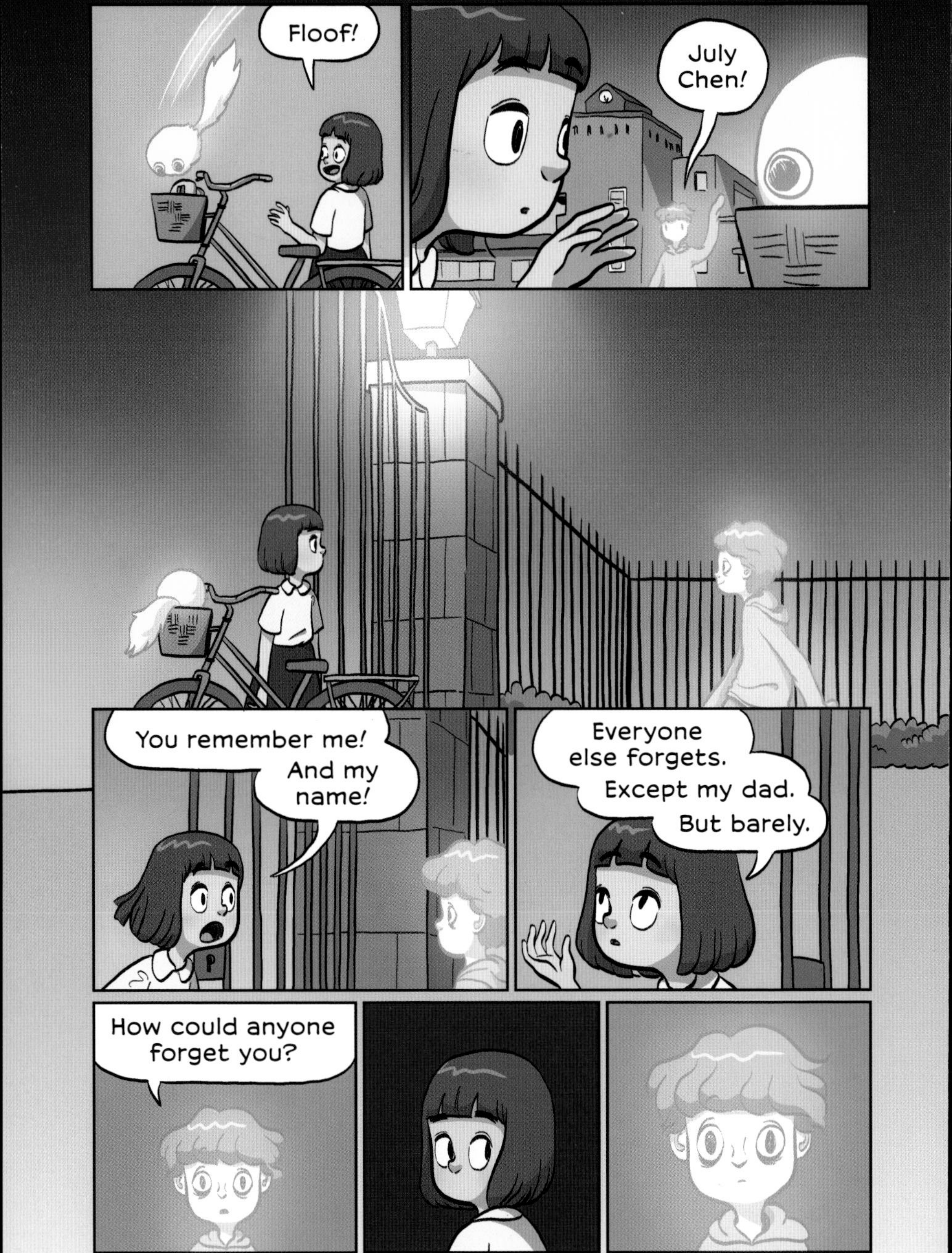

Floof!
July Chen!
You remember me!
And my name!
Everyone else forgets.
Except my dad.
But barely.
How could anyone forget you?

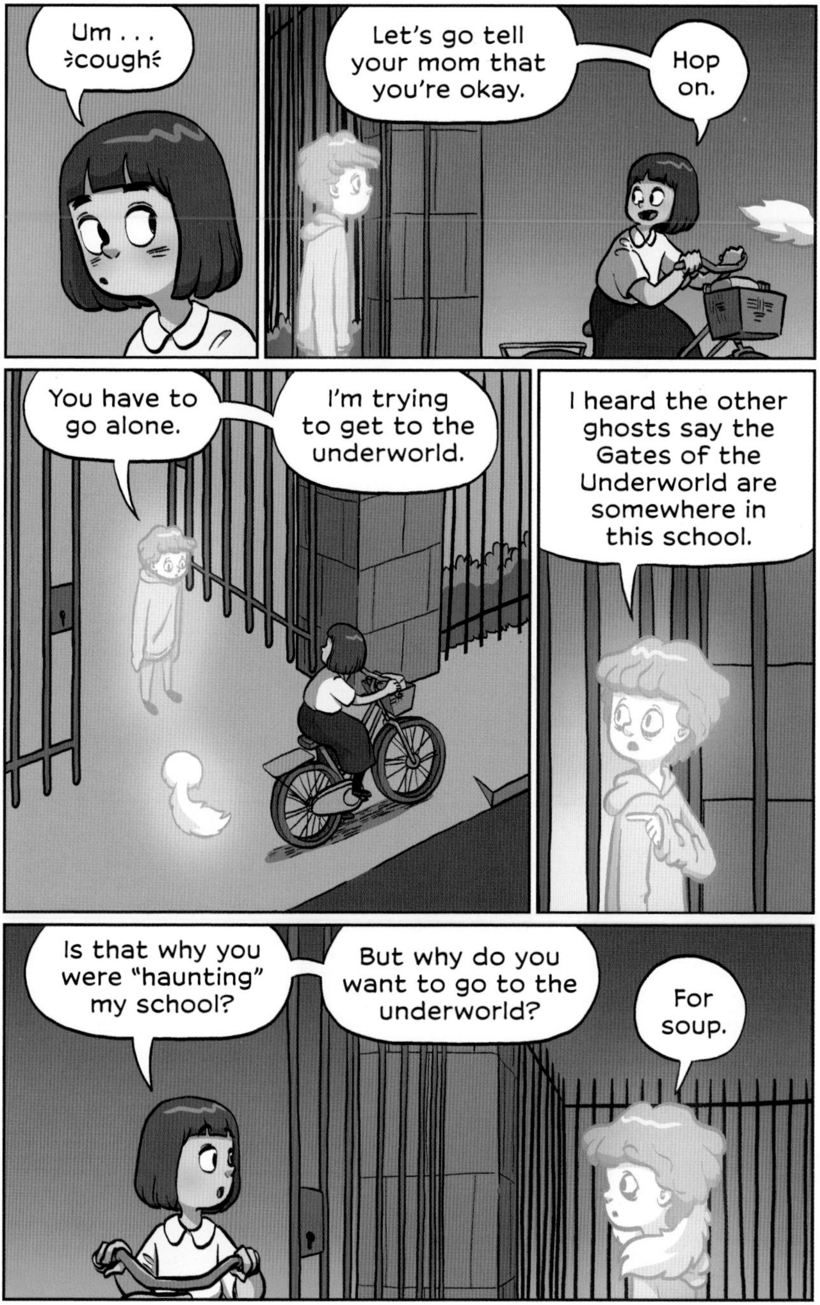
Um . . .
cough
Let's go tell your mom that you're okay.
Hop on.
You have to go alone.
I'm trying to get to the underworld.
I heard the other ghosts say the Gates of the Underworld are somewhere in this school.
Is that why you were "haunting" my school?
But why do you want to go to the underworld?
For soup.

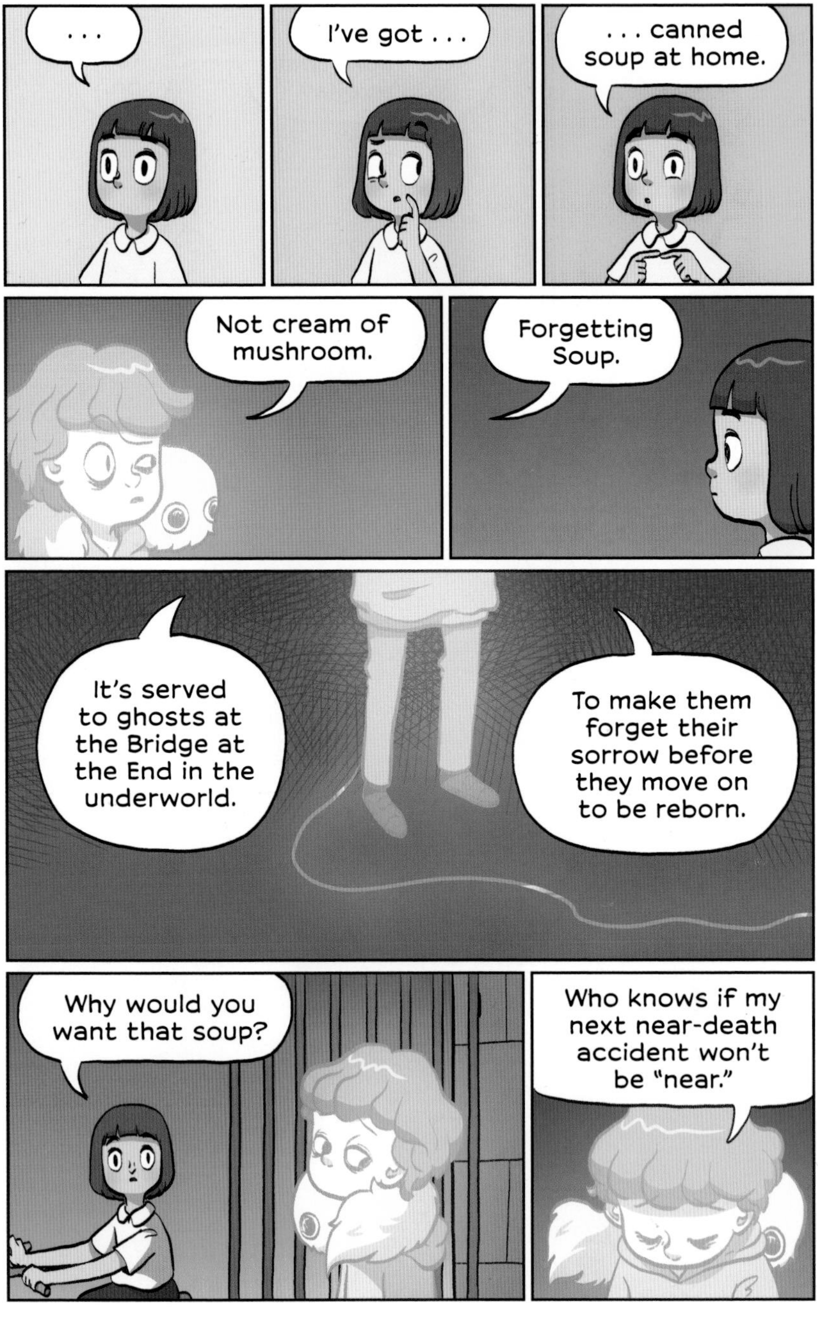
. . .
I've got . . .
. . . canned soup at home.
Not cream of mushroom.
Forgetting Soup.
It's served to ghosts at the Bridge at the End in the underworld.
To make them forget their sorrow before they move on to be reborn.
Why would you want that soup?
Who knows if my next near-death accident won't be "near."

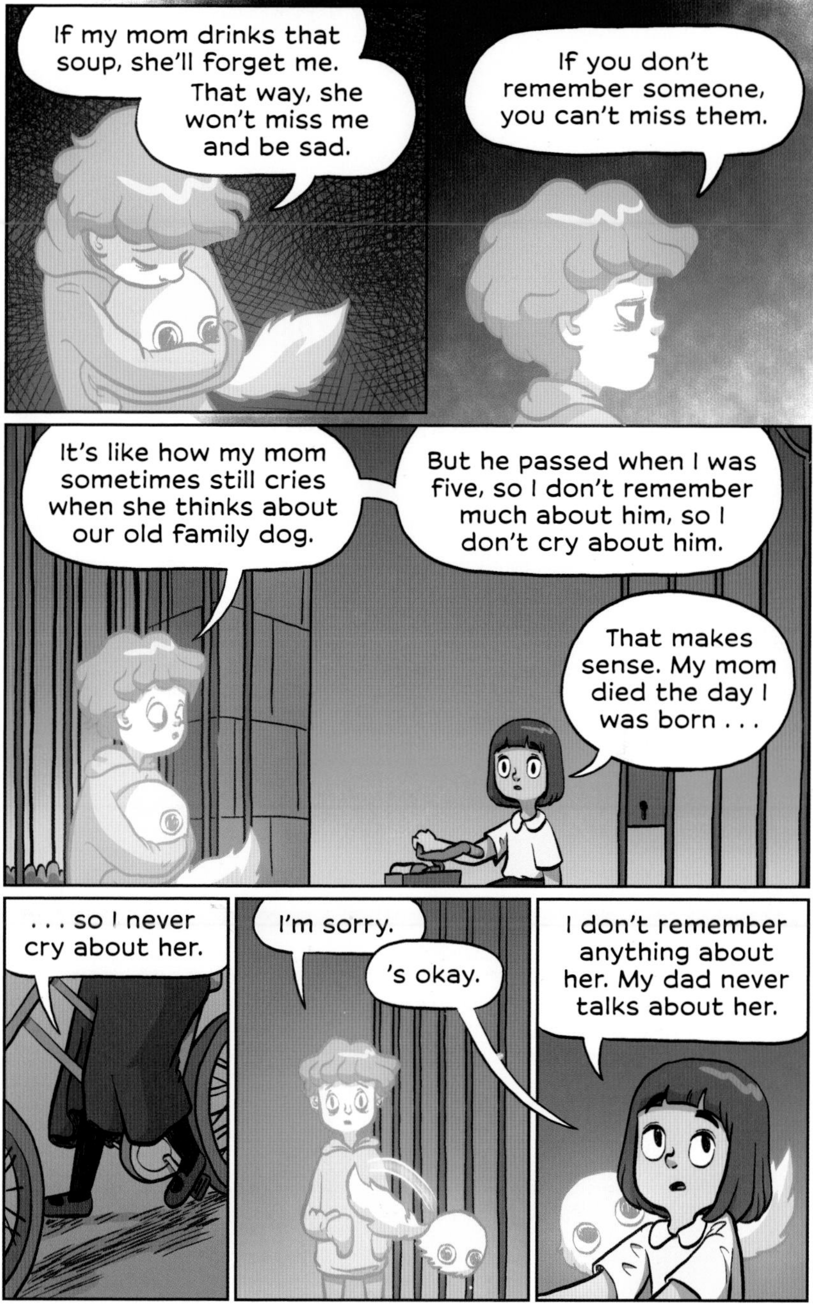
If my mom drinks that soup, she'll forget me.
That way, she won't miss me and be sad.
If you don't remember someone, you can't miss them.
It's like how my mom sometimes still cries when she thinks about our old family dog.
But he passed when I was five, so I don't remember much about him, so I don't cry about him.
That makes sense. My mom died the day I was born . . .
. . . so I never cry about her.
I'm sorry.
's okay.
I don't remember anything about her. My dad never talks about her.

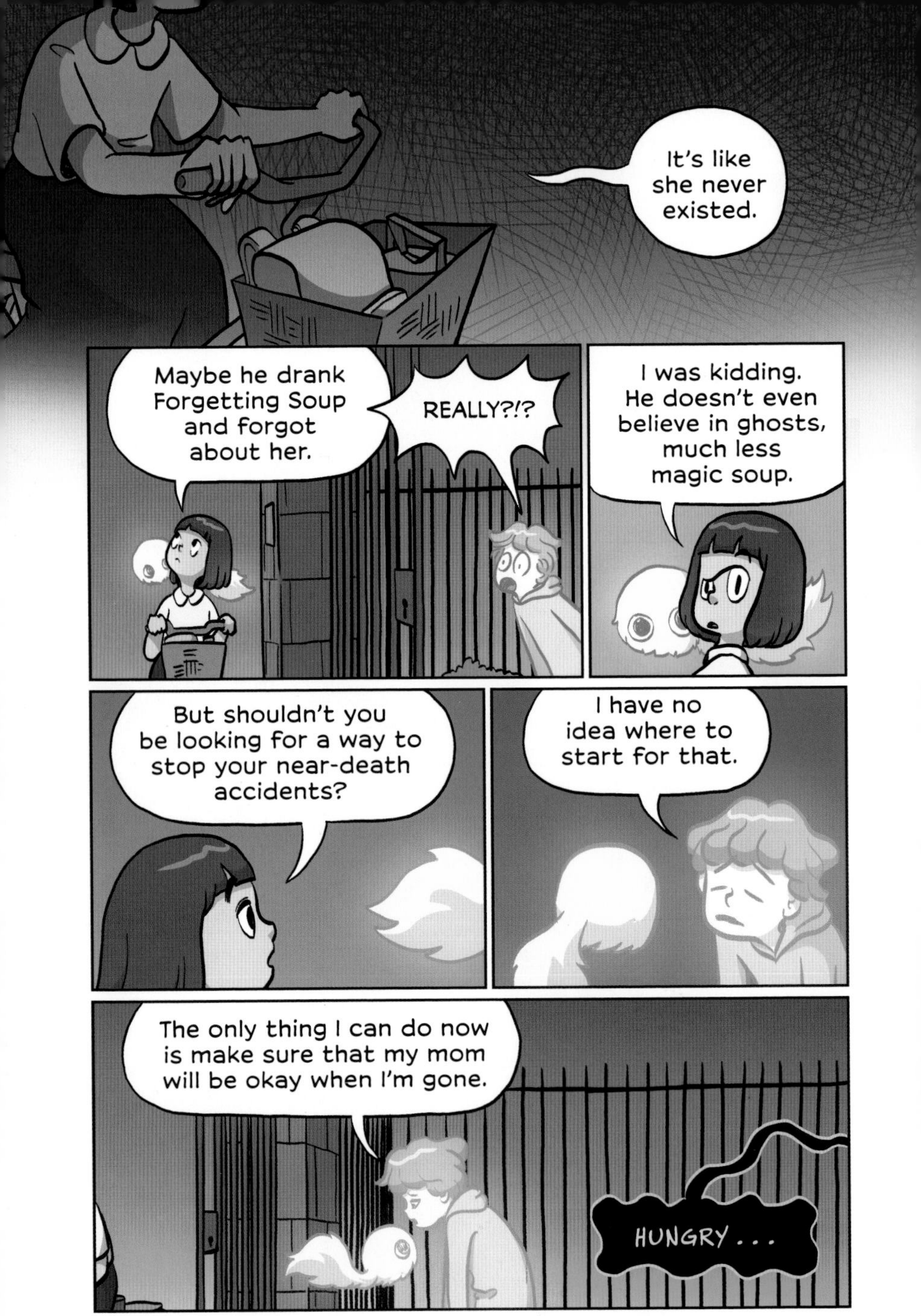
It's like she never existed.
Maybe he drank Forgetting Soup and forgot about her.
REALLY?!?
I was kidding. He doesn't even believe in ghosts, much less magic soup.
But shouldn't you be looking for a way to stop your near-death accidents?
I have no idea where to start for that.
The only thing I can do now is make sure that my mom will be okay when I'm gone.
HUNGRY . . .

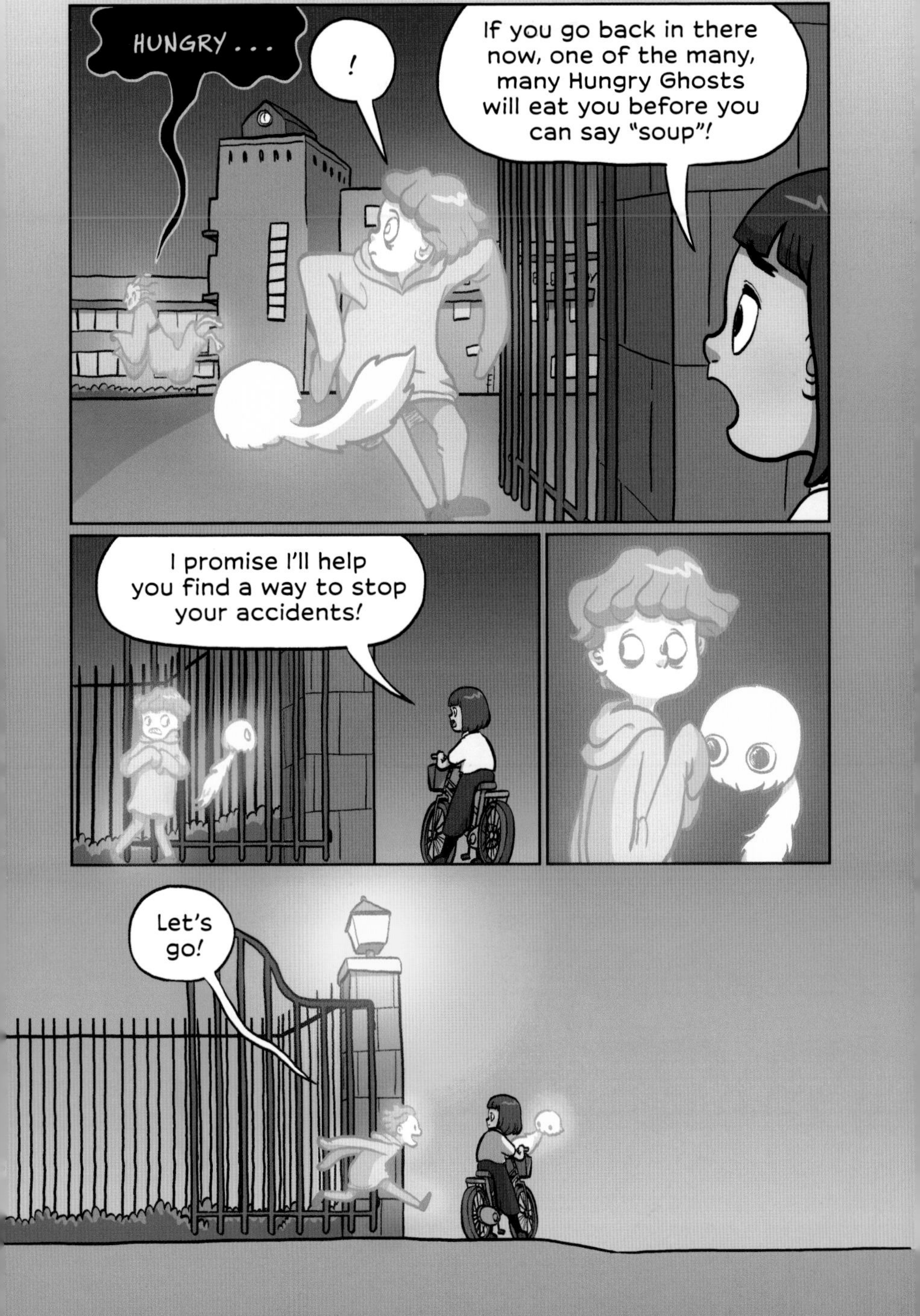
HUNGRY . . .
!
If you go back in there now, one of the many, many Hungry Ghosts will eat you before you can say "soup"!
I promise I'll help you find a way to stop your accidents!
Let's go!

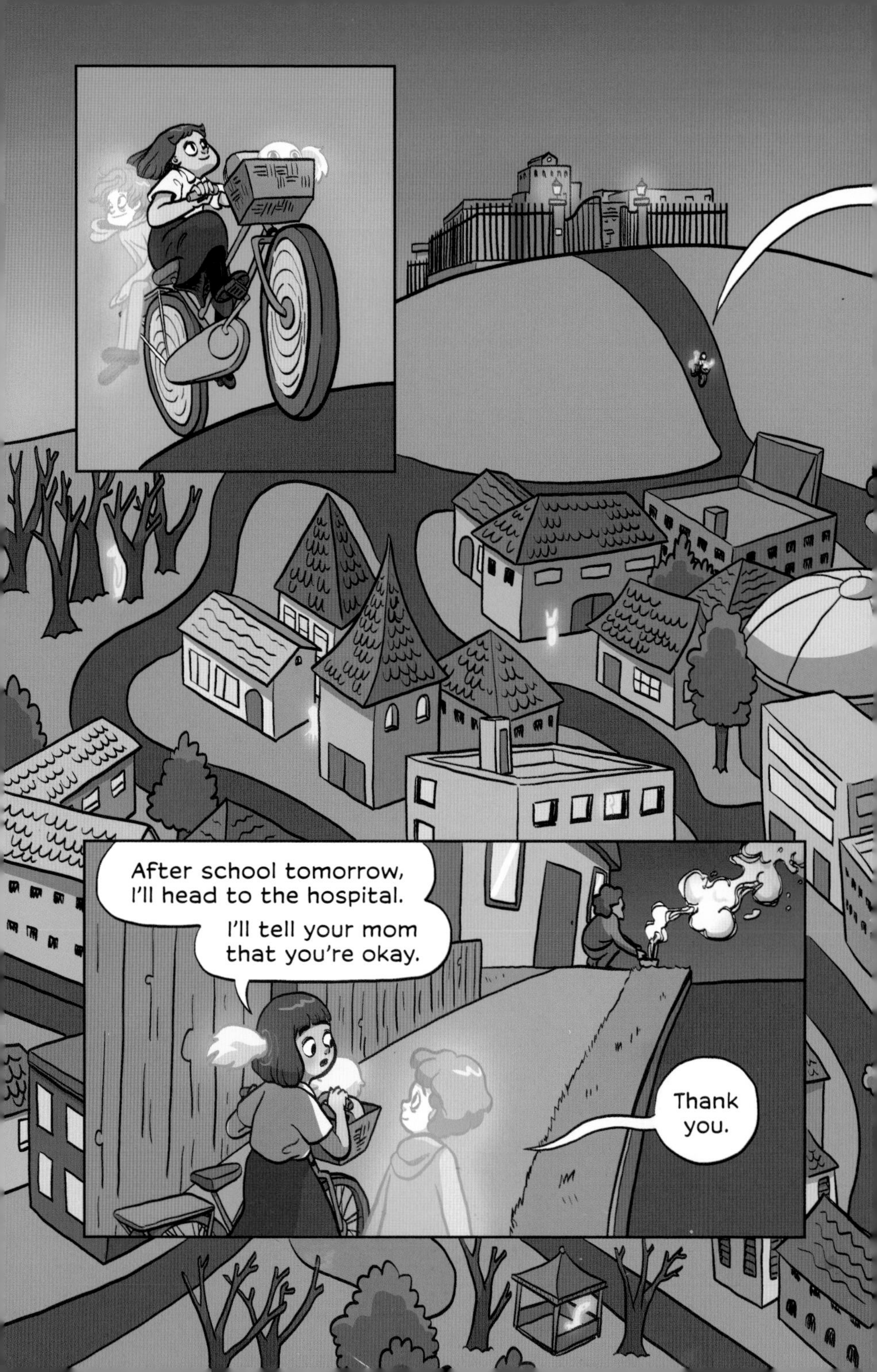
After school tomorrow, I'll head to the hospital.
I'll tell your mom that you're okay.
Thank you.

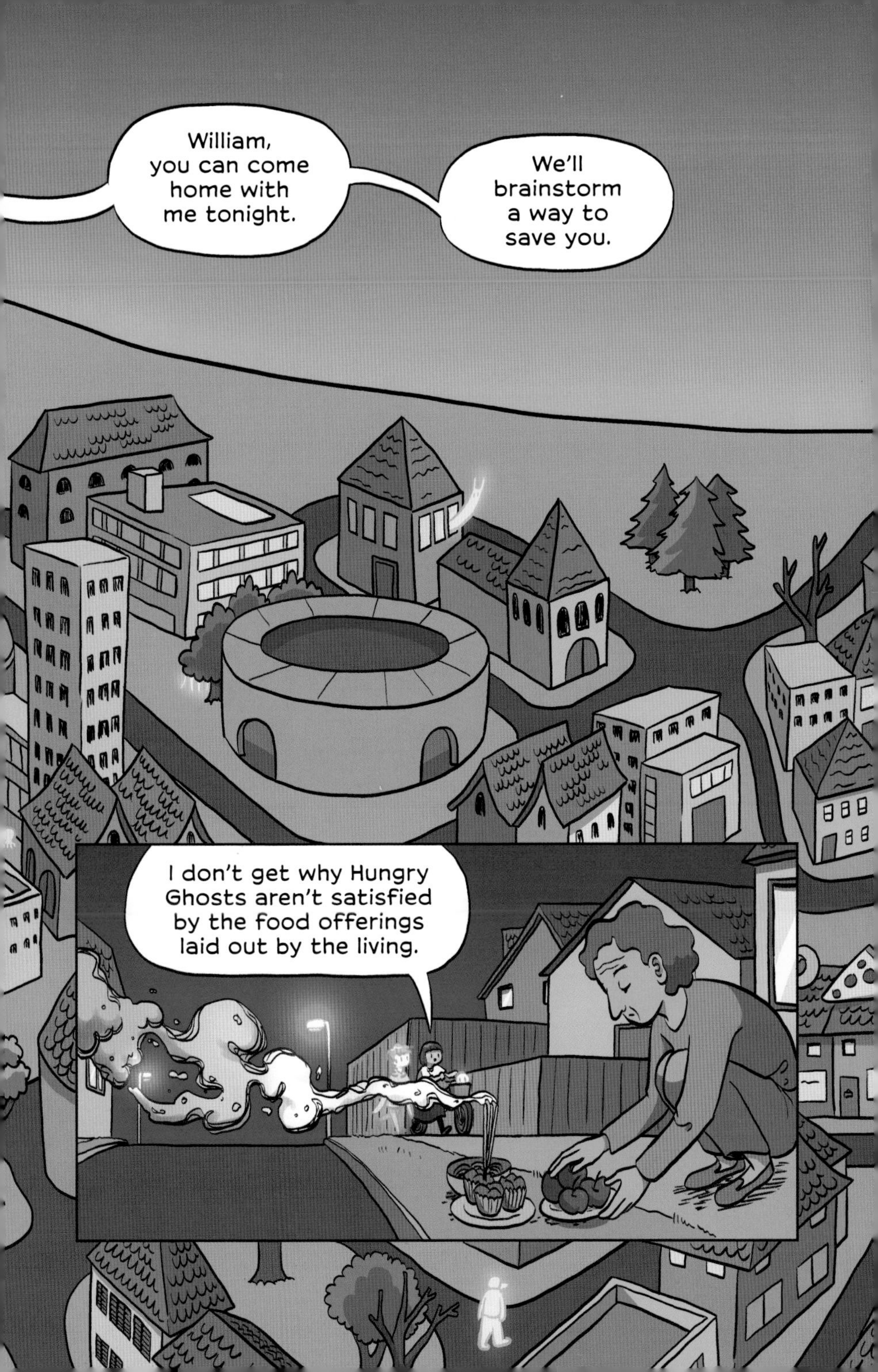
William, you can come home with me tonight.
We'll brainstorm a way to save you.
I don't get why Hungry Ghosts aren't satisfied by the food offerings laid out by the living.

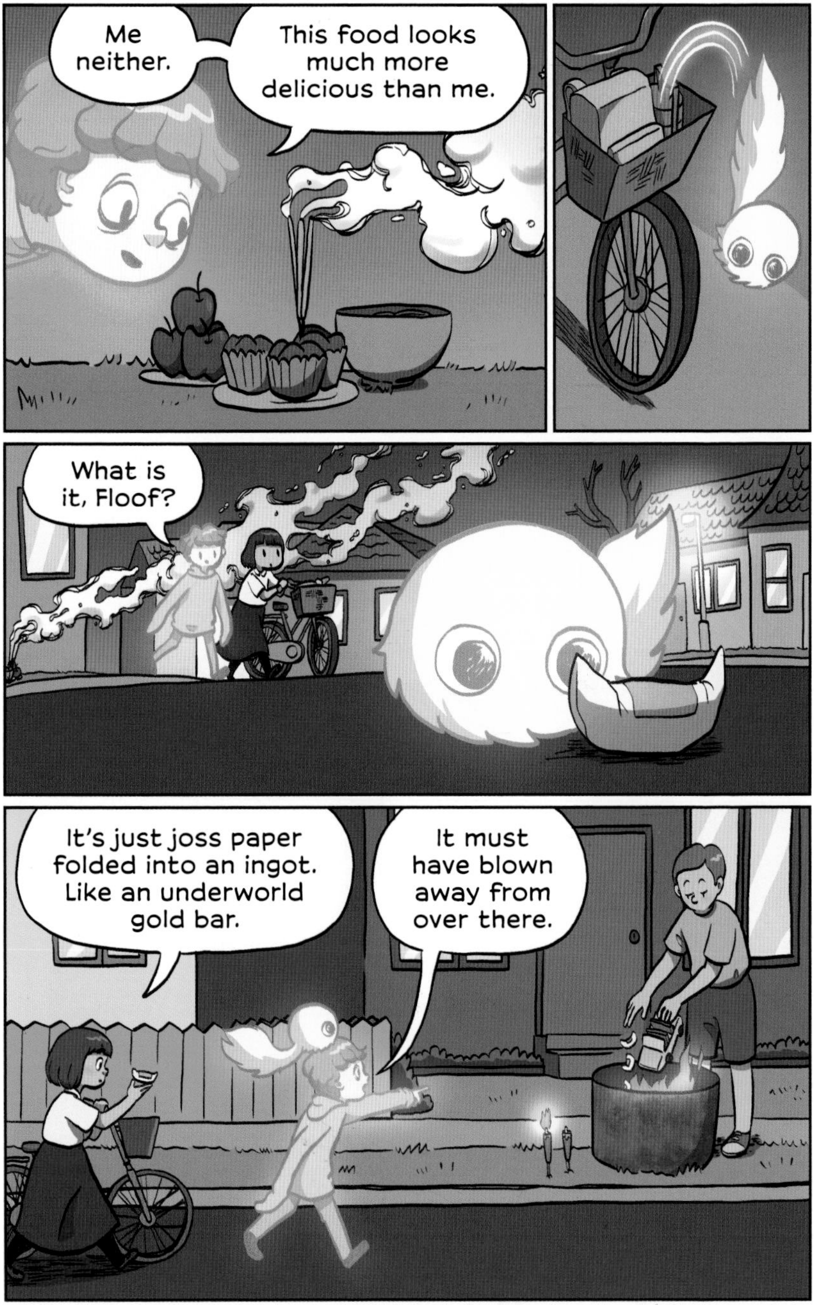
Me neither.
This food looks much more delicious than me.
What is it, Floof?
It's just joss paper folded into an ingot. Like an underworld gold bar.
It must have blown away from over there.

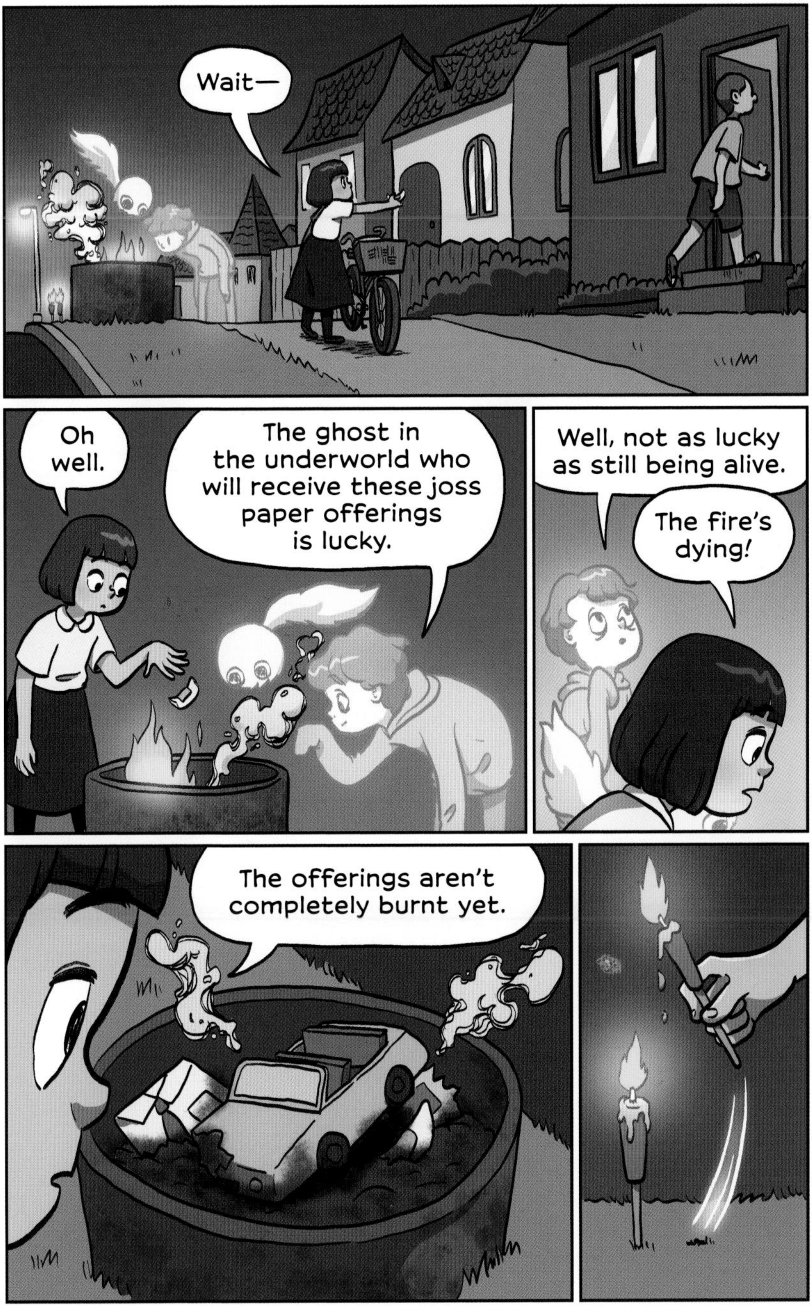
Wait—
Oh well.
The ghost in the underworld who will receive these joss paper offerings is lucky.
Well, not as lucky as still being alive.
The fire's dying!
The offerings aren't completely burnt yet.

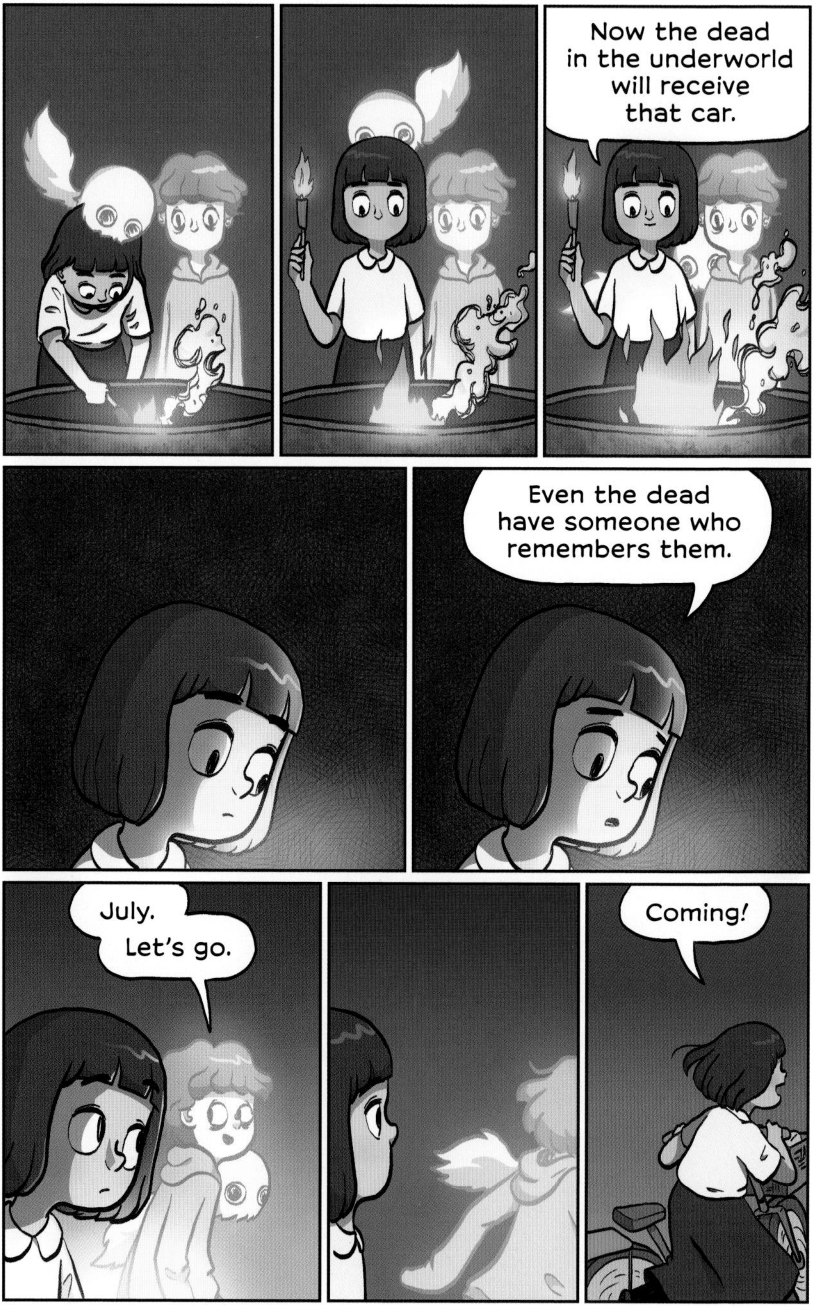
Now the dead in the underworld will receive that car.
Even the dead have someone who remembers them.
July.
Let's go.
Coming!

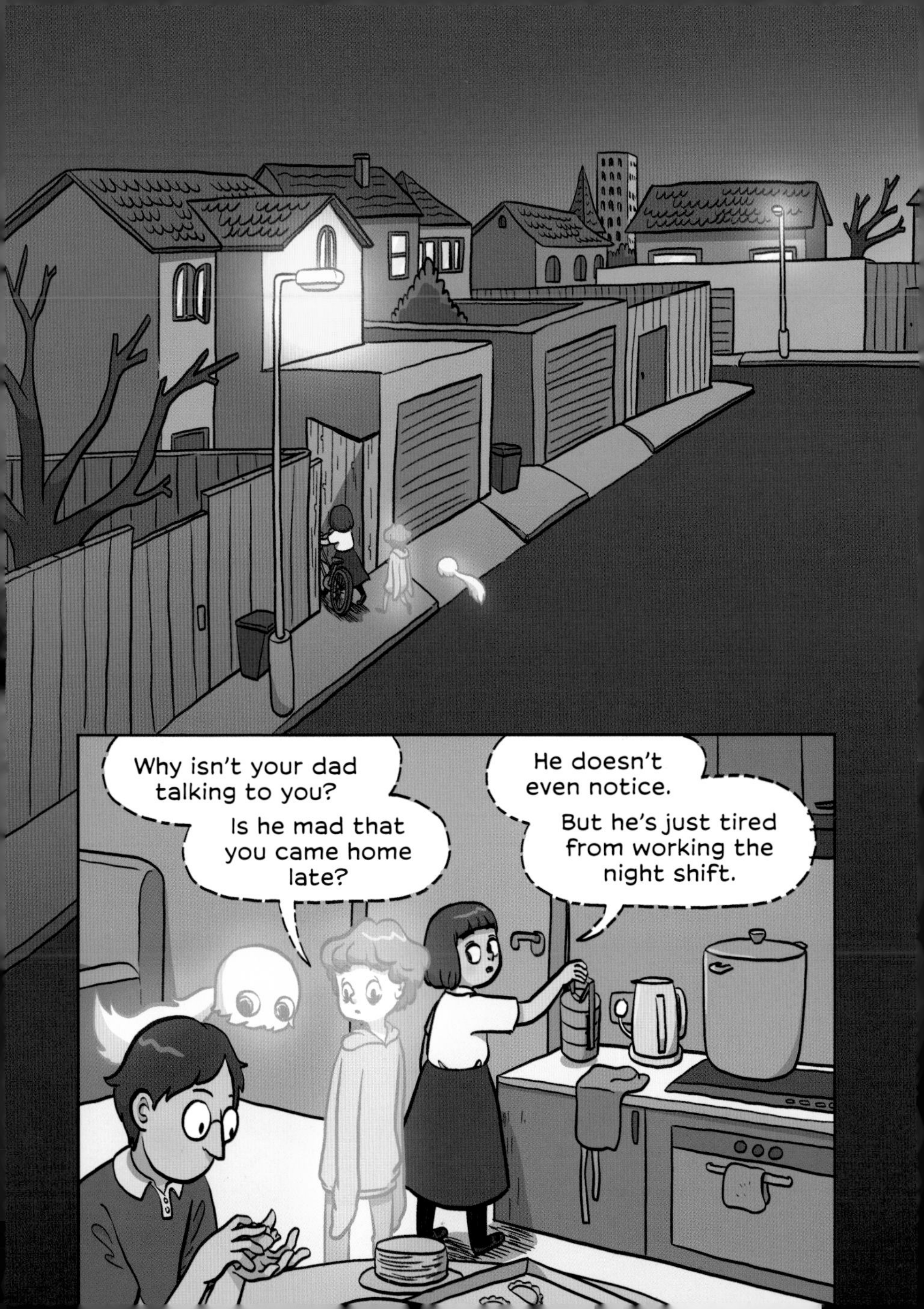
Why isn't your dad talking to you?
Is he mad that you came home late?
He doesn't even notice.
But he's just tired from working the night shift.

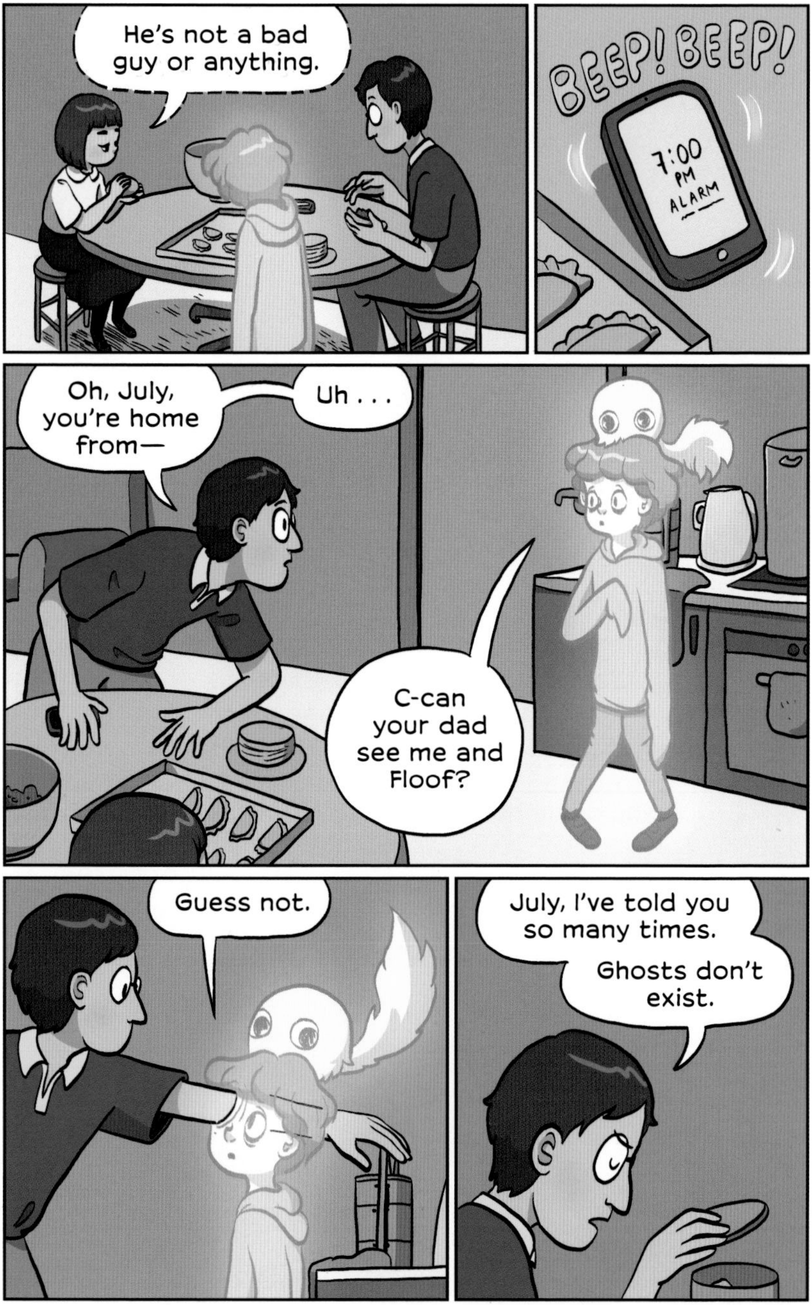
He's not a bad guy or anything.
BEEP! BEEP!
7:00 PM ALARM
Oh, July, you're home from—
Uh . . .
C-can your dad see me and Floof?
Guess not.
July, I've told you so many times.
Ghosts don't exist.

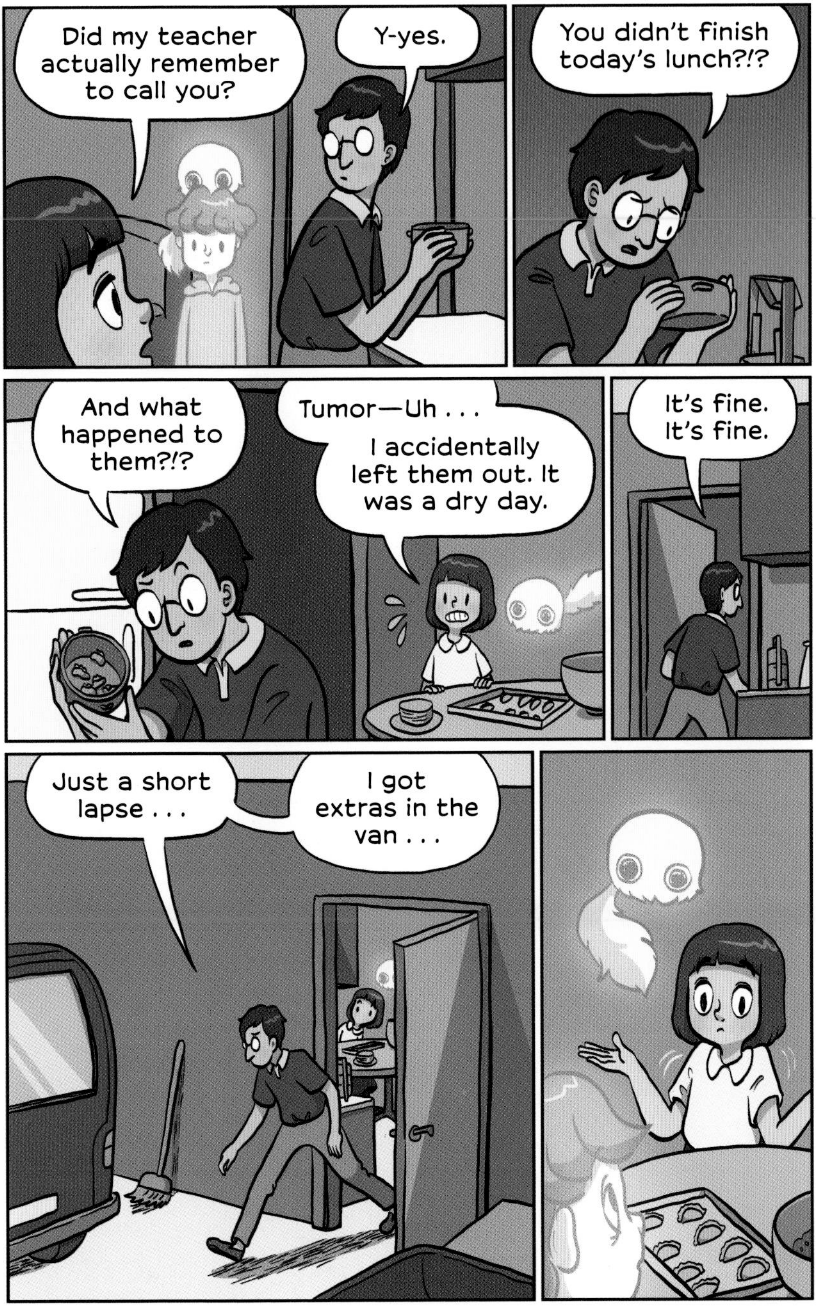
Did my teacher actually remember to call you?
Y-yes.
You didn't finish today's lunch?!?
And what happened to them?!?
Tumor—Uh . . .
I accidentally left them out. It was a dry day.
It's fine. It's fine.
Just a short lapse . . .
I got extras in the van . . .

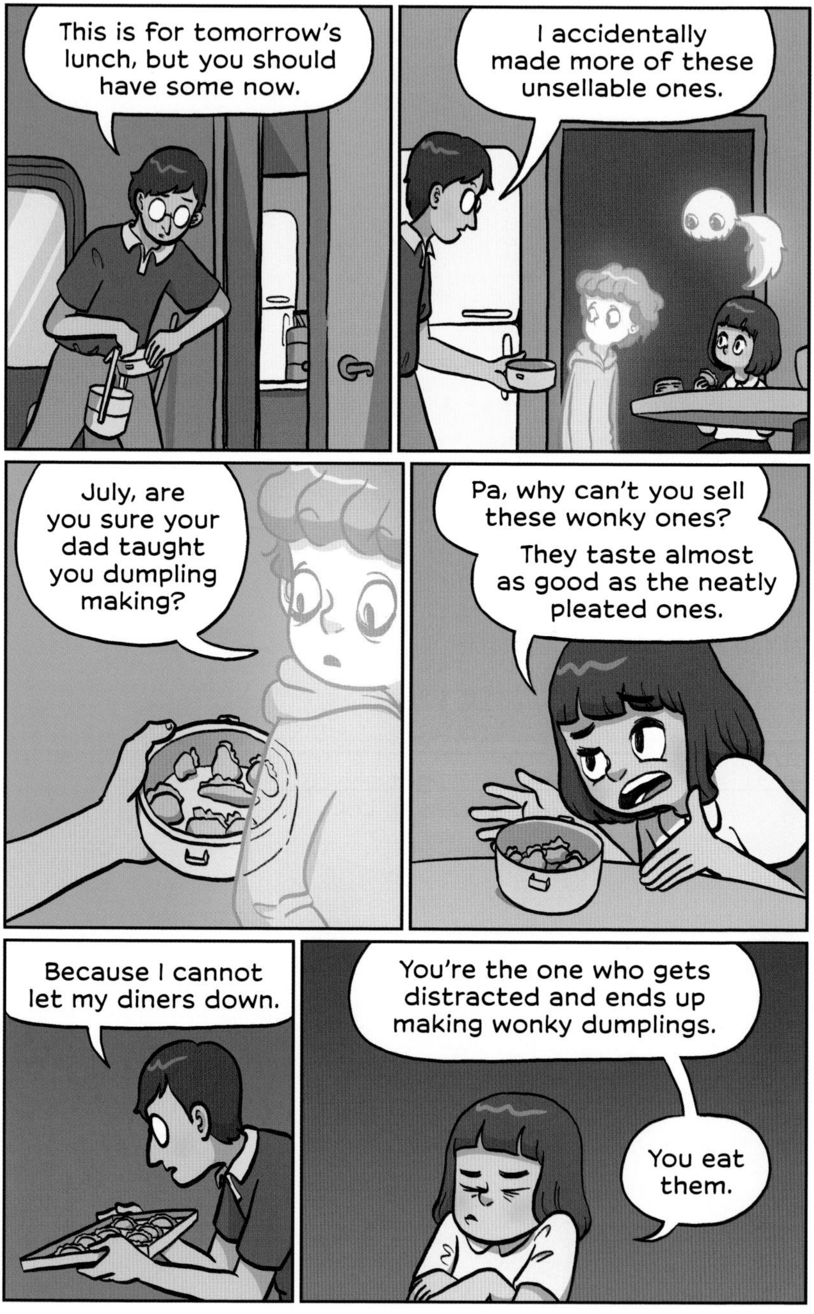
This is for tomorrow's lunch, but you should have some now.
I accidentally made more of these unsellable ones.
July, are you sure your dad taught you dumpling making?
Pa, why can't you sell these wonky ones?
They taste almost as good as the neatly pleated ones.
Because I cannot let my diners down.
You're the one who gets distracted and ends up making wonky dumplings.
You eat them.

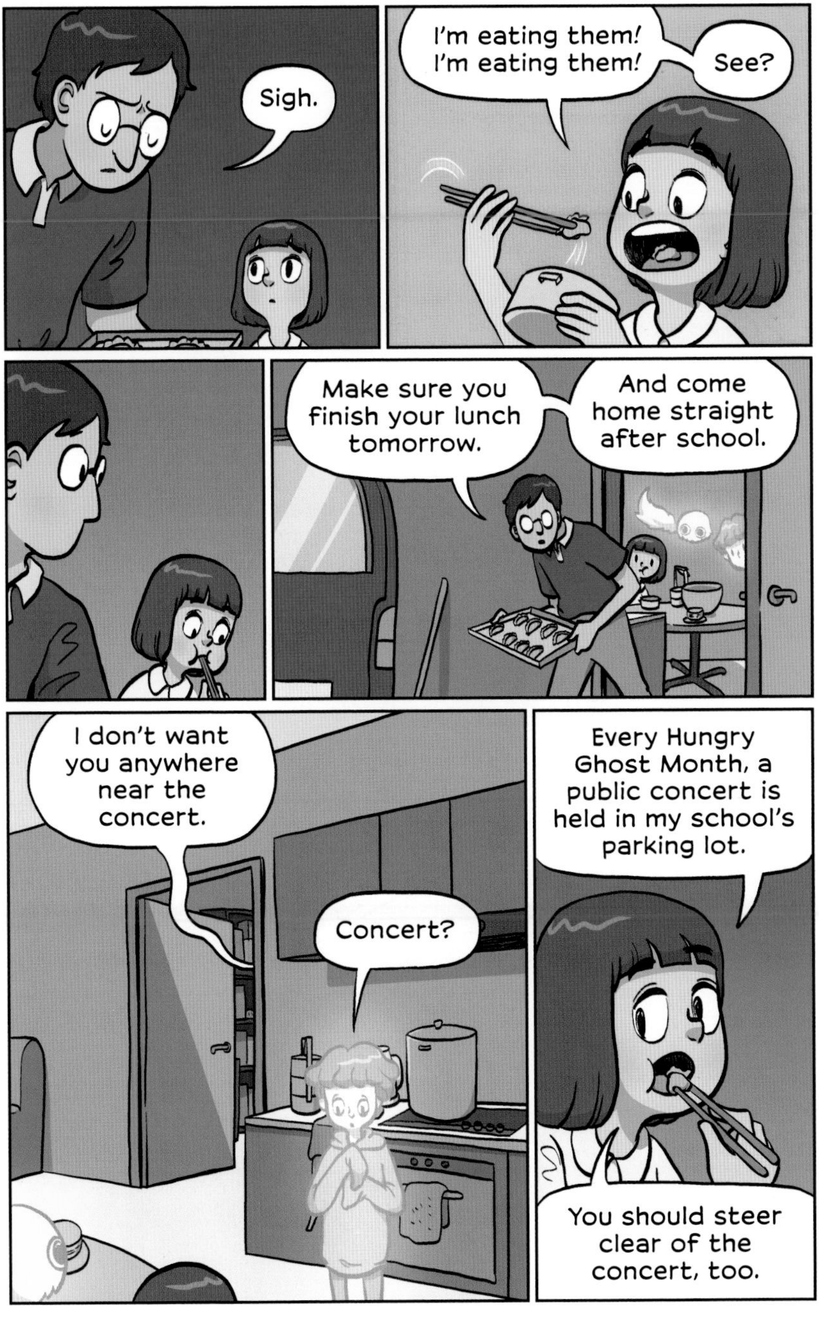
Sigh.
I'm eating them! I'm eating them!
See?
Make sure you finish your lunch tomorrow.
And come home straight after school.
I don't want you anywhere near the concert.
Concert?
Every Hungry Ghost Month, a public concert is held in my school's parking lot.
You should steer clear of the concert, too.

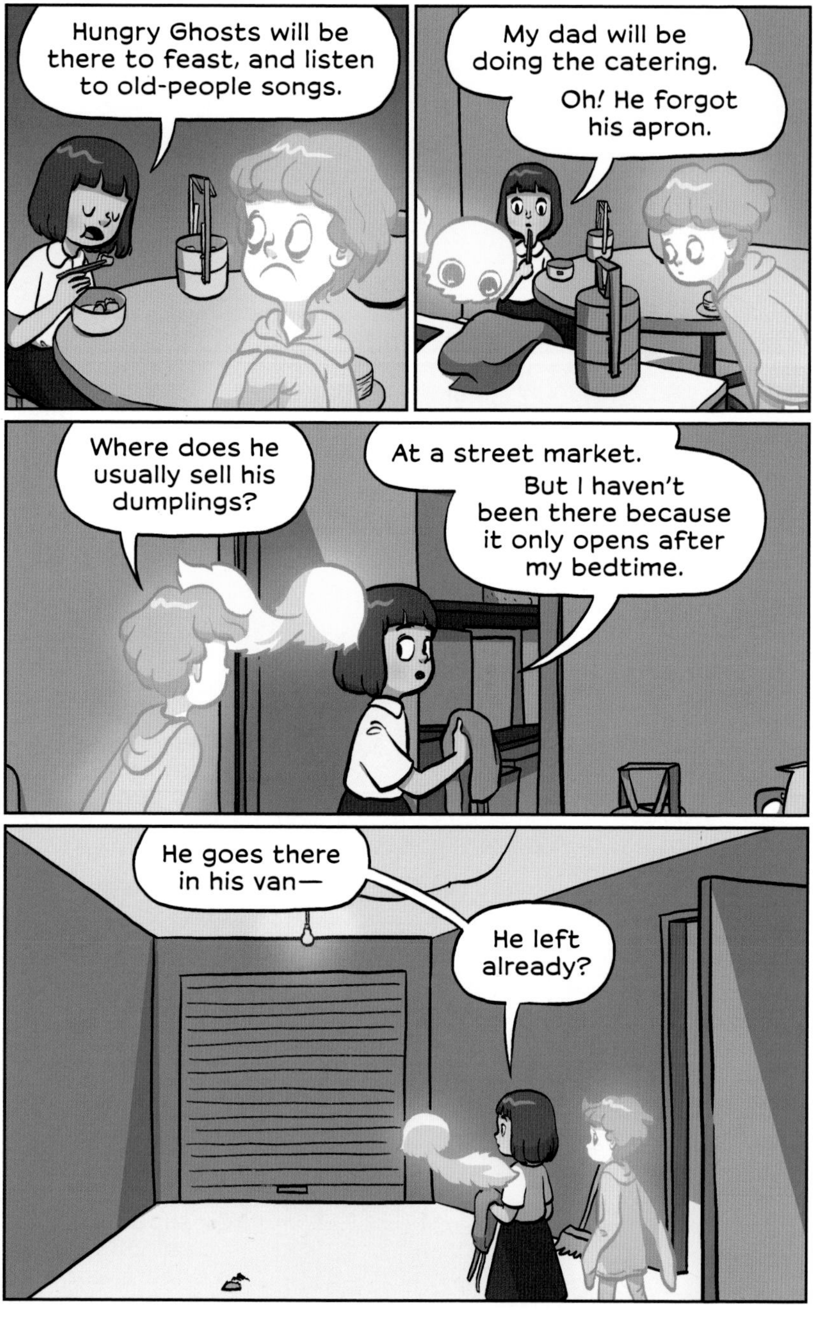
Hungry Ghosts will be there to feast, and listen to old-people songs.
My dad will be doing the catering.
Oh! He forgot his apron.
Where does he usually sell his dumplings?
At a street market.
But I haven't been there because it only opens after my bedtime.
He goes there in his van—
He left already?

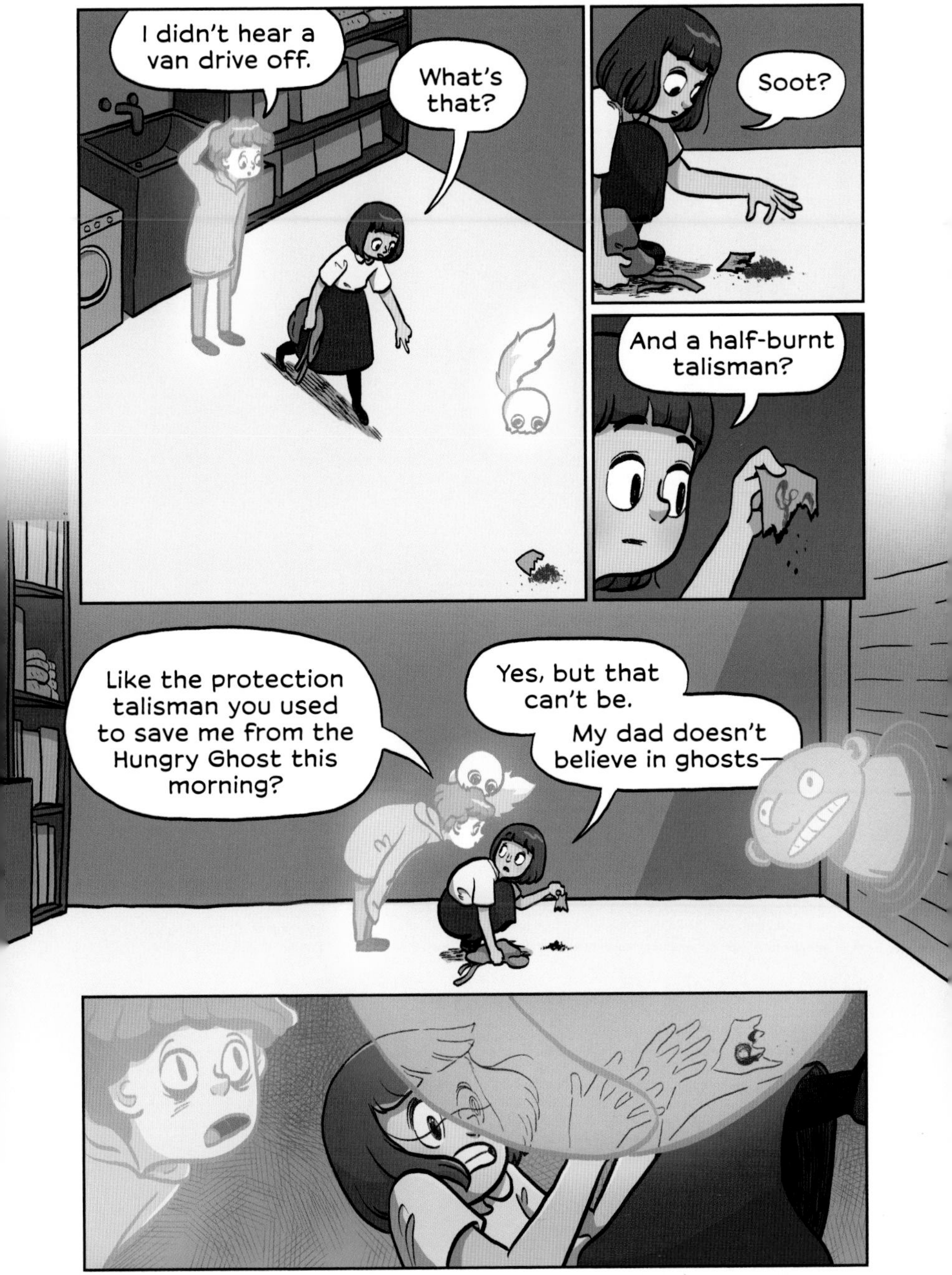
I didn't hear a van drive off.
What's that?
Soot?
And a half-burnt talisman?
Like the protection talisman you used to save me from the Hungry Ghost this morning?
Yes, but that can't be.
My dad doesn't believe in ghosts—

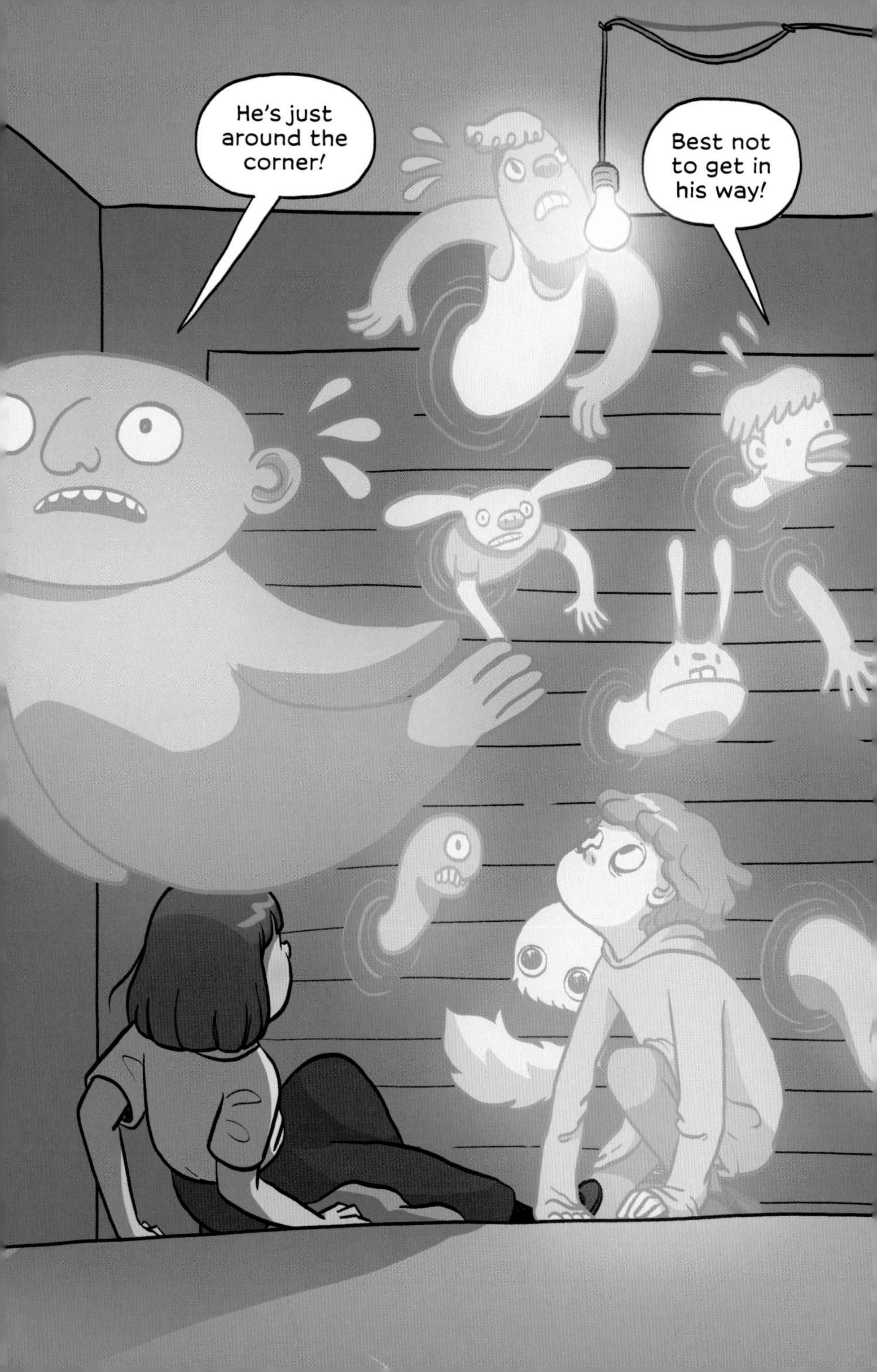
He's just around the corner!
Best not to get in his way!

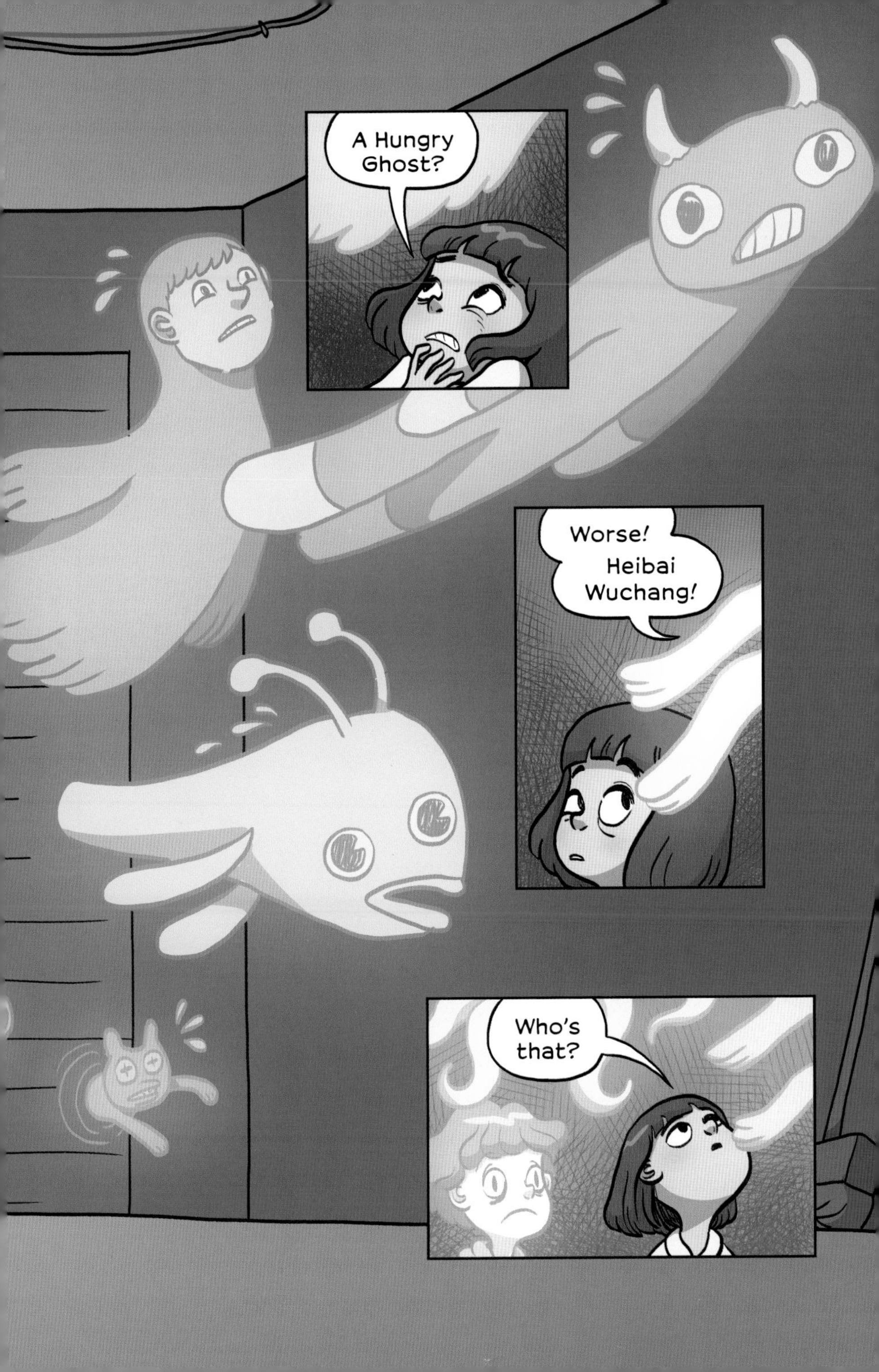
A Hungry Ghost?
Worse! Heibai Wuchang!
Who's that?

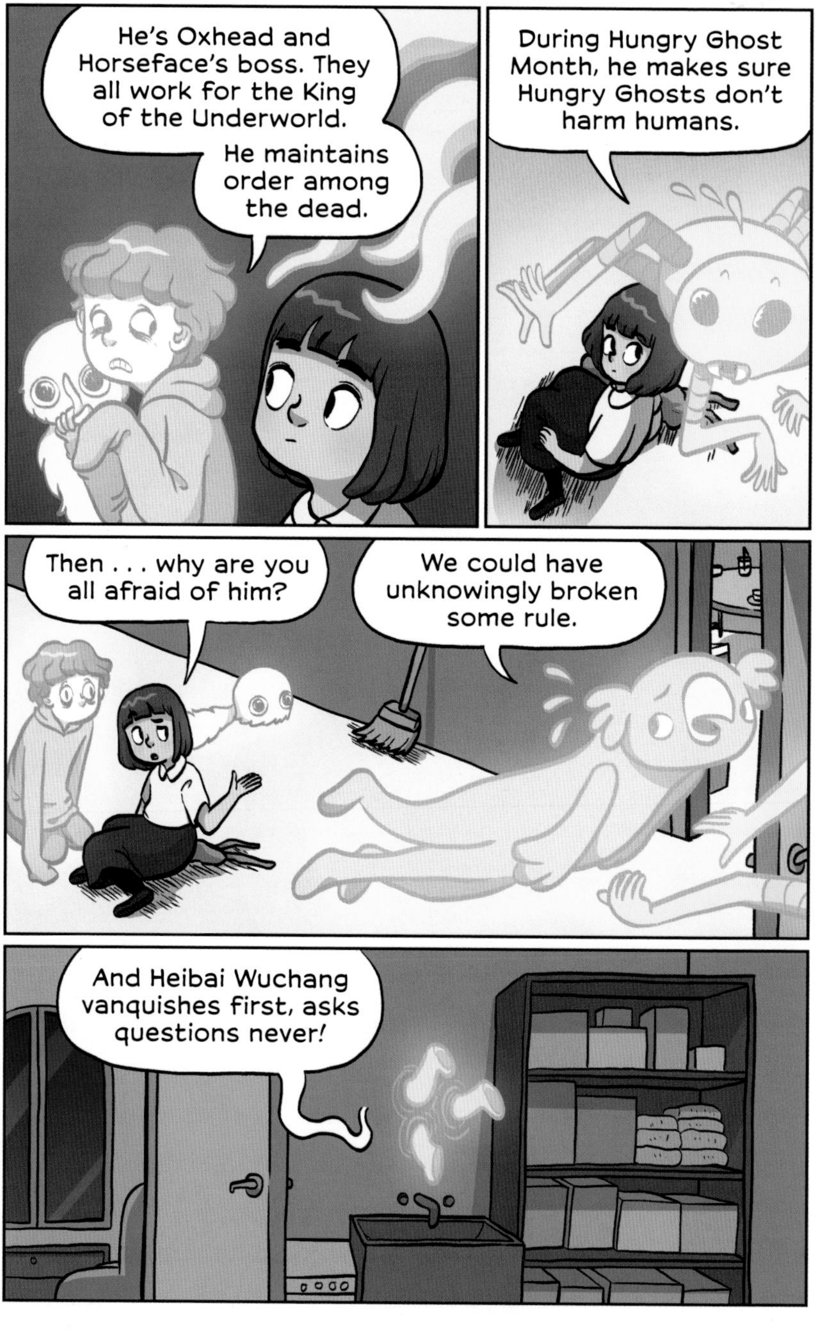
He's Oxhead and Horseface's boss. They all work for the King of the Underworld.
He maintains order among the dead.
During Hungry Ghost Month, he makes sure Hungry Ghosts don't harm humans.
Then . . . why are you all afraid of him?
We could have unknowingly broken some rule.
And Heibai Wuchang vanquishes first, asks questions never!

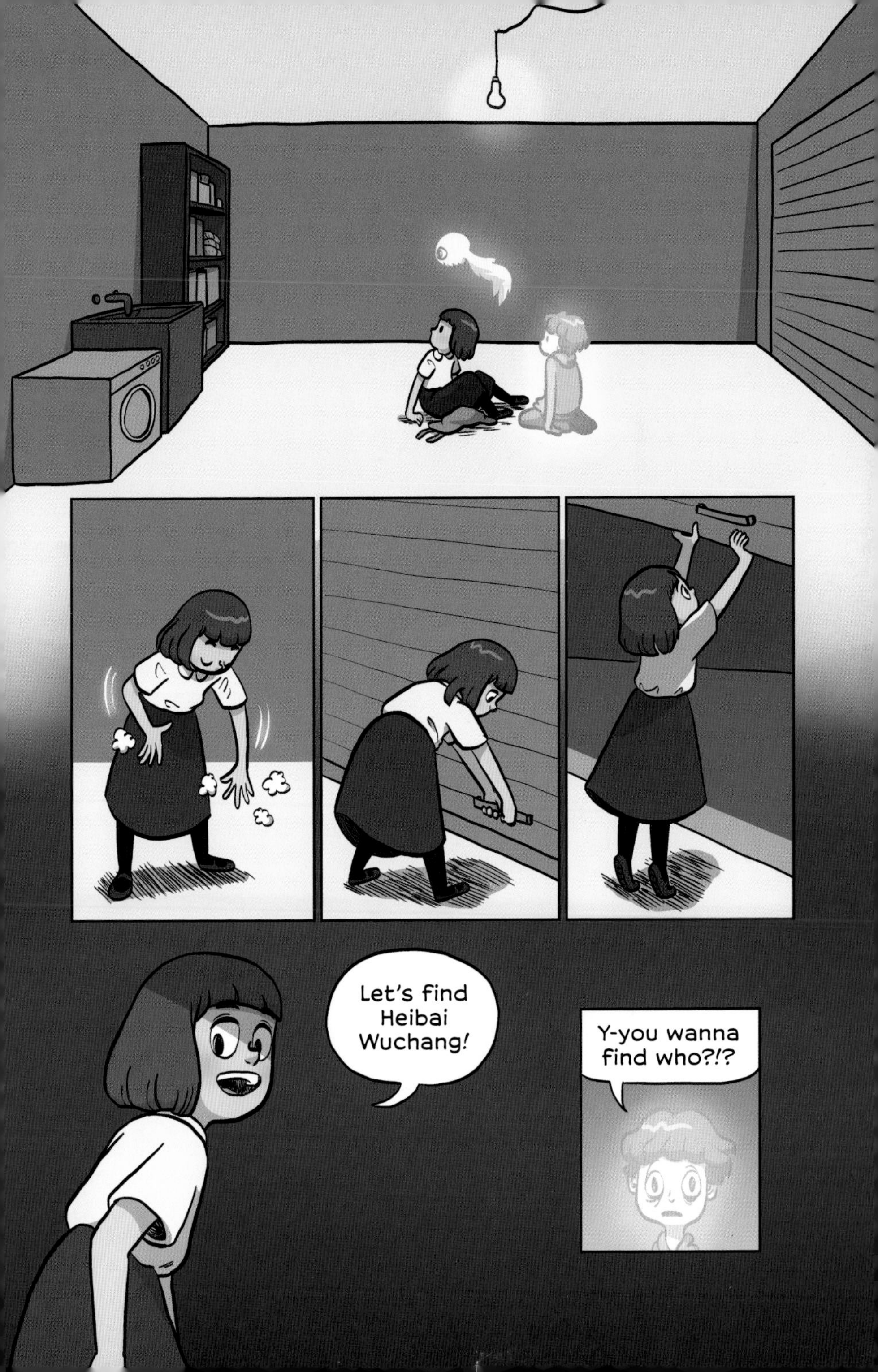
Let's find Heibai Wuchang!
Y-you wanna find who?!?

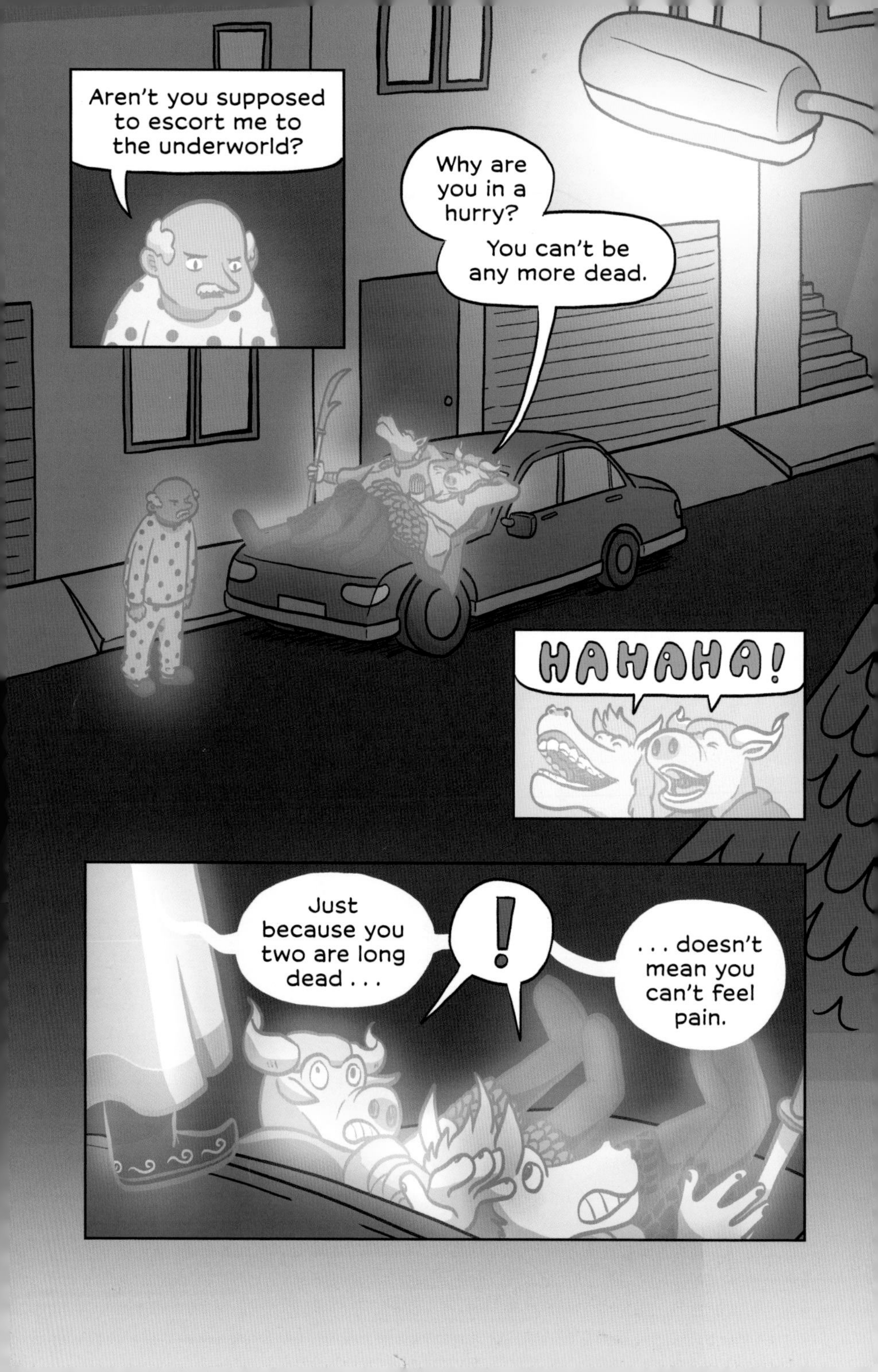
Aren't you supposed to escort me to the underworld?
Why are you in a hurry?
You can't be any more dead.
HAHAHA!
Just because you two are long dead . . .
!
. . . doesn't mean you can't feel pain.

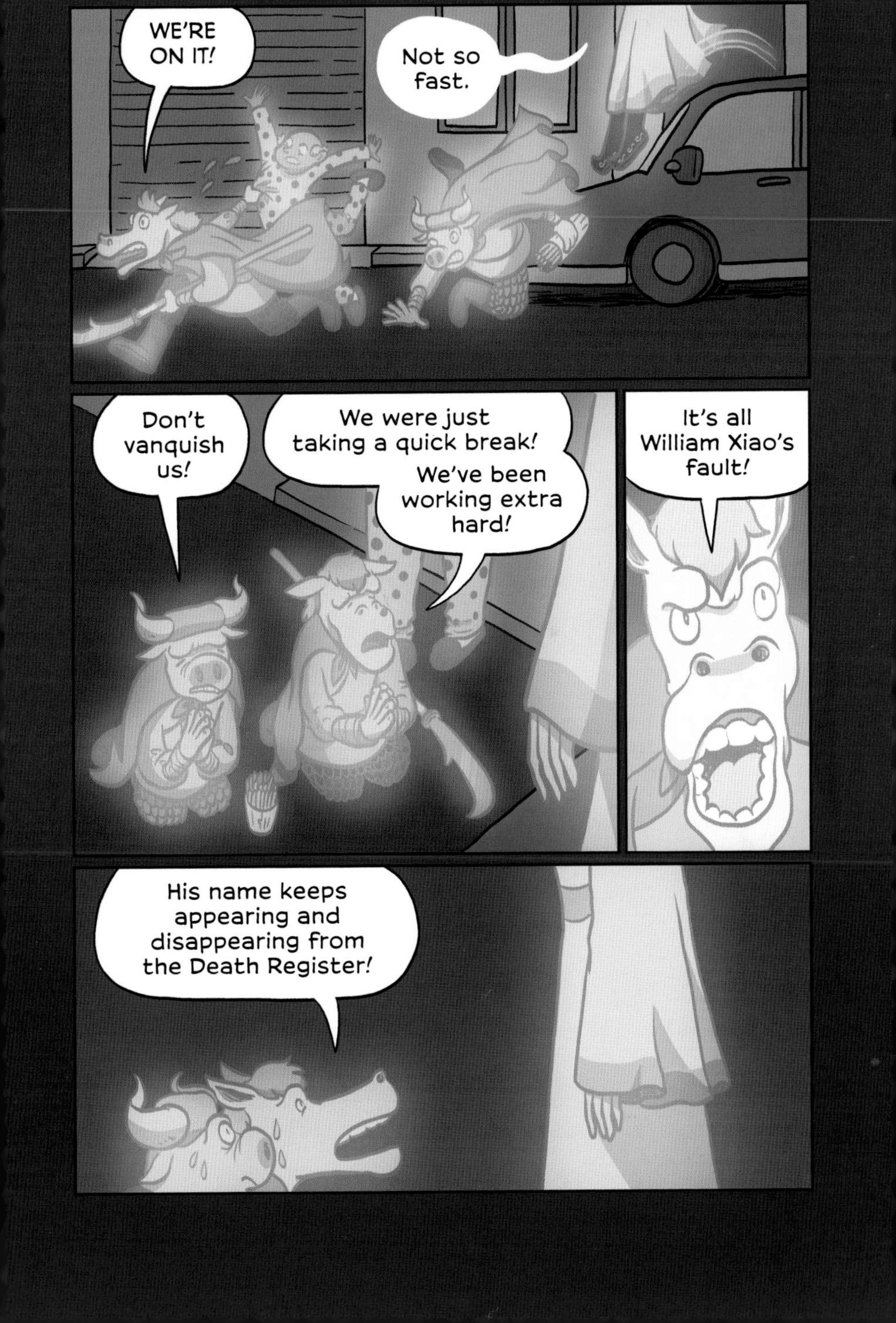
WE'RE ON IT!
Not so fast.
Don't vanquish us!
We were just taking a quick break!
We've been working extra hard!
It's all William Xiao's fault!
His name keeps appearing and disappearing from the Death Register!

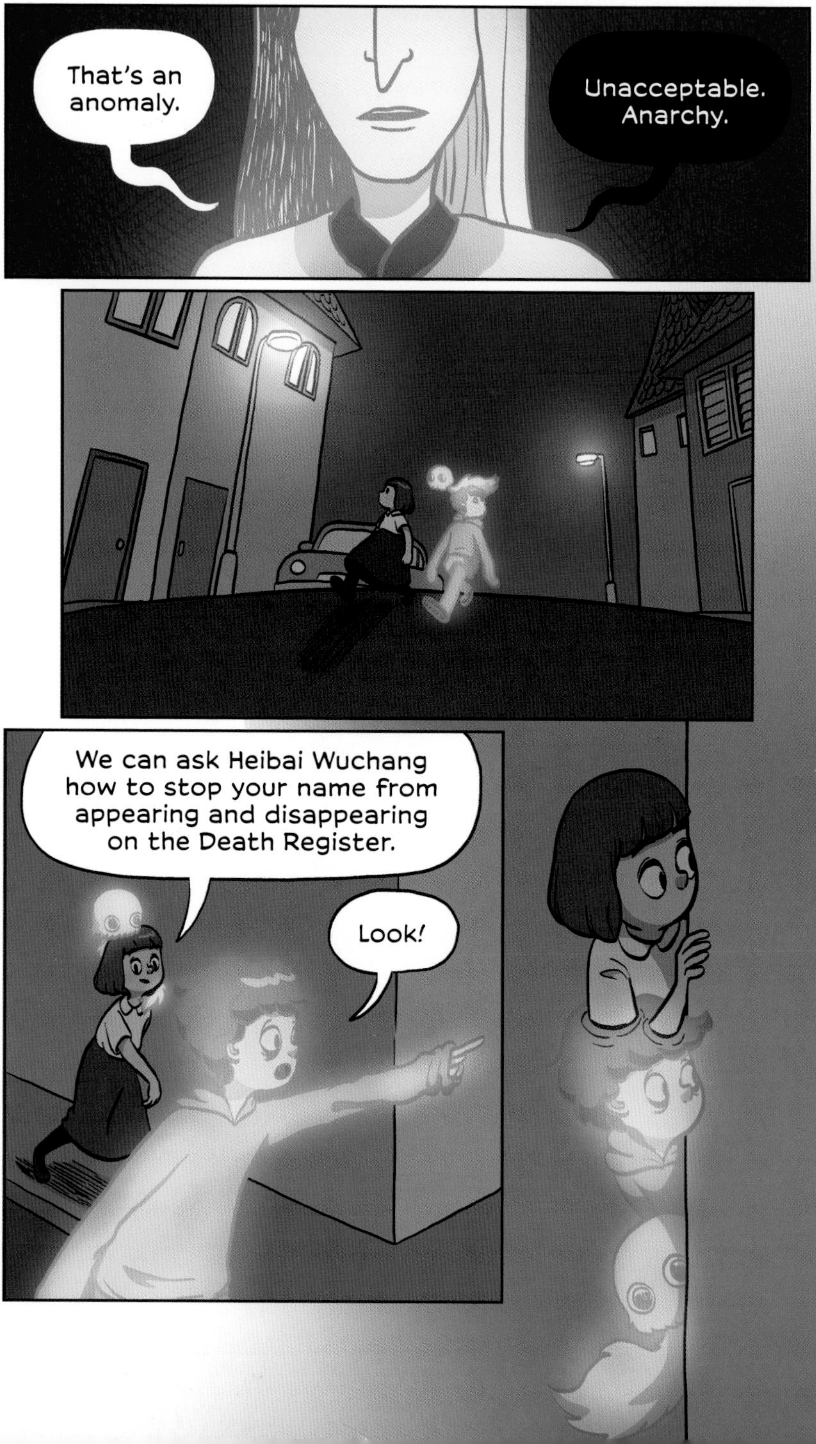
That's an anomaly.
Unacceptable. Anarchy.
We can ask Heibai Wuchang how to stop your name from appearing and disappearing on the Death Register.
Look!

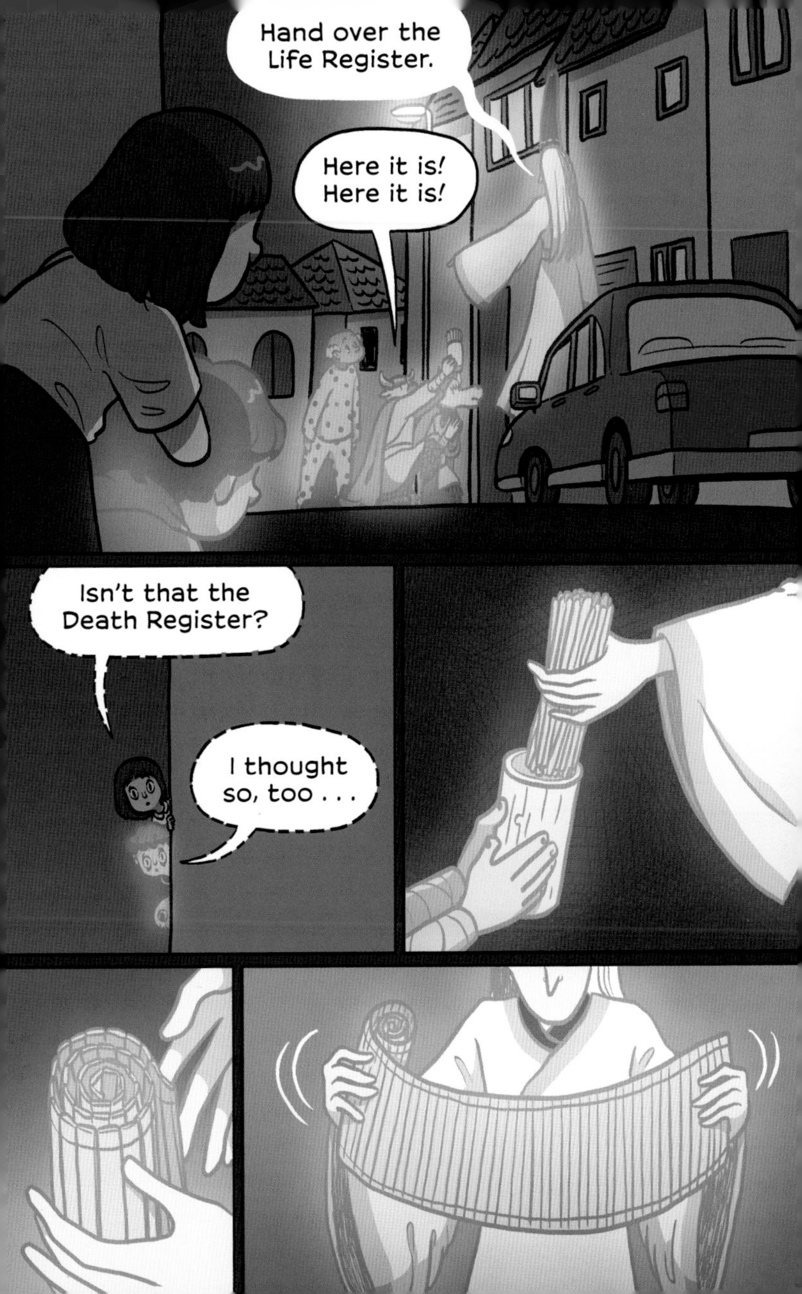

Hand over the Life Register.
Here it is! Here it is!
Isn't that the Death Register?
I thought so, too . . .

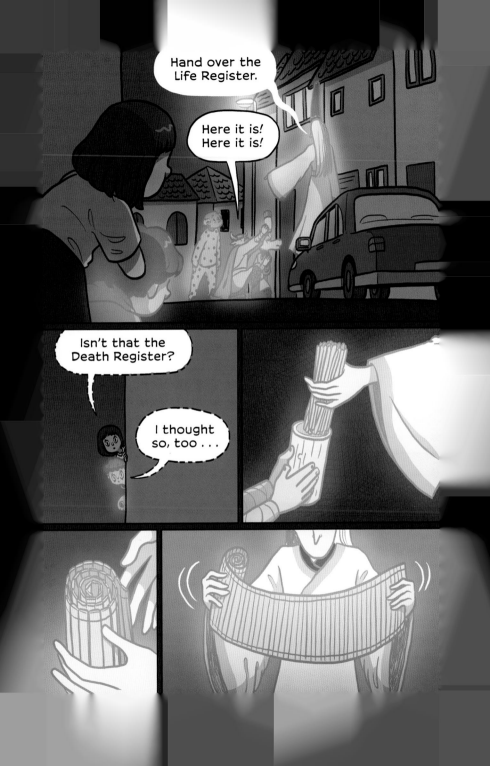

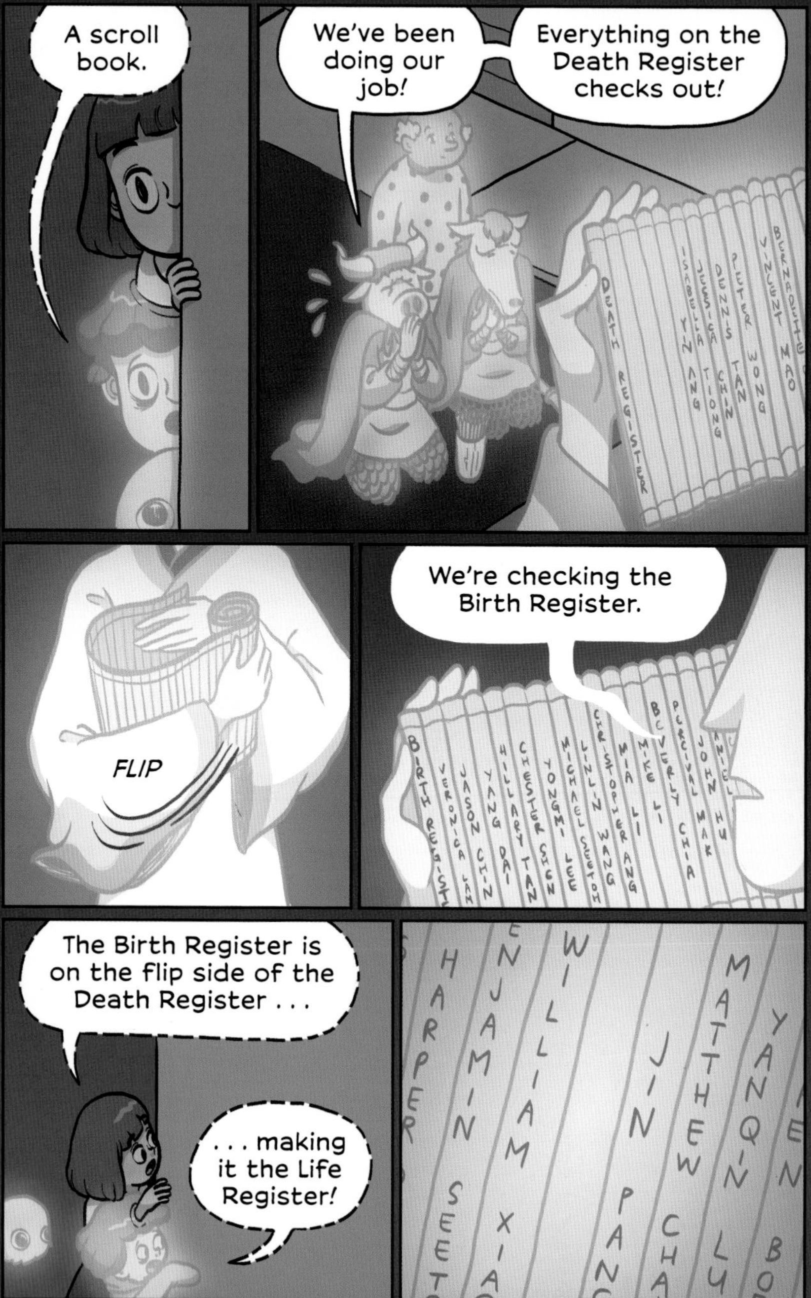
A scroll book.
We've been doing our job!
Everything on the Death Register checks out!
FLIP
We're checking the Birth Register.
The Birth Register is on the flip side of the Death Register . . .
. . . making it the Life Register!

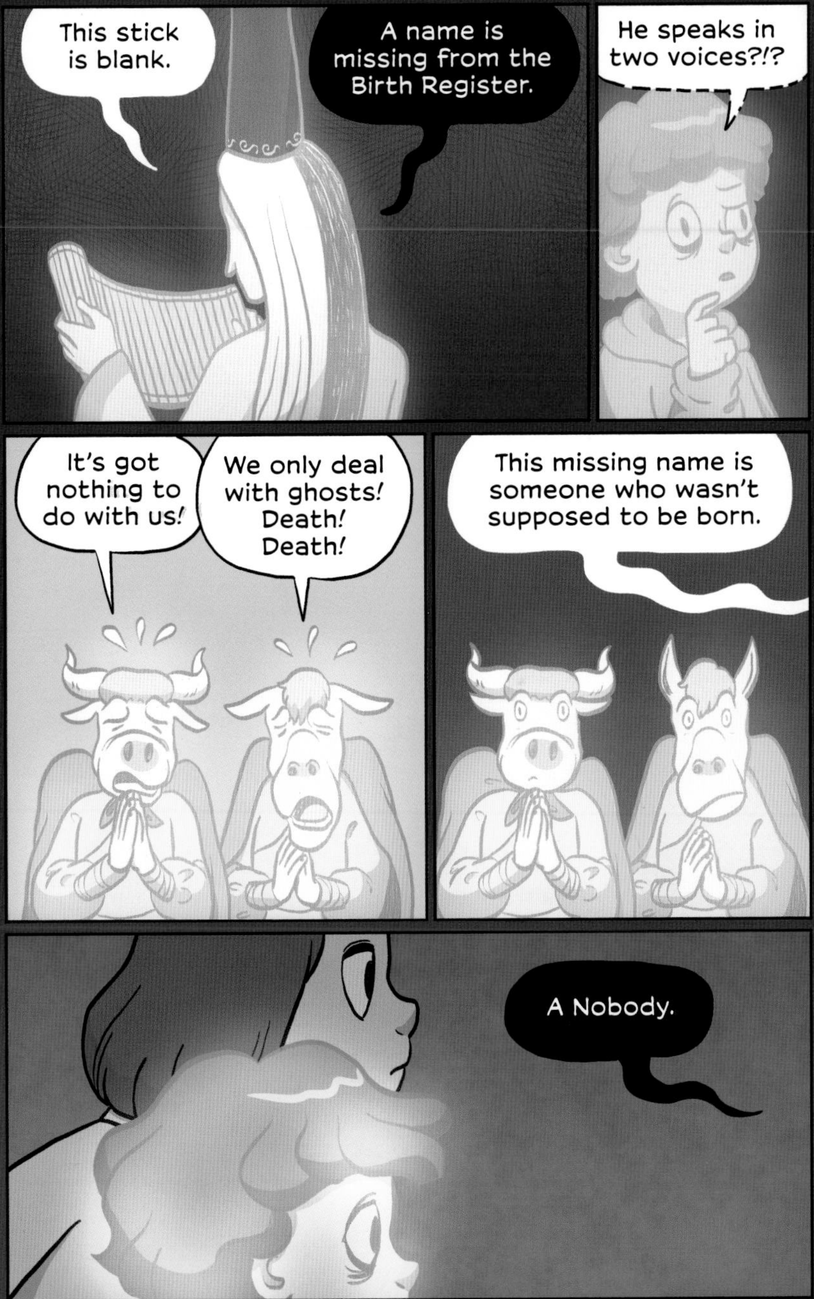
This stick is blank.
A name is missing from the Birth Register.
He speaks in two voices?!?
It's got nothing to do with us!
We only deal with ghosts! Death! Death!
This missing name is someone who wasn't supposed to be born.
A Nobody.

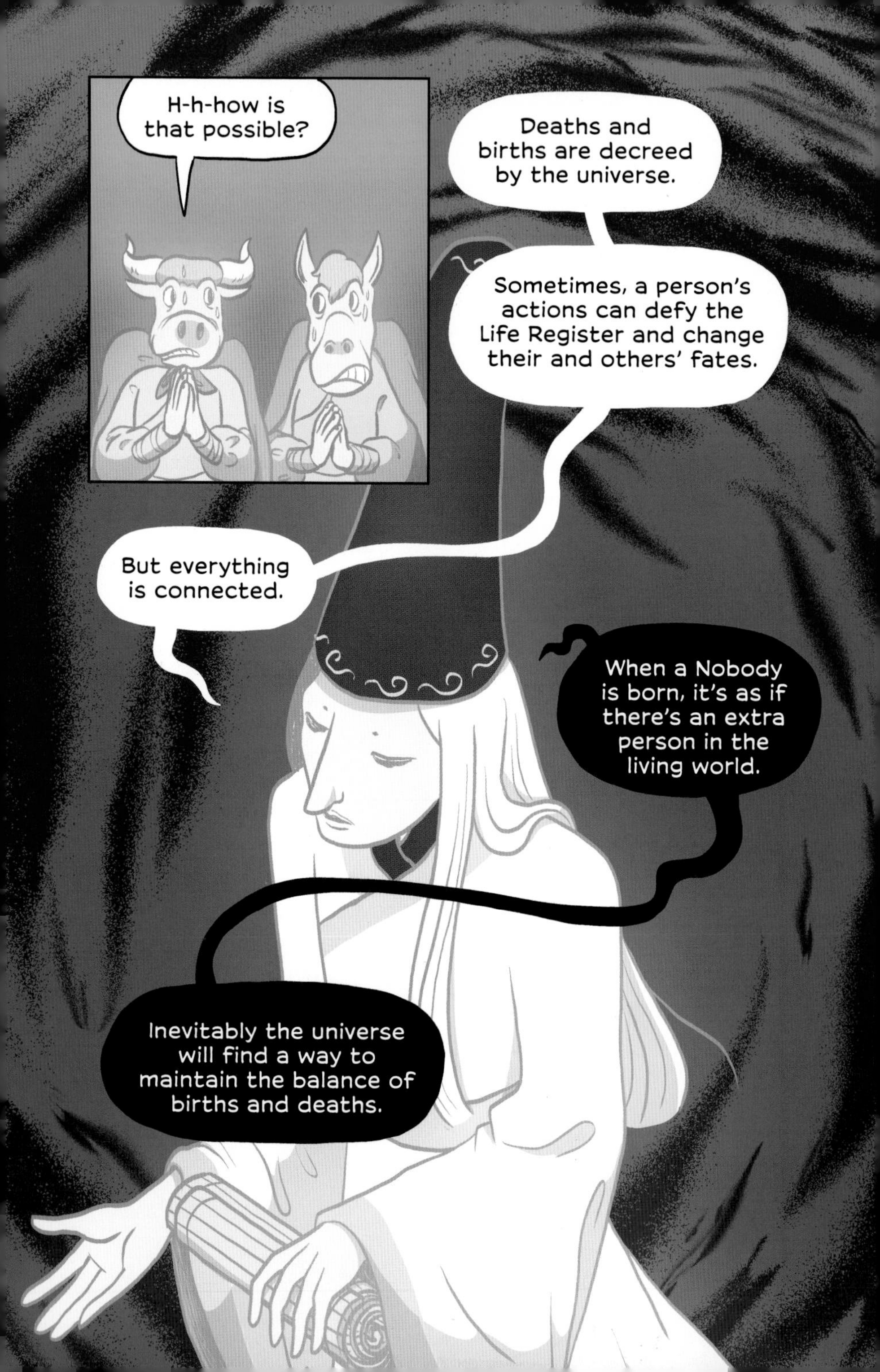
H-h-how is that possible?
Deaths and births are decreed by the universe.
Sometimes, a person's actions can defy the Life Register and change their and others' fates.
But everything is connected.
When a Nobody is born, it's as if there's an extra person in the living world.
Inevitably the universe will find a way to maintain the balance of births and deaths.

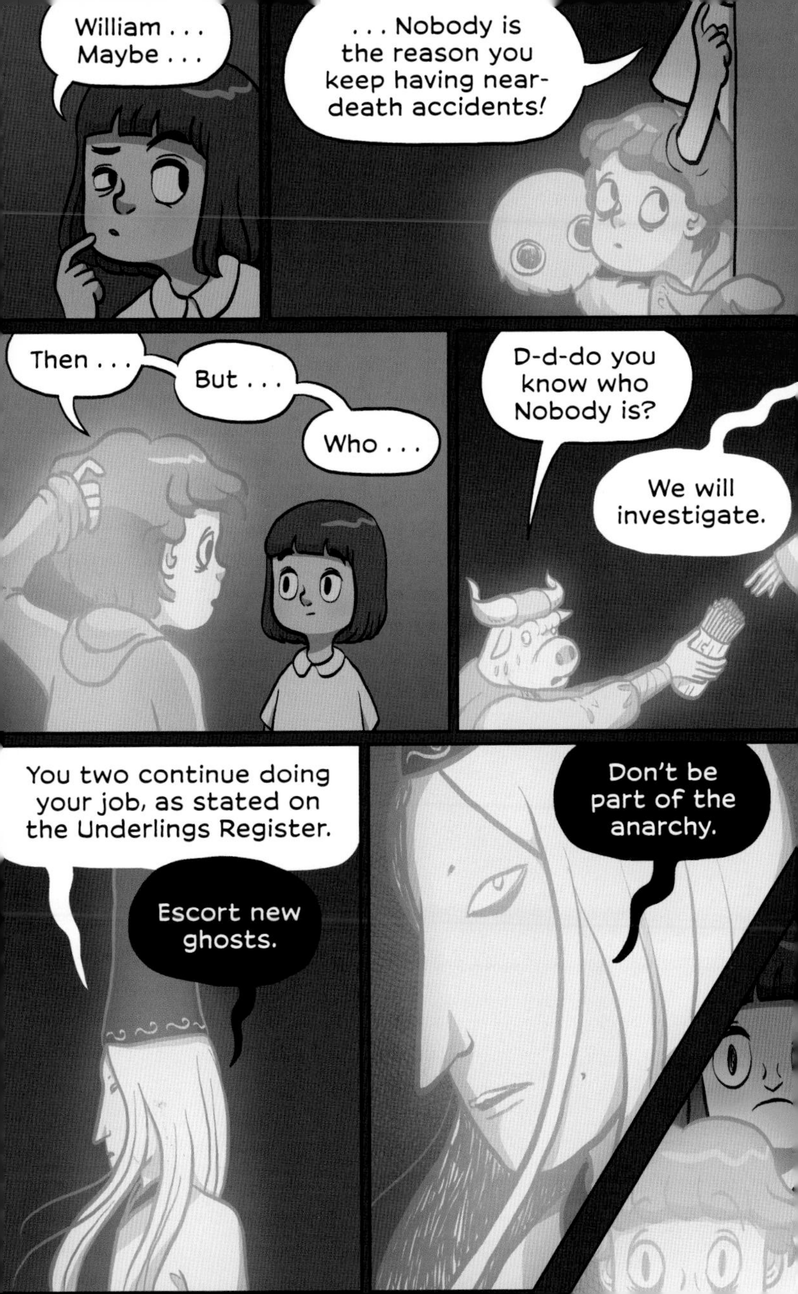
William . . .
Maybe . . .
. . . Nobody is the reason you keep having near-death accidents!
Then . . .
But . . .
Who . . .
D-d-do you know who Nobody is?
We will investigate.
You two continue doing your job, as stated on the Underlings Register.
Escort new ghosts.
Don't be part of the anarchy.

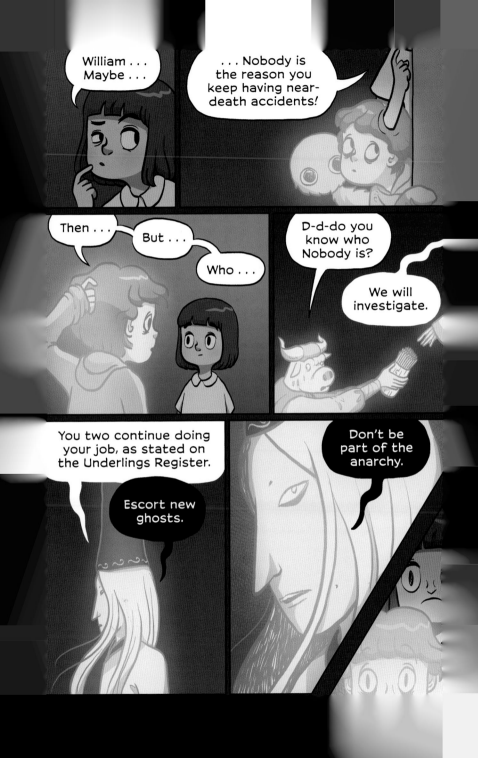

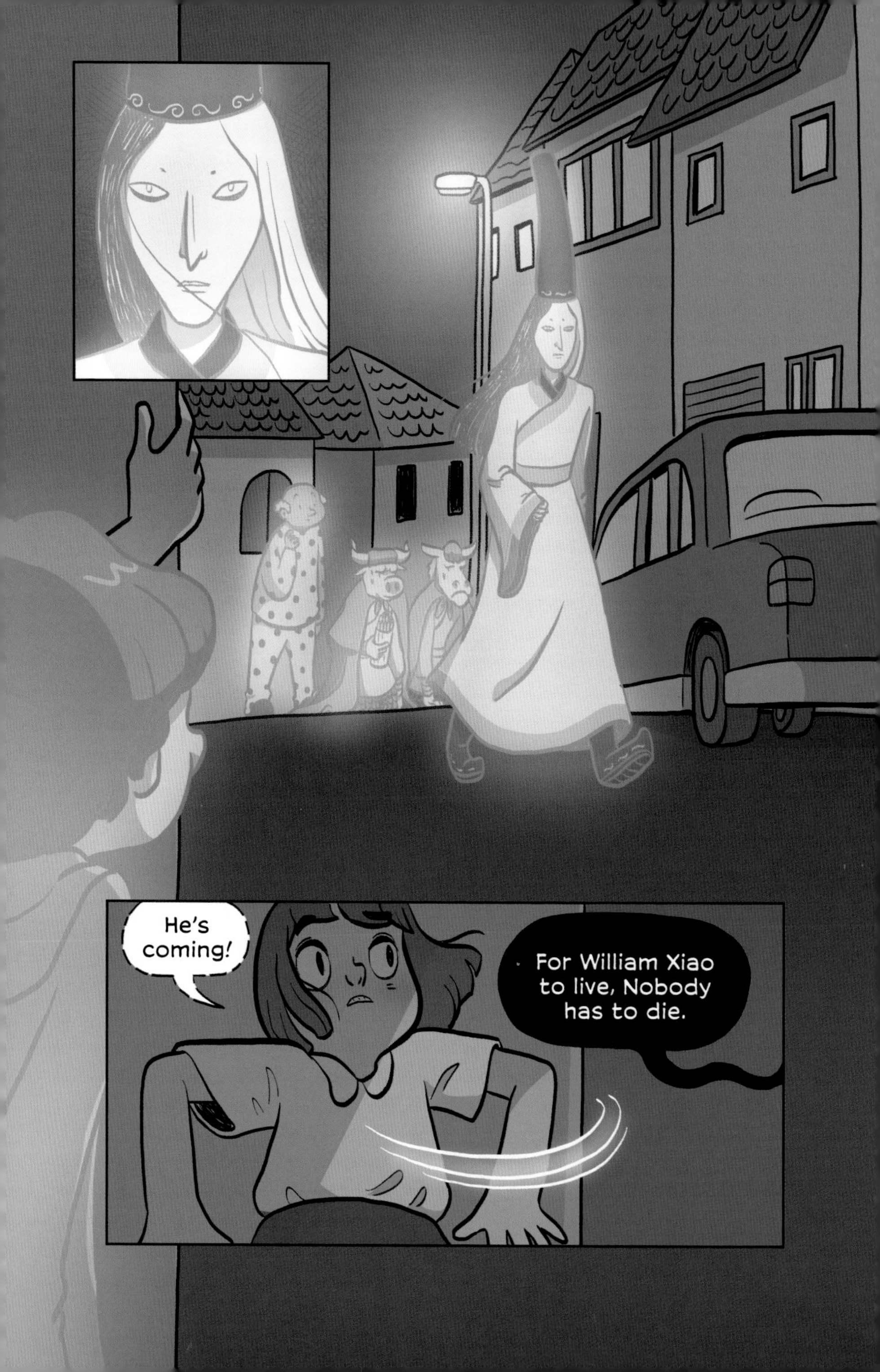
He's coming!
For William Xiao to live, Nobody has to die.

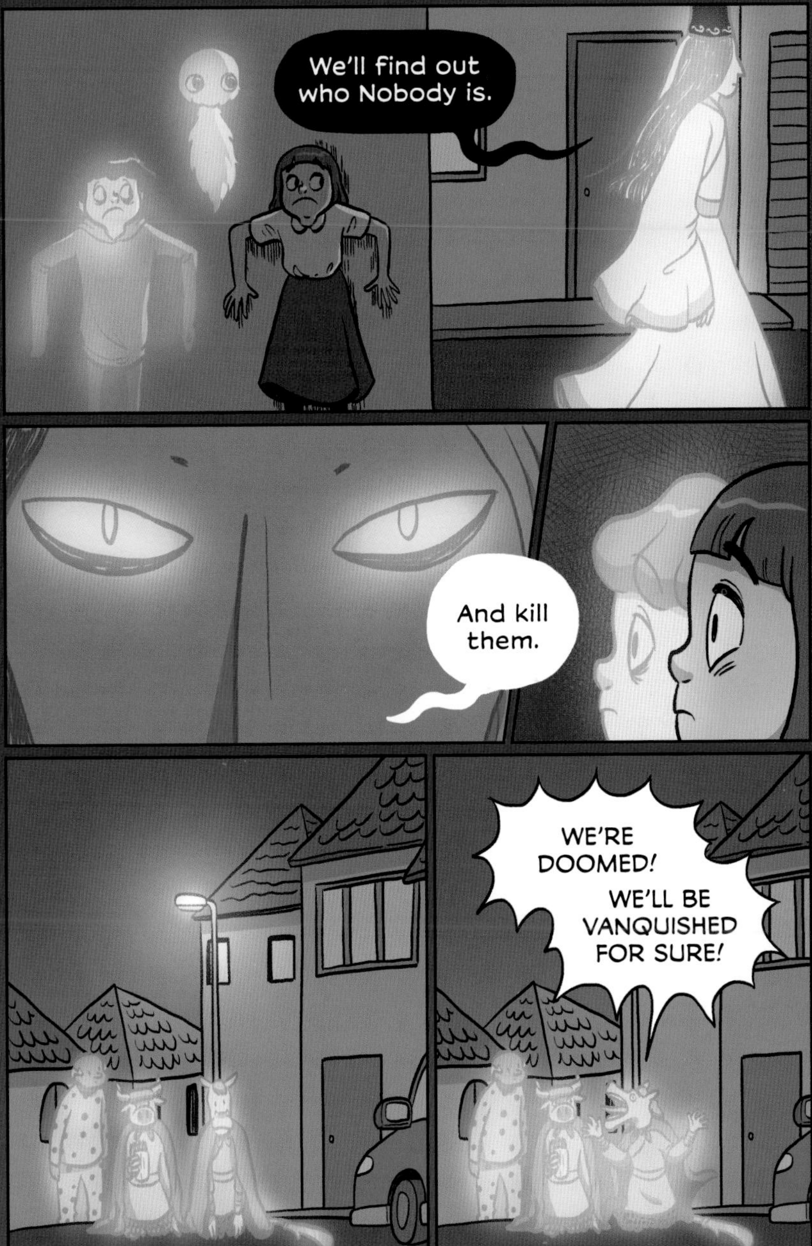
We'll find out who Nobody is.
And kill them.
WE'RE DOOMED!
WE'LL BE VANQUISHED FOR SURE!

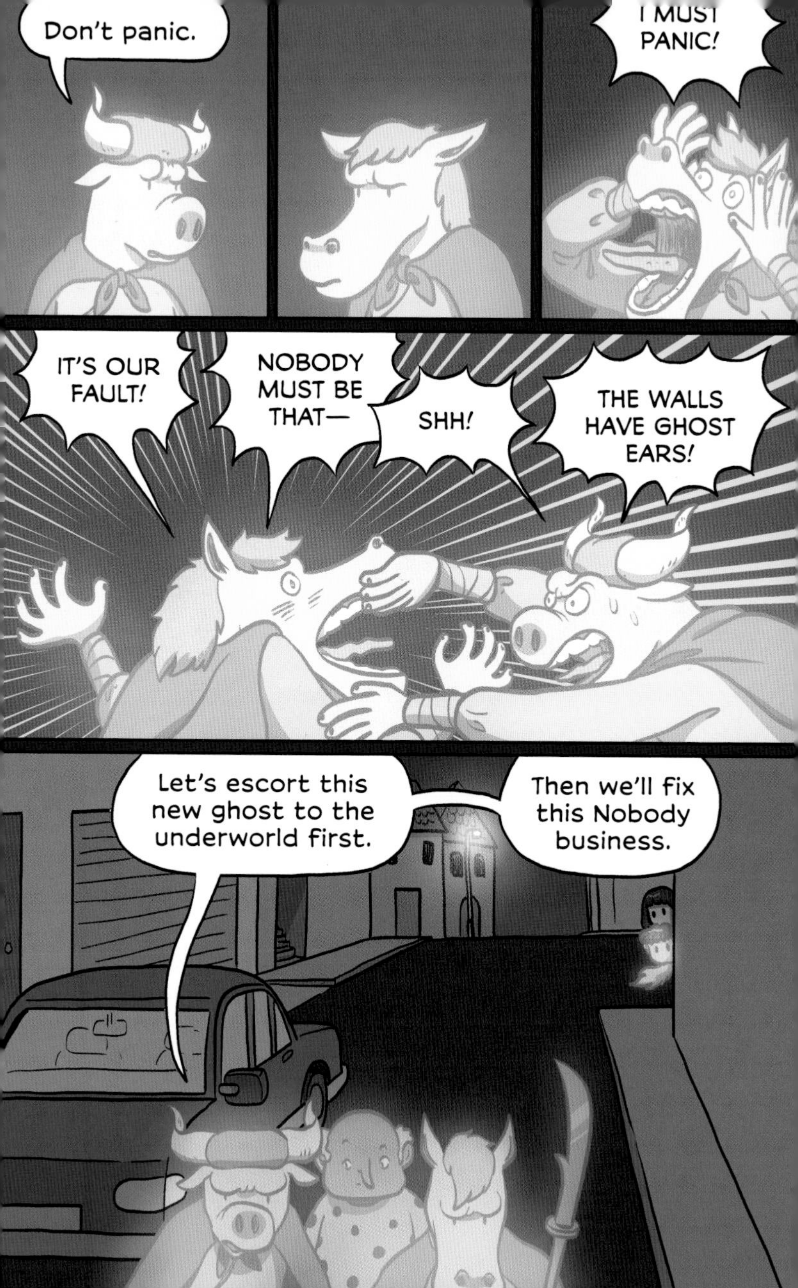
Don't panic.
I MUST PANIC!
IT'S OUR FAULT!
NOBODY MUST BE THAT—
SHH!
THE WALLS HAVE GHOST EARS!
Let's escort this new ghost to the underworld first.
Then we'll fix this Nobody business.

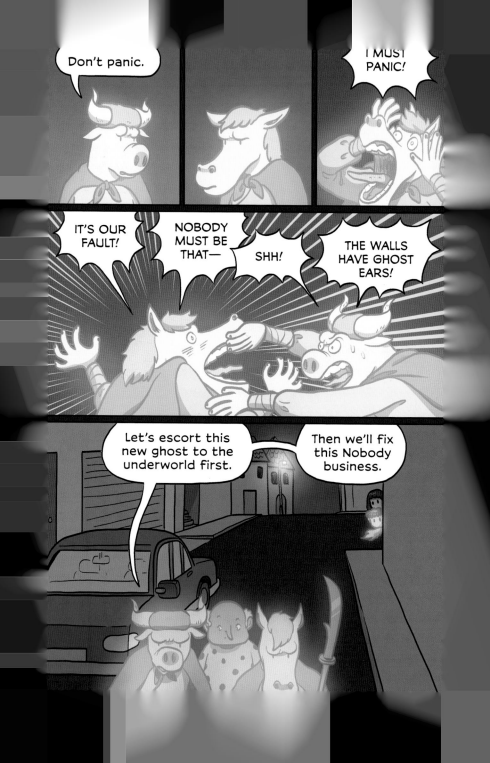

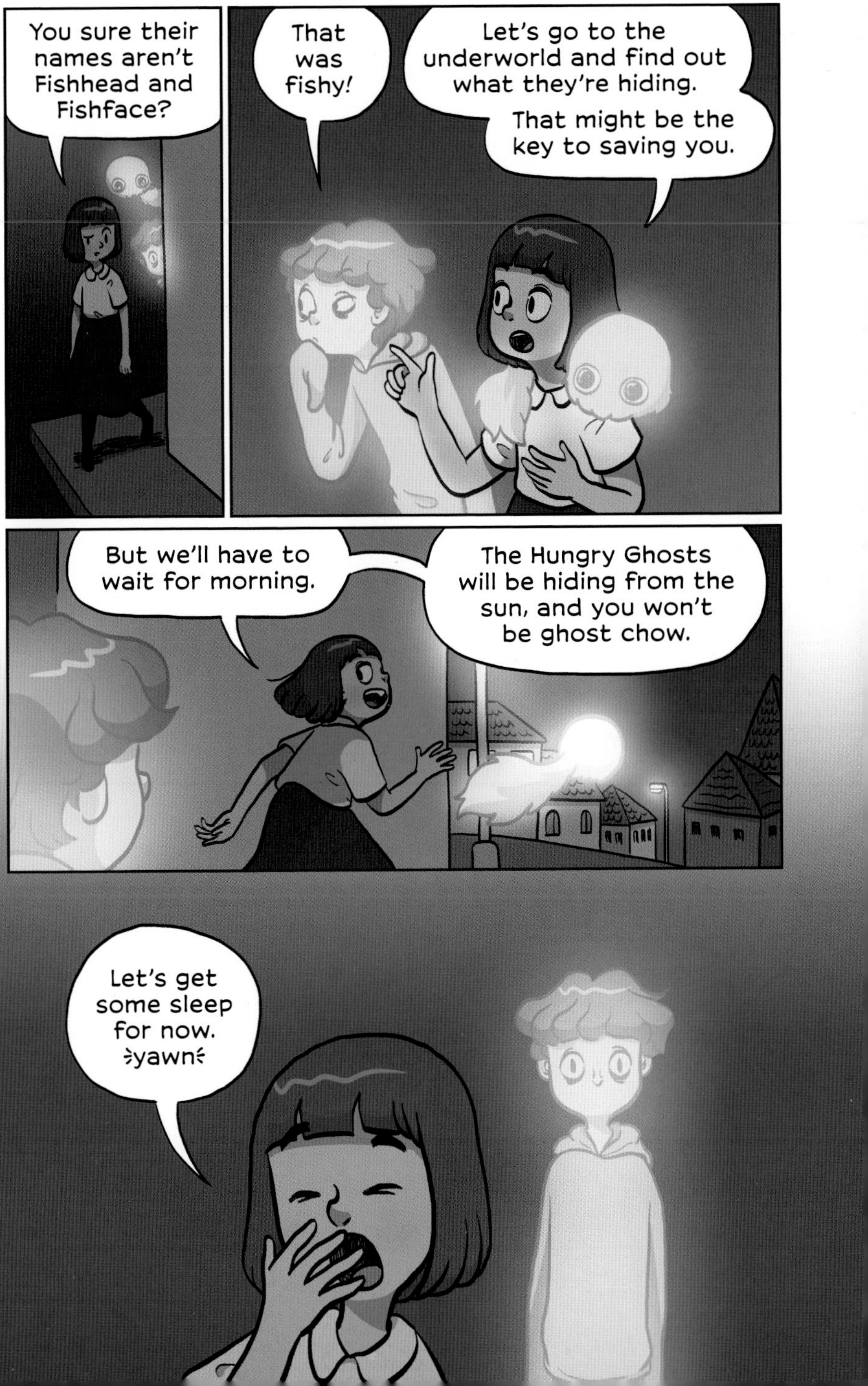
You sure their names aren't Fishhead and Fishface?
That was fishy!
Let's go to the underworld and find out what they're hiding.
That might be the key to saving you.
But we'll have to wait for morning.
The Hungry Ghosts will be hiding from the sun, and you won't be ghost chow.
Let's get some sleep for now.
⋟yawn⋞

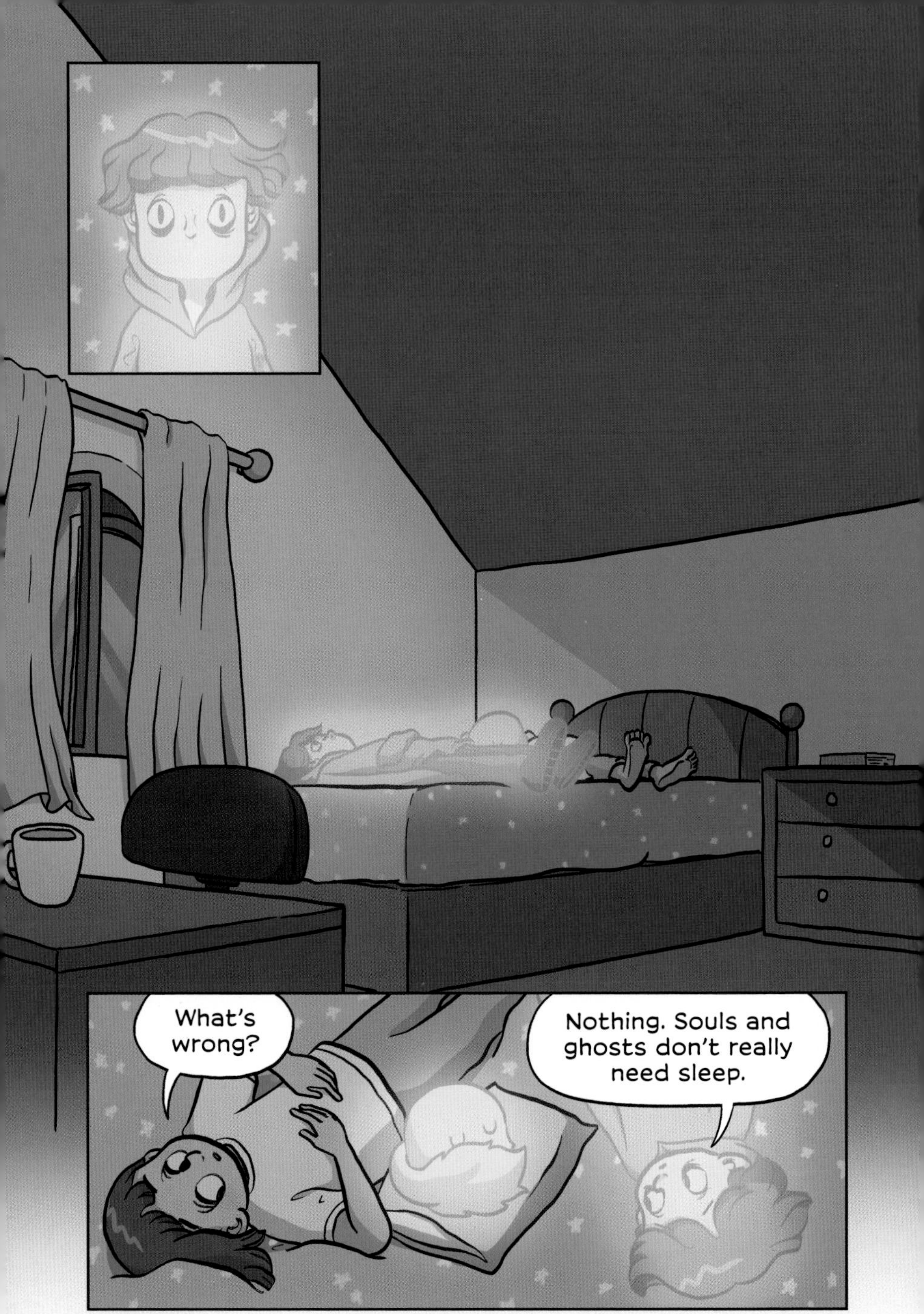
What's wrong?
Nothing. Souls and ghosts don't really need sleep.

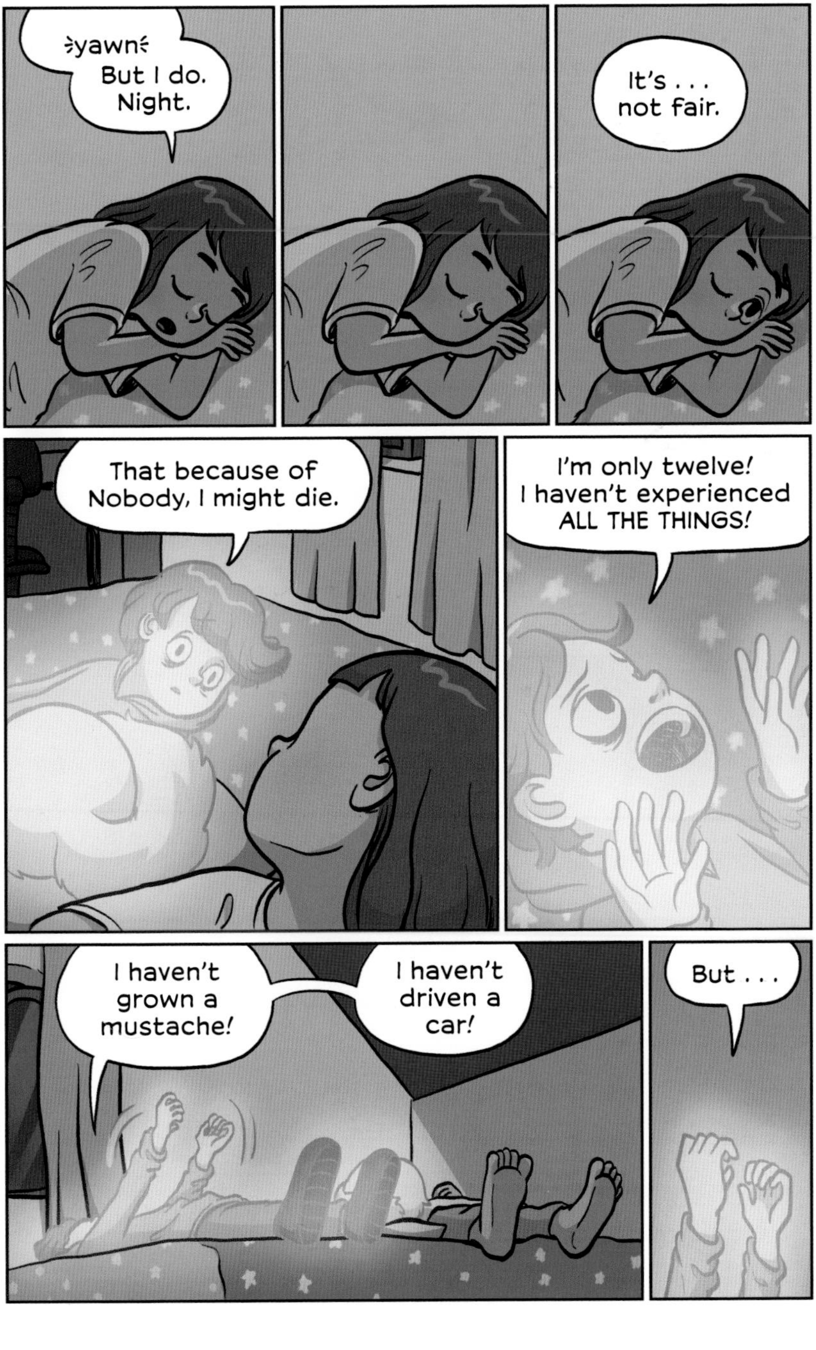

⩶yawn⩶ But I do. Night.
It's . . . not fair.
That because of Nobody, I might die.
I'm only twelve! I haven't experienced ALL THE THINGS!
I haven't grown a mustache!
I haven't driven a car!
But . . .

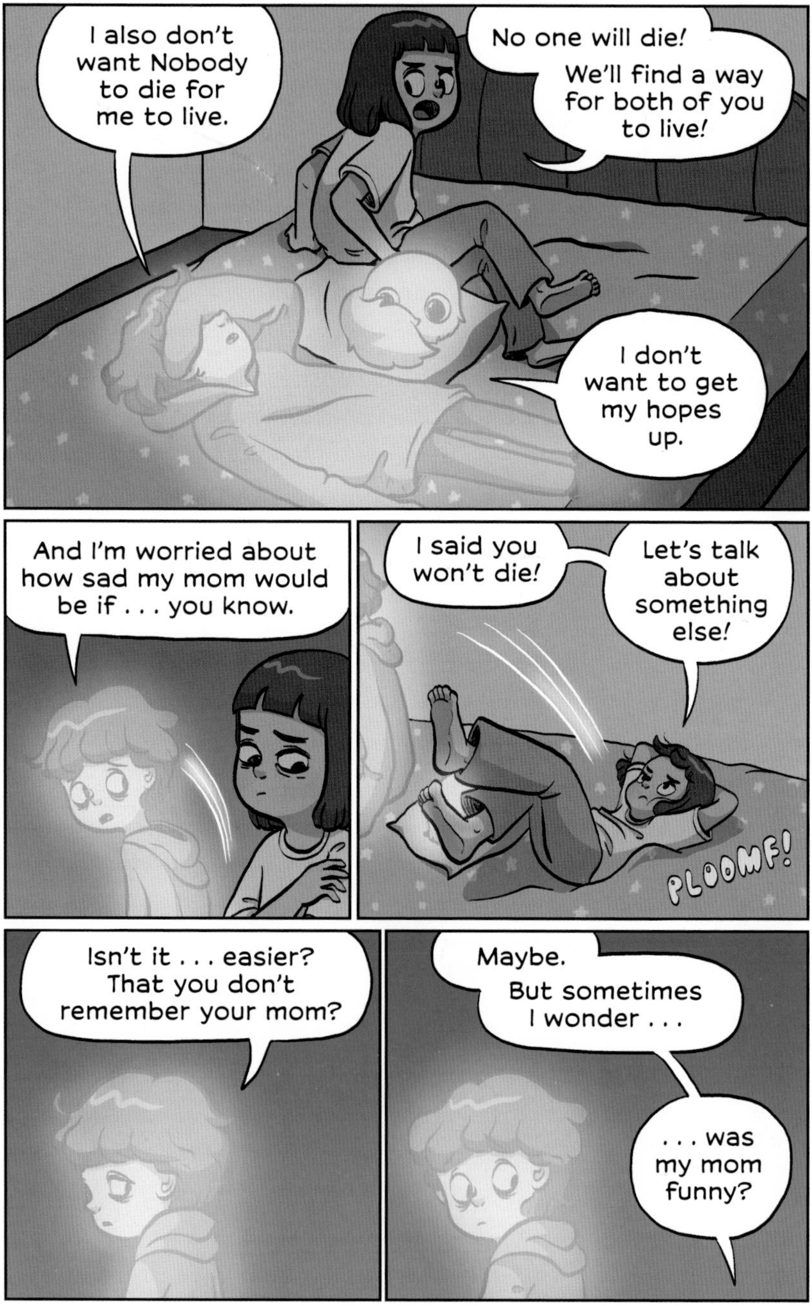
I also don't want Nobody to die for me to live.
No one will die!
We'll find a way for both of you to live!
I don't want to get my hopes up.
And I'm worried about how sad my mom would be if . . . you know.
I said you won't die!
Let's talk about something else!
PLOOMF!
Isn't it . . . easier? That you don't remember your mom?
Maybe.
But sometimes I wonder . . .
. . . was my mom funny?

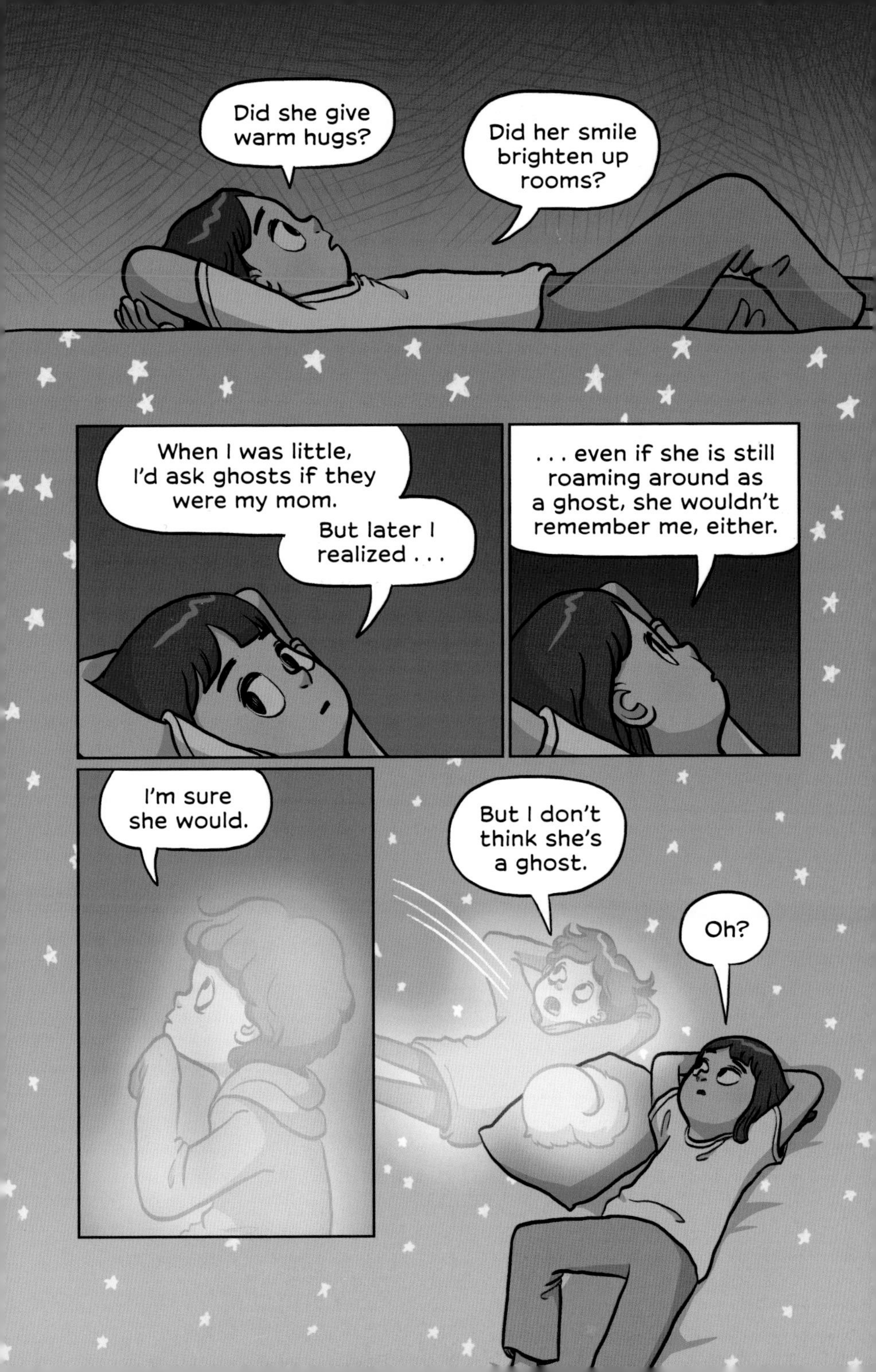
Did she give warm hugs?
Did her smile brighten up rooms?
When I was little, I'd ask ghosts if they were my mom.
But later I realized . . .
. . . even if she is still roaming around as a ghost, she wouldn't remember me, either.
I'm sure she would.
But I don't think she's a ghost.
Oh?

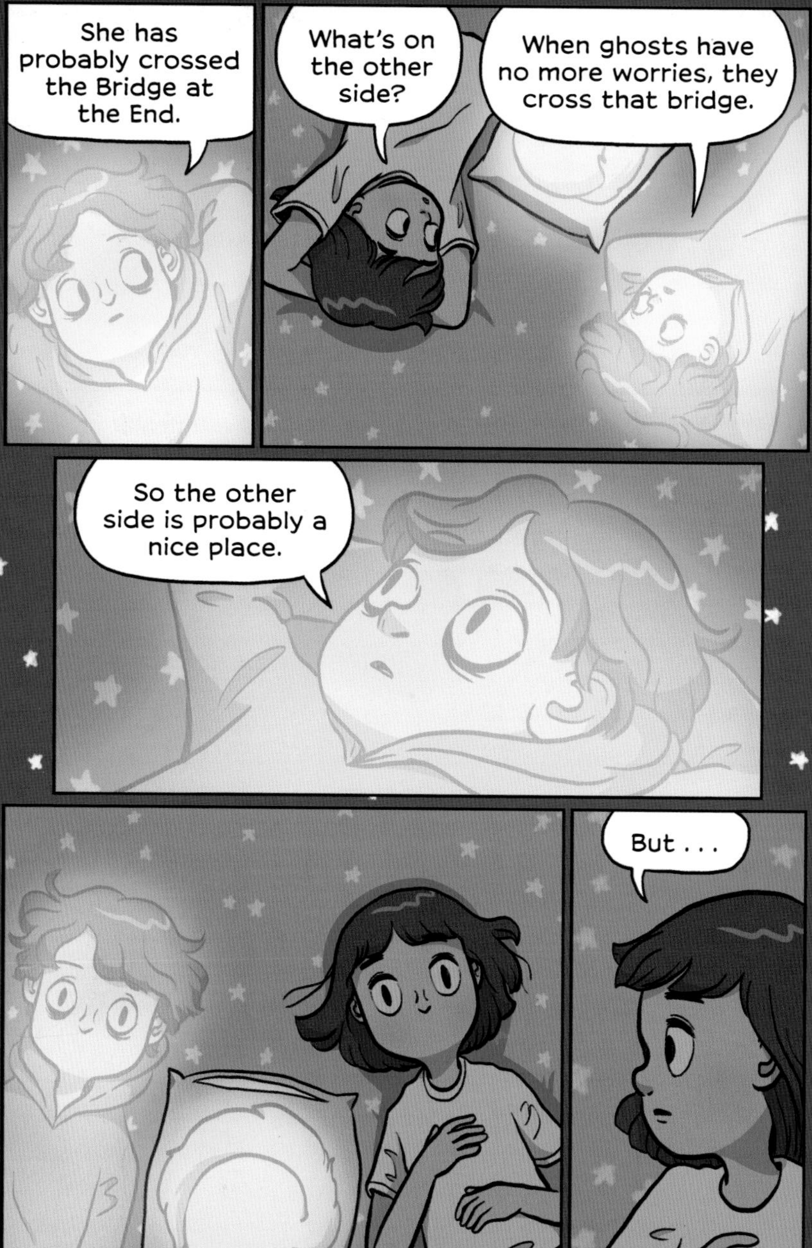
She has probably crossed the Bridge at the End.
What's on the other side?
When ghosts have no more worries, they cross that bridge.
So the other side is probably a nice place.
But . . .

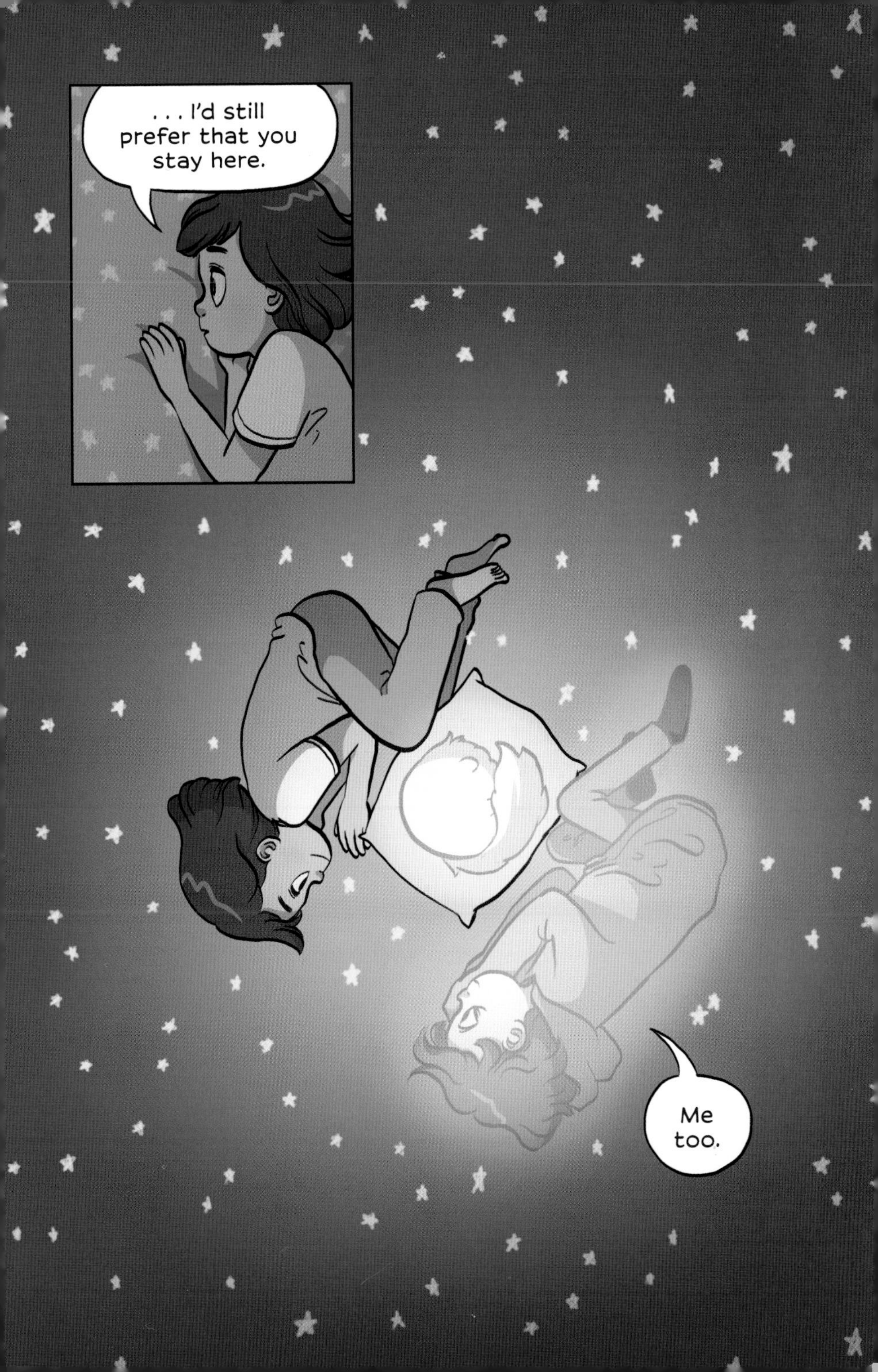
. . . I'd still prefer that you stay here.
Me too.

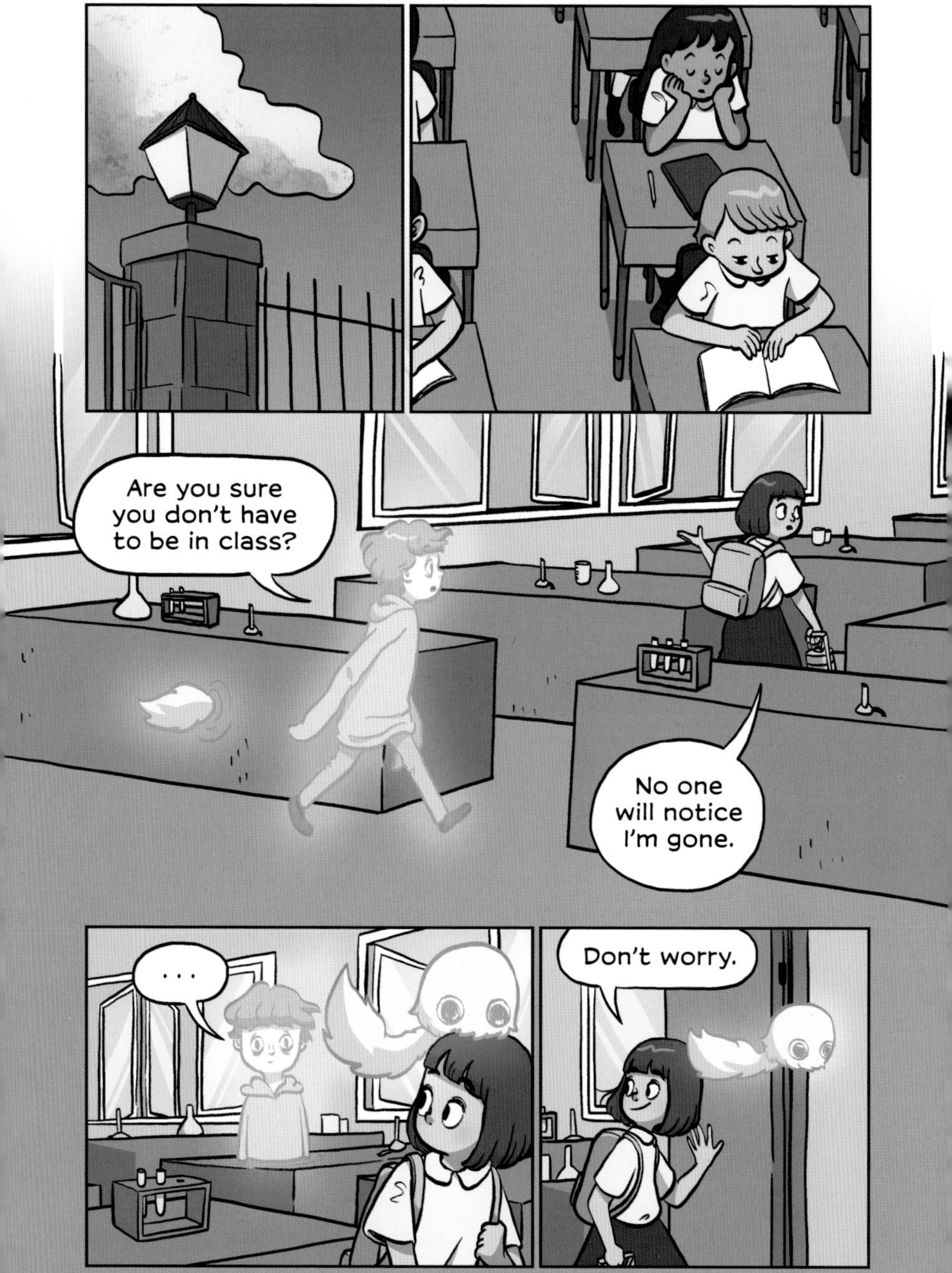
Are you sure you don't have to be in class?
No one will notice I'm gone.
. . .
Don't worry.

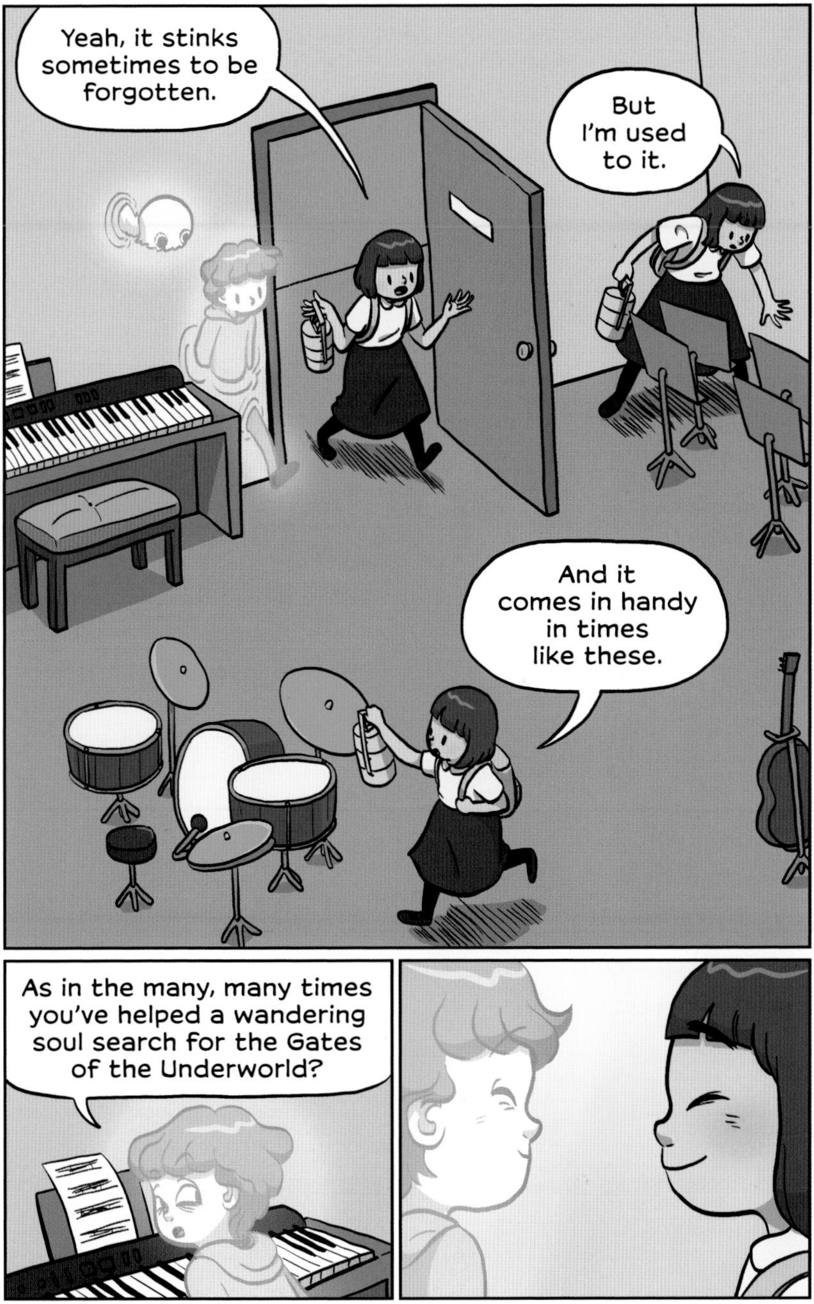
Yeah, it stinks sometimes to be forgotten.
But I'm used to it.
And it comes in handy in times like these.
As in the many, many times you've helped a wandering soul search for the Gates of the Underworld?

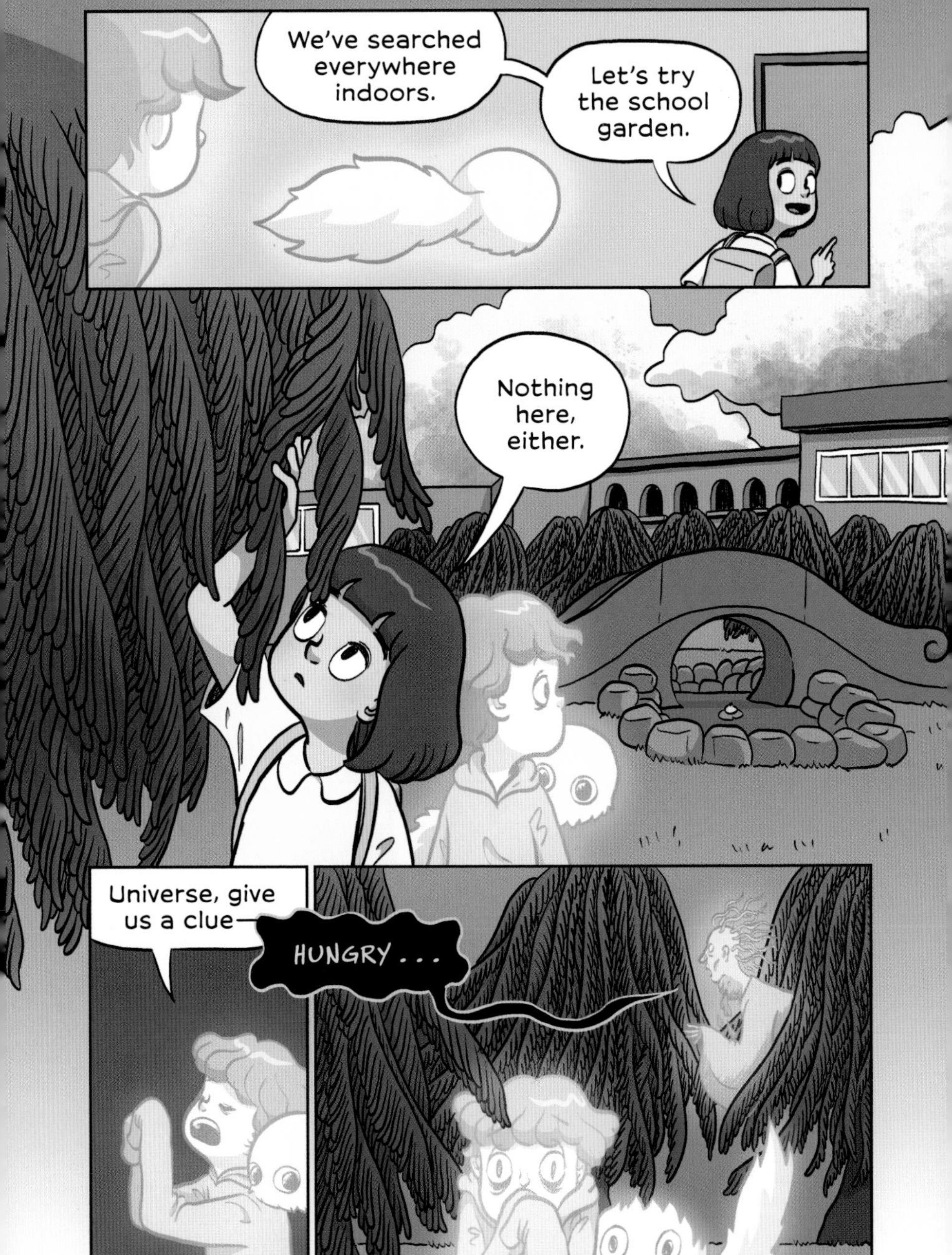
We've searched everywhere indoors.
Let's try the school garden.
Nothing here, either.
Universe, give us a clue—
HUNGRY . . .

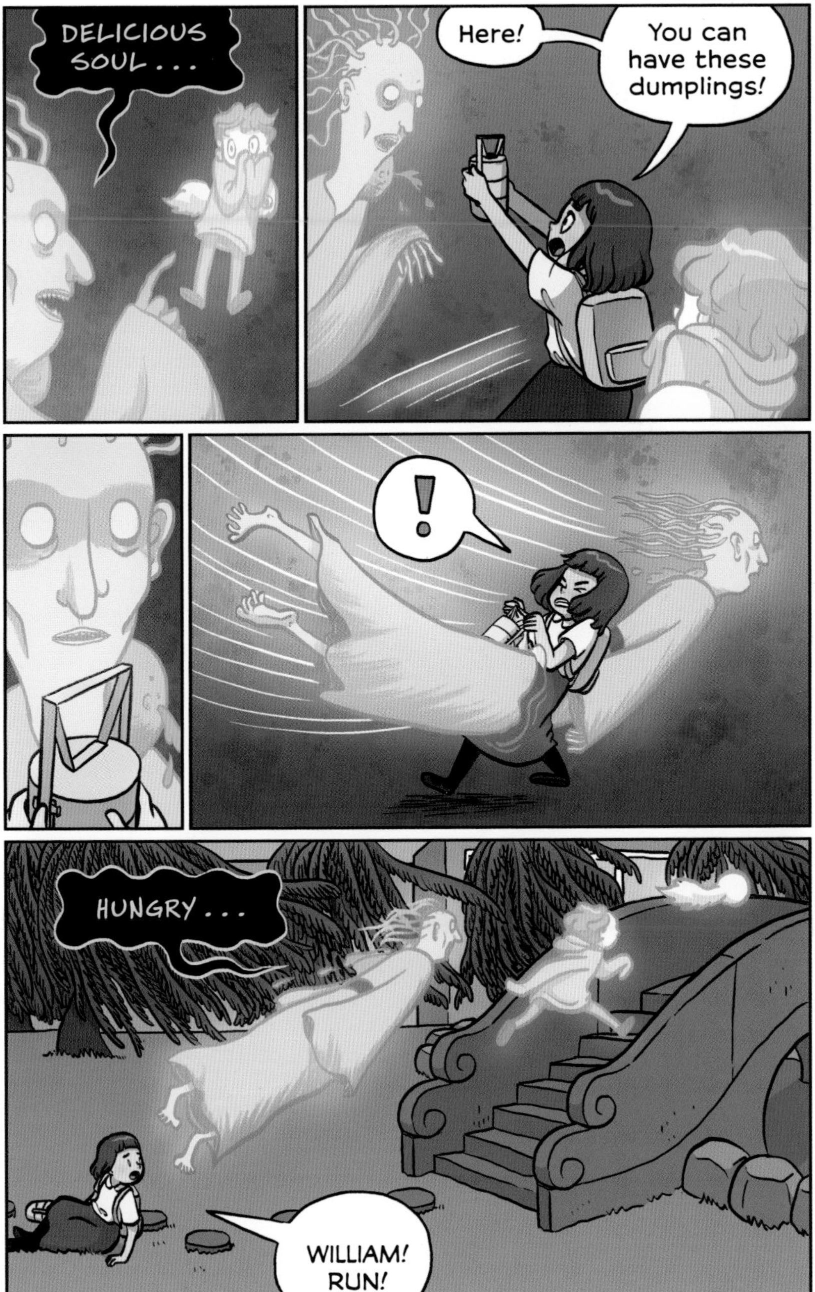
DELICIOUS SOUL . . .
Here!
You can have these dumplings!
!
HUNGRY . . .
WILLIAM! RUN!

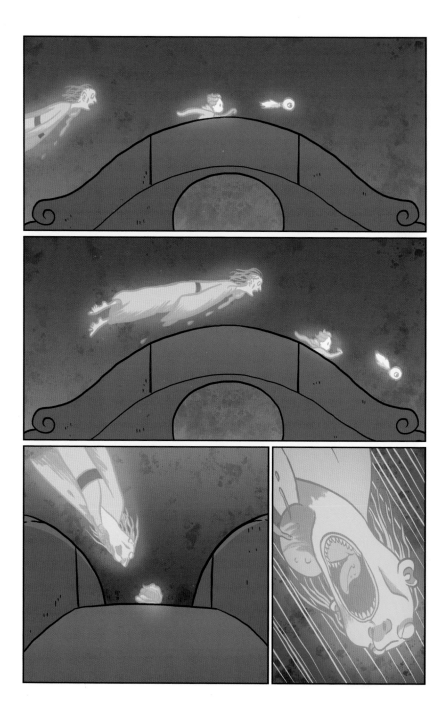

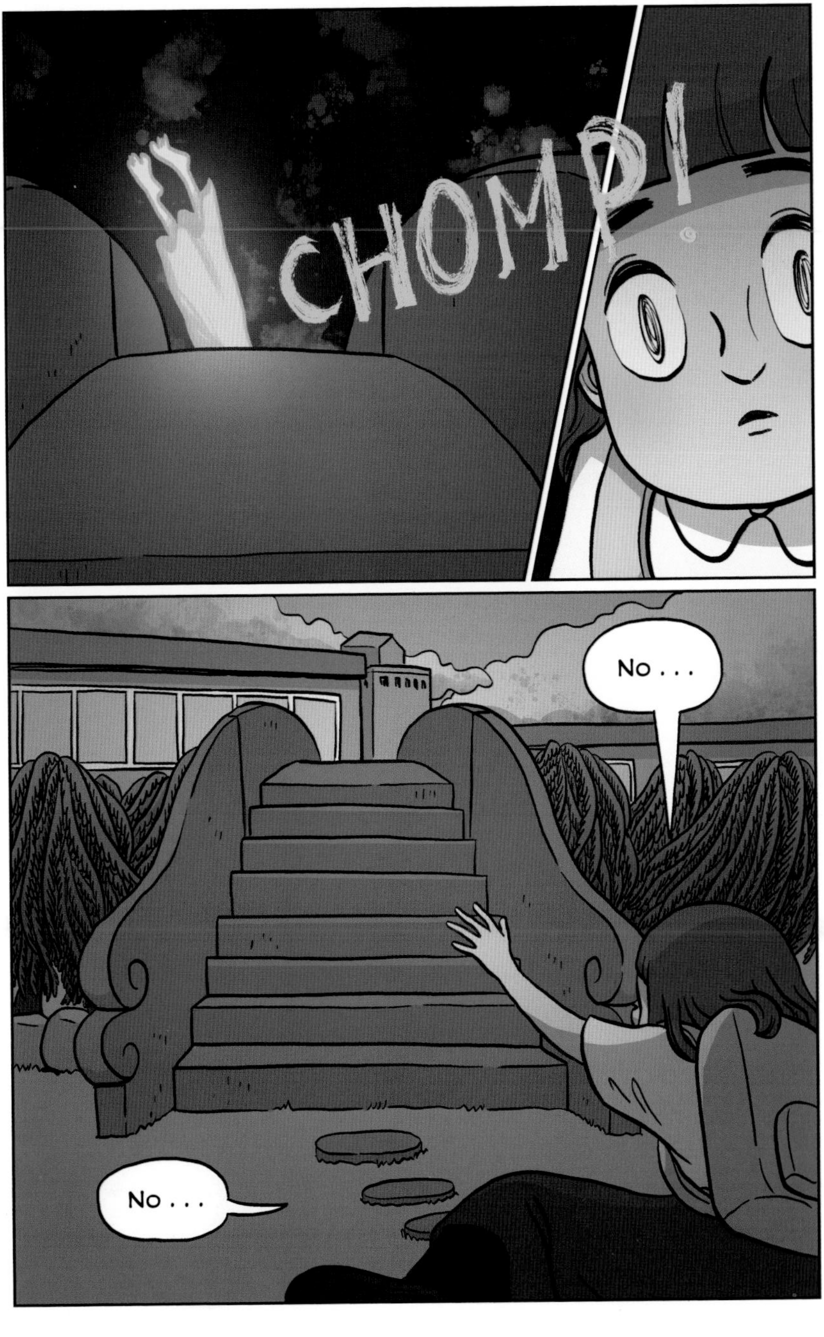
CHOMP!
No . . .
No . . .

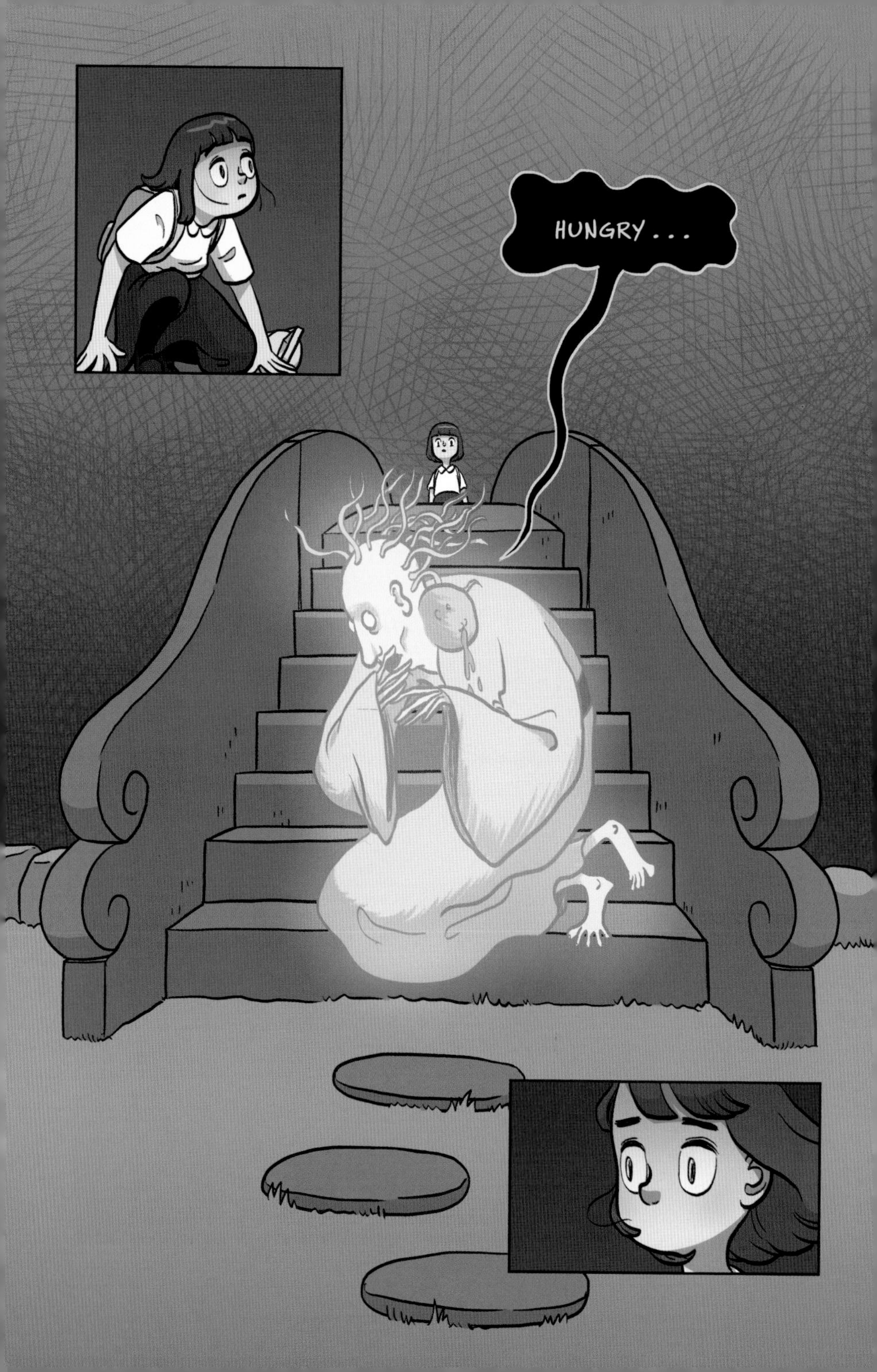
HUNGRY . . .

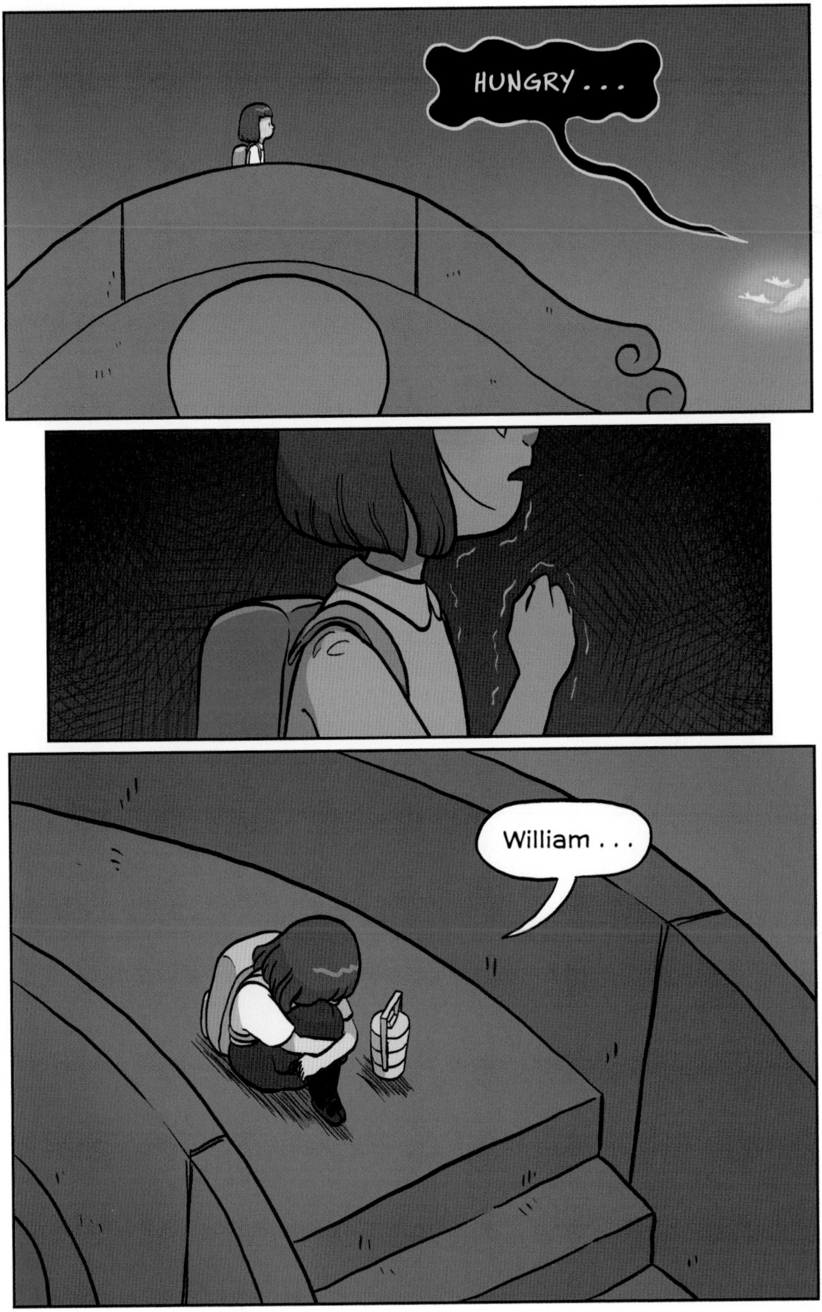
HUNGRY . . .
William . . .

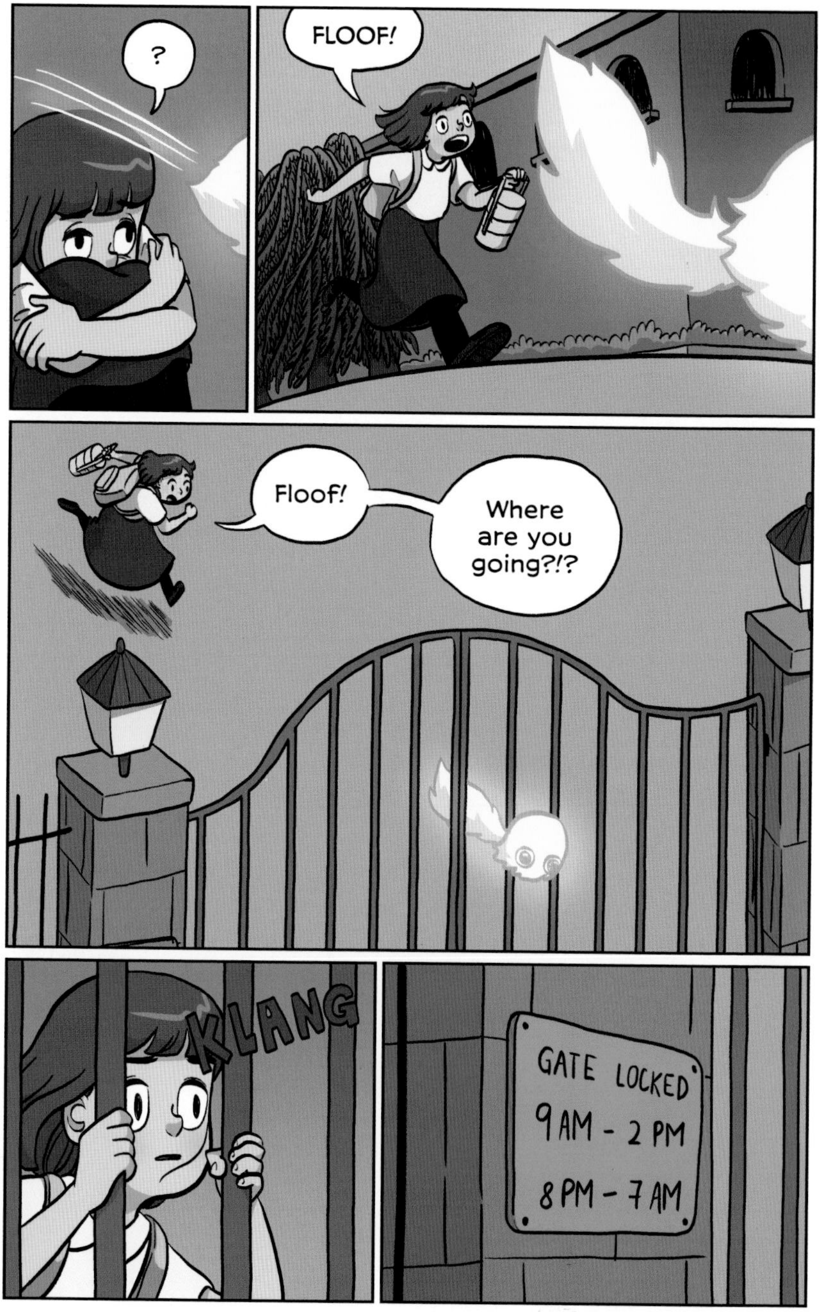
?
FLOOF!
Floof!
Where are you going?!?
KLANG
GATE LOCKED
9 AM - 2 PM
8 PM - 7 AM

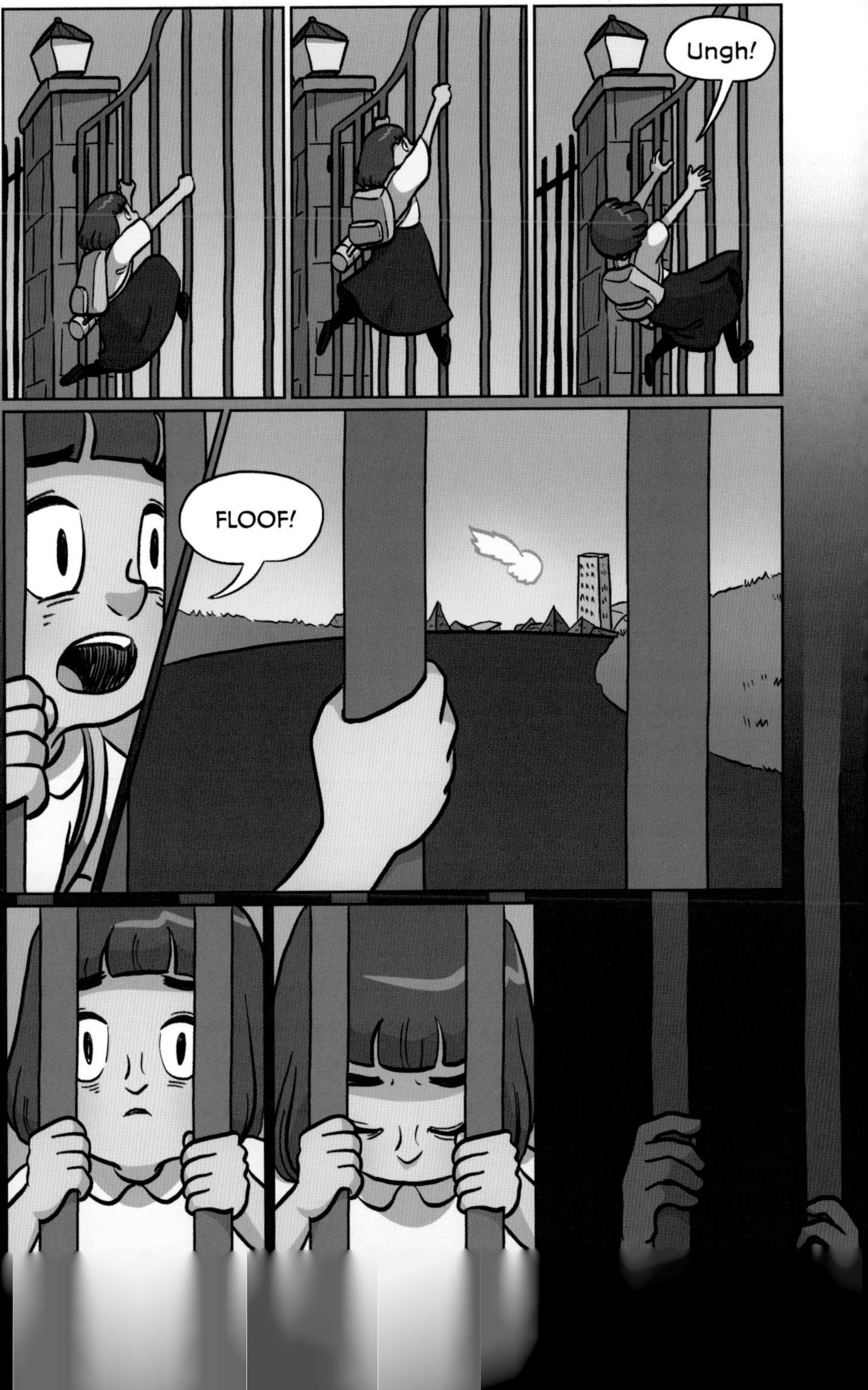
Ungh!
FLOOF!

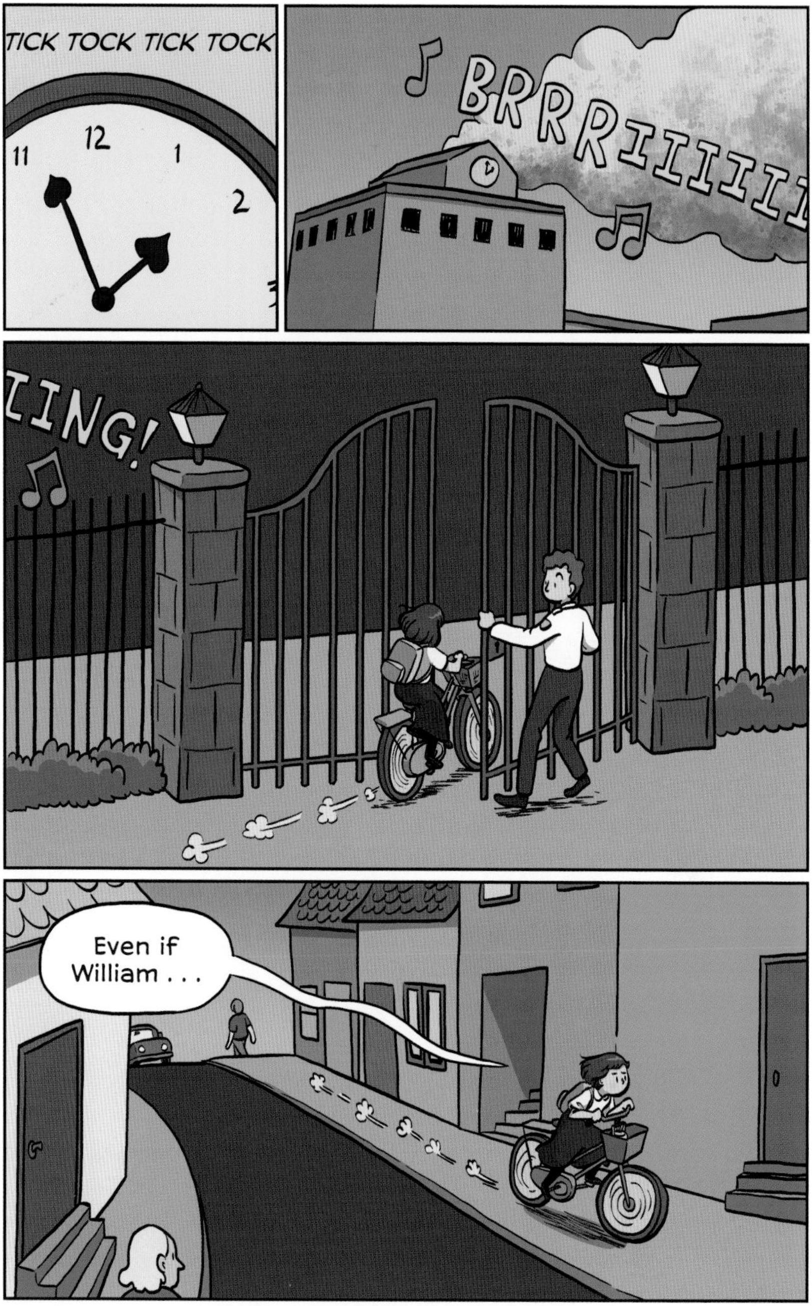
TICK TOCK TICK TOCK
BRRRIIIIII
IING!
Even if William . . .

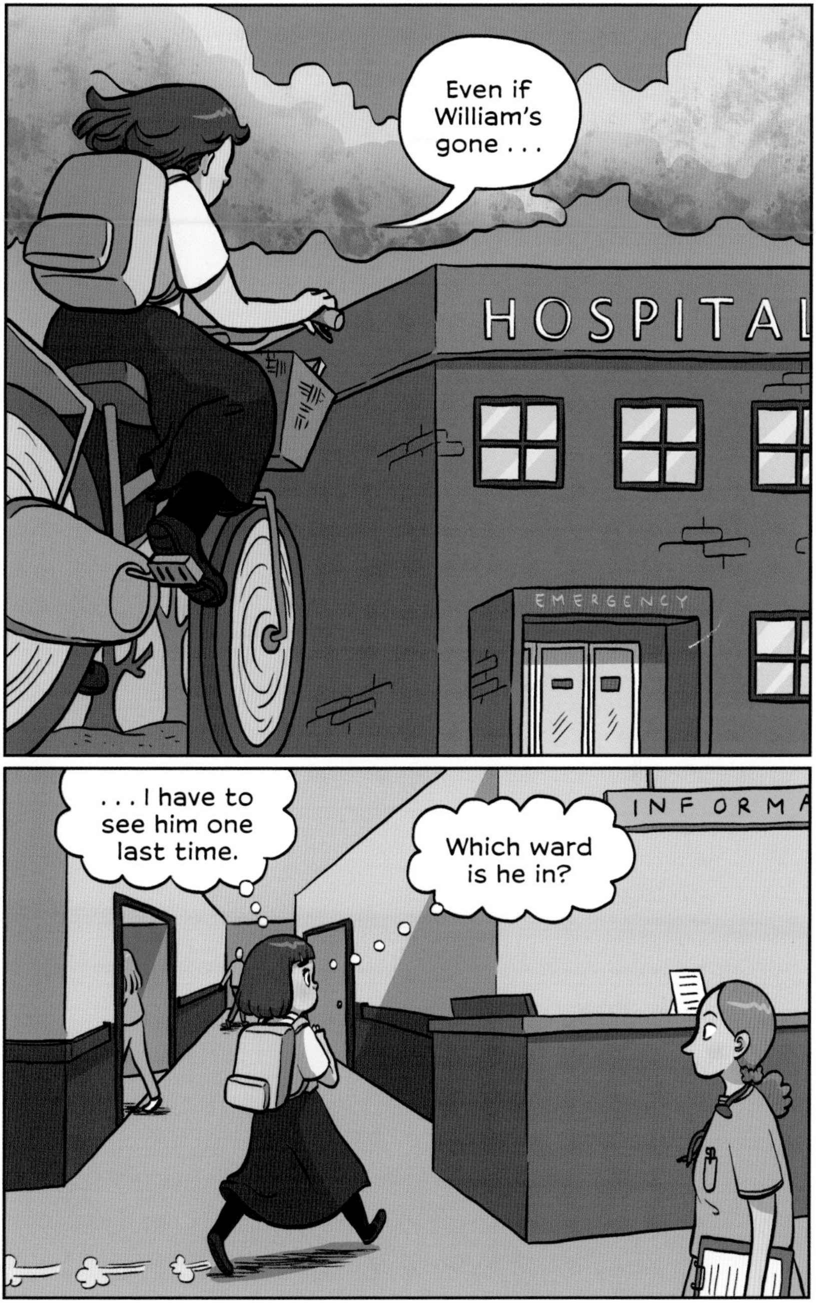
Even if William's gone . . .
HOSPITAL
EMERGENCY
. . . I have to see him one last time.
INFORMA
Which ward is he in?

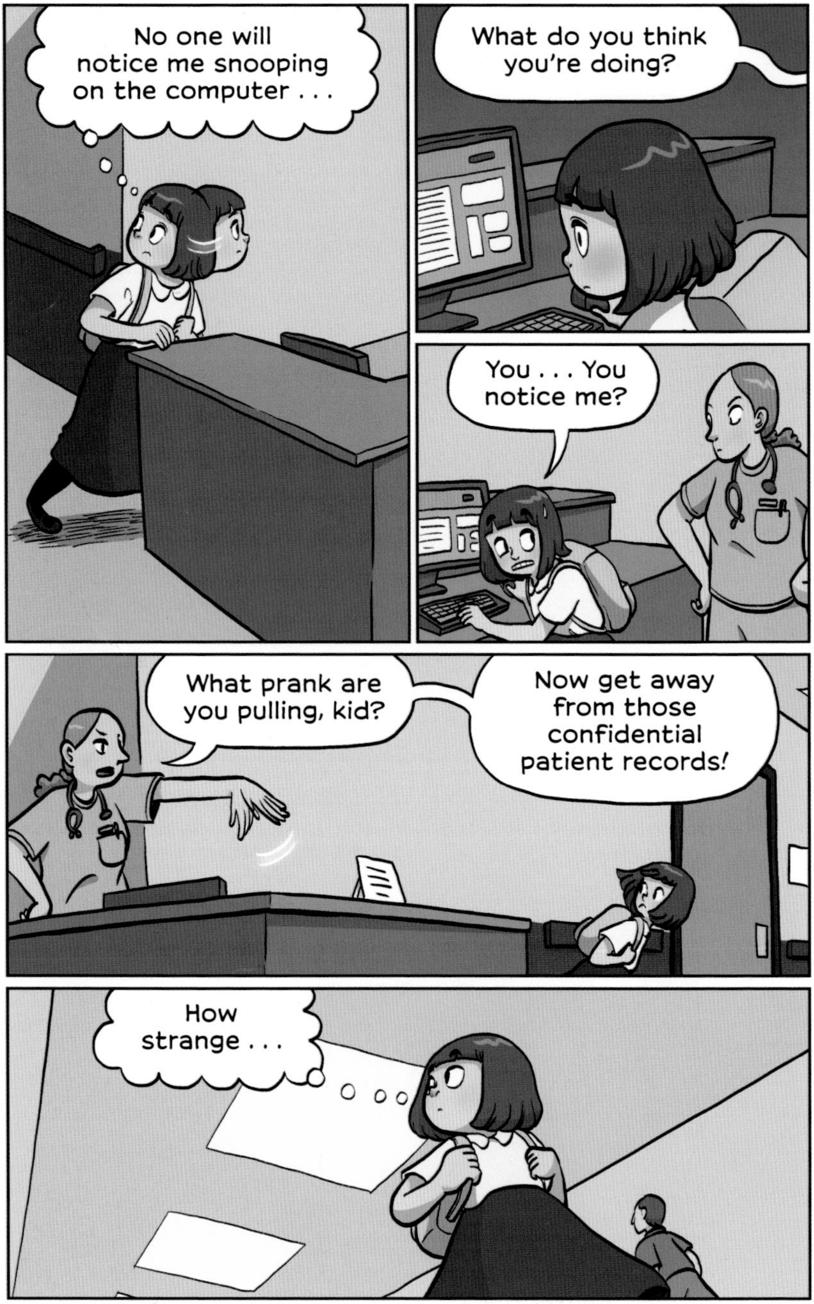
No one will notice me snooping on the computer . . .
What do you think you're doing?
You . . . You notice me?
What prank are you pulling, kid?
Now get away from those confidential patient records!
How strange . . .

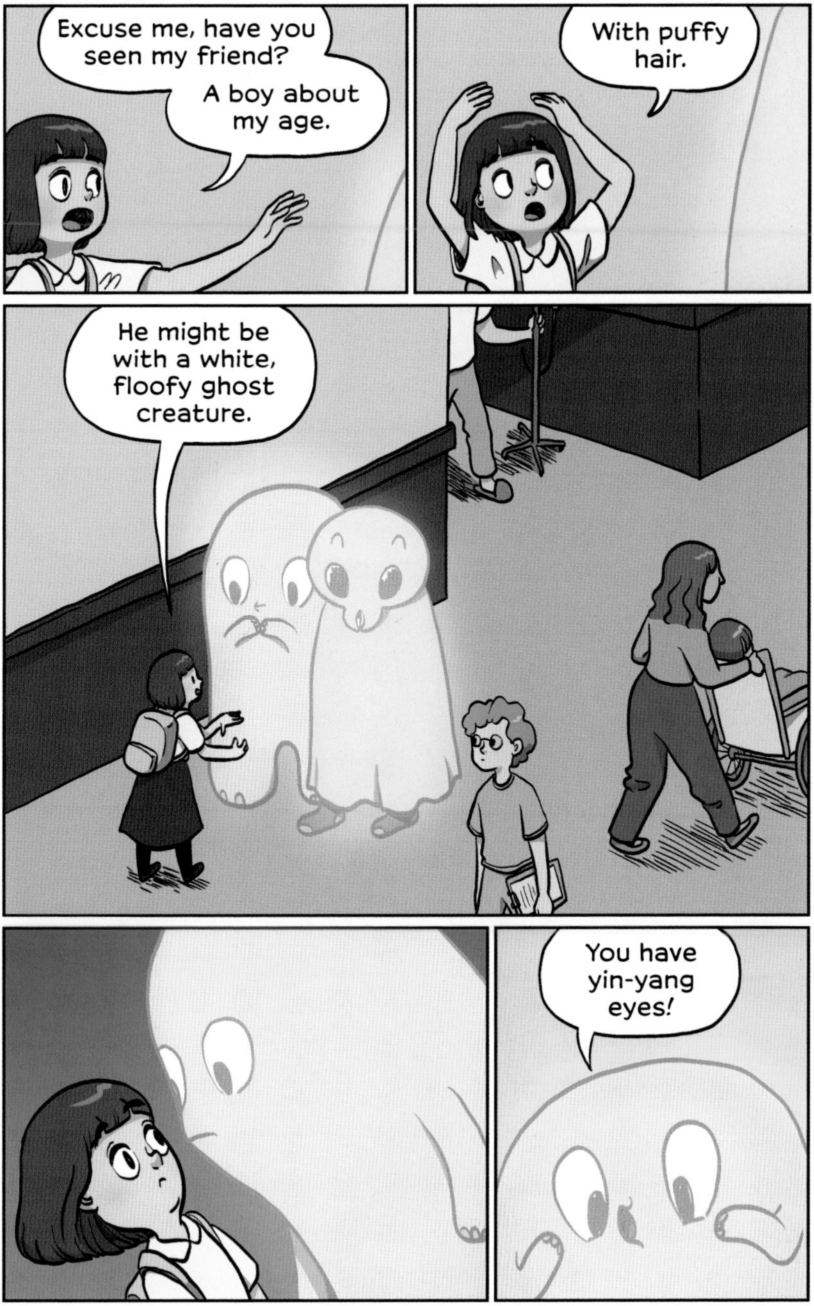

Excuse me, have you seen my friend?
A boy about my age.
With puffy hair.
He might be with a white, floofy ghost creature.
You have yin-yang eyes!

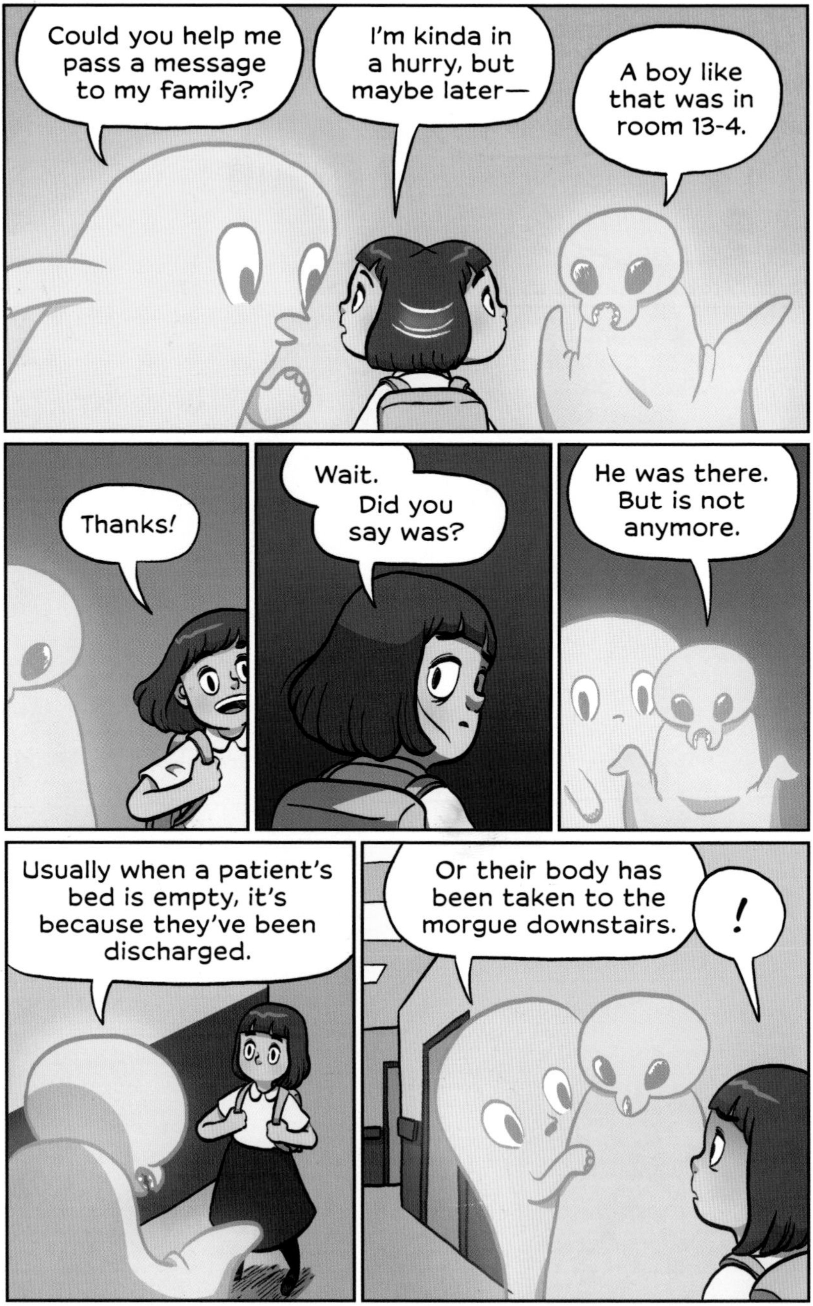
Could you help me pass a message to my family?
I'm kinda in a hurry, but maybe later—
A boy like that was in room 13-4.
Thanks!
Wait. Did you say was?
He was there. But is not anymore.
Usually when a patient's bed is empty, it's because they've been discharged.
Or their body has been taken to the morgue downstairs.
!

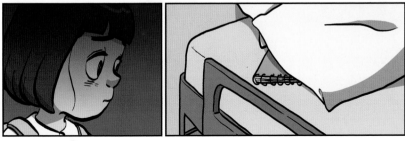

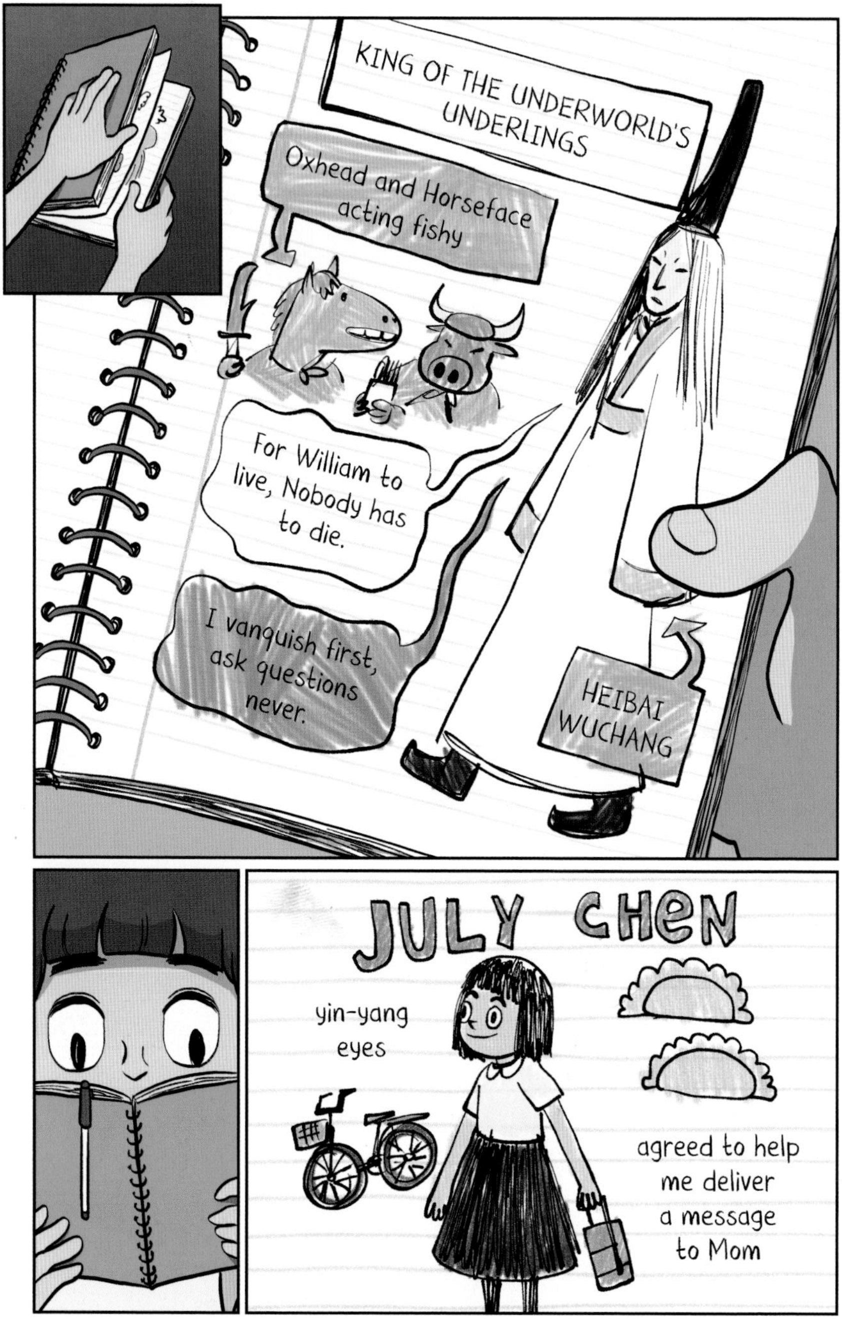
KING OF THE UNDERWORLD'S UNDERLINGS
Oxhead and Horseface acting fishy
For William to live, Nobody has to die.
I vanquish first, ask questions never.
HEIBAI WUCHANG
JULY CHEN
yin-yang eyes
agreed to help me deliver a message to Mom

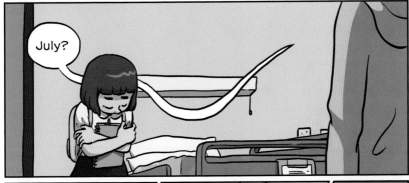

July?

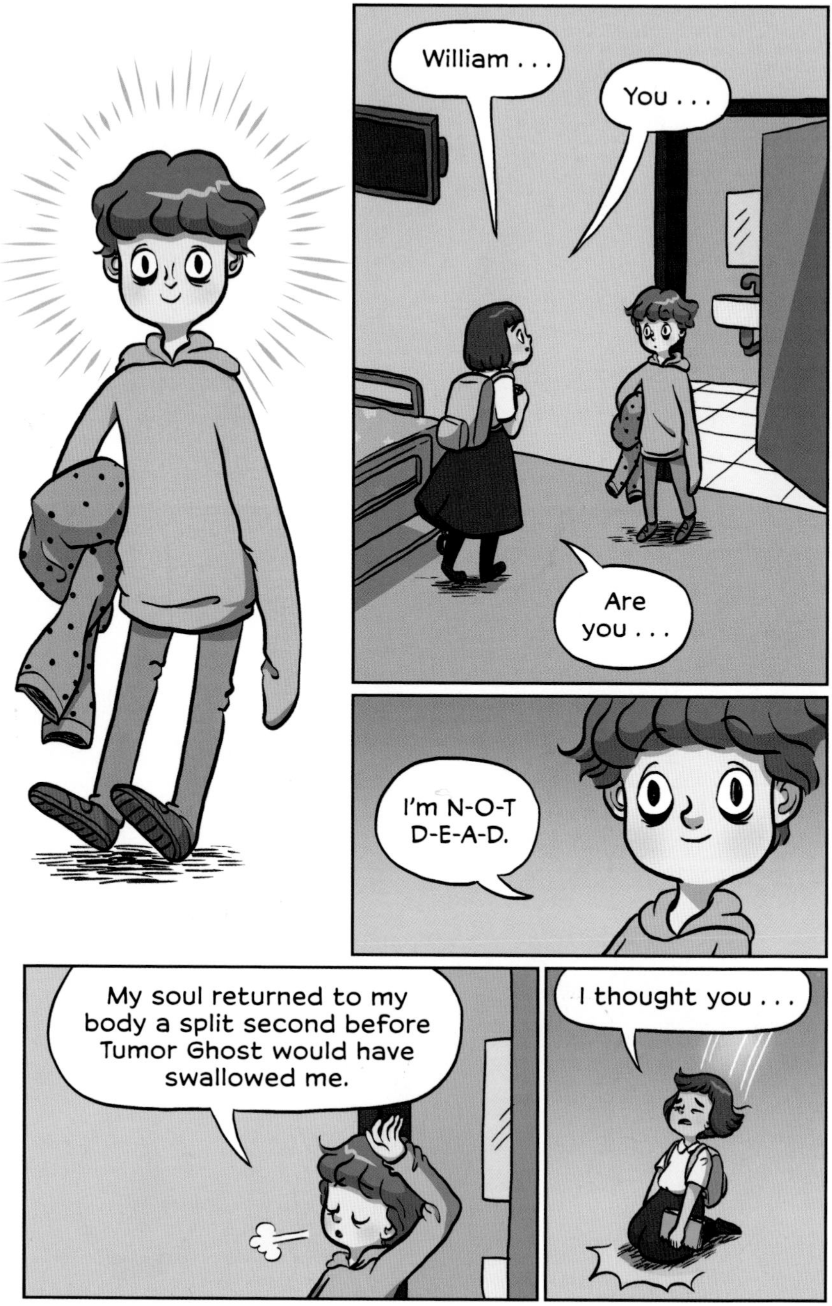
William . . .
You . . .
Are you . . .
I'm N-O-T D-E-A-D.
My soul returned to my body a split second before Tumor Ghost would have swallowed me.
I thought you . . .

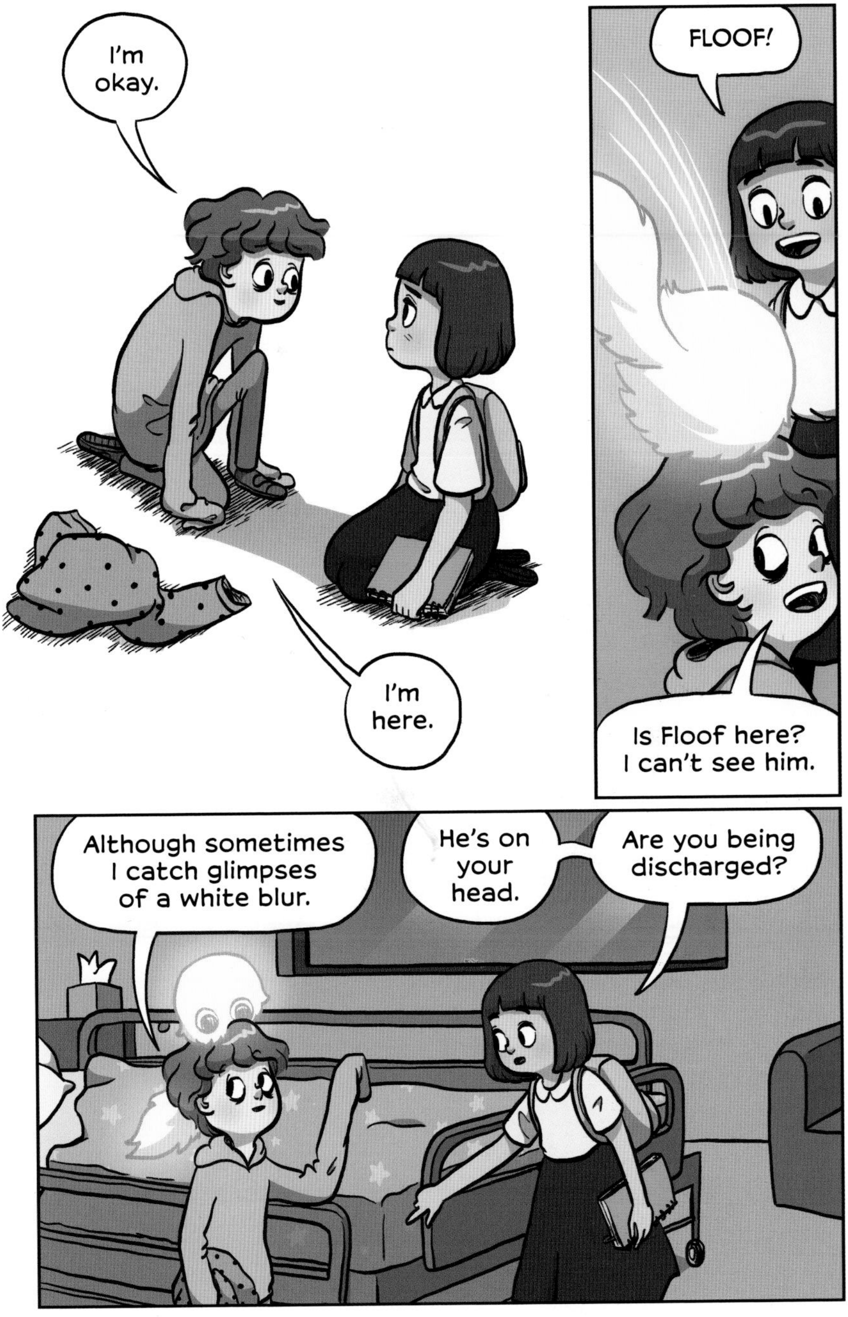
I'm okay.
I'm here.
FLOOF!
Is Floof here? I can't see him.
Although sometimes I catch glimpses of a white blur.
He's on your head.
Are you being discharged?

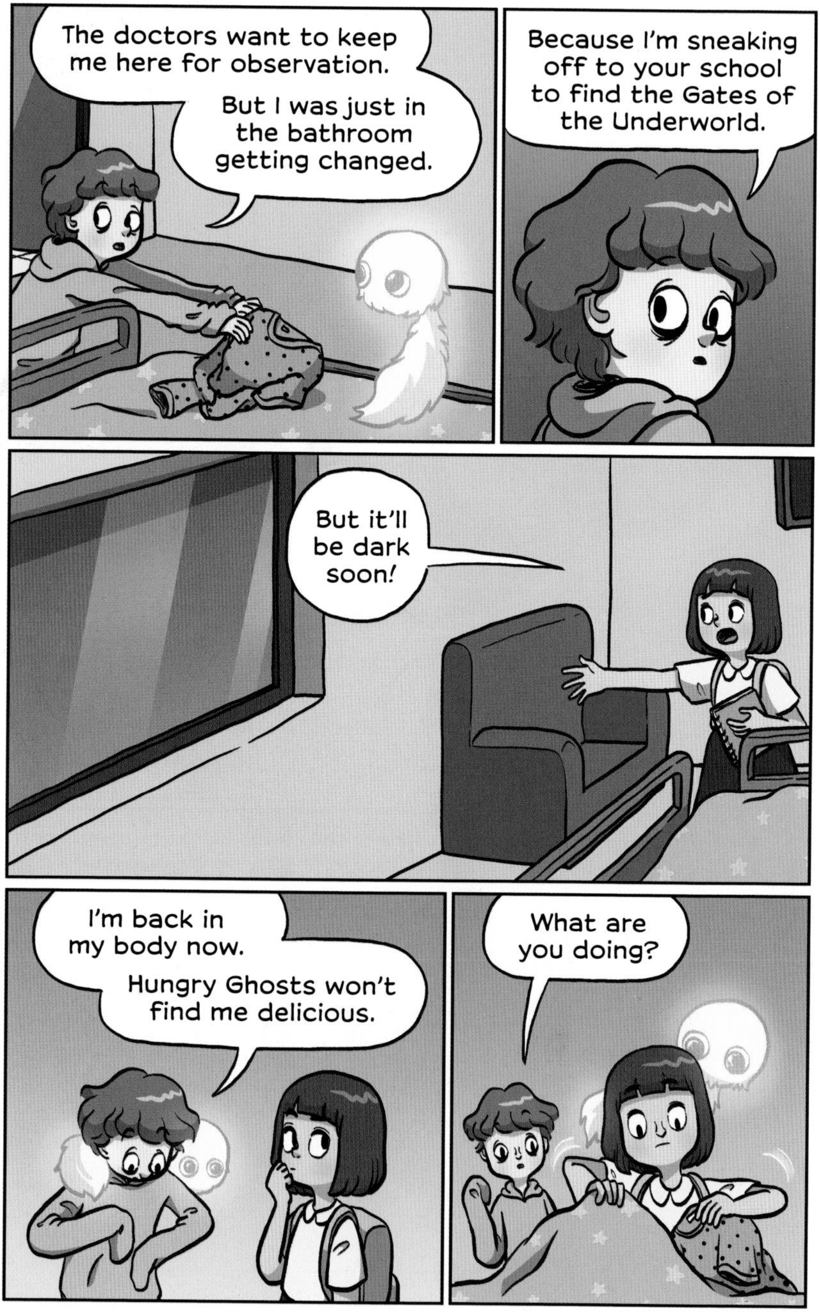
The doctors want to keep me here for observation.
But I was just in the bathroom getting changed.
Because I'm sneaking off to your school to find the Gates of the Underworld.
But it'll be dark soon!
I'm back in my body now.
Hungry Ghosts won't find me delicious.
What are you doing?

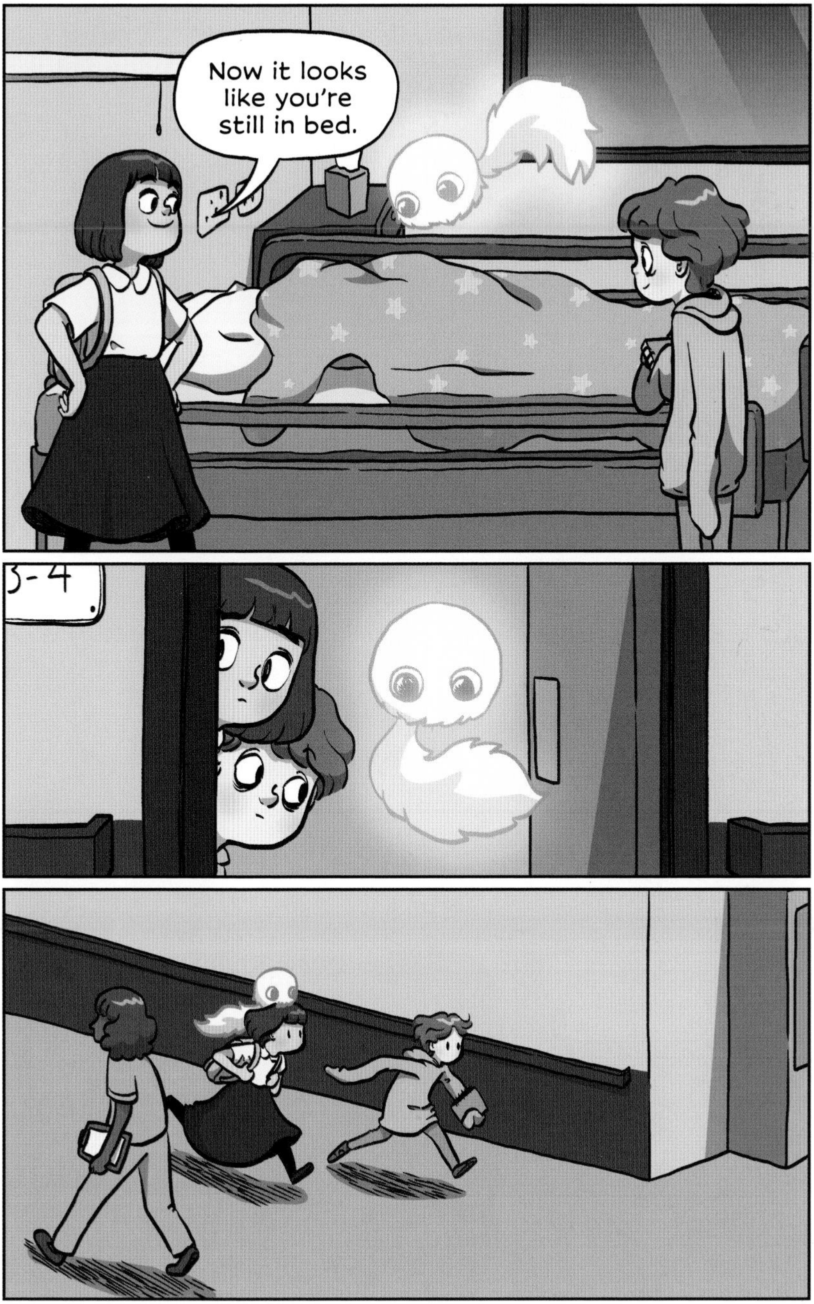
Now it looks like you're still in bed.
3-4

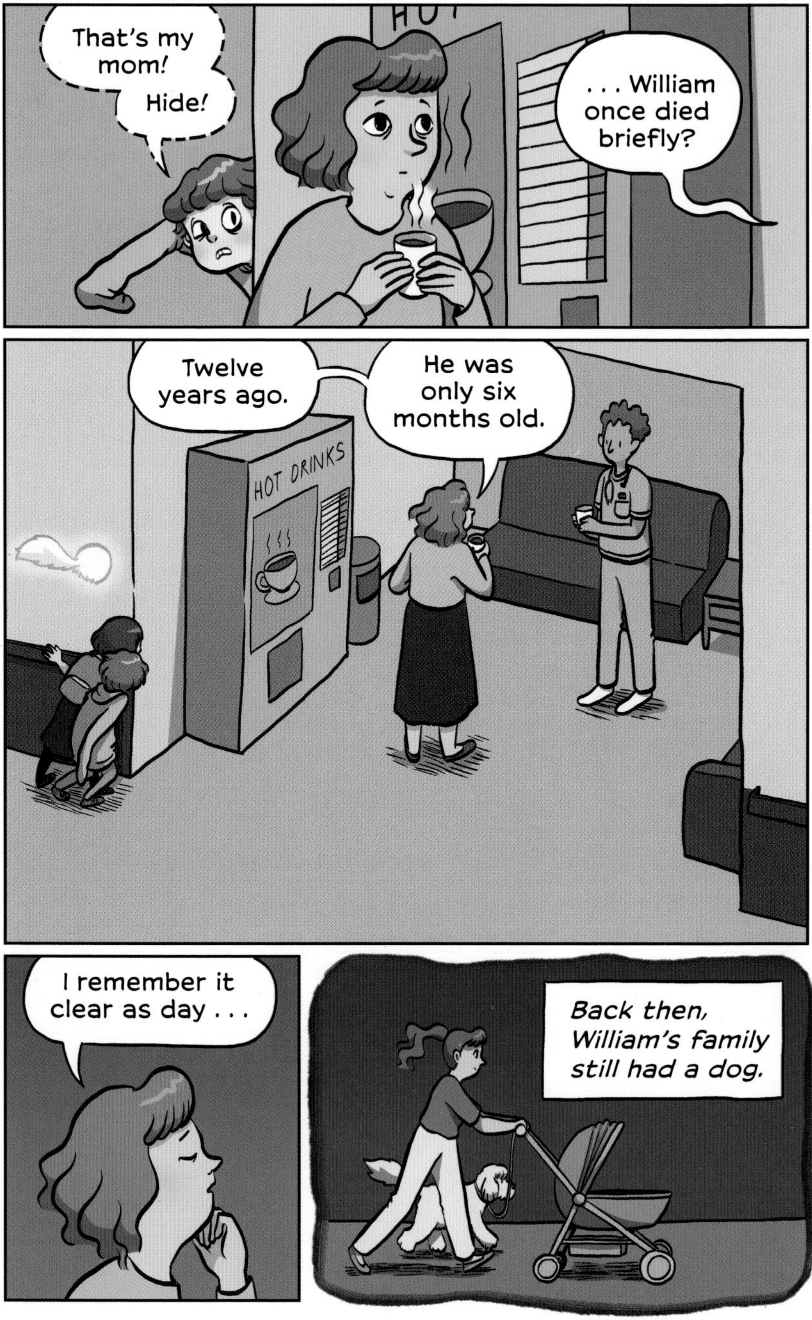
That's my mom! Hide!
. . . William once died briefly?
Twelve years ago.
He was only six months old.
HOT DRINKS
I remember it clear as day . . .
Back then, William's family still had a dog.

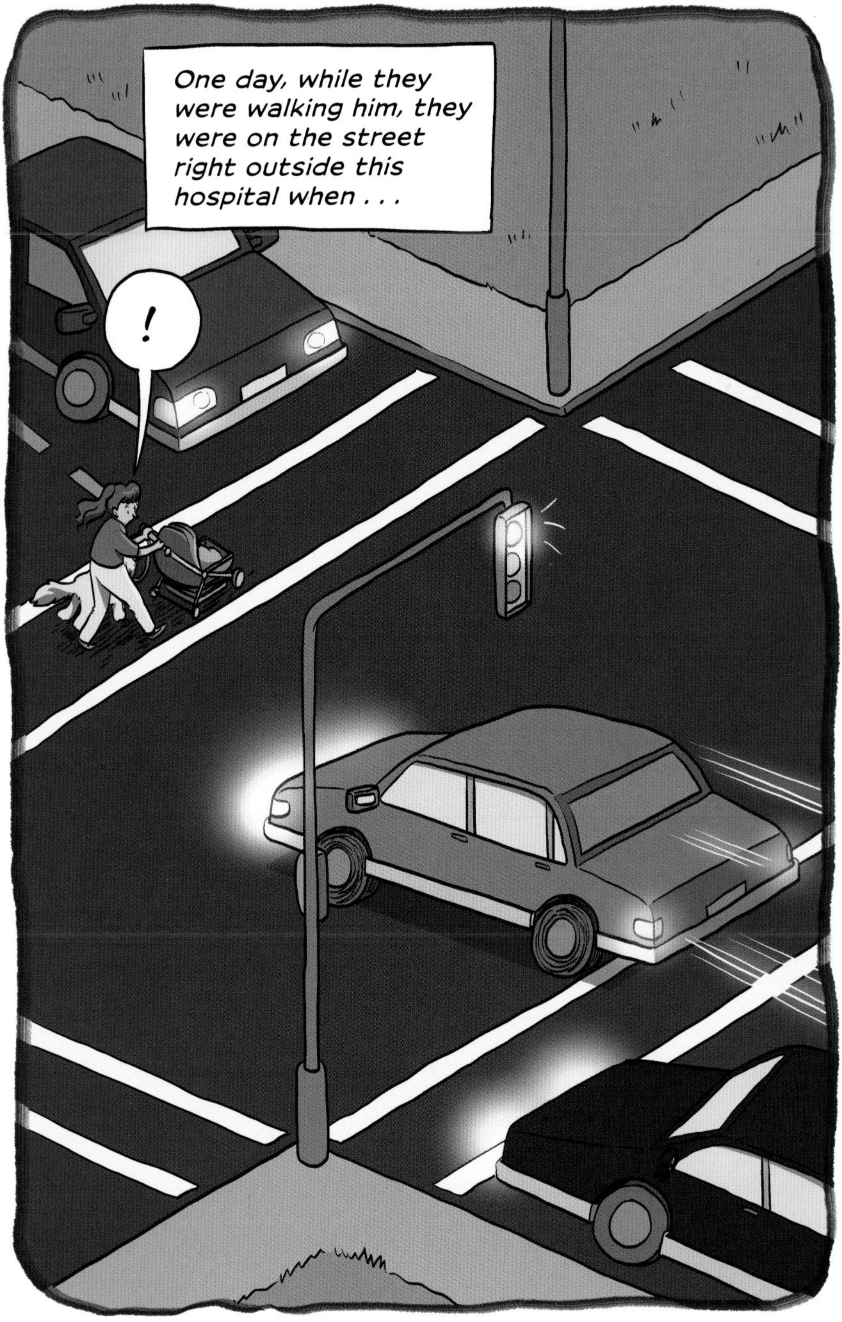
One day, while they were walking him, they were on the street right outside this hospital when . . .
!

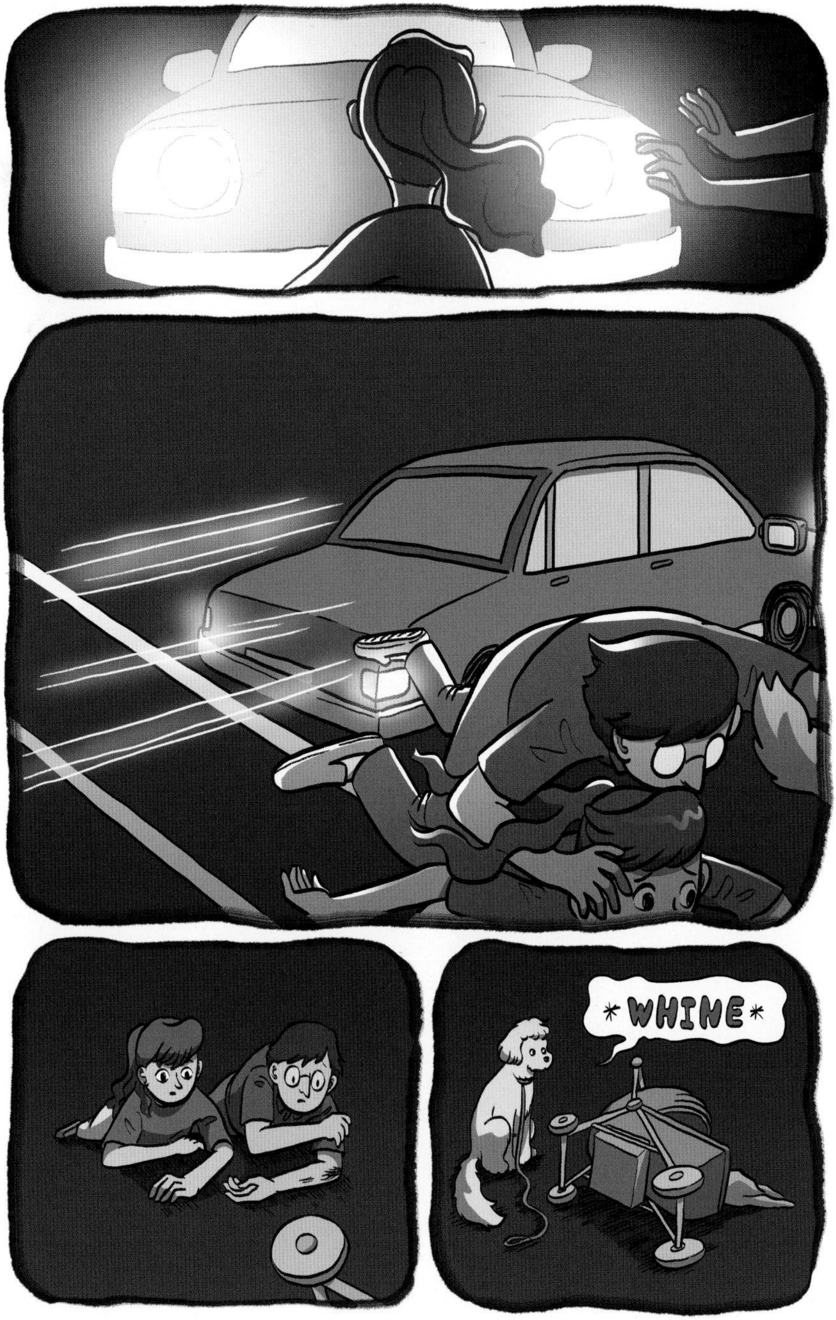
WHINE

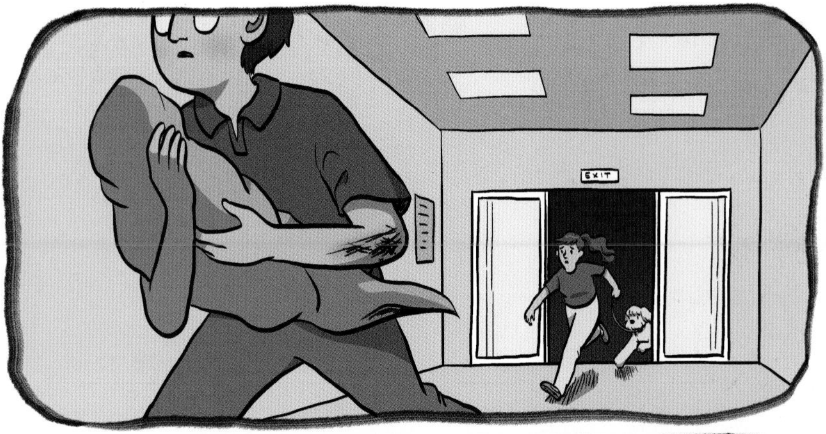

EXIT

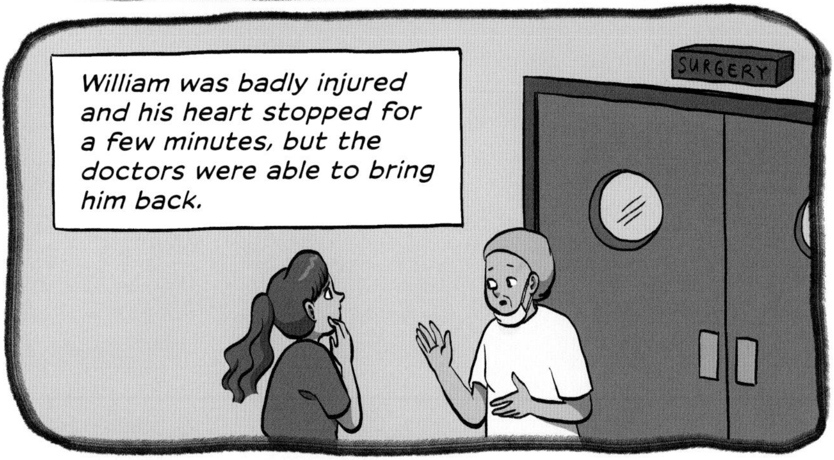

William was badly injured and his heart stopped for a few minutes, but the doctors were able to bring him back.
SURGERY

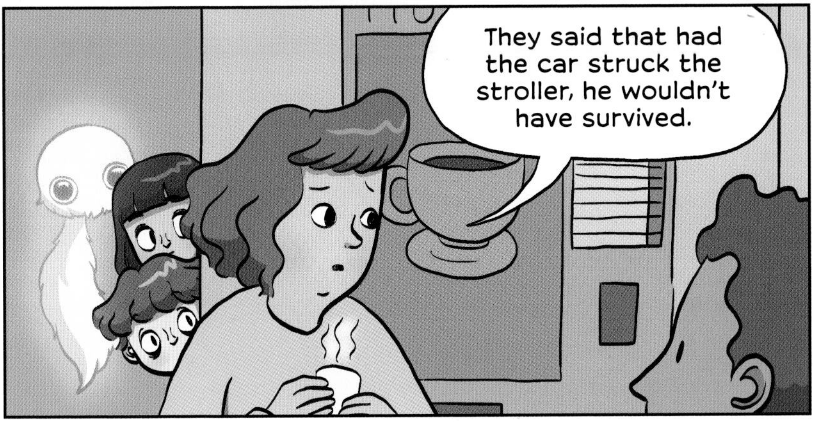

They said that had the car struck the stroller, he wouldn't have survived.

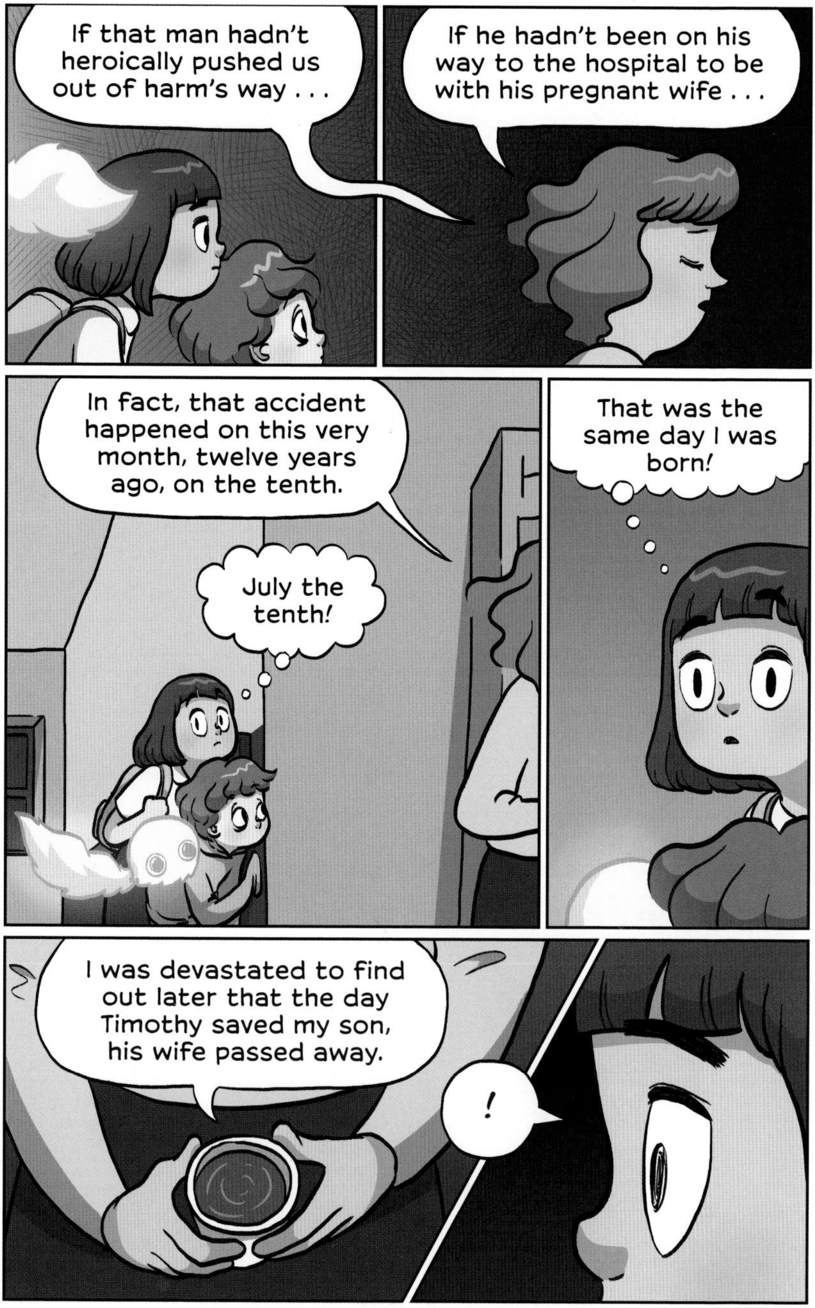
If that man hadn't heroically pushed us out of harm's way . . .
If he hadn't been on his way to the hospital to be with his pregnant wife . . .
In fact, that accident happened on this very month, twelve years ago, on the tenth.
July the tenth!
That was the same day I was born!
I was devastated to find out later that the day Timothy saved my son, his wife passed away.
!

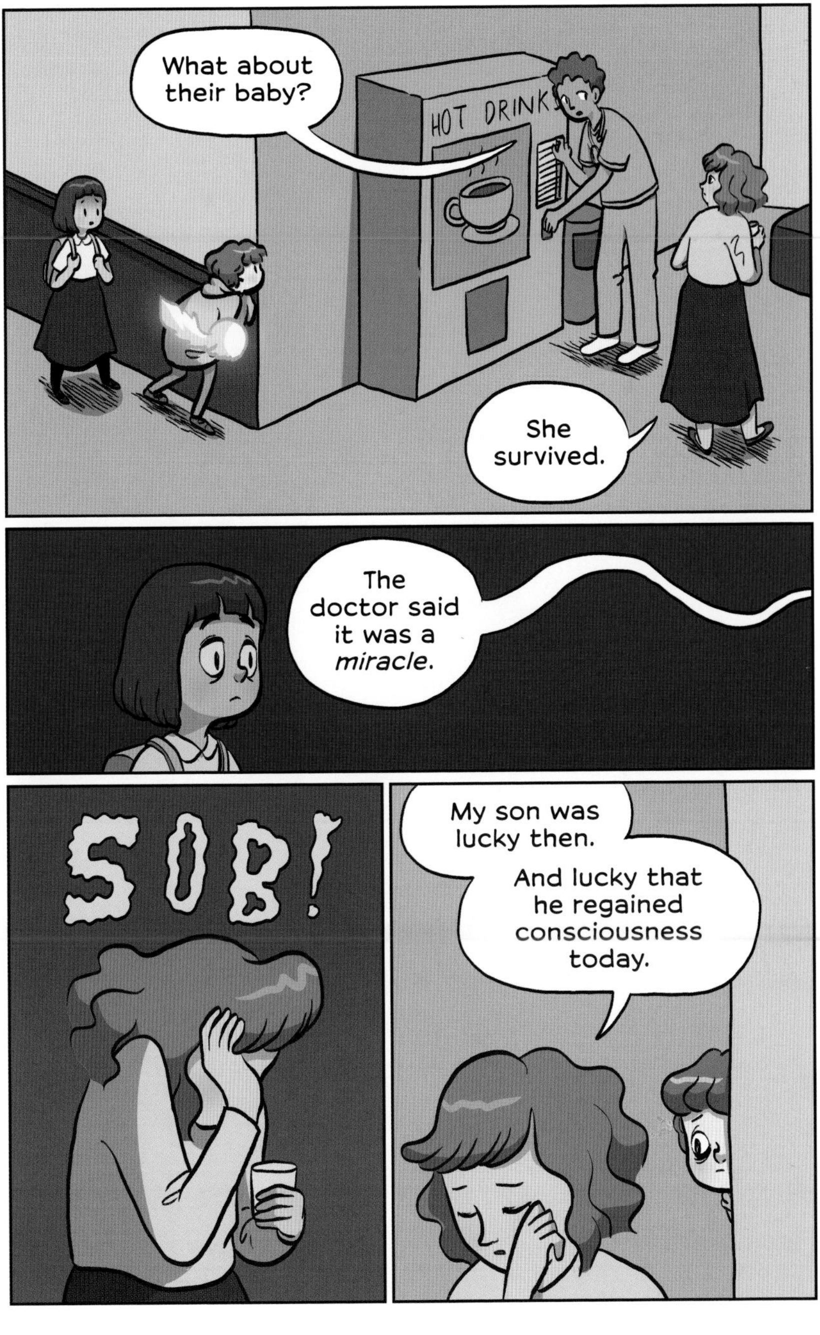
What about their baby?
HOT DRINKS
She survived.
The doctor said it was a *miracle*.
SOB!
My son was lucky then.
And lucky that he regained consciousness today.

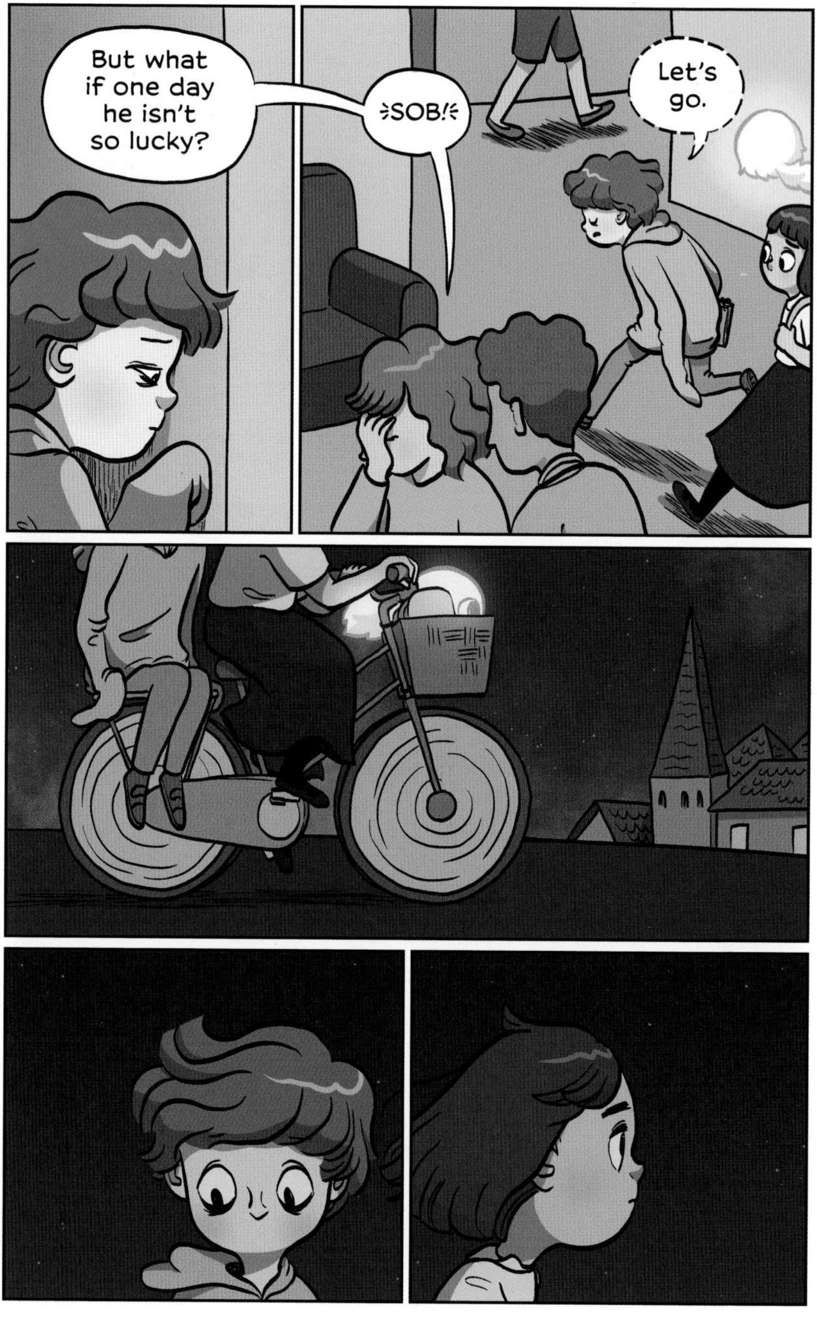
But what if one day he isn't so lucky?
SOB!
Let's go.

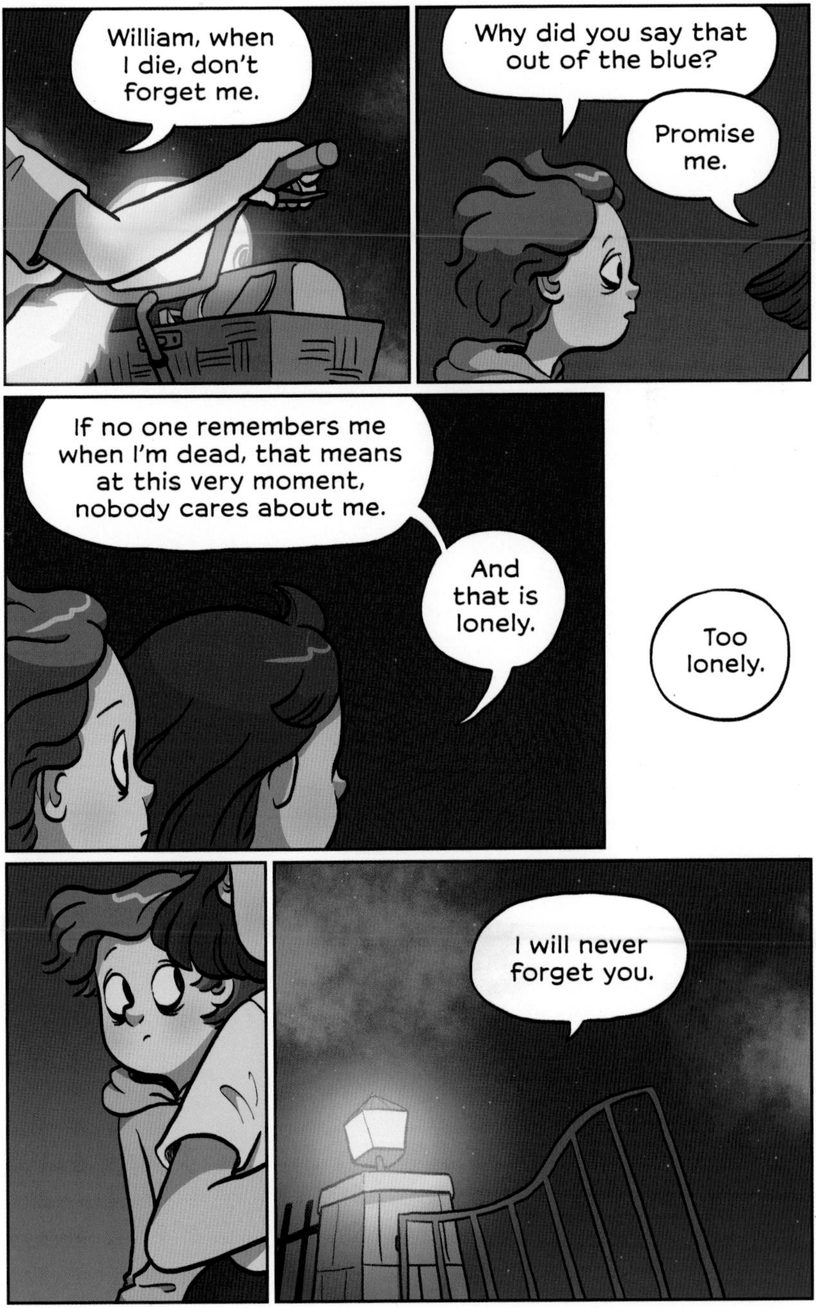
William, when I die, don't forget me.
Why did you say that out of the blue?
Promise me.
If no one remembers me when I'm dead, that means at this very moment, nobody cares about me.
And that is lonely.
Too lonely.
I will never forget you.

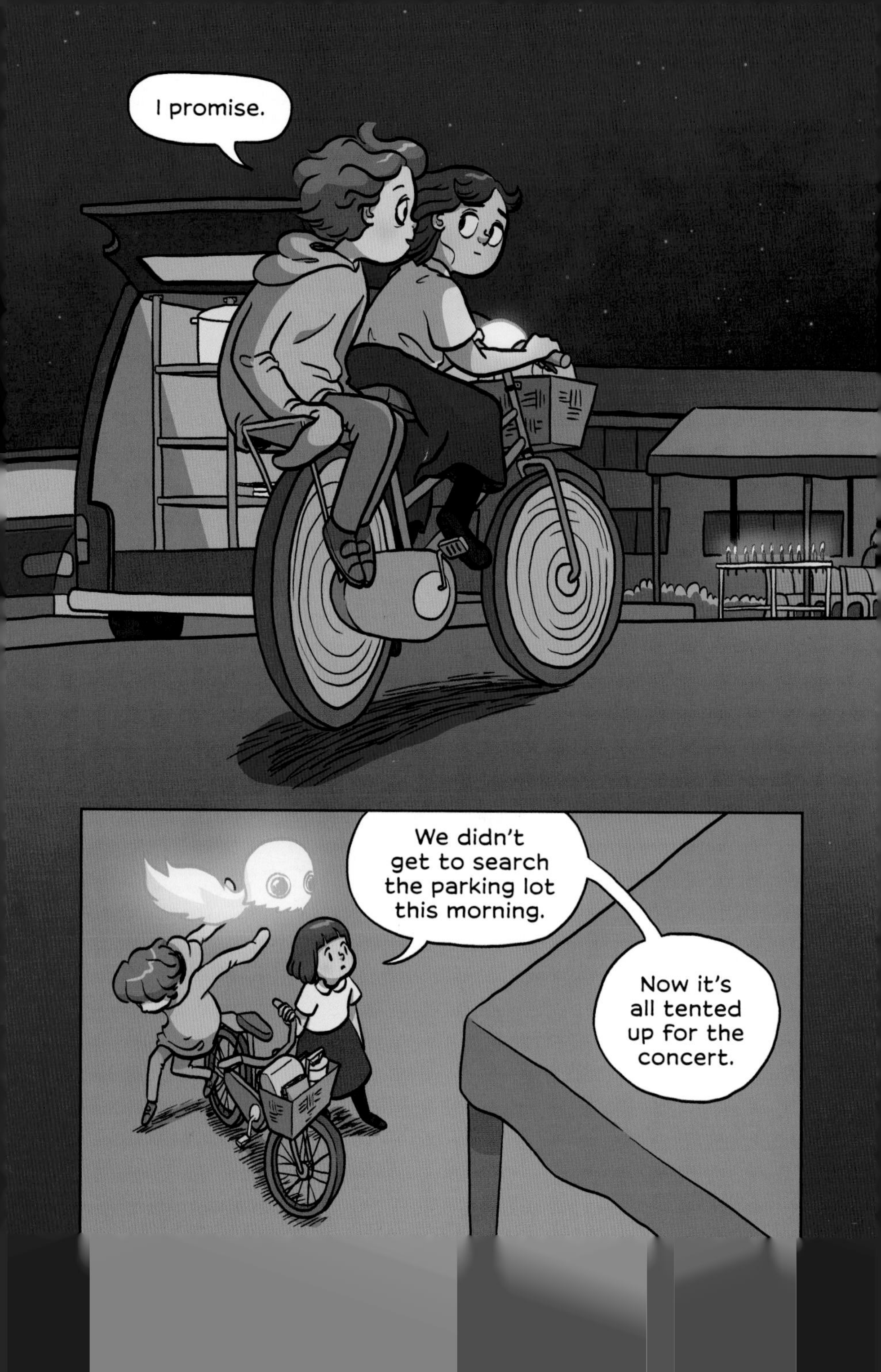
I promise.
We didn't get to search the parking lot this morning.
Now it's all tented up for the concert.

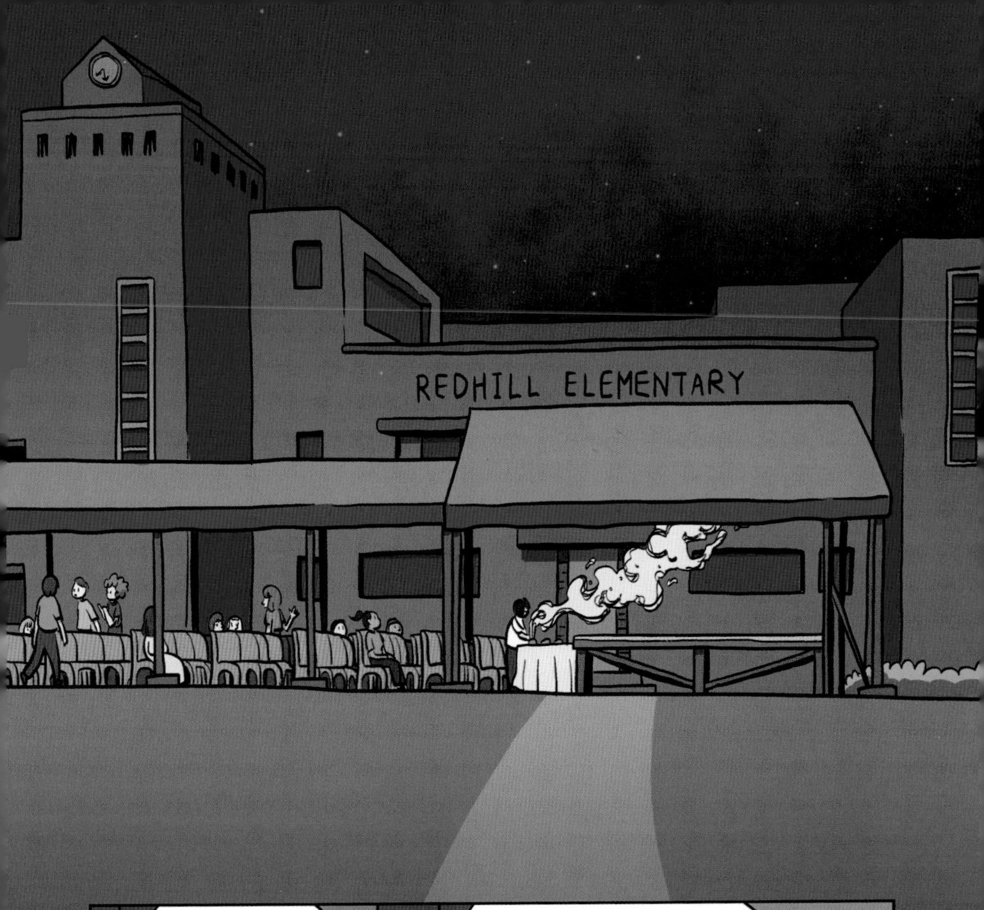
REDHILL ELEMENTARY

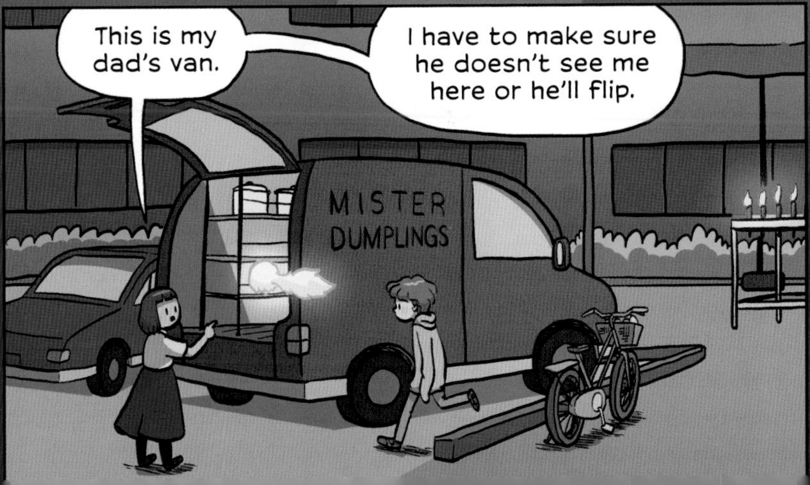
This is my dad's van.
I have to make sure he doesn't see me here or he'll flip.
MISTER DUMPLINGS

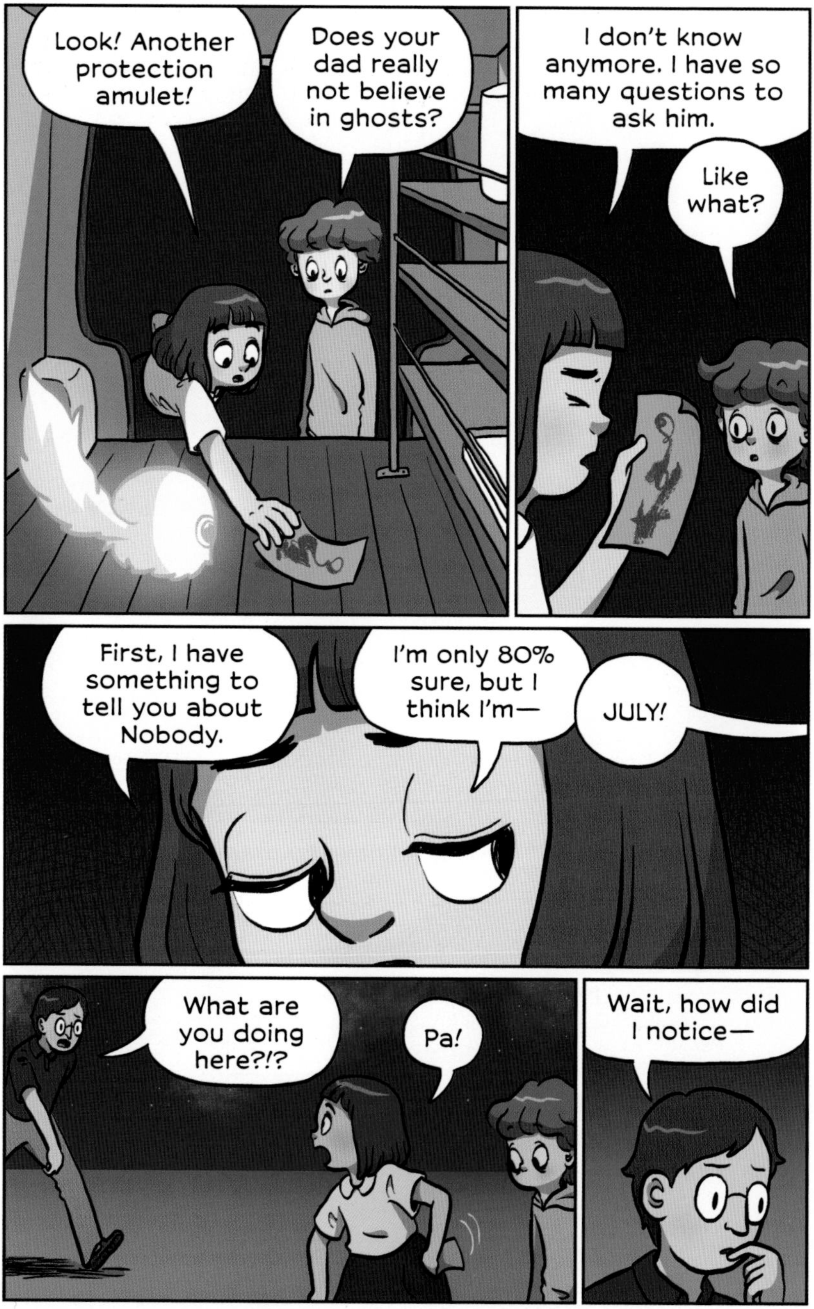
Look! Another protection amulet!
Does your dad really not believe in ghosts?
I don't know anymore. I have so many questions to ask him.
Like what?
First, I have something to tell you about Nobody.
I'm only 80% sure, but I think I'm—
JULY!
What are you doing here?!?
Pa!
Wait, how did I notice—

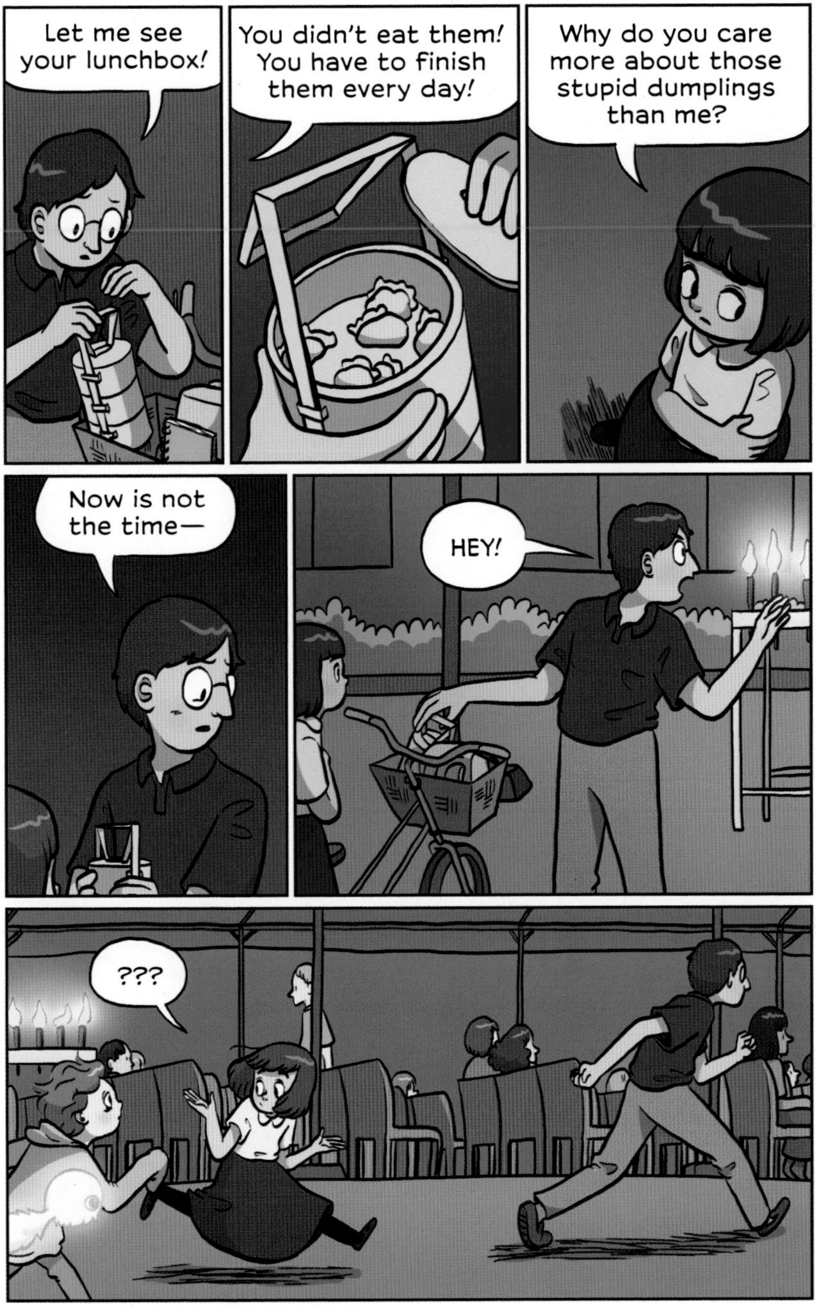
Let me see your lunchbox!
You didn't eat them! You have to finish them every day!
Why do you care more about those stupid dumplings than me?
Now is not the time—
HEY!
???

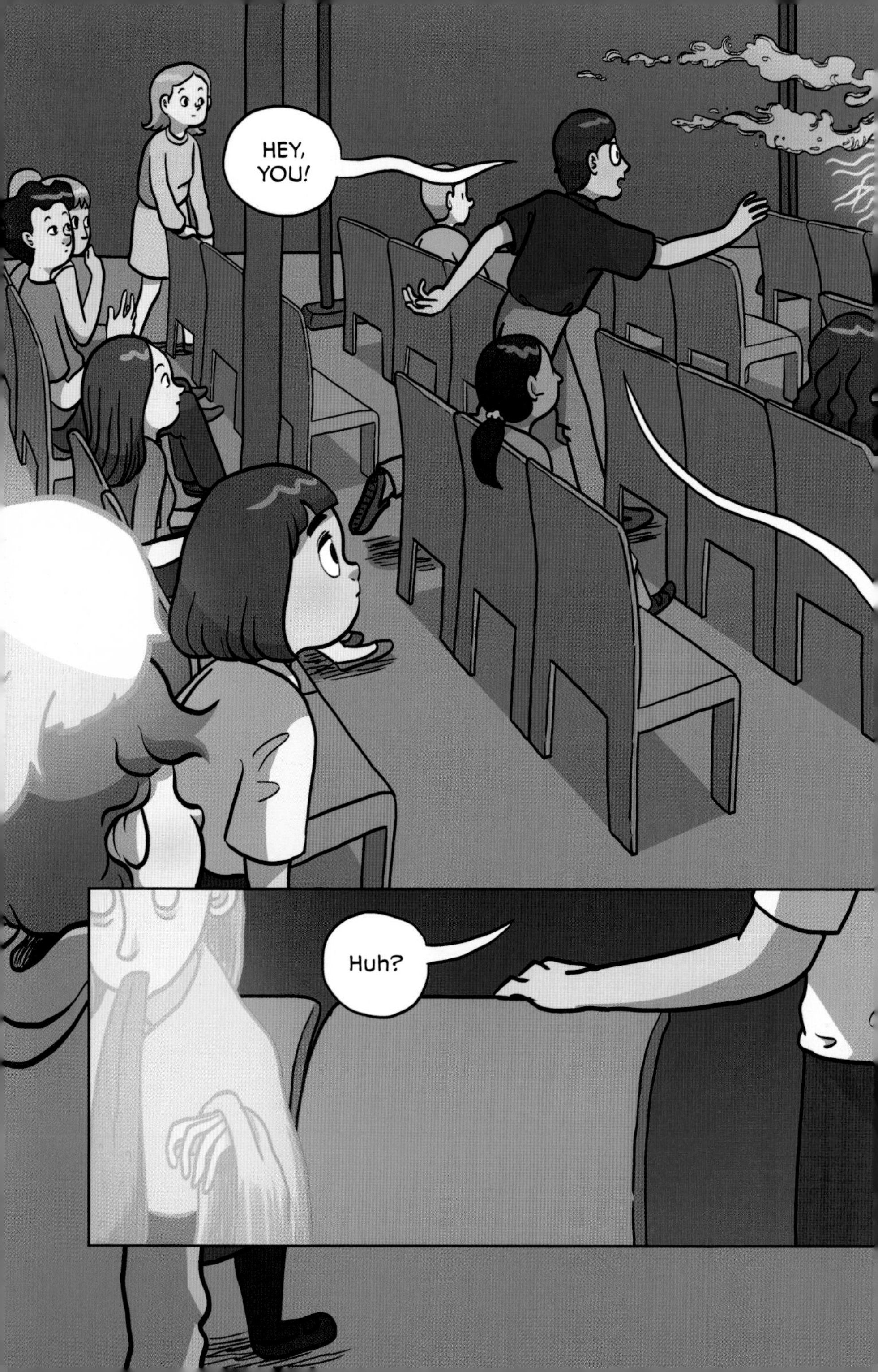
HEY, YOU!
Huh?

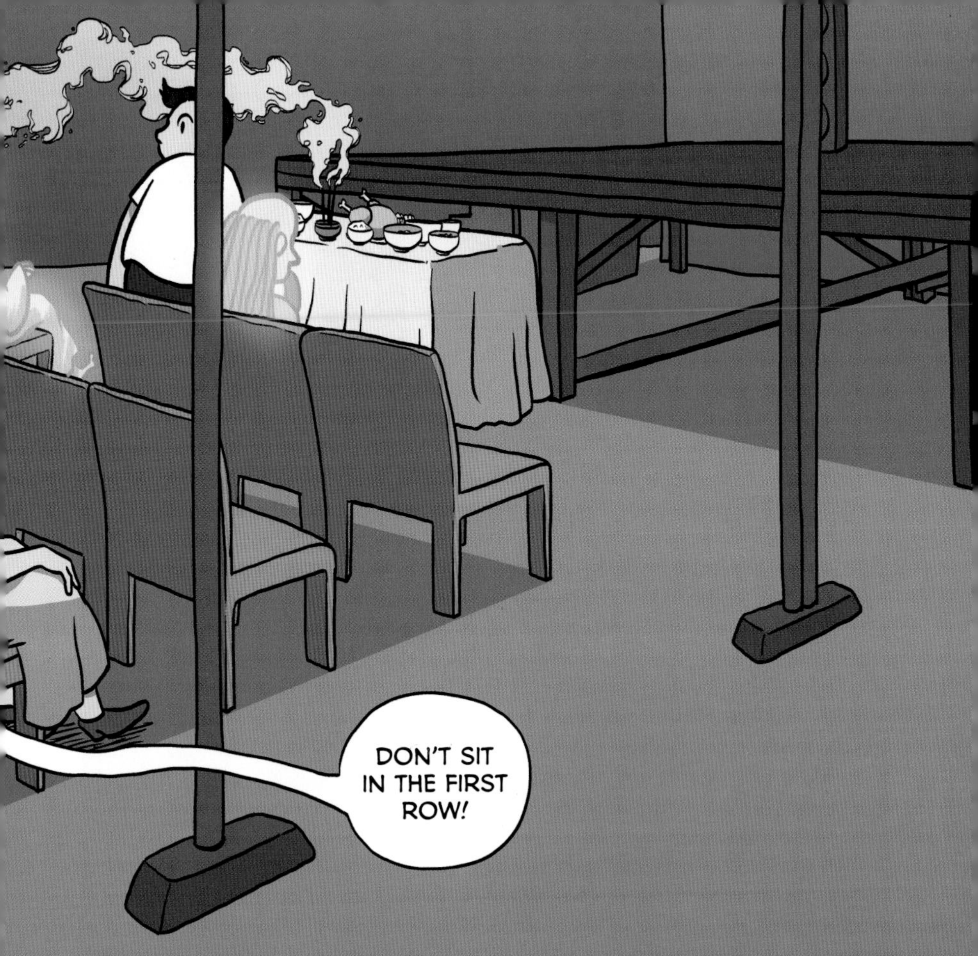
DON'T SIT IN THE FIRST ROW!

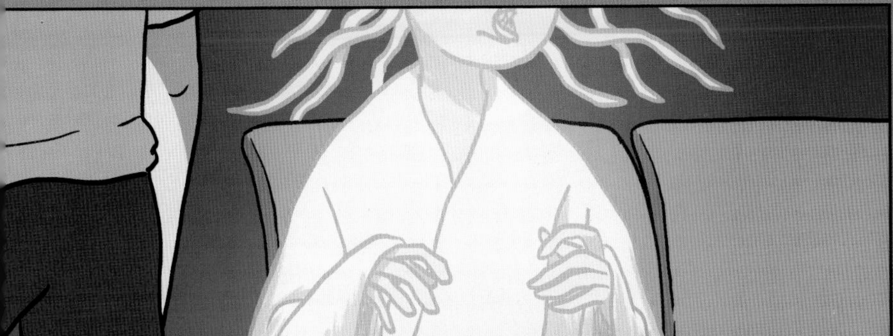

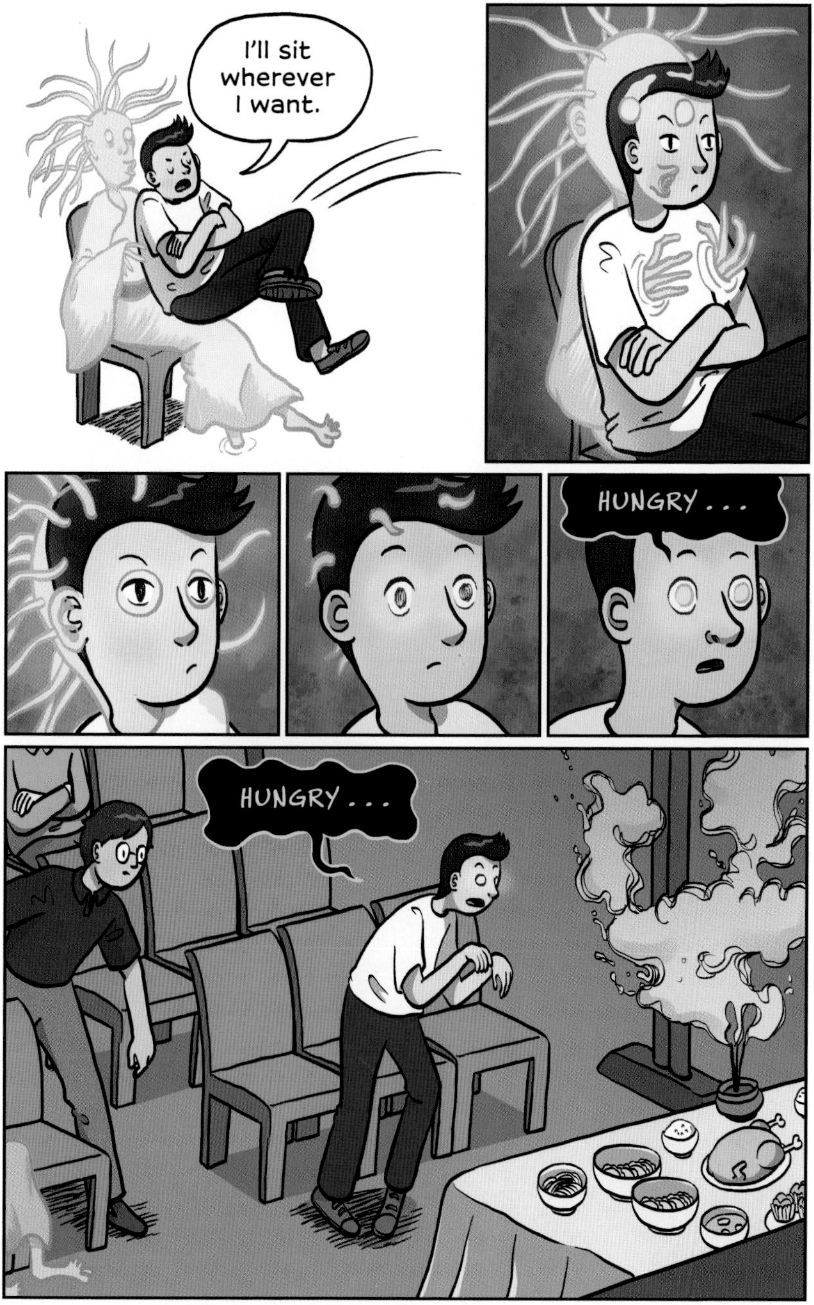
I'll sit wherever I want.
HUNGRY . . .
HUNGRY . . .

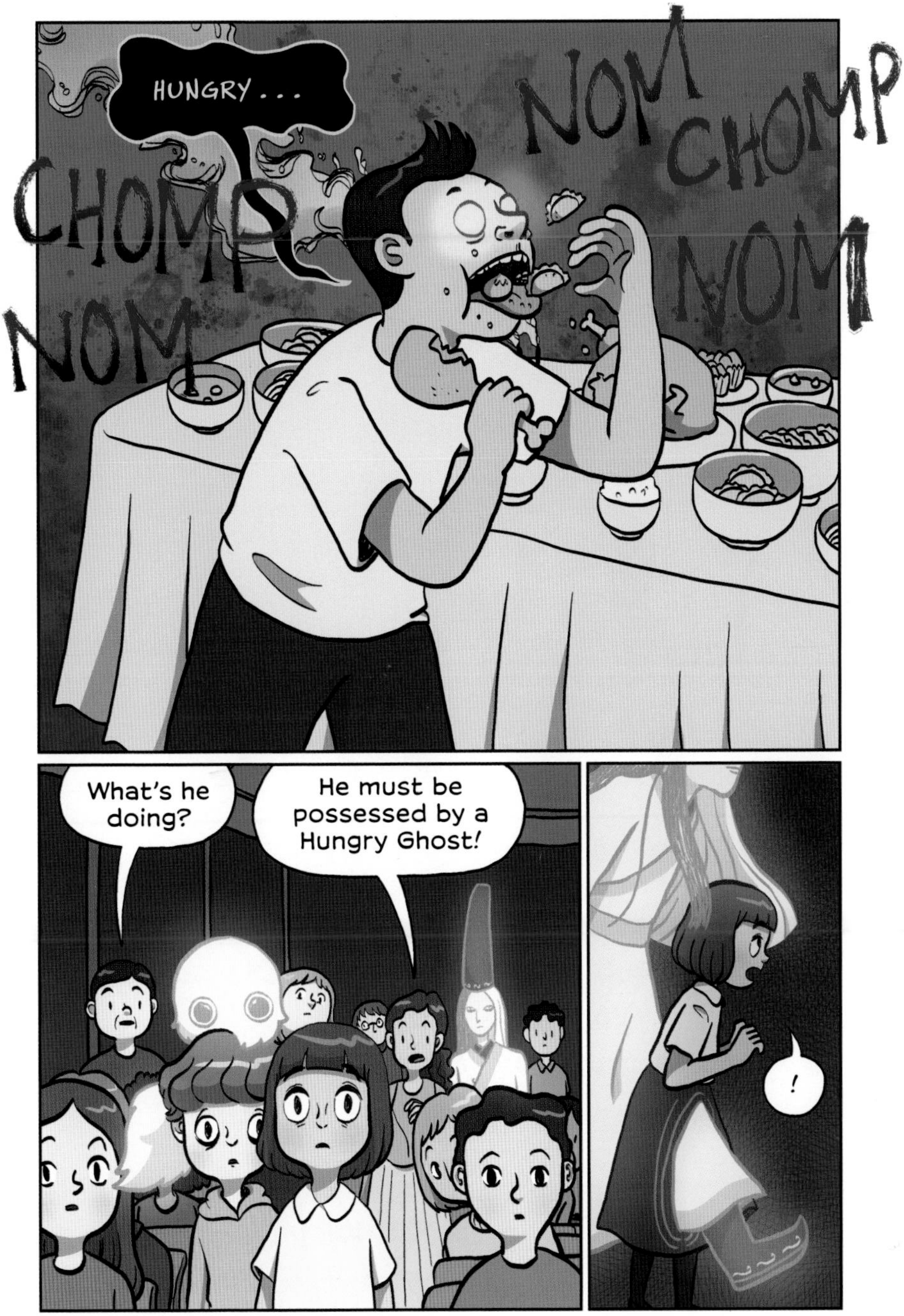
HUNGRY . . .
CHOMP
NOM
NOM
CHOMP
NOM
What's he doing?
He must be possessed by a Hungry Ghost!
!

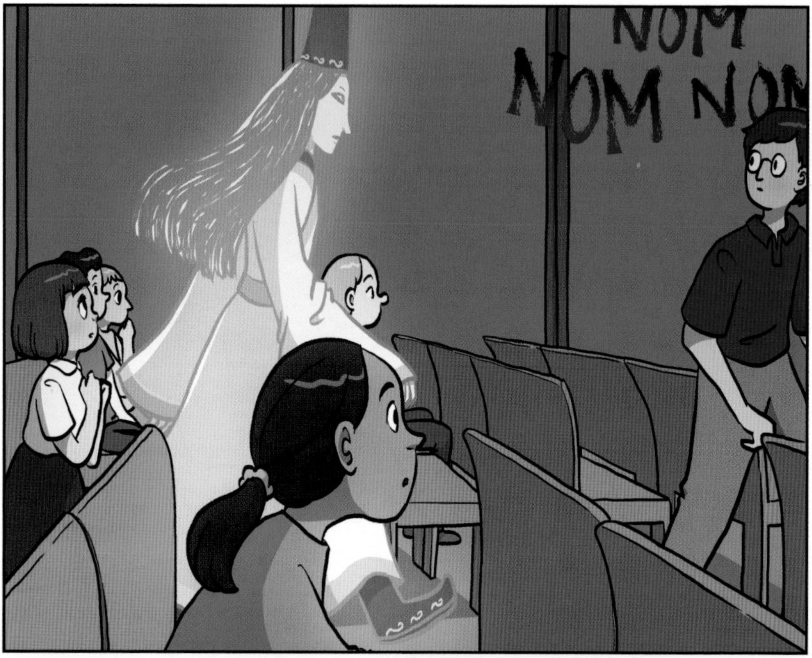
NOM
NOM NOM

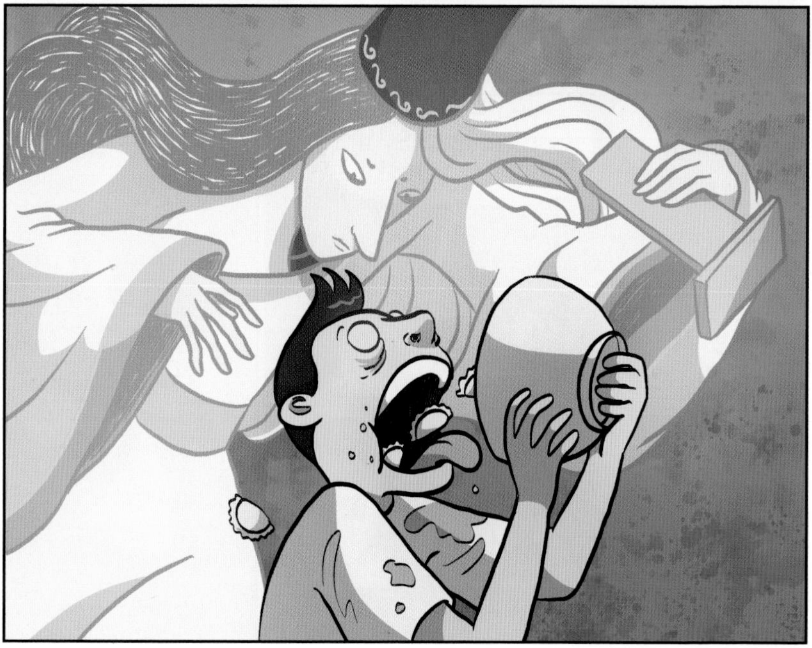

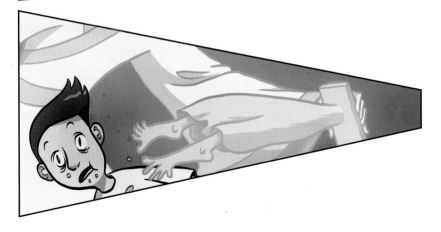

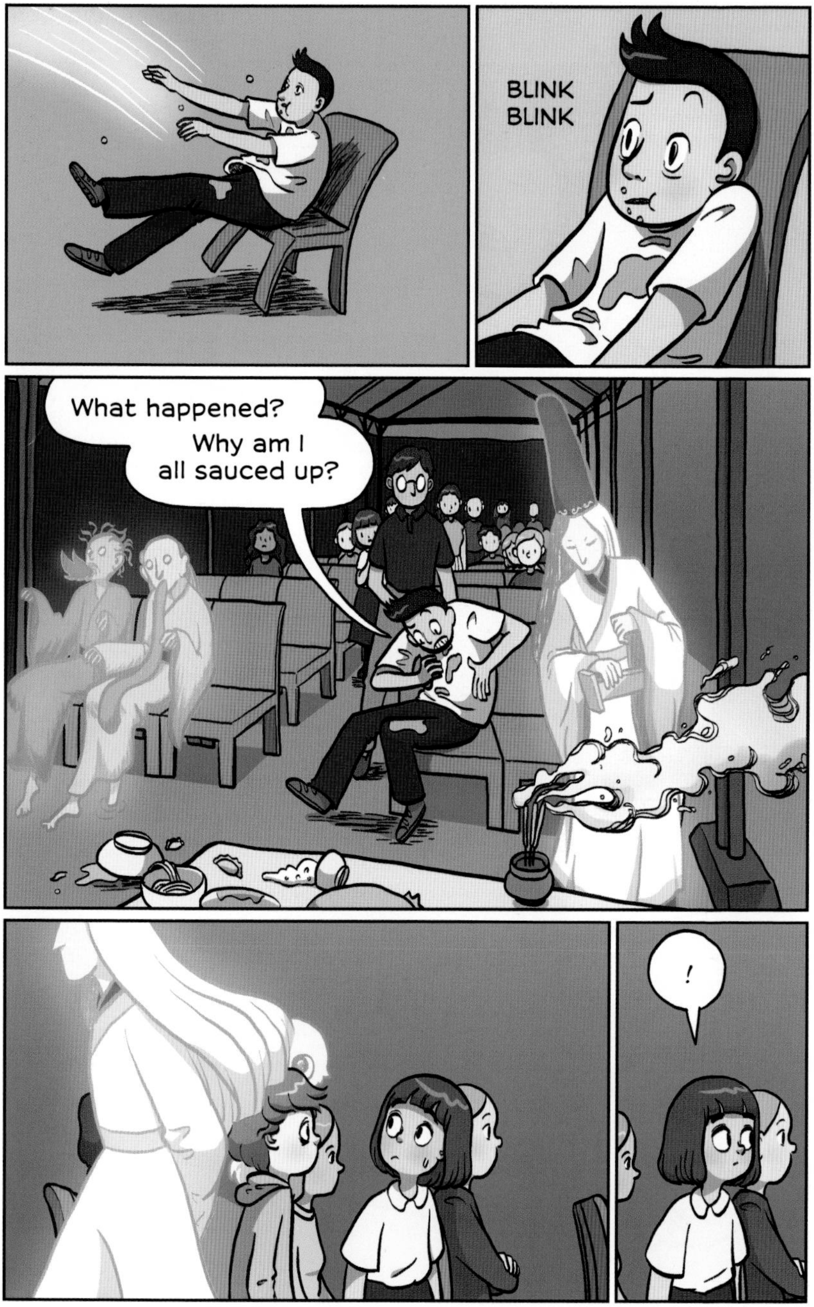
BLINK
BLINK
What happened?
Why am I all sauced up?
!

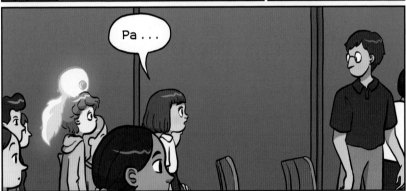

Pa . . .

. . . you can see Heibai Wuchang. You can see ghosts.

G-ghosts don't exist.

Why was THIS in your van?!?

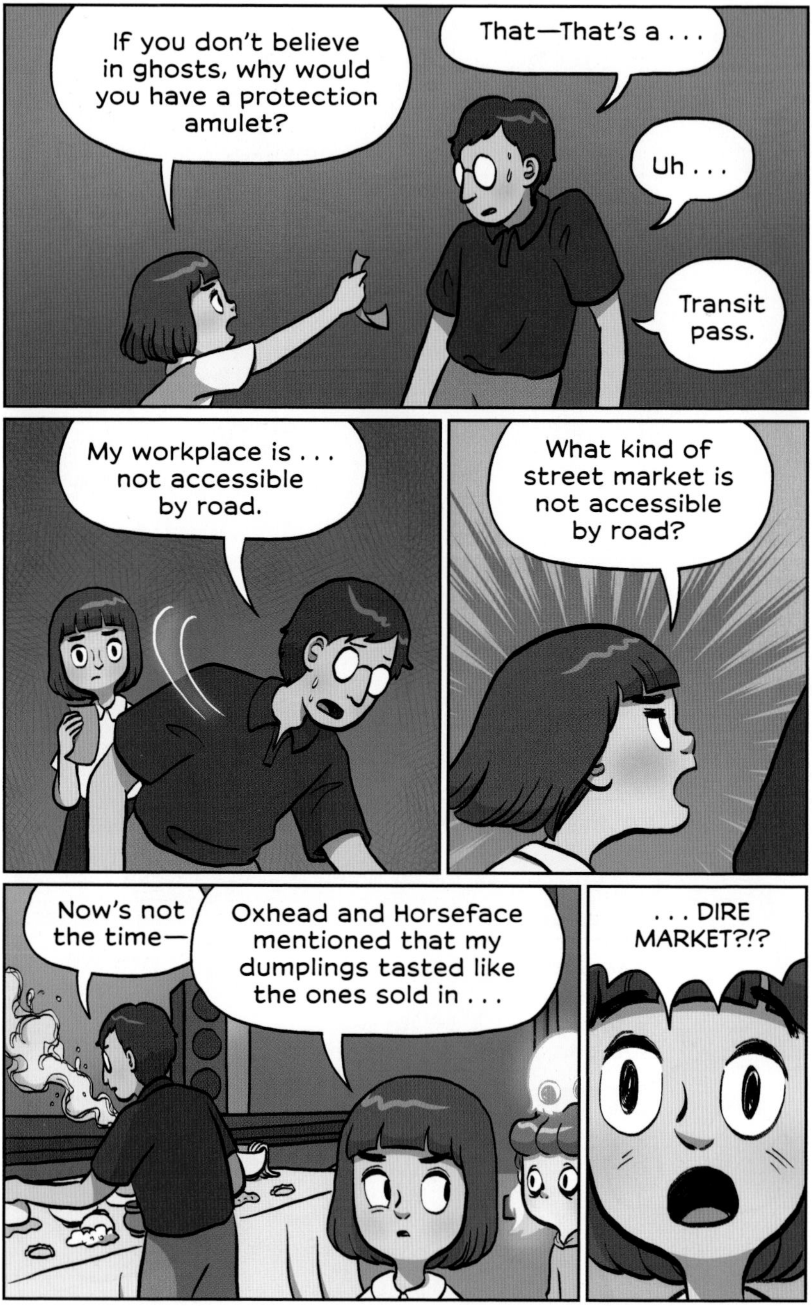
If you don't believe in ghosts, why would you have a protection amulet?
That—That's a . . .
Uh . . .
Transit pass.
My workplace is . . . not accessible by road.
What kind of street market is not accessible by road?
Now's not the time—
Oxhead and Horseface mentioned that my dumplings tasted like the ones sold in . . .
. . . DIRE MARKET?!?

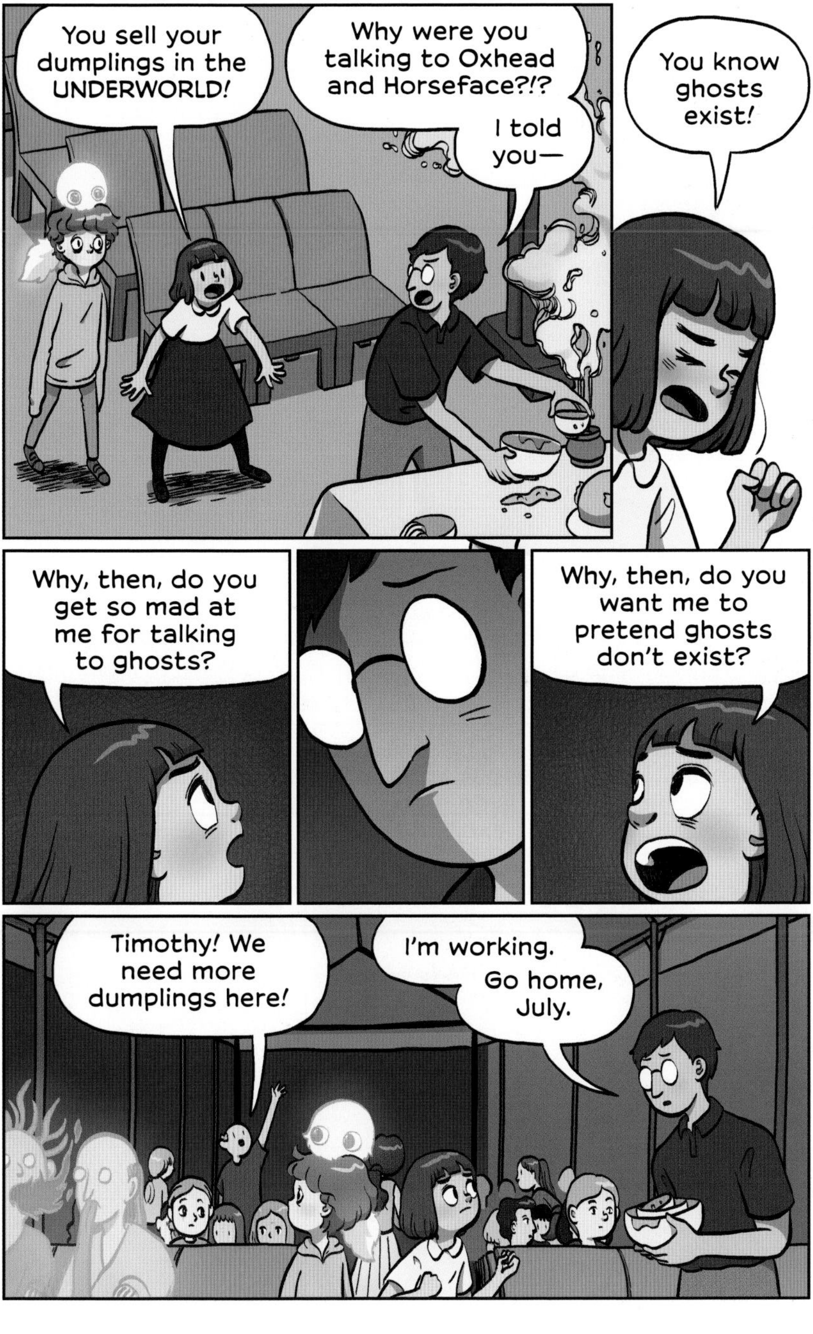
You sell your dumplings in the UNDERWORLD!
Why were you talking to Oxhead and Horseface?!?
I told you—
You know ghosts exist!
Why, then, do you get so mad at me for talking to ghosts?
Why, then, do you want me to pretend ghosts don't exist?
Timothy! We need more dumplings here!
I'm working.
Go home, July.

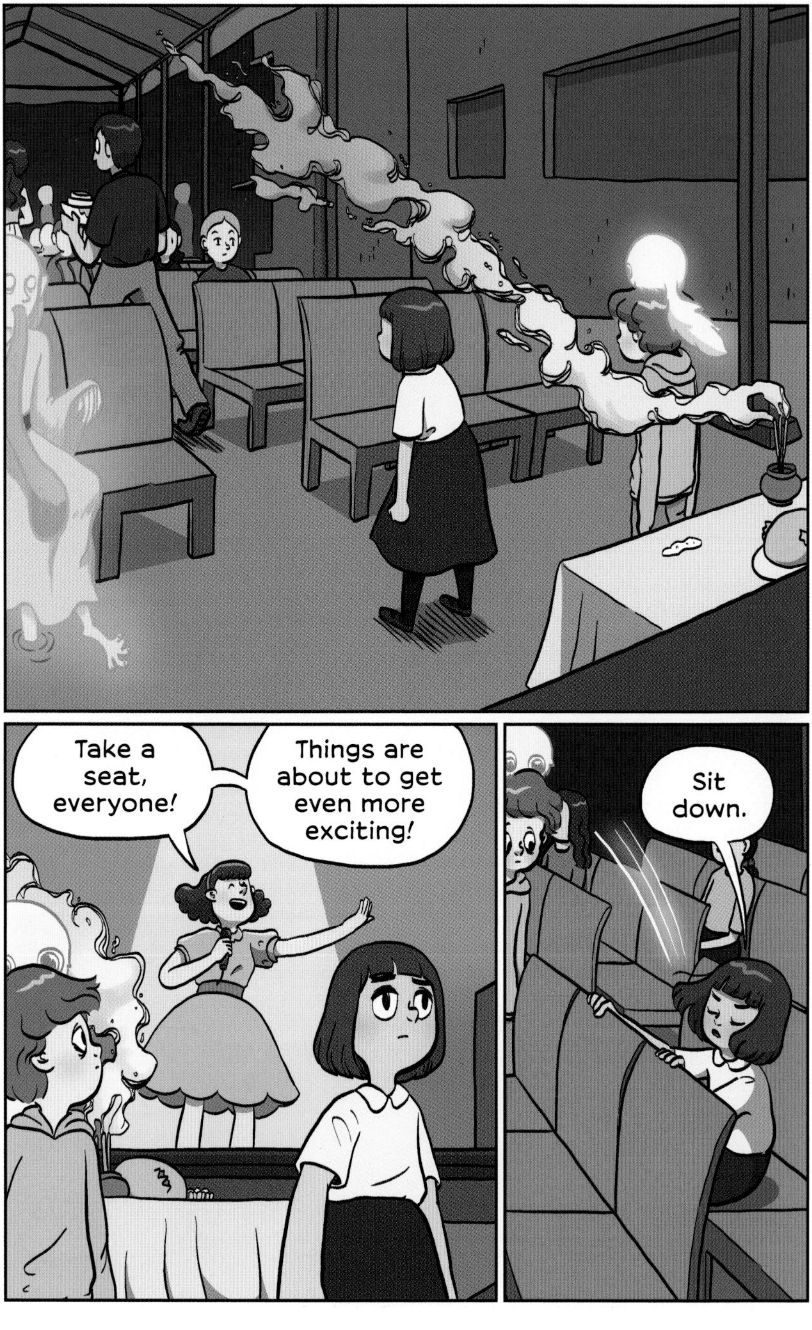
Take a seat, everyone!
Things are about to get even more exciting!
Sit down.

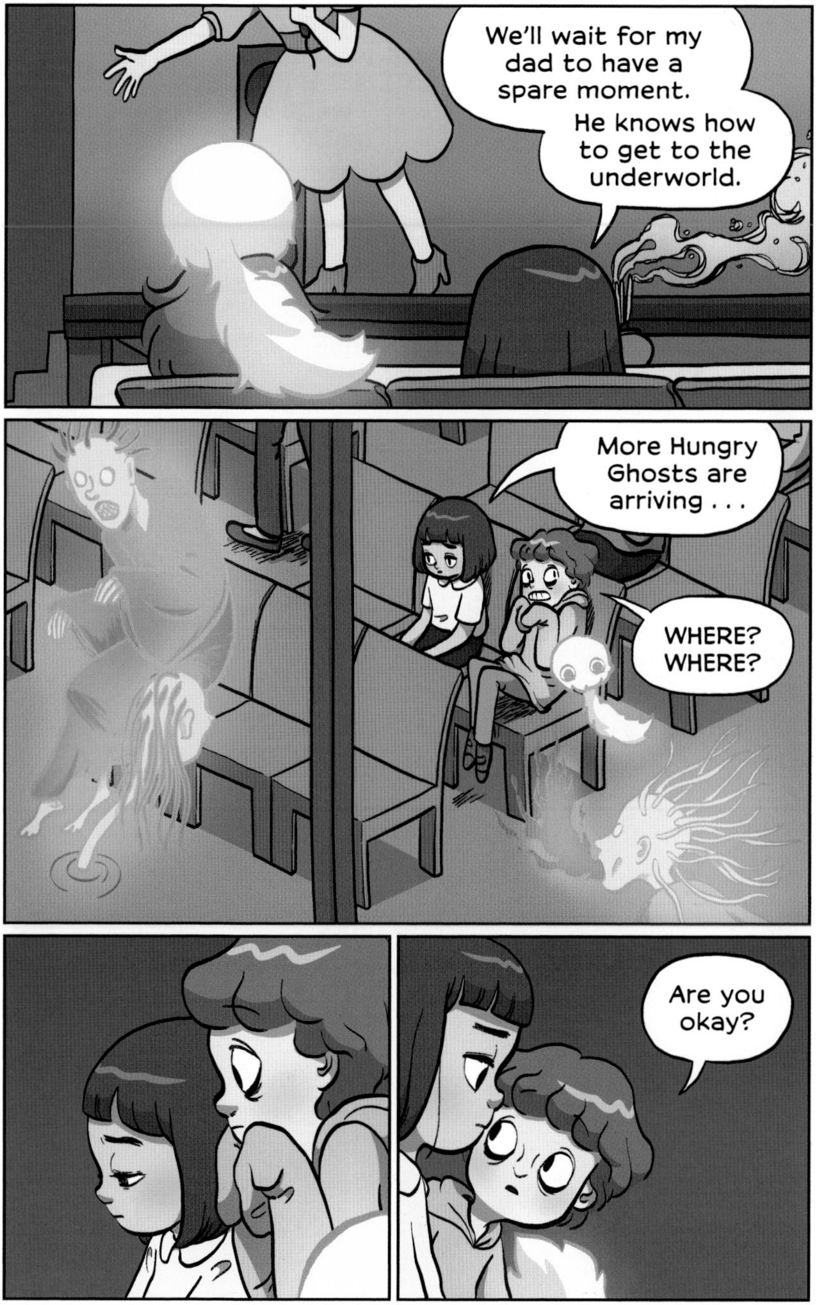
We'll wait for my dad to have a spare moment.
He knows how to get to the underworld.
More Hungry Ghosts are arriving . . .
WHERE? WHERE?
Are you okay?

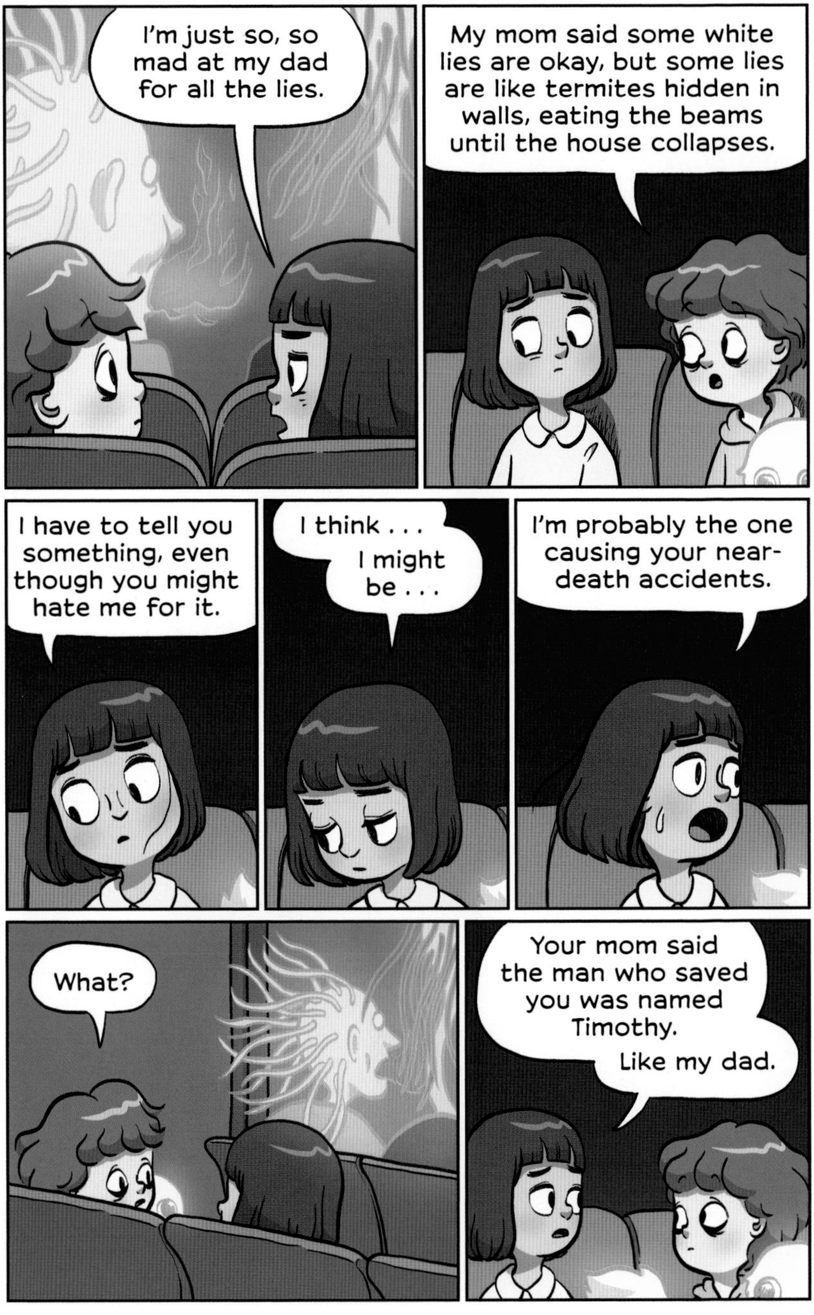
I'm just so, so mad at my dad for all the lies.
My mom said some white lies are okay, but some lies are like termites hidden in walls, eating the beams until the house collapses.
I have to tell you something, even though you might hate me for it.
I think . . .
I might be . . .
I'm probably the one causing your near-death accidents.
What?
Your mom said the man who saved you was named Timothy.
Like my dad.

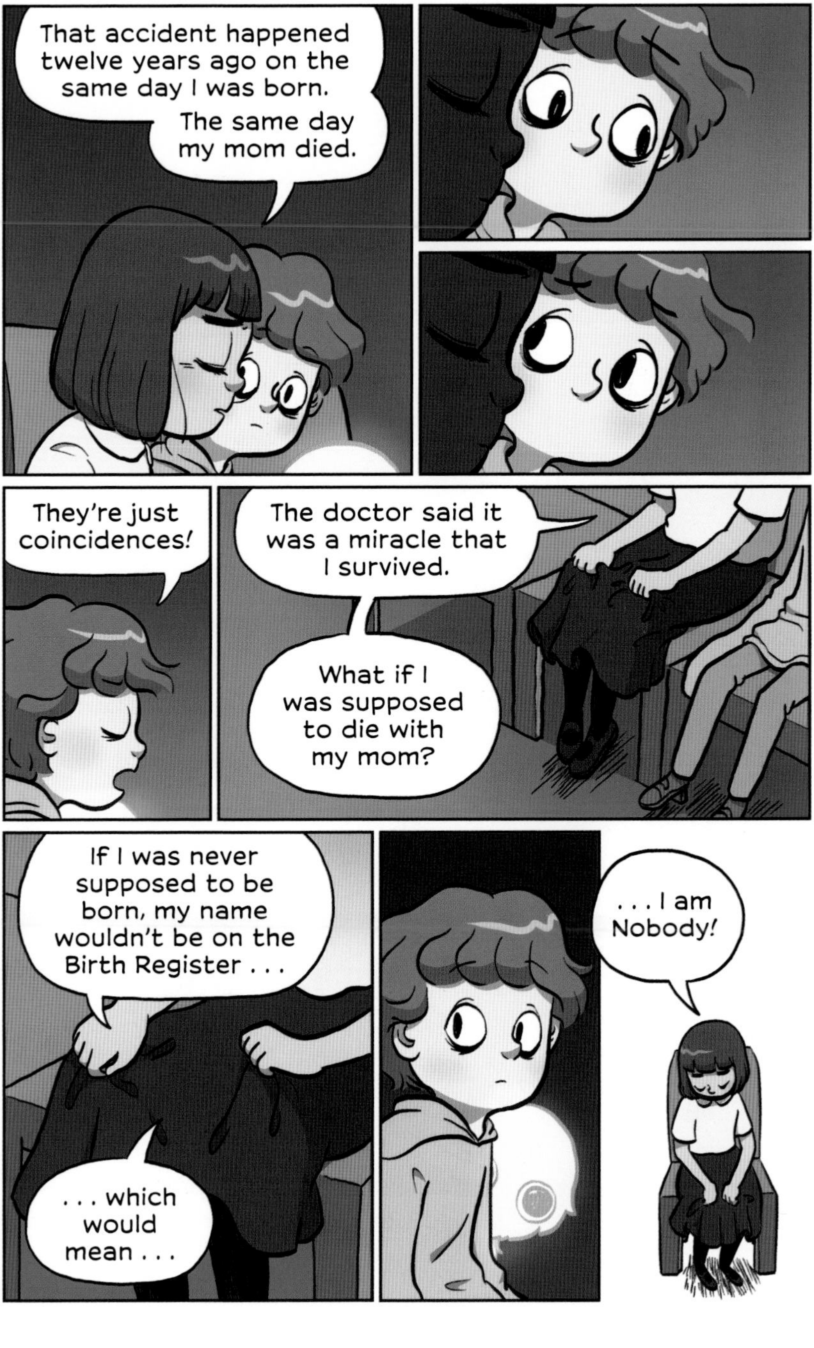
That accident happened twelve years ago on the same day I was born.
The same day my mom died.
They're just coincidences!
The doctor said it was a miracle that I survived.
What if I was supposed to die with my mom?
If I was never supposed to be born, my name wouldn't be on the Birth Register . . .
. . . which would mean . . .
. . . I am Nobody!

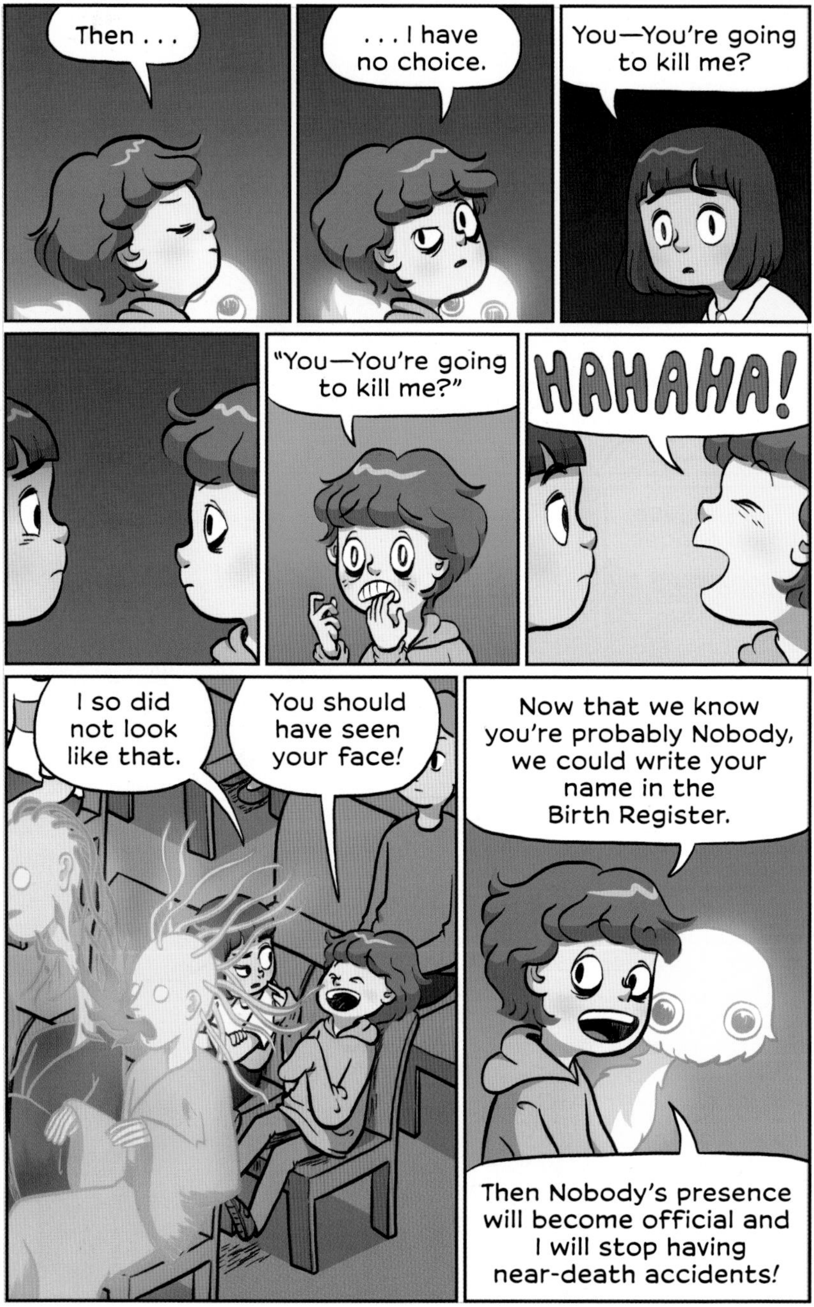
Then . . .
. . . I have no choice.
You—You're going to kill me?
"You—You're going to kill me?"
HAHAHA!
I so did not look like that.
You should have seen your face!
Now that we know you're probably Nobody, we could write your name in the Birth Register.
Then Nobody's presence will become official and I will stop having near-death accidents!

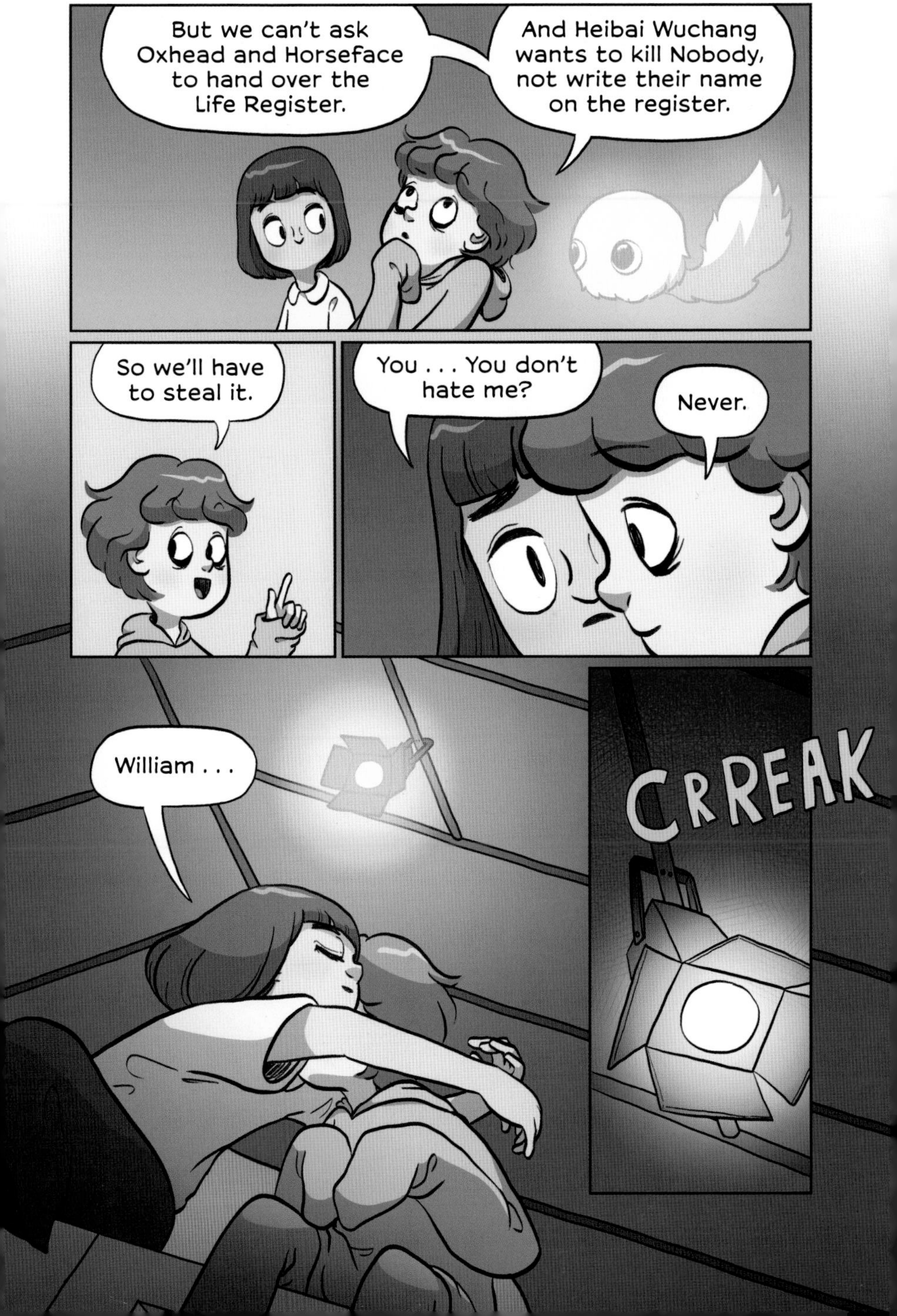
But we can't ask Oxhead and Horseface to hand over the Life Register.
And Heibai Wuchang wants to kill Nobody, not write their name on the register.
So we'll have to steal it.
You . . . You don't hate me?
Never.
William . . .
CRREAK

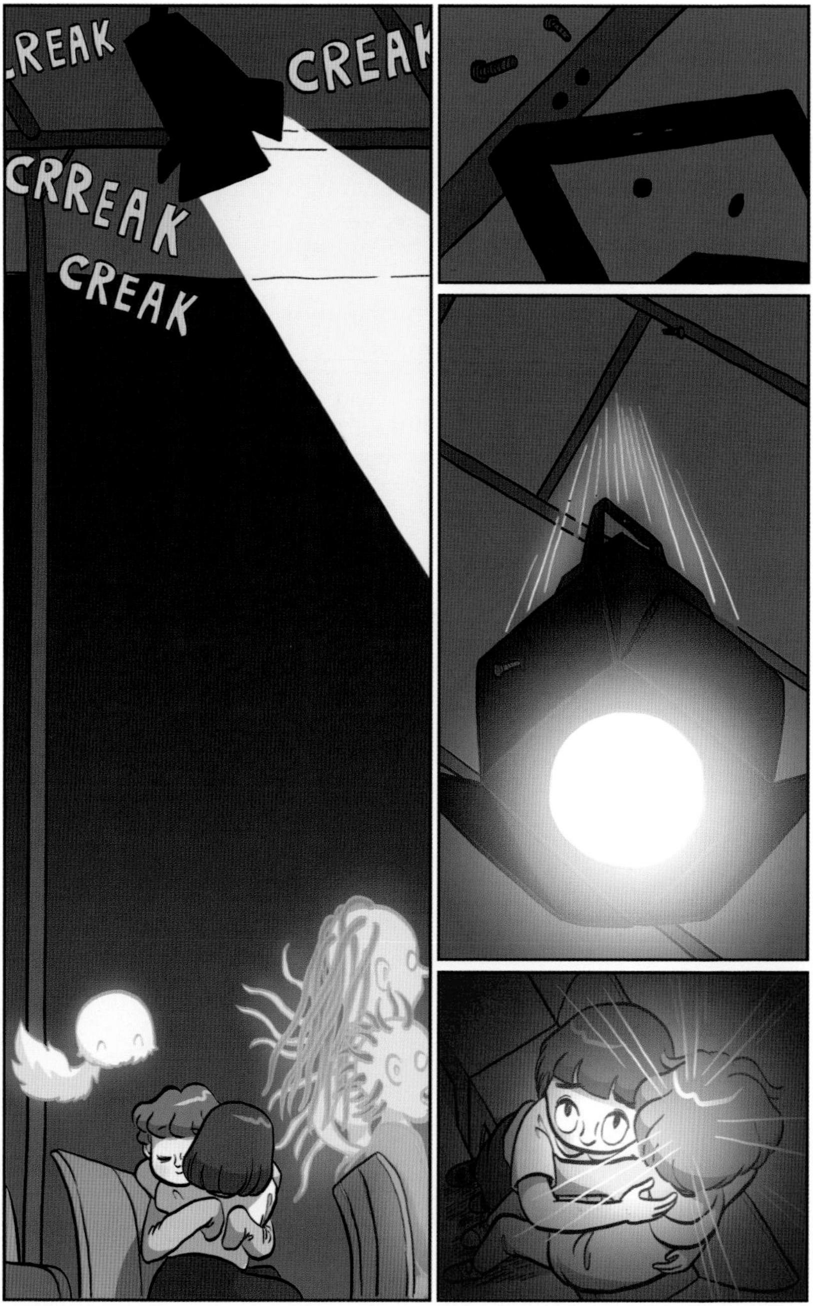

REAK
CREAK
CRREAK
CREAK

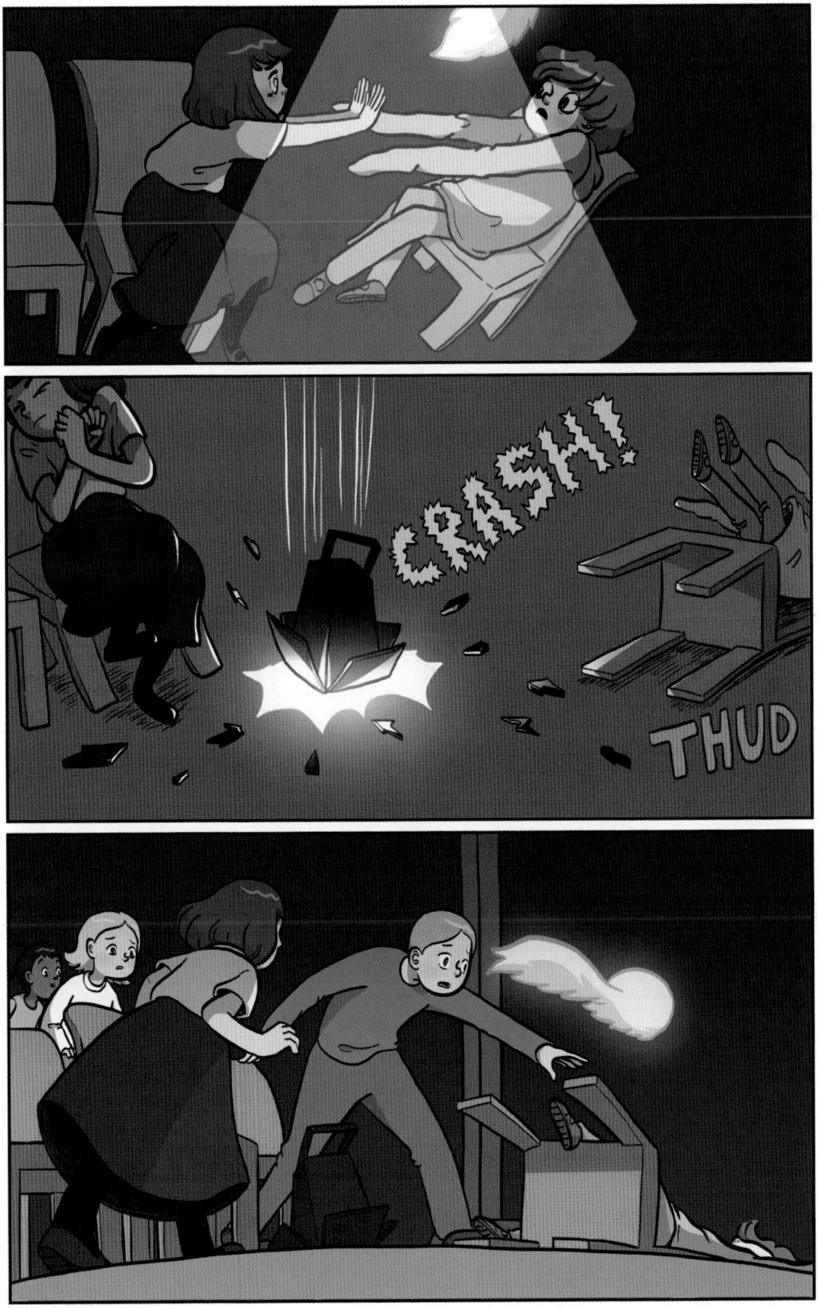
CRASH!
THUD

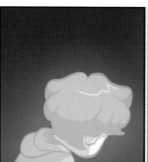

He's breathing!

Hold on, kid! The ambulance is on its way!

I'm still alive!

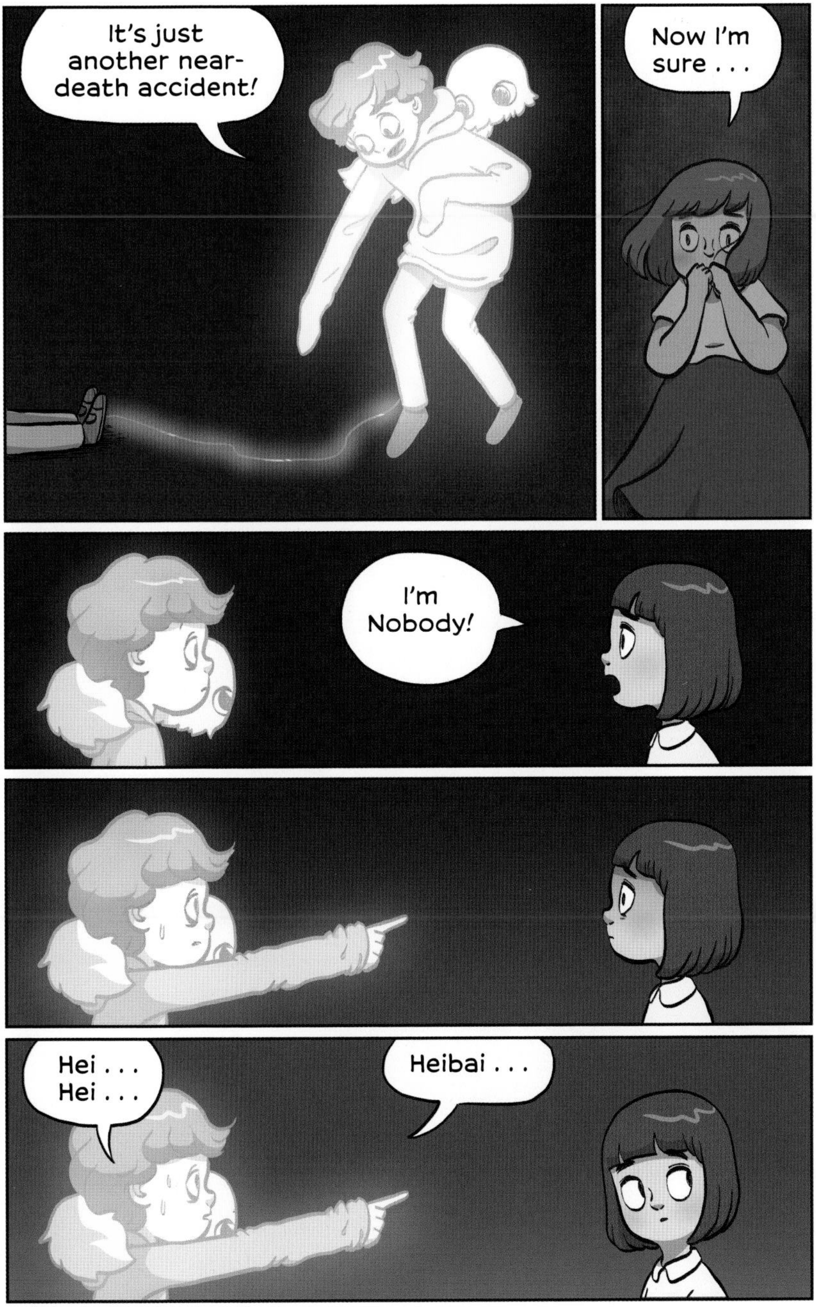
It's just another near-death accident!
Now I'm sure . . .
I'm Nobody!
Hei . . .
Hei . . .
Heibai . . .

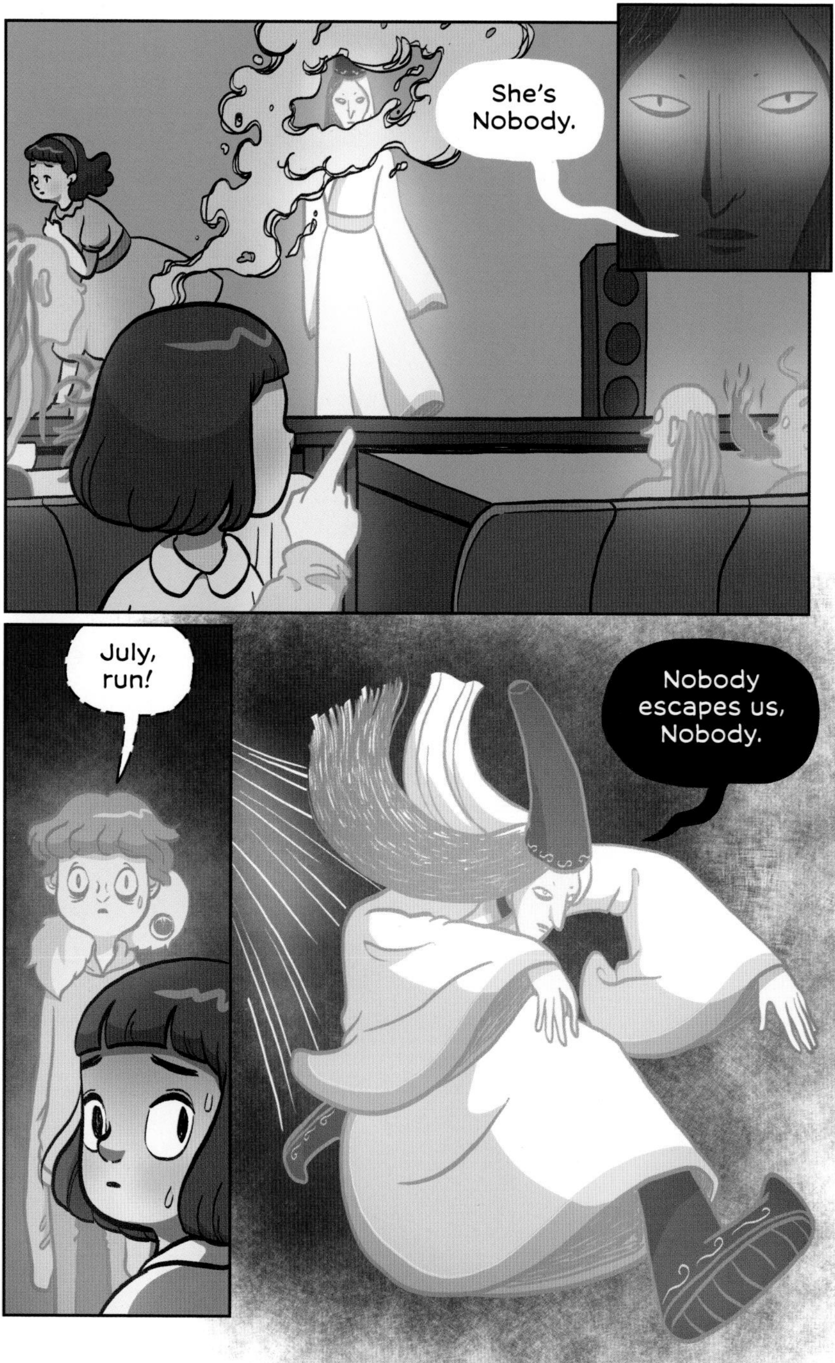
She's Nobody.
July, run!
Nobody escapes us, Nobody.

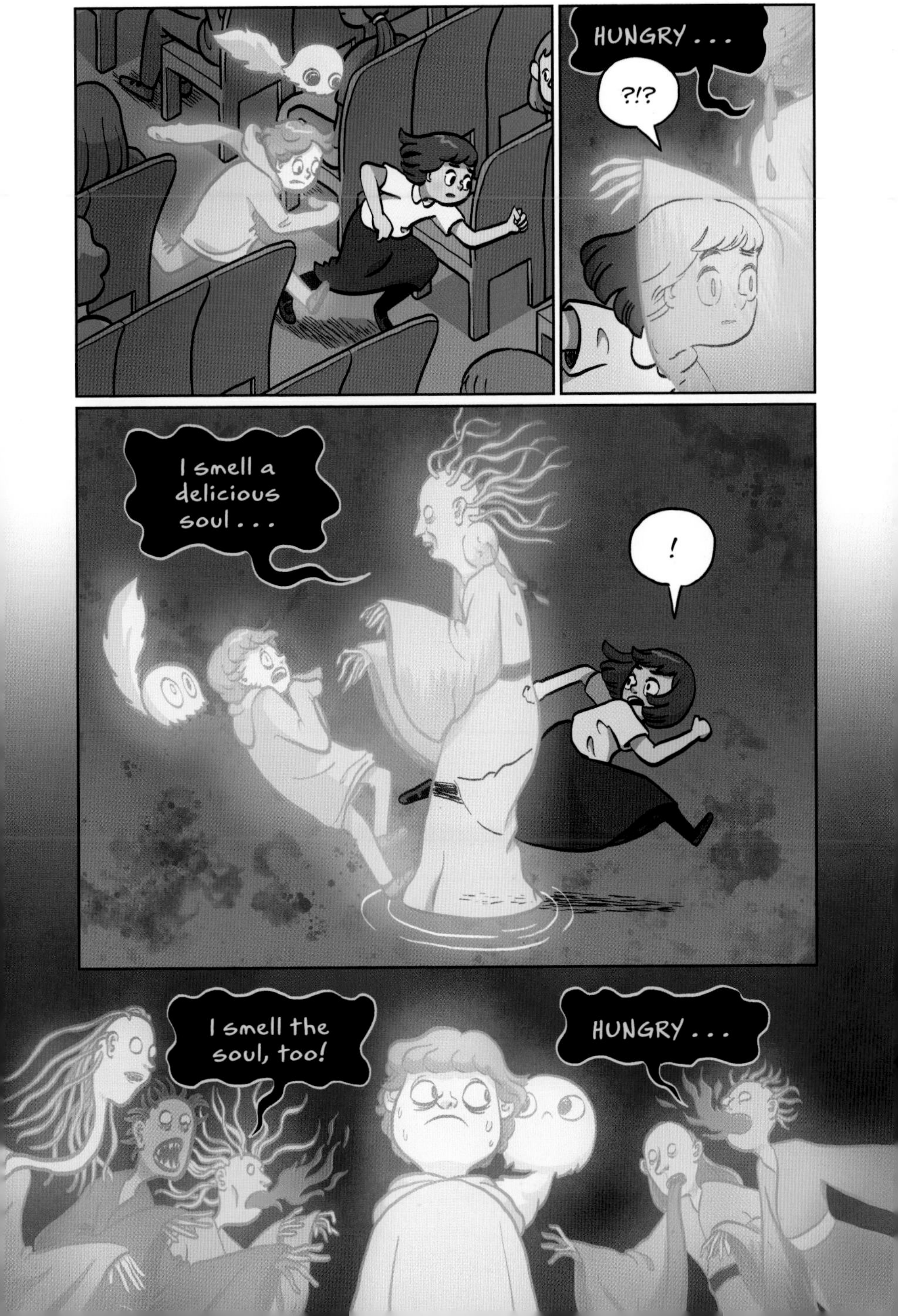
HUNGRY . . .
?!?
I smell a delicious soul . . .
!
I smell the soul, too!
HUNGRY . . .

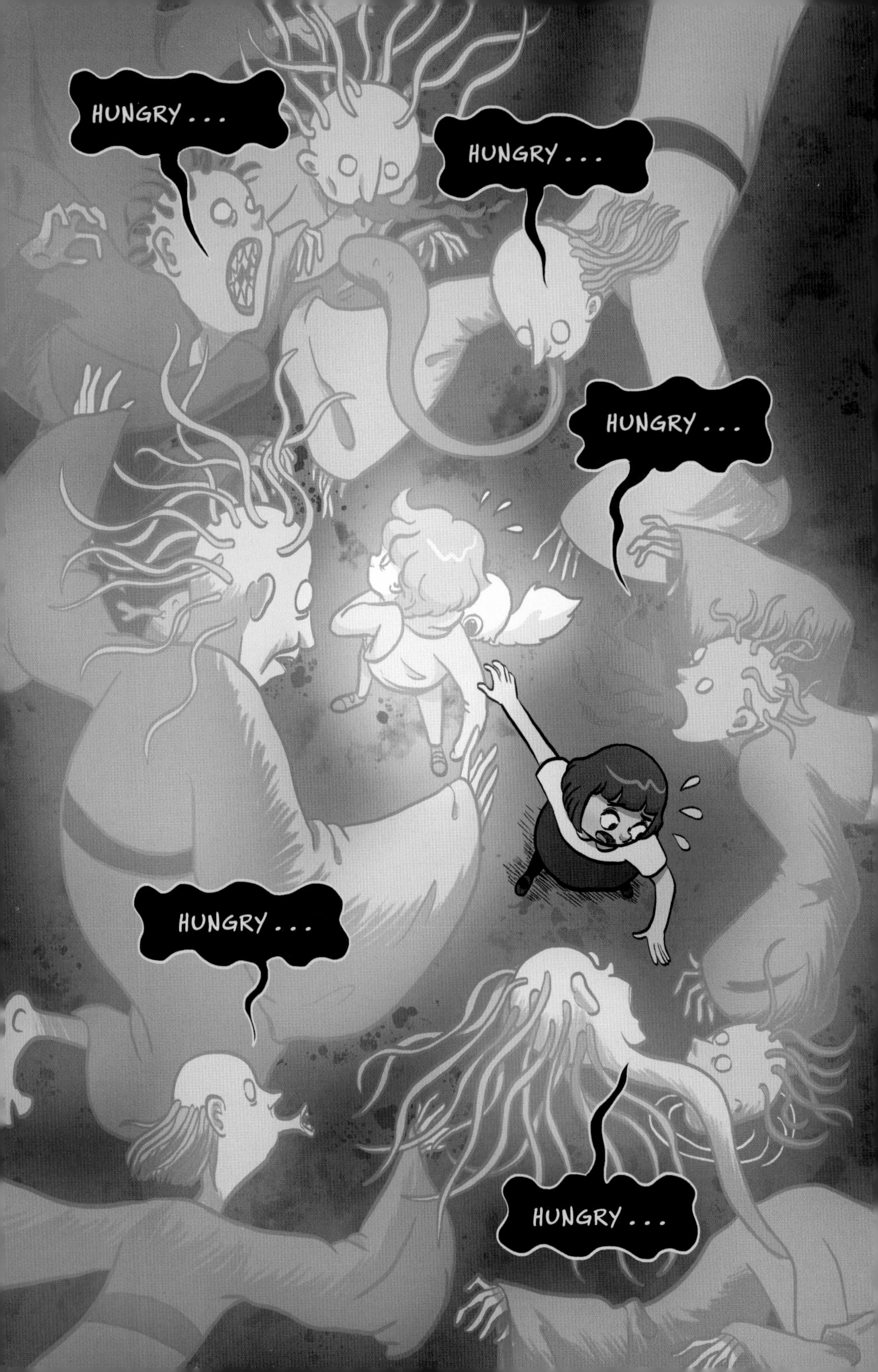
HUNGRY . . .
HUNGRY . . .
HUNGRY . . .
HUNGRY . . .
HUNGRY . . .

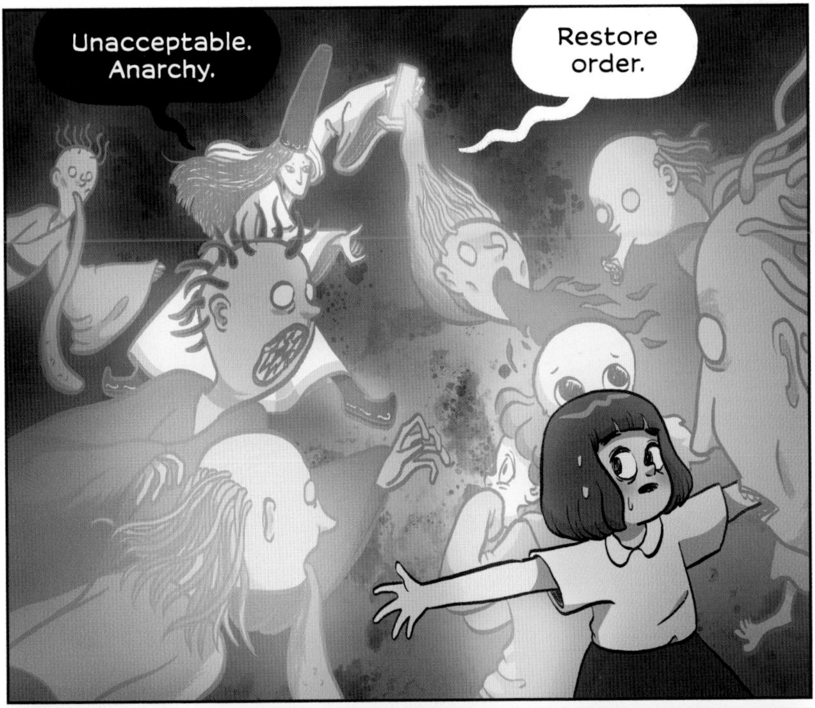
Unacceptable.
Anarchy.
Restore
order.

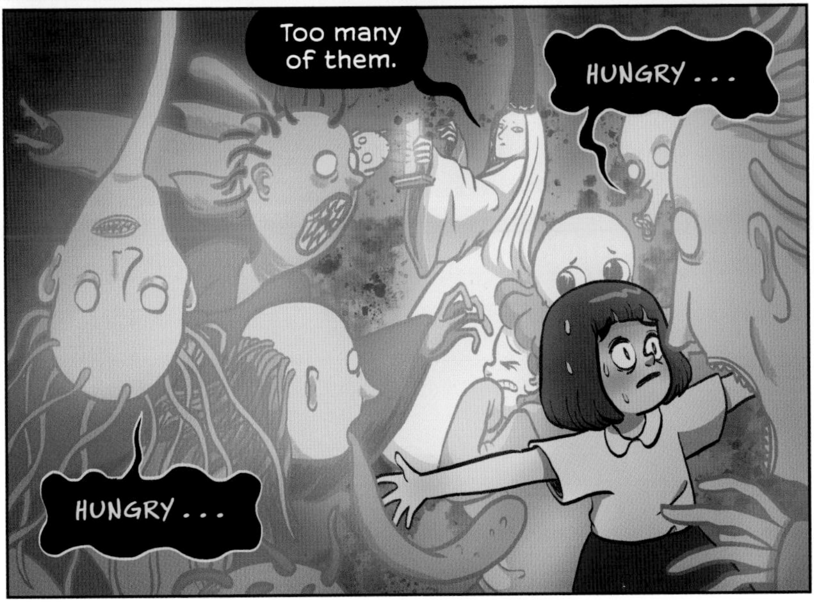
Too many
of them.
HUNGRY . . .
HUNGRY . . .

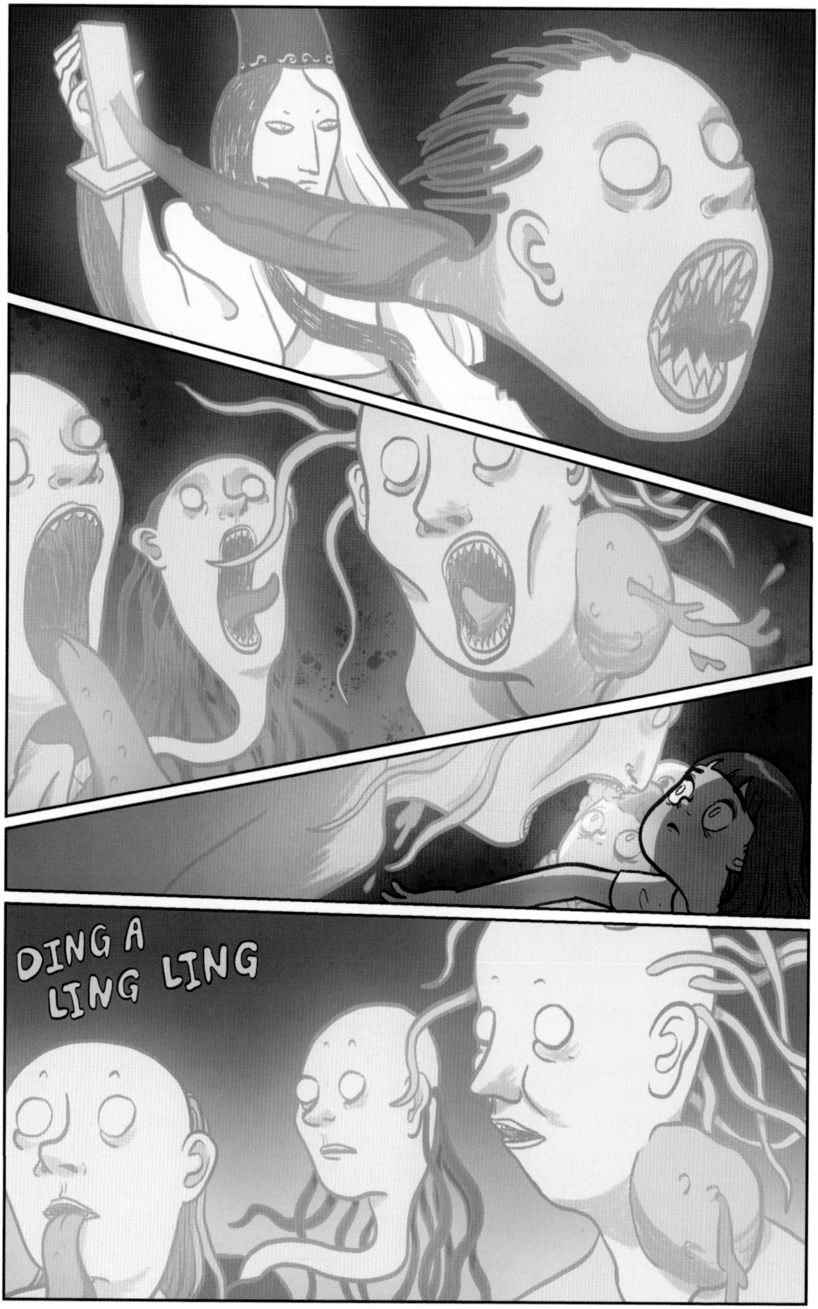
DING A LING LING

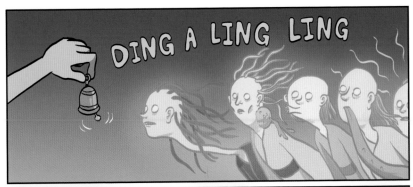

DING A LING LING

RUN, KIDS!

The bell only distracts them for a bit!

DING A LING LING

We can't outrun these Hungry Ghosts!

My dad's van!

We can't drive!

No! His van disappeared from the garage!

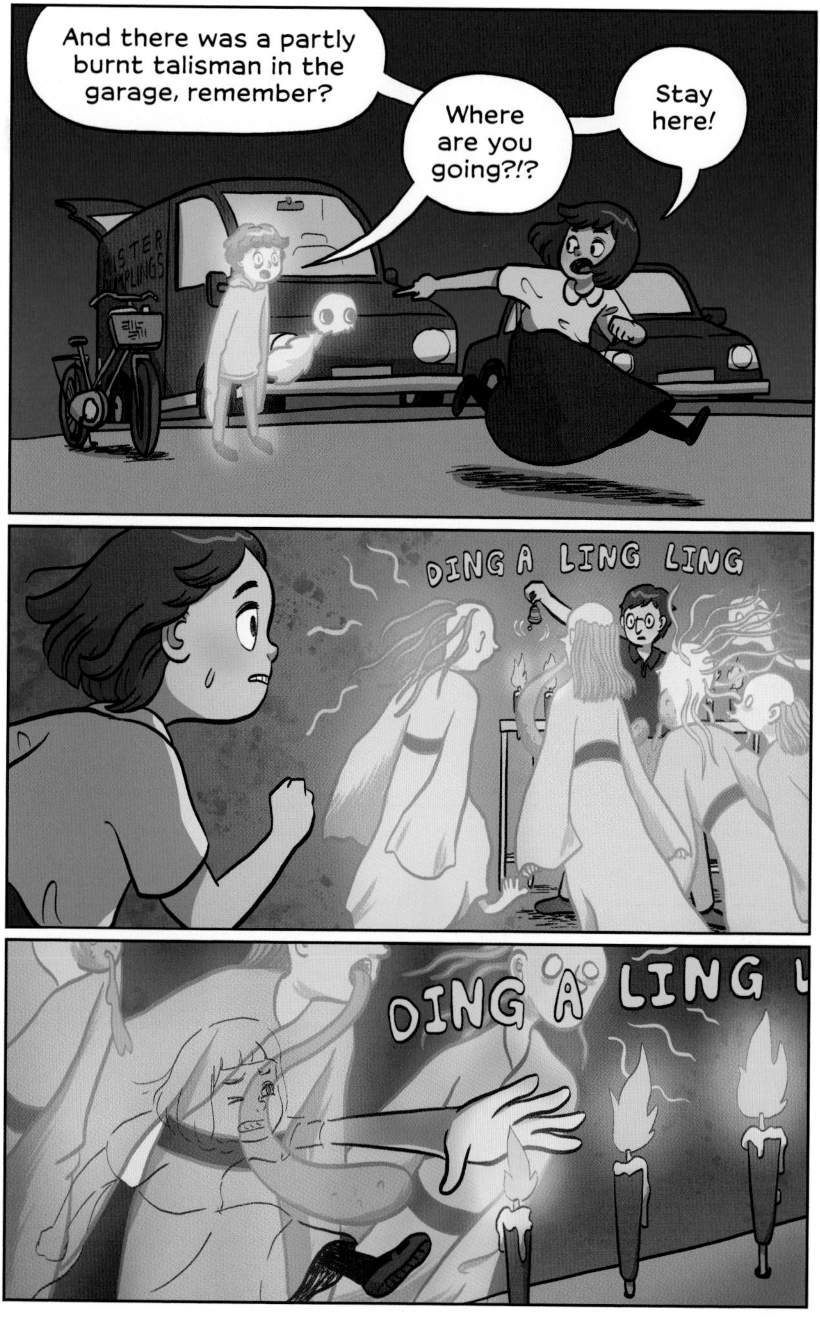
And there was a partly burnt talisman in the garage, remember?
Where are you going?!?
Stay here!
DING A LING LING
DING A LING

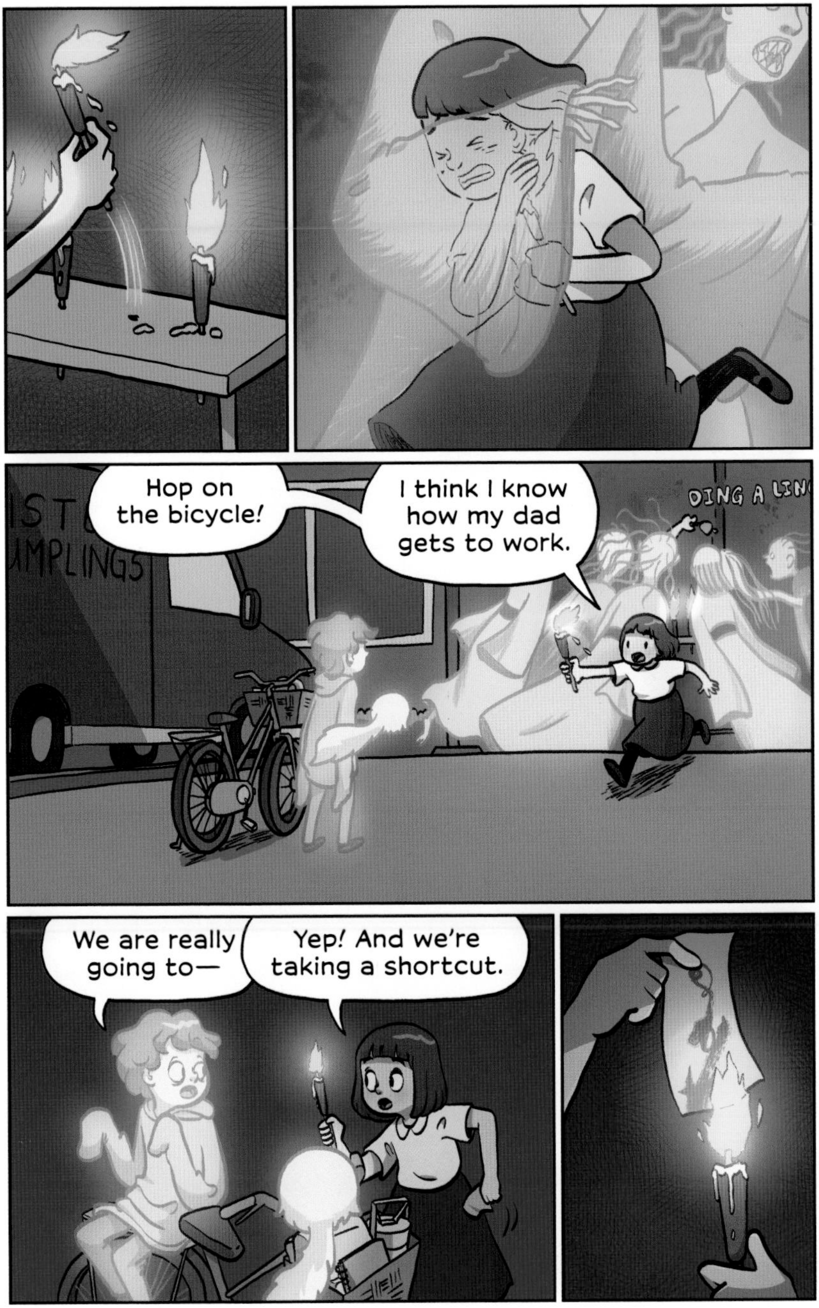
Hop on the bicycle!
I think I know how my dad gets to work.
We are really going to—
Yep! And we're taking a shortcut.

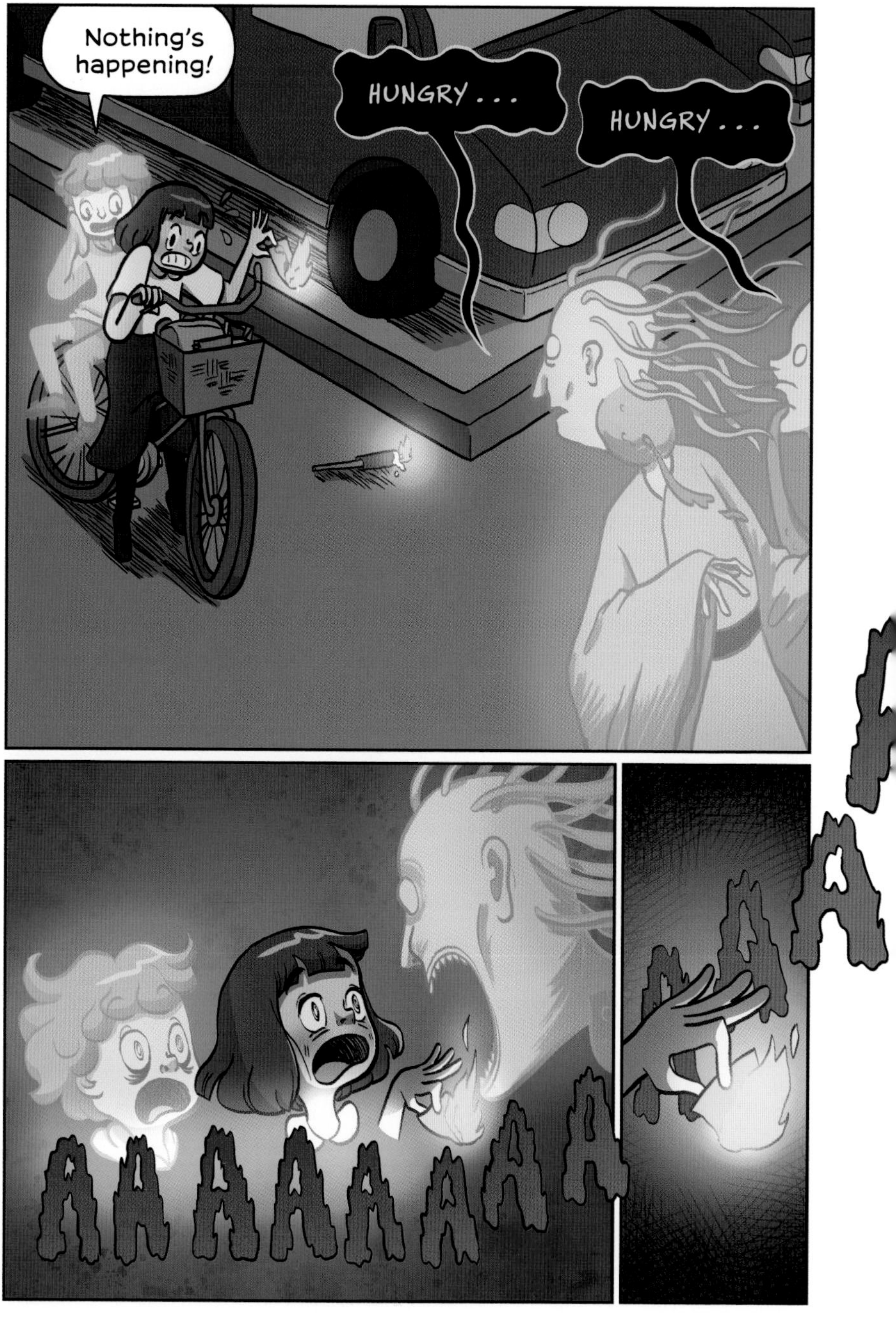
Nothing's happening!
HUNGRY . . .
HUNGRY . . .
AAAAAAAAAAAA

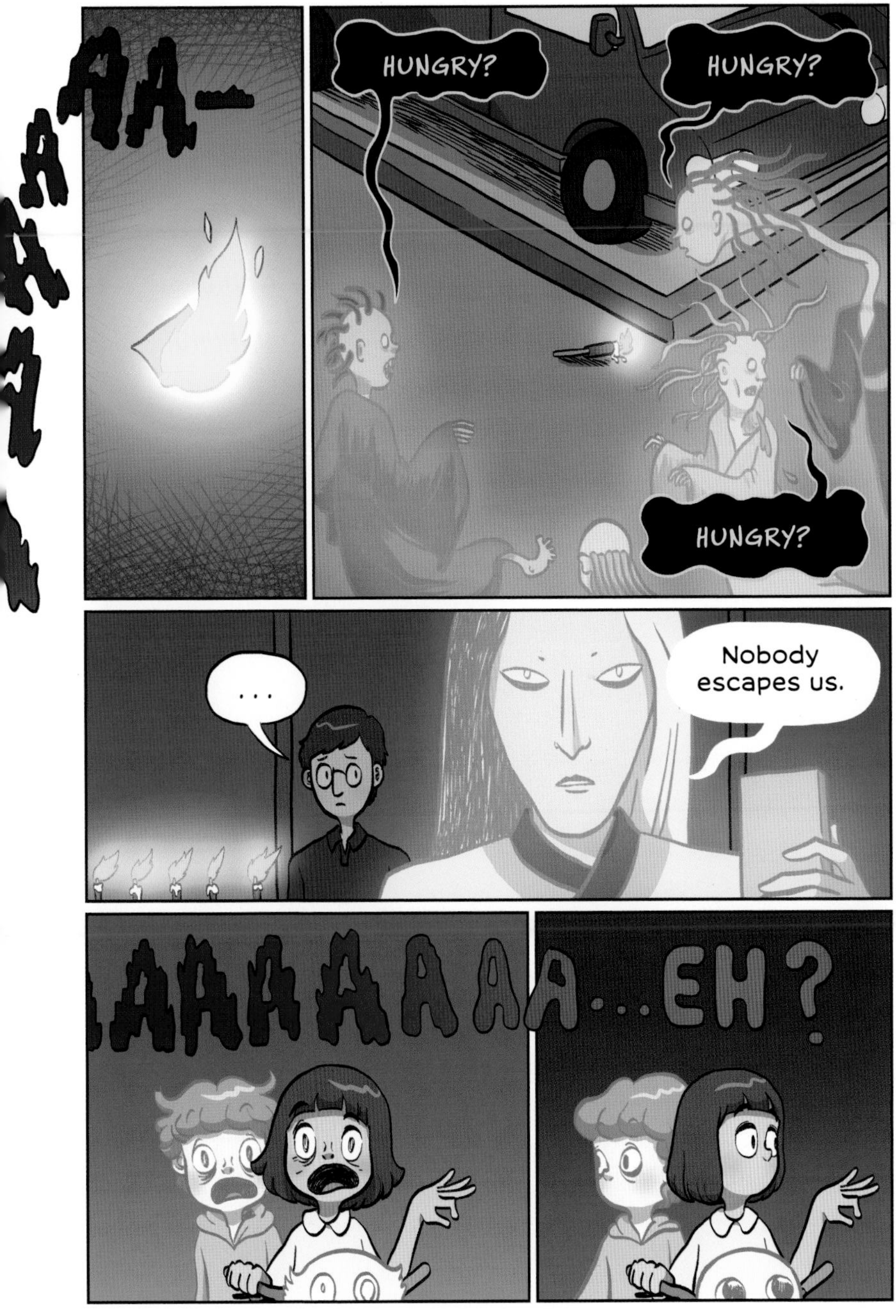
AAAAAAA—
HUNGRY?
HUNGRY?
HUNGRY?
. . .
Nobody escapes us.
AAAAAAAAAA...EH?

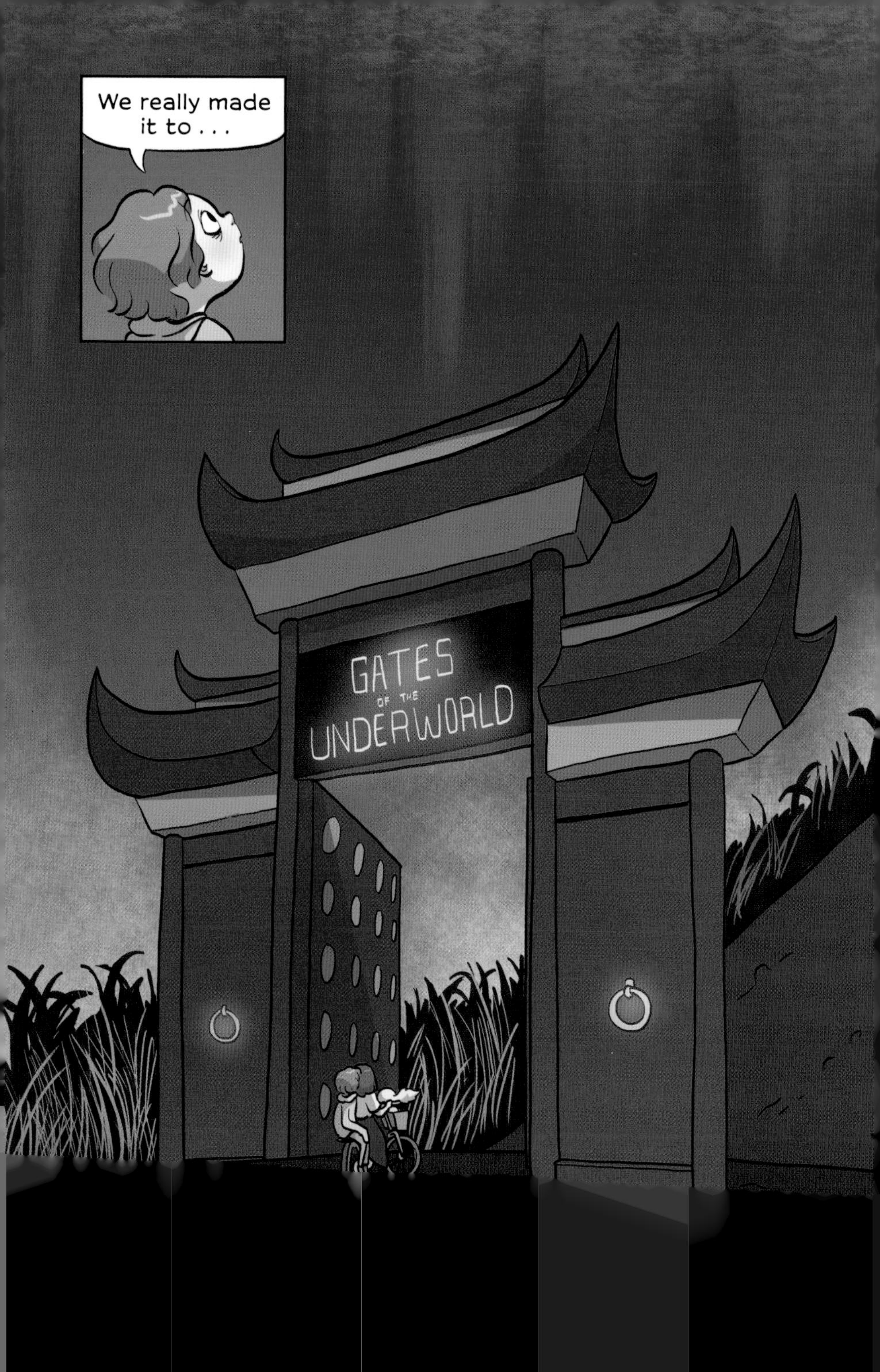
We really made it to . . .
GATES OF THE UNDERWORLD

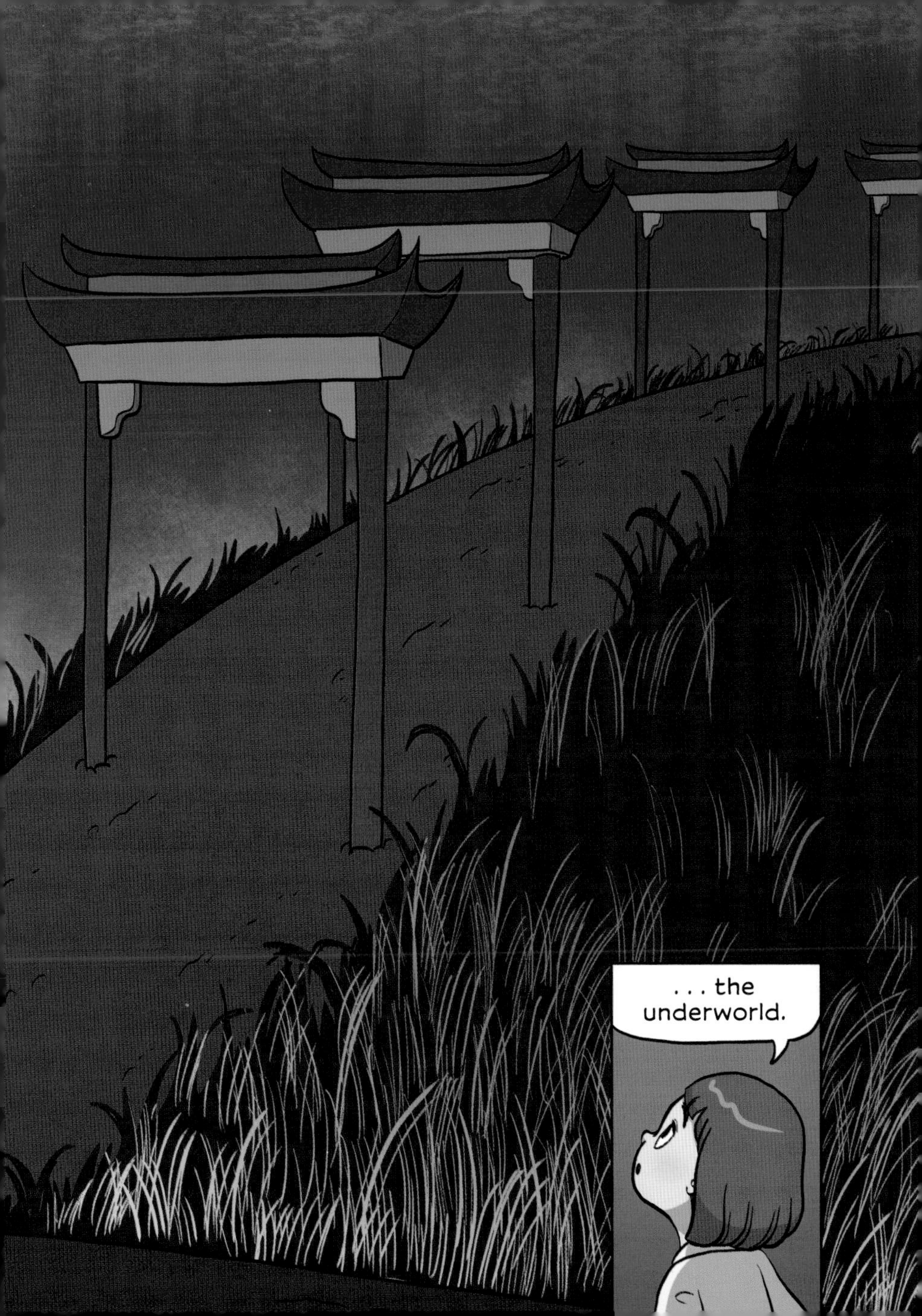
. . . the underworld.

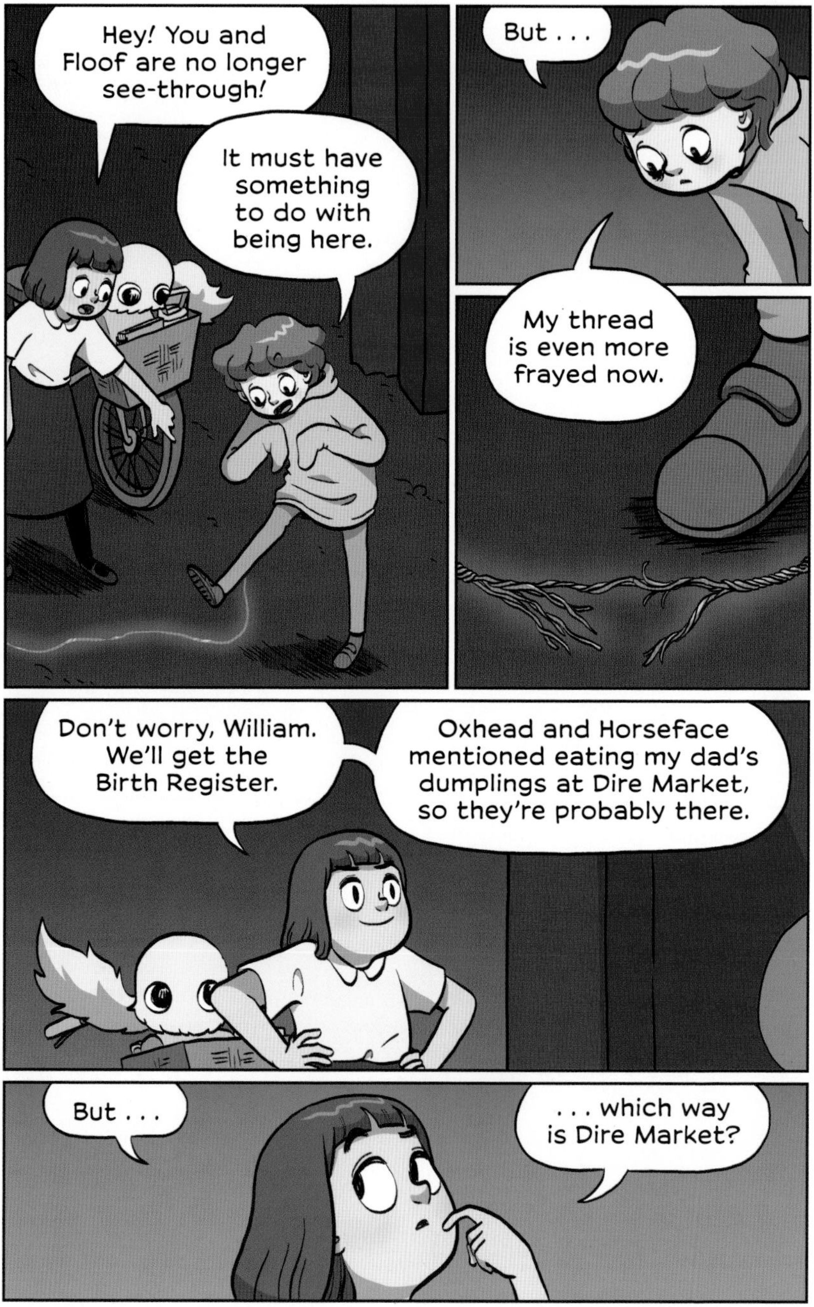
Hey! You and Floof are no longer see-through!
It must have something to do with being here.
But . . .
My thread is even more frayed now.
Don't worry, William. We'll get the Birth Register.
Oxhead and Horseface mentioned eating my dad's dumplings at Dire Market, so they're probably there.
But . . .
. . . which way is Dire Market?

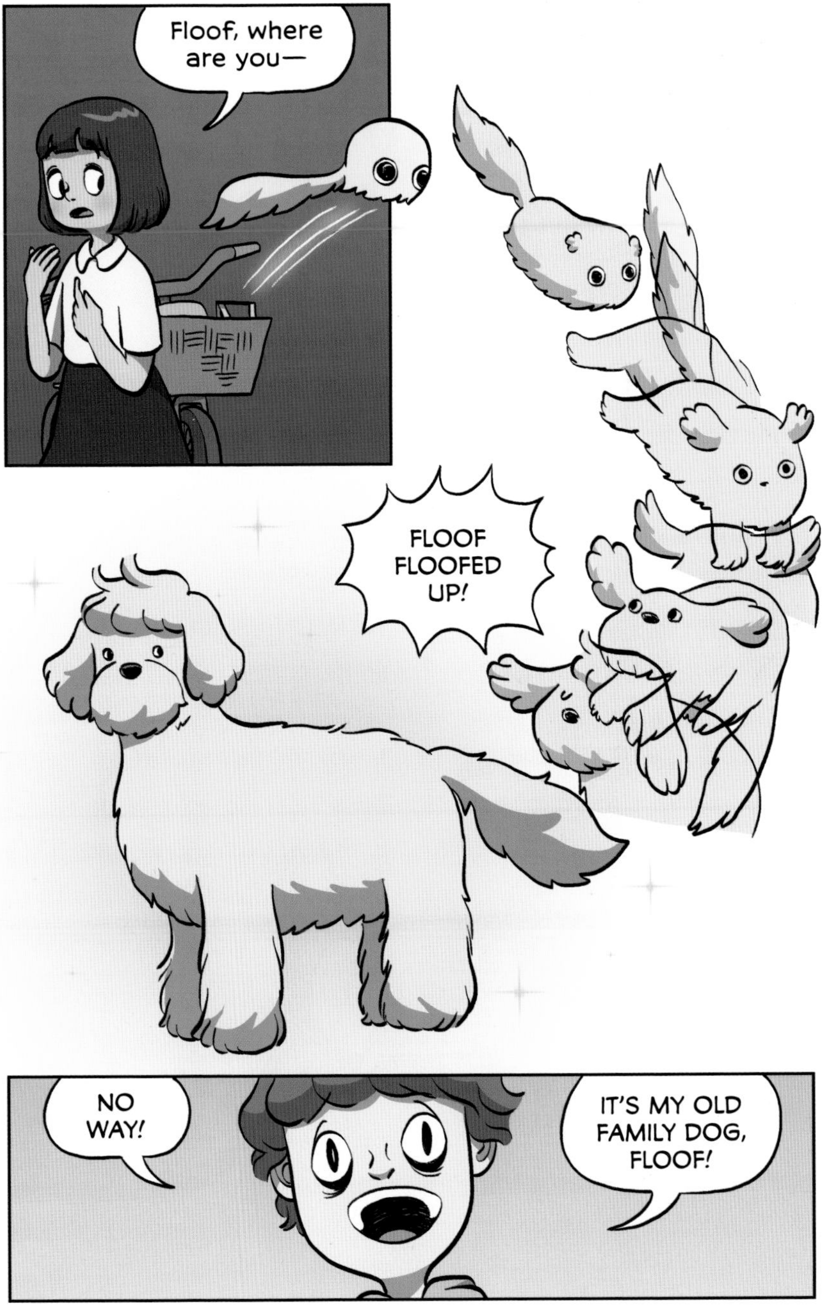
Floof, where are you—
FLOOF FLOOFED UP!
NO WAY!
IT'S MY OLD FAMILY DOG, FLOOF!

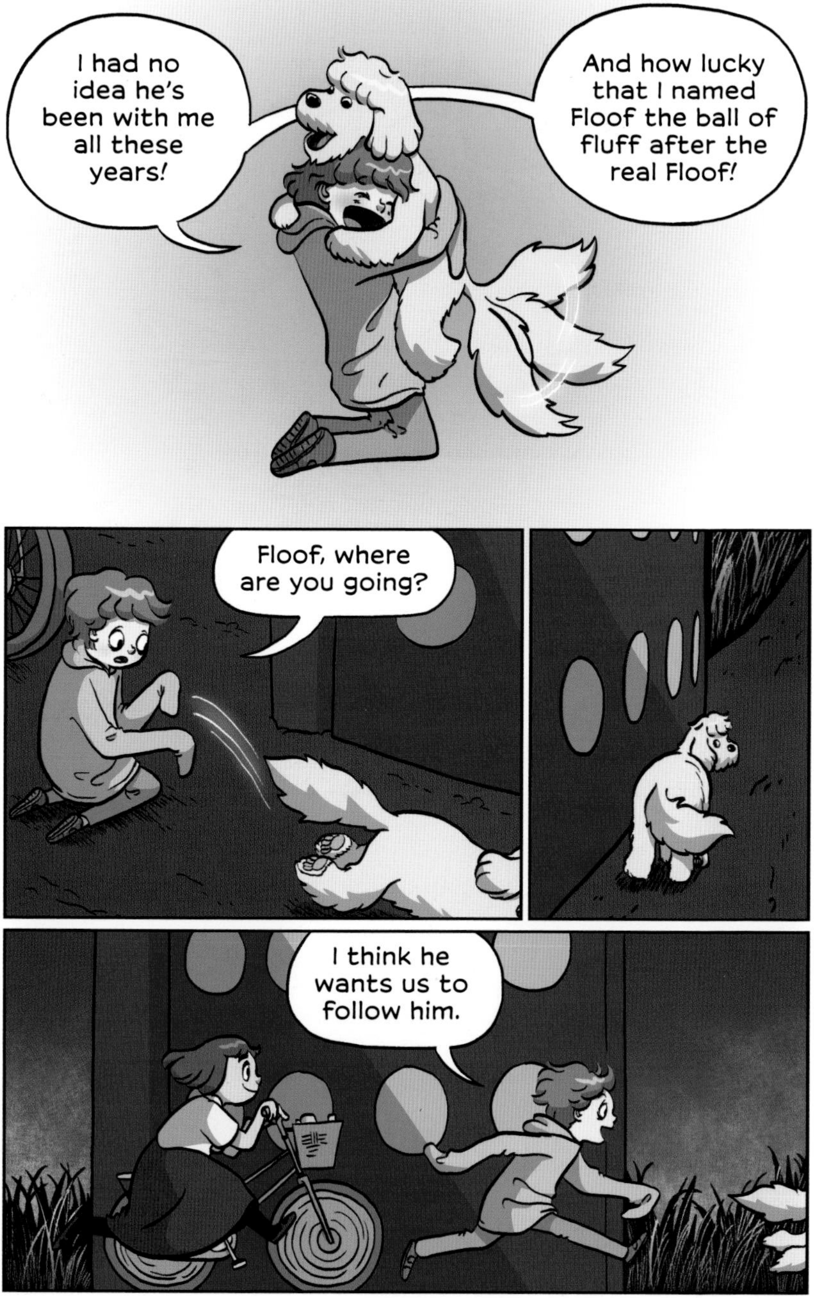
I had no idea he's been with me all these years!
And how lucky that I named Floof the ball of fluff after the real Floof!
Floof, where are you going?
I think he wants us to follow him.

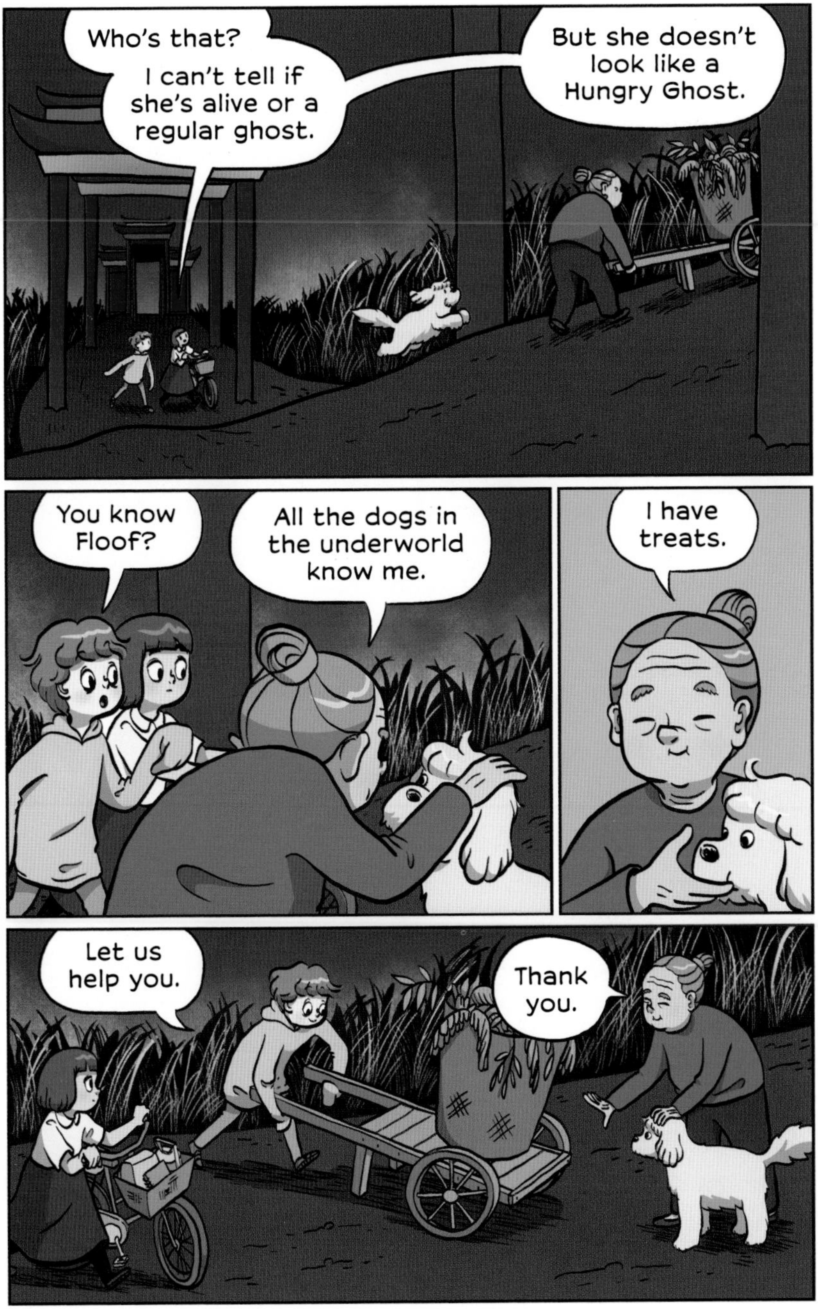
Who's that?
I can't tell if she's alive or a regular ghost.
But she doesn't look like a Hungry Ghost.
You know Floof?
All the dogs in the underworld know me.
I have treats.
Let us help you.
Thank you.

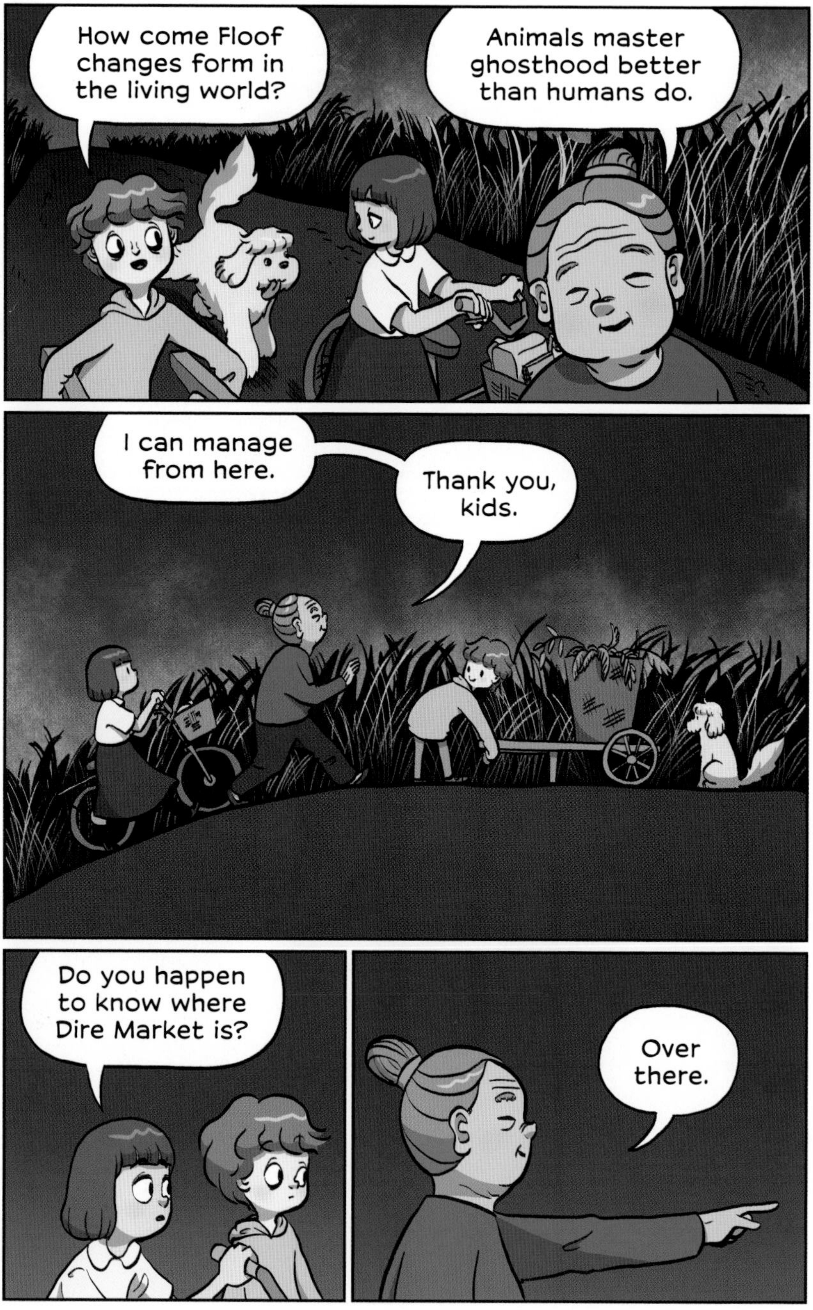
How come Floof changes form in the living world?
Animals master ghosthood better than humans do.
I can manage from here.
Thank you, kids.
Do you happen to know where Dire Market is?
Over there.

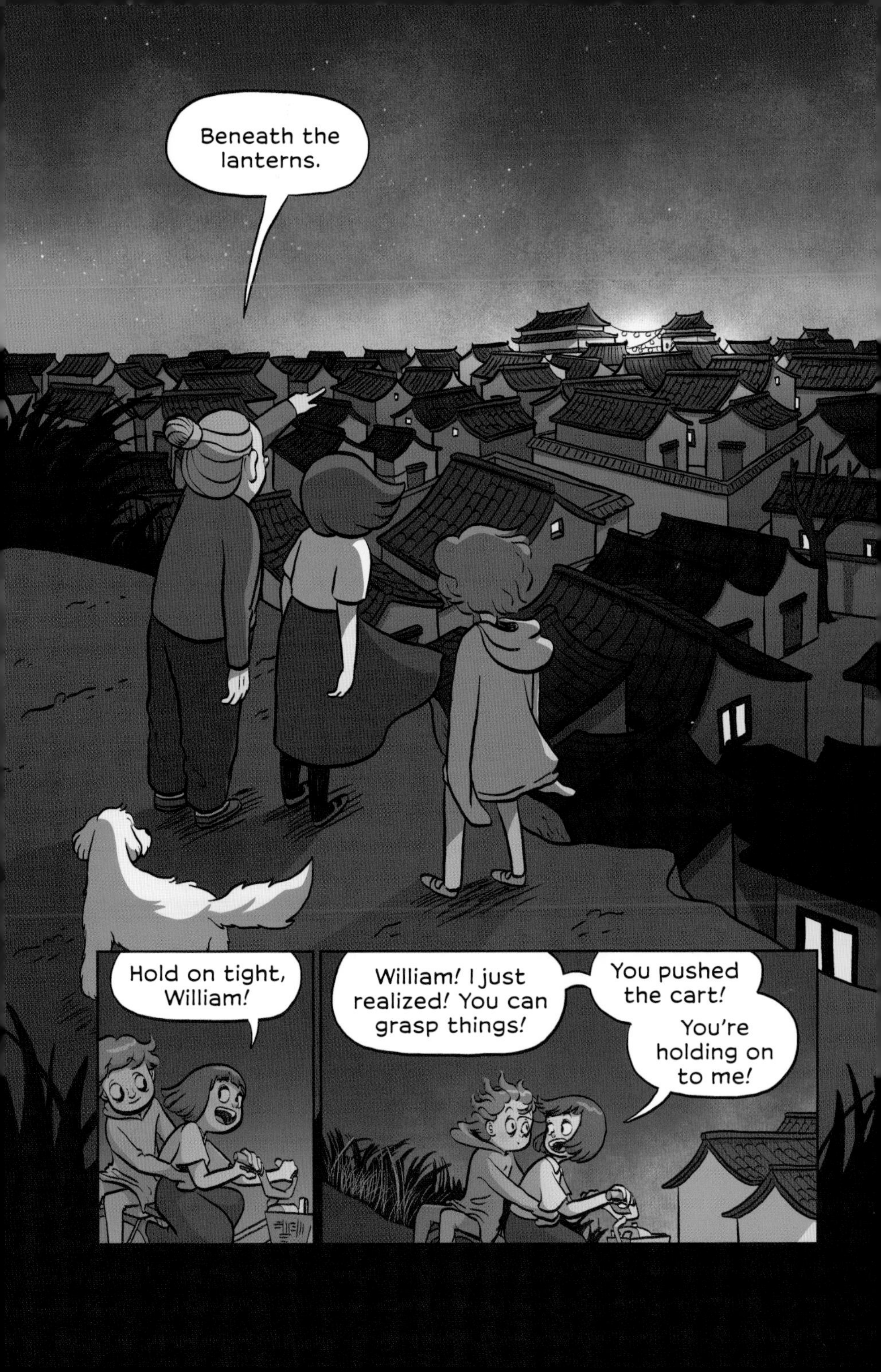
Beneath the lanterns.
Hold on tight, William!
William! I just realized! You can grasp things!
You pushed the cart!
You're holding on to me!

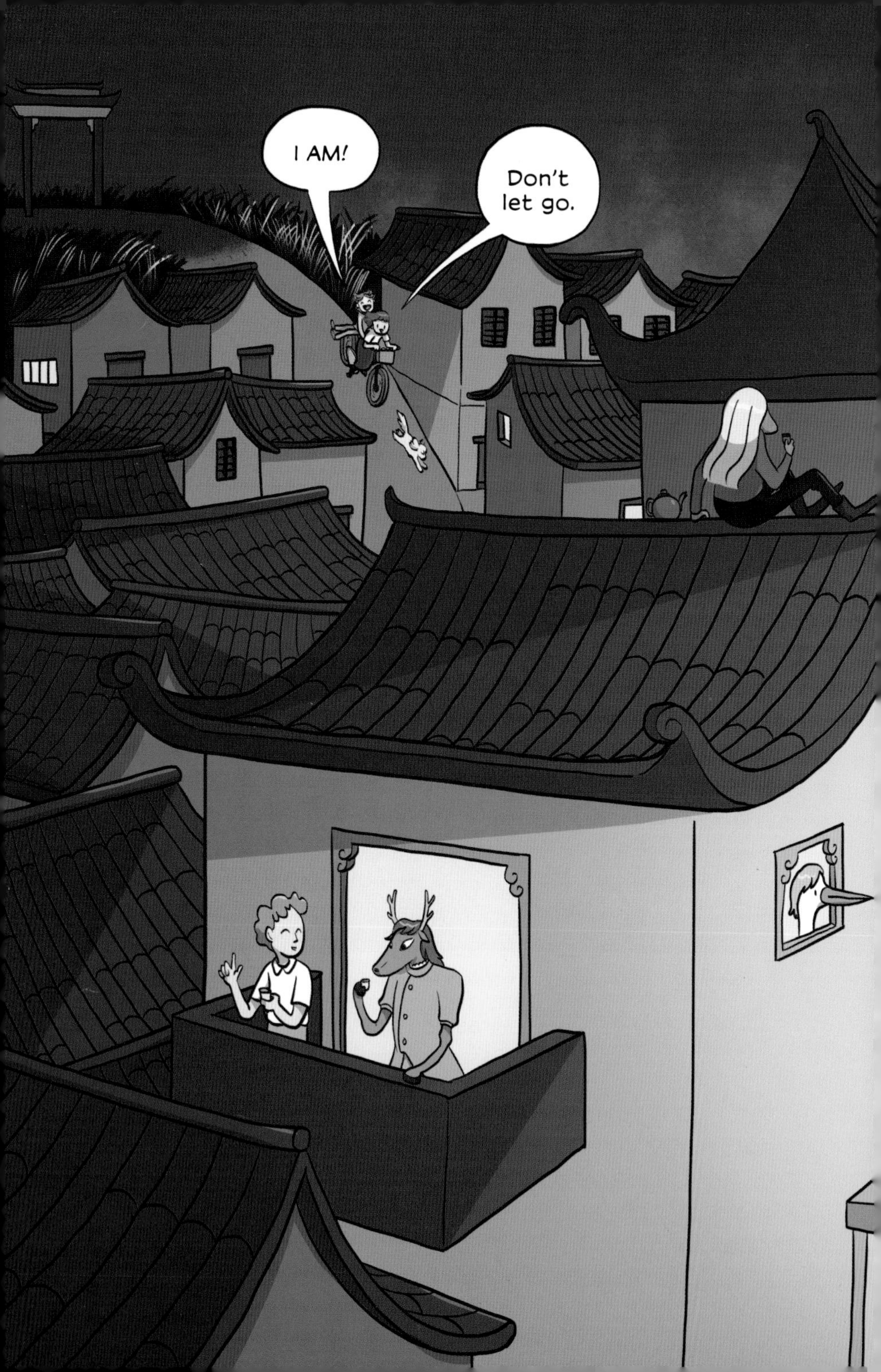
I AM!
Don't let go.

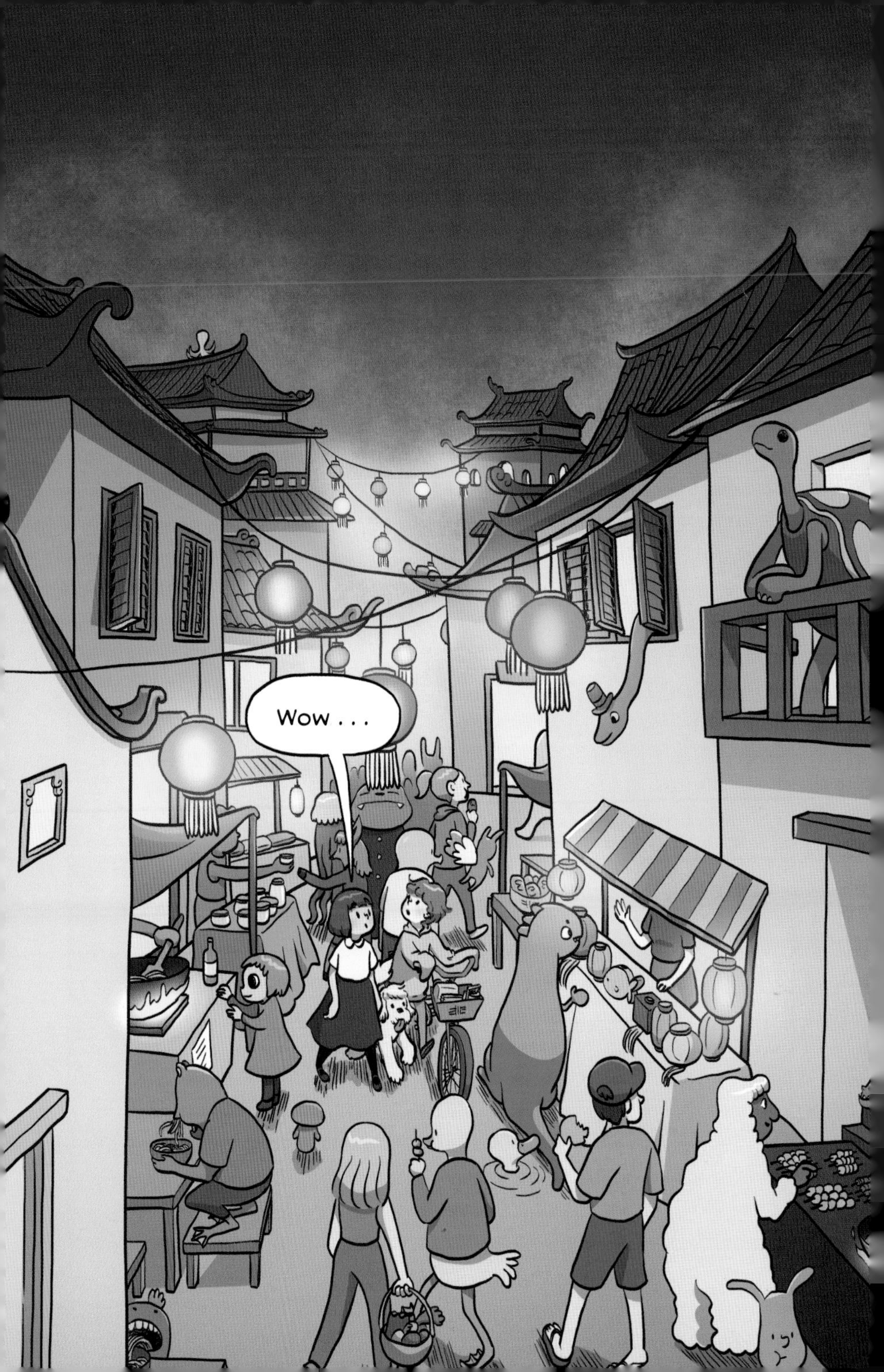
Wow . . .

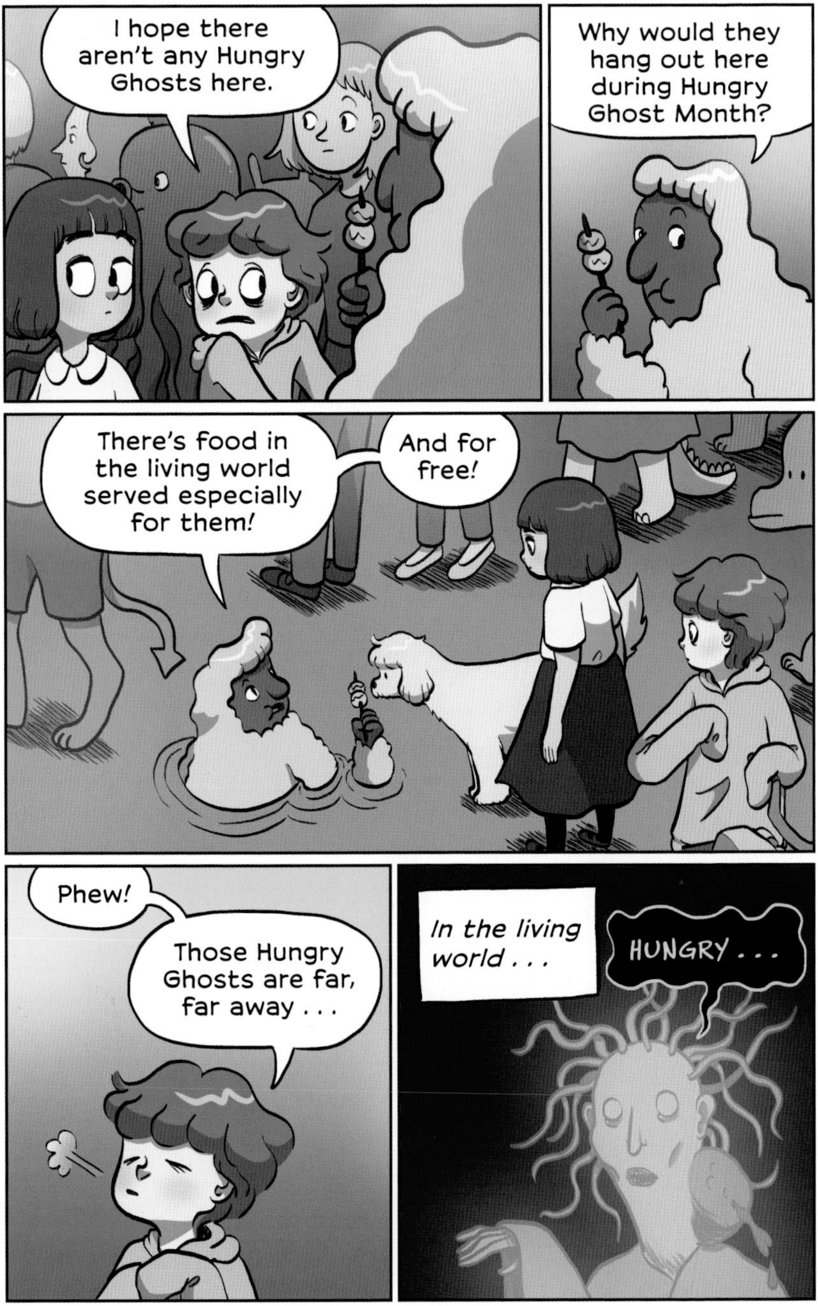
I hope there aren't any Hungry Ghosts here.
Why would they hang out here during Hungry Ghost Month?
There's food in the living world served especially for them!
And for free!
Phew!
Those Hungry Ghosts are far, far away . . .
In the living world . . .
HUNGRY . . .

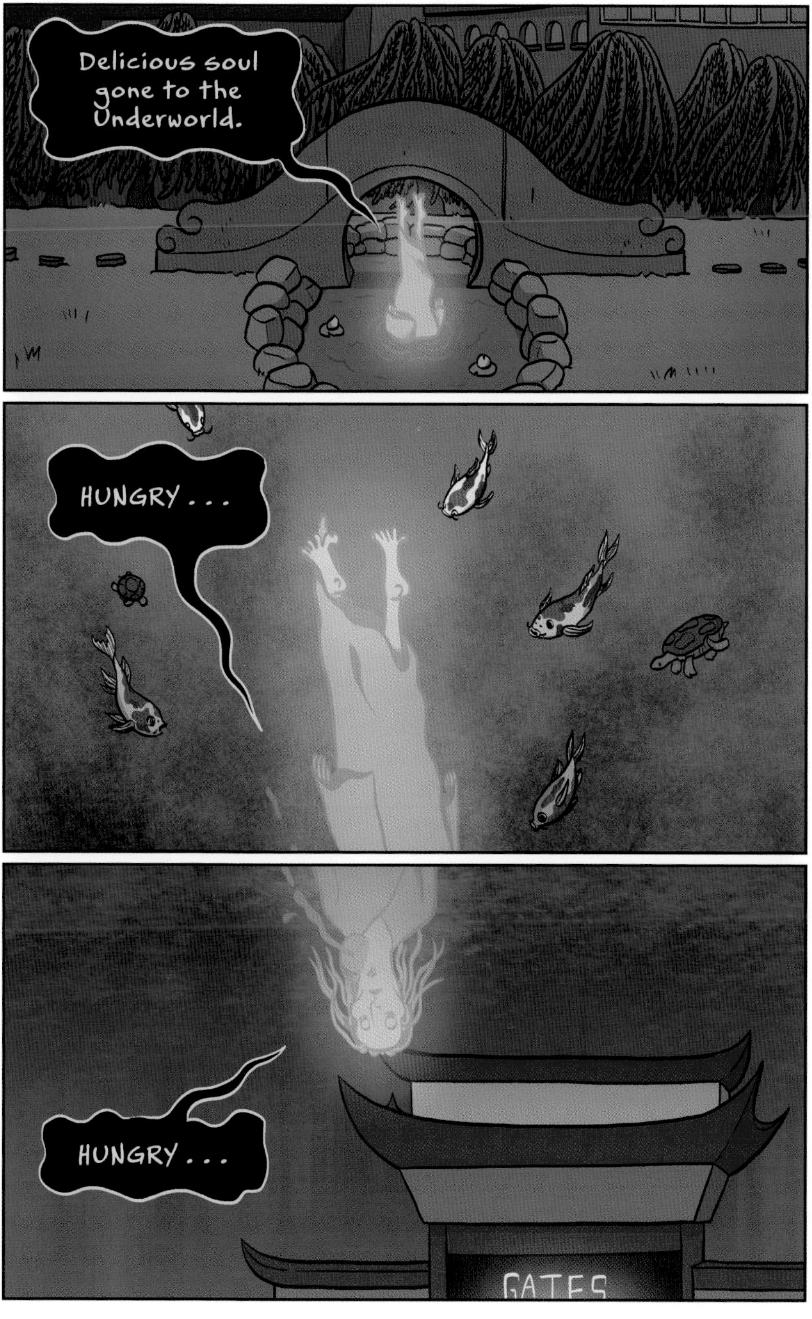
Delicious soul gone to the Underworld.
HUNGRY . . .
HUNGRY . . .
GATES

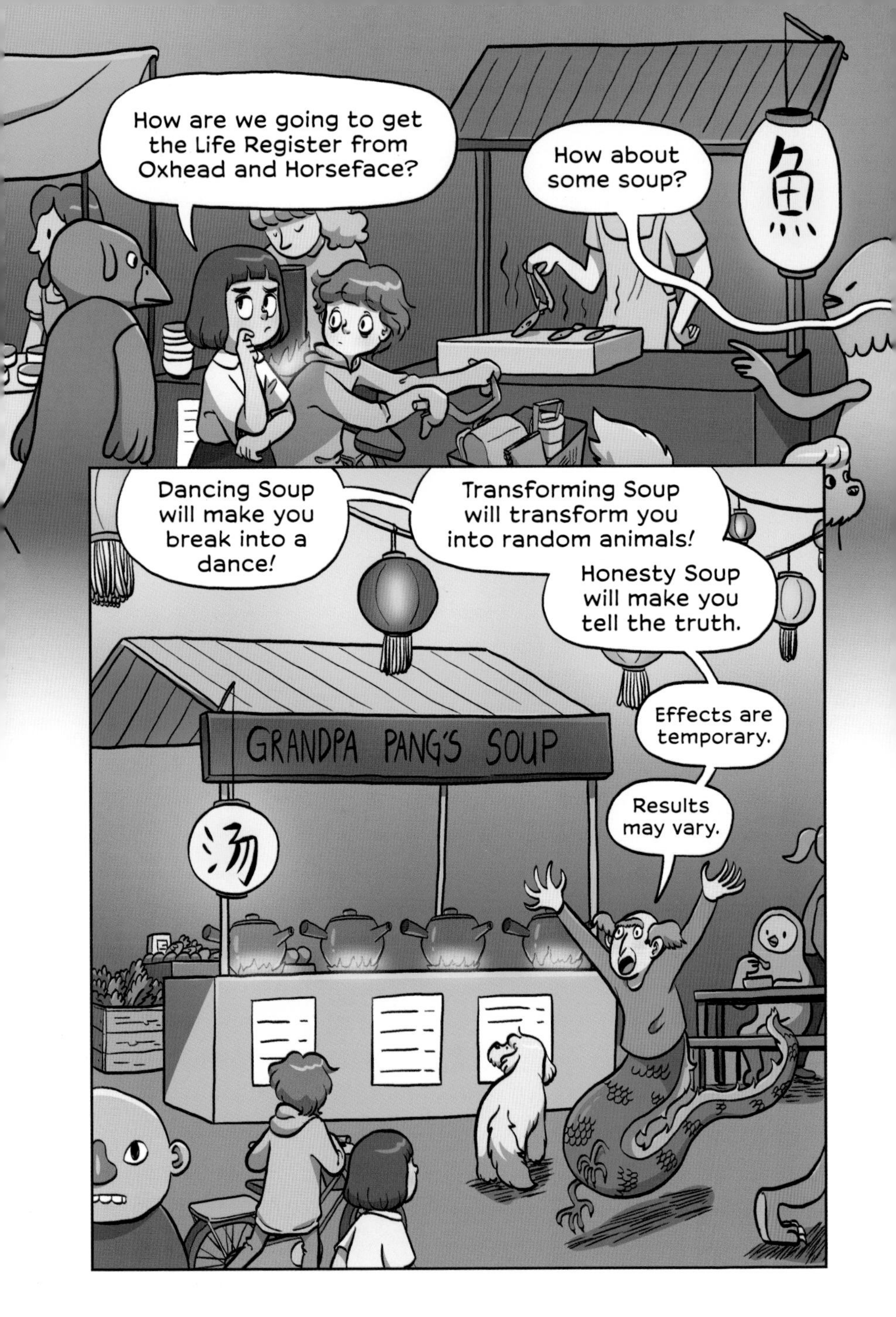
How are we going to get the Life Register from Oxhead and Horseface?
How about some soup?
魚
Dancing Soup will make you break into a dance!
Transforming Soup will transform you into random animals!
Honesty Soup will make you tell the truth.
Effects are temporary.
Results may vary.
GRANDPA PANG'S SOUP
汤

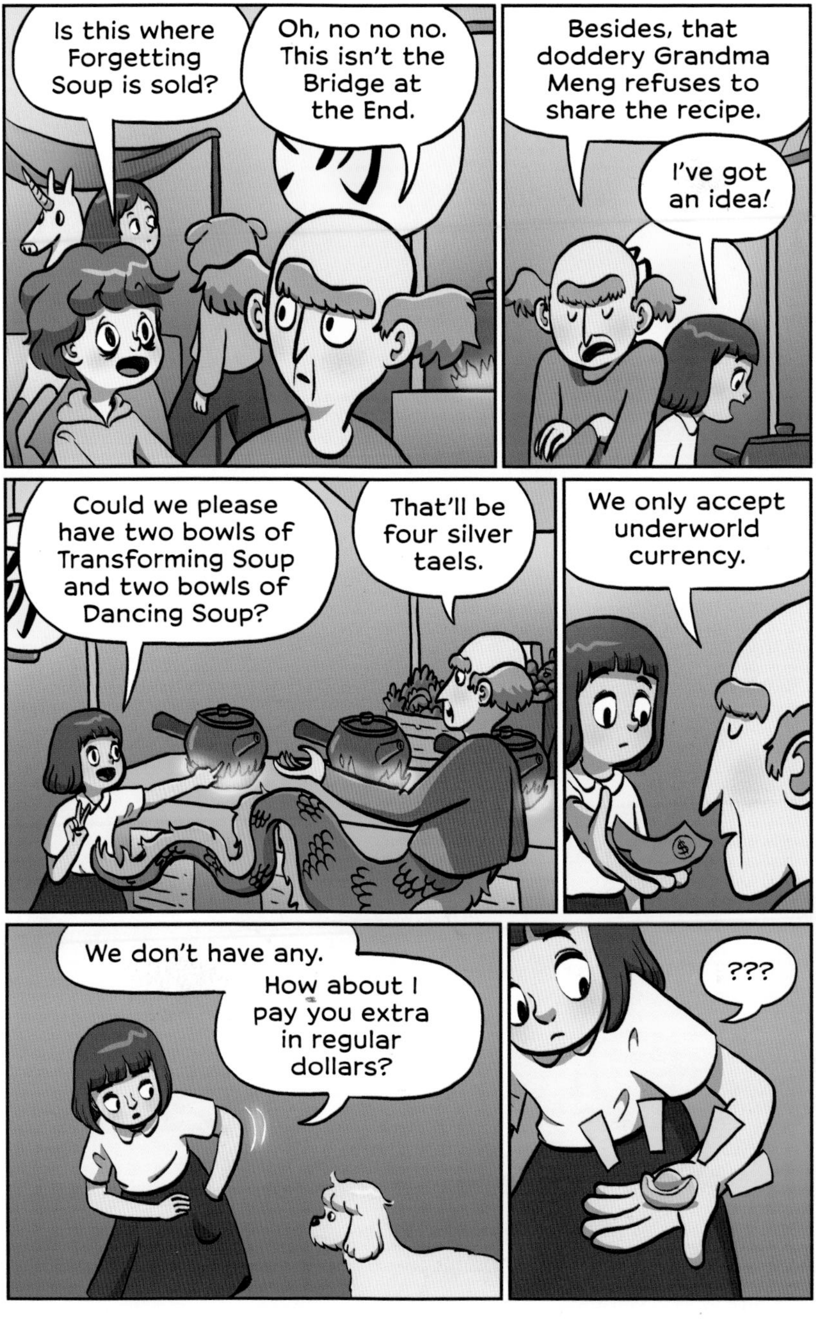
Is this where Forgetting Soup is sold?
Oh, no no no. This isn't the Bridge at the End.
Besides, that doddery Grandma Meng refuses to share the recipe.
I've got an idea!
Could we please have two bowls of Transforming Soup and two bowls of Dancing Soup?
That'll be four silver taels.
We only accept underworld currency.
We don't have any.
How about I pay you extra in regular dollars?
???

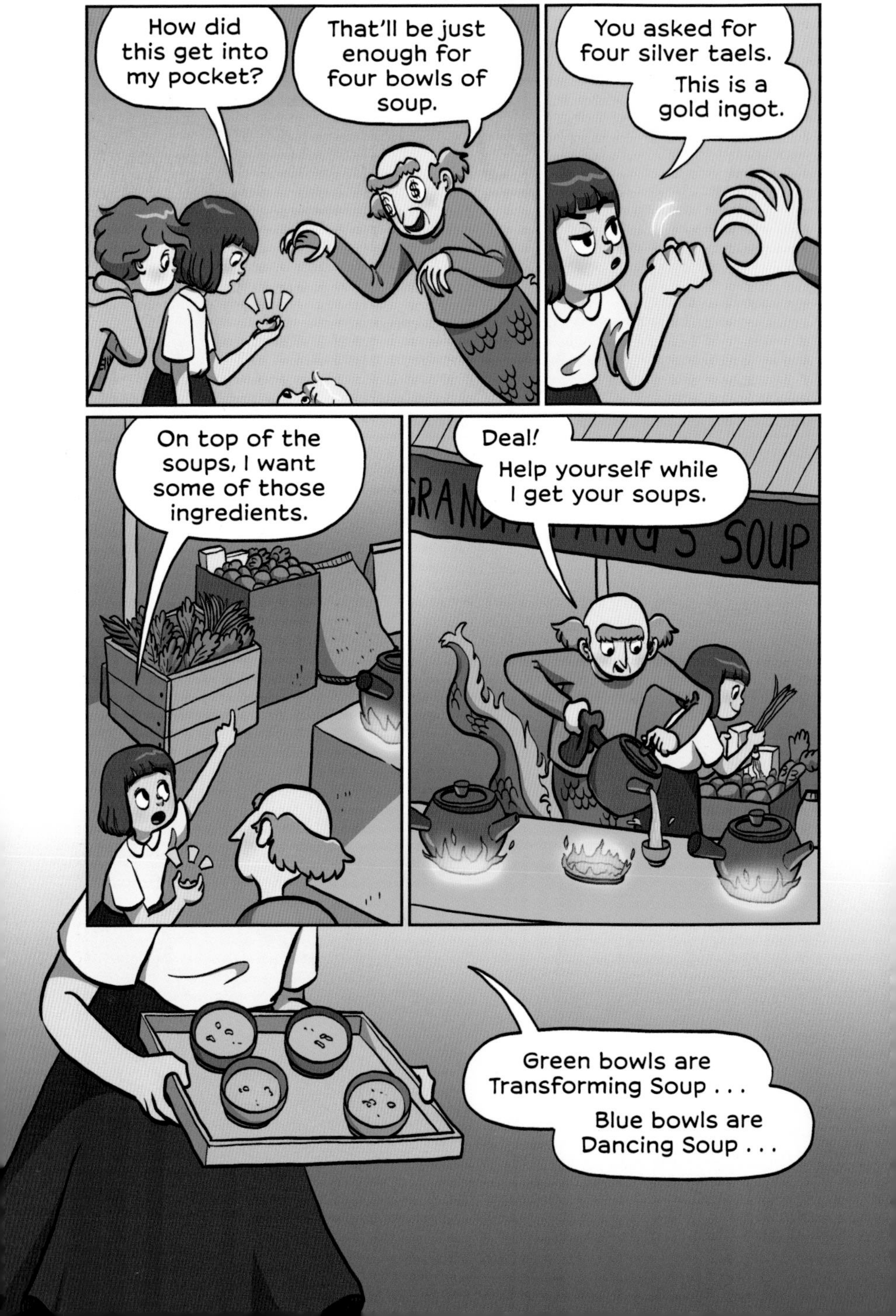

How did this get into my pocket?
That'll be just enough for four bowls of soup.
You asked for four silver taels.
This is a gold ingot.
On top of the soups, I want some of those ingredients.
Deal!
Help yourself while I get your soups.
SOUP
Green bowls are Transforming Soup . . .
Blue bowls are Dancing Soup . . .

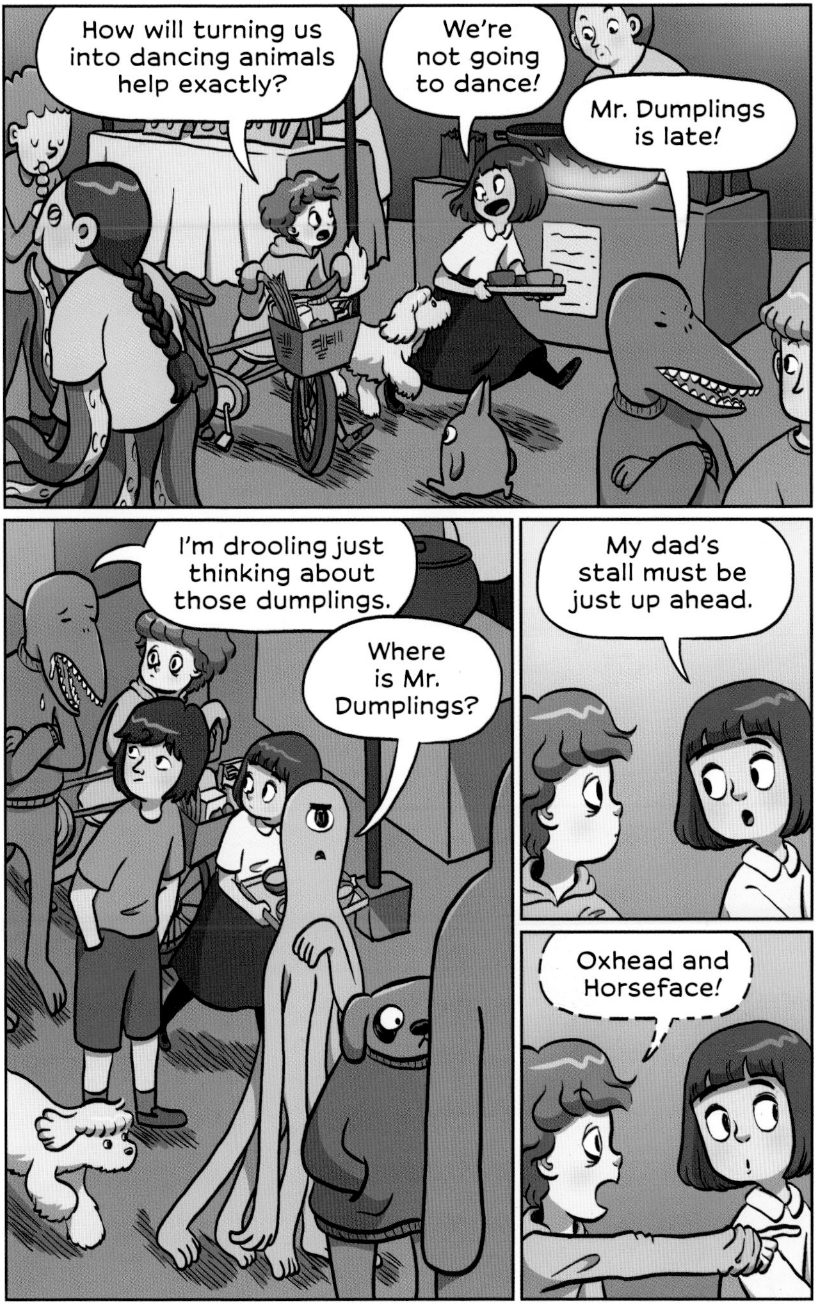
How will turning us into dancing animals help exactly?
We're not going to dance!
Mr. Dumplings is late!
I'm drooling just thinking about those dumplings.
Where is Mr. Dumplings?
My dad's stall must be just up ahead.
Oxhead and Horseface!

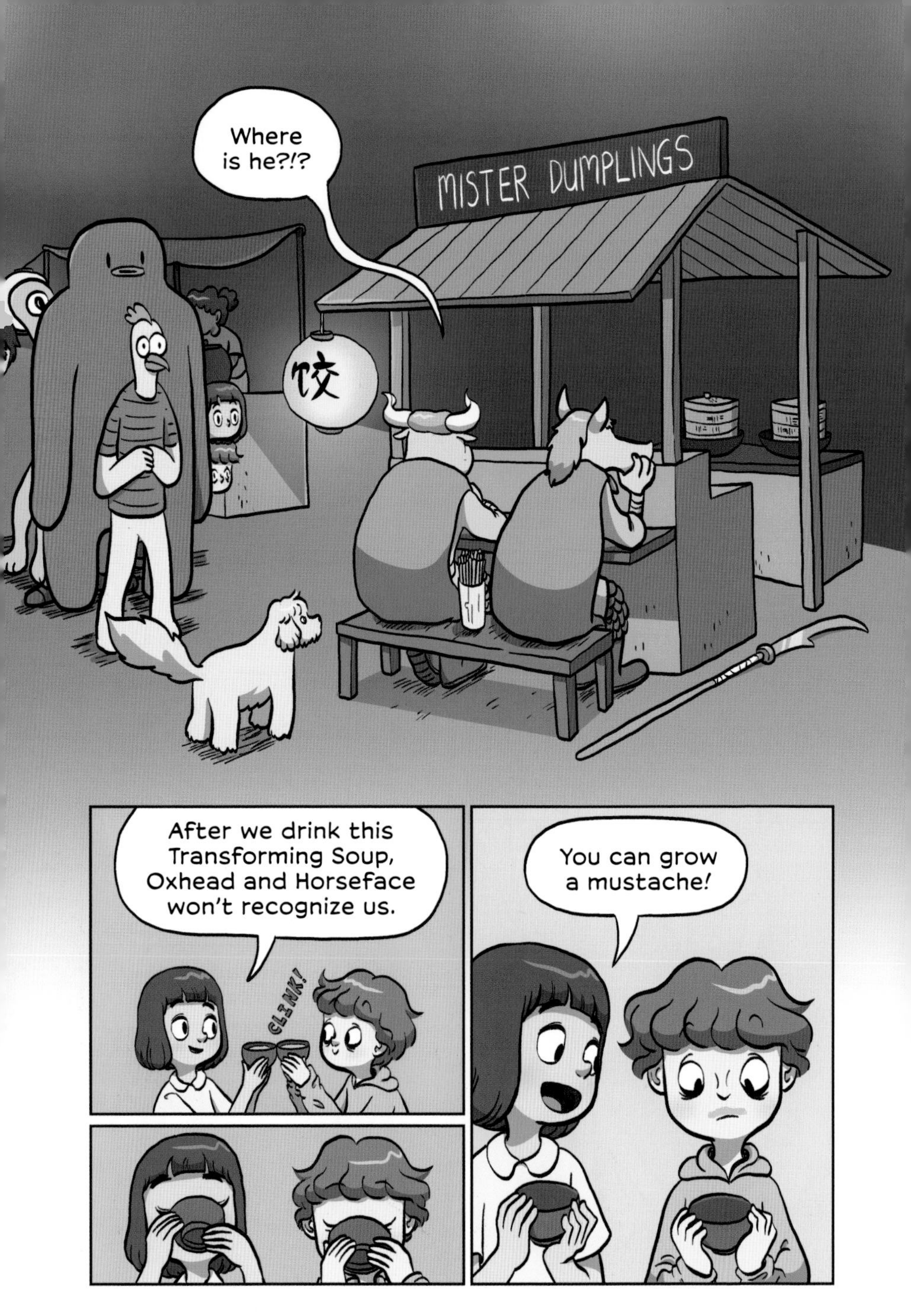
Where is he?!?
MISTER DUMPLINGS
饺
After we drink this Transforming Soup, Oxhead and Horseface won't recognize us.
CLINK!
You can grow a mustache!

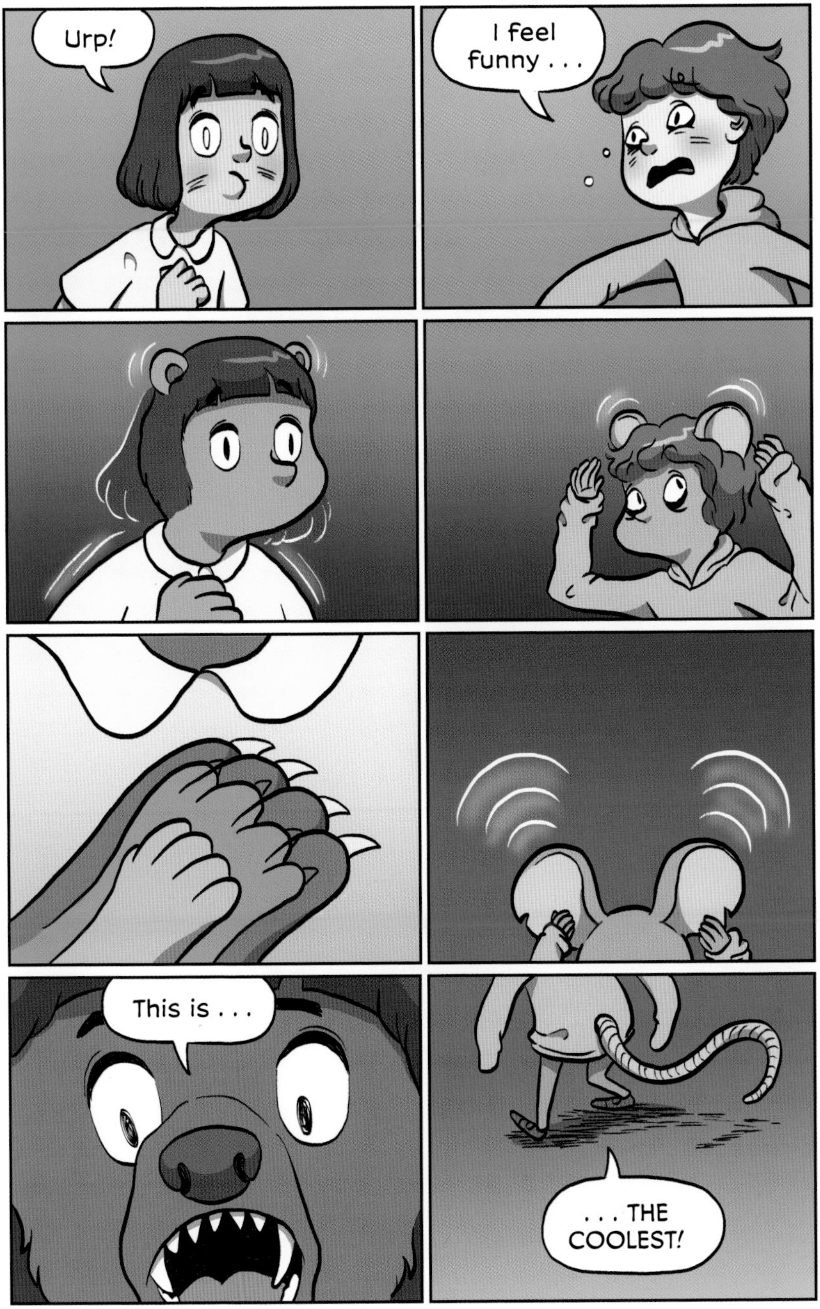
Urp!
I feel funny . . .
This is . . .
. . . THE COOLEST!

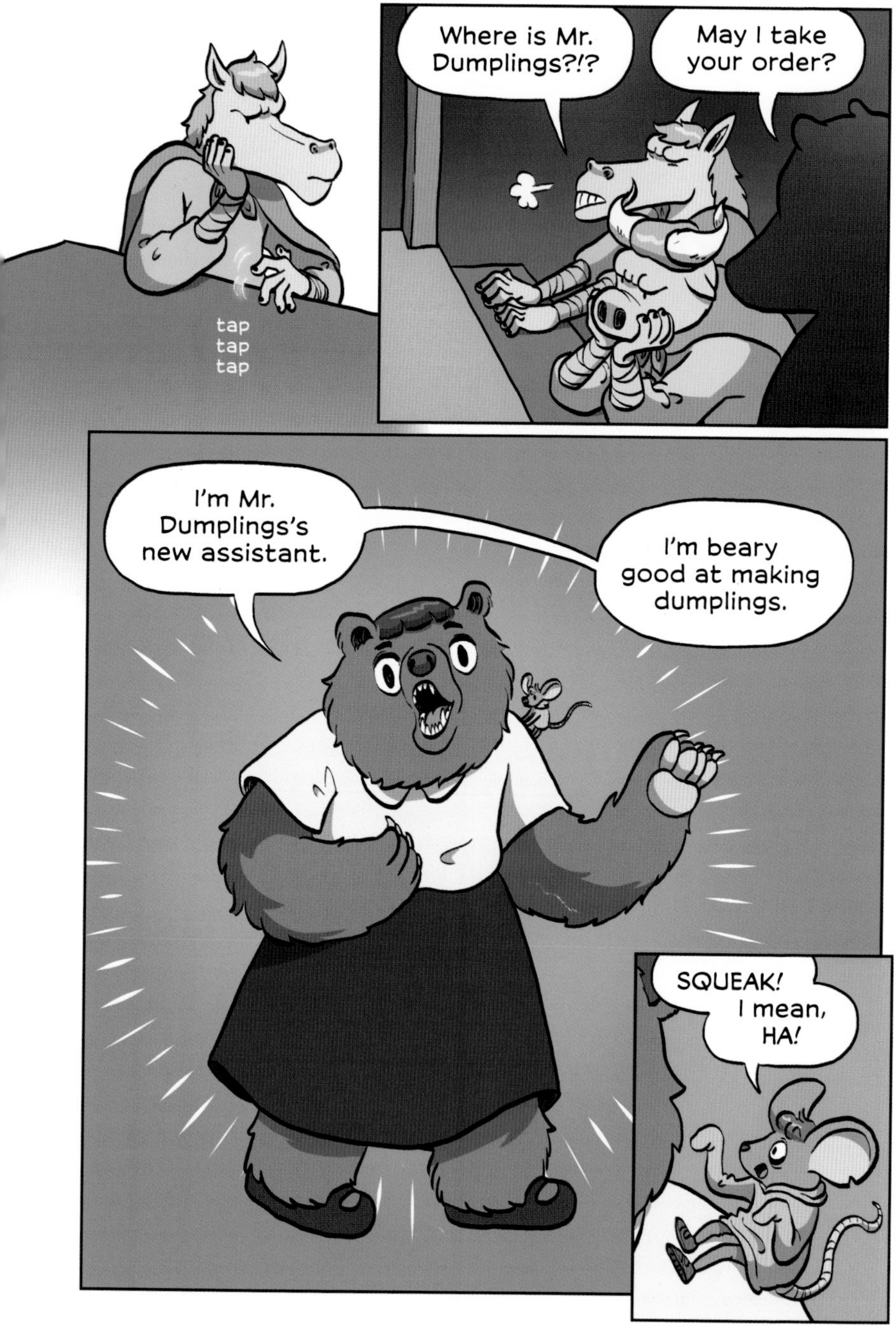
tap
tap
tap
Where is Mr. Dumplings?!?
May I take your order?
I'm Mr. Dumplings's new assistant.
I'm beary good at making dumplings.
SQUEAK! I mean, HA!

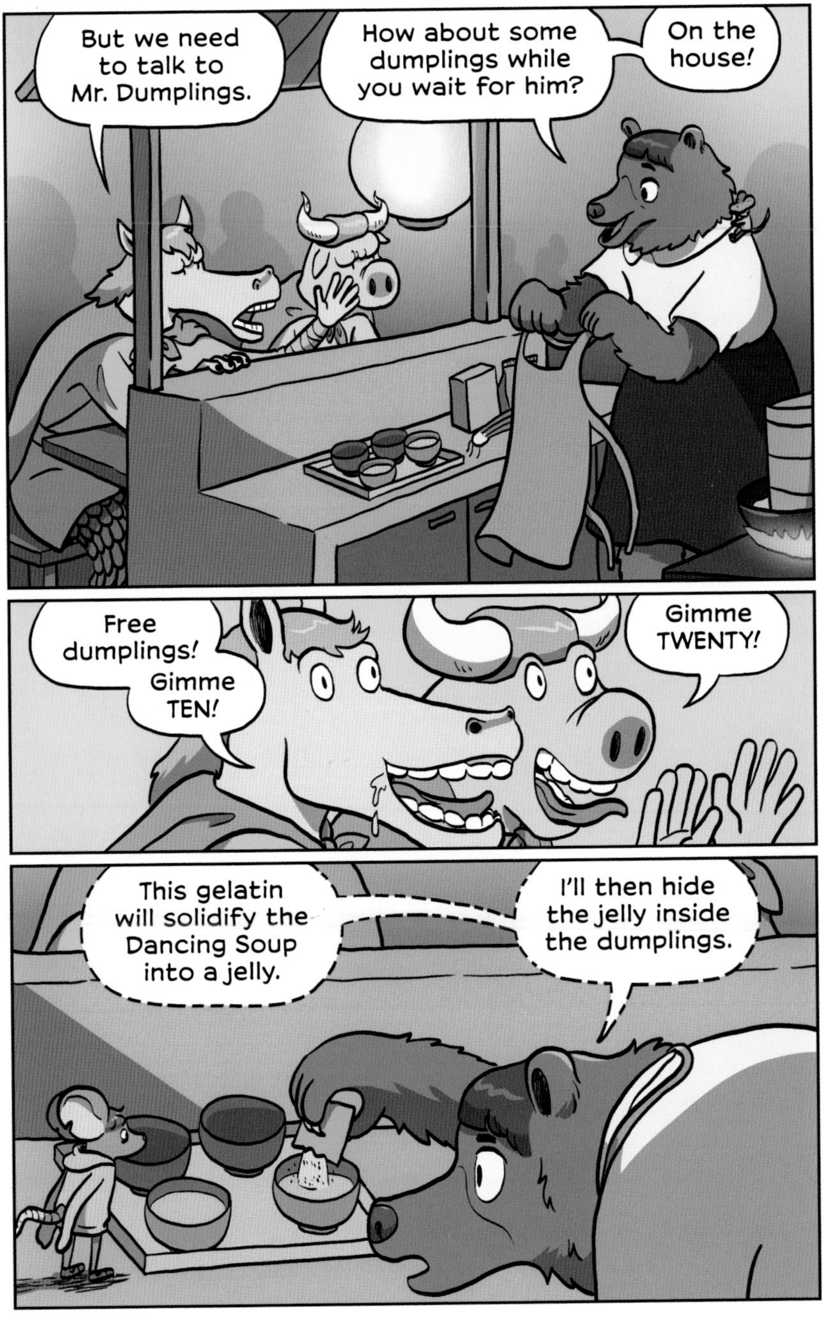
But we need to talk to Mr. Dumplings.
How about some dumplings while you wait for him?
On the house!
Free dumplings! Gimme TEN!
Gimme TWENTY!
This gelatin will solidify the Dancing Soup into a jelly.
I'll then hide the jelly inside the dumplings.

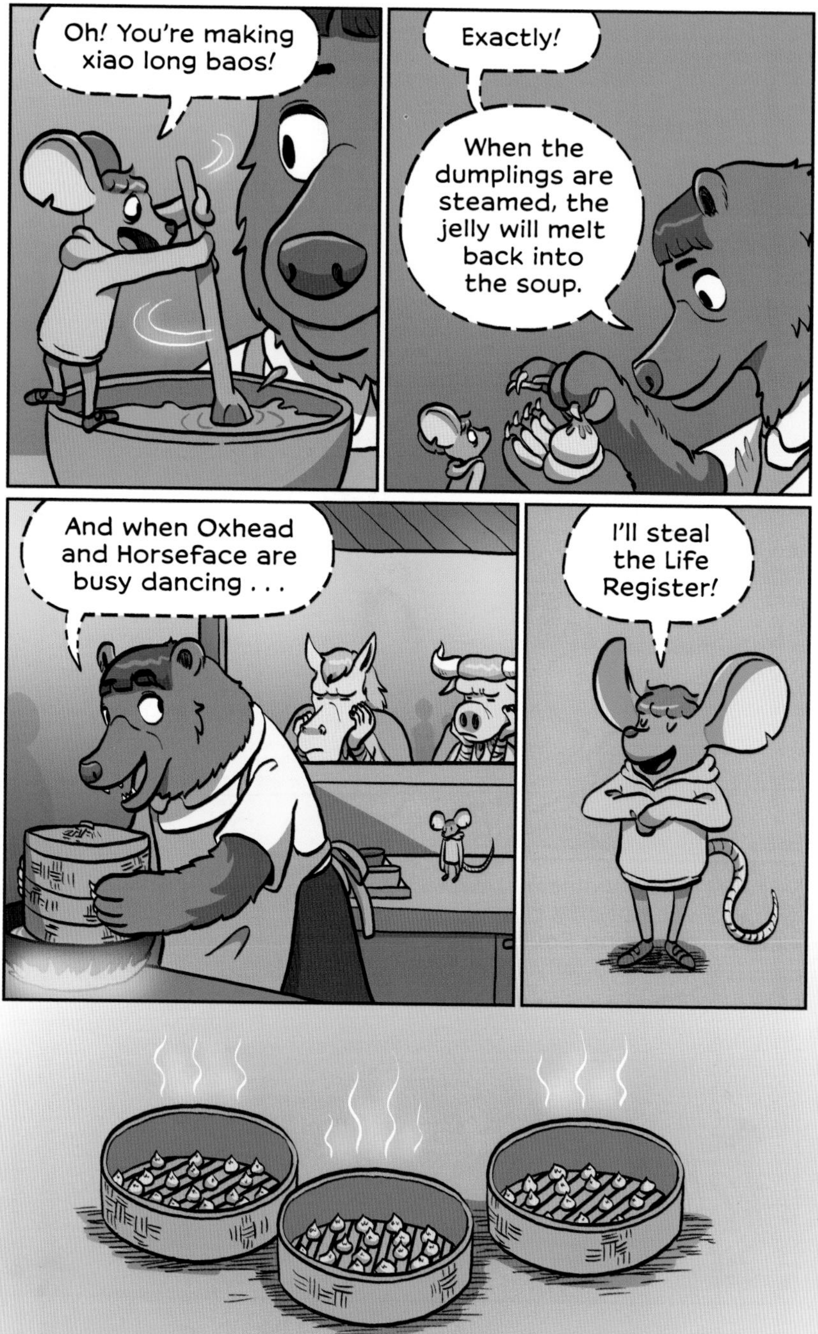
Oh! You're making xiao long baos!
Exactly!
When the dumplings are steamed, the jelly will melt back into the soup.
And when Oxhead and Horseface are busy dancing . . .
I'll steal the Life Register!

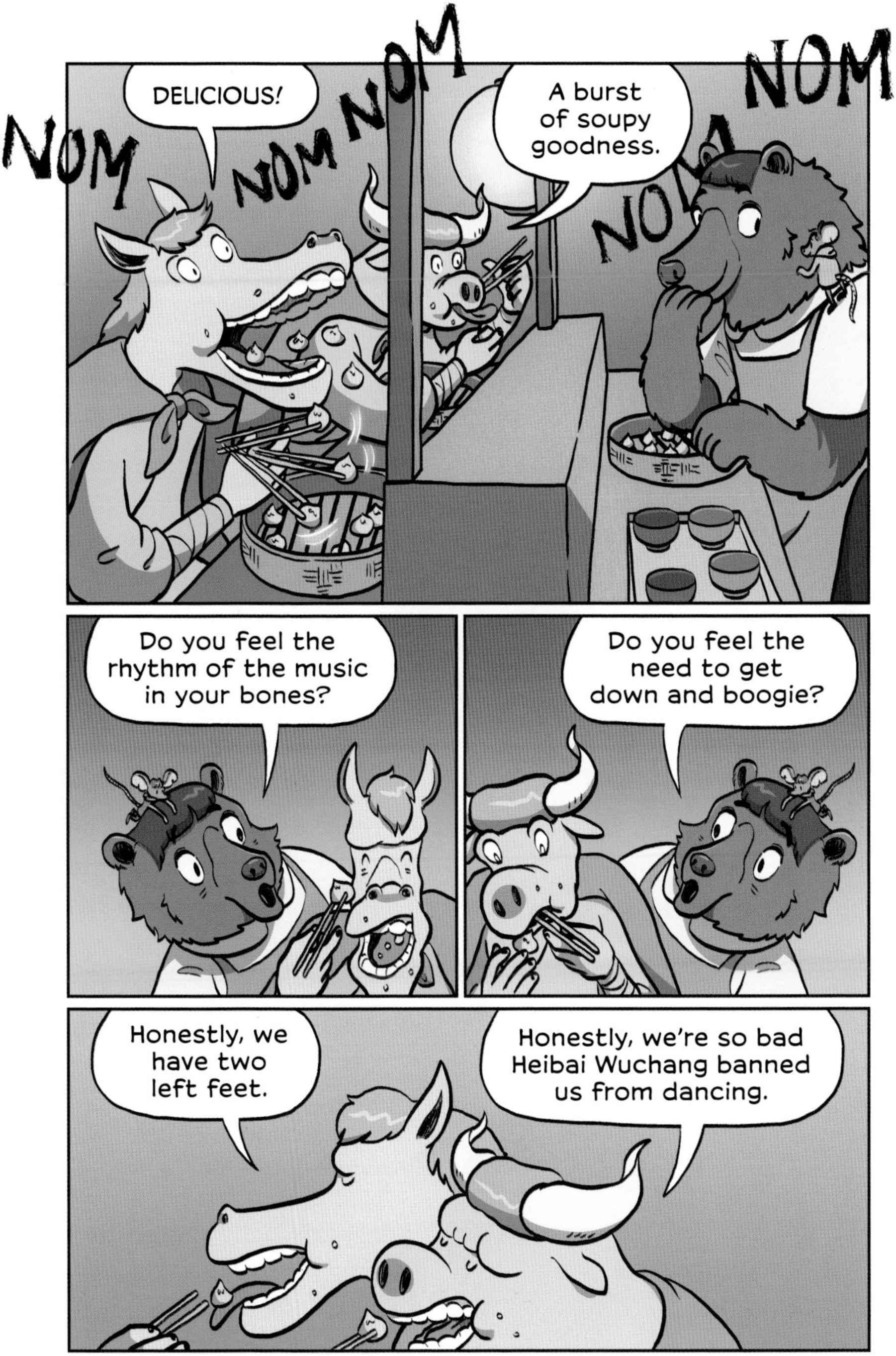

NOM
DELICIOUS!
NOM NOM NOM
A burst of soupy goodness.
NOM NOM
Do you feel the rhythm of the music in your bones?
Do you feel the need to get down and boogie?
Honestly, we have two left feet.
Honestly, we're so bad Heibai Wuchang banned us from dancing.

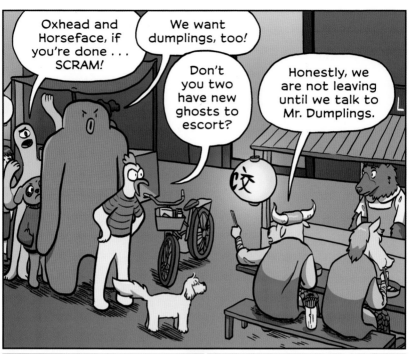

Oxhead and Horseface, if you're done . . . SCRAM!

We want dumplings, too!

Don't you two have new ghosts to escort?

Honestly, we are not leaving until we talk to Mr. Dumplings.

Oxhead and Horseface were evil when they were alive, too.

That's why the King of the Underworld made them ghost-collectors as a punishment.

And now they're here every night, demanding free dumplings from Mr. Dumplings!

Honestly, we have a deal with Mr. Dumplings.

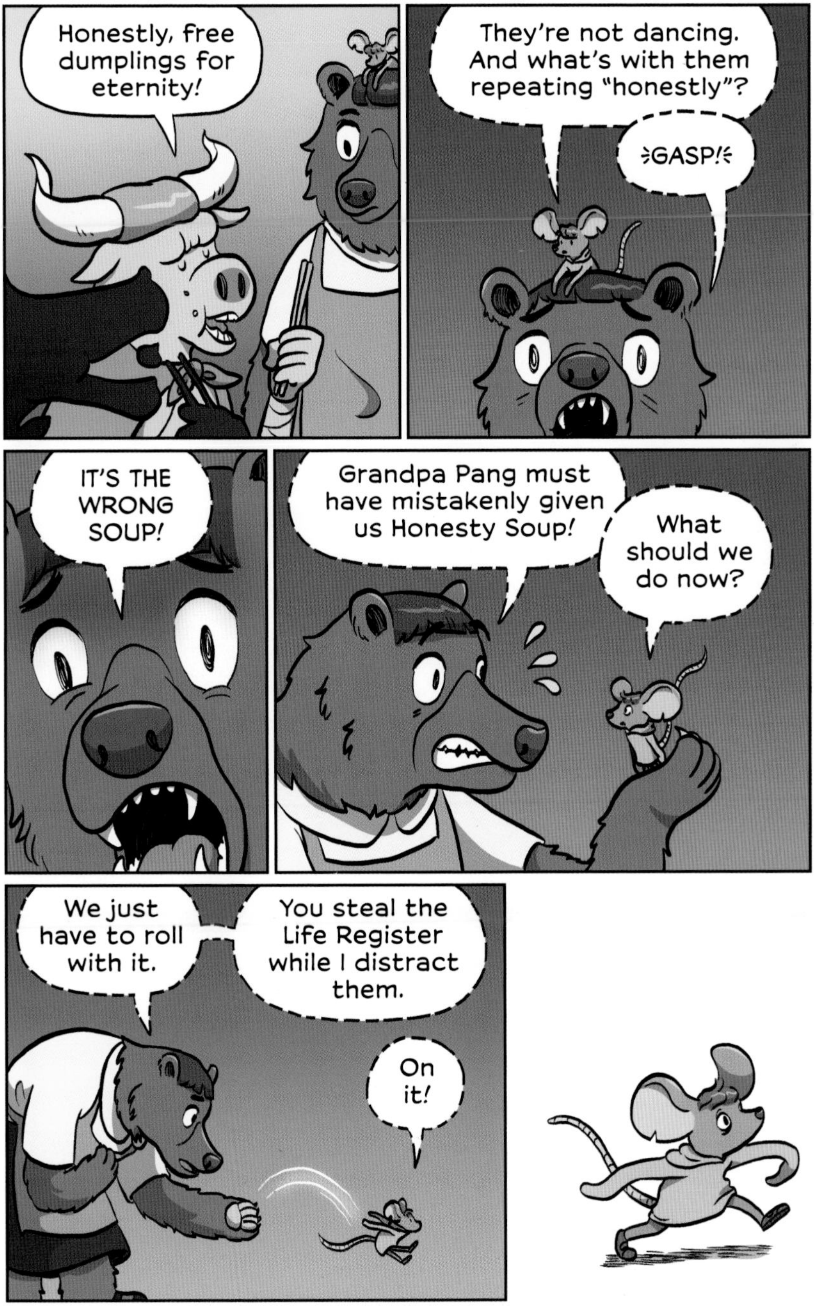
Honestly, free dumplings for eternity!
They're not dancing. And what's with them repeating "honestly"?
GASP!
IT'S THE WRONG SOUP!
Grandpa Pang must have mistakenly given us Honesty Soup!
What should we do now?
We just have to roll with it.
You steal the Life Register while I distract them.
On it!

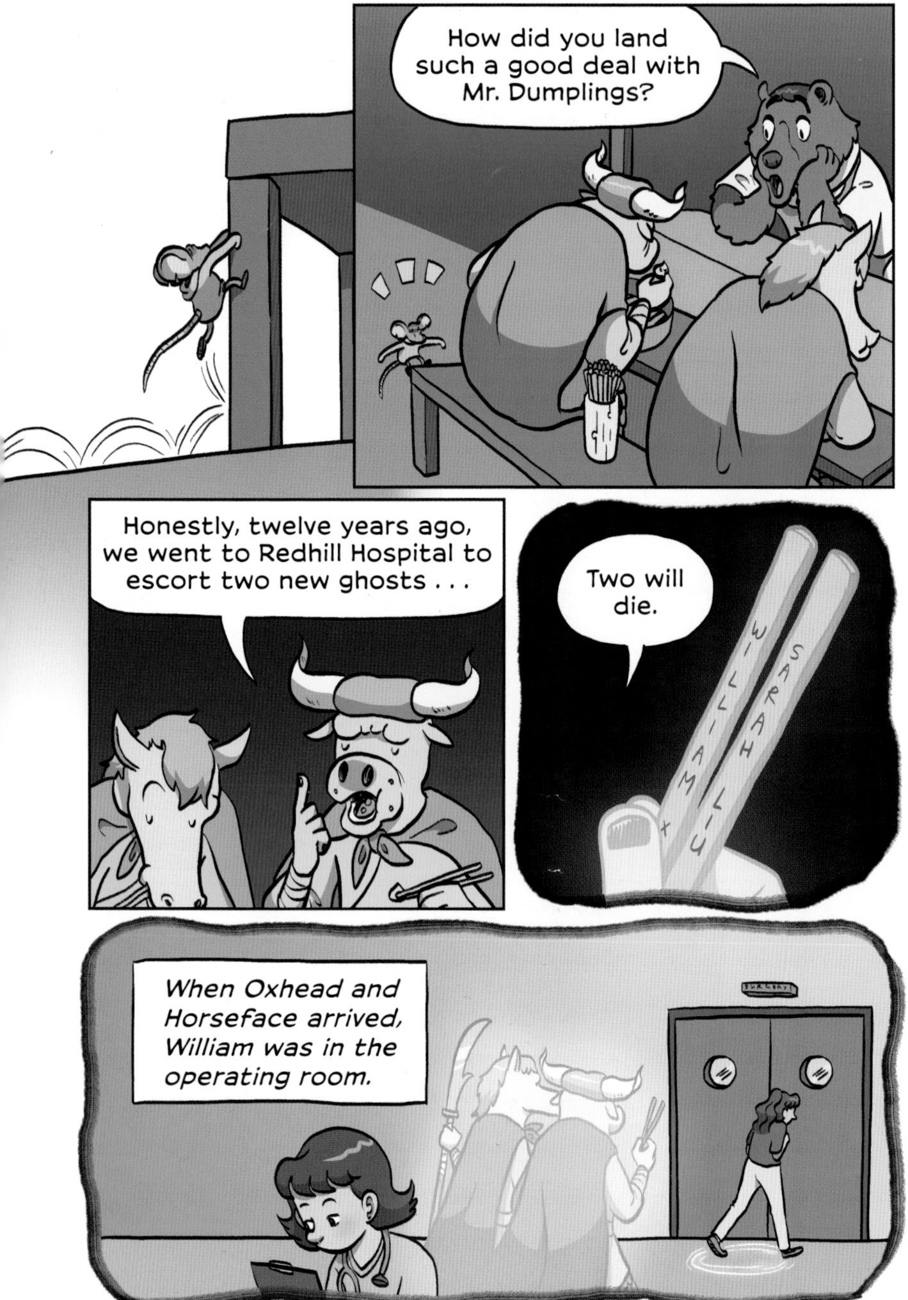
How did you land such a good deal with Mr. Dumplings?
Honestly, twelve years ago, we went to Redhill Hospital to escort two new ghosts . . .
Two will die.
WILLIAM
SARAH LIU
When Oxhead and Horseface arrived, William was in the operating room.

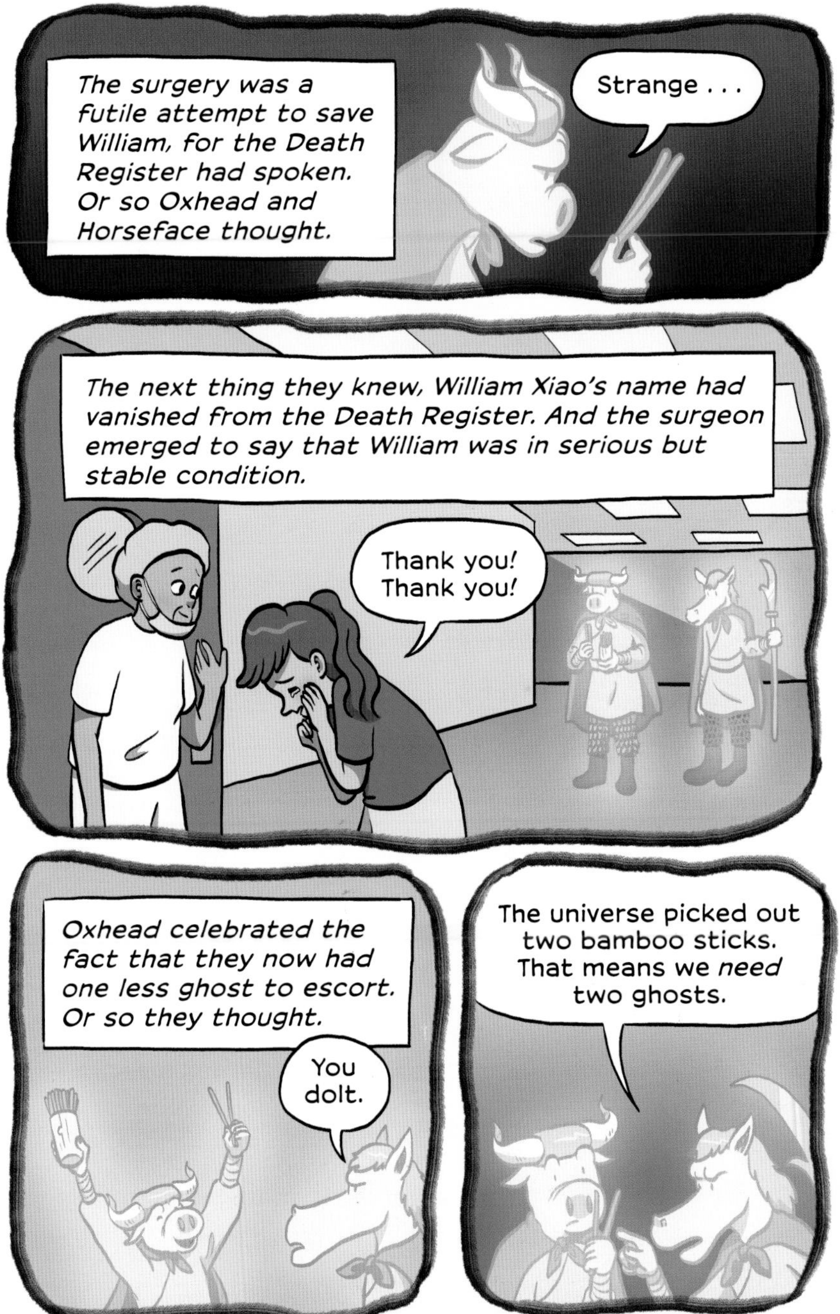
The surgery was a futile attempt to save William, for the Death Register had spoken. Or so Oxhead and Horseface thought.
Strange . . .
The next thing they knew, William Xiao's name had vanished from the Death Register. And the surgeon emerged to say that William was in serious but stable condition.
Thank you! Thank you!
Oxhead celebrated the fact that they now had one less ghost to escort. Or so they thought.
You dolt.
The universe picked out two bamboo sticks. That means we *need* two ghosts.

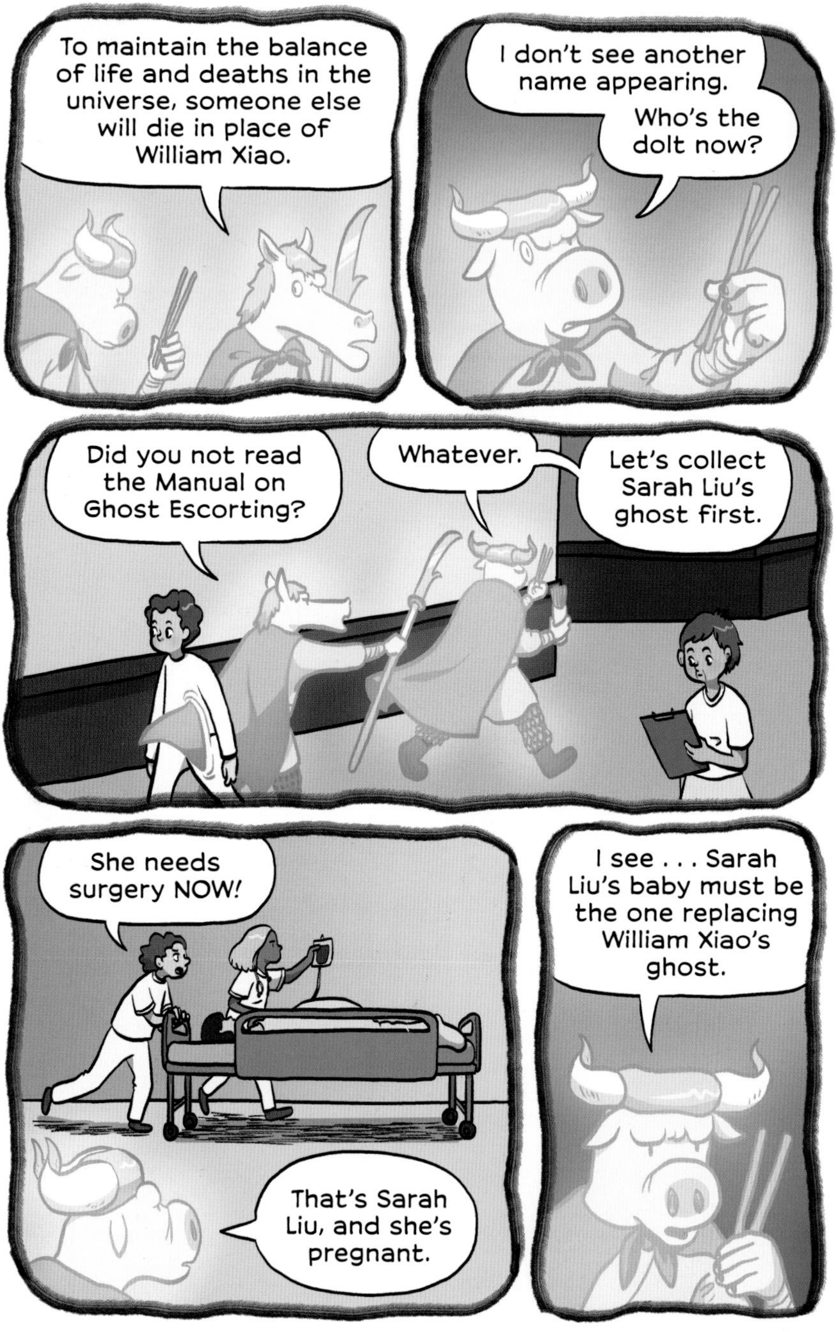
To maintain the balance of life and deaths in the universe, someone else will die in place of William Xiao.
I don't see another name appearing.
Who's the dolt now?
Did you not read the Manual on Ghost Escorting?
Whatever.
Let's collect Sarah Liu's ghost first.
She needs surgery NOW!
That's Sarah Liu, and she's pregnant.
I see . . . Sarah Liu's baby must be the one replacing William Xiao's ghost.

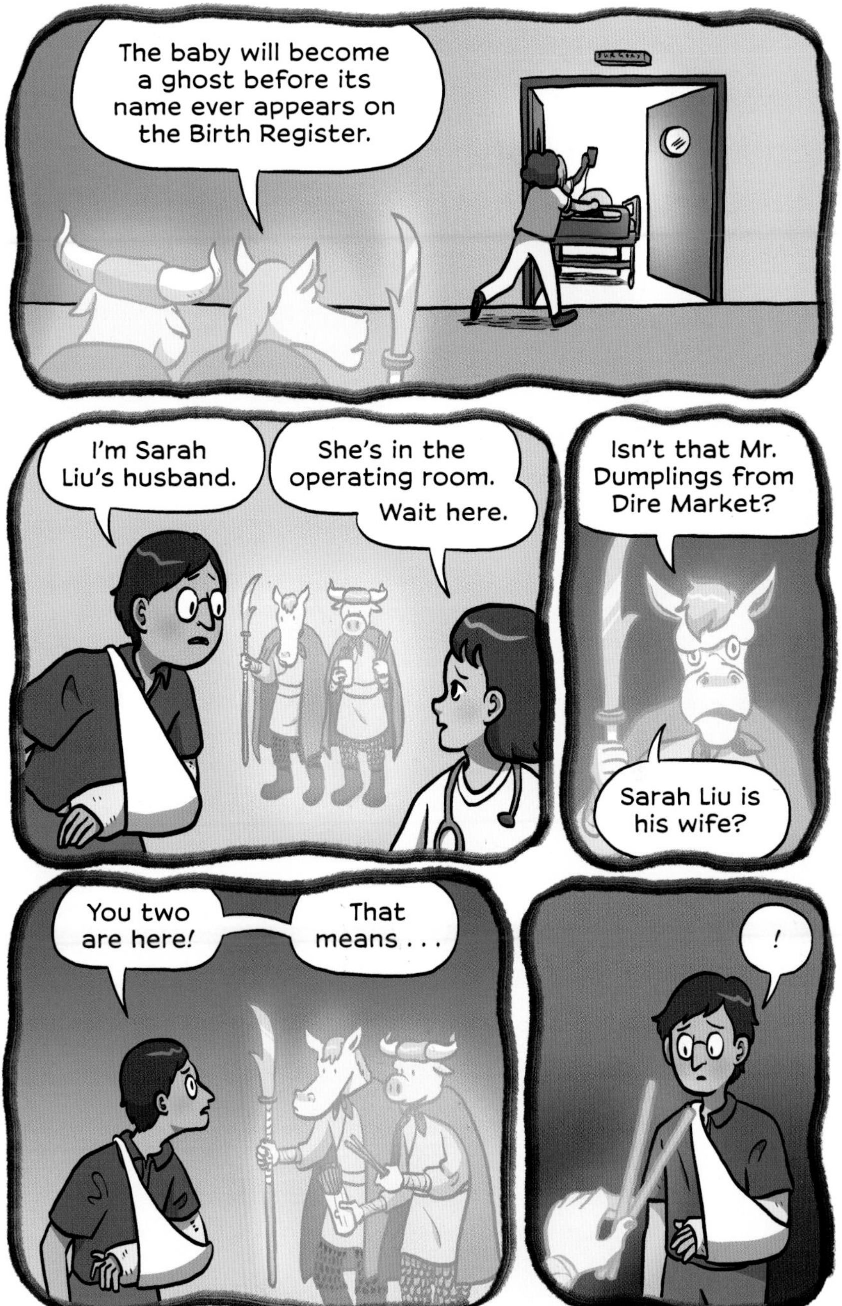
The baby will become a ghost before its name ever appears on the Birth Register.
I'm Sarah Liu's husband.
She's in the operating room.
Wait here.
Isn't that Mr. Dumplings from Dire Market?
Sarah Liu is his wife?
You two are here!
That means . . .
!

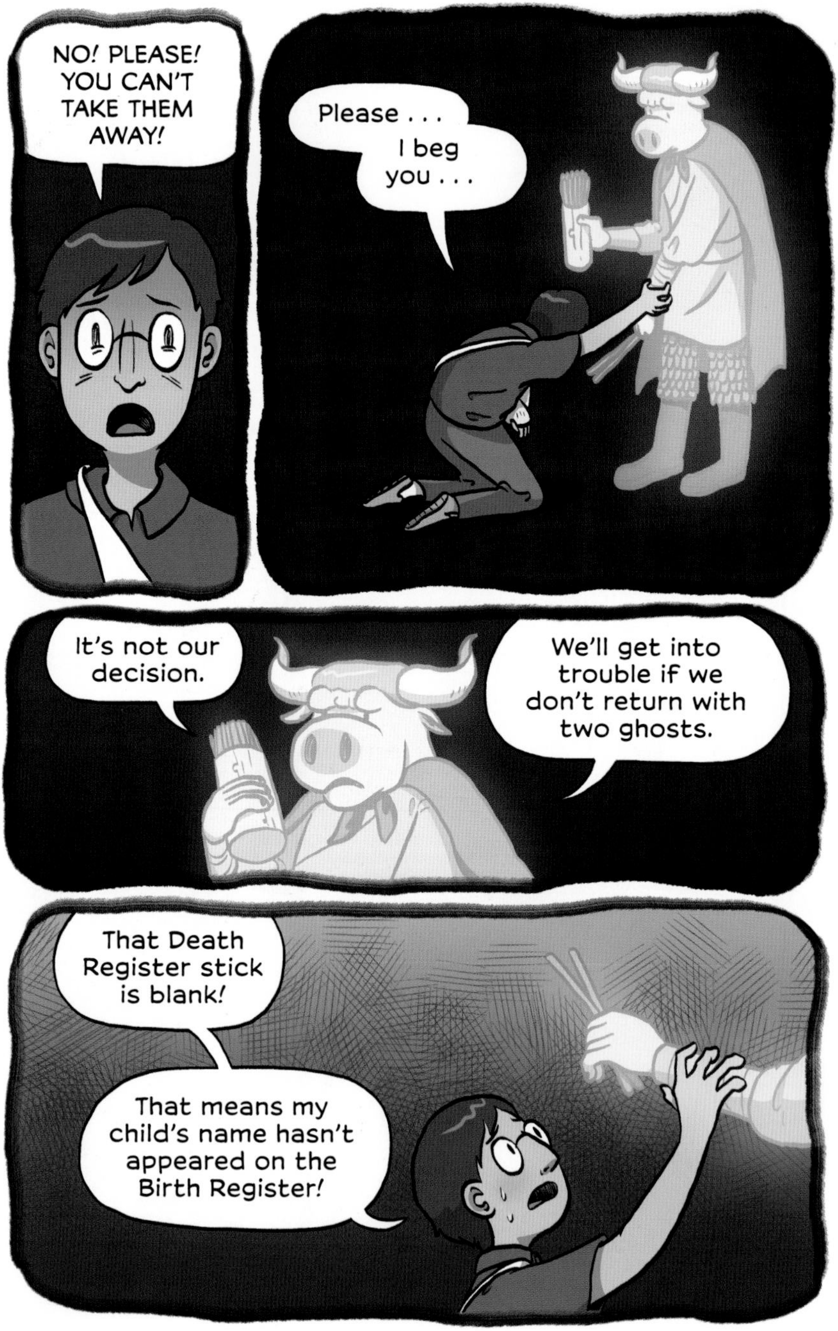
NO! PLEASE! YOU CAN'T TAKE THEM AWAY!
Please . . .
I beg you . . .
It's not our decision.
We'll get into trouble if we don't return with two ghosts.
That Death Register stick is blank!
That means my child's name hasn't appeared on the Birth Register!

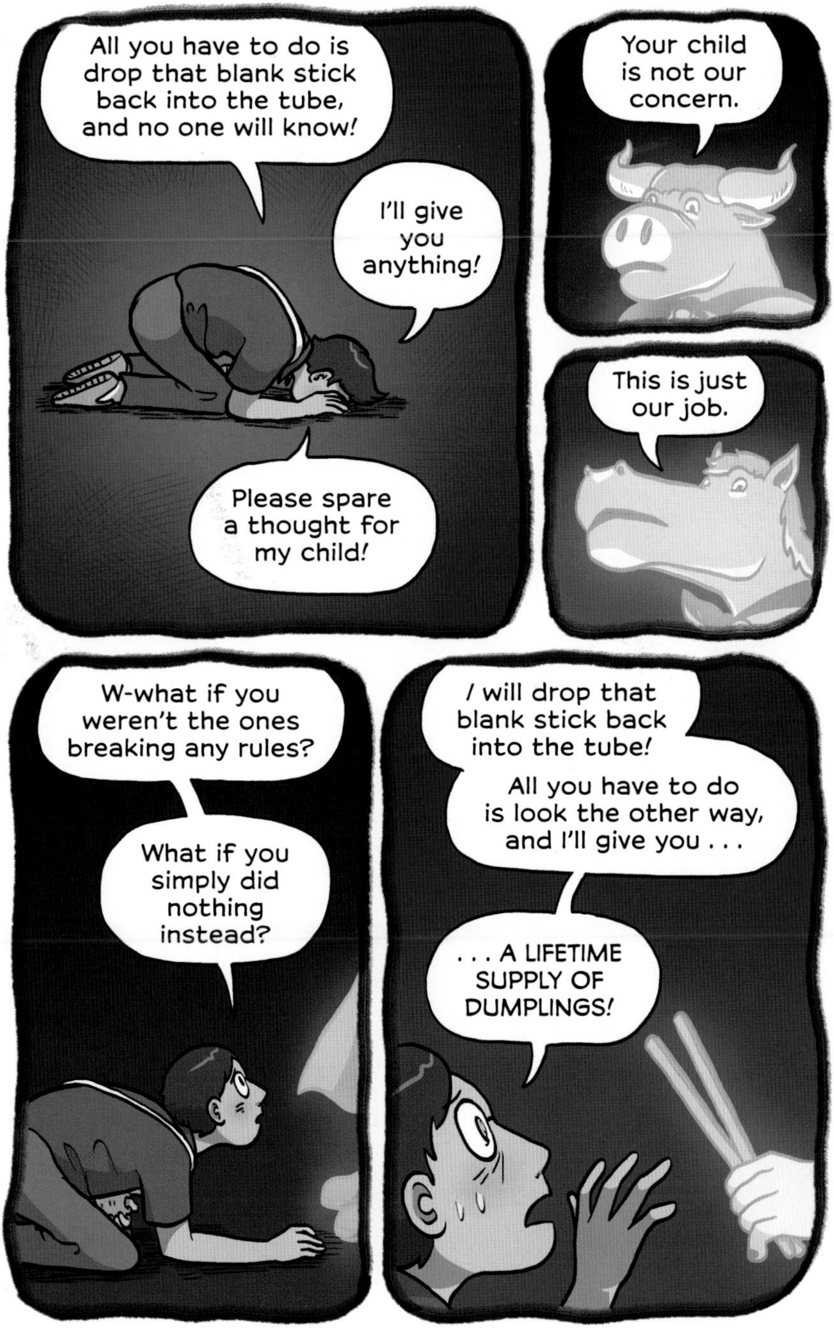
All you have to do is drop that blank stick back into the tube, and no one will know!
I'll give you anything!
Please spare a thought for my child!
Your child is not our concern.
This is just our job.
W-what if you weren't the ones breaking any rules?
What if you simply did nothing instead?
I will drop that blank stick back into the tube!
All you have to do is look the other way, and I'll give you . . .
. . . A LIFETIME SUPPLY OF DUMPLINGS!

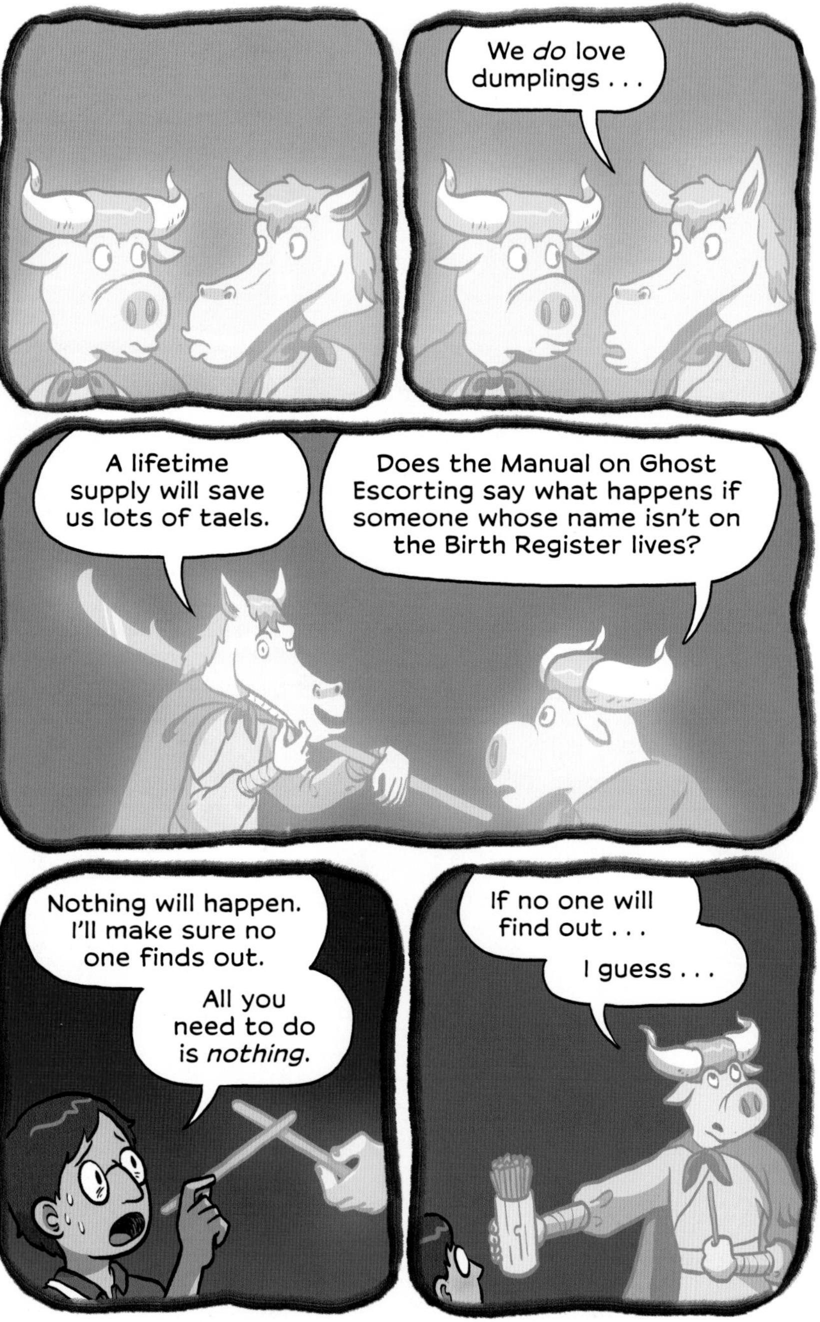
We *do* love dumplings . . .
A lifetime supply will save us lots of taels.
Does the Manual on Ghost Escorting say what happens if someone whose name isn't on the Birth Register lives?
Nothing will happen. I'll make sure no one finds out.
All you need to do is *nothing*.
If no one will find out . . .
I guess . . .

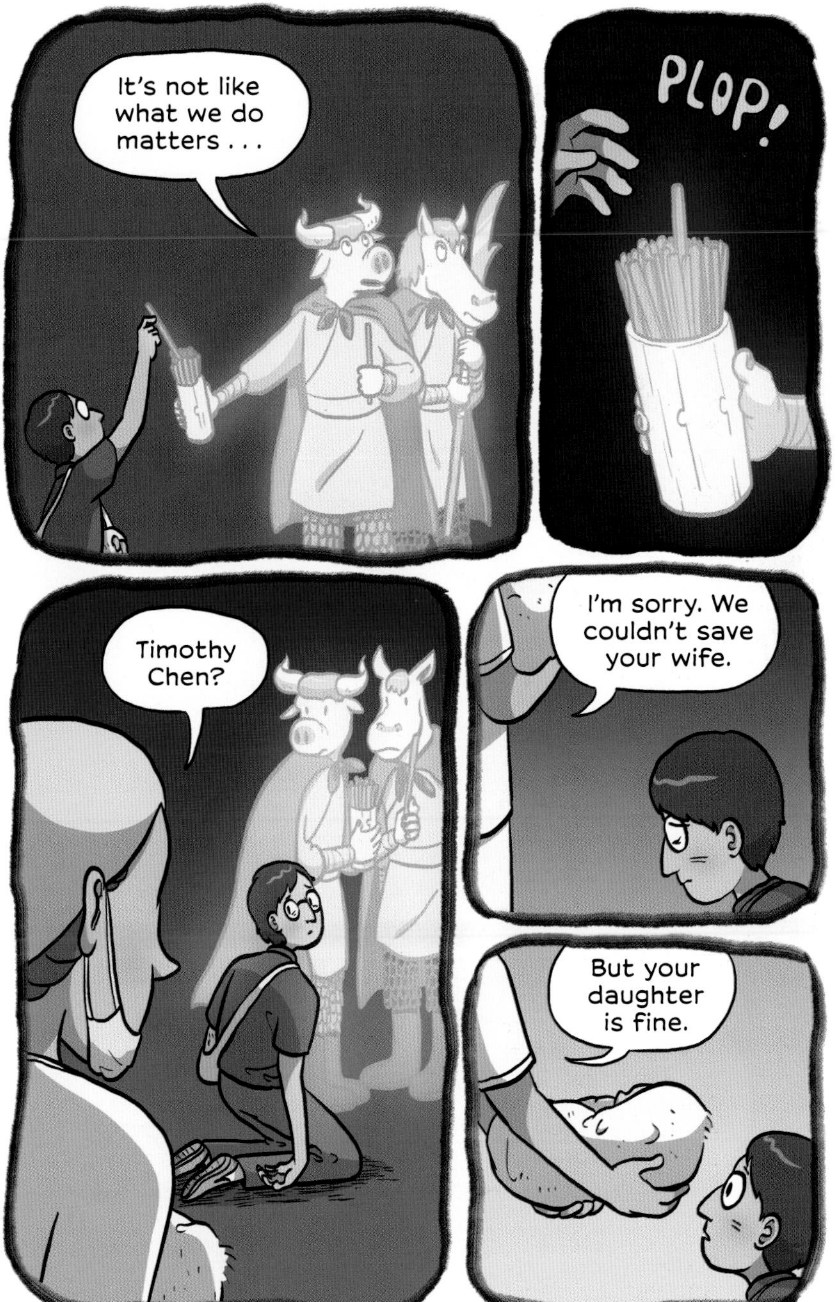
It's not like what we do matters . . .
PLOP!
Timothy Chen?
I'm sorry. We couldn't save your wife.
But your daughter is fine.

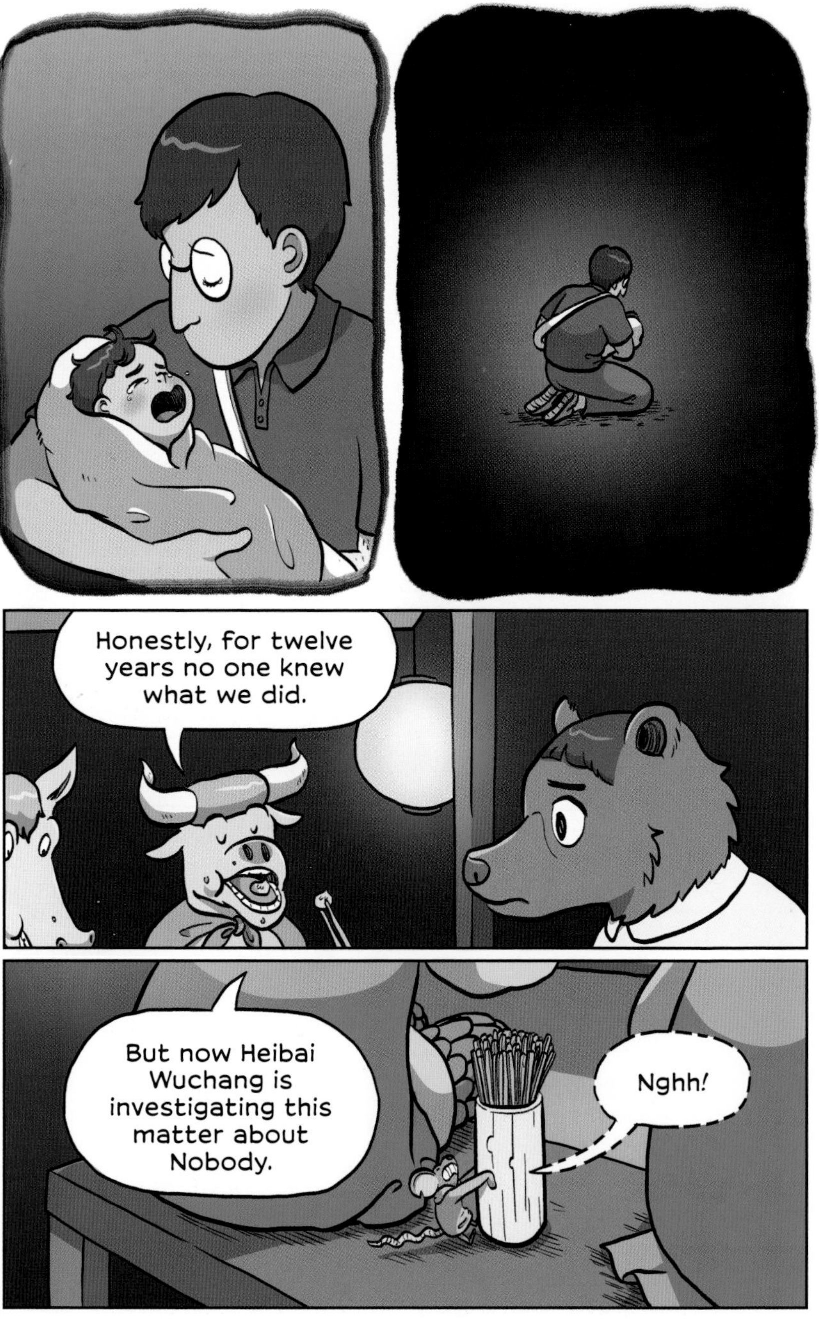
Honestly, for twelve years no one knew what we did.
But now Heibai Wuchang is investigating this matter about Nobody.
Nghh!

Honestly, we have to warn Mr. Dumplings to keep his mouth shut.

Honestly, we thought not collecting that baby's soul was no big deal, but turns out it was a HUGE MISTAKE.

Honestly, we accepted a bribe.

That's a big no-no.

Honestly, it'll be okay, because no one knows but us two.

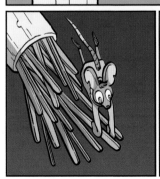

And Mr. Dumplings—

CLACK!

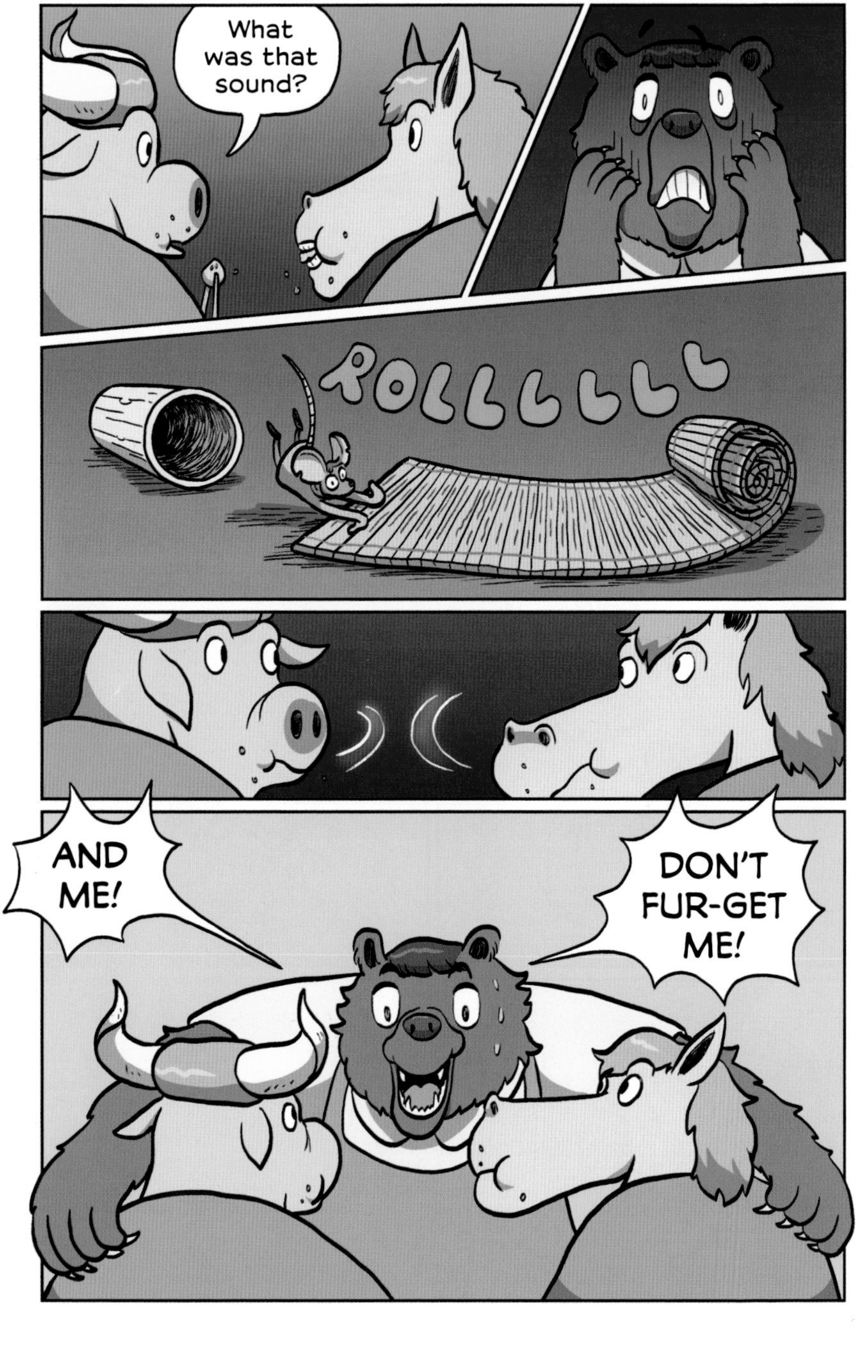
What was that sound?
ROLLLLLL
AND ME!
DON'T FUR-GET ME!

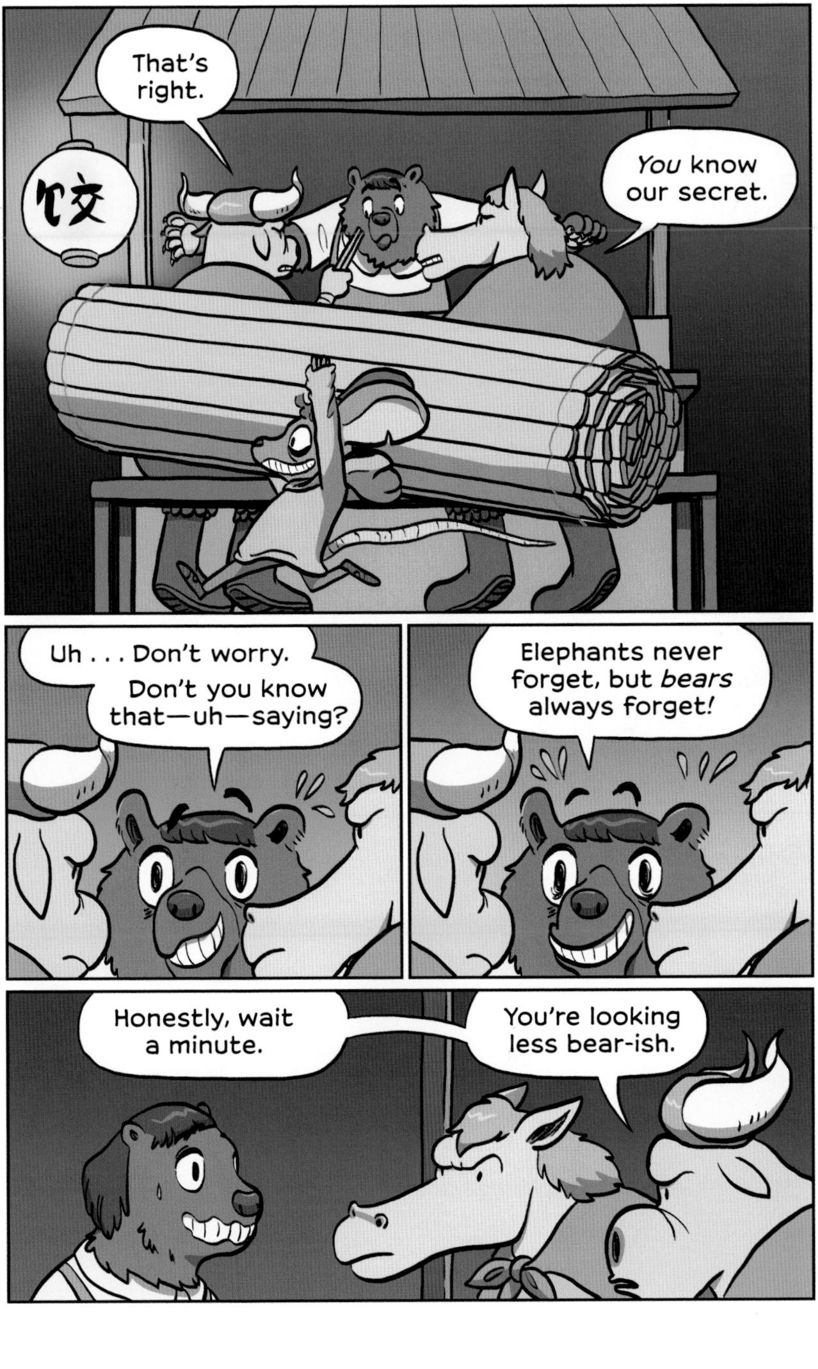
饺
That's right.
You know our secret.
Uh . . . Don't worry.
Don't you know that—uh—saying?
Elephants never forget, but *bears* always forget!
Honestly, wait a minute.
You're looking less bear-ish.

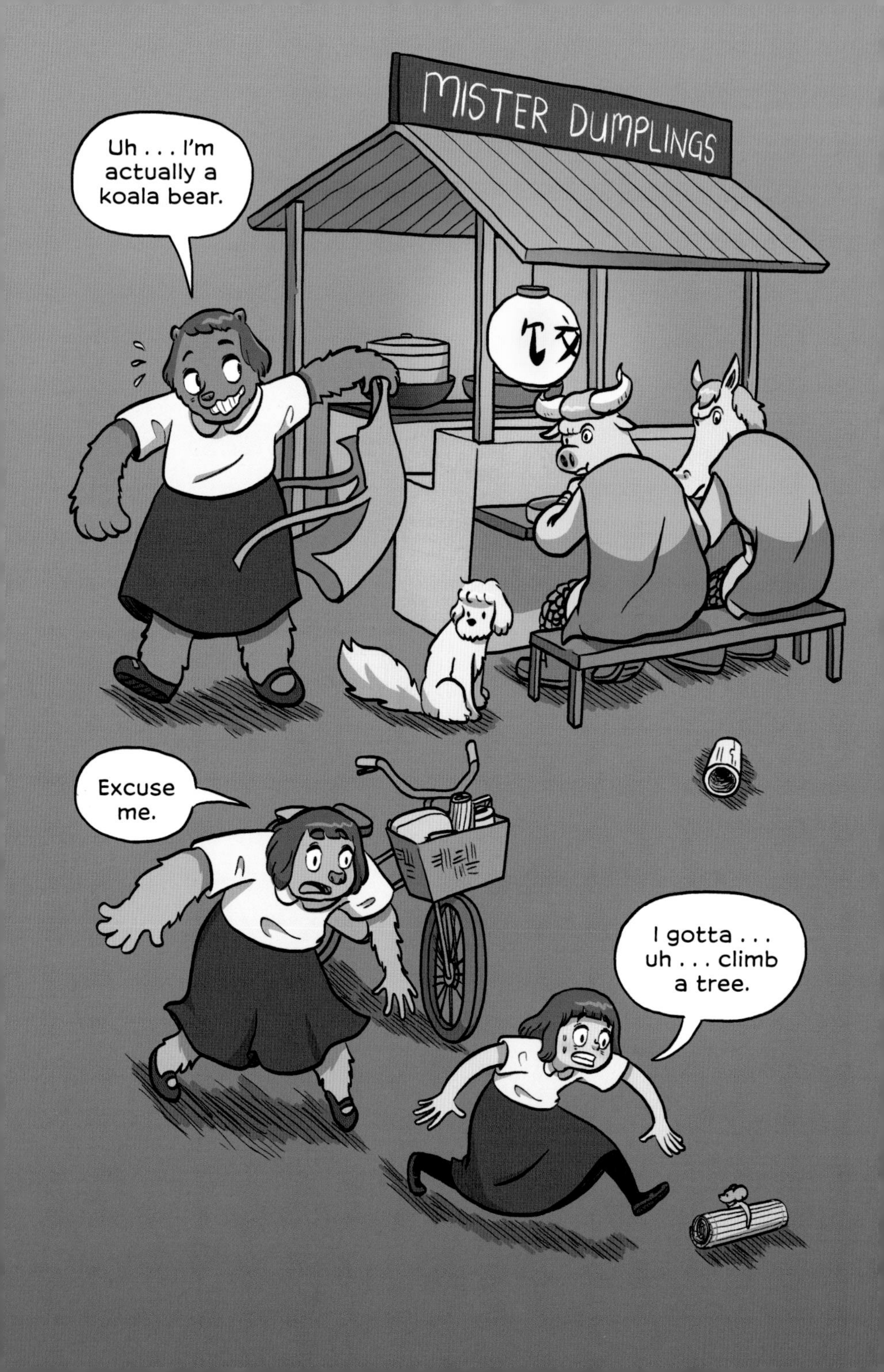
MISTER DUMPLINGS
Uh . . . I'm actually a koala bear.
Excuse me.
I gotta . . . uh . . . climb a tree.

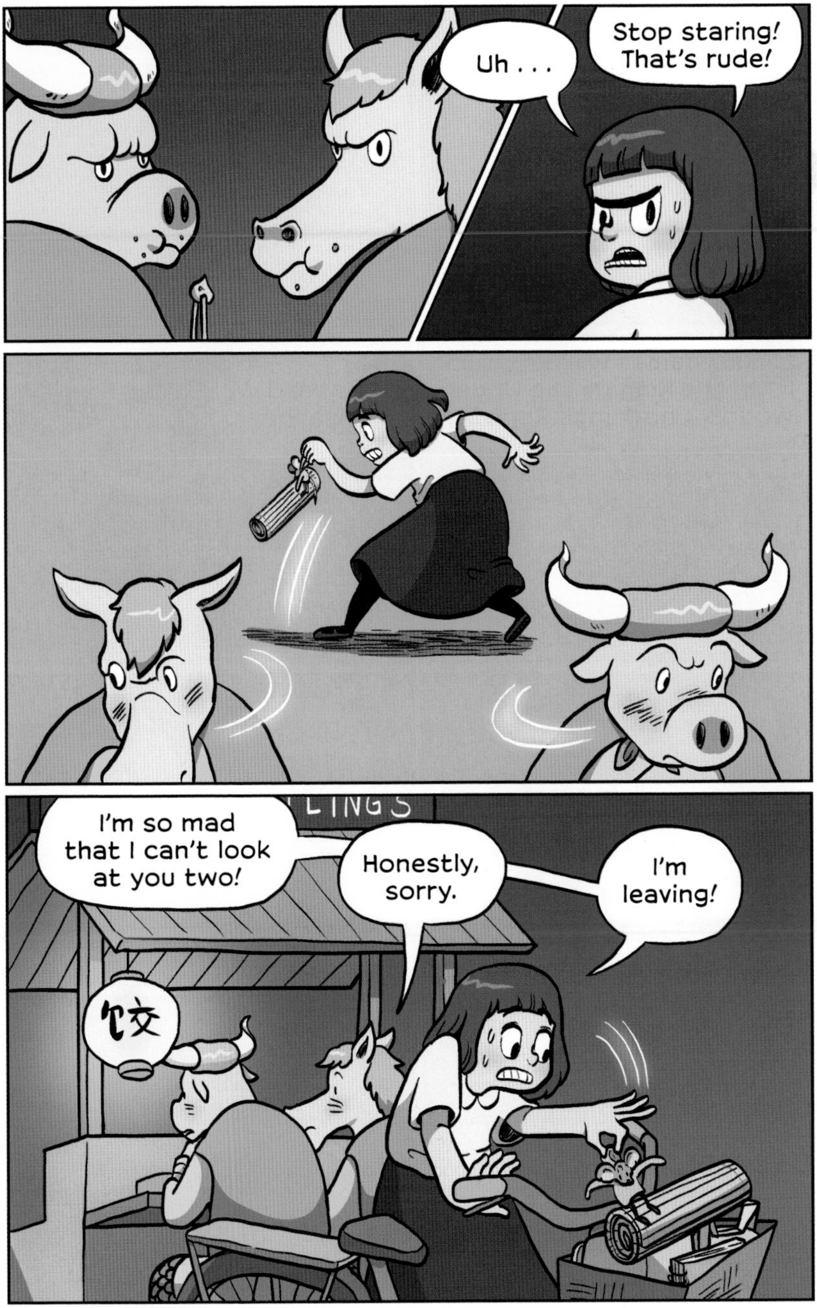
Uh . . .
Stop staring! That's rude!
LINGS
I'm so mad that I can't look at you two!
Honestly, sorry.
I'm leaving!
饺

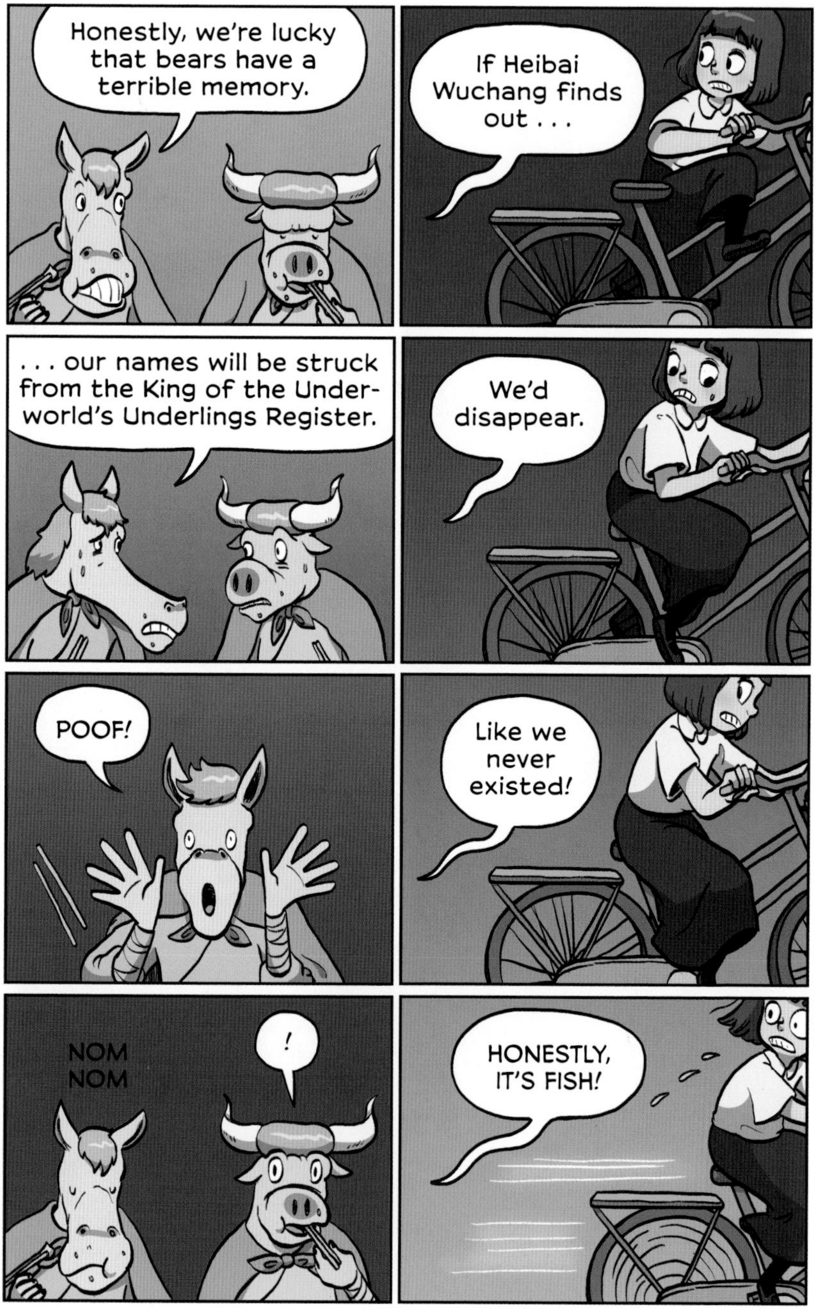
Honestly, we're lucky that bears have a terrible memory.
If Heibai Wuchang finds out . . .
. . . our names will be struck from the King of the Underworld's Underlings Register.
We'd disappear.
POOF!
Like we never existed!
NOM NOM
!
HONESTLY, IT'S FISH!

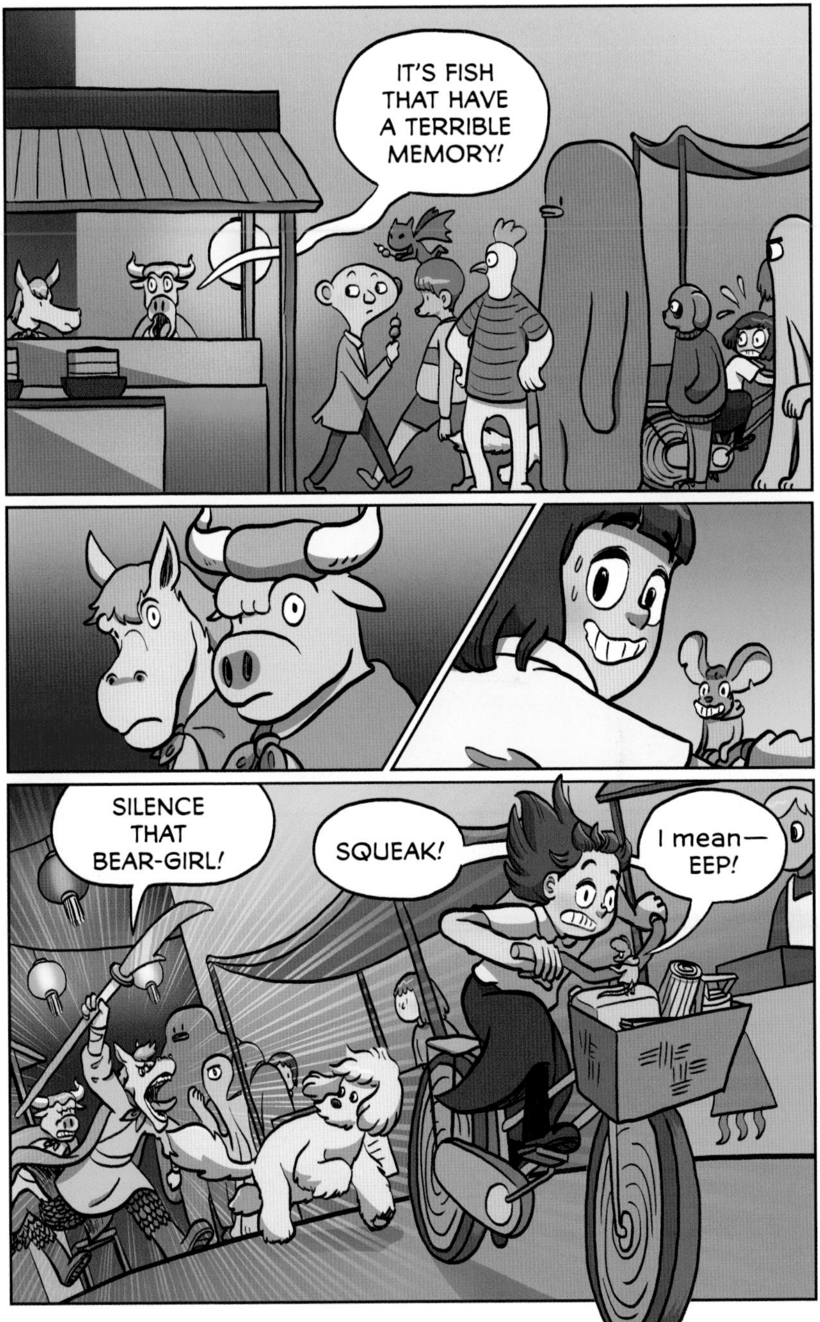
IT'S FISH THAT HAVE A TERRIBLE MEMORY!
SILENCE THAT BEAR-GIRL!
SQUEAK!
I mean—EEP!

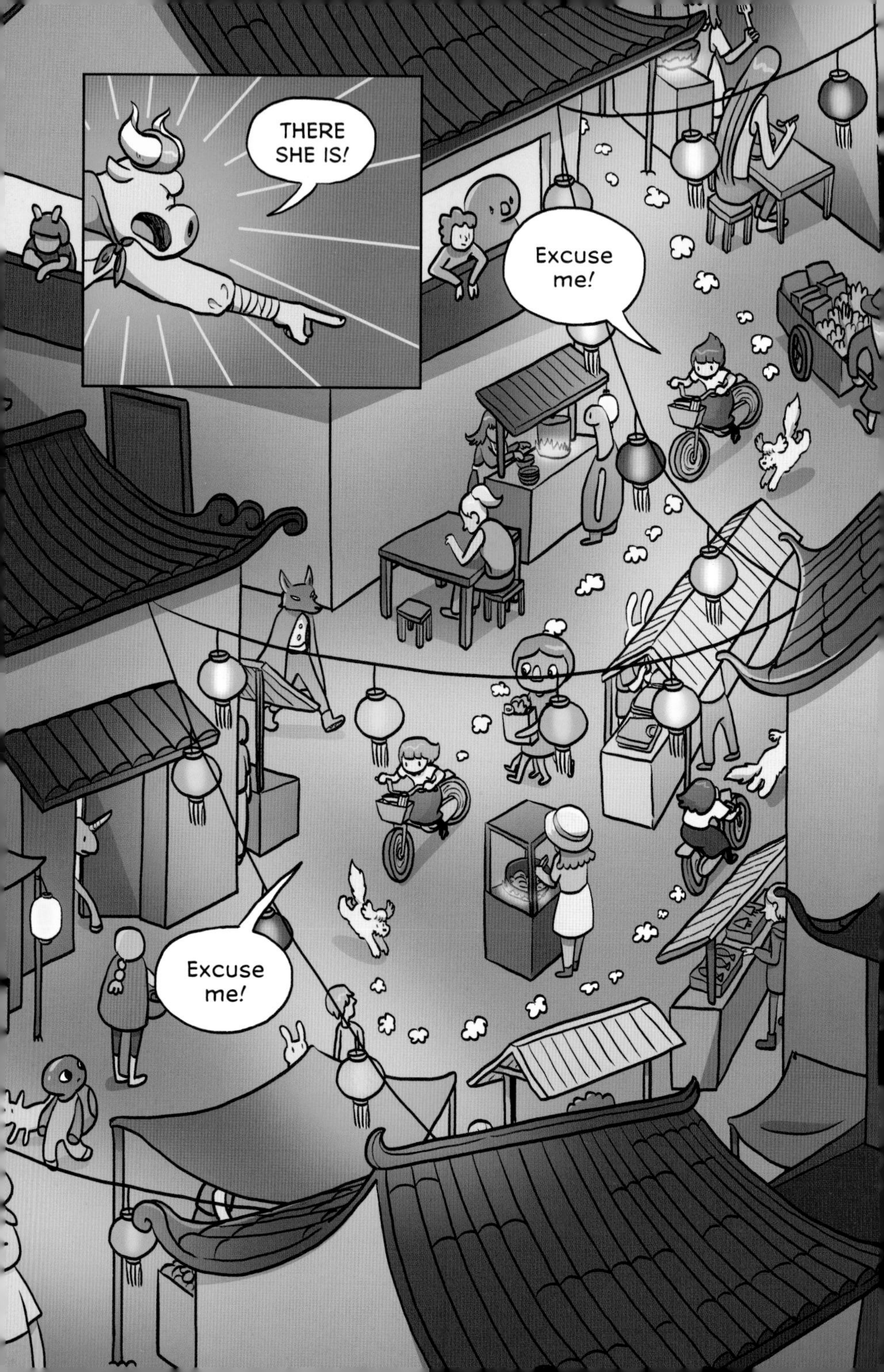
THERE SHE IS!
Excuse me!
Excuse me!

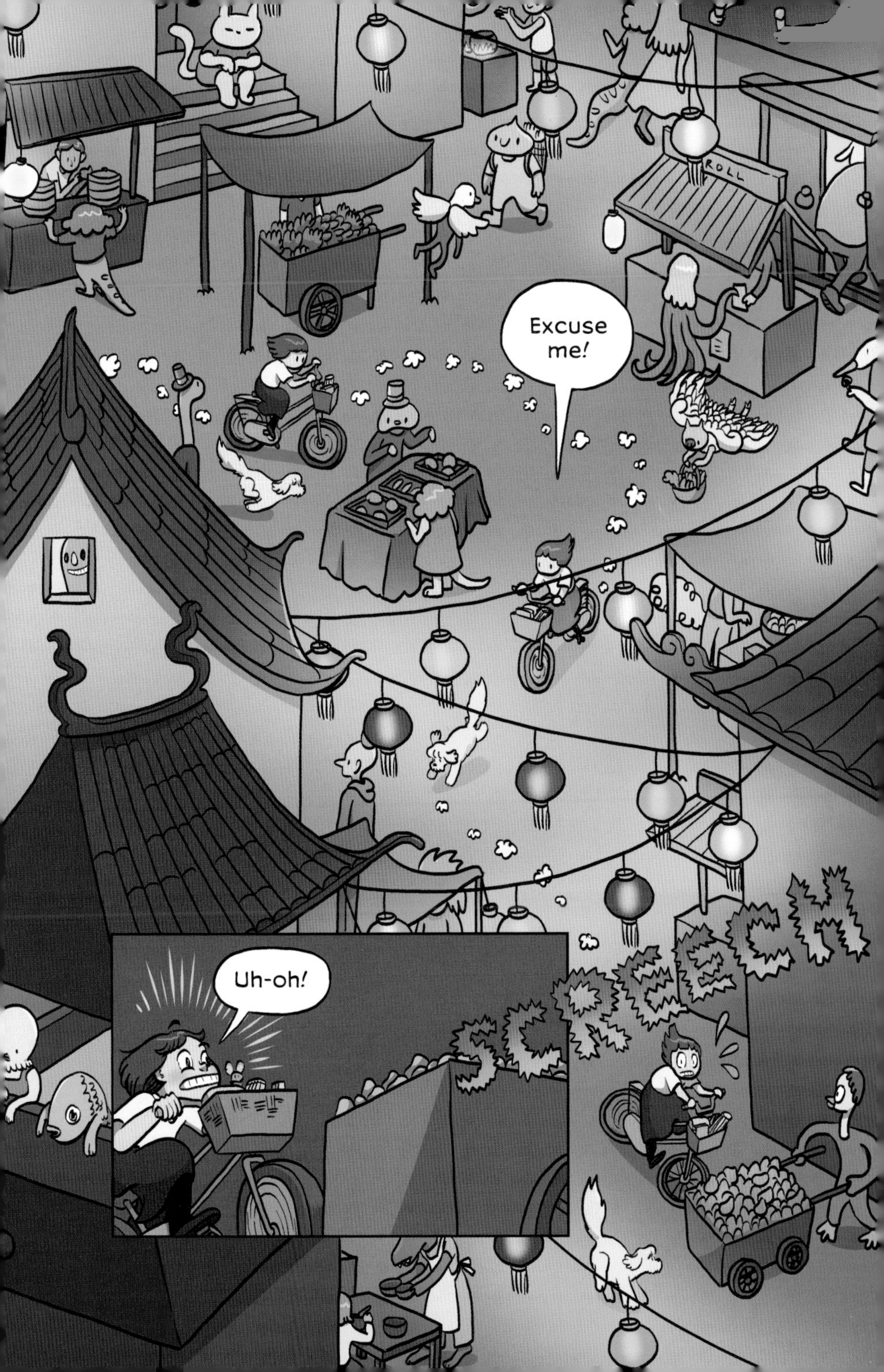
Excuse me!
Uh-oh!
SCREECH

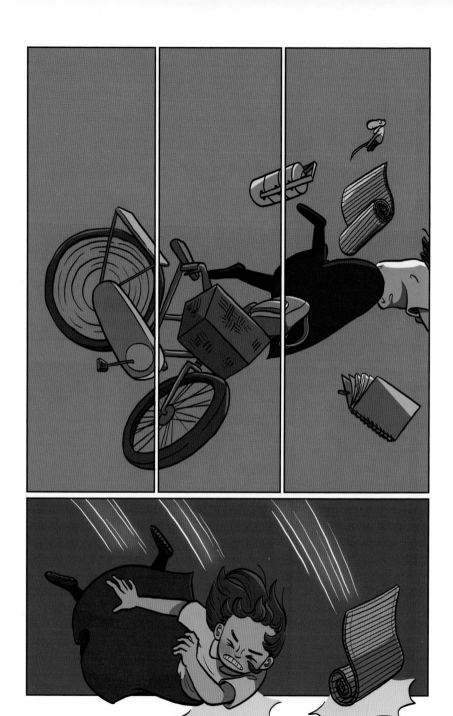

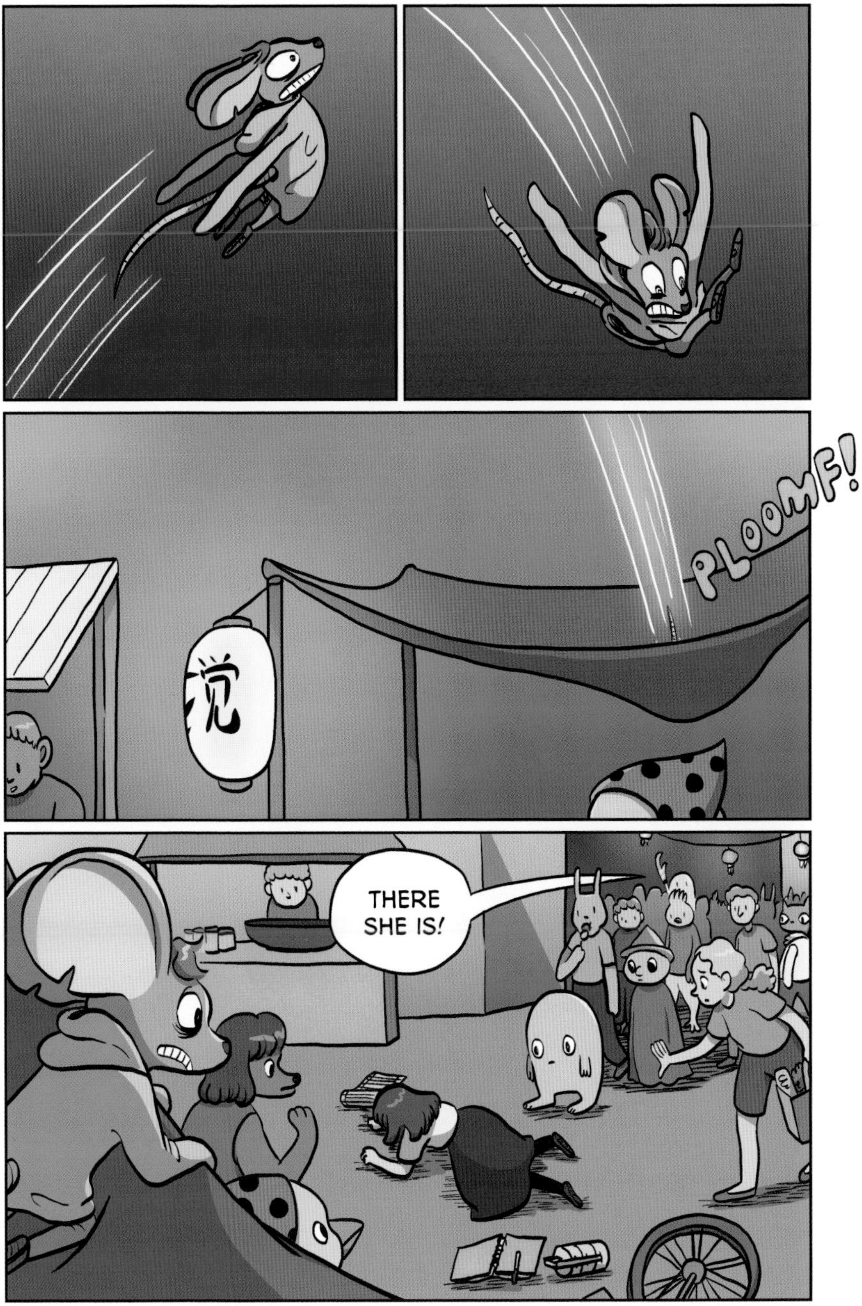
PLOOMF!
THERE SHE IS!

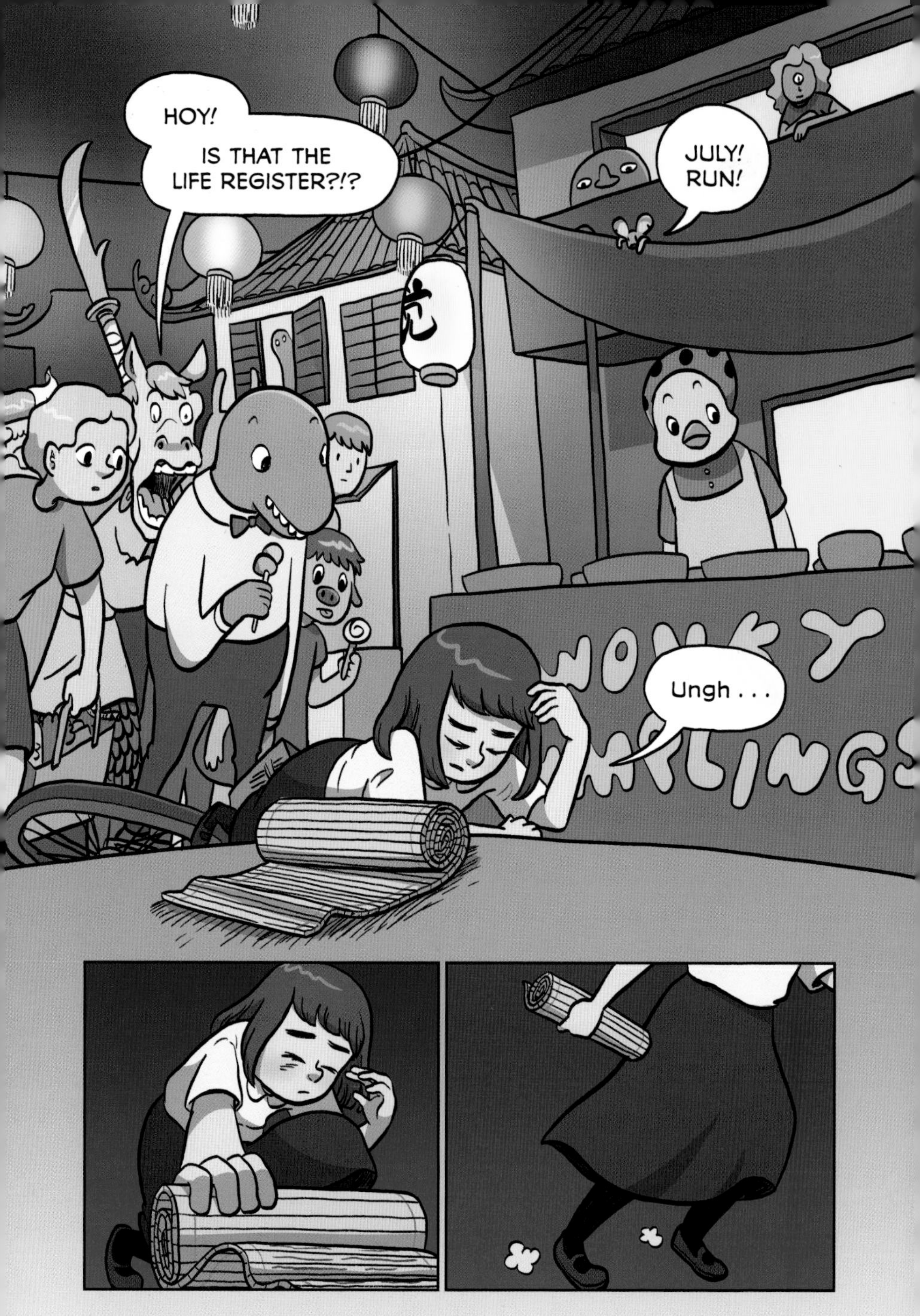
HOY!
IS THAT THE LIFE REGISTER?!?
JULY! RUN!
Ungh . . .

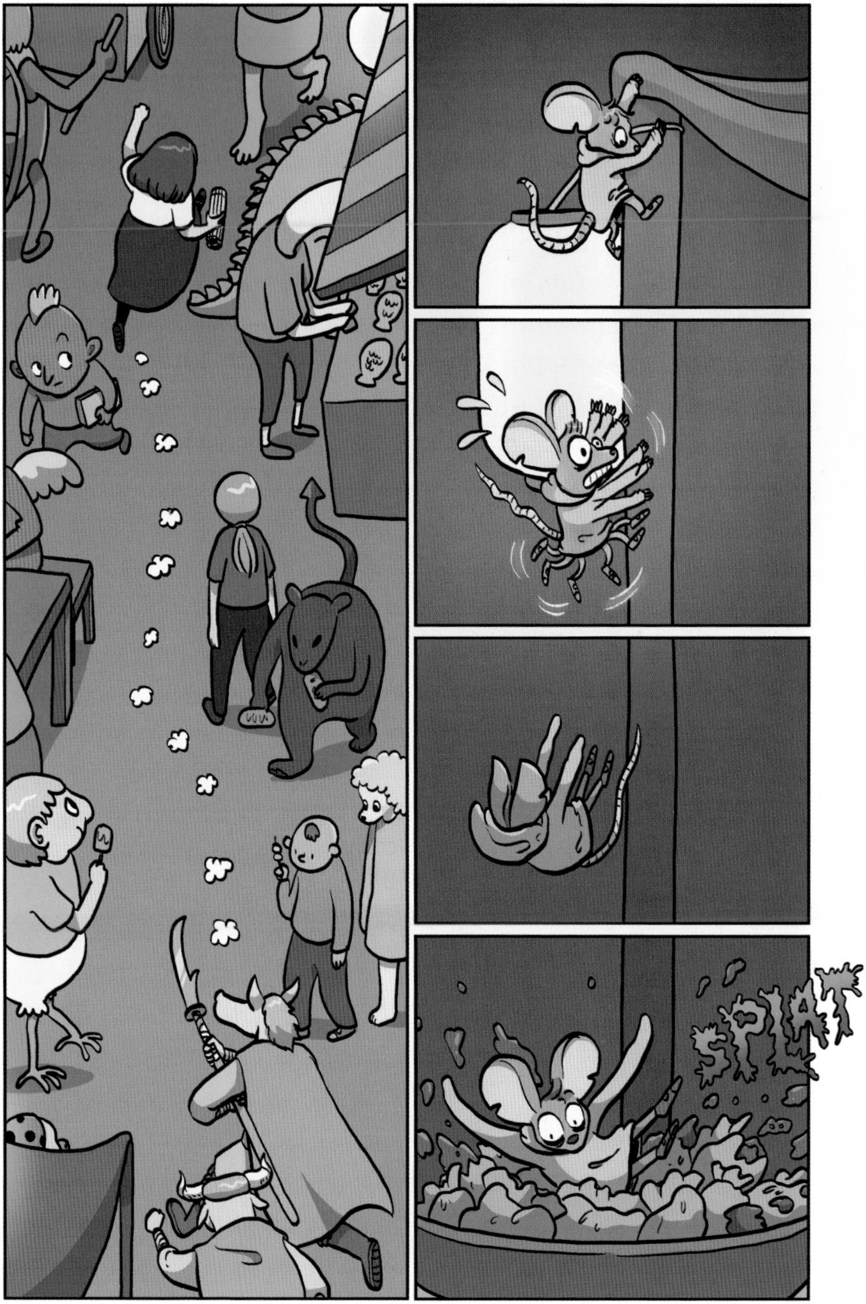
SPLAT

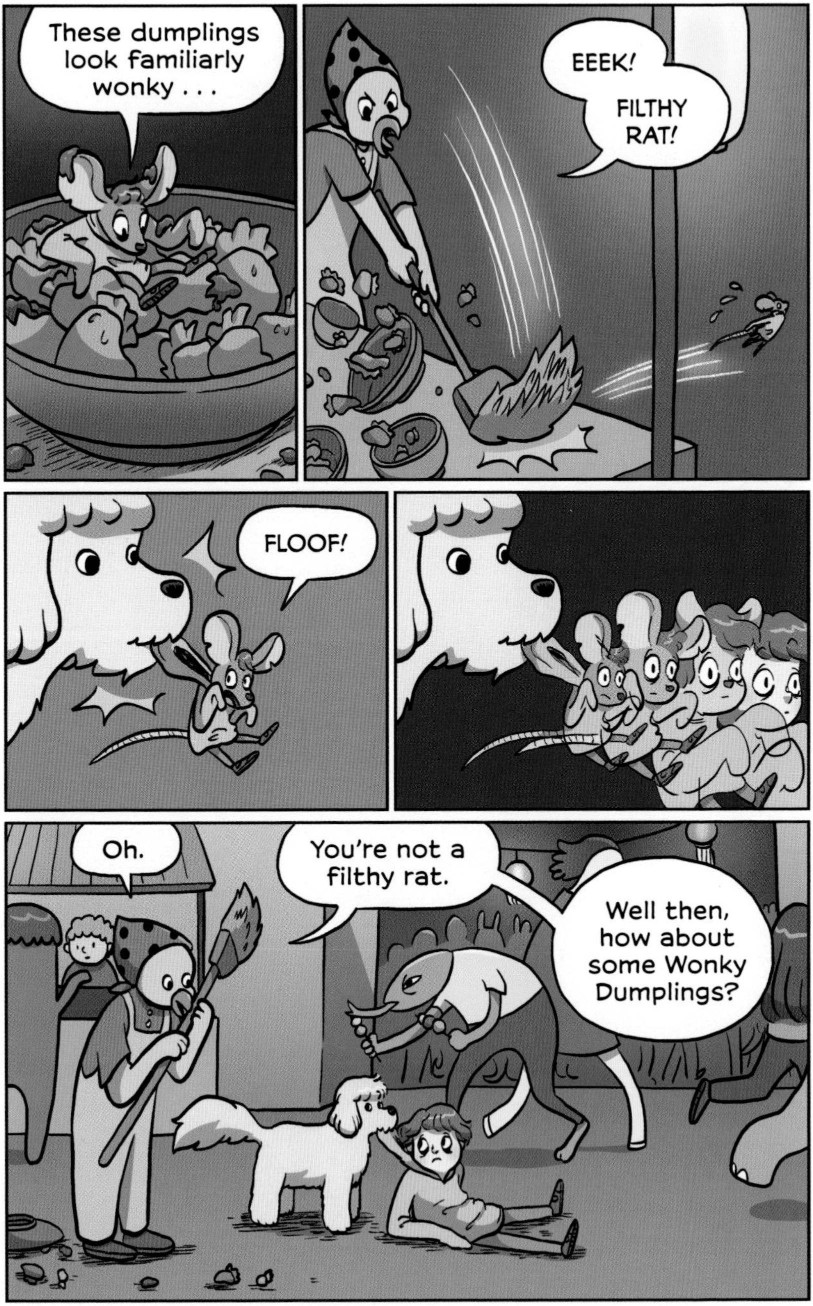
These dumplings look familiarly wonky . . .
EEEK!
FILTHY RAT!
FLOOF!
Oh.
You're not a filthy rat.
Well then, how about some Wonky Dumplings?

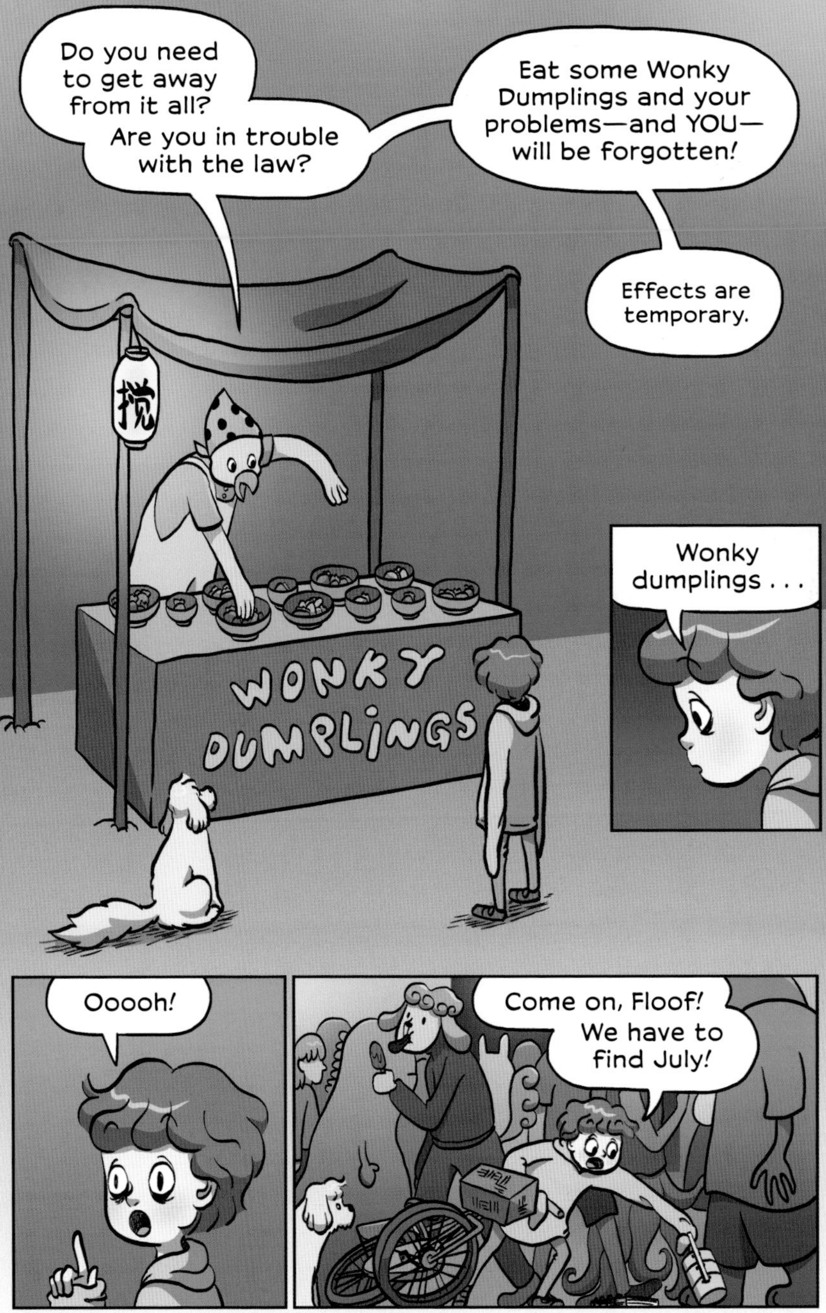
Do you need to get away from it all?
Are you in trouble with the law?
Eat some Wonky Dumplings and your problems—and YOU—will be forgotten!
Effects are temporary.
搅
WONKY DUMPLINGS
Wonky dumplings . . .
Ooooh!
Come on, Floof! We have to find July!

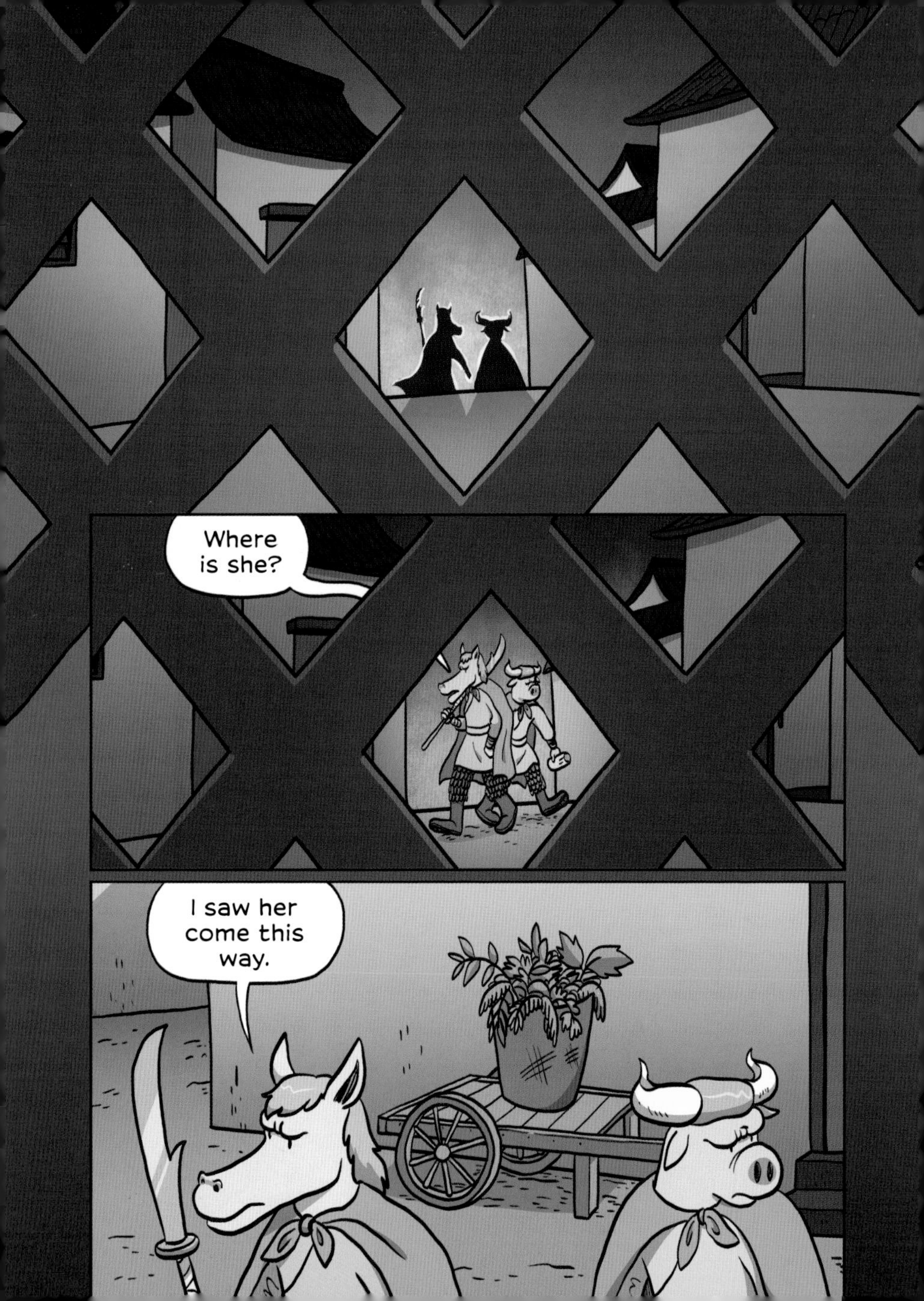
Where is she?
I saw her come this way.

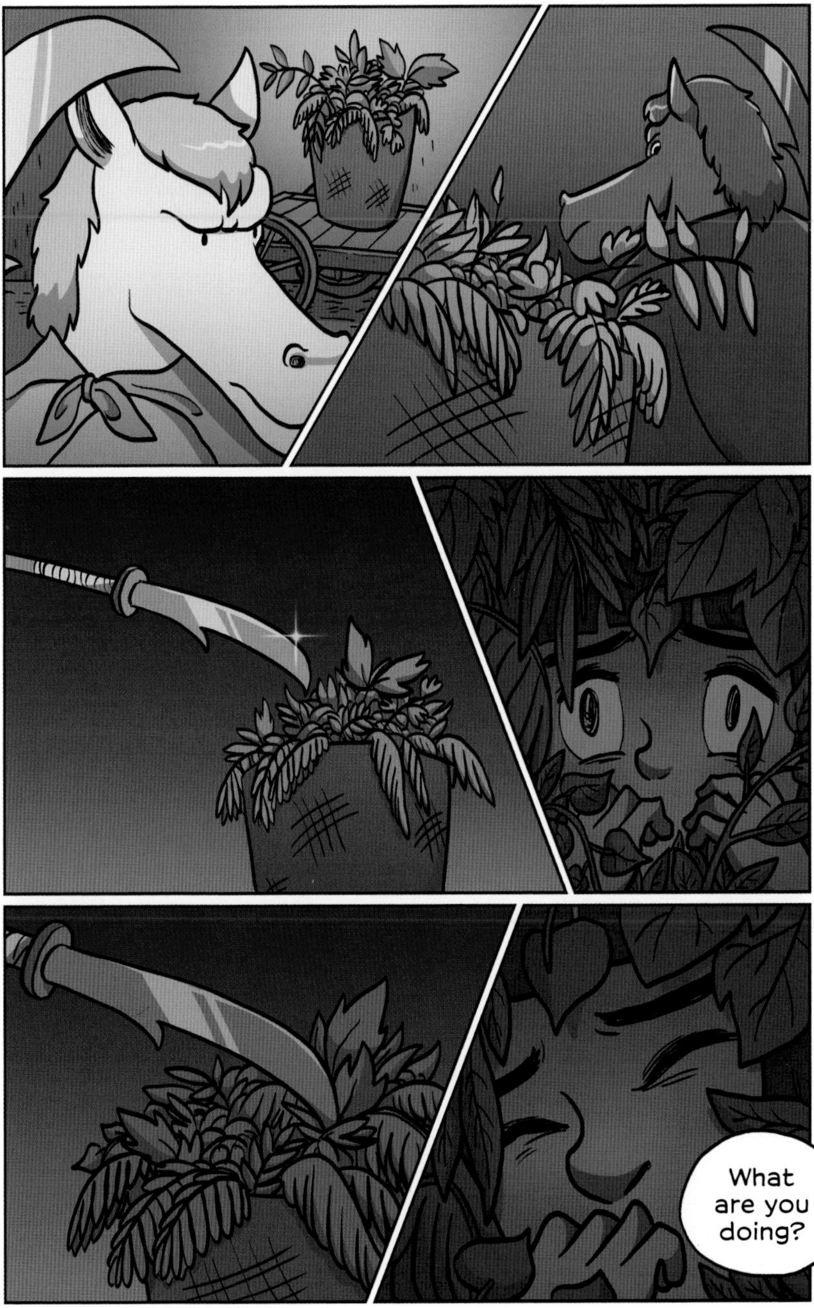
What are you doing?

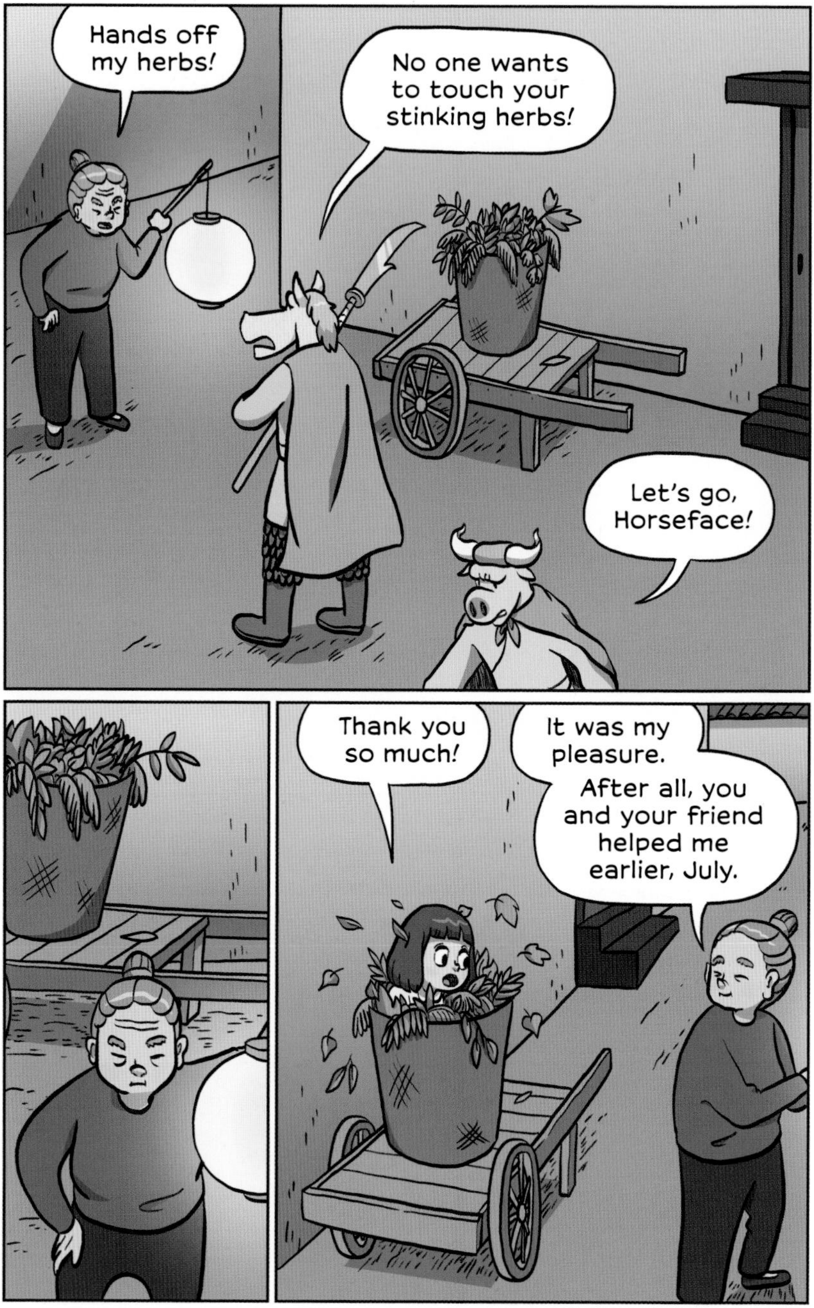

Hands off my herbs!
No one wants to touch your stinking herbs!
Let's go, Horseface!
Thank you so much!
It was my pleasure.
After all, you and your friend helped me earlier, July.

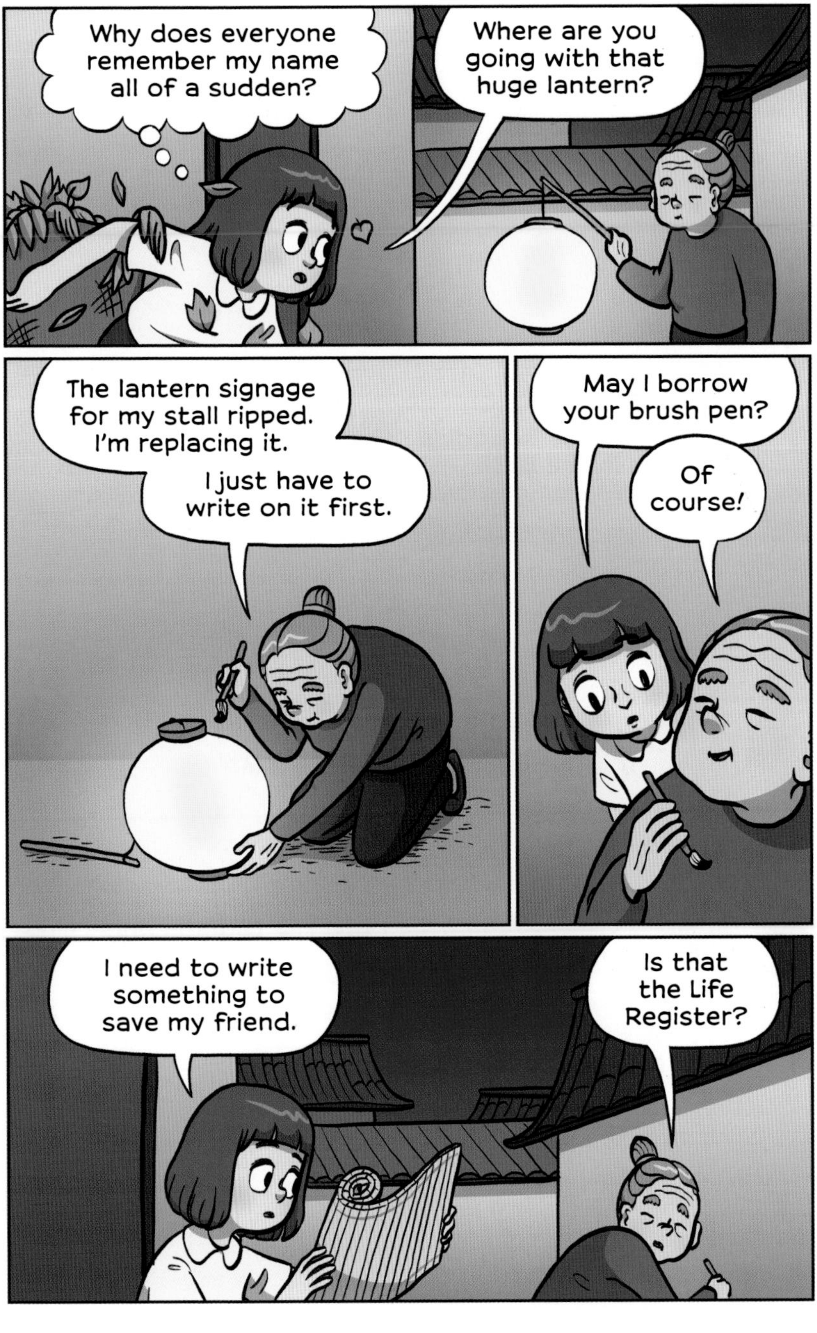
Why does everyone remember my name all of a sudden?
Where are you going with that huge lantern?
The lantern signage for my stall ripped. I'm replacing it.
I just have to write on it first.
May I borrow your brush pen?
Of course!
I need to write something to save my friend.
Is that the Life Register?

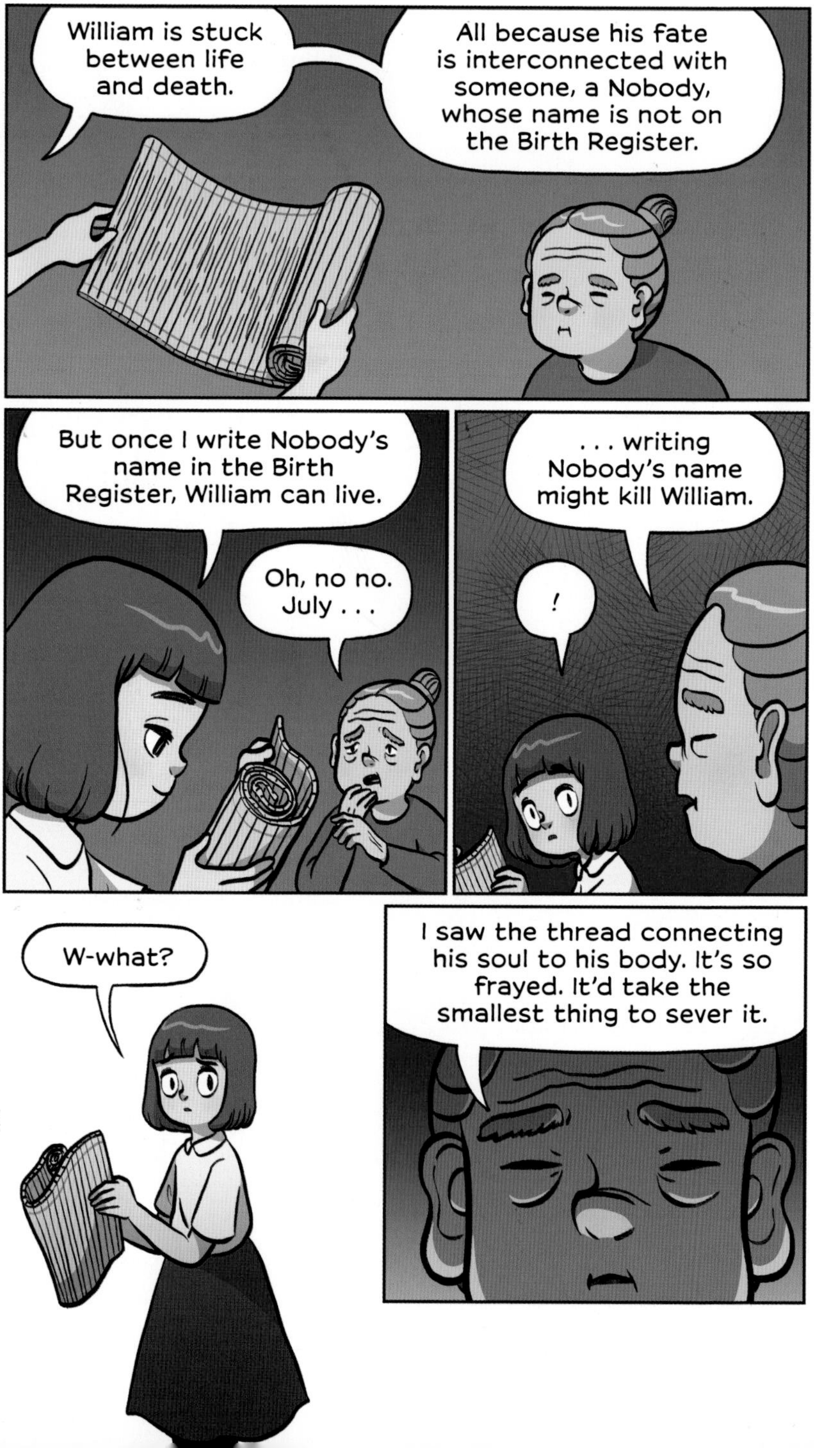
William is stuck between life and death.
All because his fate is interconnected with someone, a Nobody, whose name is not on the Birth Register.
But once I write Nobody's name in the Birth Register, William can live.
Oh, no no. July . . .
. . . writing Nobody's name might kill William.
!
W-what?
I saw the thread connecting his soul to his body. It's so frayed. It'd take the smallest thing to sever it.

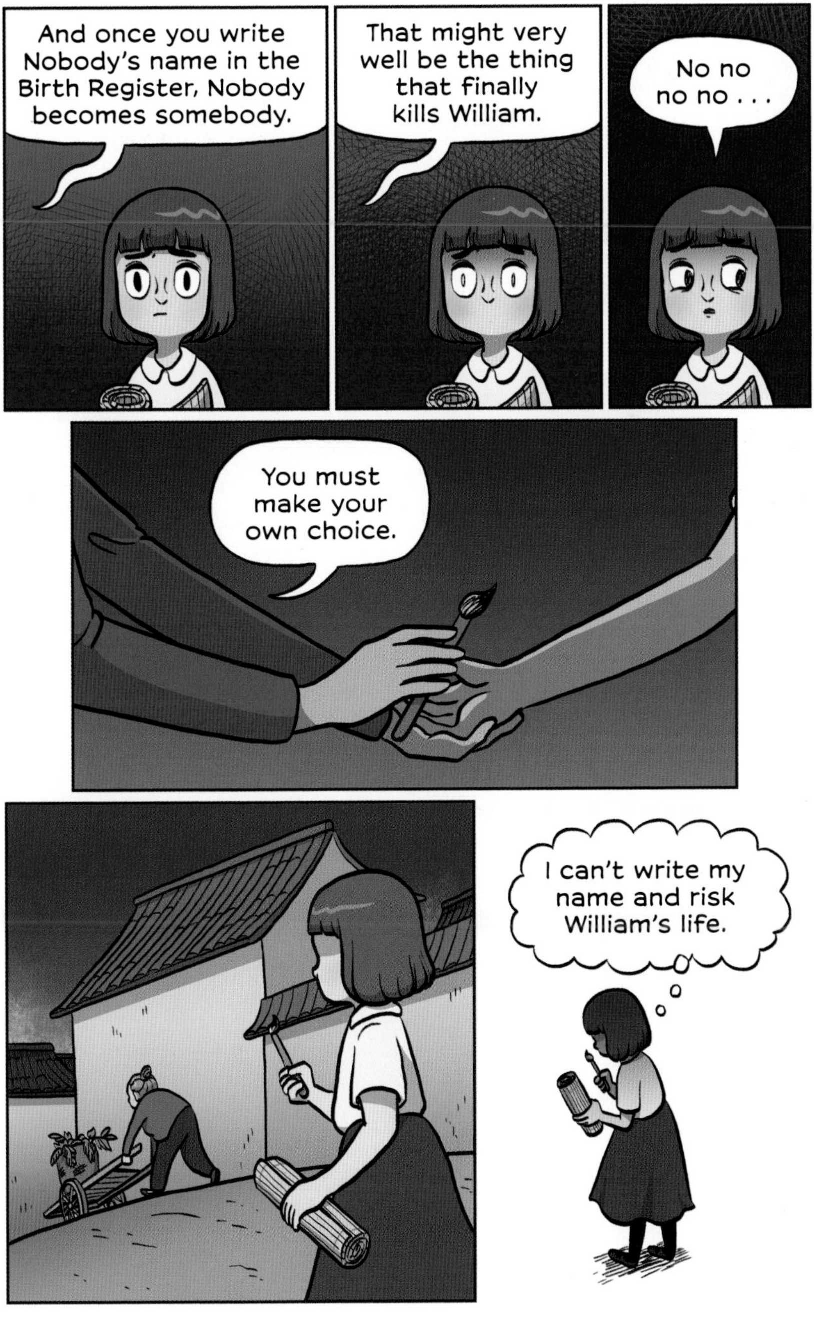

And once you write Nobody's name in the Birth Register, Nobody becomes somebody.
That might very well be the thing that finally kills William.
No no no no . . .
You must make your own choice.
I can't write my name and risk William's life.

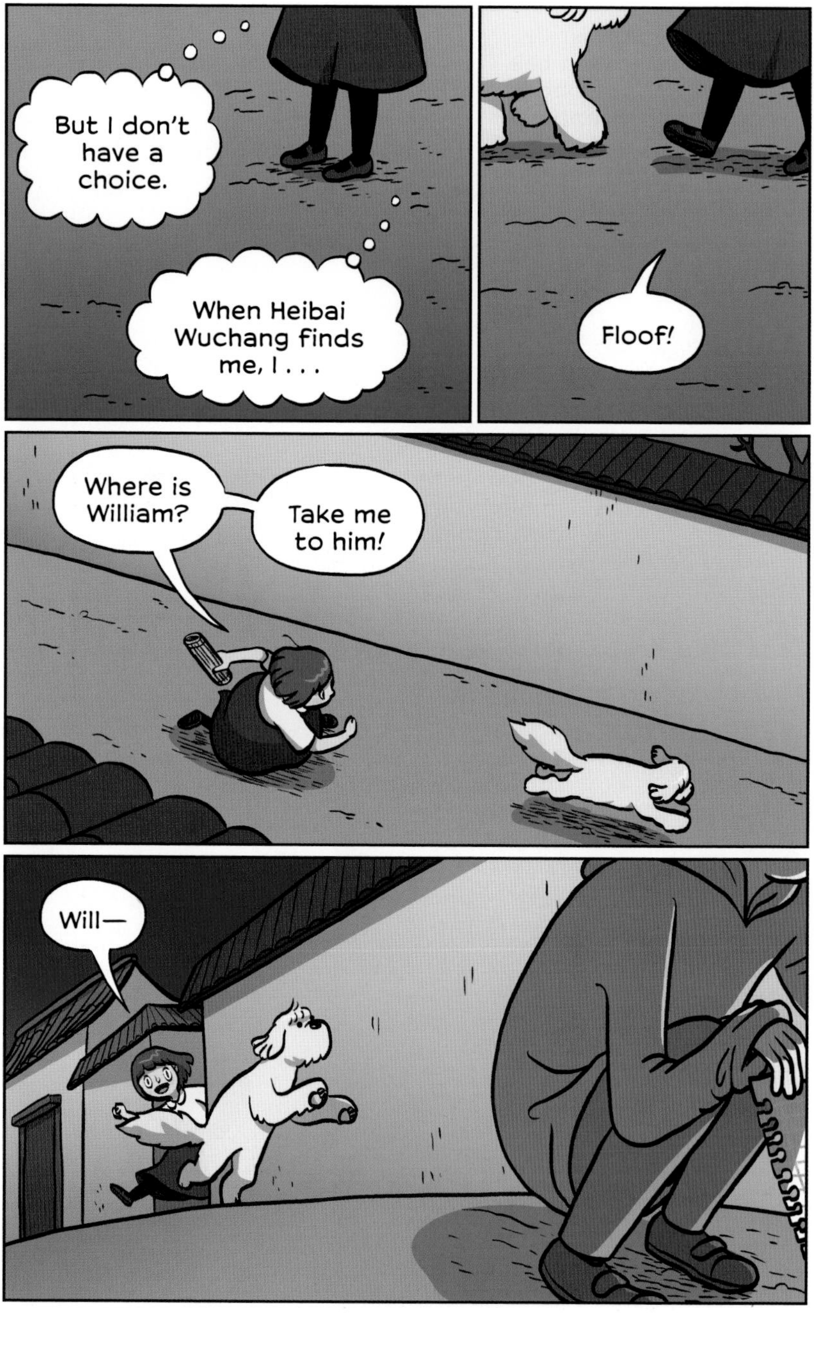
But I don't have a choice.
When Heibai Wuchang finds me, I . . .
Floof!
Where is William?
Take me to him!
Will—

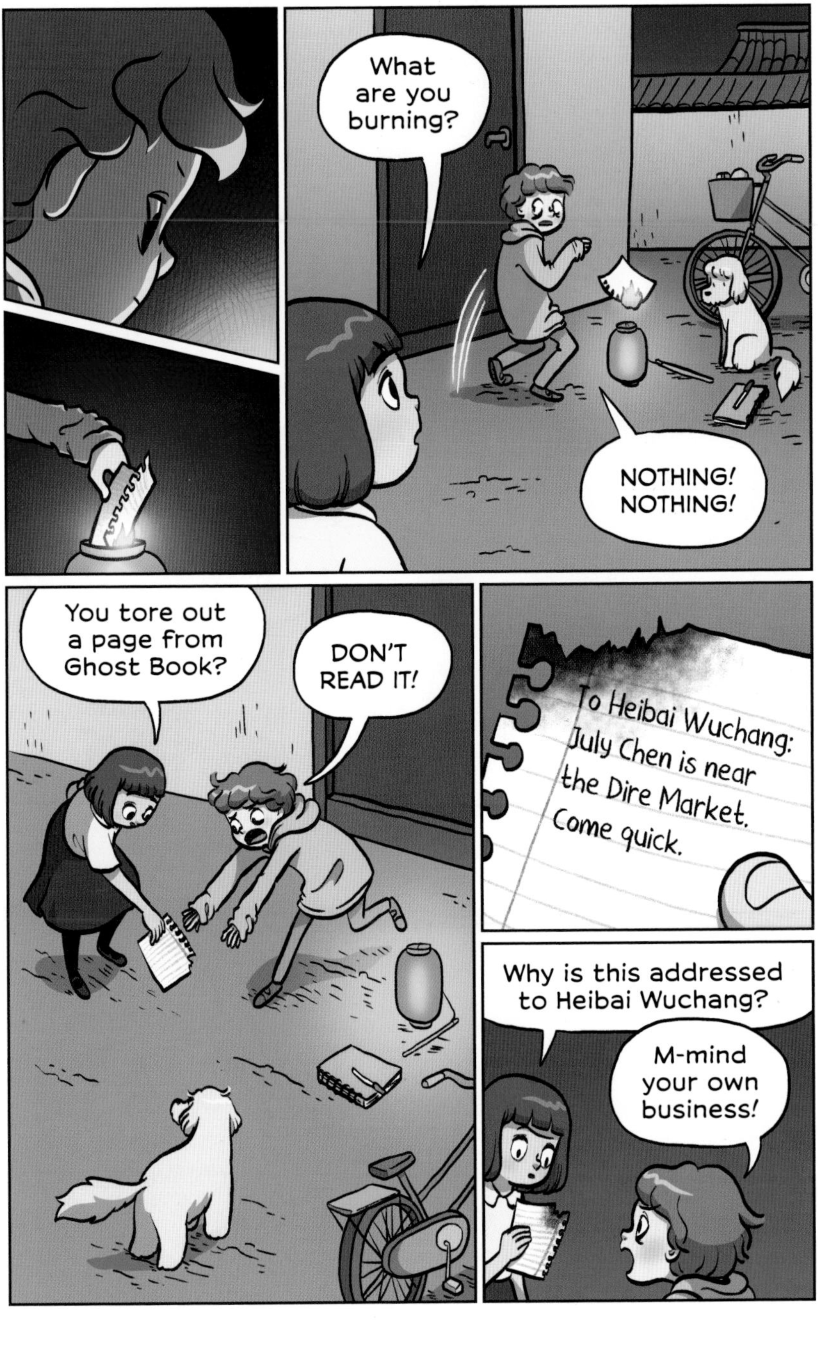
What are you burning?
NOTHING! NOTHING!
You tore out a page from Ghost Book?
DON'T READ IT!
To Heibai Wuchang: July Chen is near the Dire Market. Come quick.
Why is this addressed to Heibai Wuchang?
M-mind your own business!

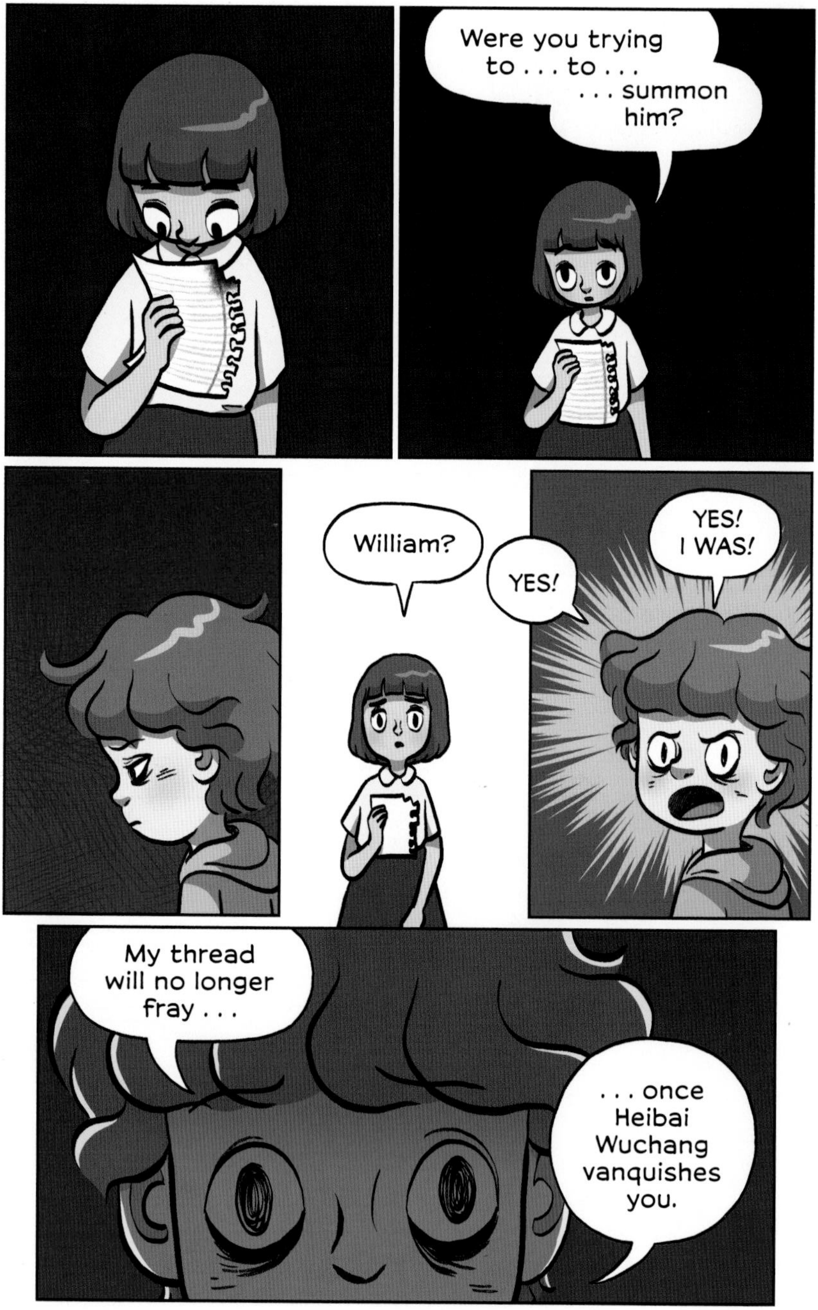
Were you trying to . . . to . . . . . . summon him?
William?
YES!
YES! I WAS!
My thread will no longer fray . . .
. . . once Heibai Wuchang vanquishes you.

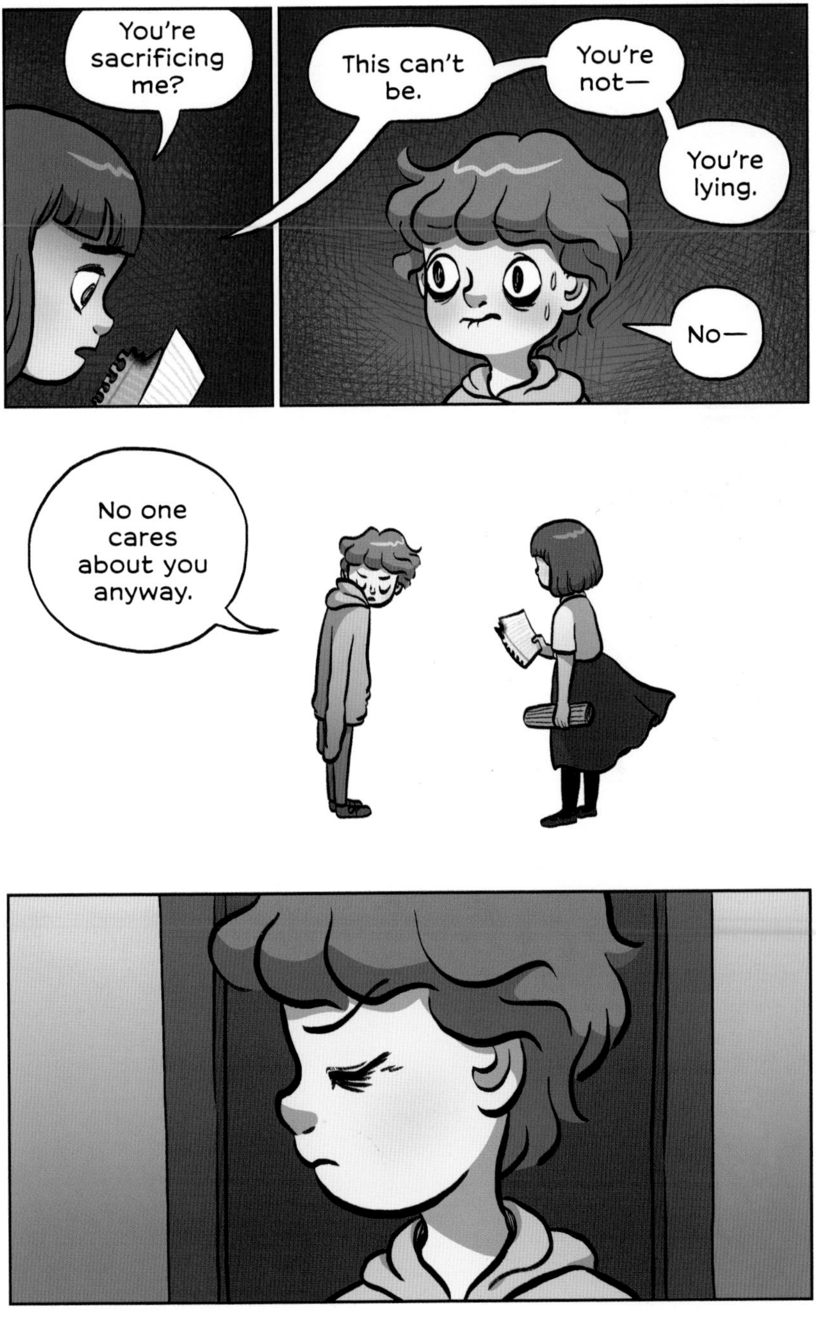
You're sacrificing me?
This can't be.
You're not—
You're lying.
No—
No one cares about you anyway.

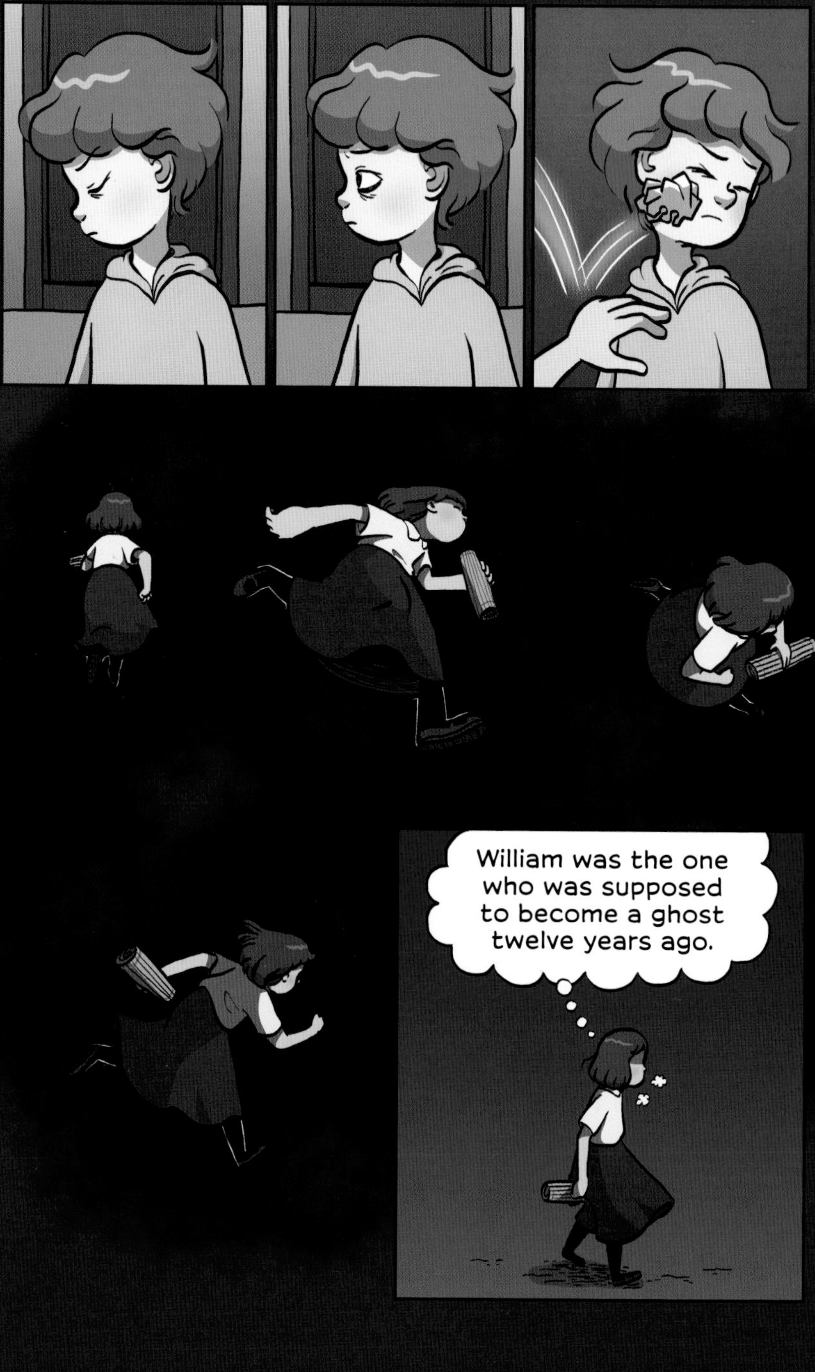
William was the one who was supposed to become a ghost twelve years ago.

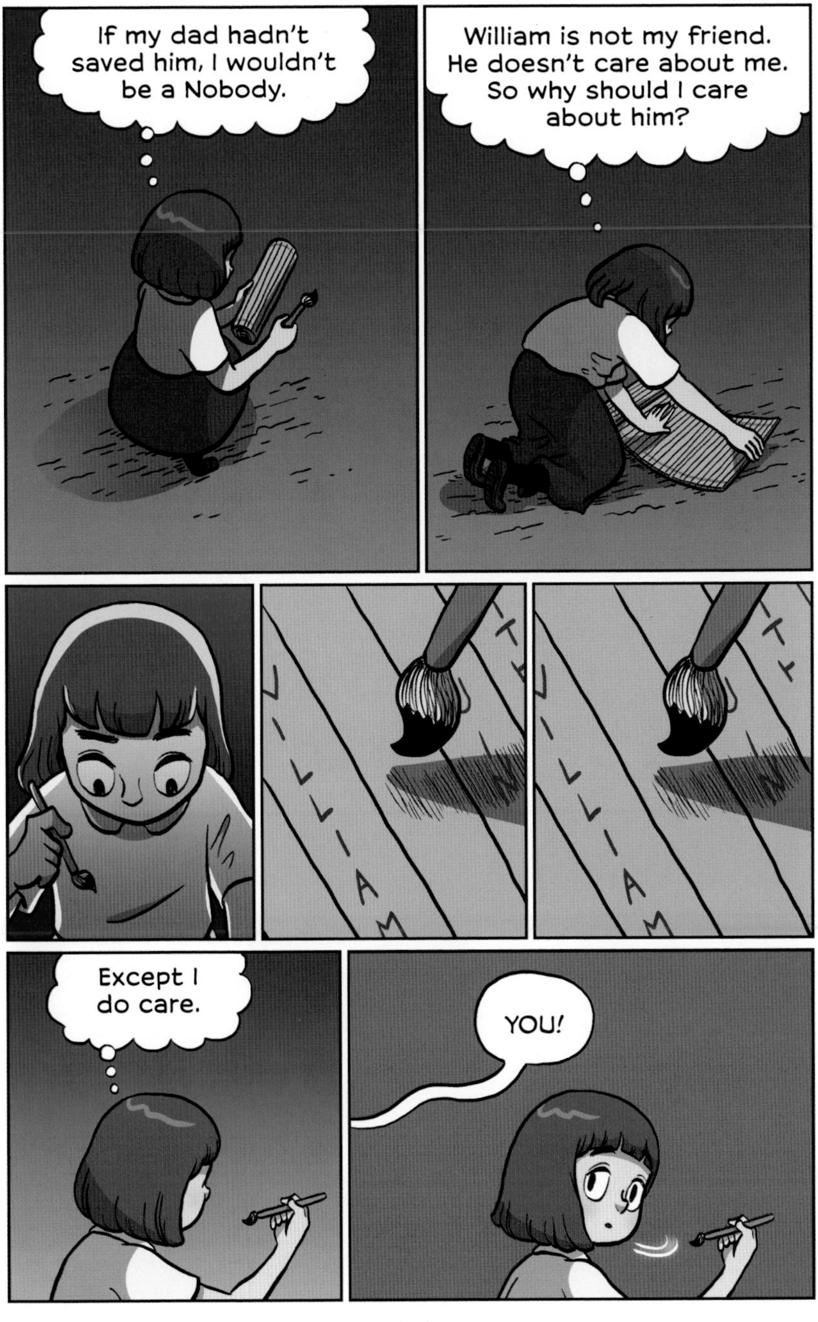
If my dad hadn't saved him, I wouldn't be a Nobody.
William is not my friend. He doesn't care about me. So why should I care about him?
WILLIAM
Except I do care.
YOU!

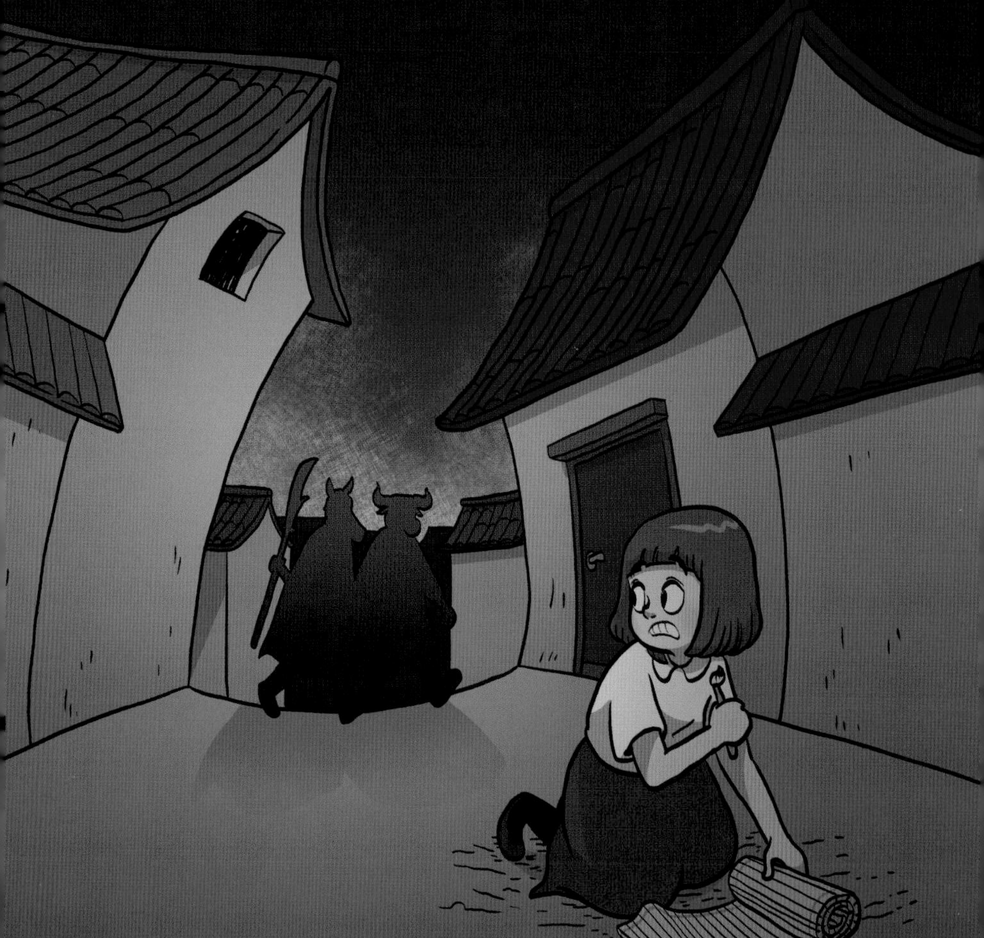

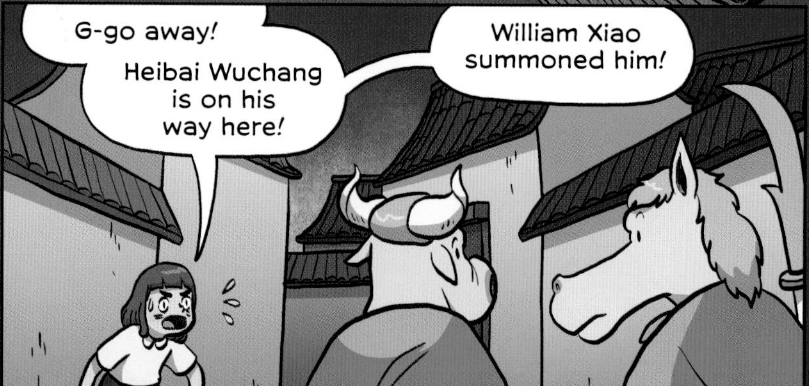
G-go away!
Heibai Wuchang is on his way here!
William Xiao summoned him!

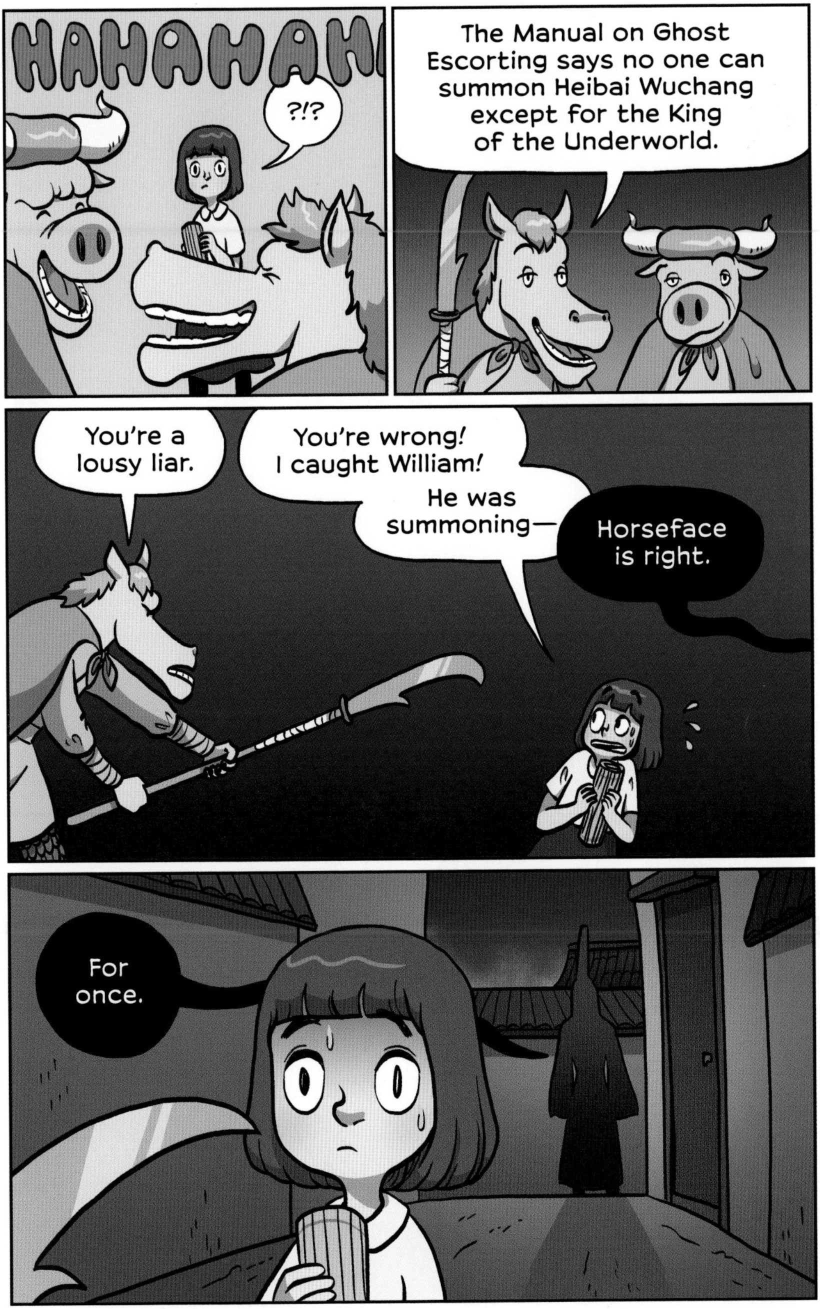
HAHAHAH
?!?
The Manual on Ghost Escorting says no one can summon Heibai Wuchang except for the King of the Underworld.
You're a lousy liar.
You're wrong! I caught William!
He was summoning—
Horseface is right.
For once.

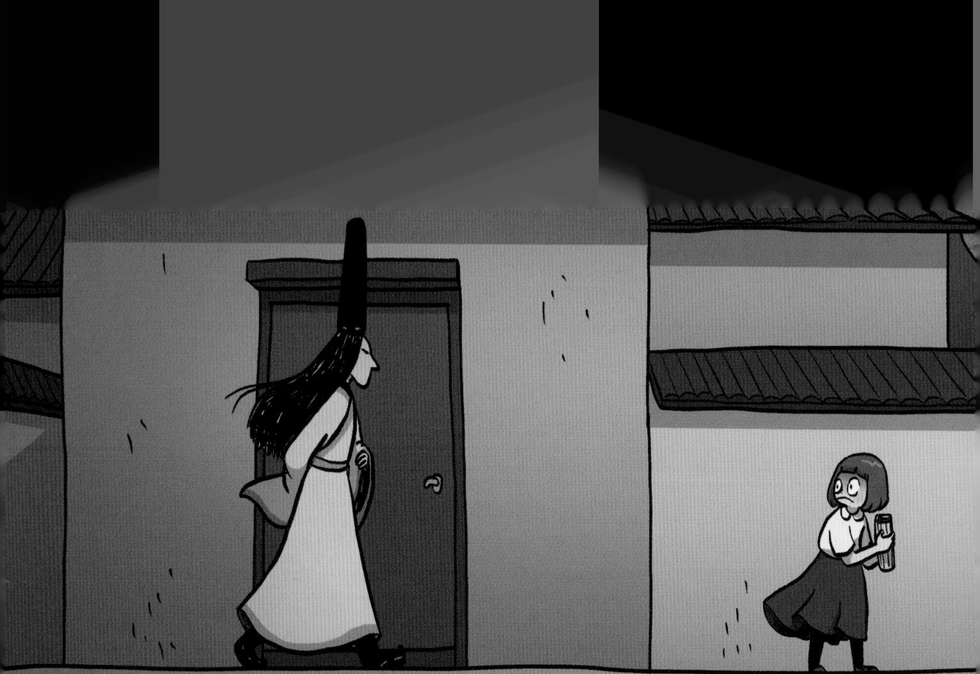

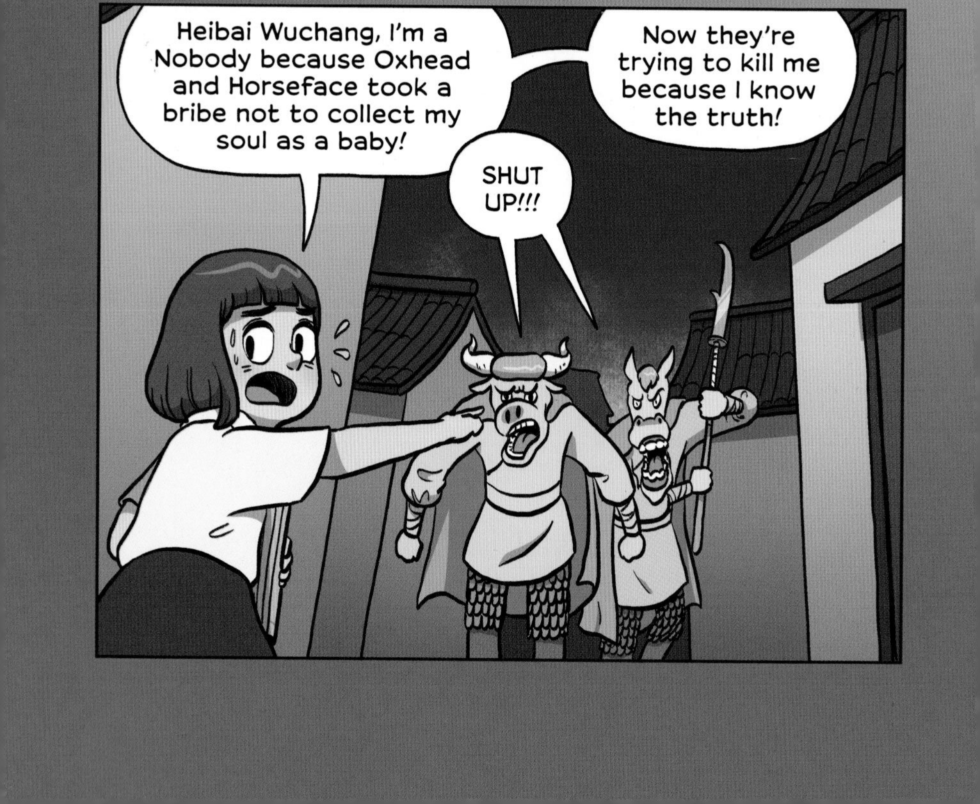
Heibai Wuchang, I'm a Nobody because Oxhead and Horseface took a bribe not to collect my soul as a baby!
Now they're trying to kill me because I know the truth!
SHUT UP!!!

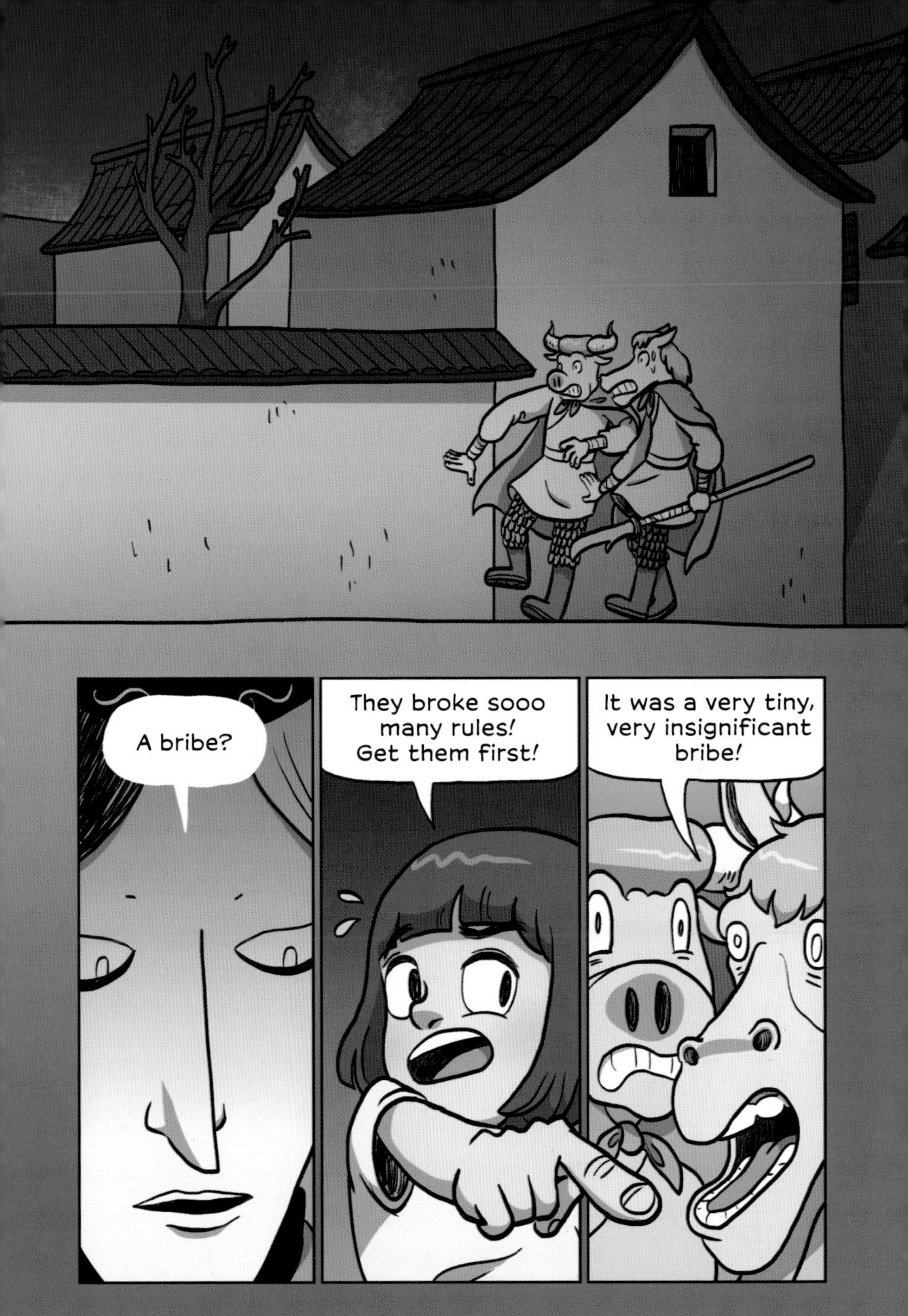
A bribe?
They broke sooo many rules! Get them first!
It was a very tiny, very insignificant bribe!

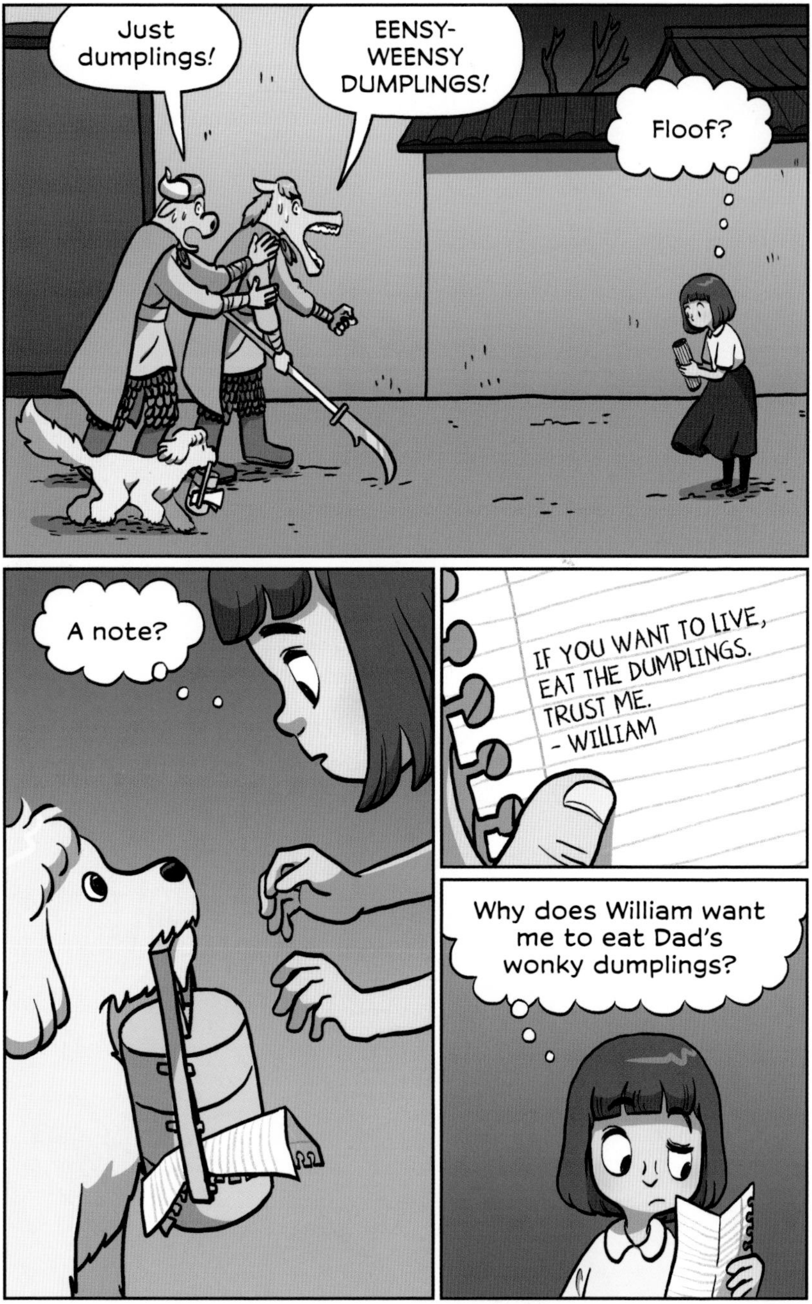
Just dumplings!
EENSY-WEENSY DUMPLINGS!
Floof?
A note?
IF YOU WANT TO LIVE, EAT THE DUMPLINGS. TRUST ME. - WILLIAM
Why does William want me to eat Dad's wonky dumplings?

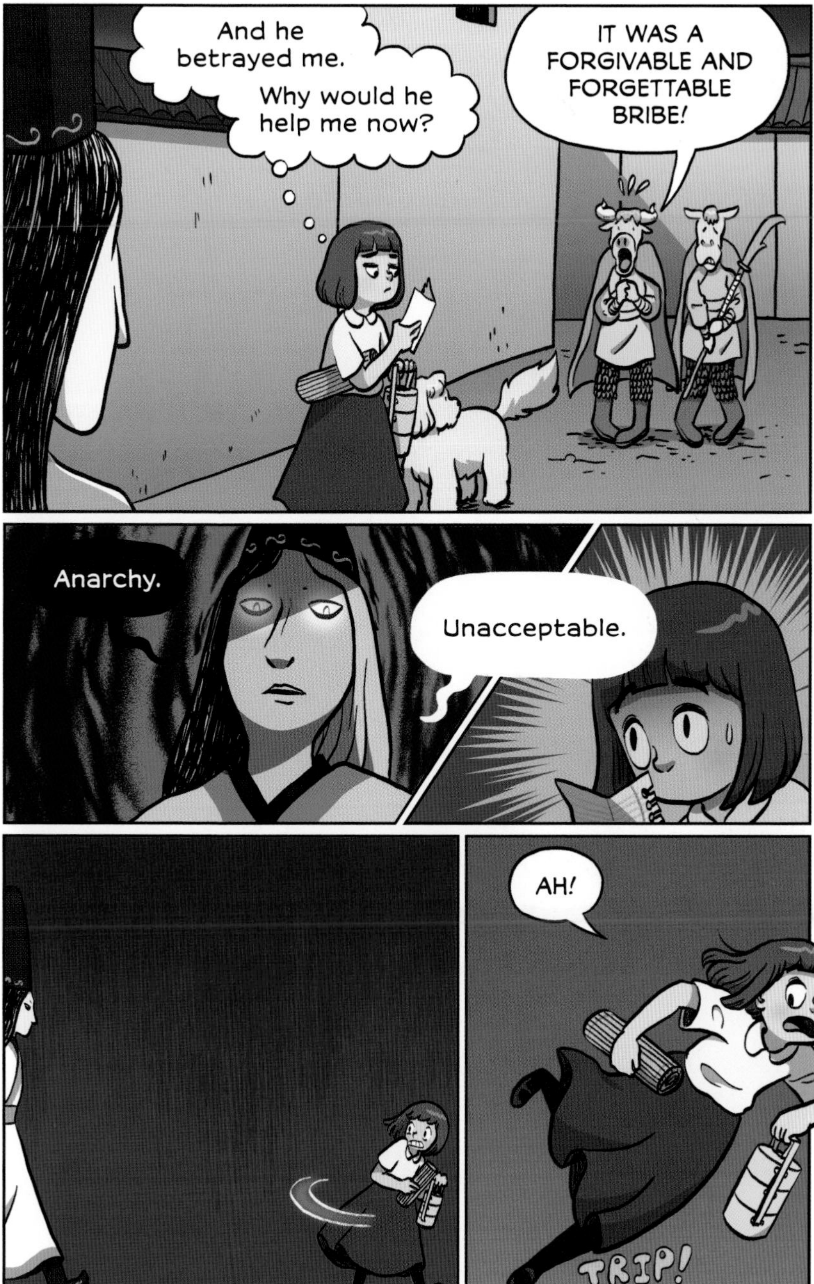
And he betrayed me.
Why would he help me now?
IT WAS A FORGIVABLE AND FORGETTABLE BRIBE!
Anarchy.
Unacceptable.
AH!
TRIP!

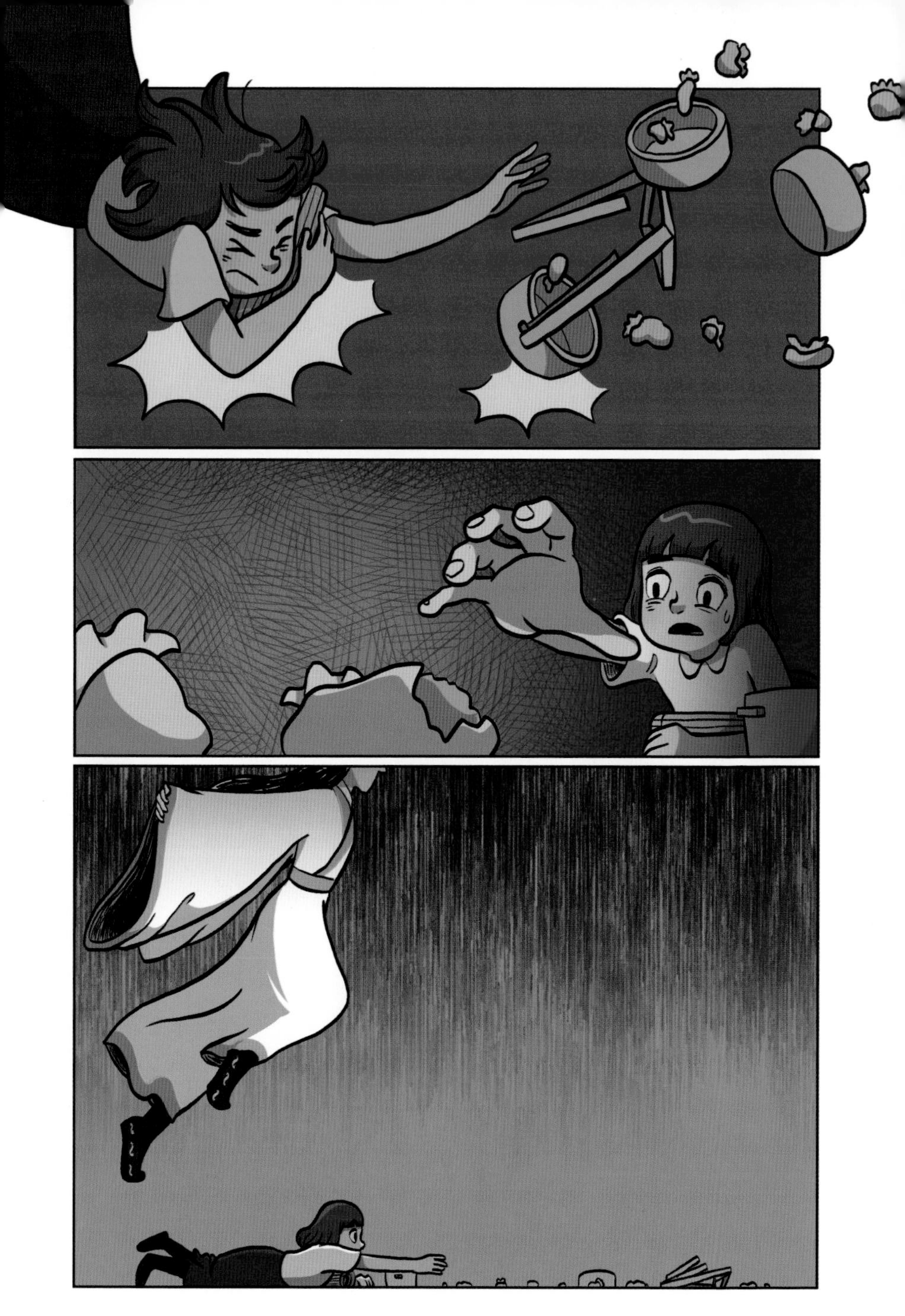

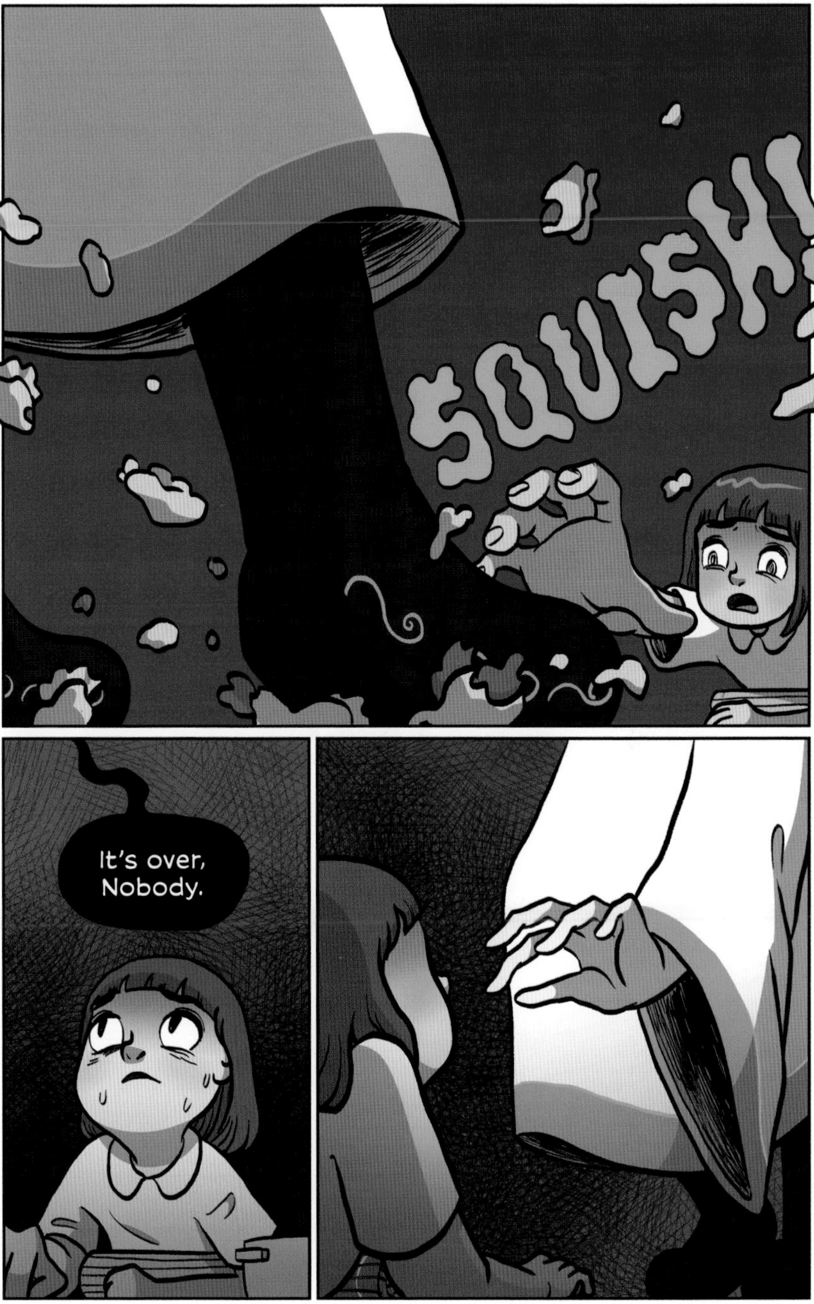
SQUISH!!
It's over,
Nobody.

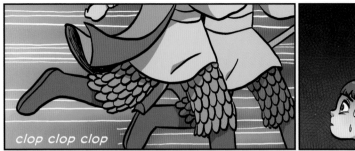

clop clop clop

PLEASE FORGIVE US!

DON'T VANQUISH US!

DON'T STRIKE OUR NAMES OFF THE UNDERLINGS REGISTER!

!

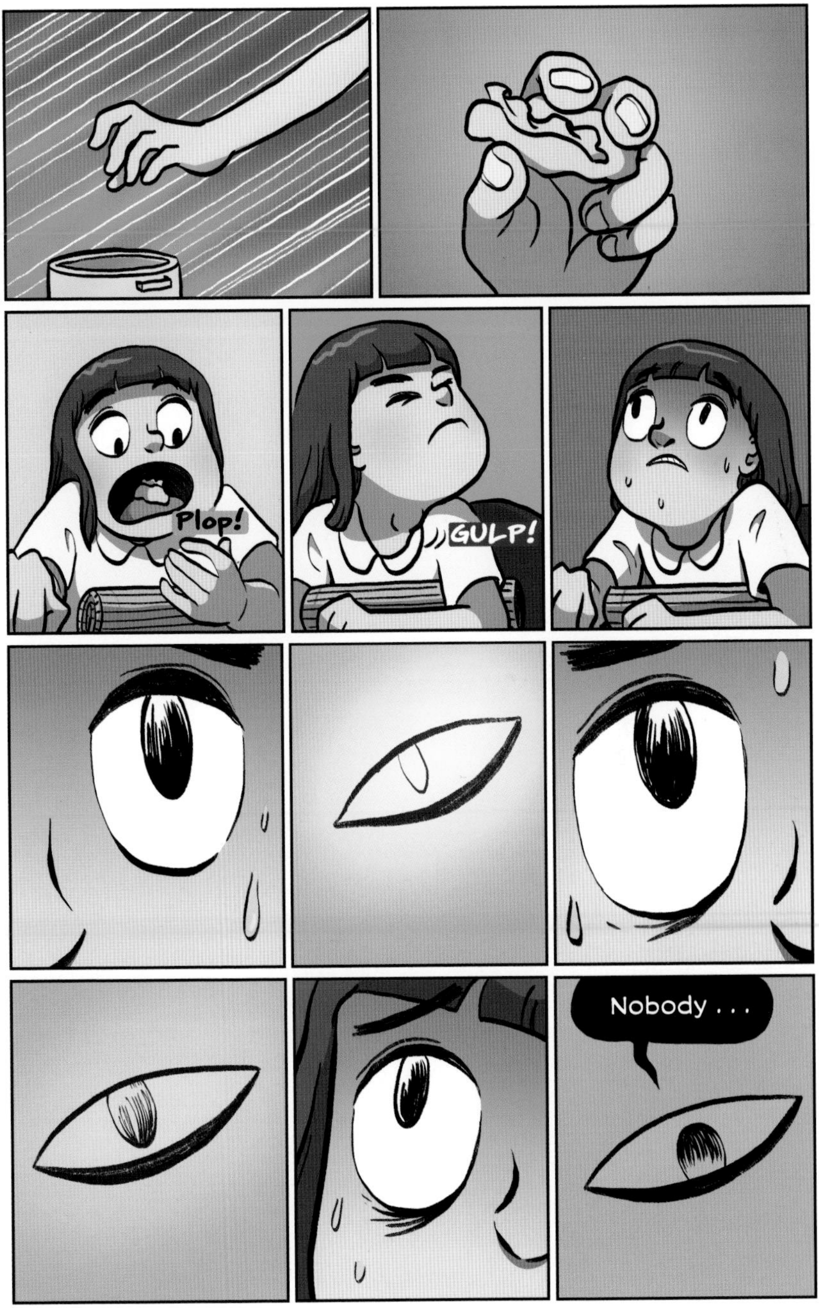
Plop!
GULP!
Nobody . . .

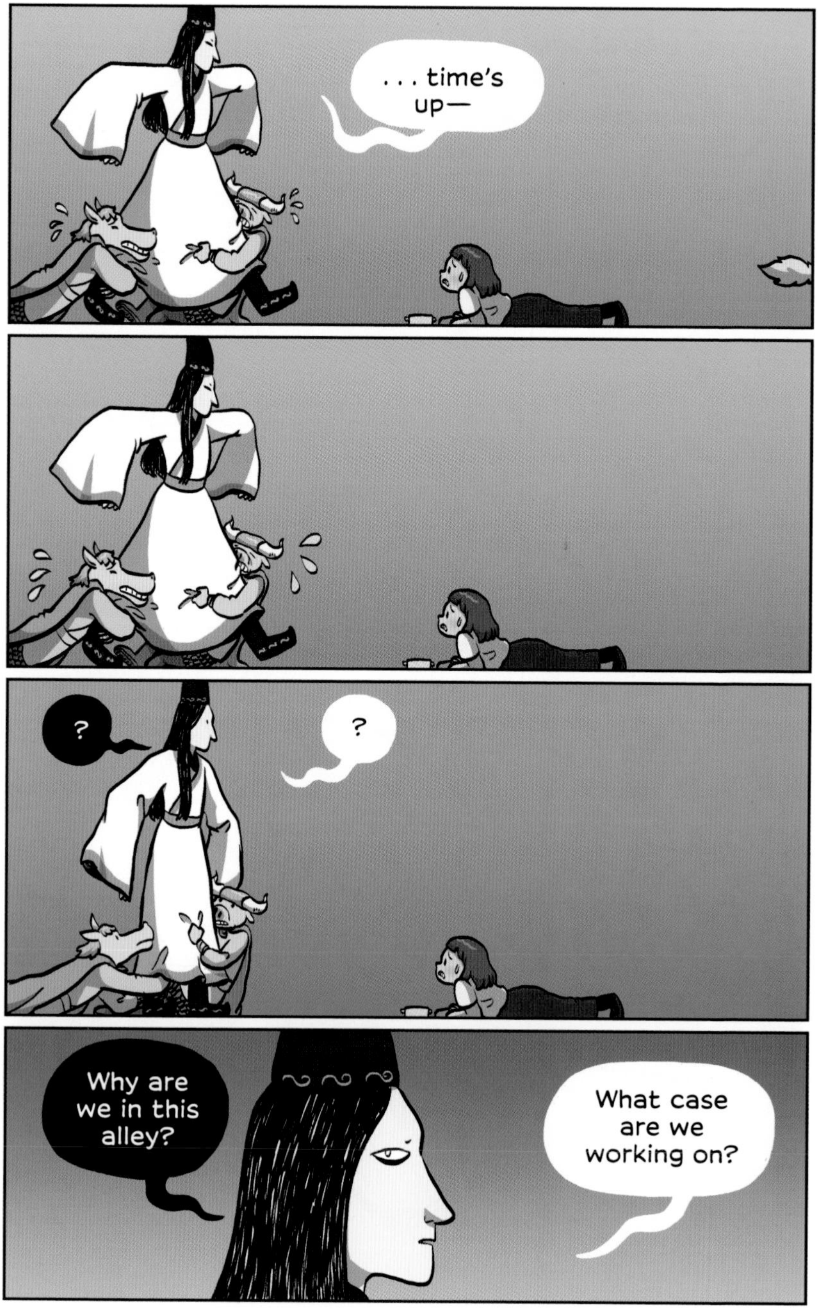
. . . time's up—
?
?
Why are we in this alley?
What case are we working on?

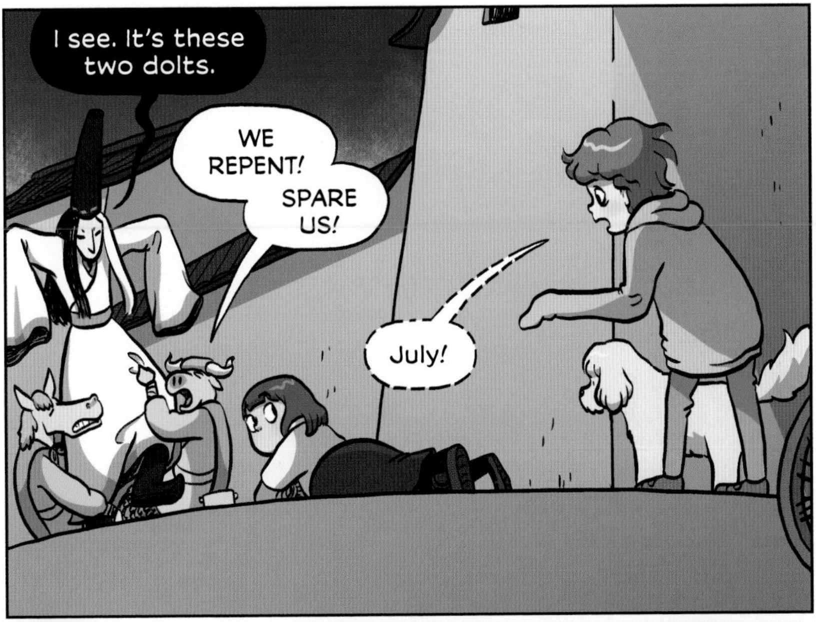
I see. It's these two dolts.
WE REPENT!
SPARE US!
July!

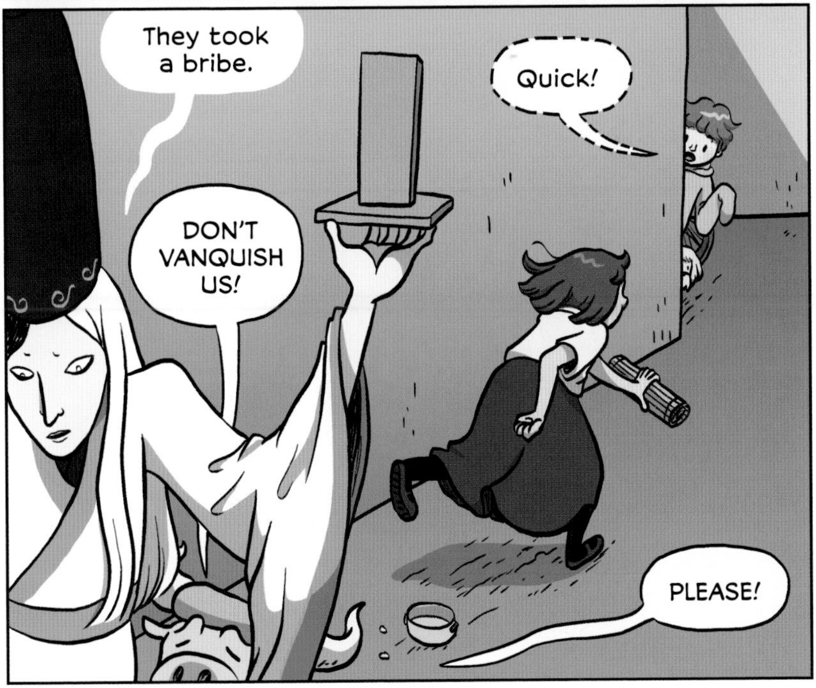
They took a bribe.
Quick!
DON'T VANQUISH US!
PLEASE!

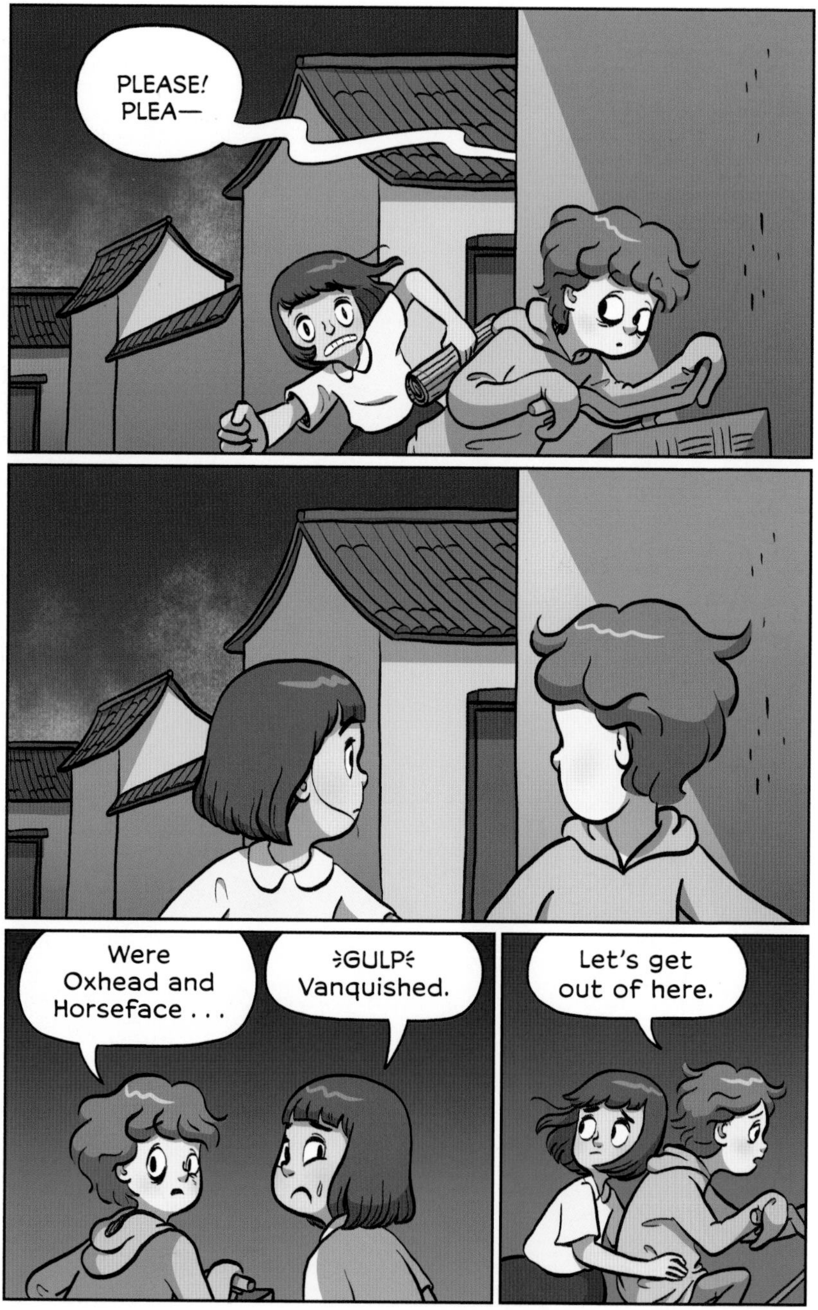
PLEASE! PLEA—
Were Oxhead and Horseface . . .
⇉GULP⇇ Vanquished.
Let's get out of here.

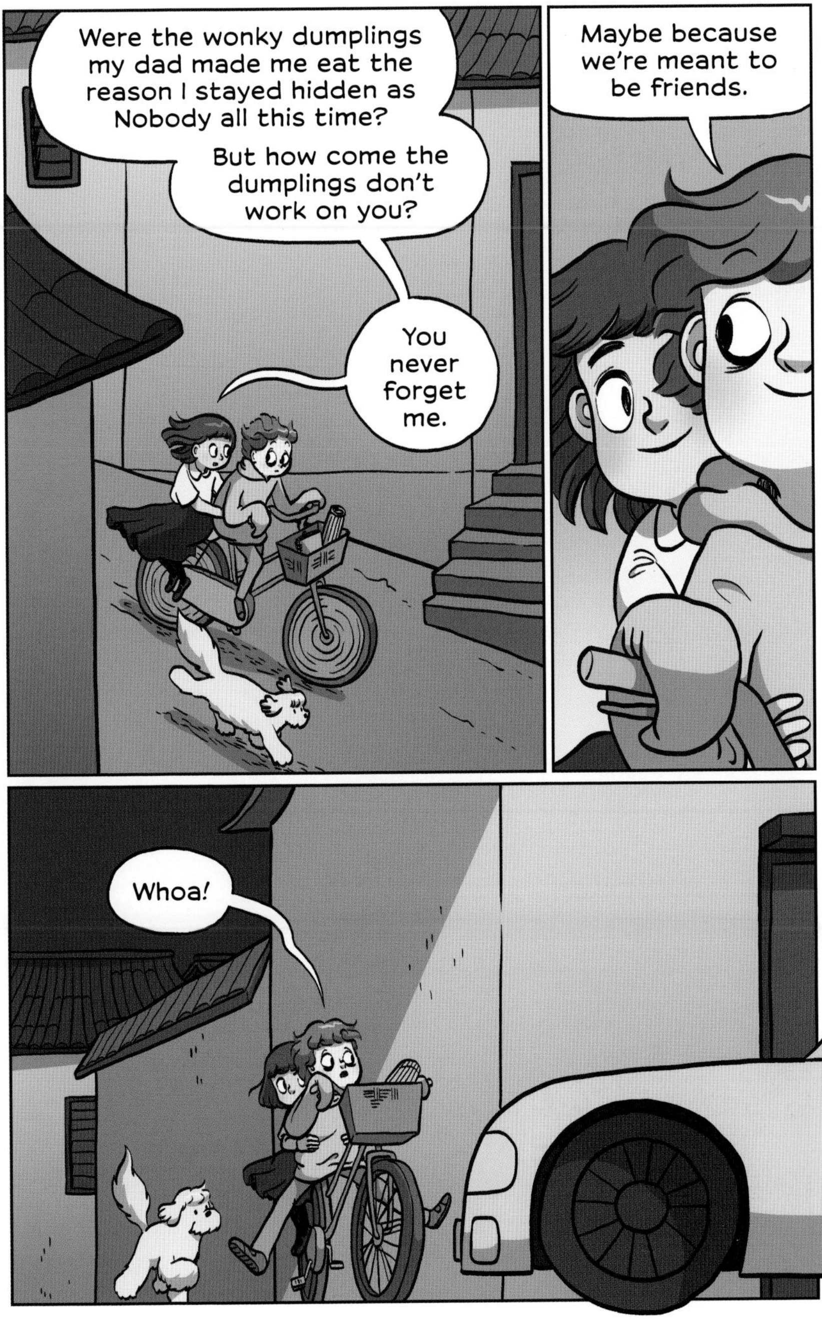
Were the wonky dumplings my dad made me eat the reason I stayed hidden as Nobody all this time?
But how come the dumplings don't work on you?
You never forget me.
Maybe because we're meant to be friends.
Whoa!

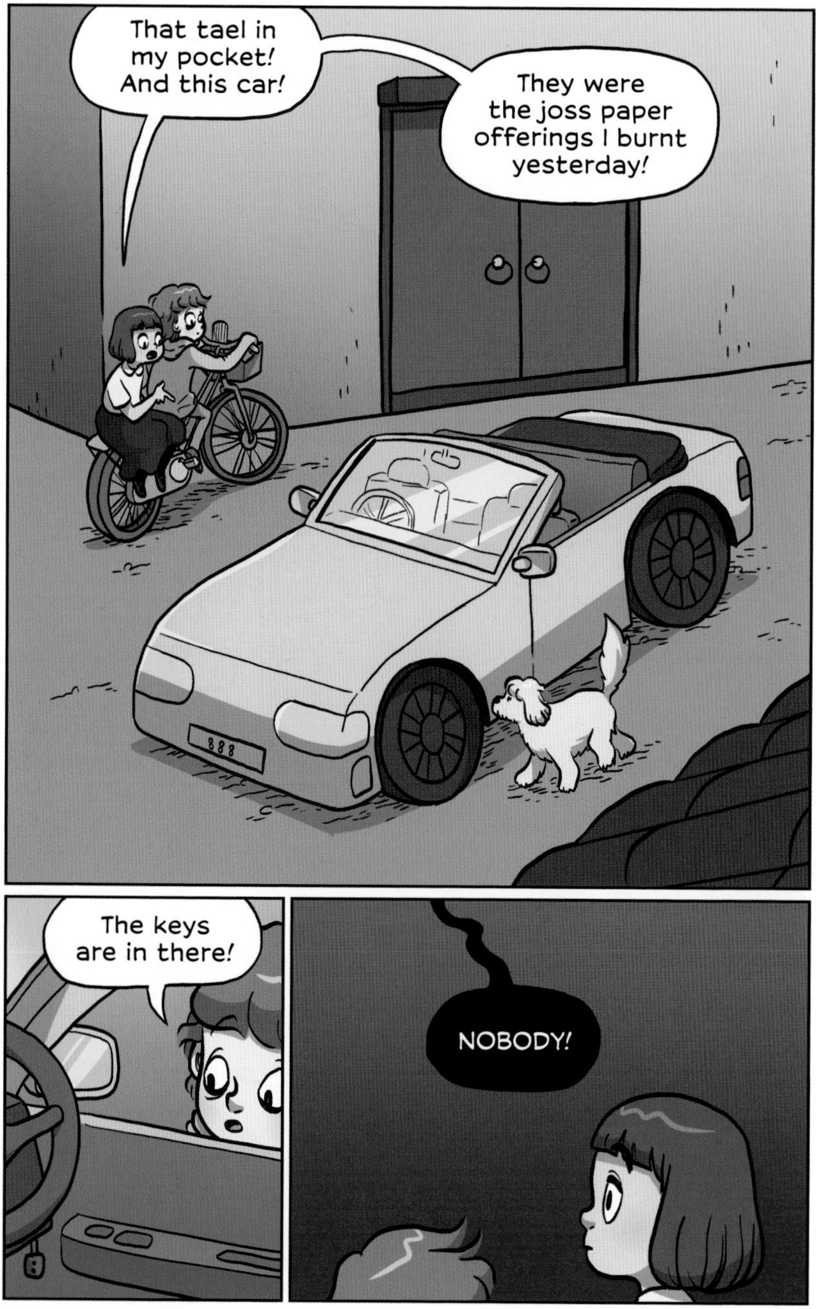
That tael in my pocket! And this car!
They were the joss paper offerings I burnt yesterday!
888
The keys are in there!
NOBODY!

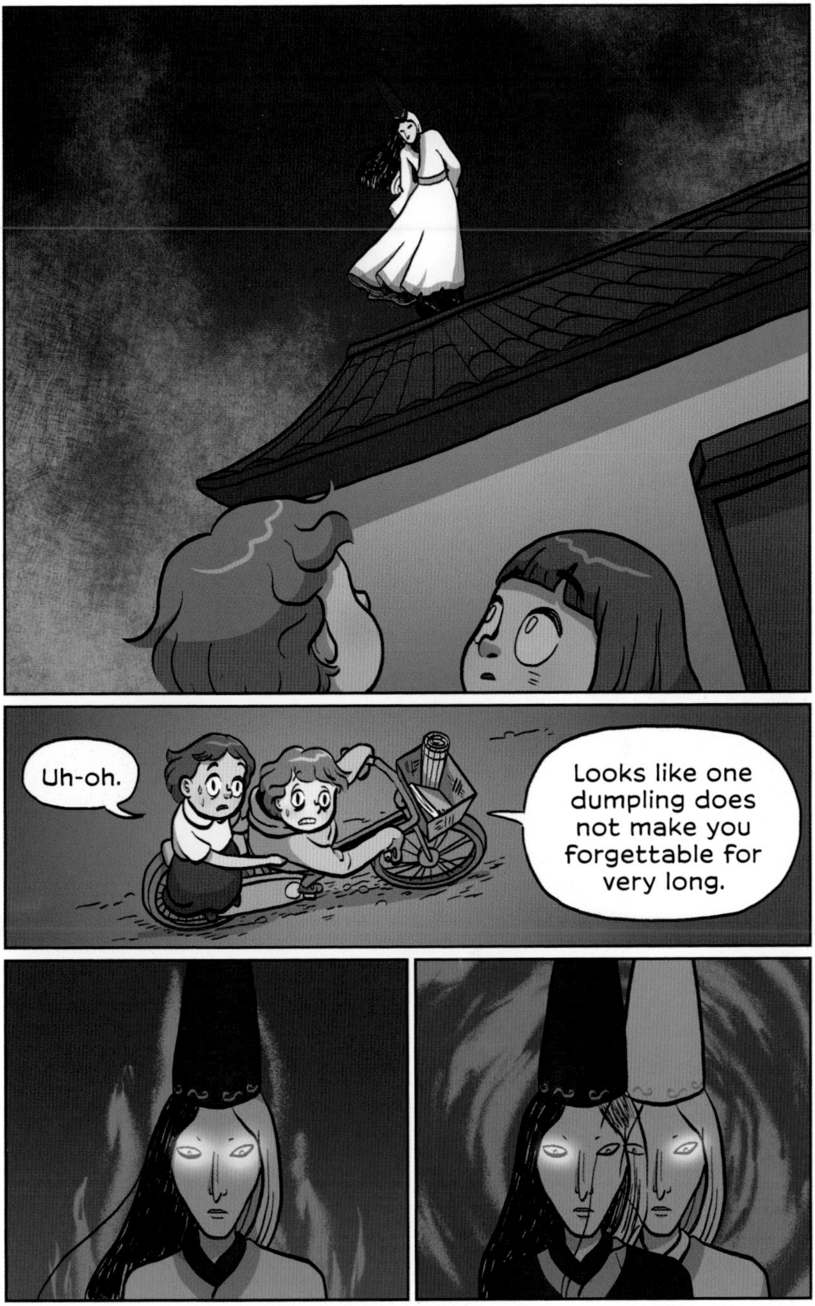
Uh-oh.
Looks like one dumpling does not make you forgettable for very long.

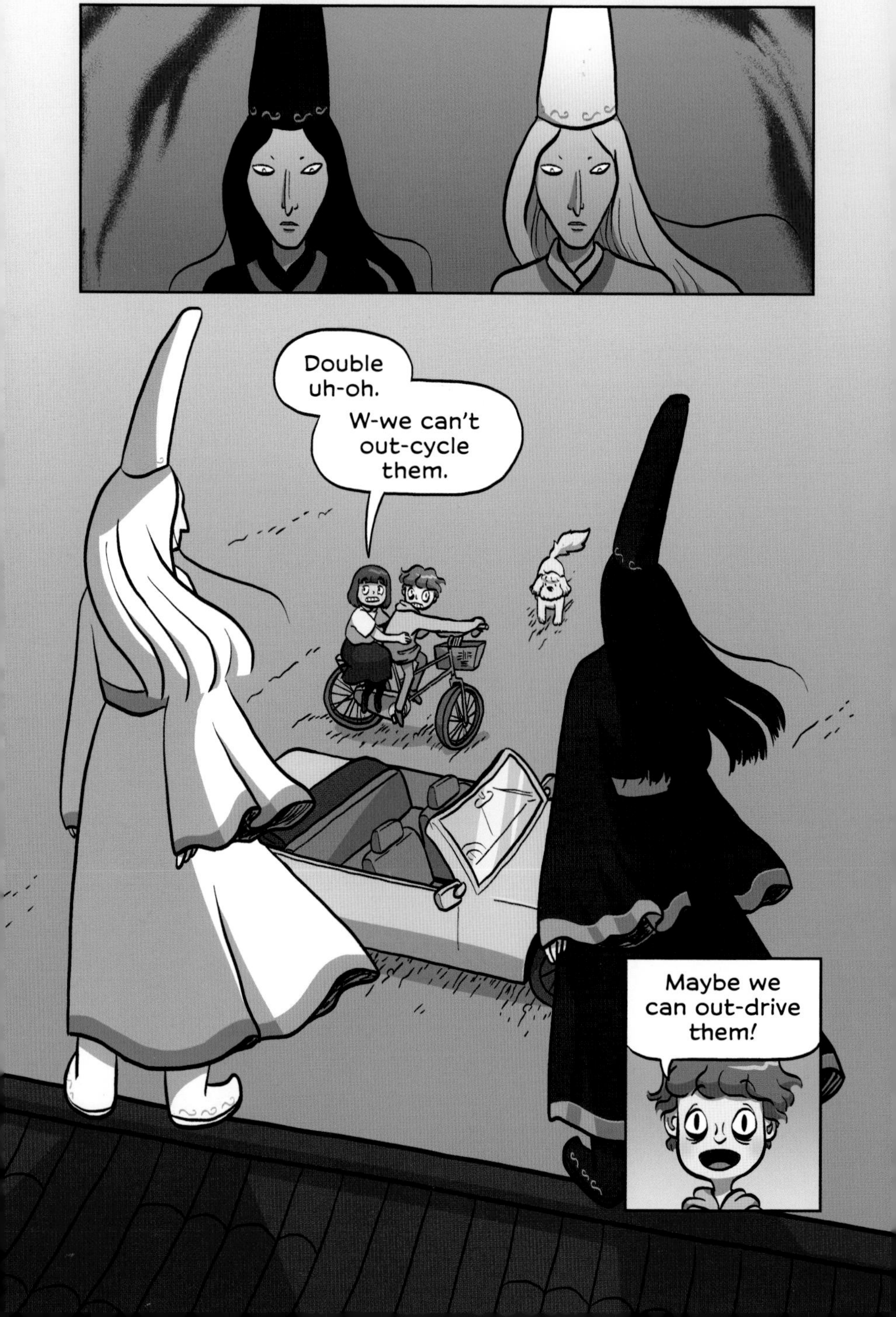
Double uh-oh.
W-we can't out-cycle them.
Maybe we can out-drive them!

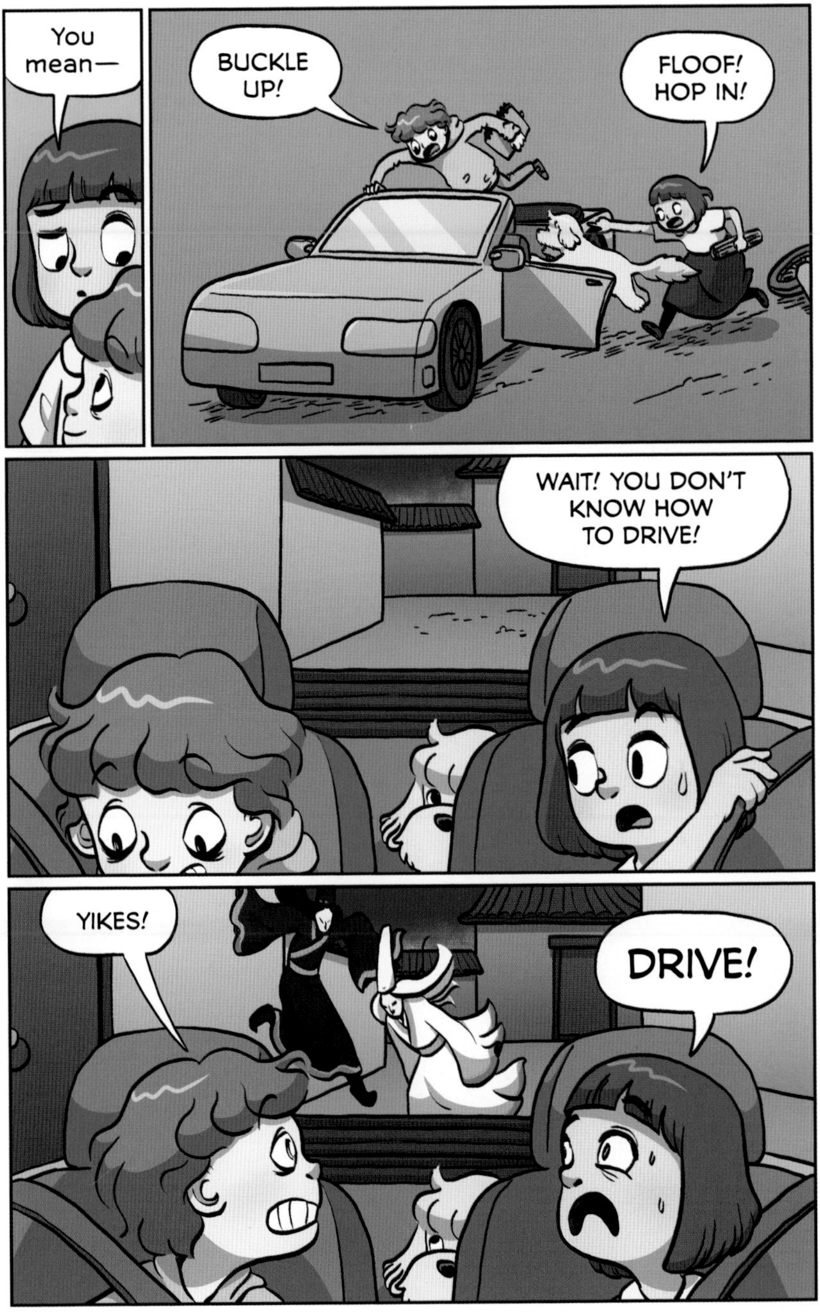
You mean—
BUCKLE UP!
FLOOF! HOP IN!
WAIT! YOU DON'T KNOW HOW TO DRIVE!
YIKES!
DRIVE!

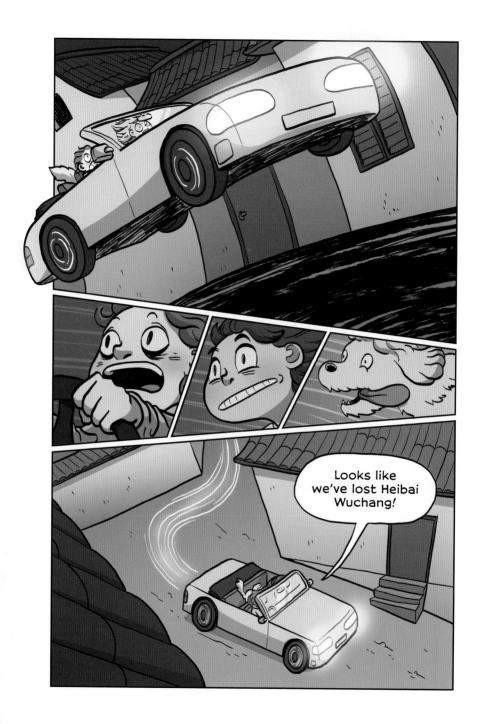

Looks like we've lost Heibai Wuchang!

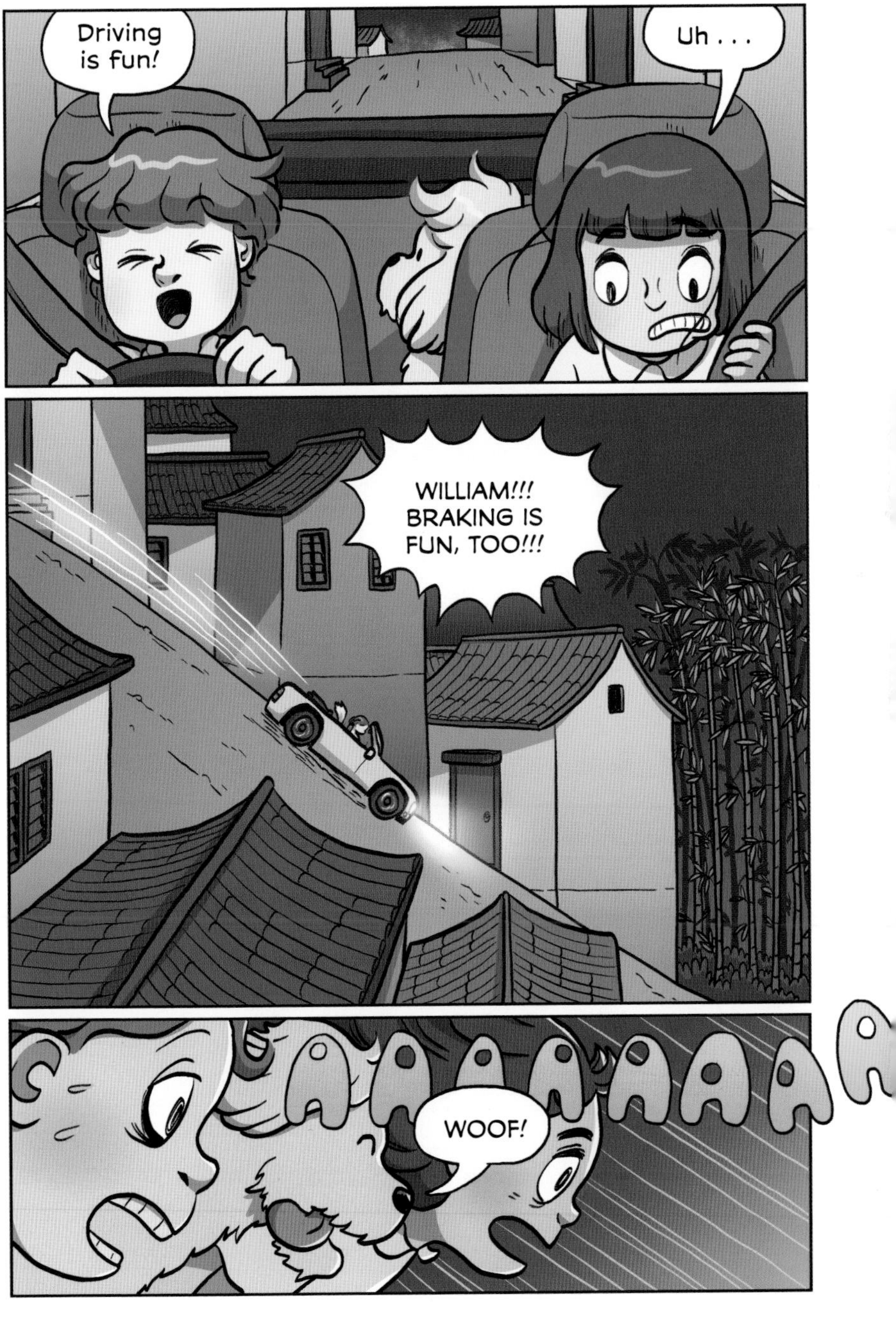
Driving is fun!
Uh . . .
WILLIAM!!! BRAKING IS FUN, TOO!!!
AAAAAAA
WOOF!

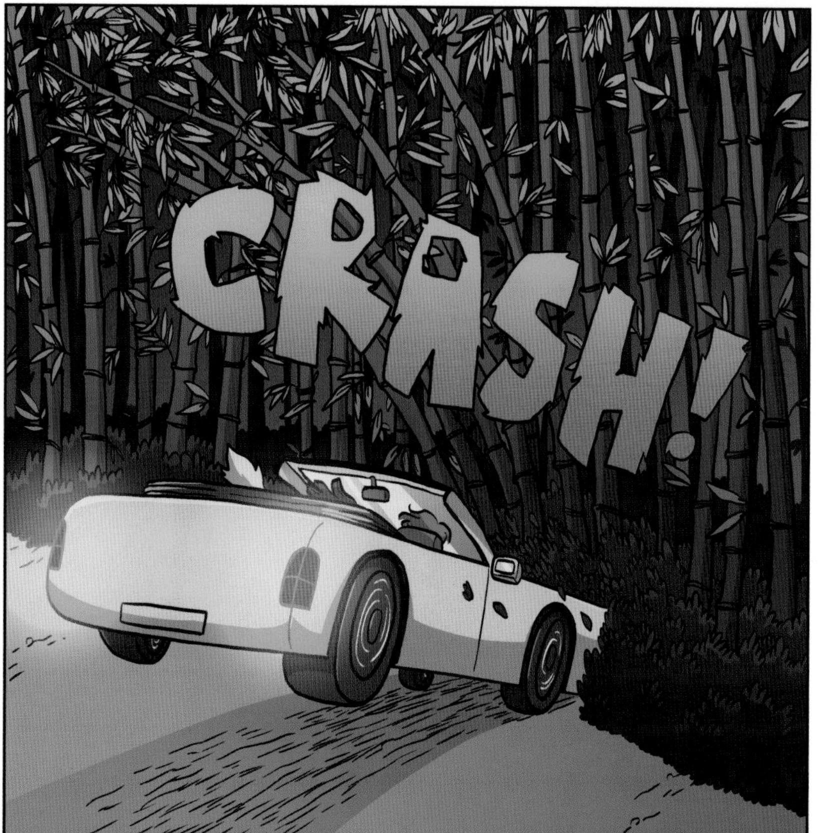
CRASH!

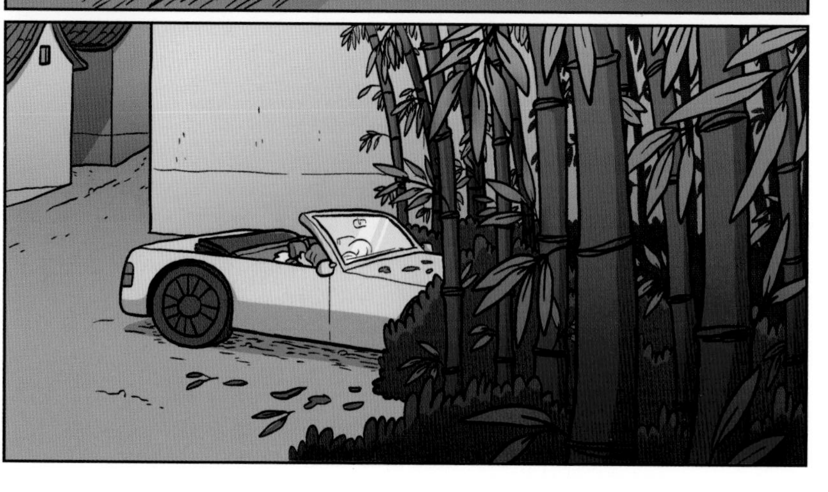

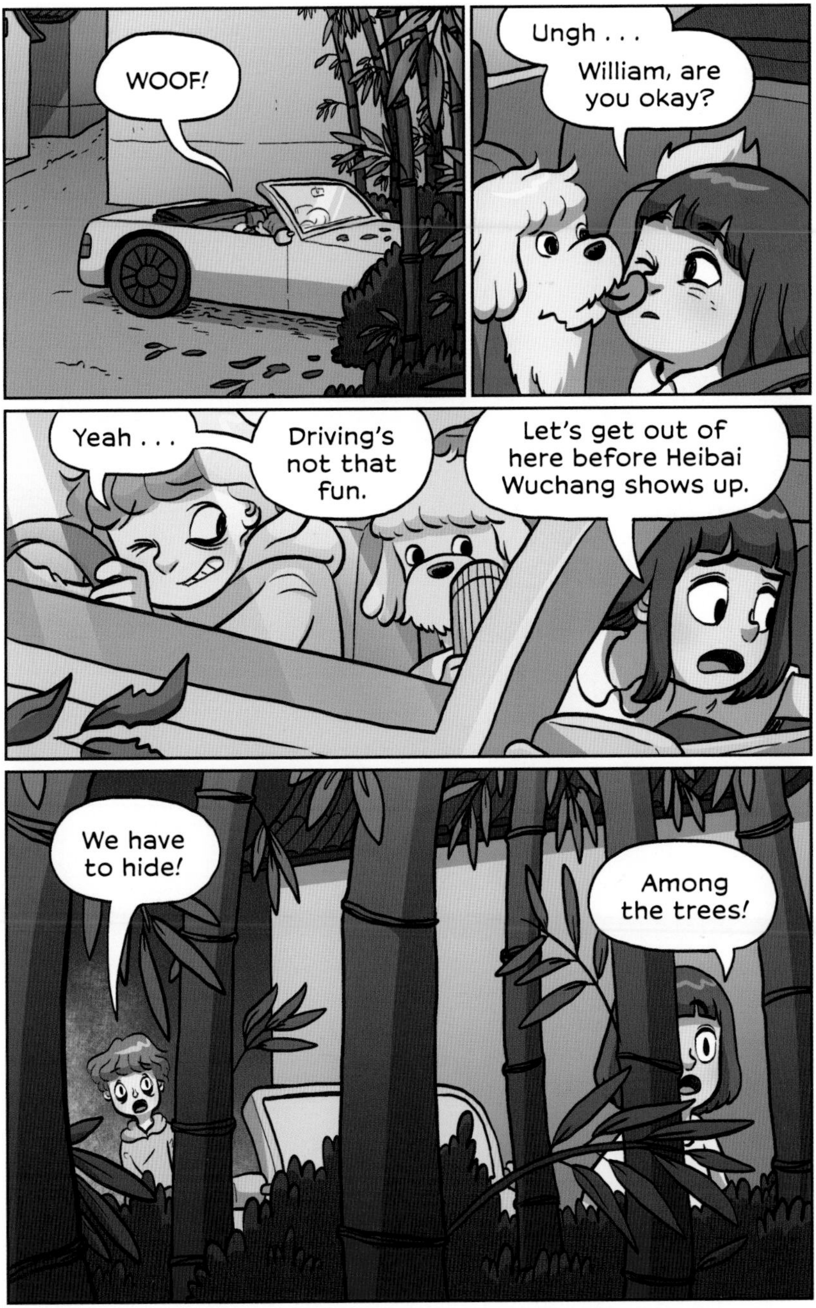
WOOF!
Ungh . . .
William, are you okay?
Yeah . . .
Driving's not that fun.
Let's get out of here before Heibai Wuchang shows up.
We have to hide!
Among the trees!

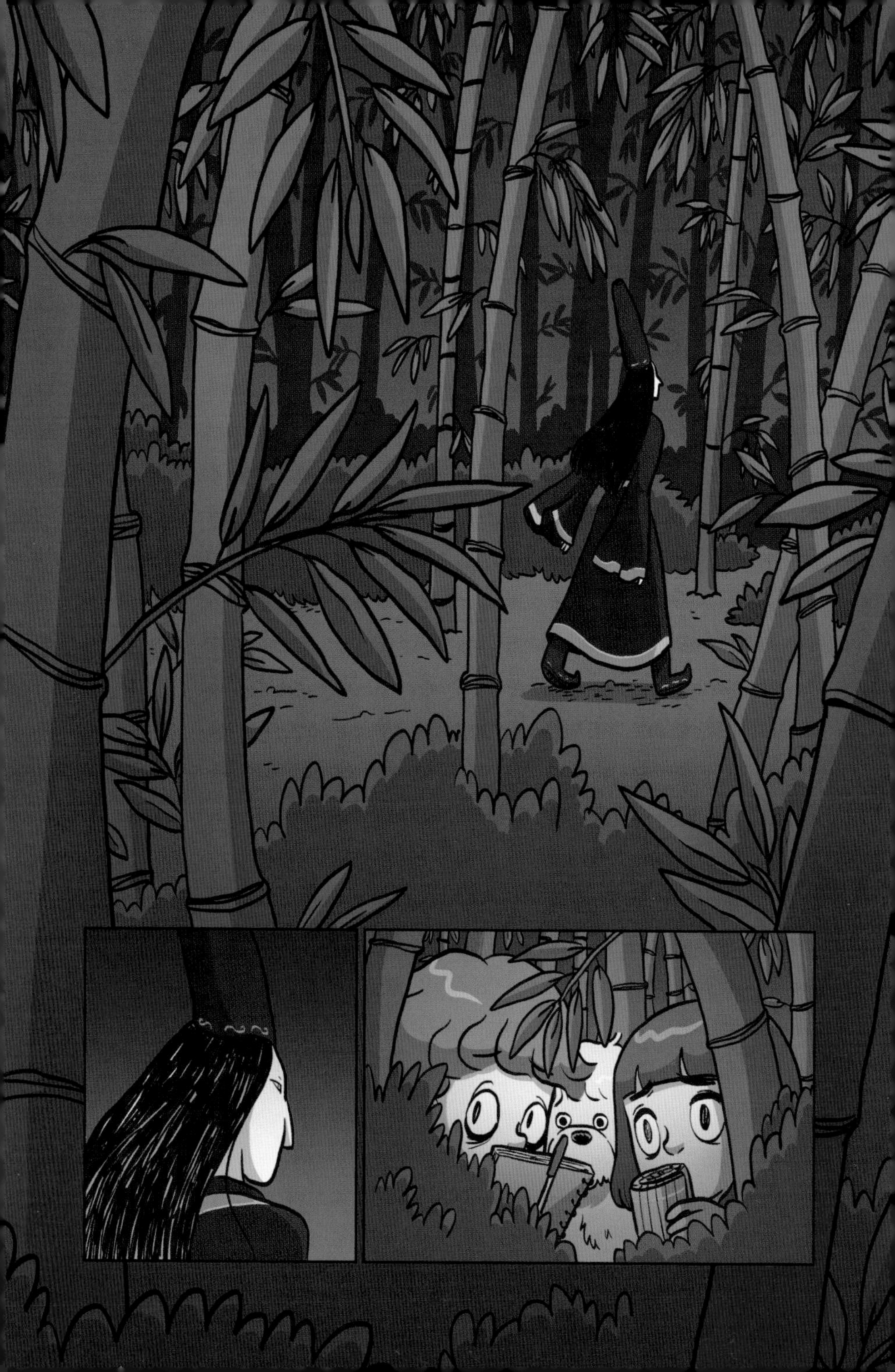

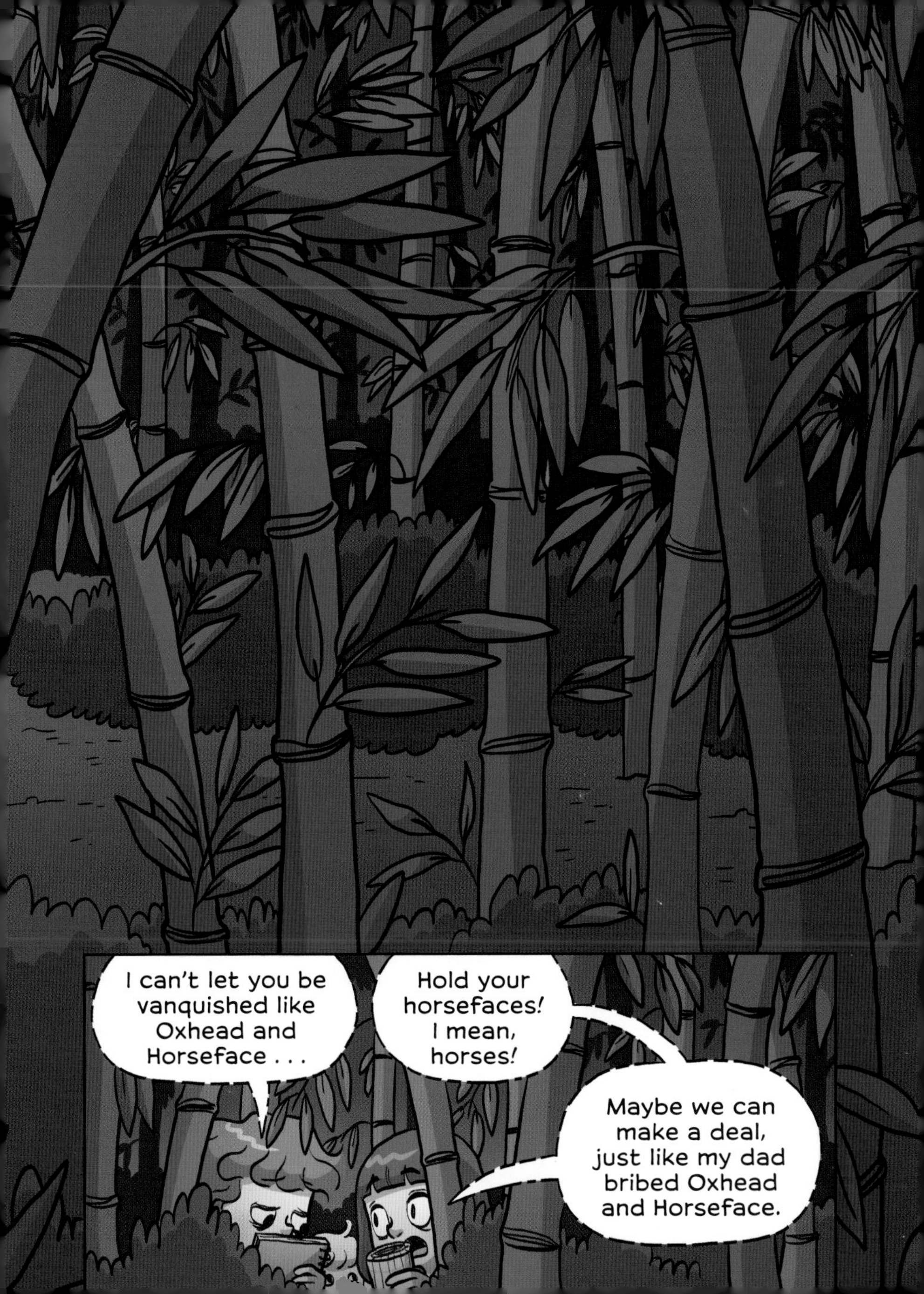
I can't let you be vanquished like Oxhead and Horseface . . .
Hold your horsefaces! I mean, horses!
Maybe we can make a deal, just like my dad bribed Oxhead and Horseface.

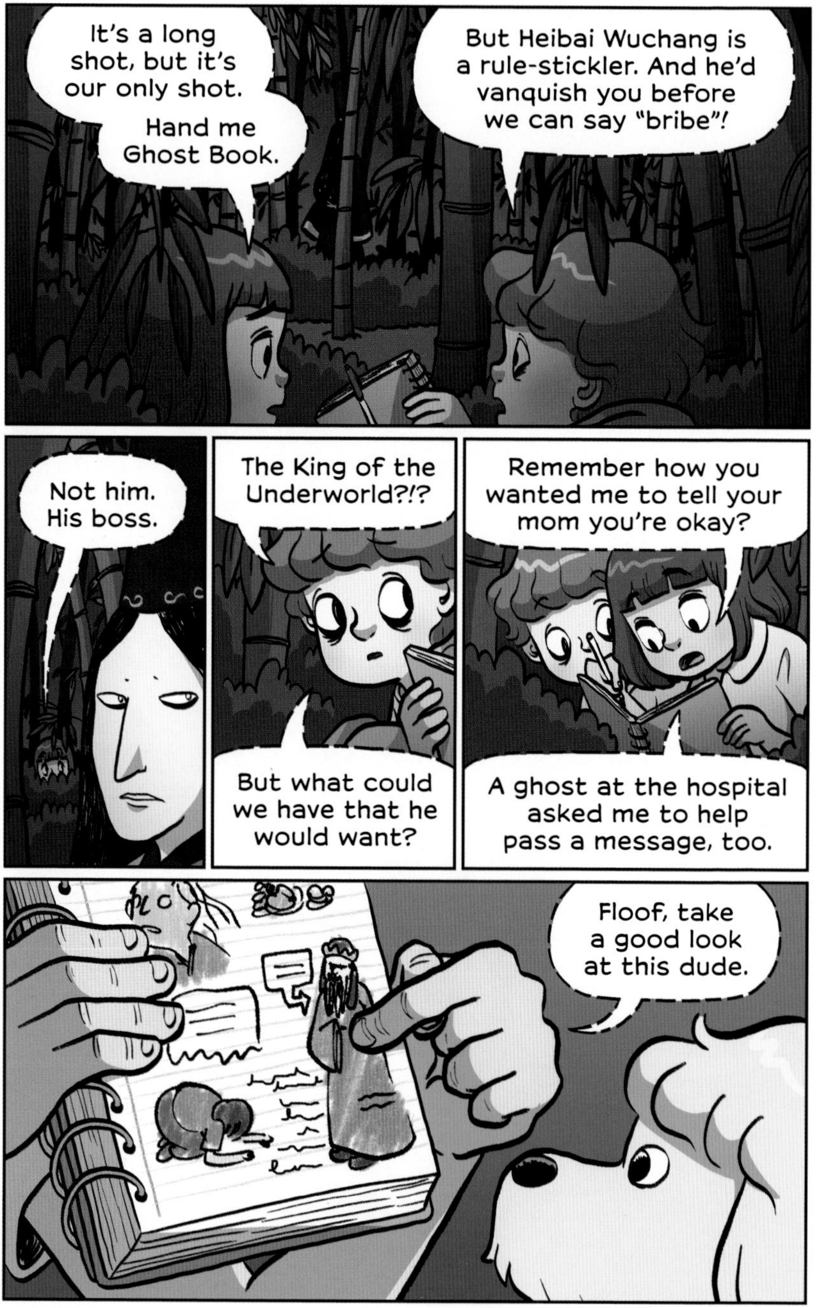
It's a long shot, but it's our only shot.
Hand me Ghost Book.
But Heibai Wuchang is a rule-stickler. And he'd vanquish you before we can say "bribe"!
Not him. His boss.
The King of the Underworld?!?
But what could we have that he would want?
Remember how you wanted me to tell your mom you're okay?
A ghost at the hospital asked me to help pass a message, too.
Floof, take a good look at this dude.

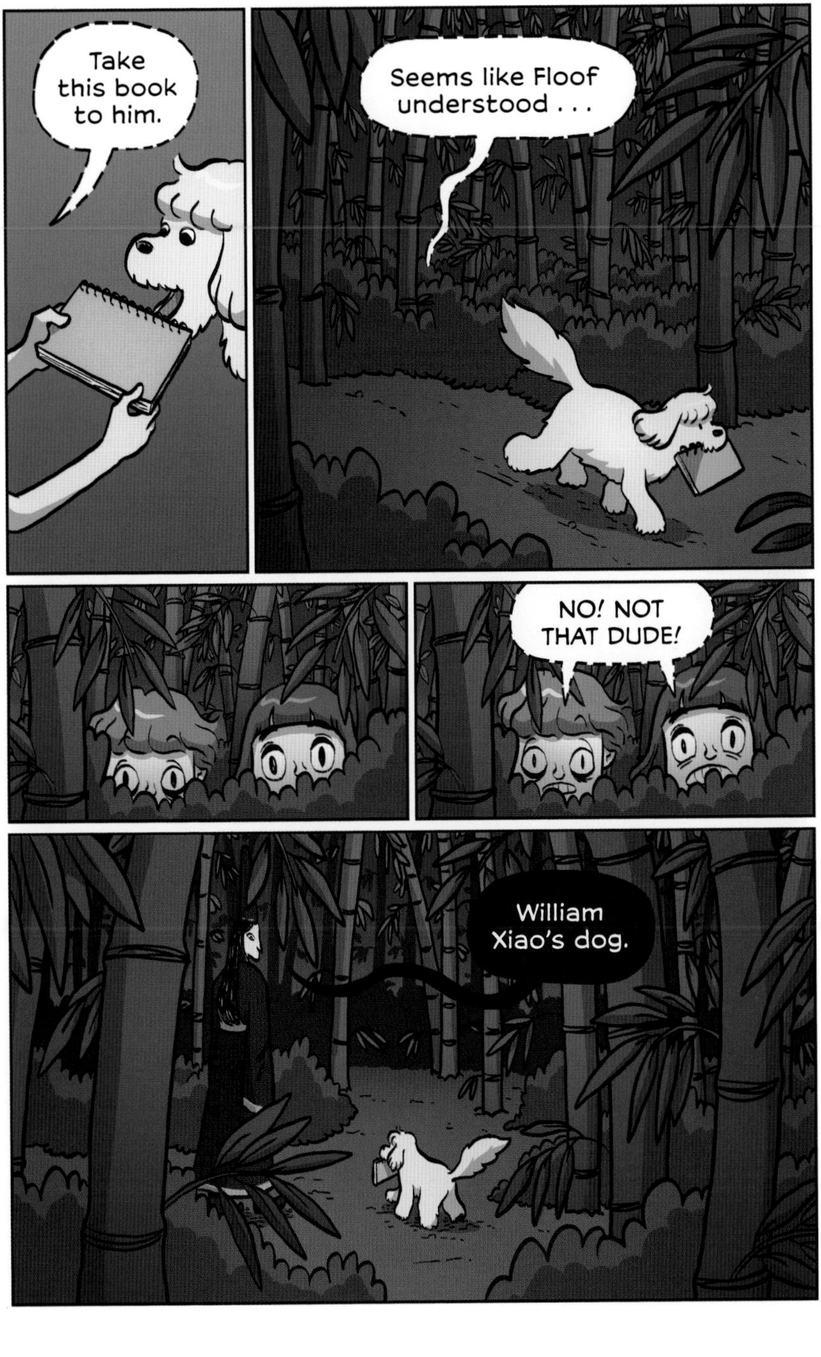
Take this book to him.
Seems like Floof understood . . .
NO! NOT THAT DUDE!
William Xiao's dog.

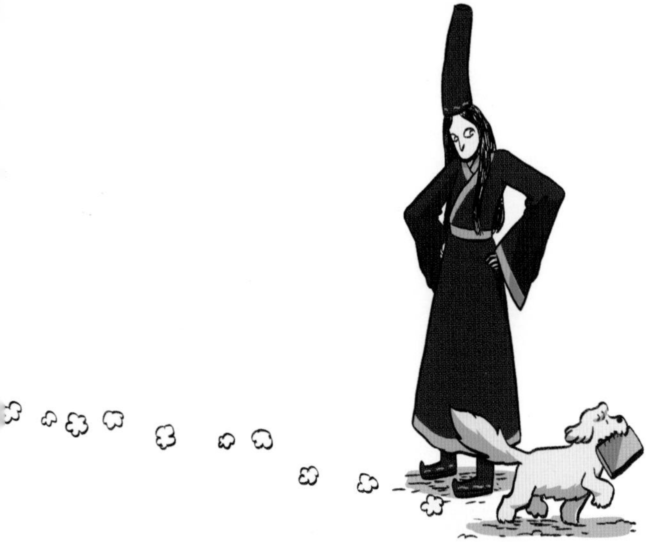

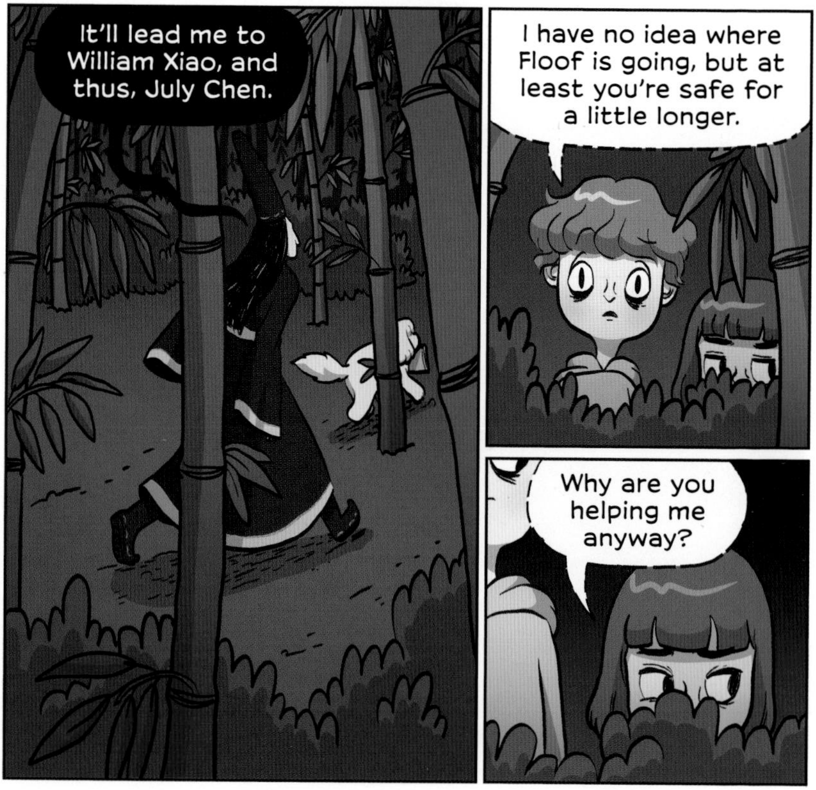
It'll lead me to William Xiao, and thus, July Chen.
I have no idea where Floof is going, but at least you're safe for a little longer.
Why are you helping me anyway?

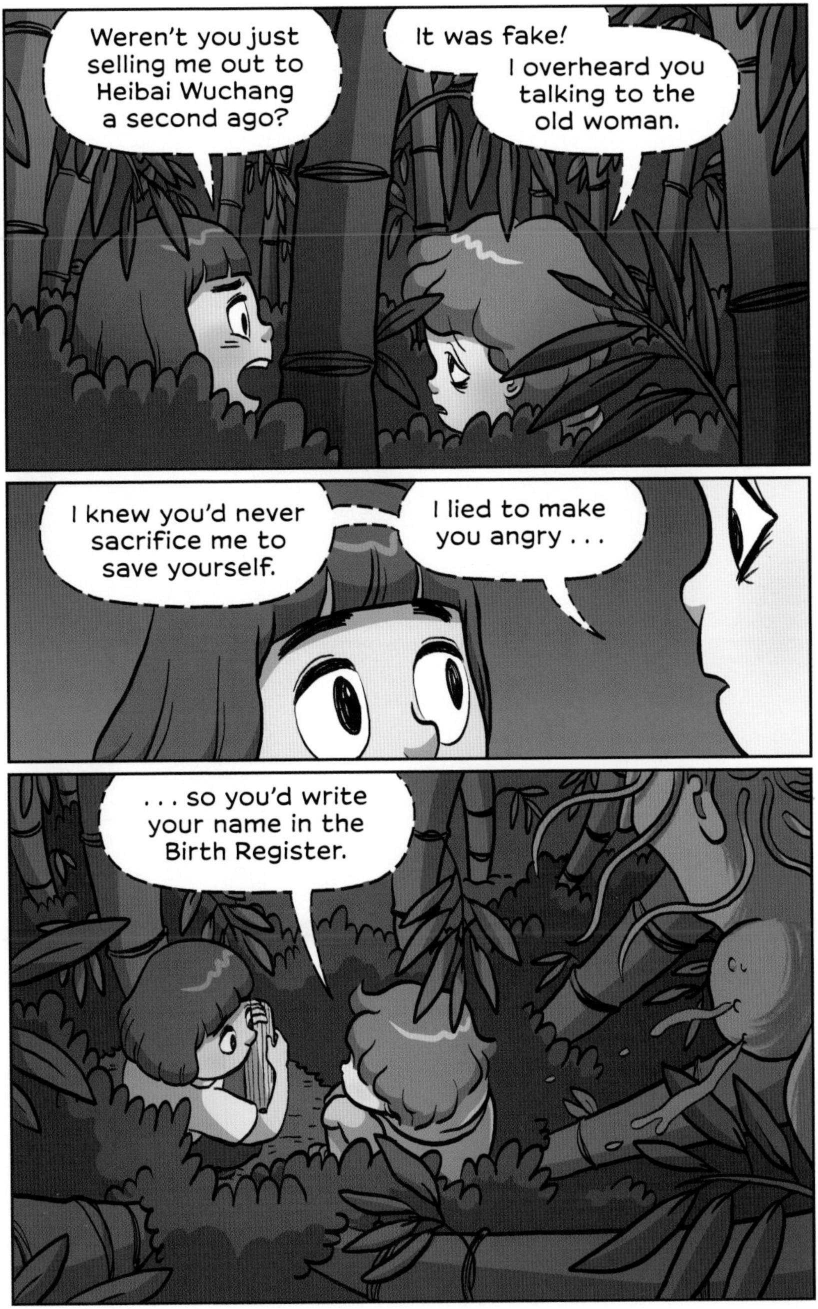
Weren't you just selling me out to Heibai Wuchang a second ago?
It was fake!
I overheard you talking to the old woman.
I knew you'd never sacrifice me to save yourself.
I lied to make you angry . . .
. . . so you'd write your name in the Birth Register.

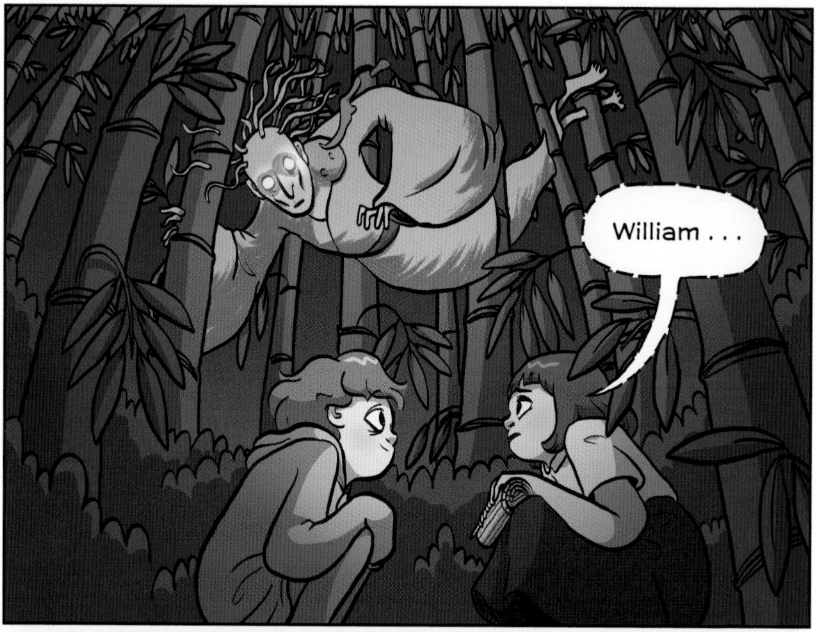
William . . .

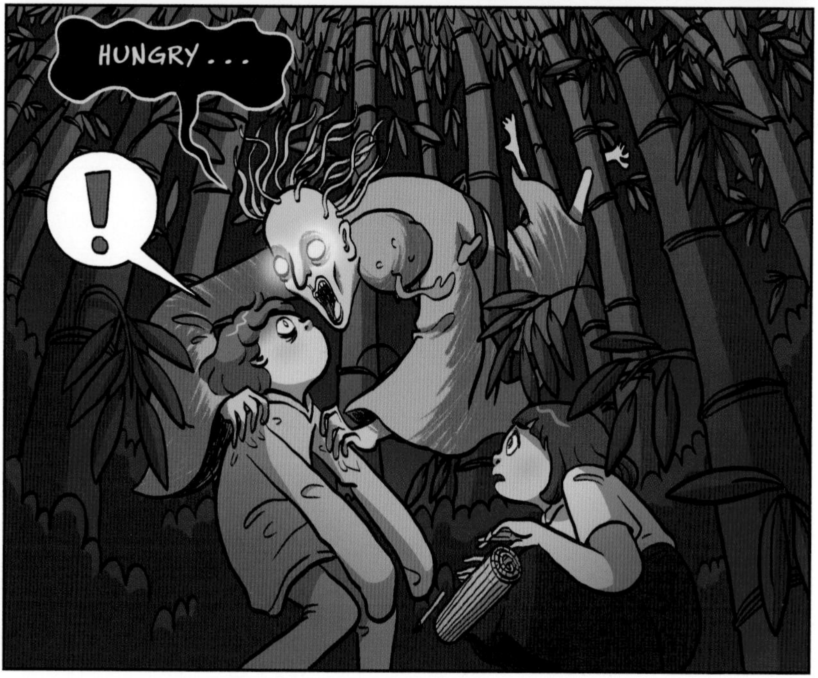
HUNGRY . . .
!

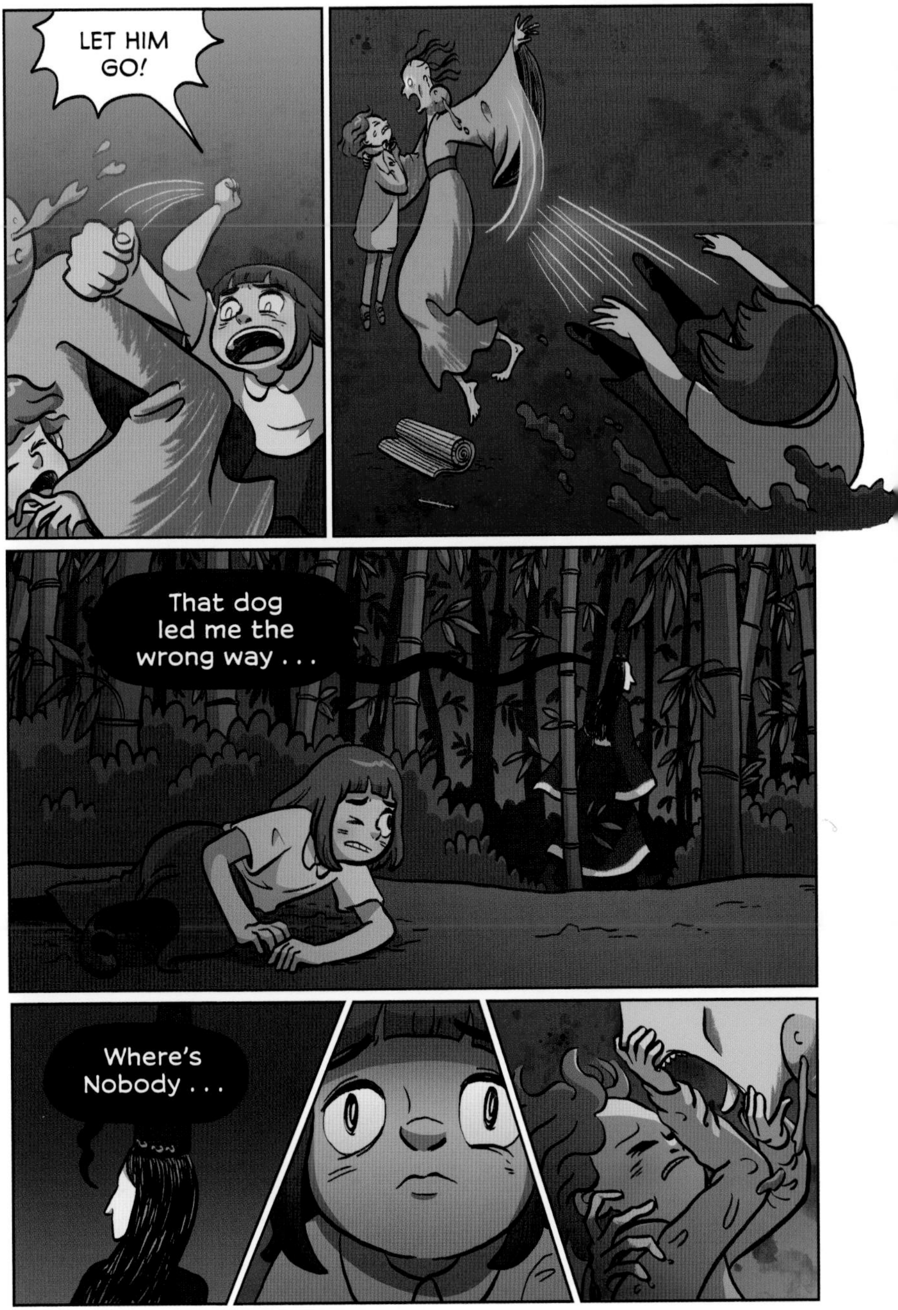
LET HIM GO!
That dog led me the wrong way . . .
Where's Nobody . . .

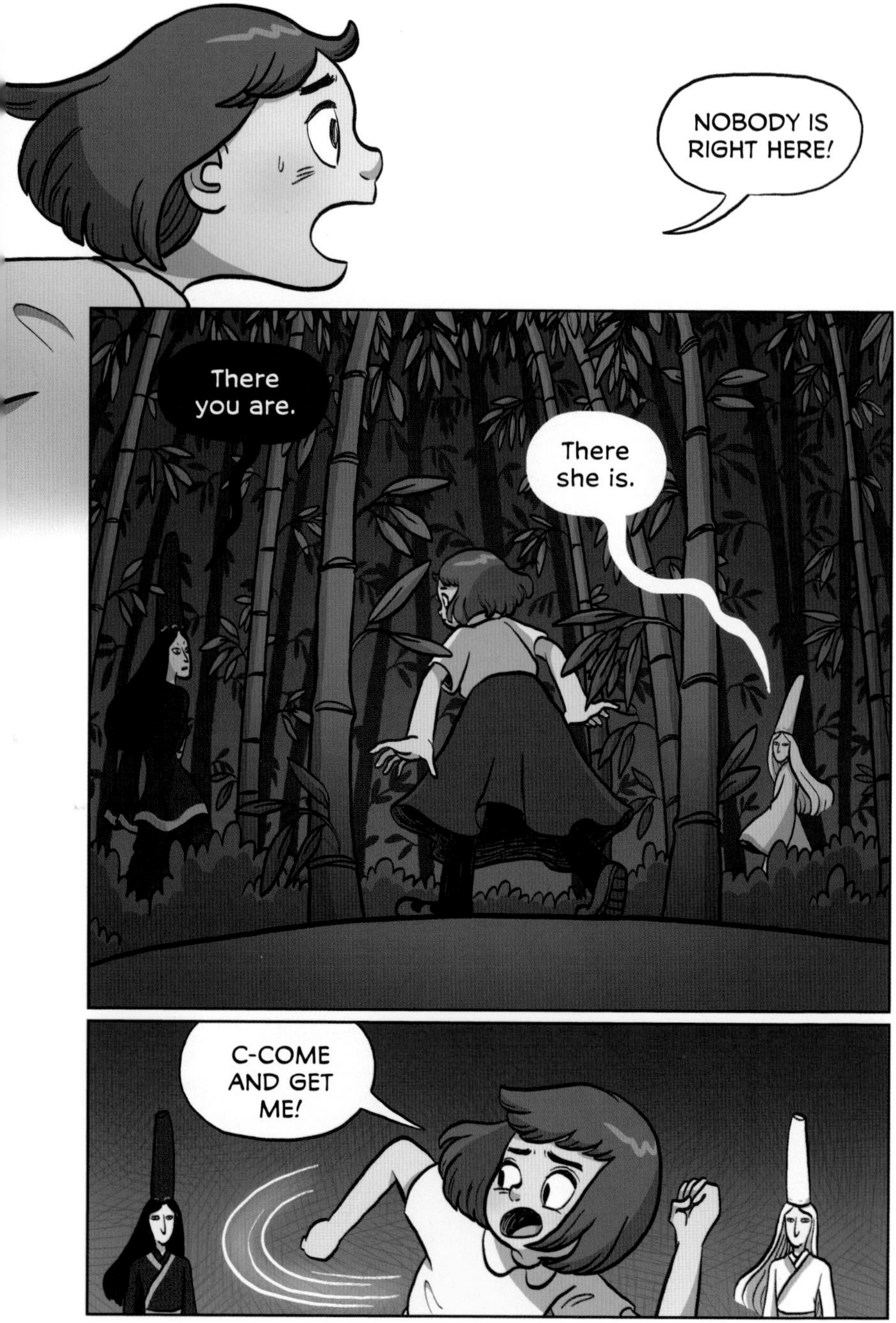
NOBODY IS RIGHT HERE!
There you are.
There she is.
C-COME AND GET ME!

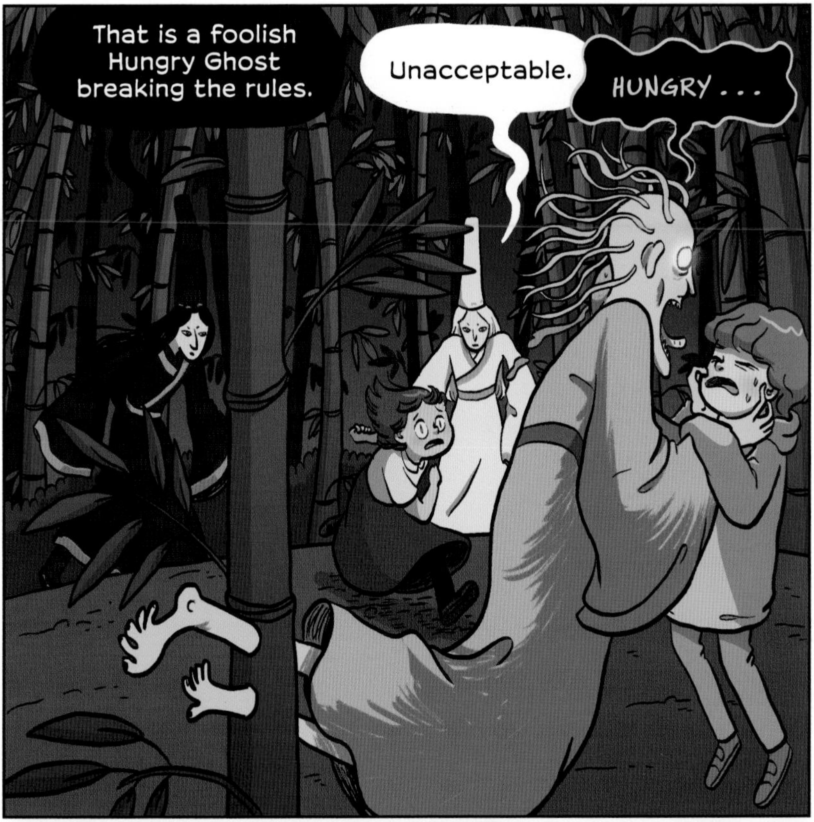
That is a foolish Hungry Ghost breaking the rules.
Unacceptable.
HUNGRY . . .

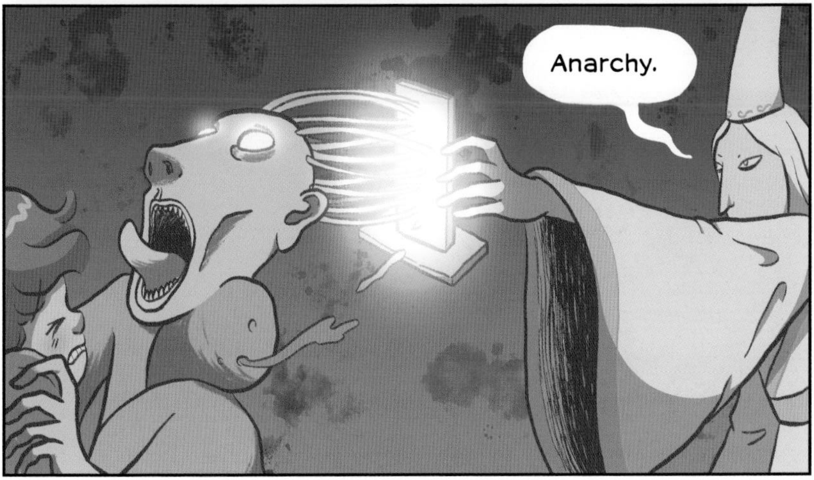
Anarchy.

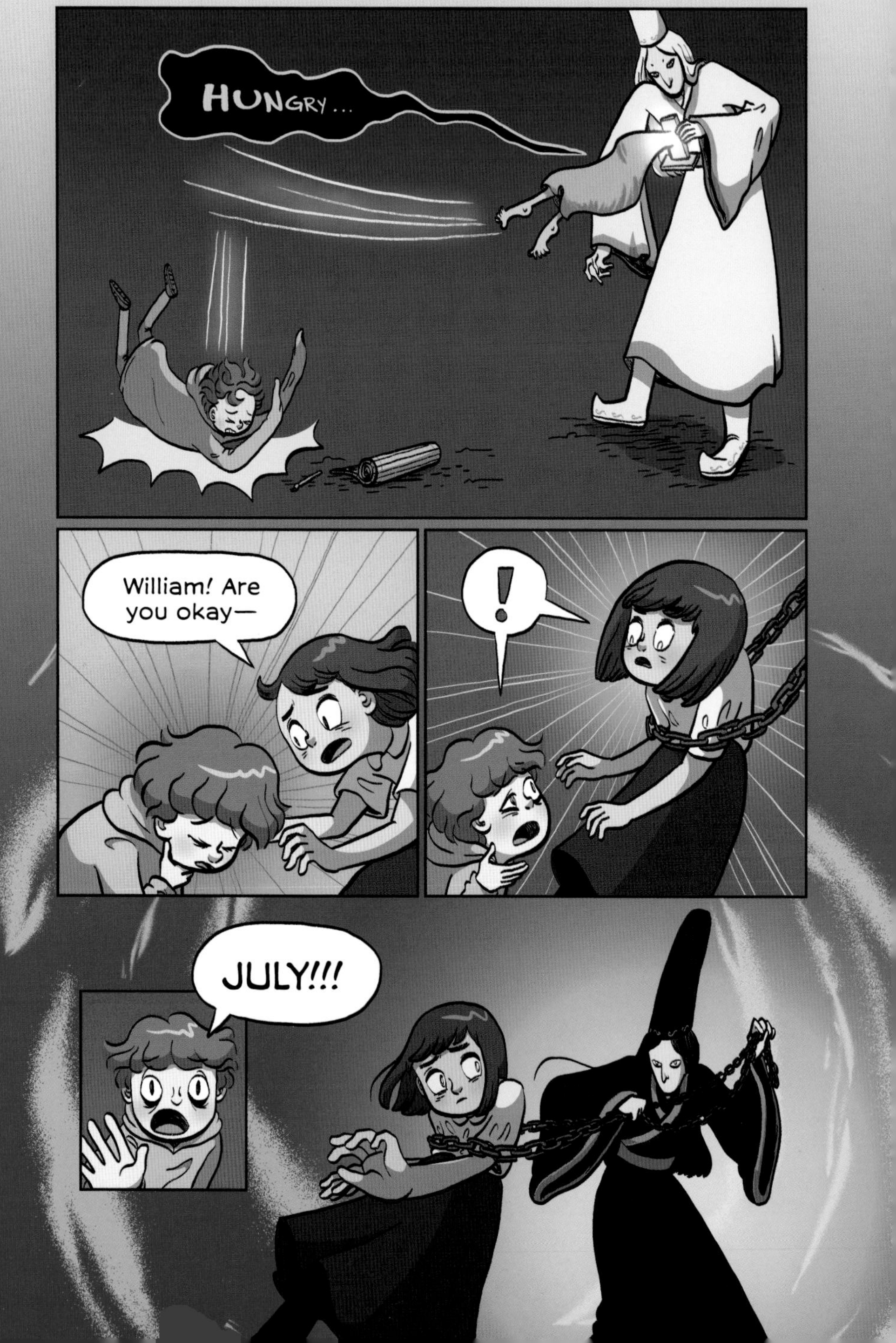
HUNGRY...
William! Are you okay—
!
JULY!!!

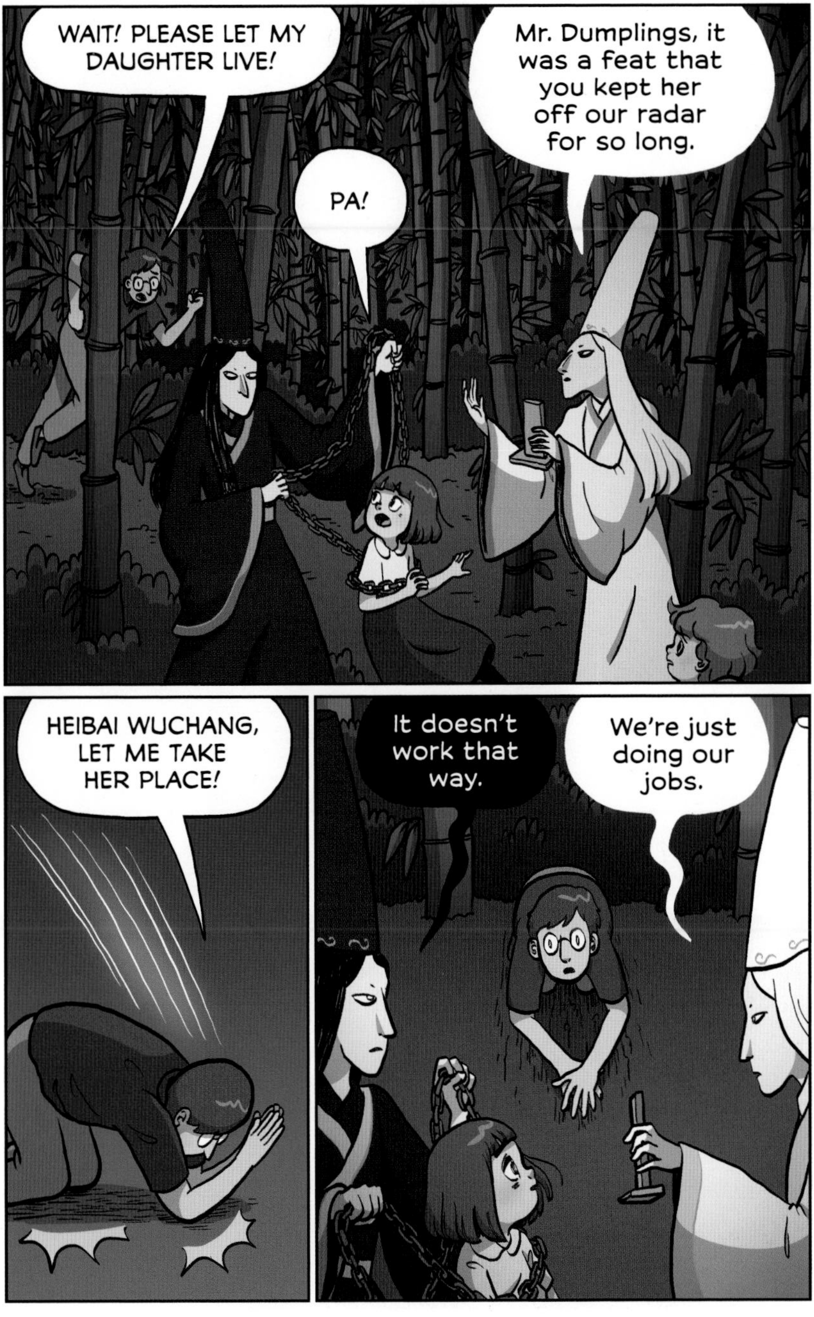
WAIT! PLEASE LET MY DAUGHTER LIVE!
PA!
Mr. Dumplings, it was a feat that you kept her off our radar for so long.
HEIBAI WUCHANG, LET ME TAKE HER PLACE!
It doesn't work that way.
We're just doing our jobs.

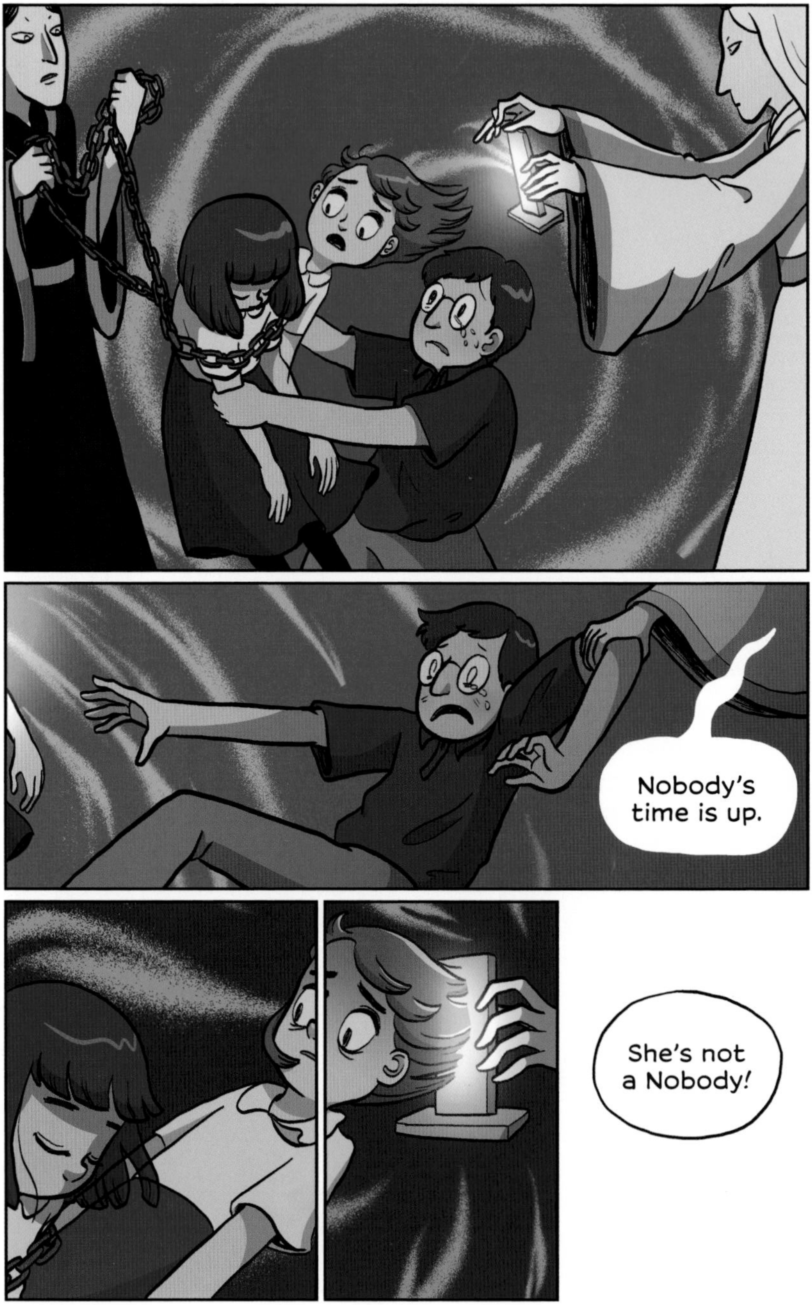
Nobody's time is up.
She's not a Nobody!

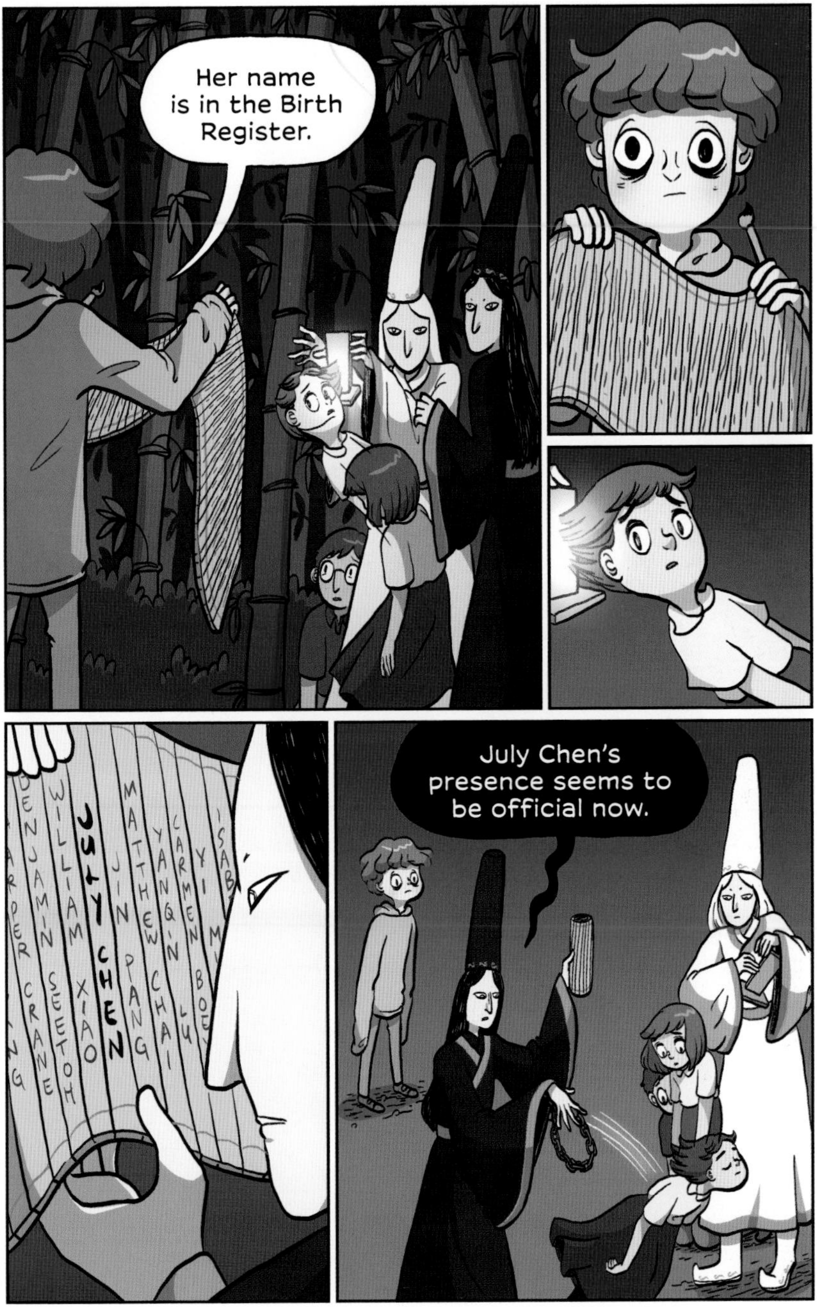
Her name is in the Birth Register.
JULY CHEN
July Chen's presence seems to be official now.

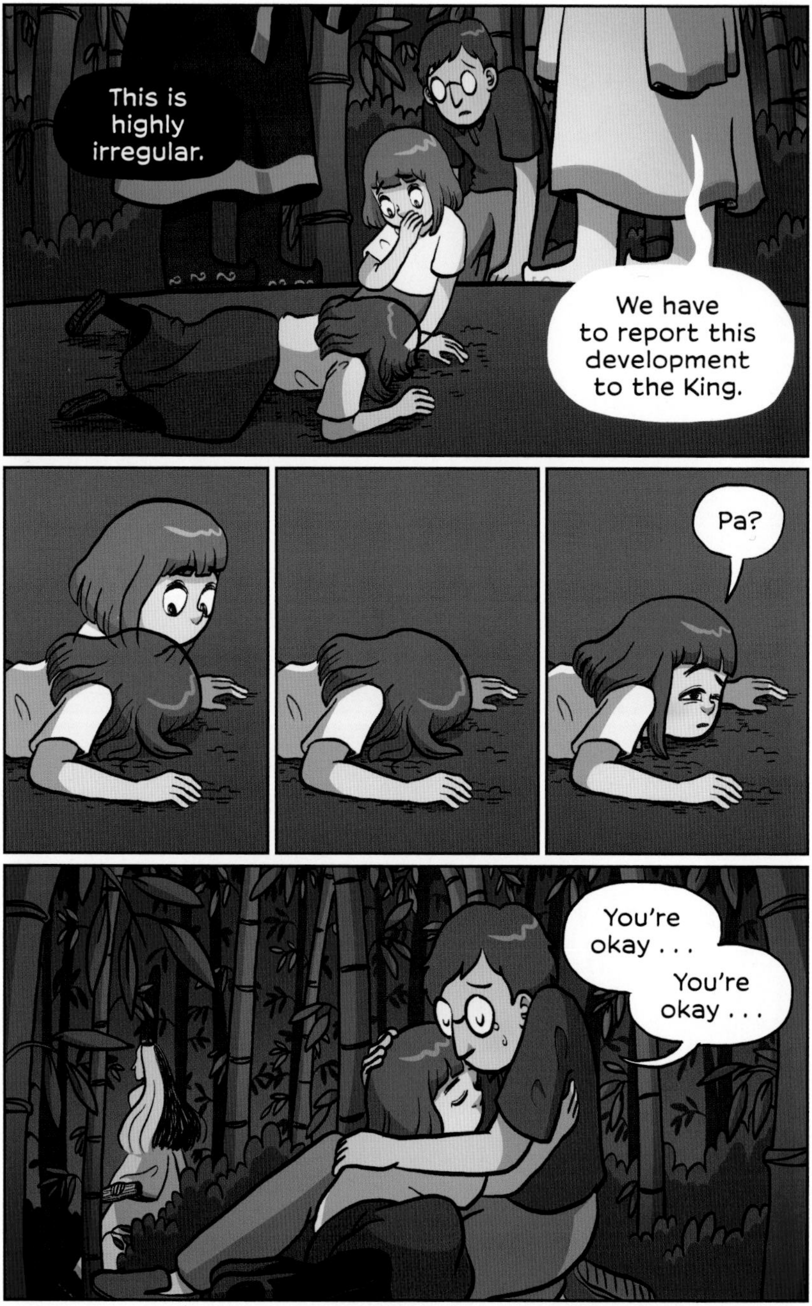
This is highly irregular.
We have to report this development to the King.
Pa?
You're okay . . .
You're okay . . .

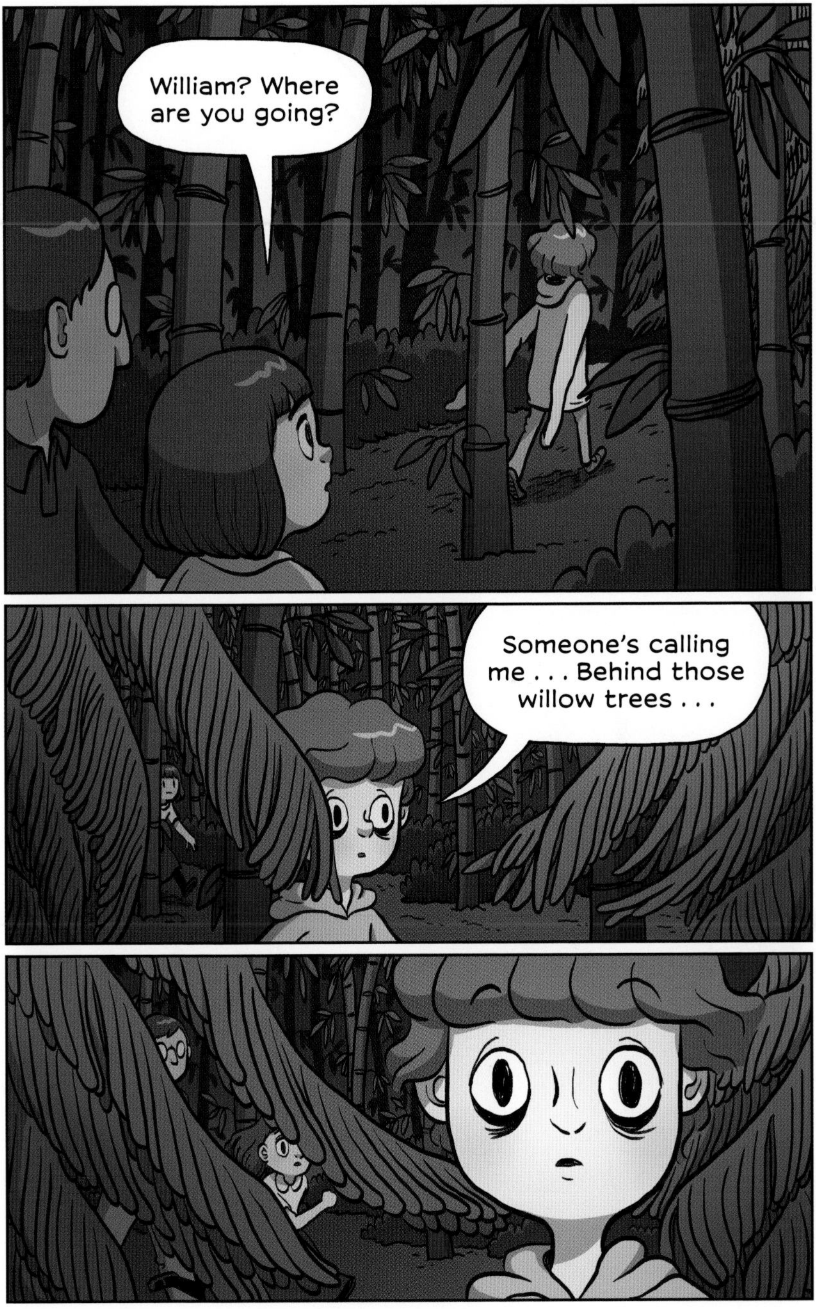
William? Where are you going?
Someone's calling me . . . Behind those willow trees . . .

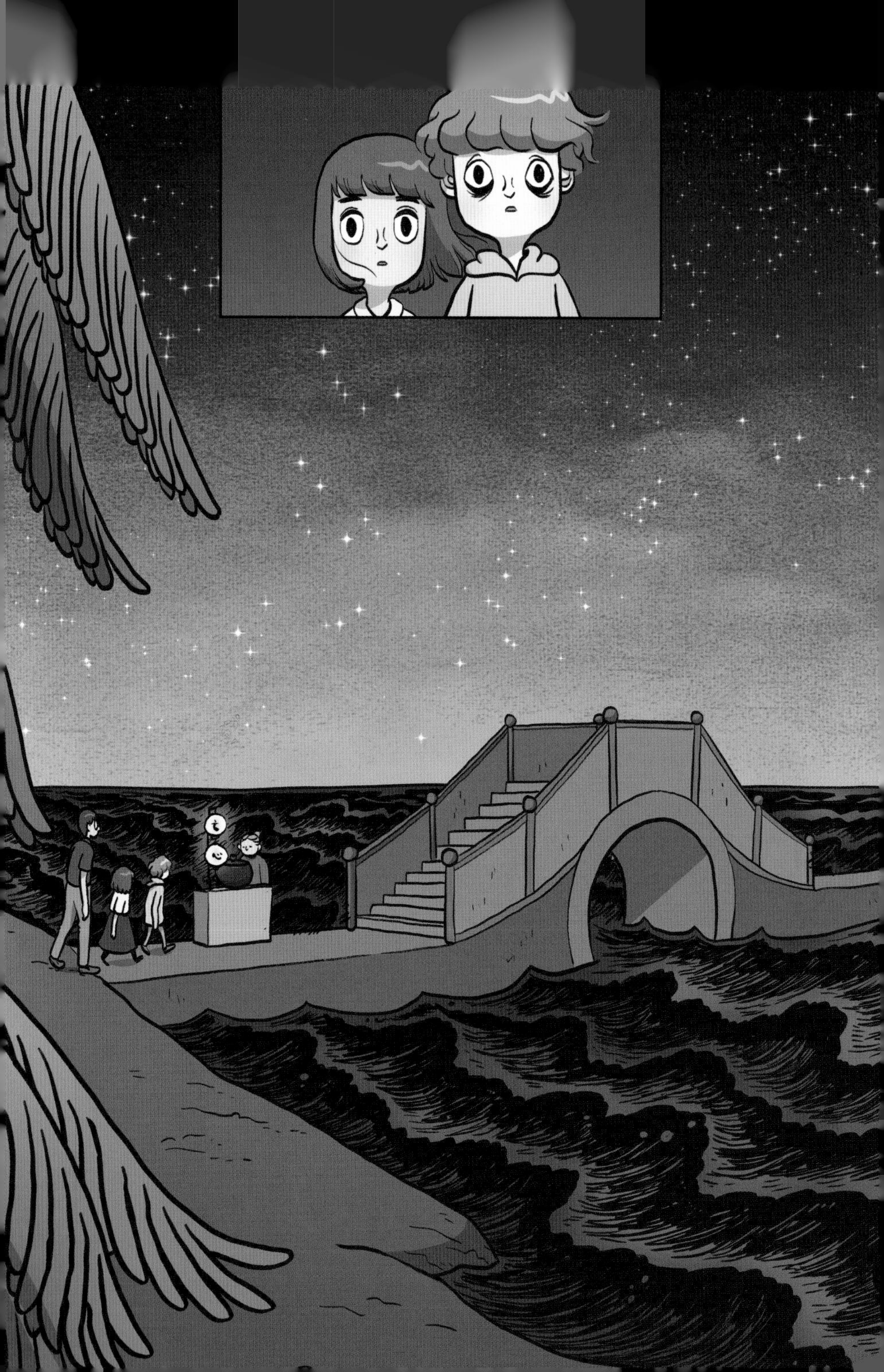

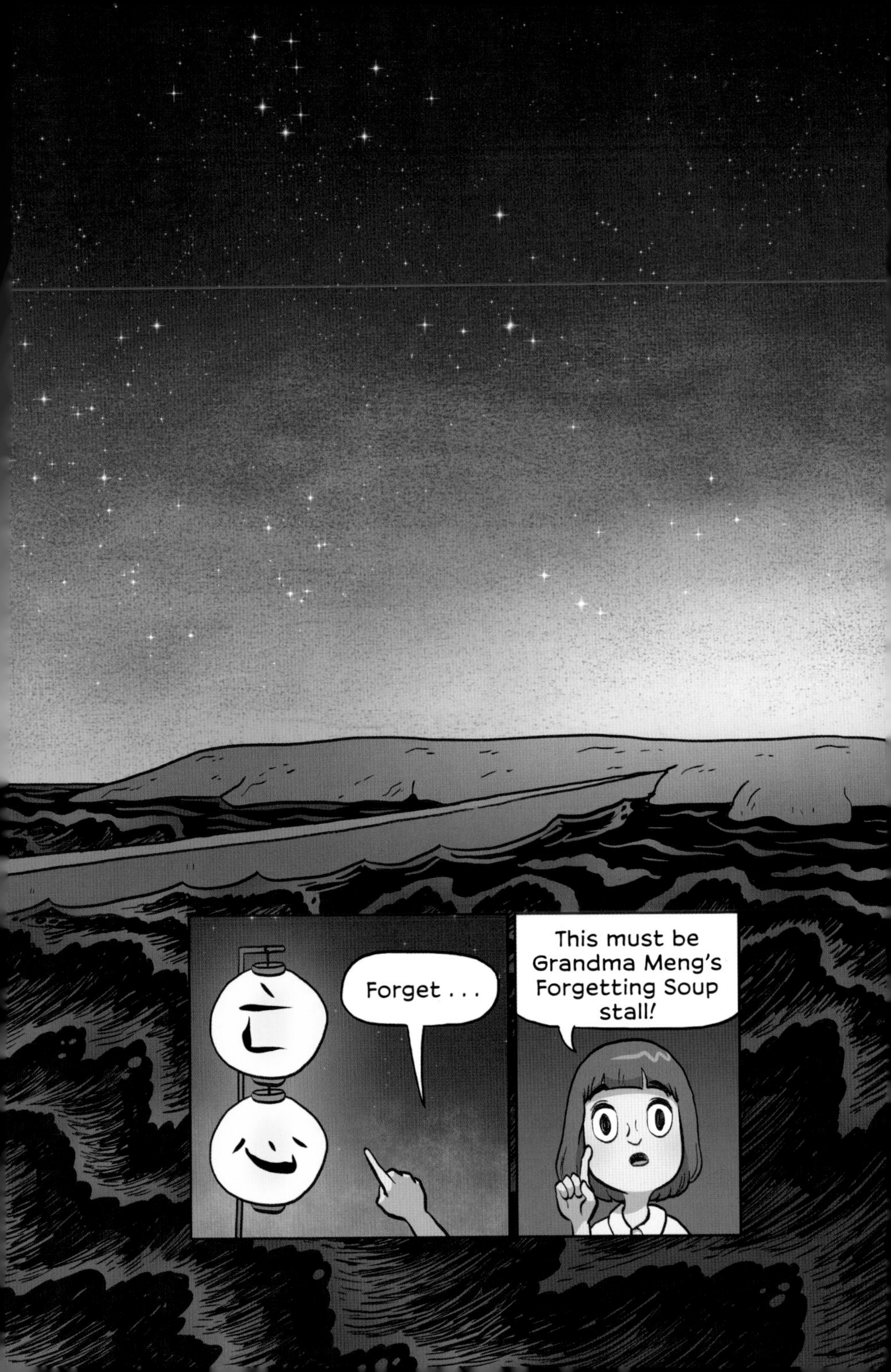
Forget . . .
This must be Grandma Meng's Forgetting Soup stall!

We meet again.
Are you Grandma Meng?!?
Yes. You're at the Bridge at the End.
The Bridge—

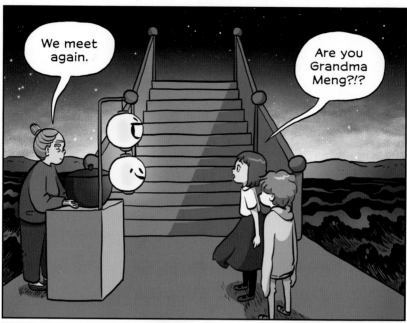

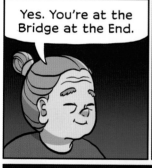

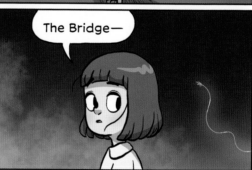

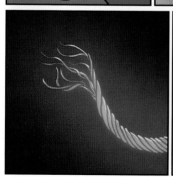

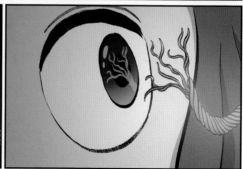

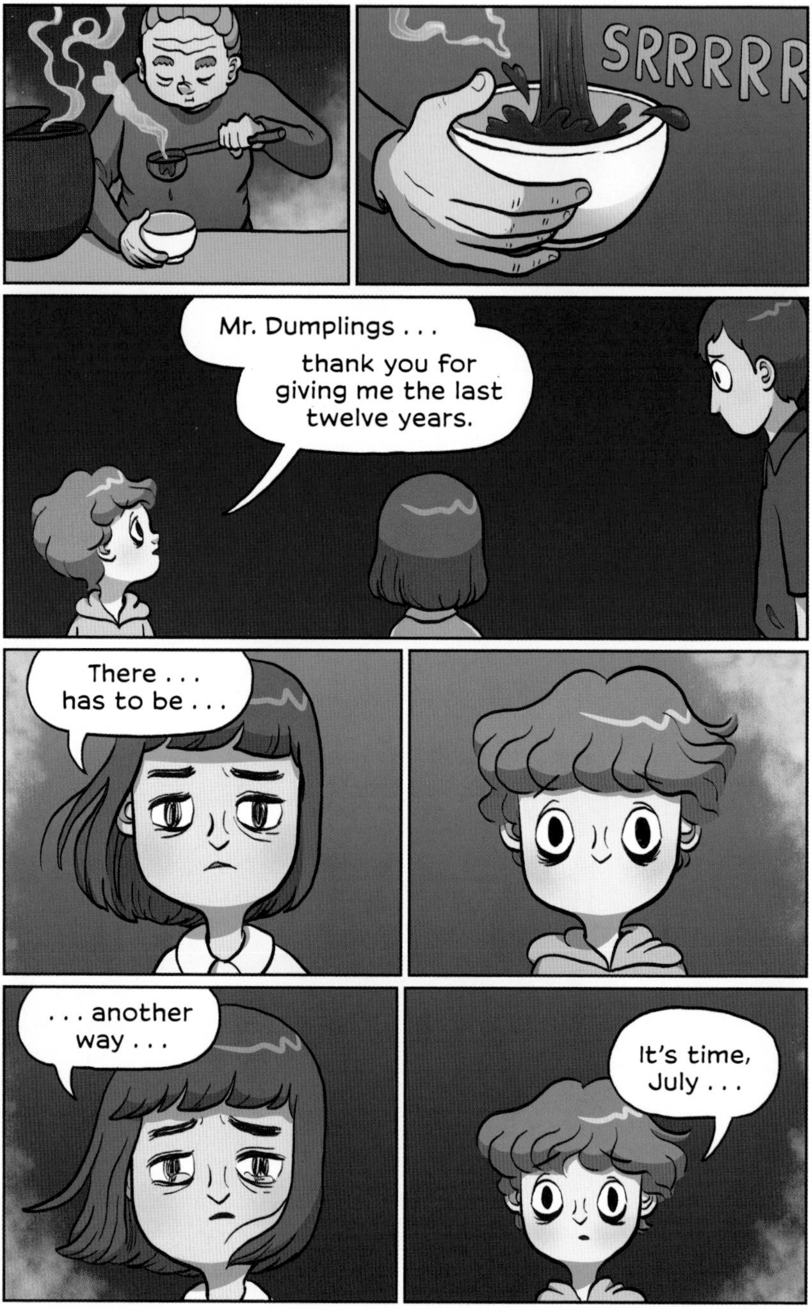
SRRRRR
Mr. Dumplings . . .
thank you for giving me the last twelve years.
There . . . has to be . . .
. . . another way . . .
It's time, July . . .

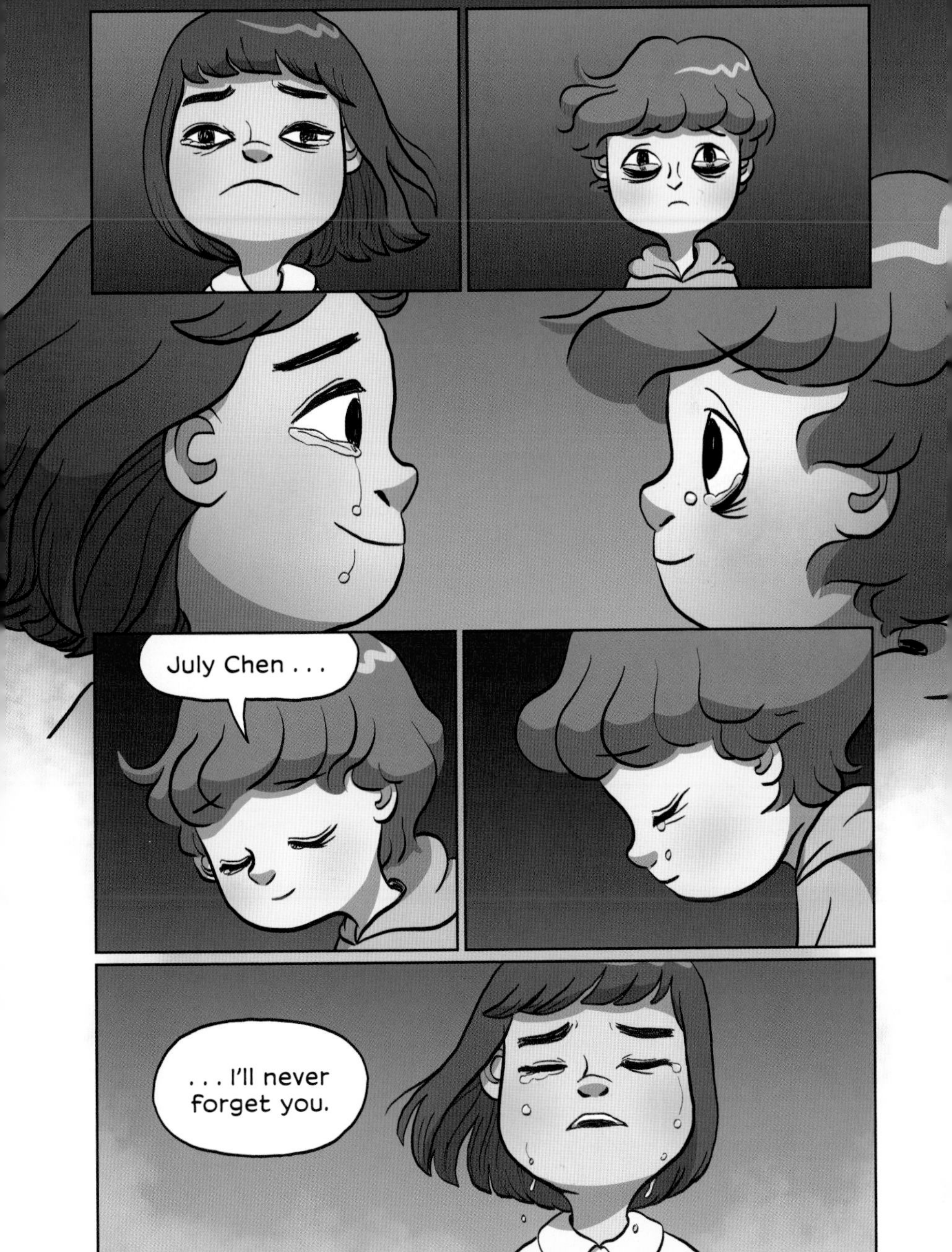
July Chen . . .
. . . I'll never forget you.

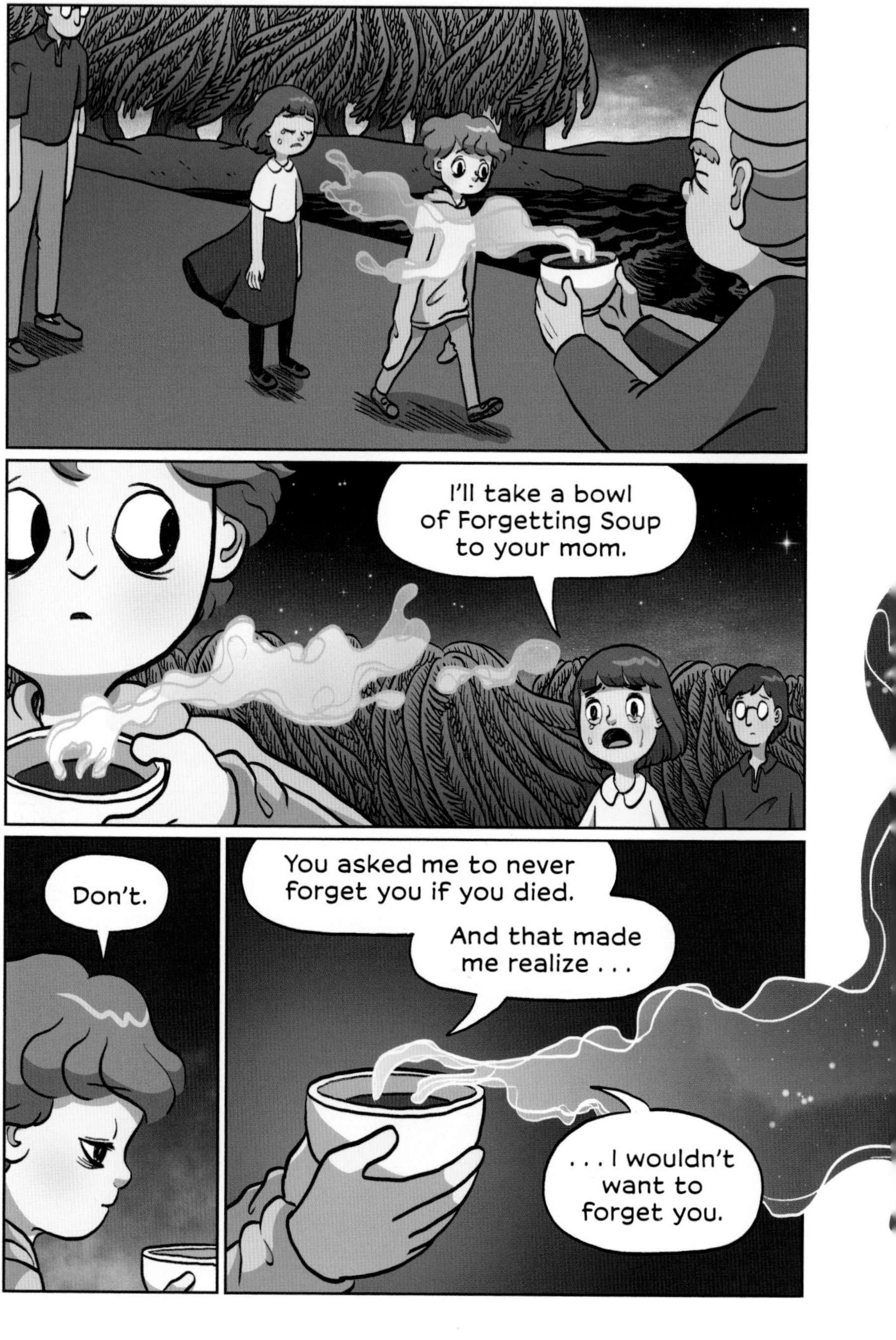
I'll take a bowl of Forgetting Soup to your mom.
Don't.
You asked me to never forget you if you died.
And that made me realize . . .
. . . I wouldn't want to forget you.

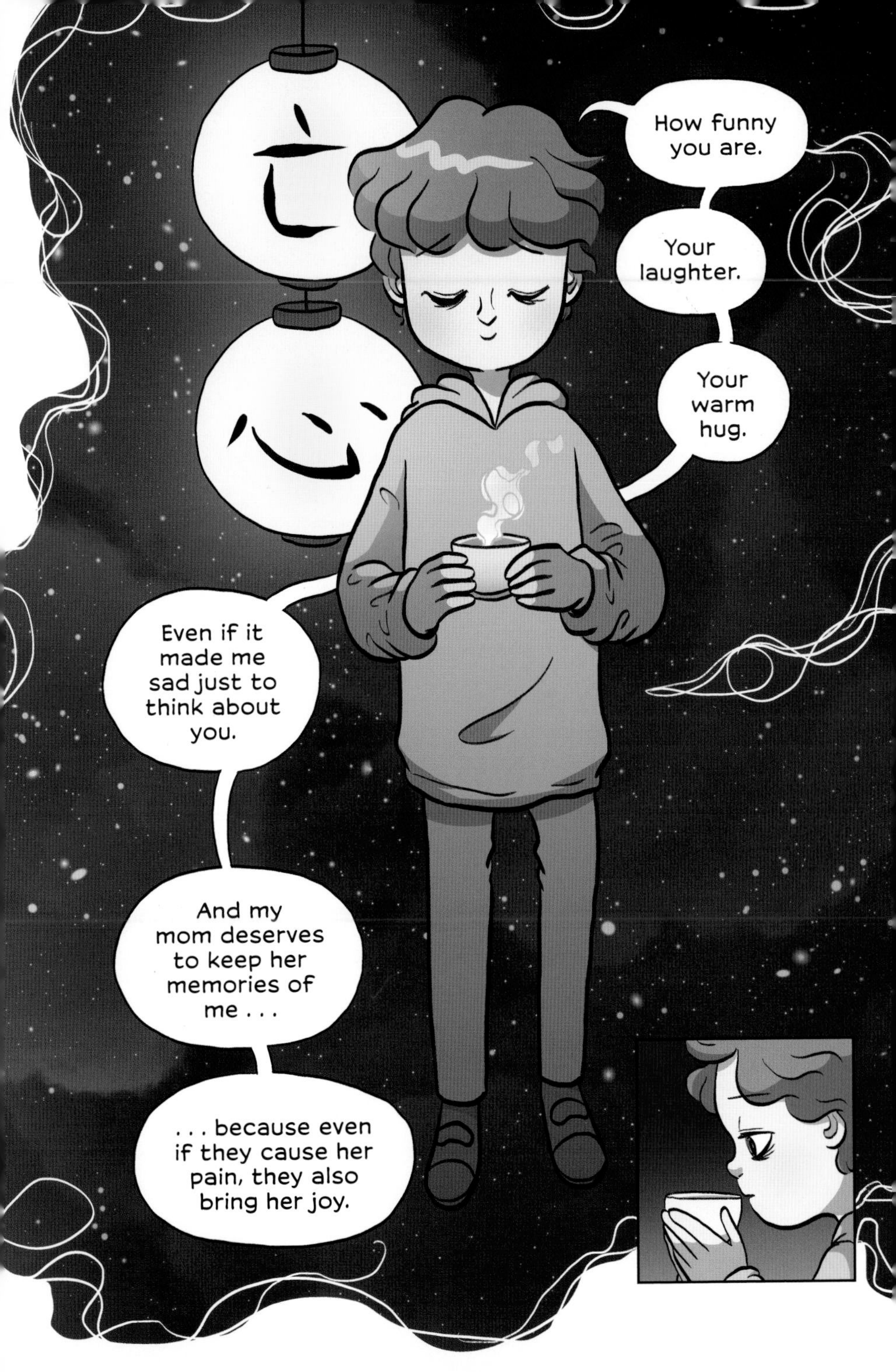
How funny you are.
Your laughter.
Your warm hug.
Even if it made me sad just to think about you.
And my mom deserves to keep her memories of me . . .
. . . because even if they cause her pain, they also bring her joy.

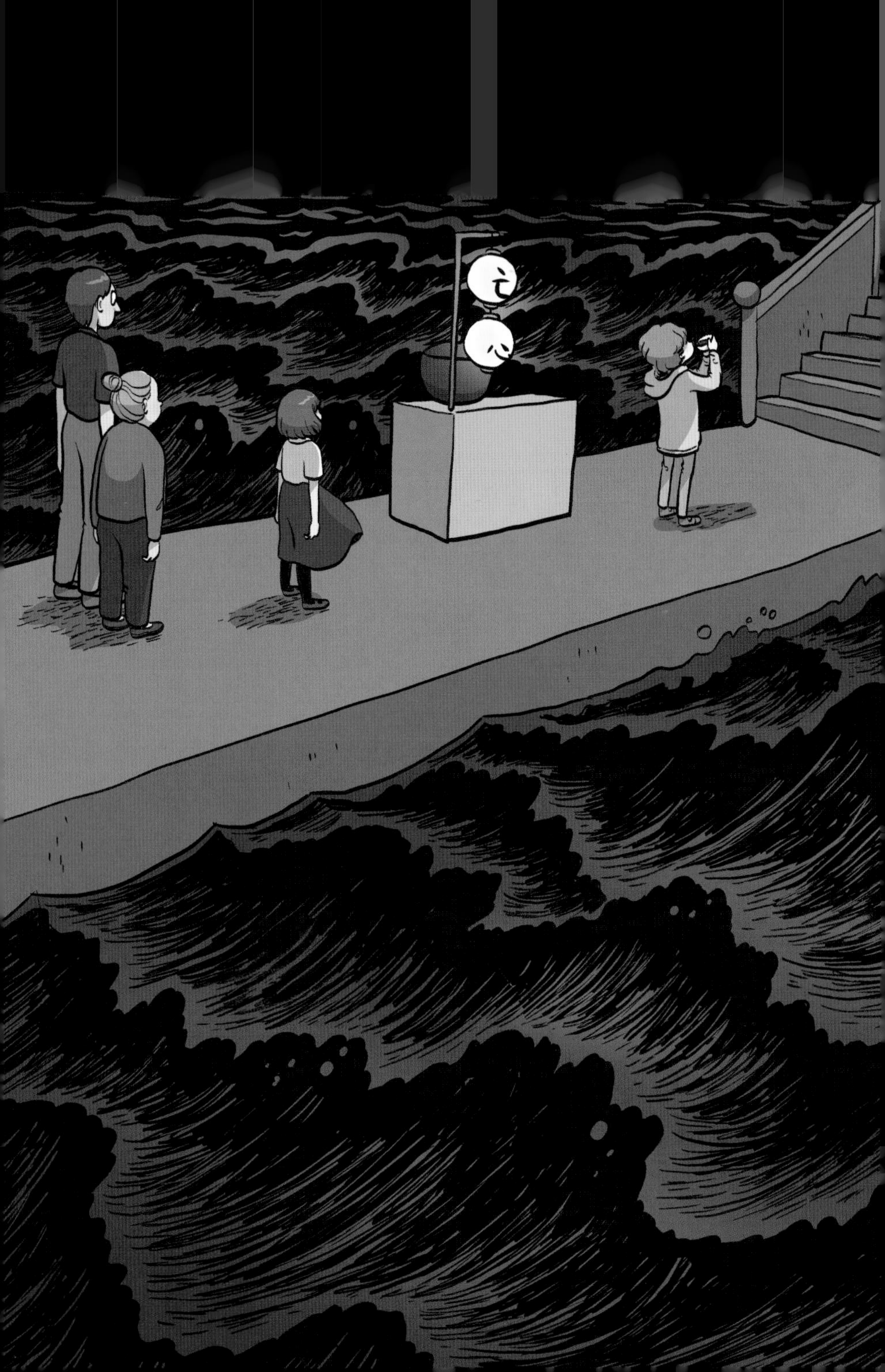

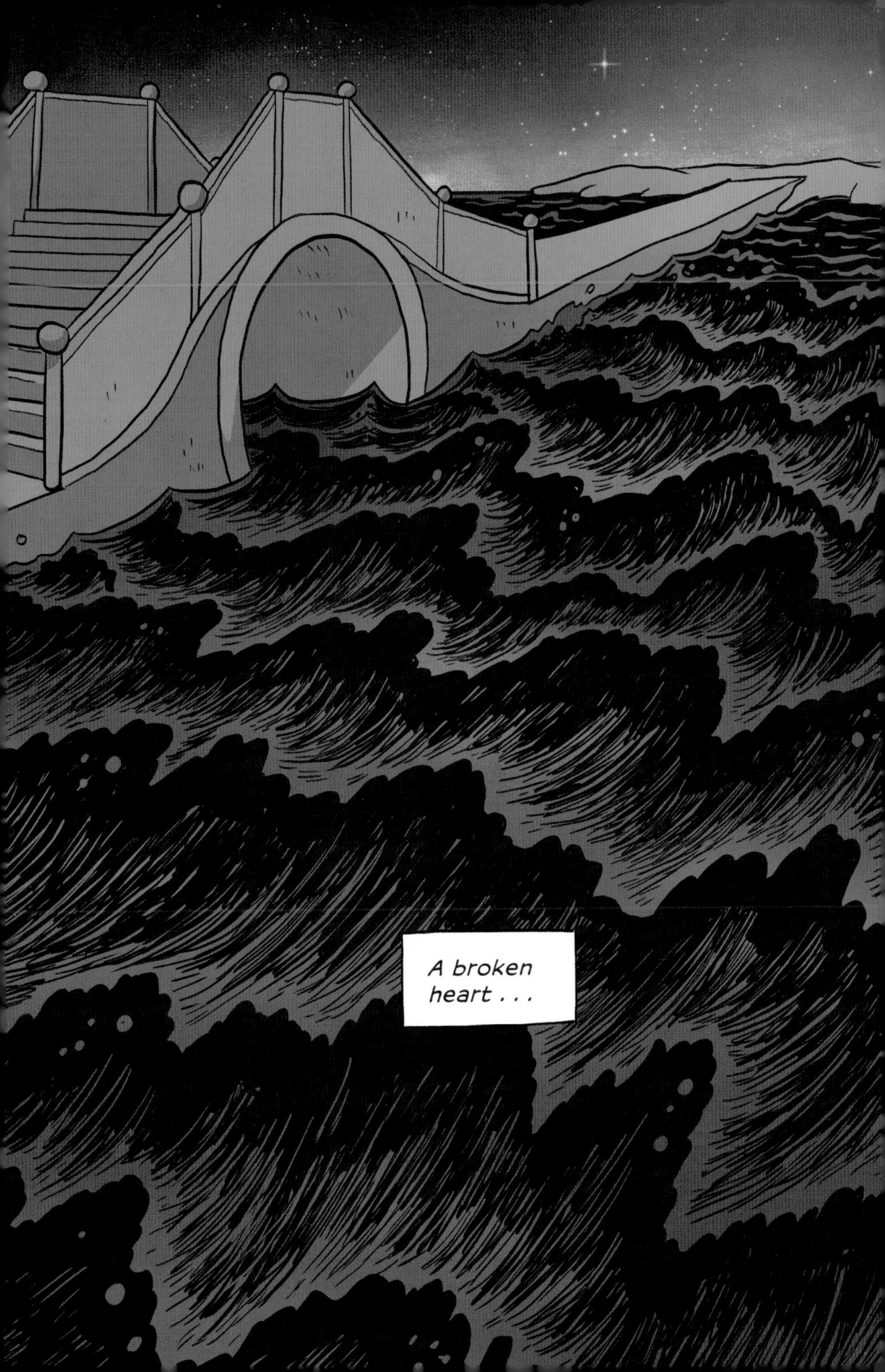
A broken heart . . .

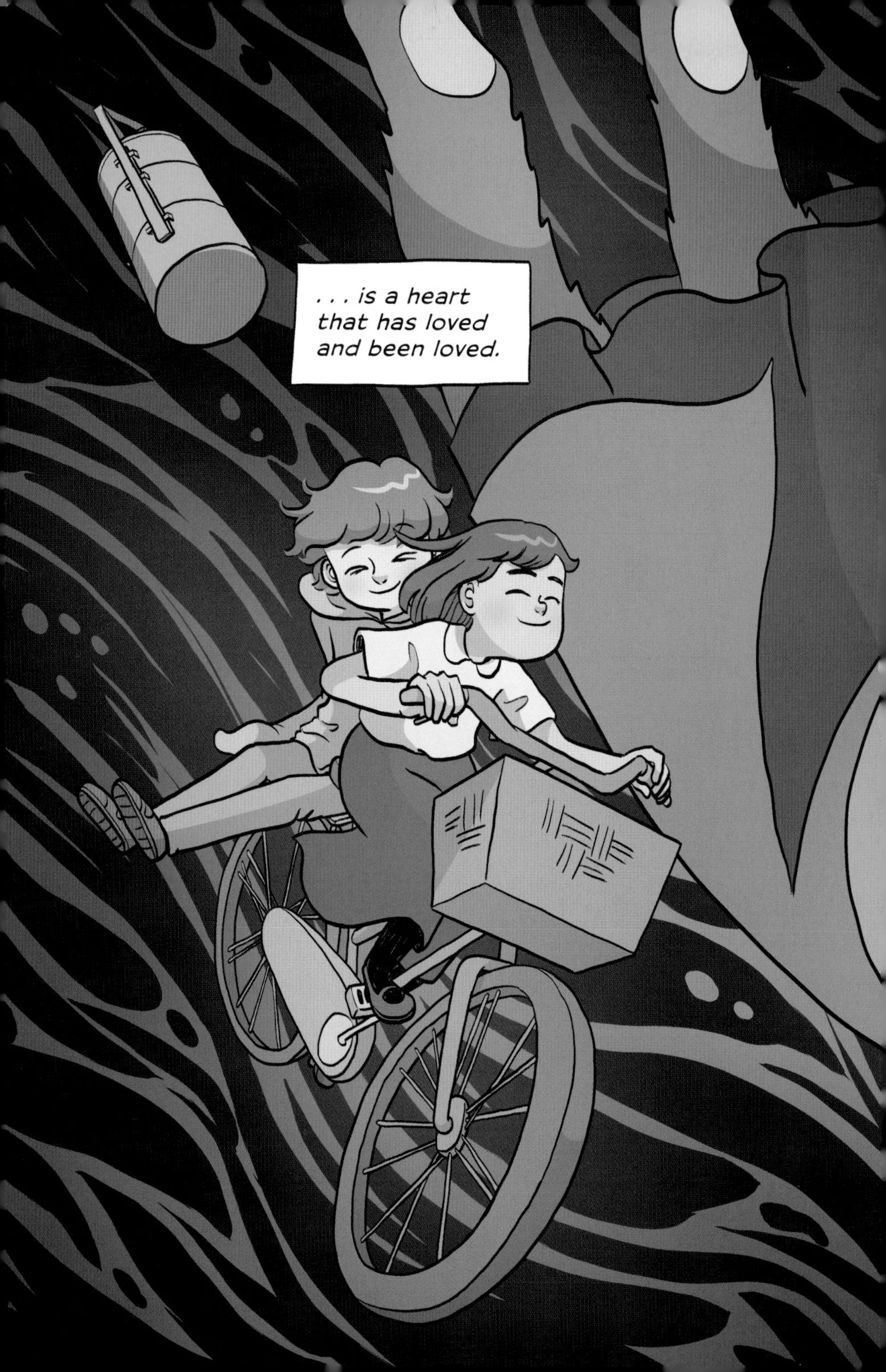
. . . is a heart
that has loved
and been loved.

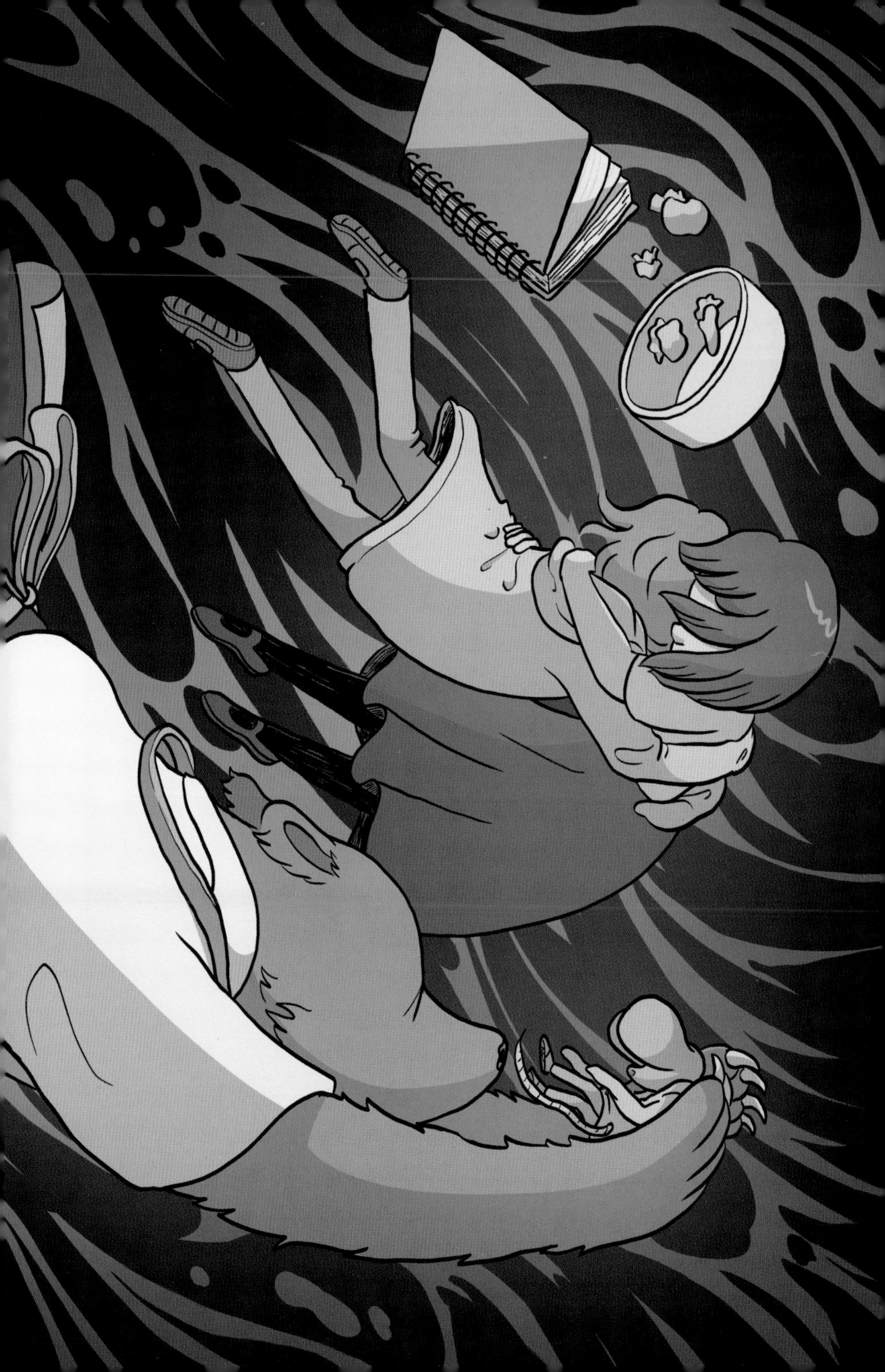

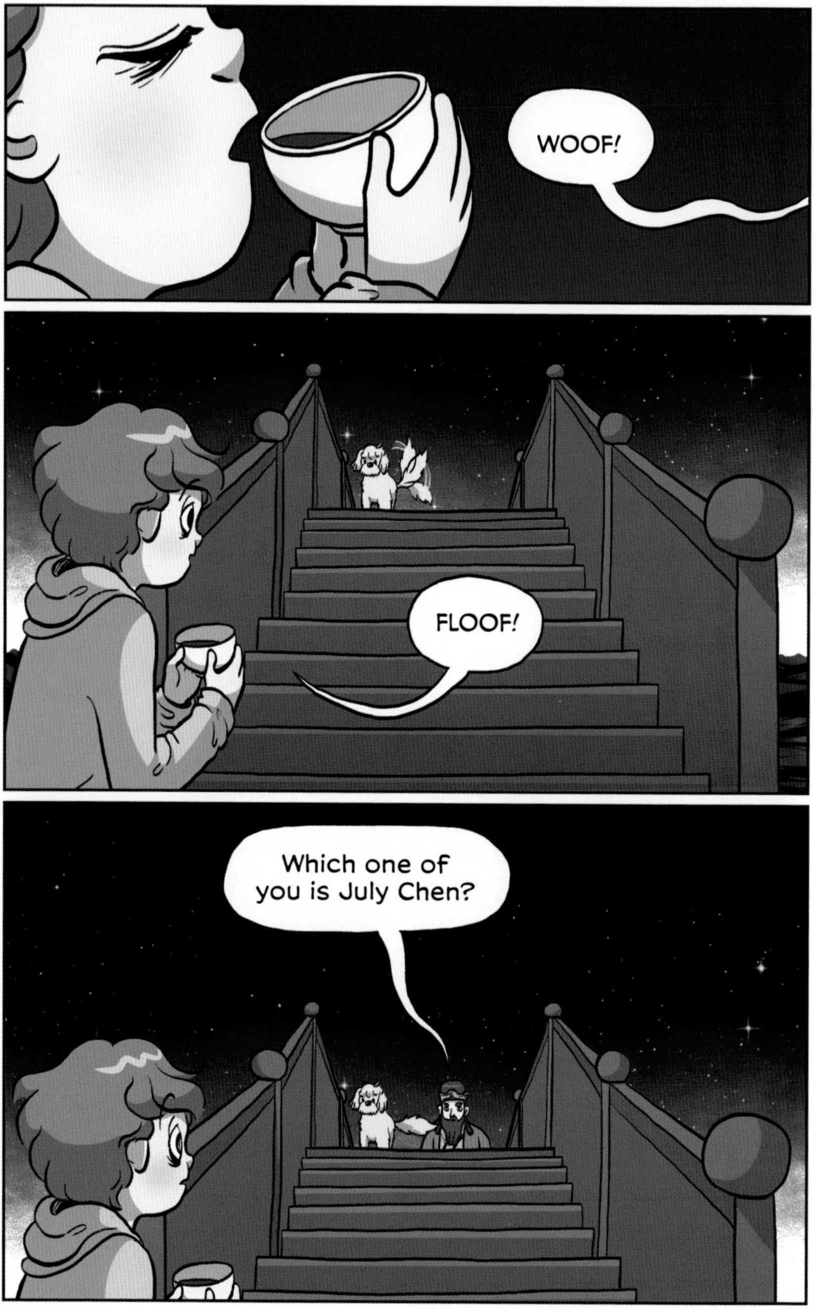
WOOF!
FLOOF!
Which one of you is July Chen?

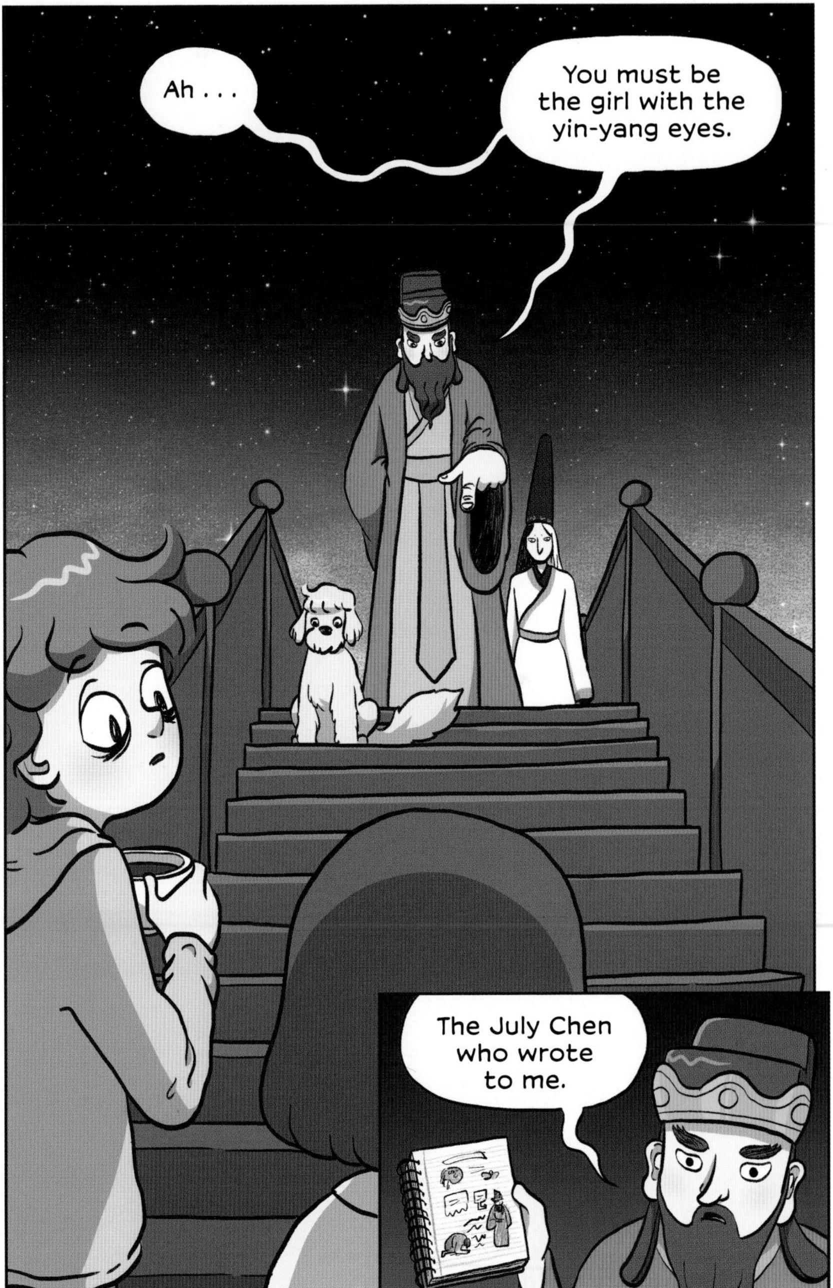

Ah . . .
You must be the girl with the yin-yang eyes.
The July Chen who wrote to me.

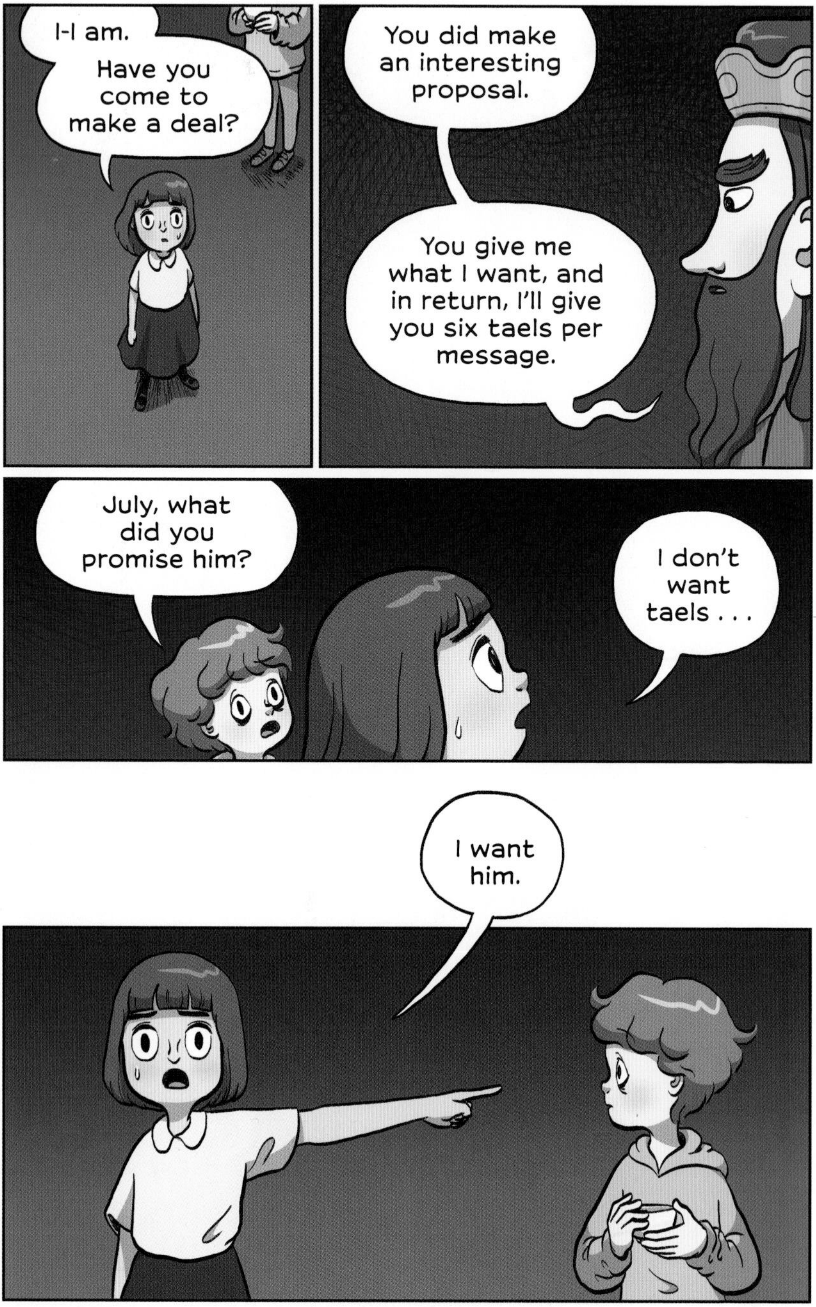
I-I am.
Have you come to make a deal?
You did make an interesting proposal.
You give me what I want, and in return, I'll give you six taels per message.
July, what did you promise him?
I don't want taels . . .
I want him.

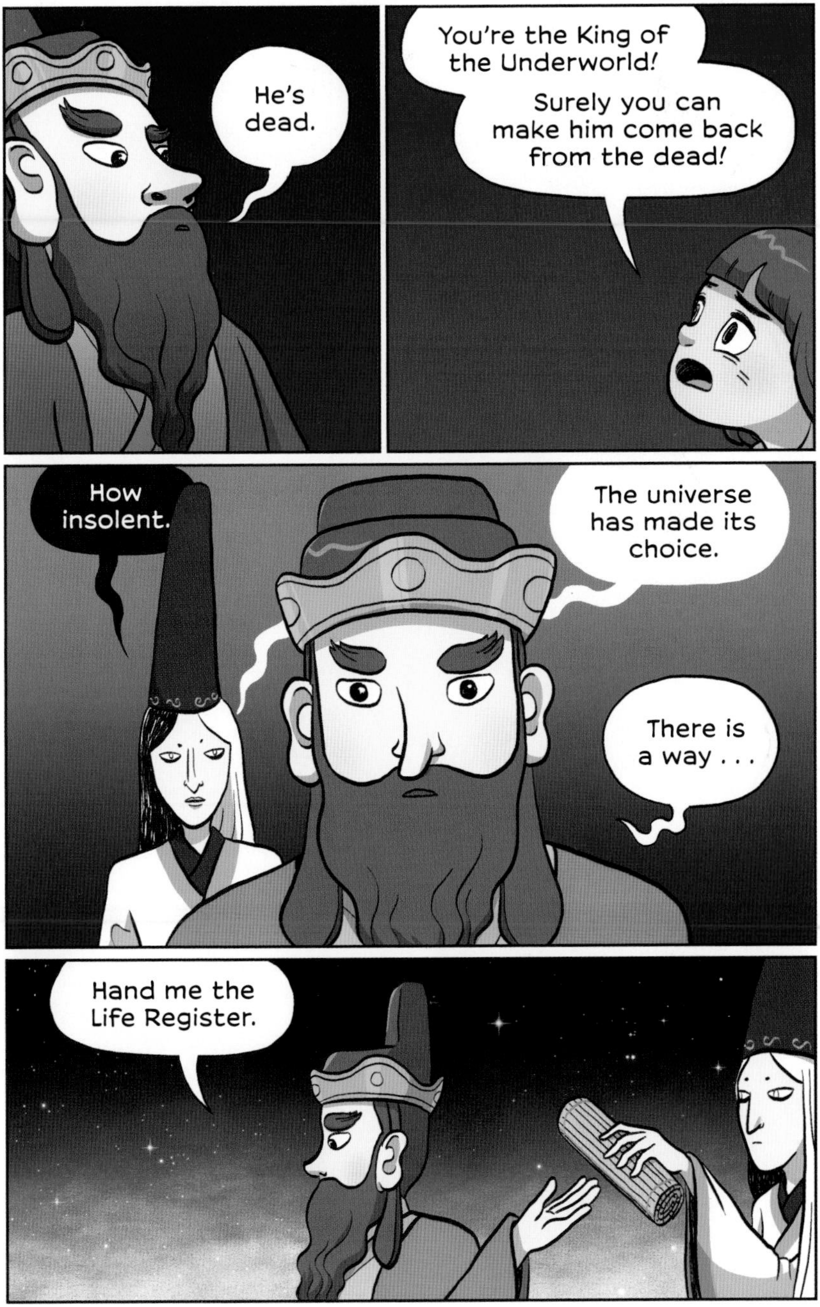
He's dead.
You're the King of the Underworld!
Surely you can make him come back from the dead!
How insolent.
The universe has made its choice.
There is a way . . .
Hand me the Life Register.

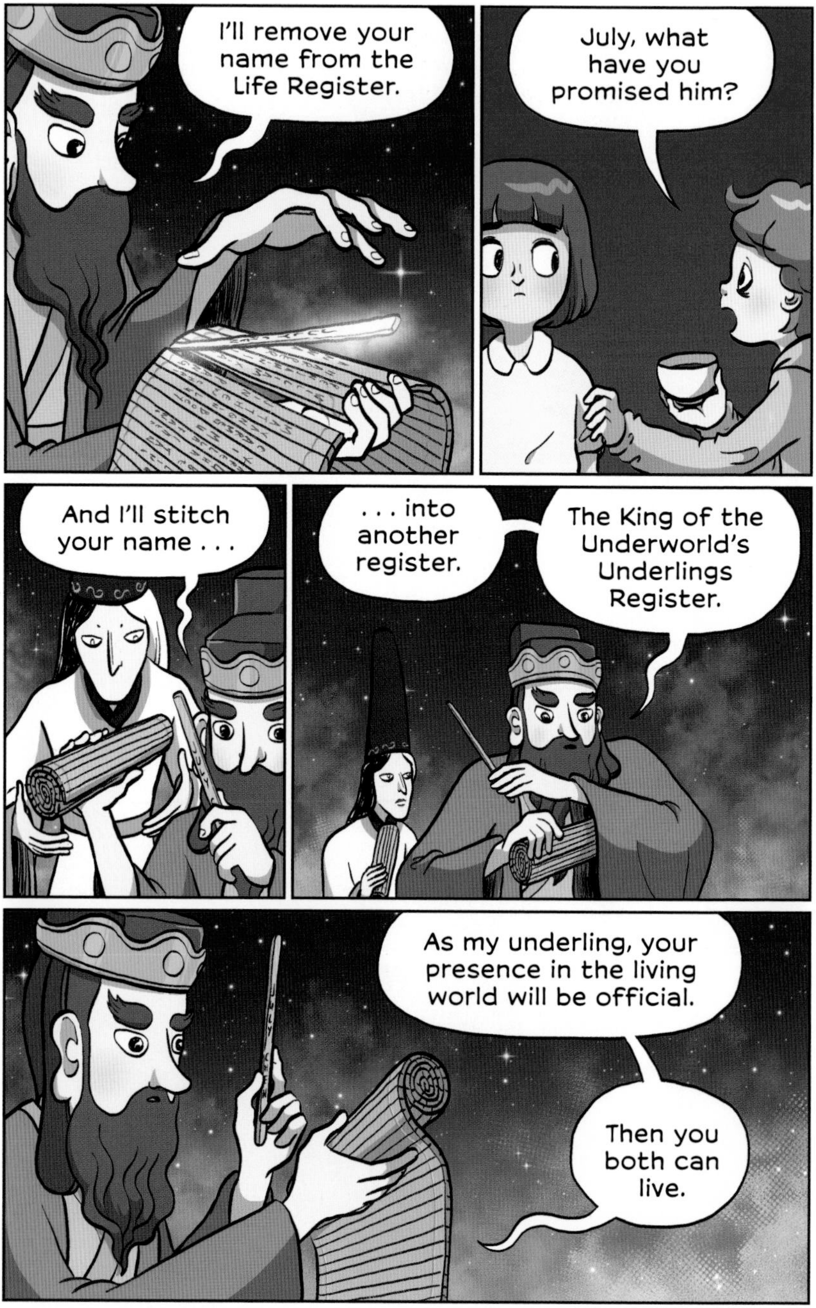
I'll remove your name from the Life Register.
July, what have you promised him?
And I'll stitch your name . . .
. . . into another register.
The King of the Underworld's Underlings Register.
As my underling, your presence in the living world will be official.
Then you both can live.

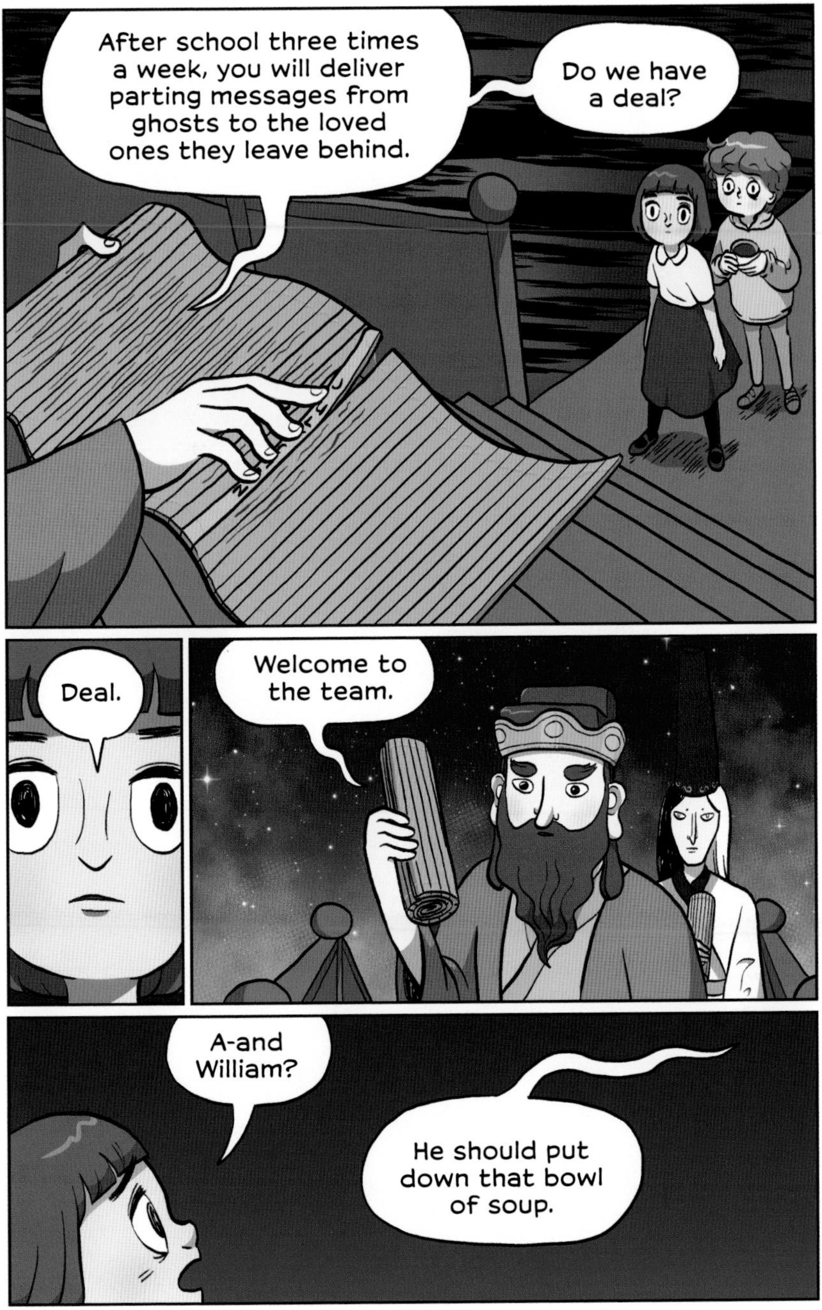
After school three times a week, you will deliver parting messages from ghosts to the loved ones they leave behind.
Do we have a deal?
Deal.
Welcome to the team.
A-and William?
He should put down that bowl of soup.

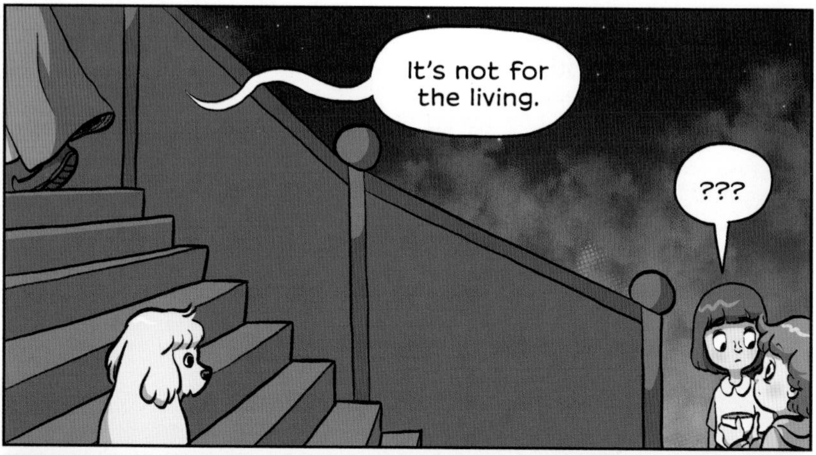
It's not for the living.
???

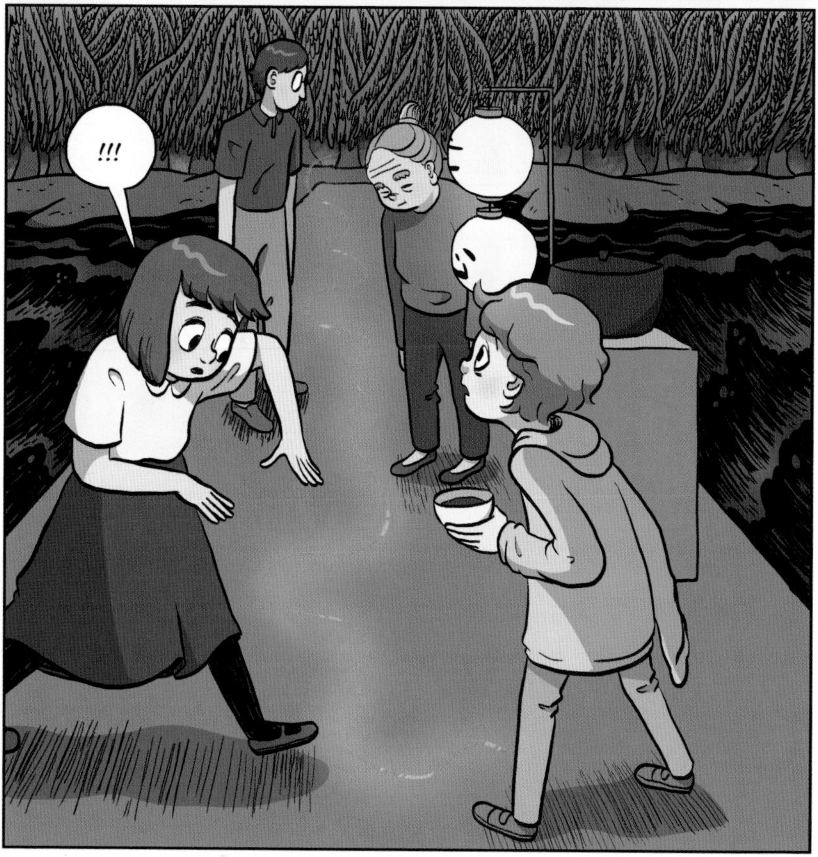
!!!

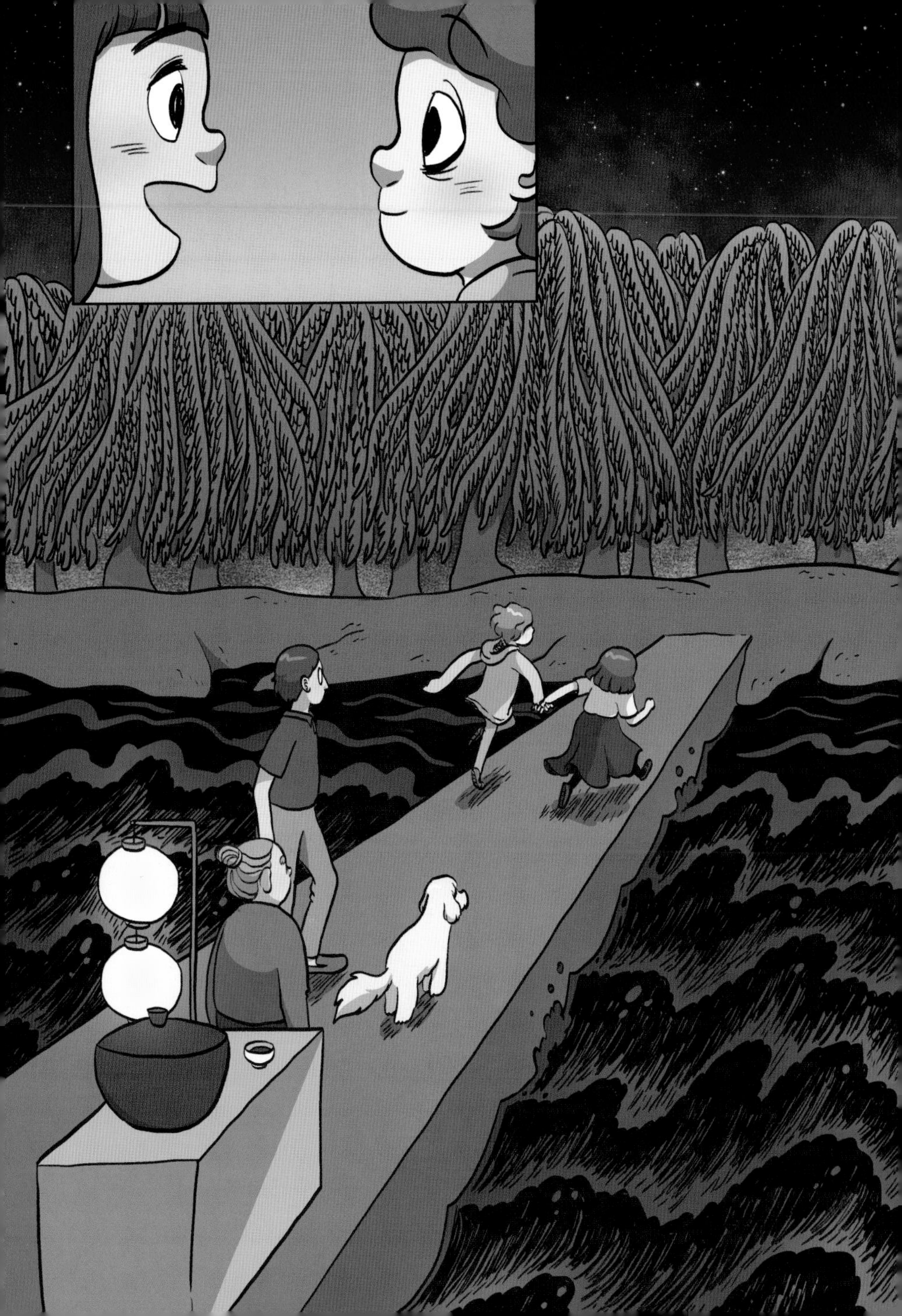

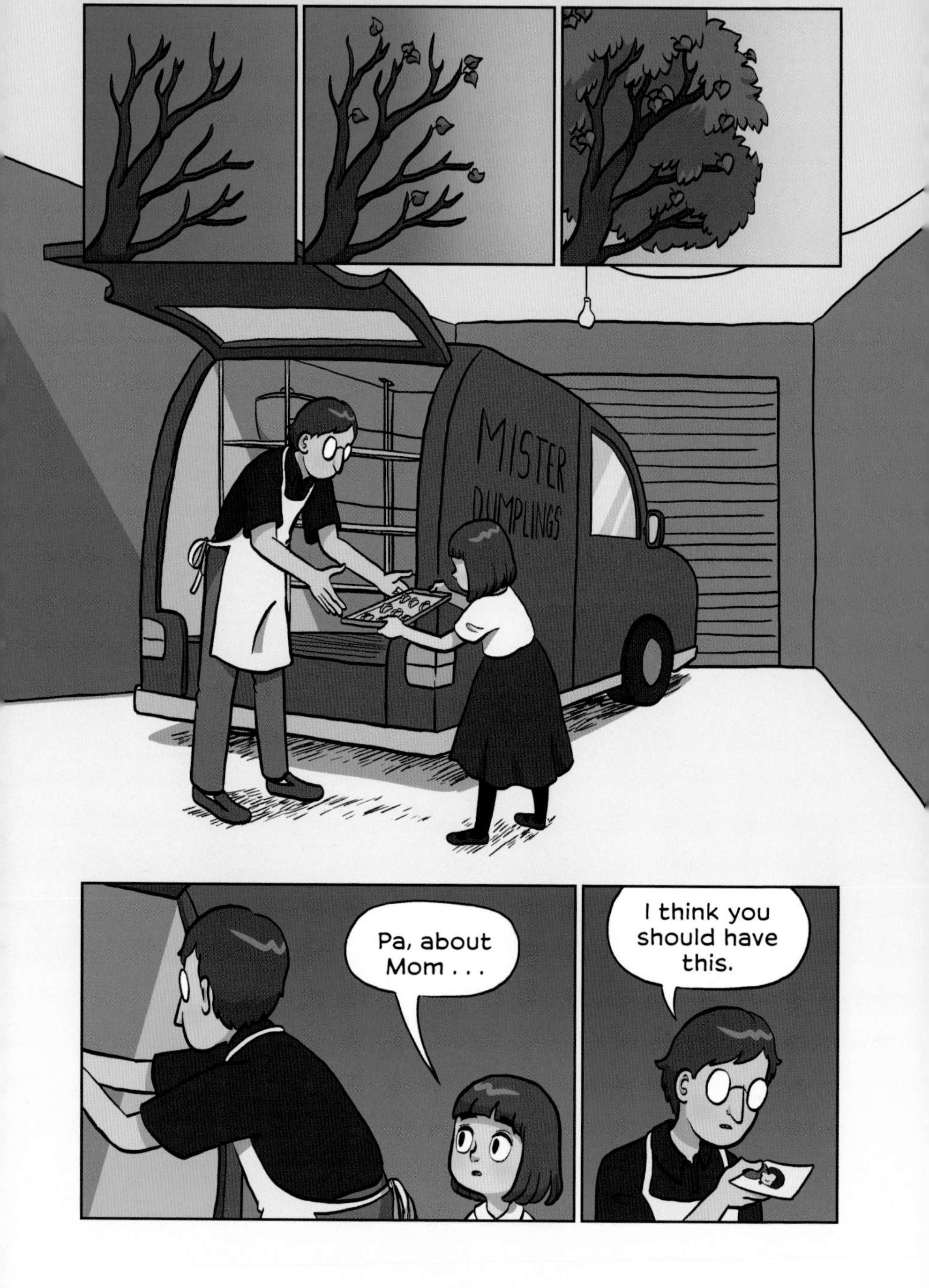
MISTER DUMPLINGS
Pa, about Mom . . .
I think you should have this.

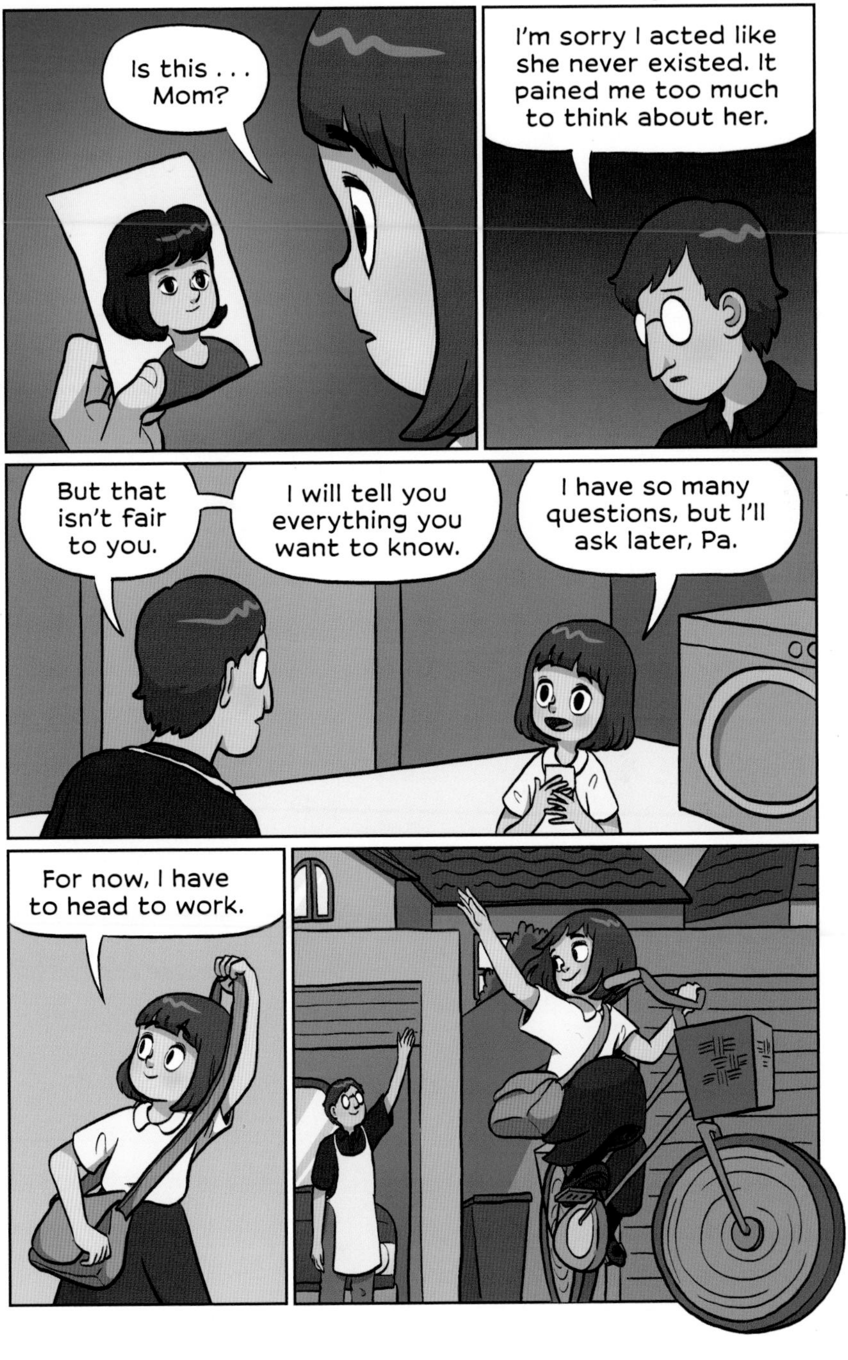
Is this . . . Mom?
I'm sorry I acted like she never existed. It pained me too much to think about her.
But that isn't fair to you.
I will tell you everything you want to know.
I have so many questions, but I'll ask later, Pa.
For now, I have to head to work.

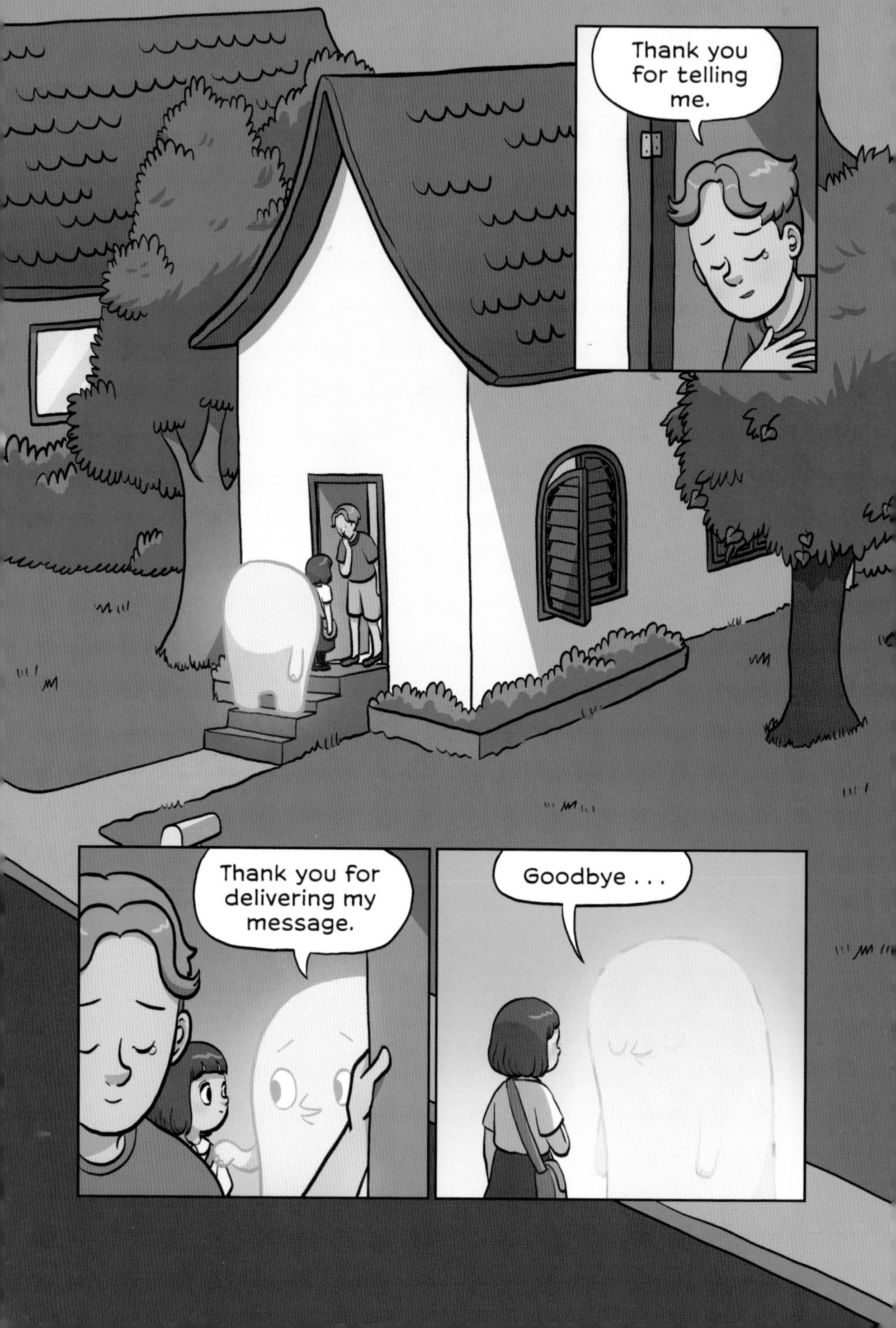
Thank you for telling me.
Thank you for delivering my message.
Goodbye . . .

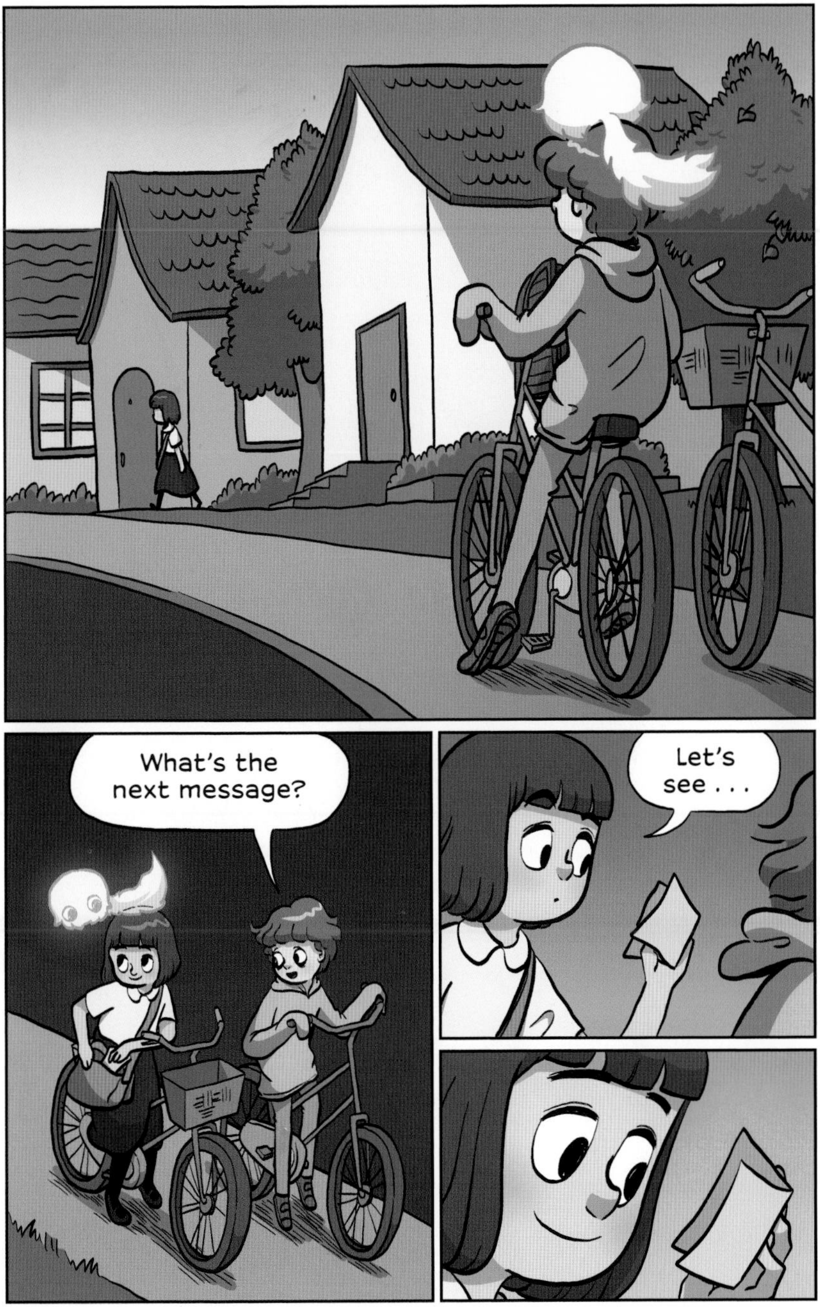
What's the next message?
Let's see . . .

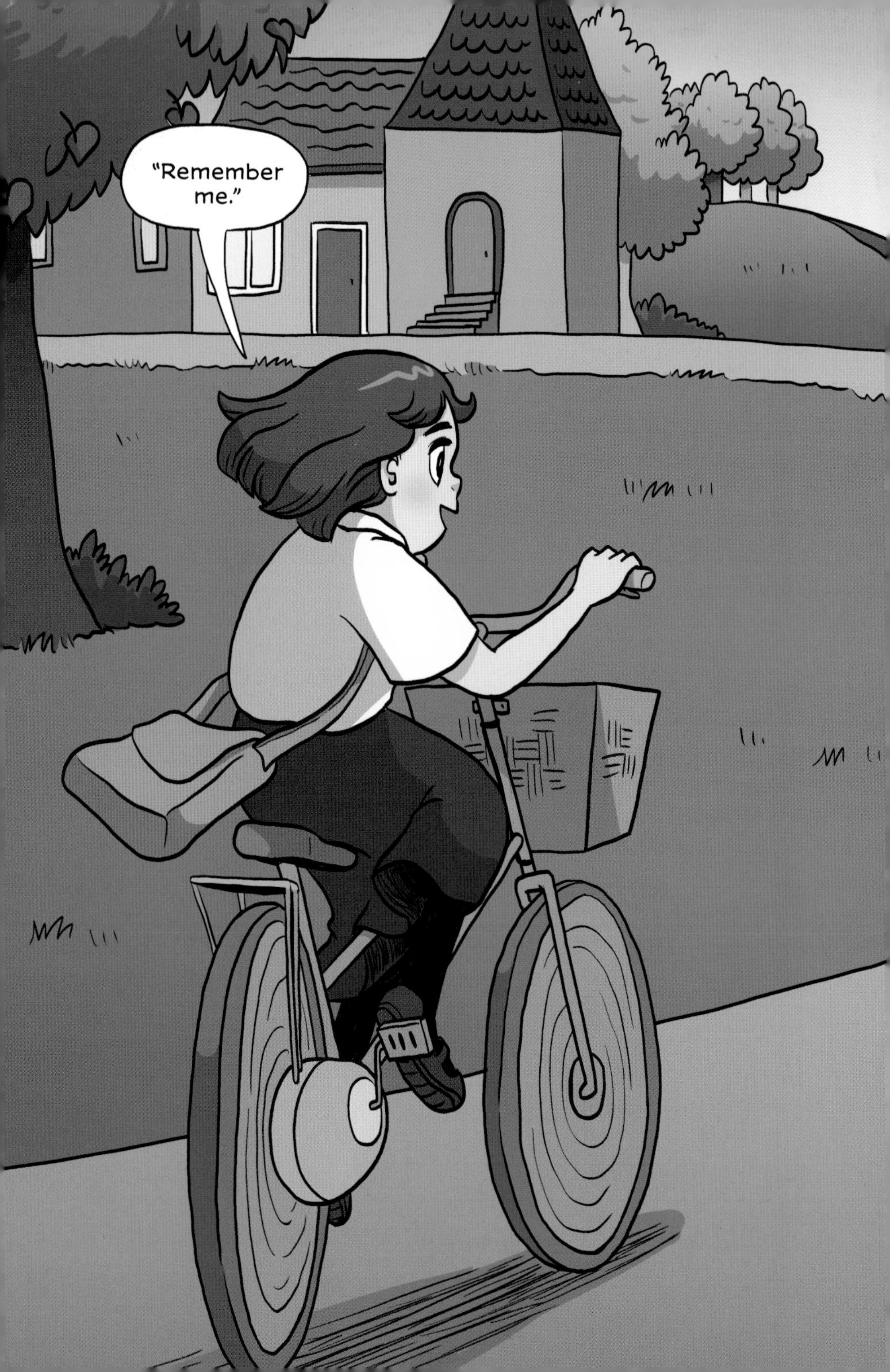
"Remember me."

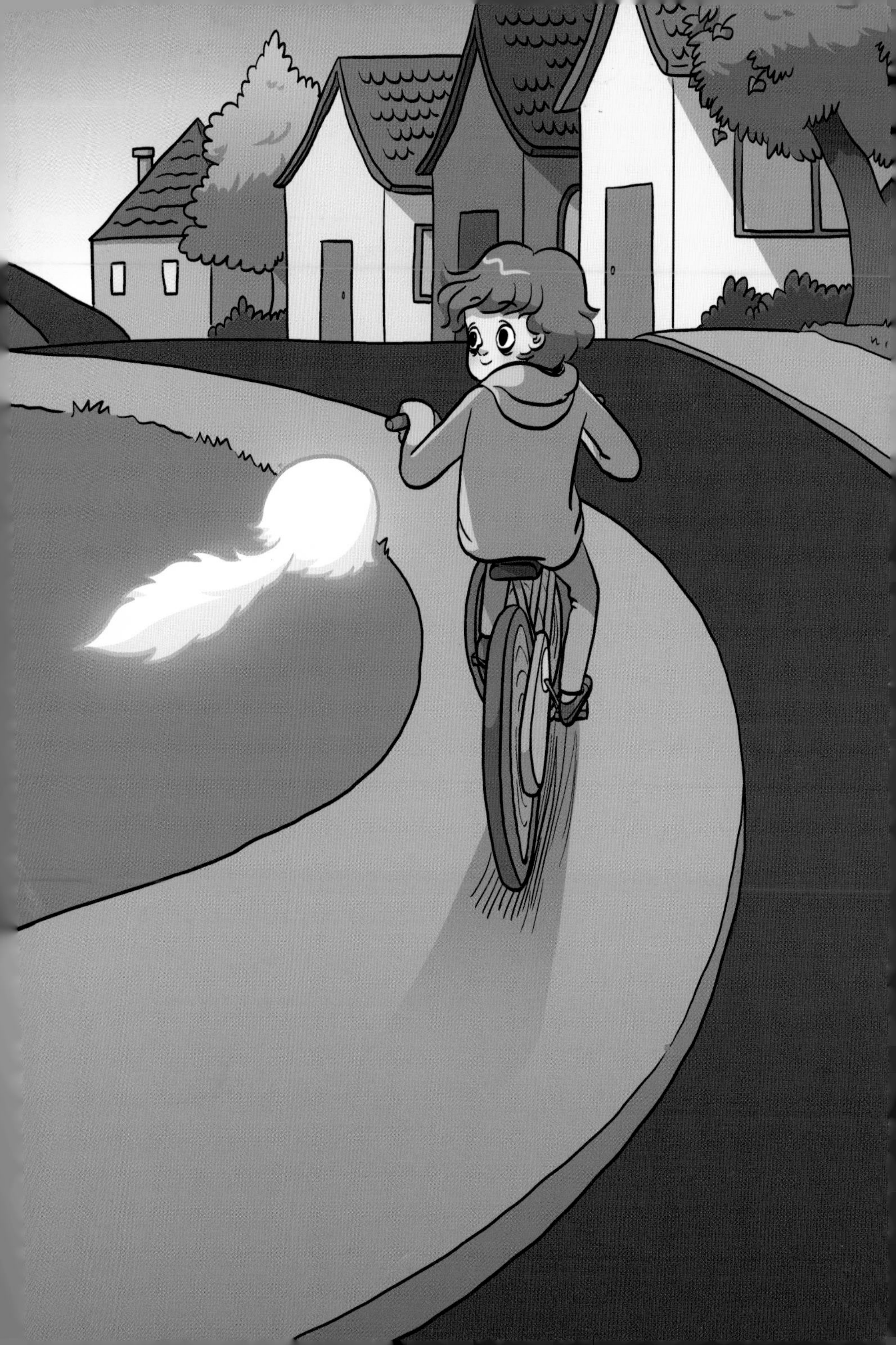

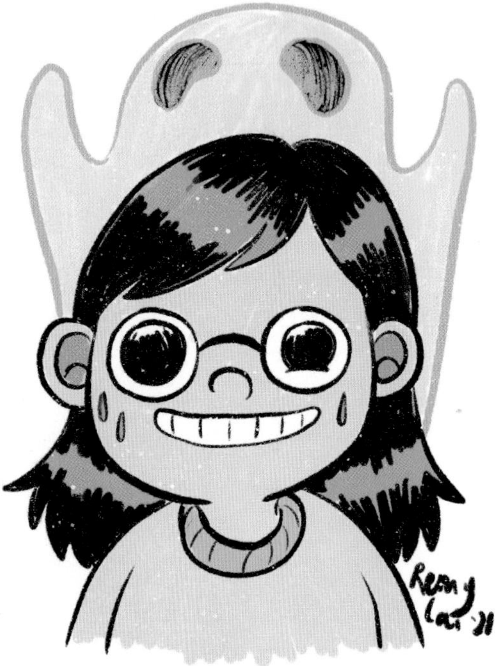
Remy
Lai '21

Remy Lai absolutely does NOT recommend truancy, but when she was in high school, she sometimes skipped school with her friends to watch horror movies in theaters that were eerily empty (because . . . um . . . everyone else was at school). She lives in Australia with her two dogs, who sometimes freak her out by barking at nothing in the corners of rooms. She is also the author of the critically acclaimed *Pie in the Sky, Fly on the Wall, Pawcasso,* and the Surviving the Wild series.

Follow Remy on Instagram at @rrremylai.

remylai.com